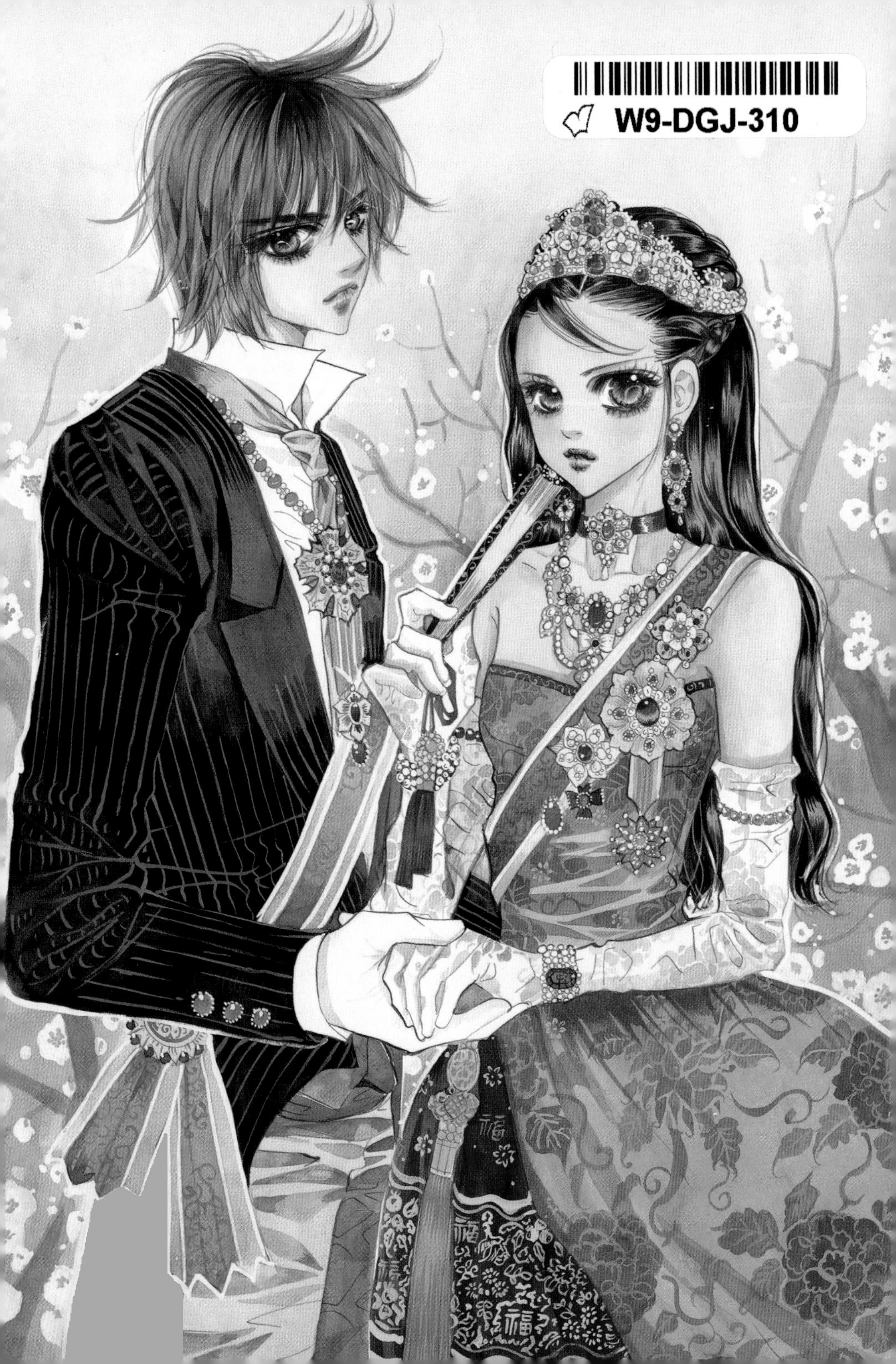

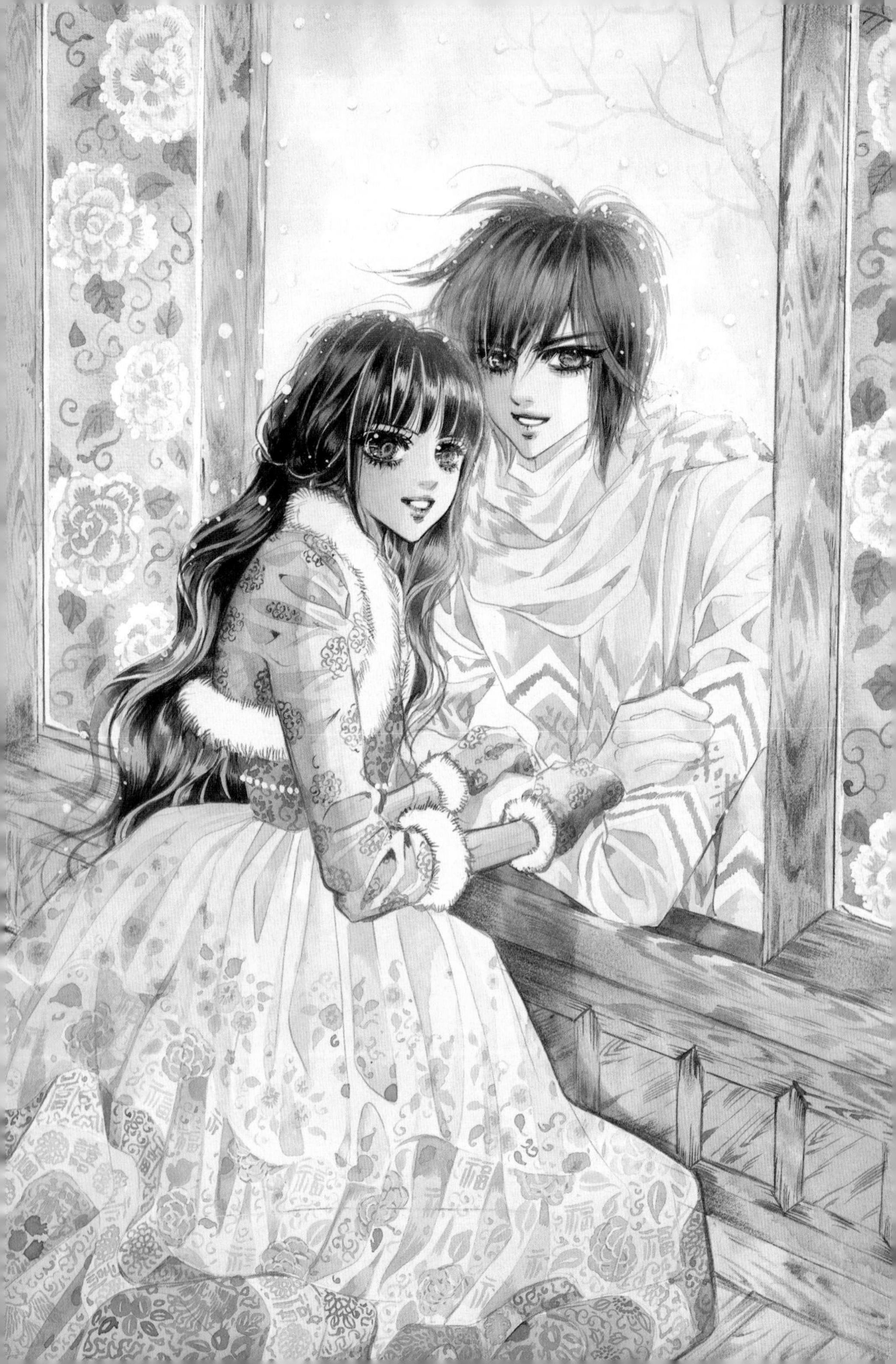

THE ROYAL PALACE Goong

vol. 15

Park SoHee

Yen Press

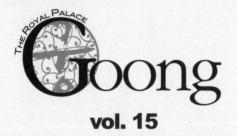

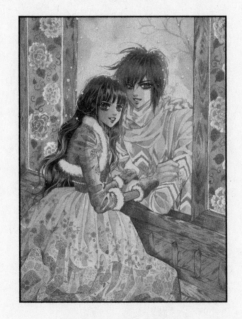

Words from the Creator

Volume 21

While I was working on Volume 21, many people who were important to me passed away. Sometimes, I want to escape to a comic world of my own making. Something I don't understand might still happen, and someone might die there too, but it would all be of my creation. My comic world wouldn't be perfect, but it would be less sad and painful. Through thick and thin, comic books remain a comfort to me.

SoHee Park

Words from the Creator

Volume 22

While I was working on Volume 22, I underwent two operations. I wasn't all that healthy to begin with, but I didn't realize that my immune system was as bad as it is. I apologize for the delay of the book. The serialization went on hiatus a few times, so the publication of Volume 22 was delayed too. My thanks go out to my editors, my friends, and my adorable assistants >puke<. But causing trouble for other people is the human way, right? I'm joking...
Anyway, I'll ply you readers with my sweet, cute kisses in a show of gratitude for your patience. Ha-ha! Are you all happy? (Huh? Is this the sound of books being torn up I hear?) Oh, stoooop it. I know you all like my kisses!!! Mwah-ha-ha-ha-ha-ha-ha...

P.S. I feel like I'm becoming more like Eunuch Kong the older I get. >sigh<

SoHee Park

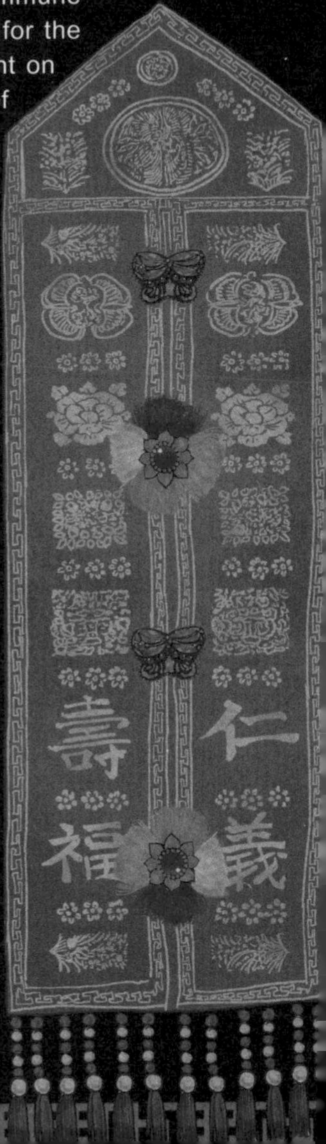
壽
仁
福
義

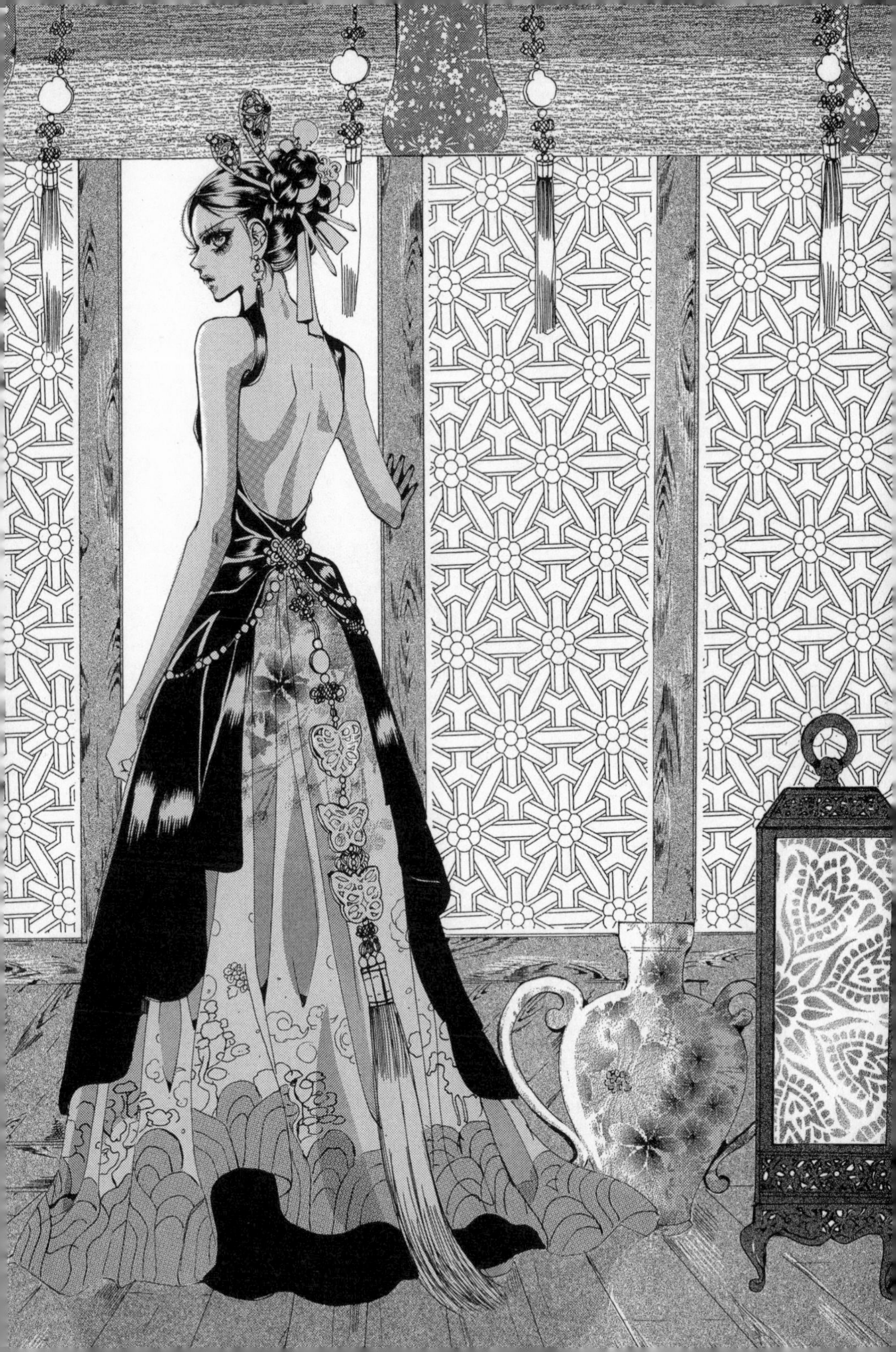

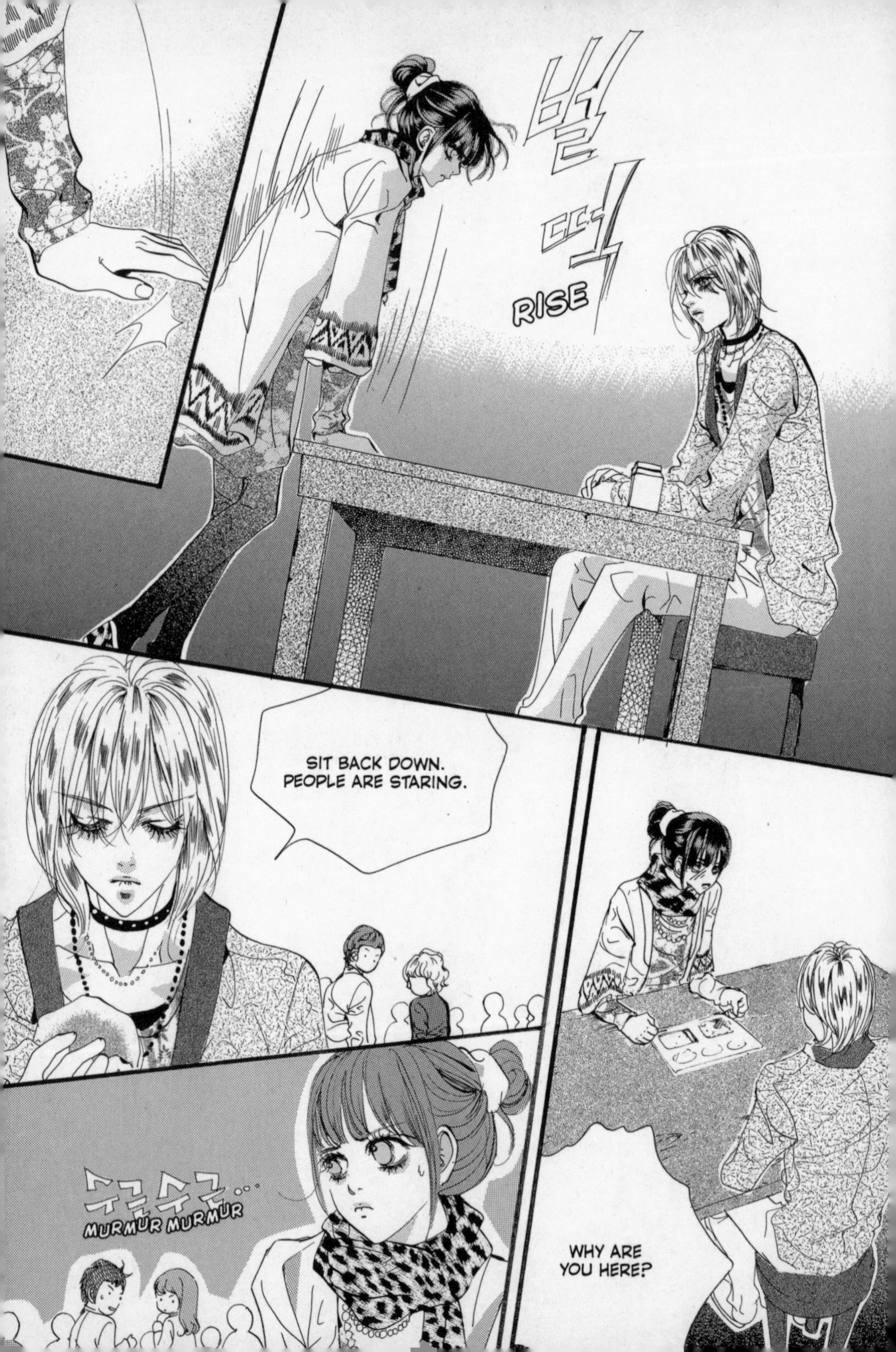

벌떡
RISE
SIT BACK DOWN. PEOPLE ARE STARING.
수군수군...
MURMUR MURMUR
WHY ARE YOU HERE?

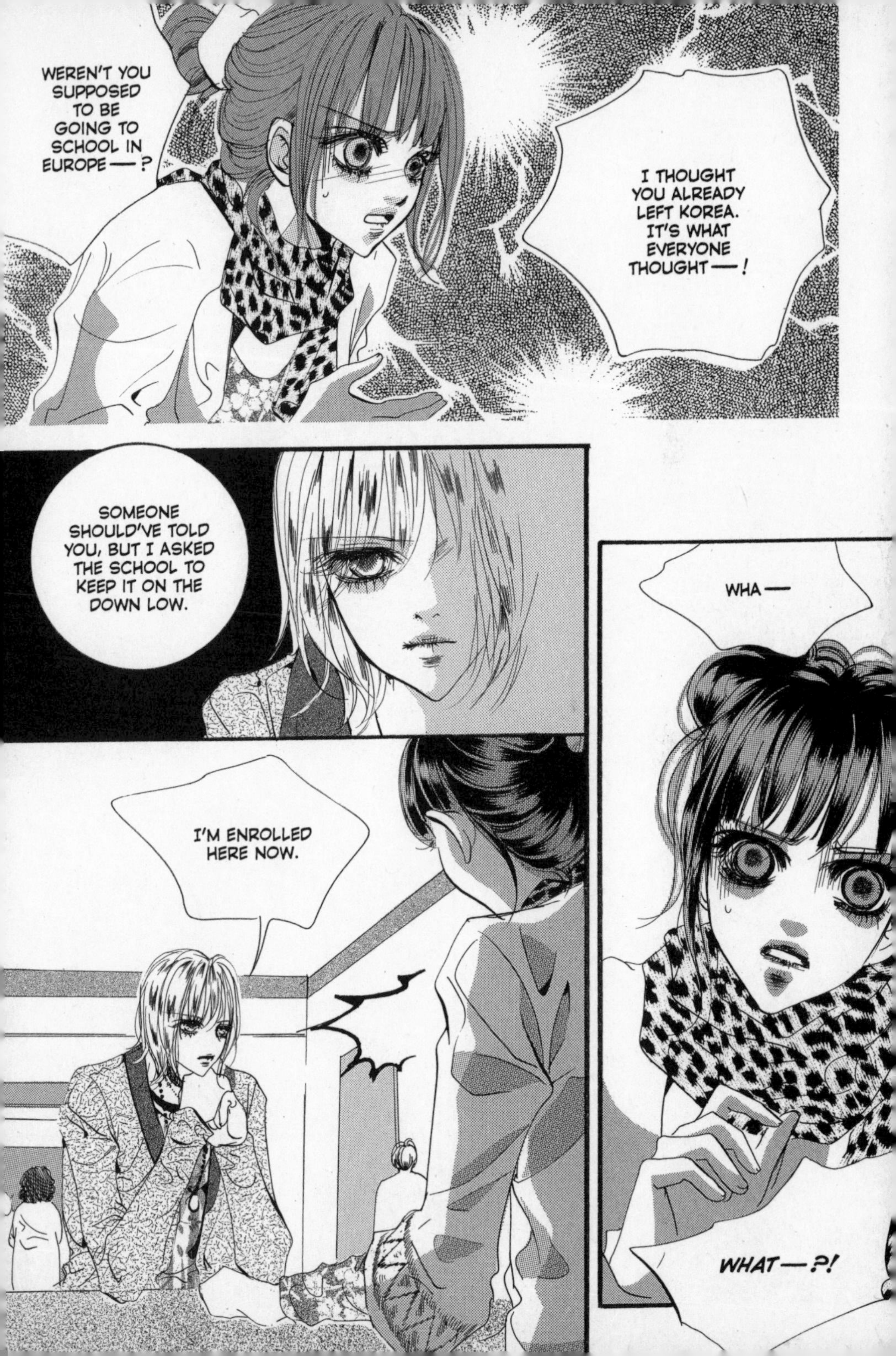
WEREN'T YOU SUPPOSED TO BE GOING TO SCHOOL IN EUROPE — ?
I THOUGHT YOU ALREADY LEFT KOREA. IT'S WHAT EVERYONE THOUGHT — !
SOMEONE SHOULD'VE TOLD YOU, BUT I ASKED THE SCHOOL TO KEEP IT ON THE DOWN LOW.
I'M ENROLLED HERE NOW.
WHA —
WHAT — ?!

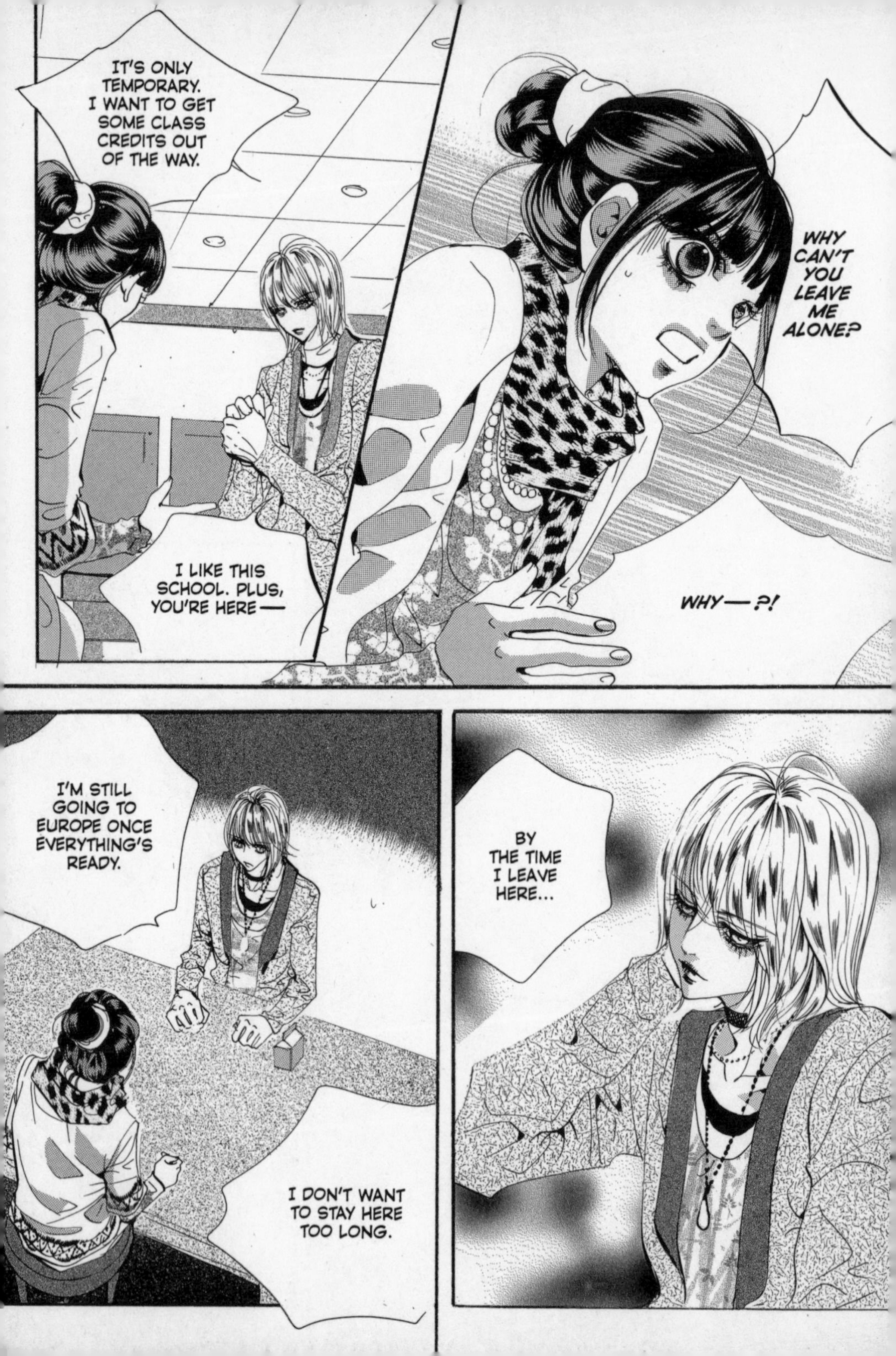
IT'S ONLY TEMPORARY. I WANT TO GET SOME CLASS CREDITS OUT OF THE WAY.
I LIKE THIS SCHOOL. PLUS, YOU'RE HERE—
WHY CAN'T YOU LEAVE ME ALONE?
WHY—?!
I'M STILL GOING TO EUROPE ONCE EVERYTHING'S READY.
I DON'T WANT TO STAY HERE TOO LONG.
BY THE TIME I LEAVE HERE...

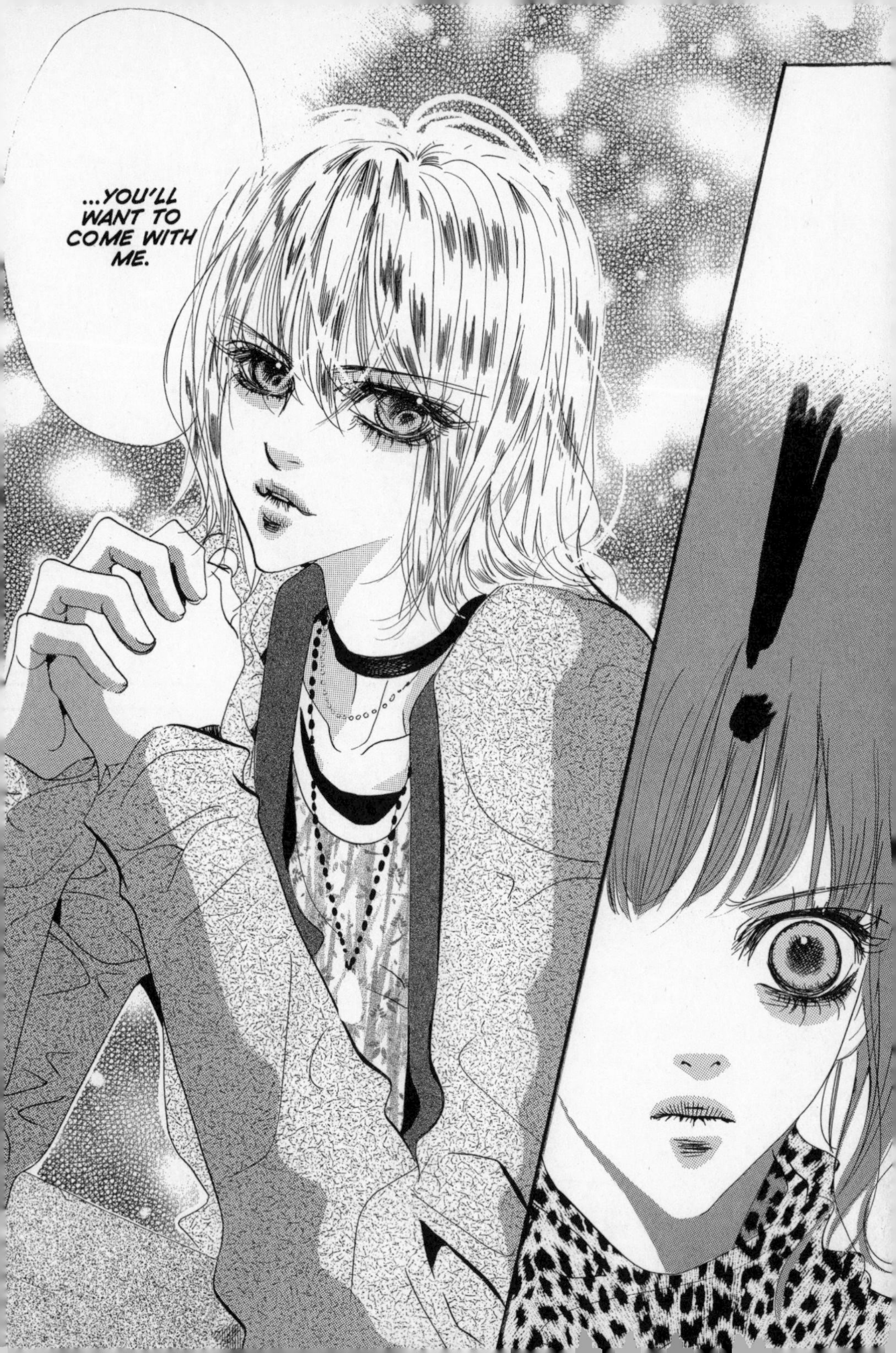
...YOU'LL WANT TO COME WITH ME.

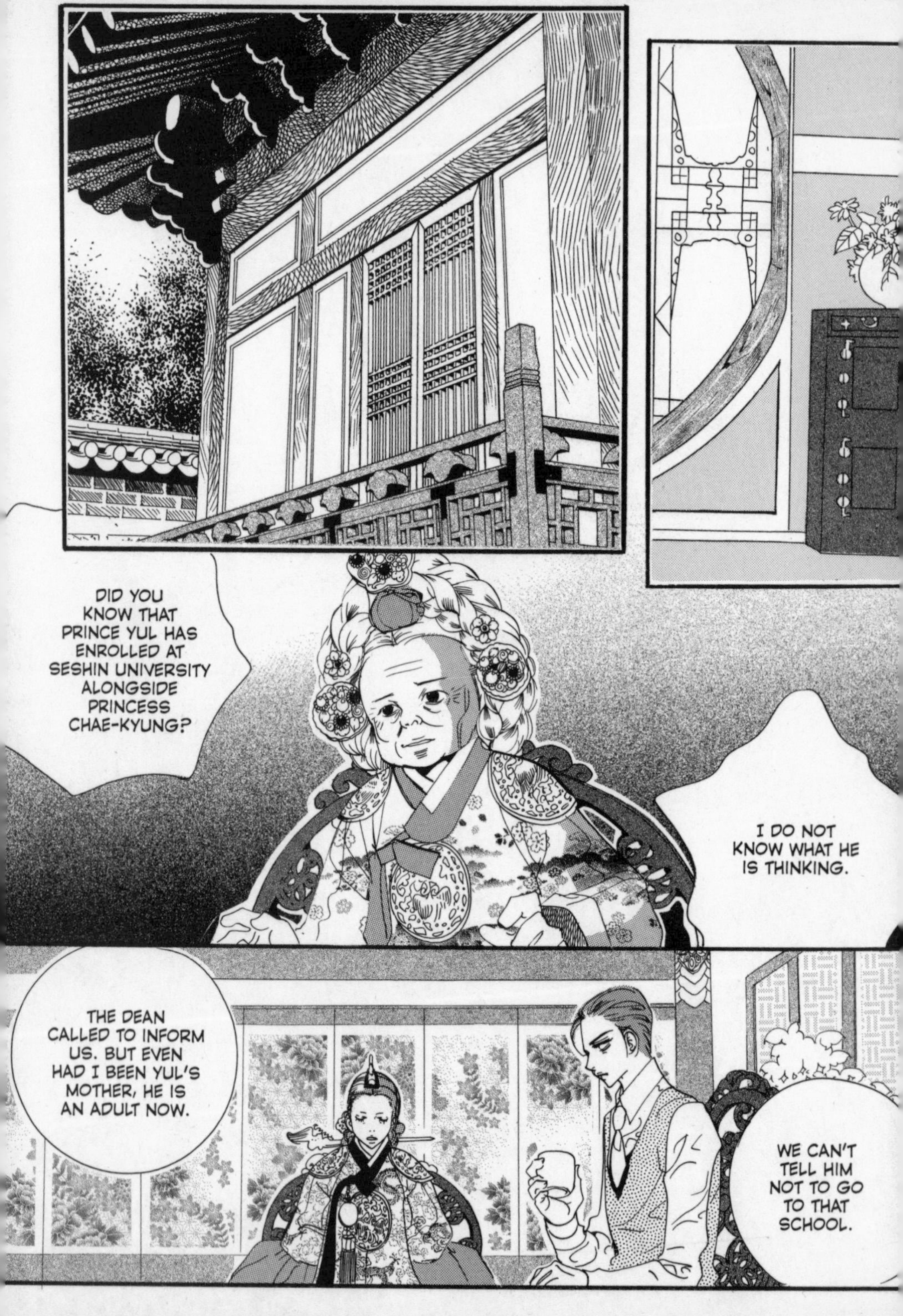
DID YOU KNOW THAT PRINCE YUL HAS ENROLLED AT SESHIN UNIVERSITY ALONGSIDE PRINCESS CHAE-KYUNG?
I DO NOT KNOW WHAT HE IS THINKING.
THE DEAN CALLED TO INFORM US. BUT EVEN HAD I BEEN YUL'S MOTHER, HE IS AN ADULT NOW.
WE CAN'T TELL HIM NOT TO GO TO THAT SCHOOL.

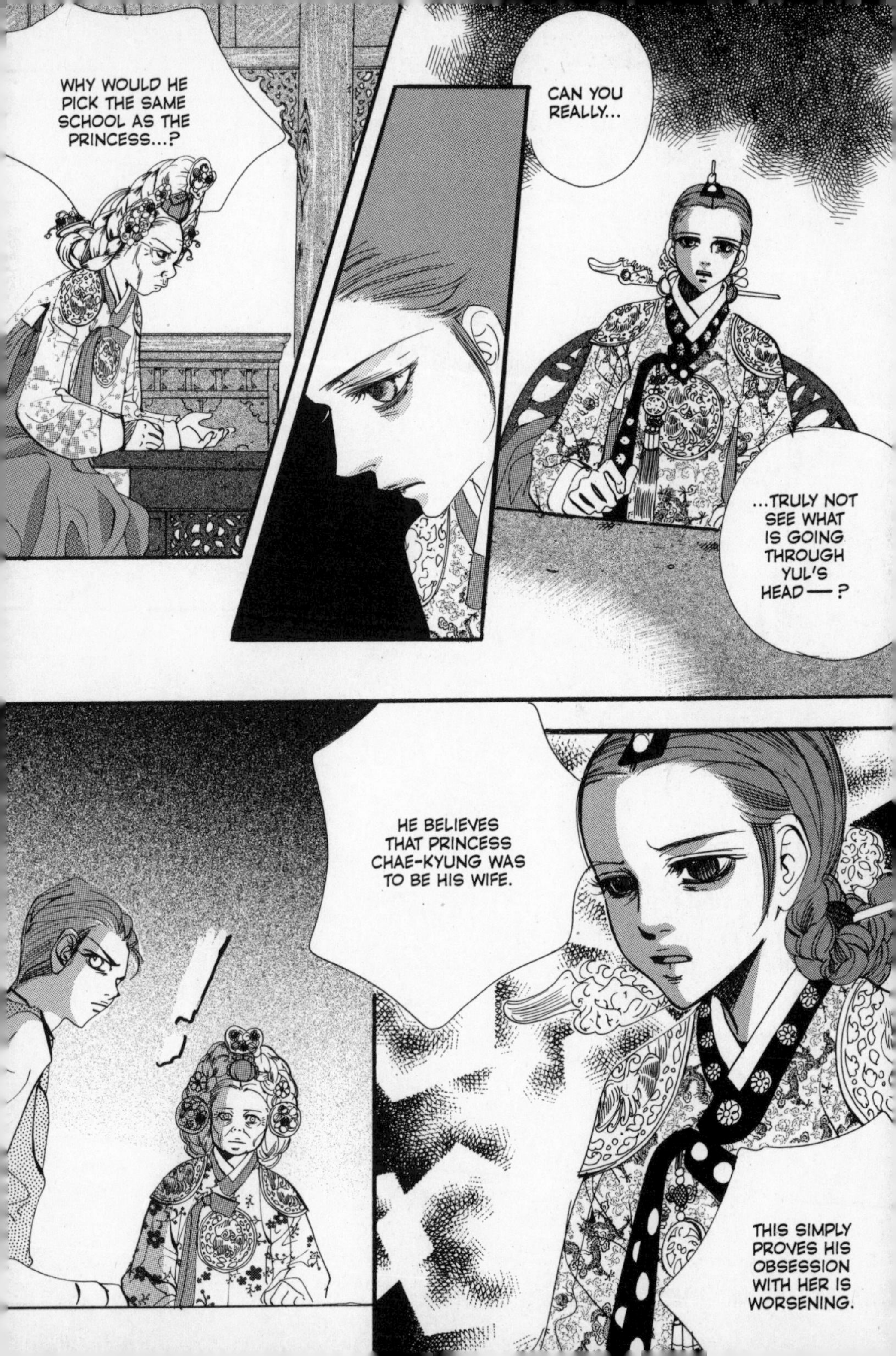
WHY WOULD HE PICK THE SAME SCHOOL AS THE PRINCESS...?
CAN YOU REALLY...
...TRULY NOT SEE WHAT IS GOING THROUGH YUL'S HEAD—?
HE BELIEVES THAT PRINCESS CHAE-KYUNG WAS TO BE HIS WIFE.
THIS SIMPLY PROVES HIS OBSESSION WITH HER IS WORSENING.

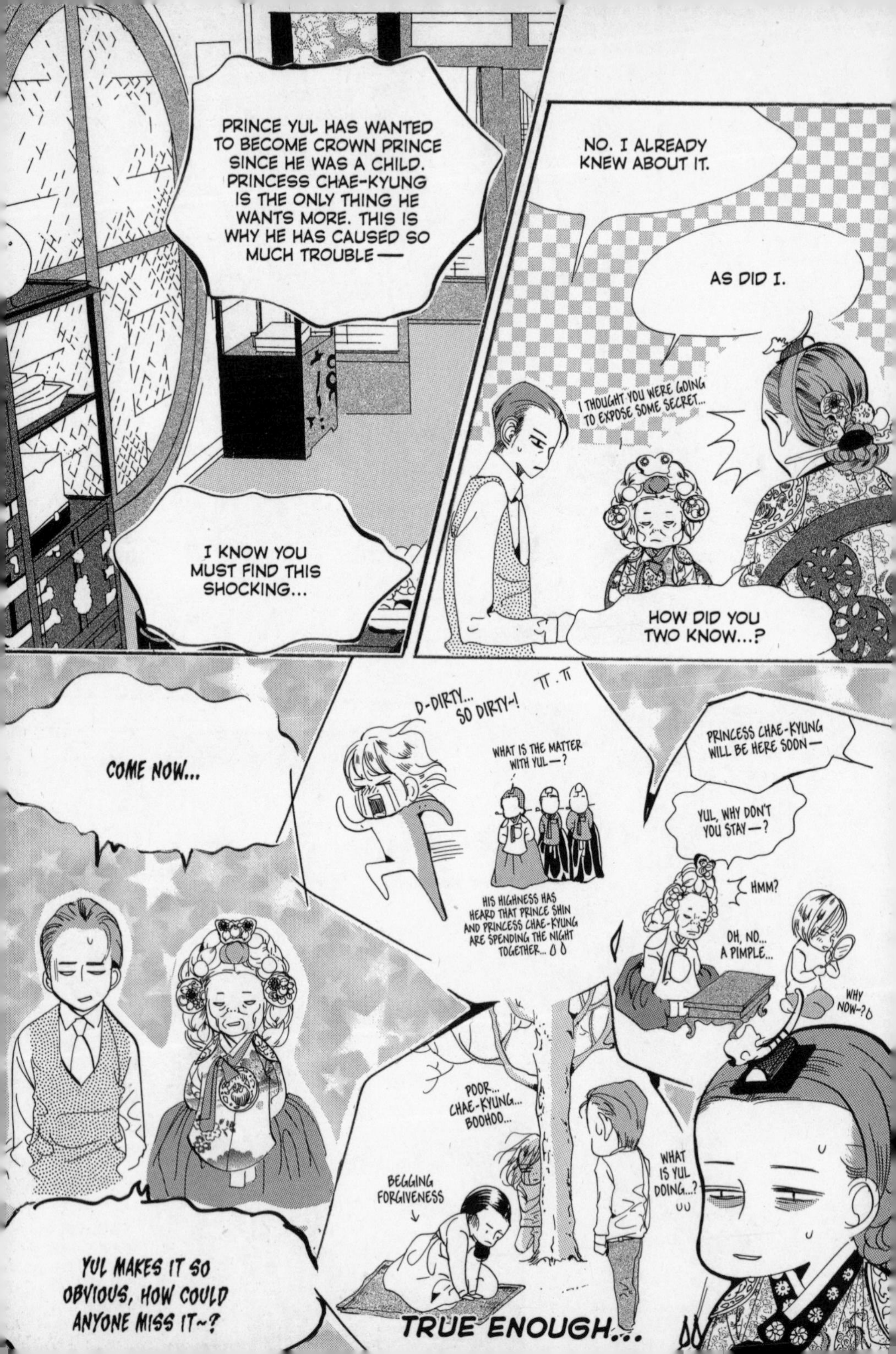

PRINCE YUL HAS WANTED TO BECOME CROWN PRINCE SINCE HE WAS A CHILD. PRINCESS CHAE-KYUNG IS THE ONLY THING HE WANTS MORE. THIS IS WHY HE HAS CAUSED SO MUCH TROUBLE—
I KNOW YOU MUST FIND THIS SHOCKING...
NO. I ALREADY KNEW ABOUT IT.
AS DID I.
I THOUGHT YOU WERE GOING TO EXPOSE SOME SECRET...
HOW DID YOU TWO KNOW...?
COME NOW...
D-DIRTY... SO DIRTY-!
TT . TT
WHAT IS THE MATTER WITH YUL—?
HIS HIGHNESS HAS HEARD THAT PRINCE SHIN AND PRINCESS CHAE-KYUNG ARE SPENDING THE NIGHT TOGETHER...
PRINCESS CHAE-KYUNG WILL BE HERE SOON—
YUL, WHY DON'T YOU STAY—?
HMM?
OH, NO... A PIMPLE...
WHY NOW-?
YUL MAKES IT SO OBVIOUS, HOW COULD ANYONE MISS IT~?
POOR... CHAE-KYUNG... BOOHOO...
BEGGING FORGIVENESS
WHAT IS YUL DOING...?
TRUE ENOUGH...

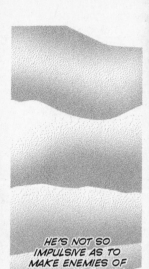

WHAT IS IT THAT YUL REALLY WANTS...?

HE'S NOT SO IMPULSIVE AS TO MAKE ENEMIES OF THE ROYAL FAMILY FOR NO REASON.

NOW THAT SHIN HAS DECIDED TO RECONCILE WITH PRINCESS CHAE-KYUNG, YUL'S NEXT MOVE IS HARD TO READ...

HONESTLY...

...I CAN'T FATHOM YUL'S TWISTED WAY OF THINKING—

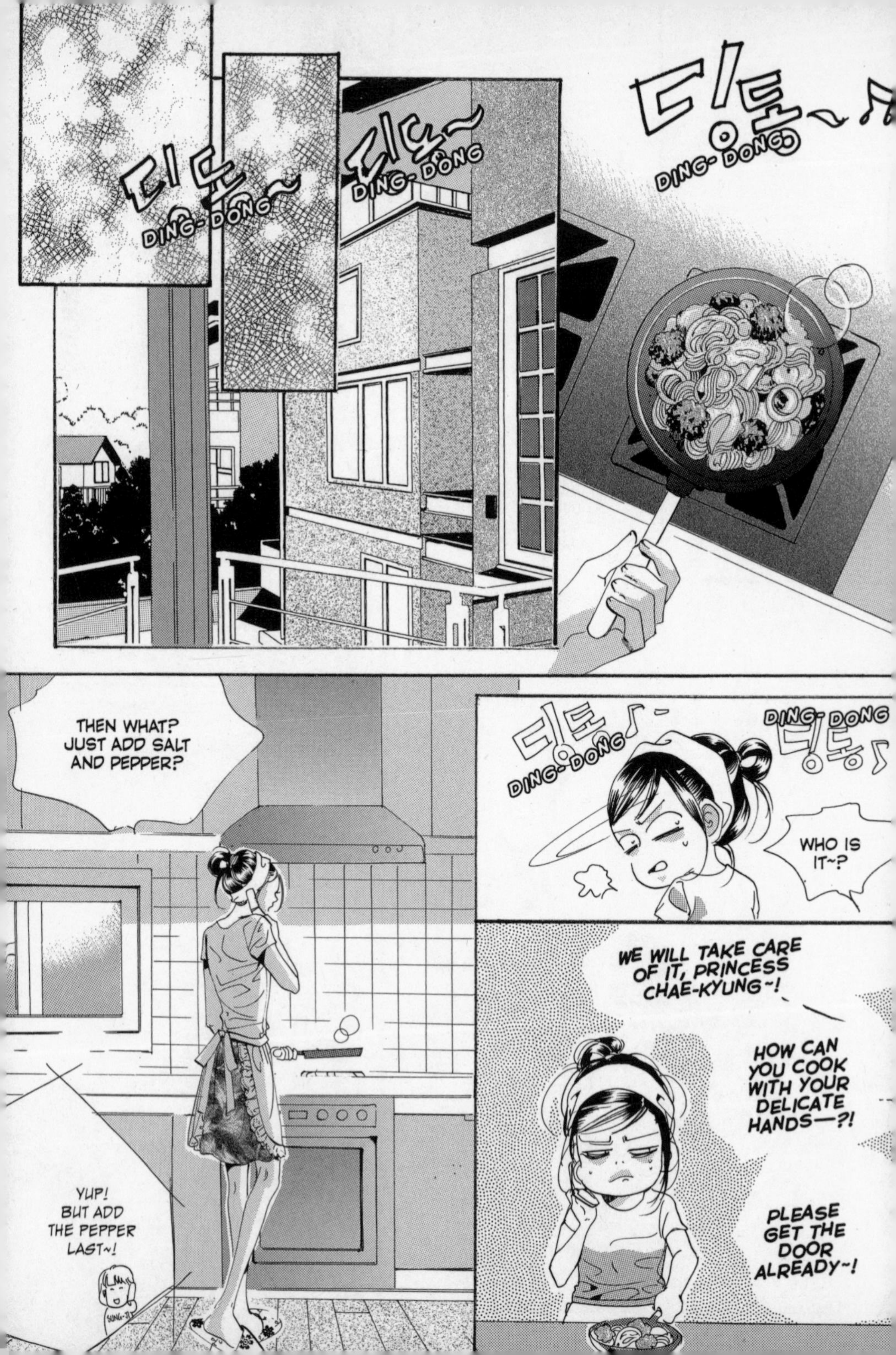
딩동~
DING-DONG
딩동~
DING-DONG
딩동~♪
DING-DONG
THEN WHAT? JUST ADD SALT AND PEPPER?
YUP! BUT ADD THE PEPPER LAST~!
딩동♪~
DING-DONG
DING-DONG
딩동♪
WHO IS IT~?
WE WILL TAKE CARE OF IT, PRINCESS CHAE-KYUNG~!
HOW CAN YOU COOK WITH YOUR DELICATE HANDS—?!
PLEASE GET THE DOOR ALREADY~!

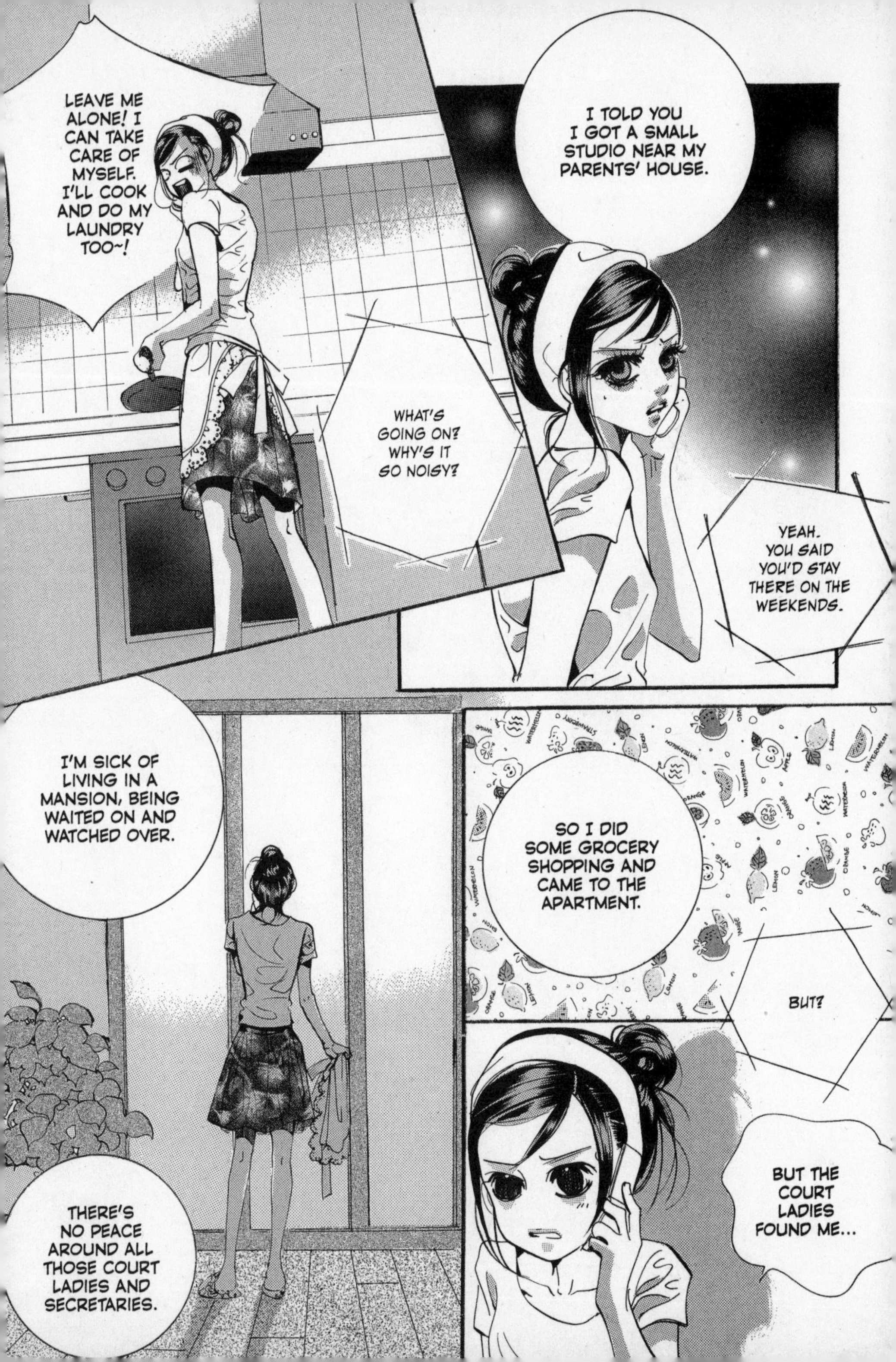
LEAVE ME ALONE! I CAN TAKE CARE OF MYSELF. I'LL COOK AND DO MY LAUNDRY TOO~!
WHAT'S GOING ON? WHY'S IT SO NOISY?
I TOLD YOU I GOT A SMALL STUDIO NEAR MY PARENTS' HOUSE.
YEAH. YOU SAID YOU'D STAY THERE ON THE WEEKENDS.
I'M SICK OF LIVING IN A MANSION, BEING WAITED ON AND WATCHED OVER.
THERE'S NO PEACE AROUND ALL THOSE COURT LADIES AND SECRETARIES.
SO I DID SOME GROCERY SHOPPING AND CAME TO THE APARTMENT.
BUT?
BUT THE COURT LADIES FOUND ME...

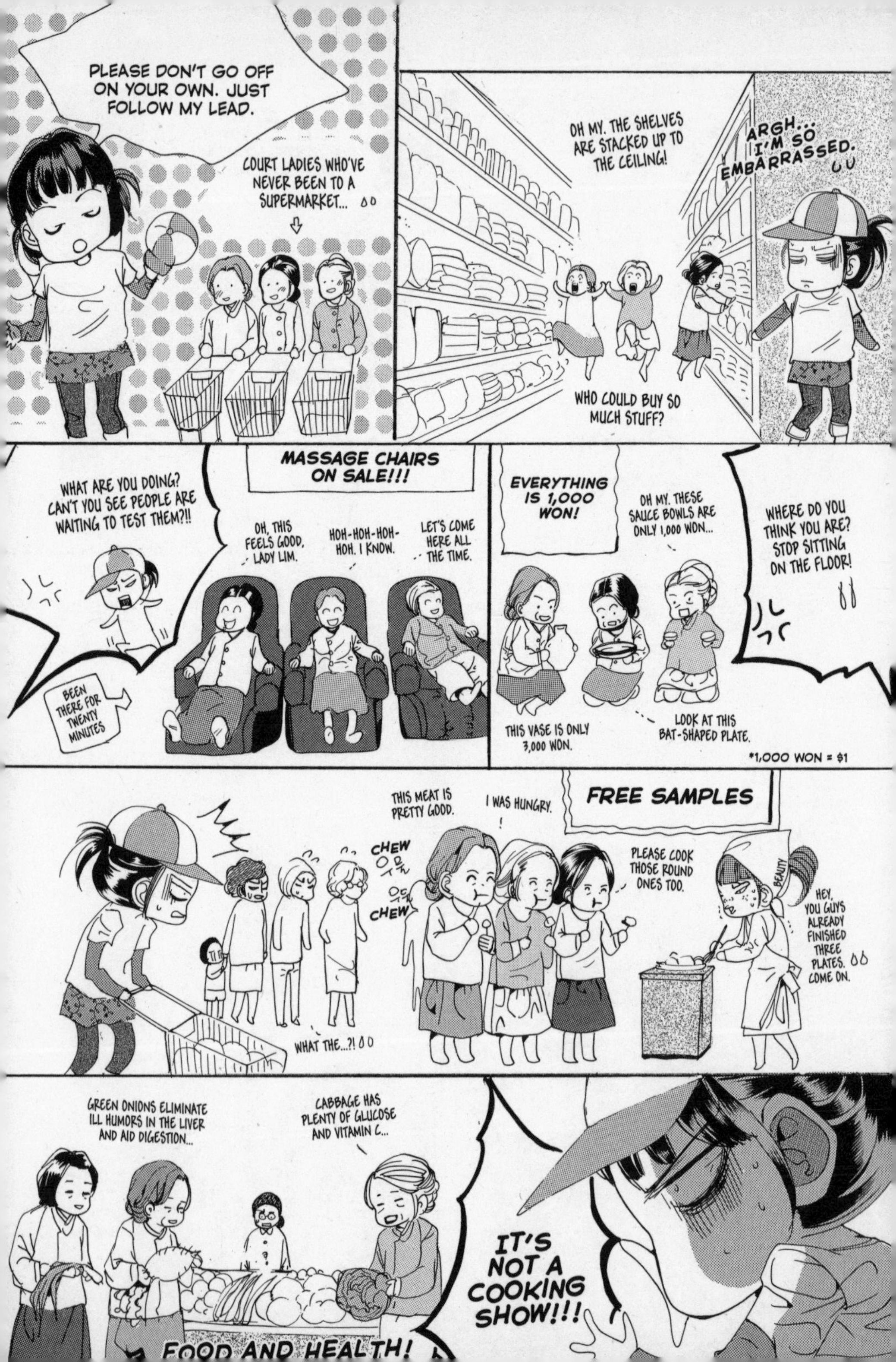
PLEASE DON'T GO OFF ON YOUR OWN. JUST FOLLOW MY LEAD.
COURT LADIES WHO'VE NEVER BEEN TO A SUPERMARKET...
OH MY. THE SHELVES ARE STACKED UP TO THE CEILING!
ARGH... I'M SO EMBARRASSED.
WHO COULD BUY SO MUCH STUFF?
MASSAGE CHAIRS ON SALE!!!
WHAT ARE YOU DOING? CAN'T YOU SEE PEOPLE ARE WAITING TO TEST THEM?!!
OH, THIS FEELS GOOD, LADY LIM.
HOH-HOH-HOH-HOH. I KNOW.
LET'S COME HERE ALL THE TIME.
BEEN THERE FOR TWENTY MINUTES
EVERYTHING IS 1,000 WON!
OH MY. THESE SAUCE BOWLS ARE ONLY 1,000 WON...
WHERE DO YOU THINK YOU ARE? STOP SITTING ON THE FLOOR!
THIS VASE IS ONLY 3,000 WON.
LOOK AT THIS BAT-SHAPED PLATE.
*1,000 WON = $1
THIS MEAT IS PRETTY GOOD.
I WAS HUNGRY.
FREE SAMPLES
CHEW
CHEW
PLEASE COOK THOSE ROUND ONES TOO.
BEAUTY
HEY, YOU GUYS ALREADY FINISHED THREE PLATES. COME ON.
WHAT THE...?!
GREEN ONIONS ELIMINATE ILL HUMORS IN THE LIVER AND AID DIGESTION...
CABBAGE HAS PLENTY OF GLUCOSE AND VITAMIN C...
IT'S NOT A COOKING SHOW!!!
FOOD AND HEALTH!

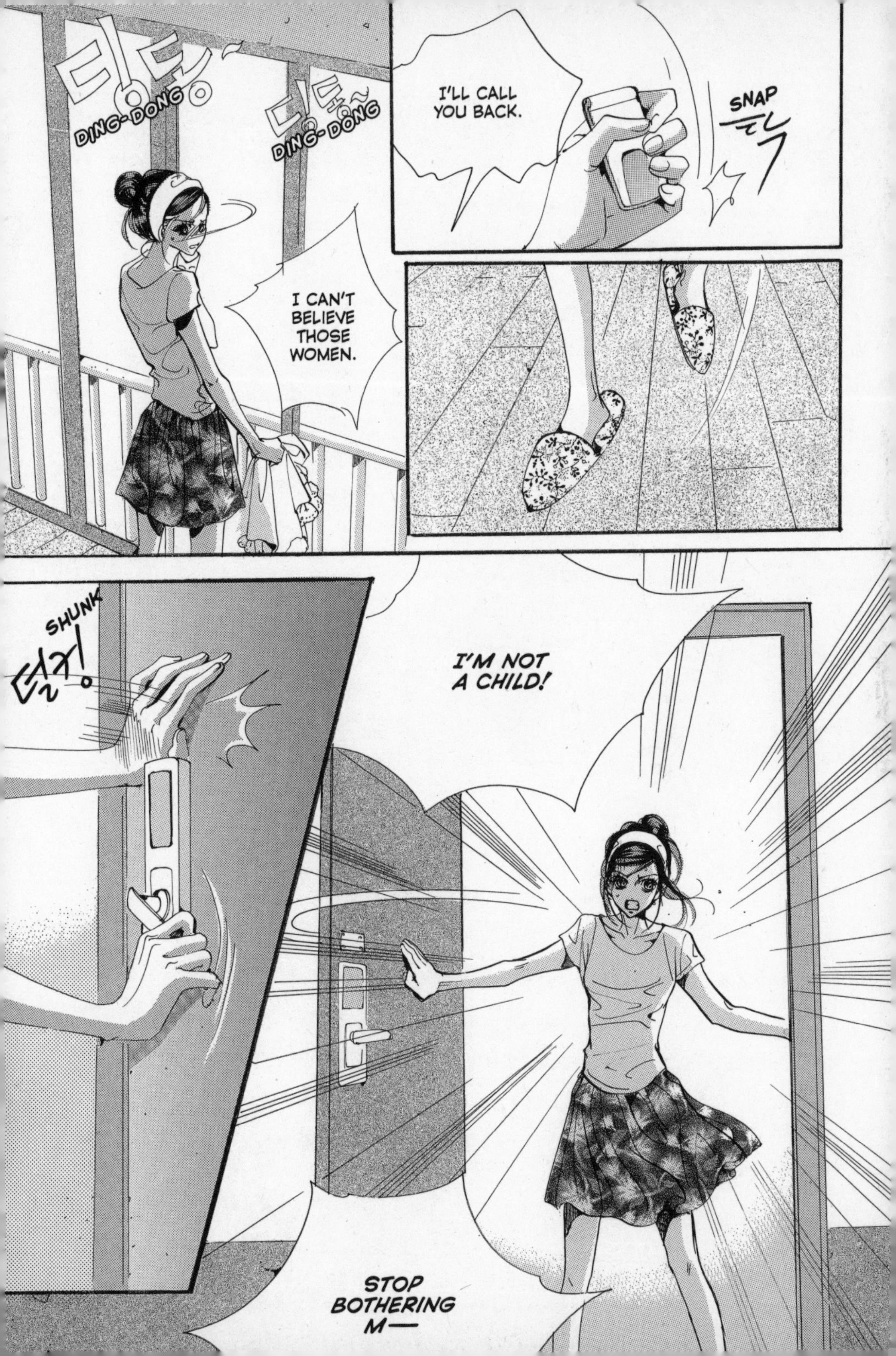
DING-DONG
DING-DONG
I CAN'T BELIEVE THOSE WOMEN.
I'LL CALL YOU BACK.
SNAP
SHUNK
I'M NOT A CHILD!
STOP BOTHERING M—

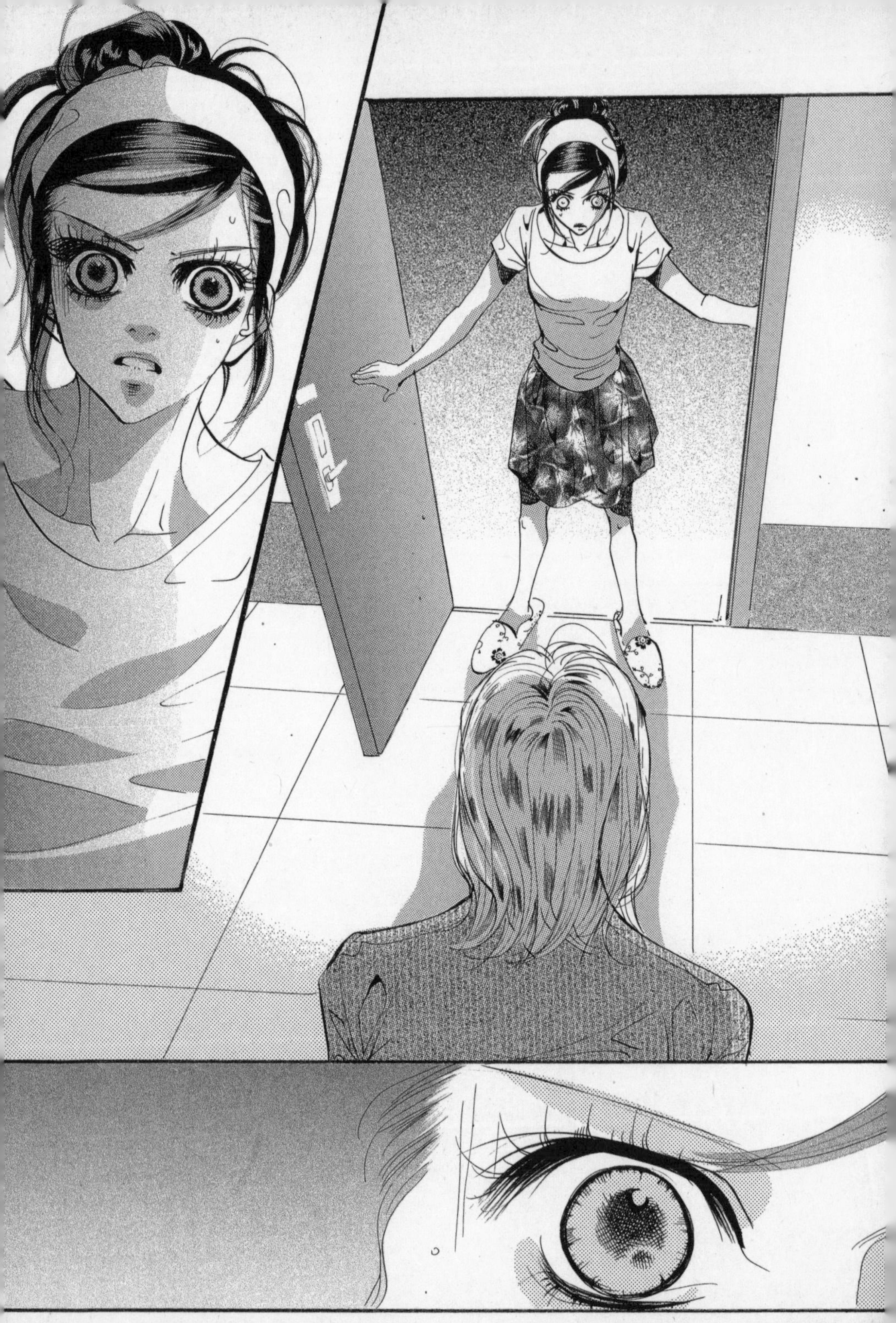

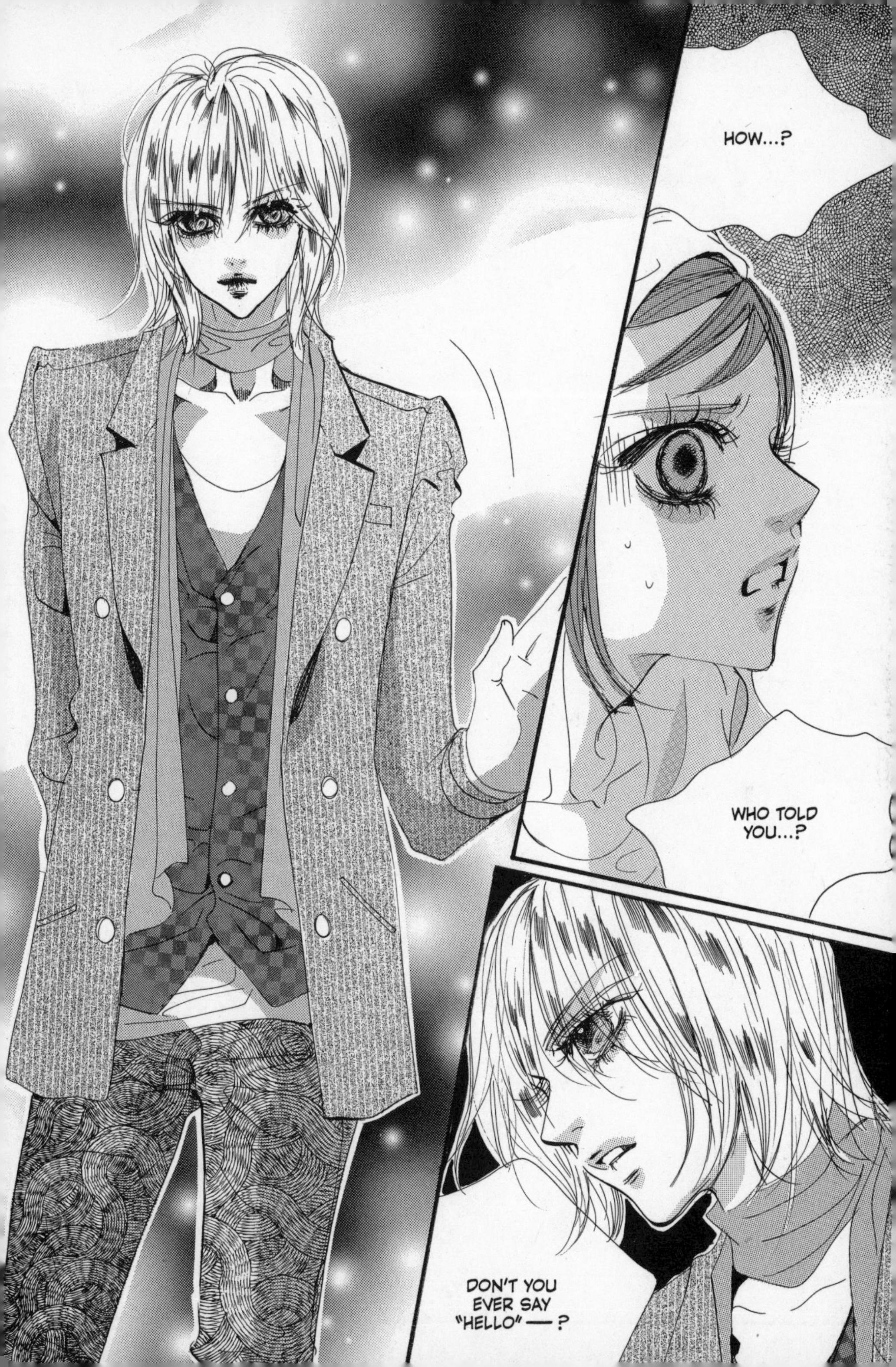
HOW...?
WHO TOLD YOU...?
DON'T YOU EVER SAY "HELLO"—?

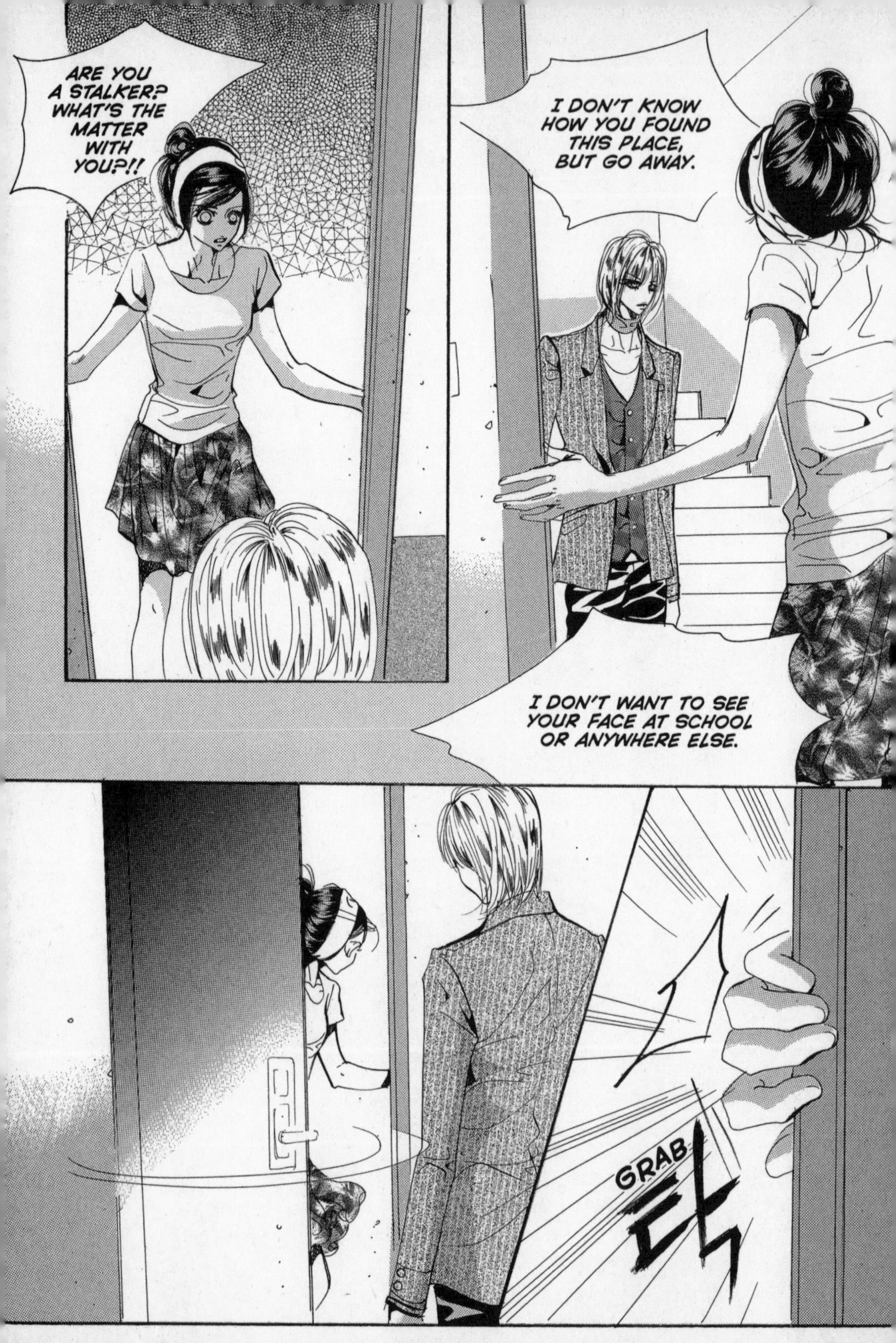
ARE YOU A STALKER? WHAT'S THE MATTER WITH YOU?!!
I DON'T KNOW HOW YOU FOUND THIS PLACE, BUT GO AWAY.
I DON'T WANT TO SEE YOUR FACE AT SCHOOL OR ANYWHERE ELSE.
GRAB

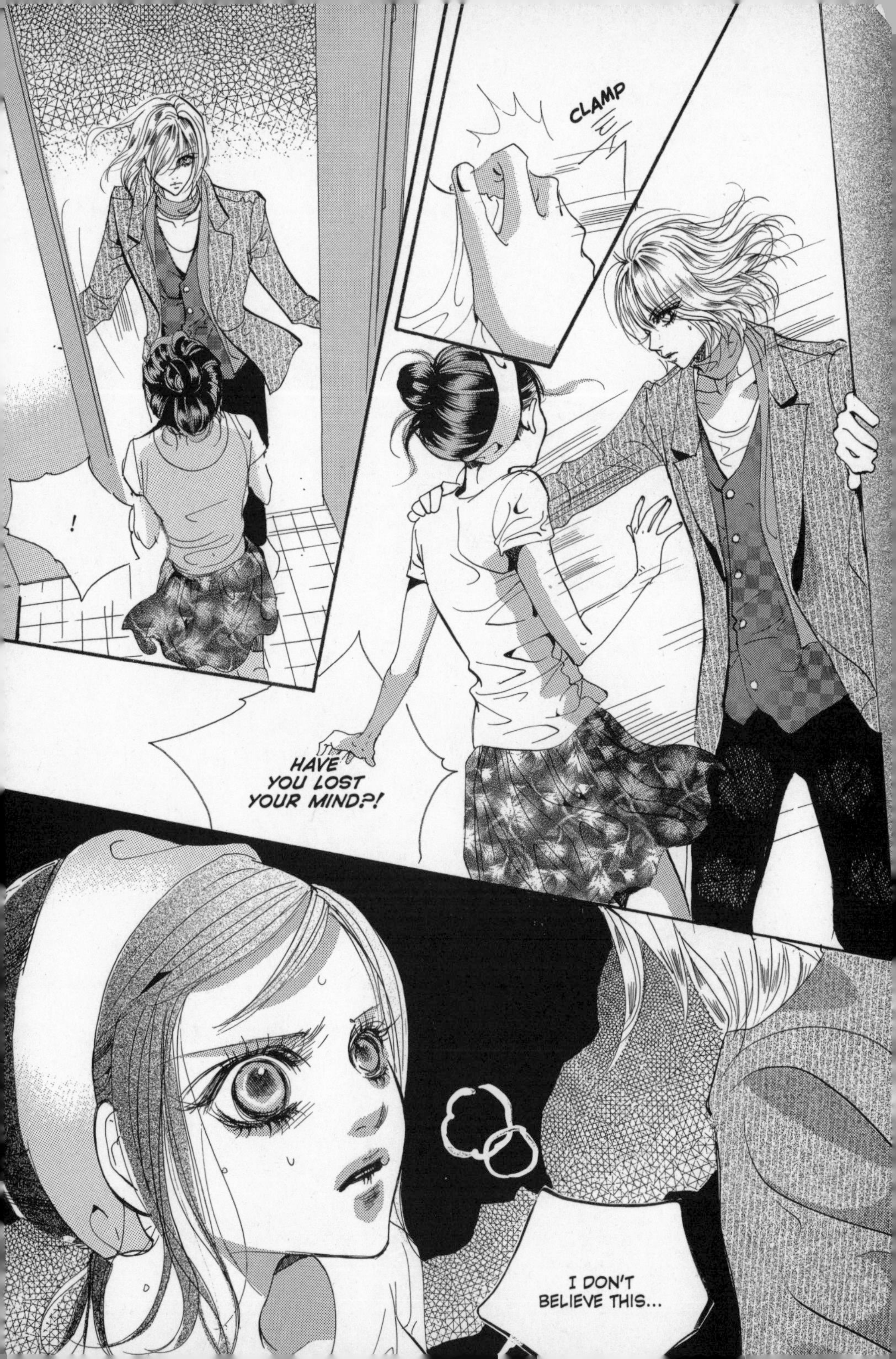
!
CLAMP
HAVE YOU LOST YOUR MIND?!
I DON'T BELIEVE THIS...

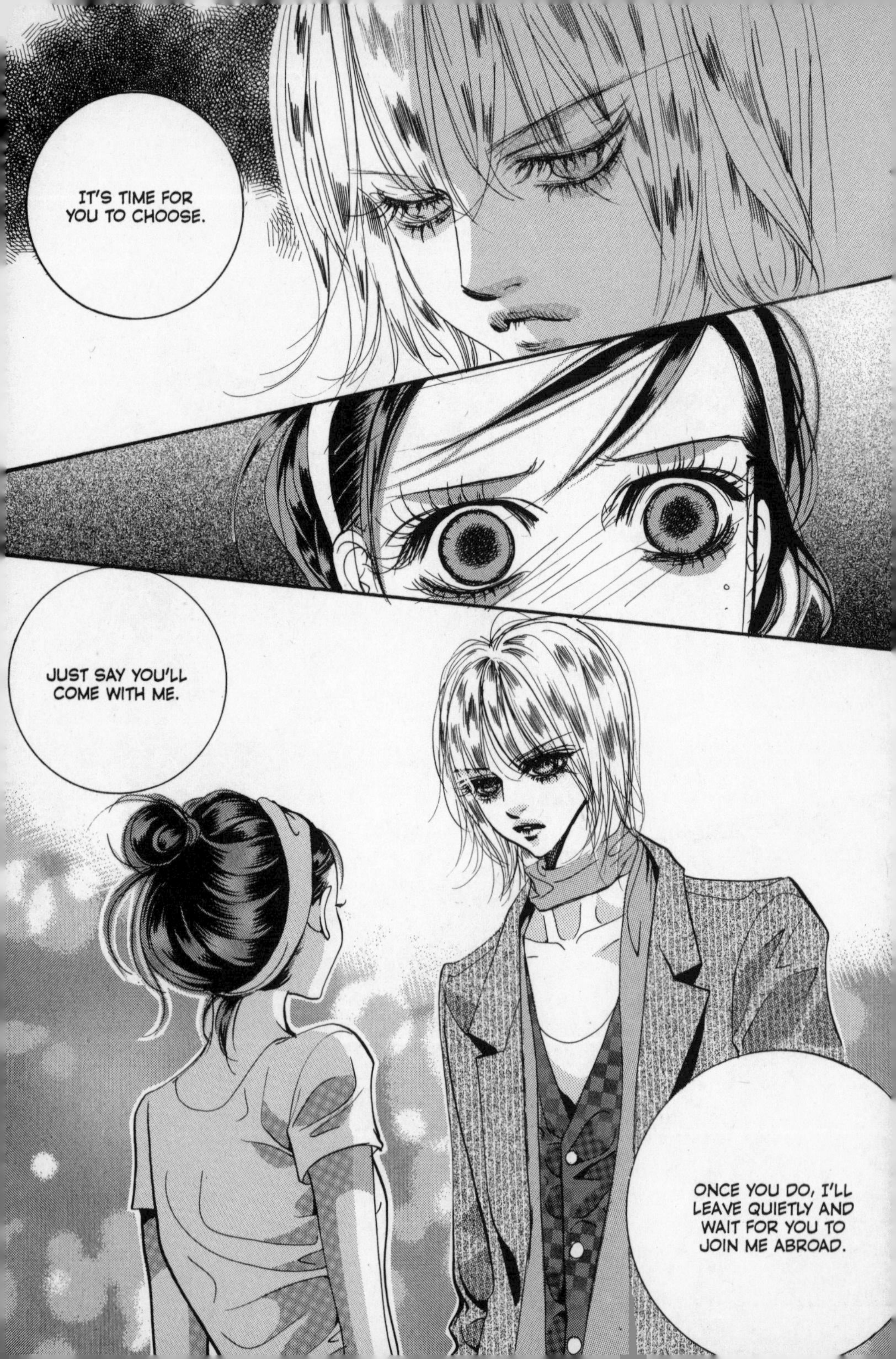
IT'S TIME FOR YOU TO CHOOSE.
JUST SAY YOU'LL COME WITH ME.
ONCE YOU DO, I'LL LEAVE QUIETLY AND WAIT FOR YOU TO JOIN ME ABROAD.

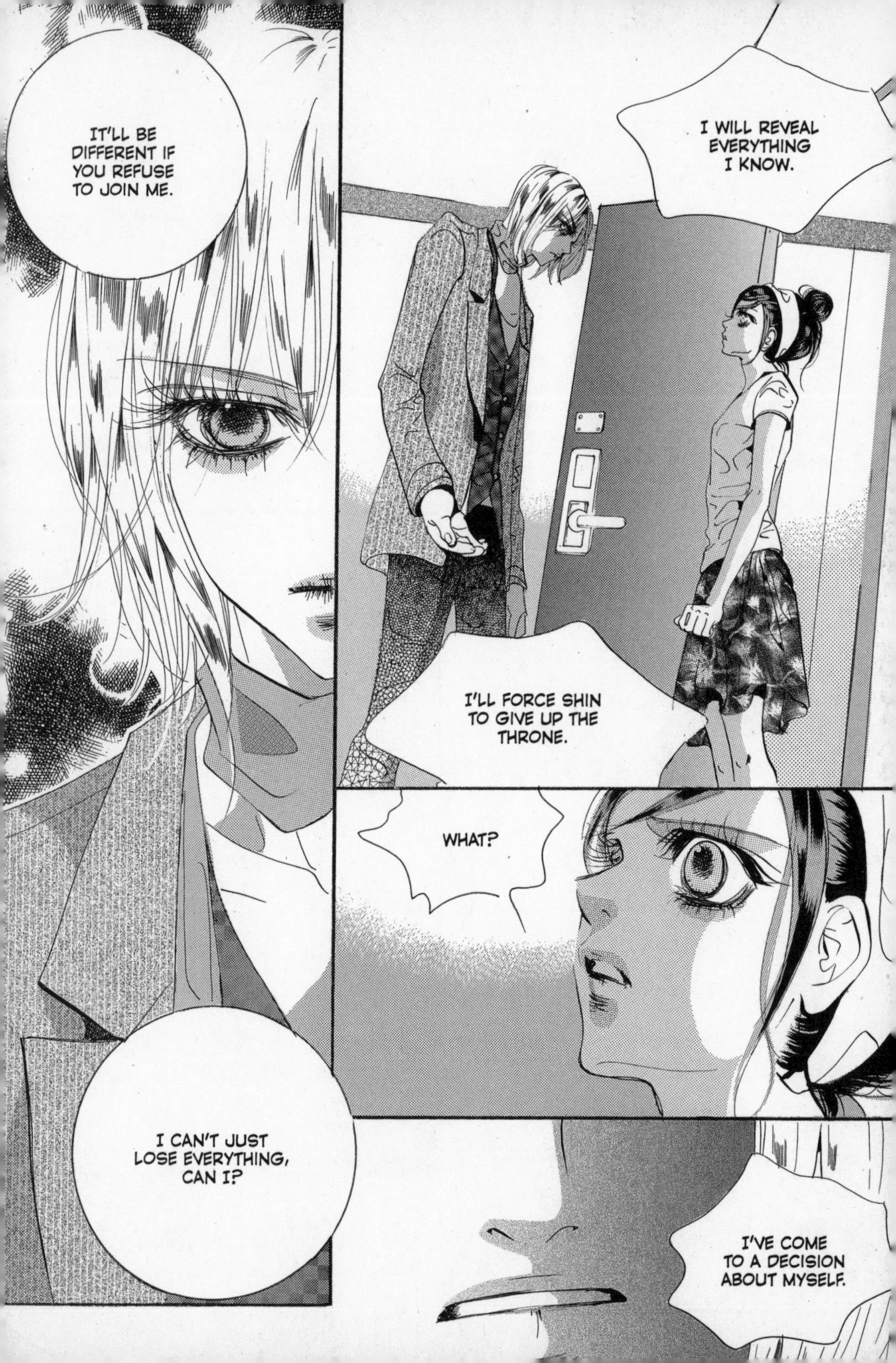
IT'LL BE DIFFERENT IF YOU REFUSE TO JOIN ME.
I CAN'T JUST LOSE EVERYTHING, CAN I?
I WILL REVEAL EVERYTHING I KNOW.
I'LL FORCE SHIN TO GIVE UP THE THRONE.
WHAT?
I'VE COME TO A DECISION ABOUT MYSELF.

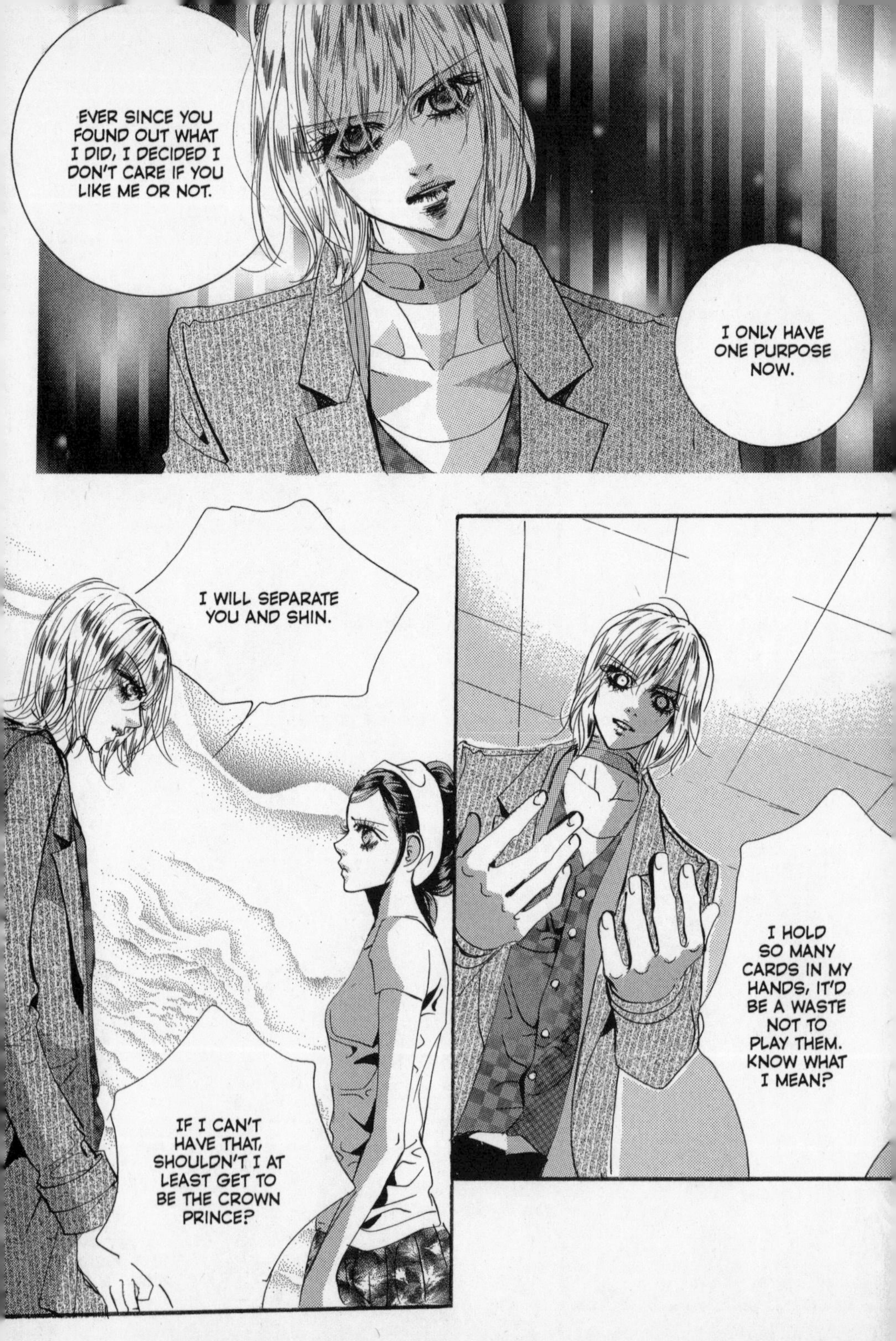
EVER SINCE YOU FOUND OUT WHAT I DID, I DECIDED I DON'T CARE IF YOU LIKE ME OR NOT.
I ONLY HAVE ONE PURPOSE NOW.
I WILL SEPARATE YOU AND SHIN.
IF I CAN'T HAVE THAT, SHOULDN'T I AT LEAST GET TO BE THE CROWN PRINCE?
I HOLD SO MANY CARDS IN MY HANDS, IT'D BE A WASTE NOT TO PLAY THEM. KNOW WHAT I MEAN?

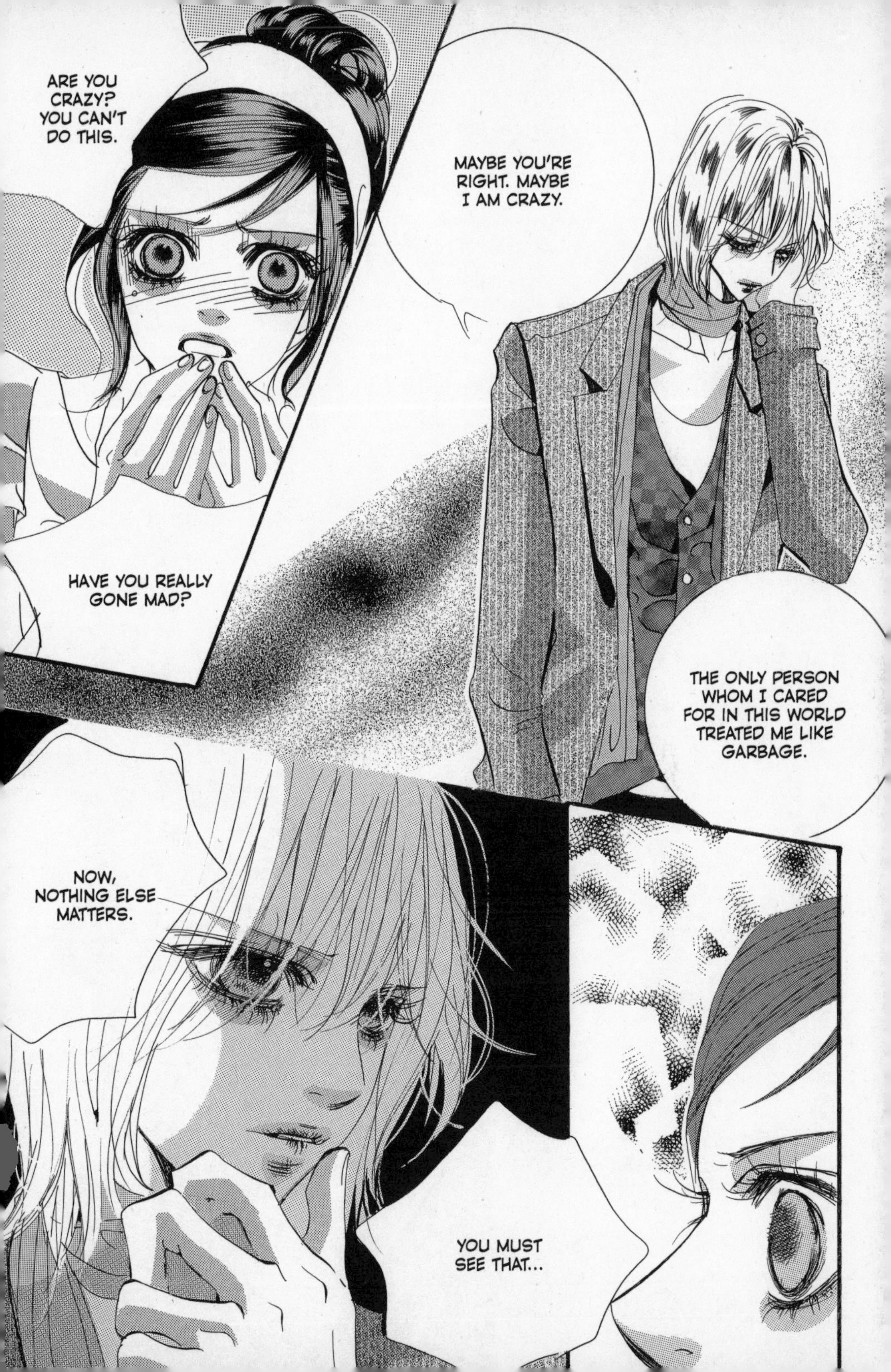
ARE YOU CRAZY? YOU CAN'T DO THIS.
HAVE YOU REALLY GONE MAD?
MAYBE YOU'RE RIGHT. MAYBE I AM CRAZY.
THE ONLY PERSON WHOM I CARED FOR IN THIS WORLD TREATED ME LIKE GARBAGE.
NOW, NOTHING ELSE MATTERS.
YOU MUST SEE THAT...

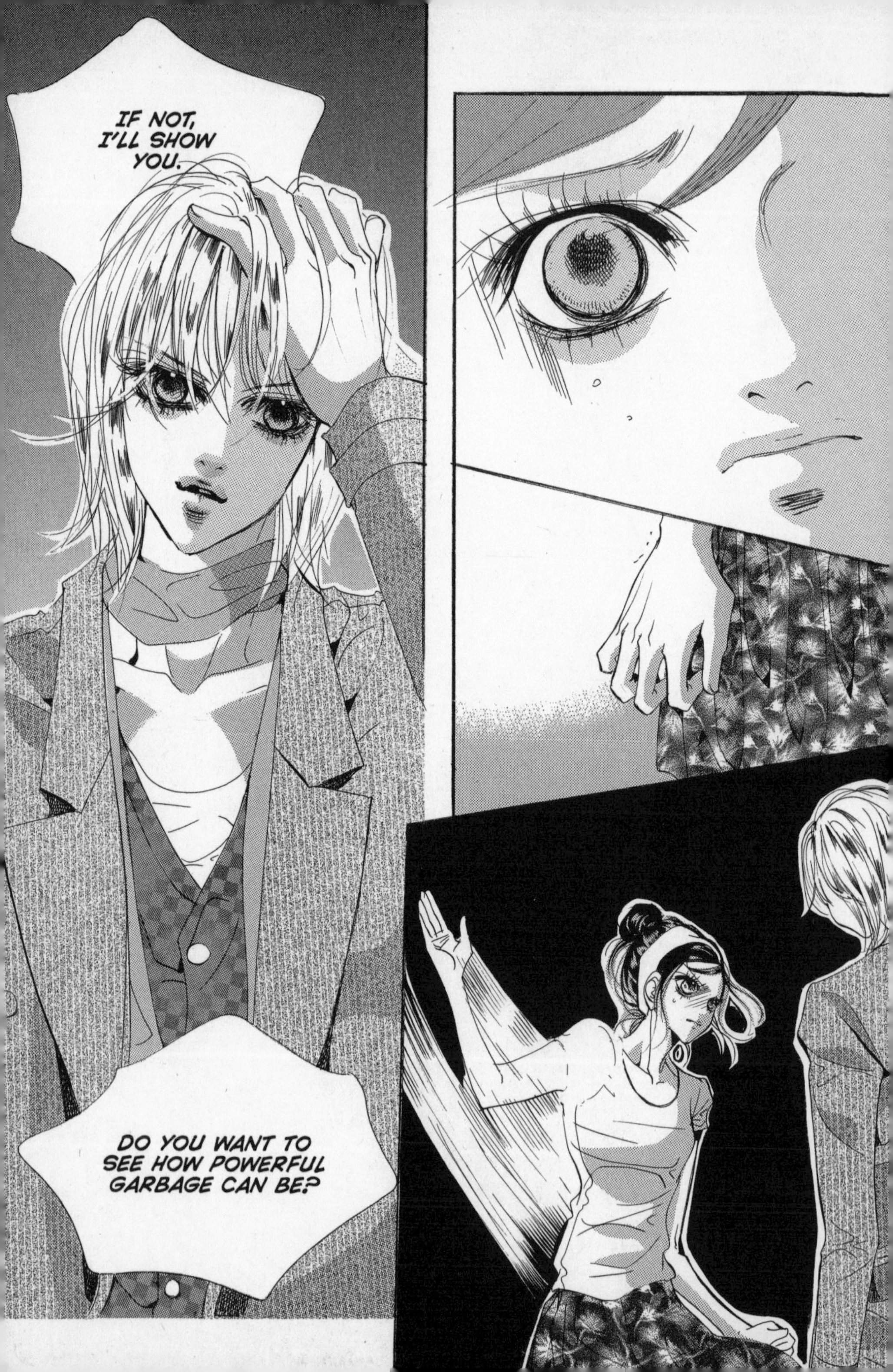
IF NOT, I'LL SHOW YOU.
DO YOU WANT TO SEE HOW POWERFUL GARBAGE CAN BE?

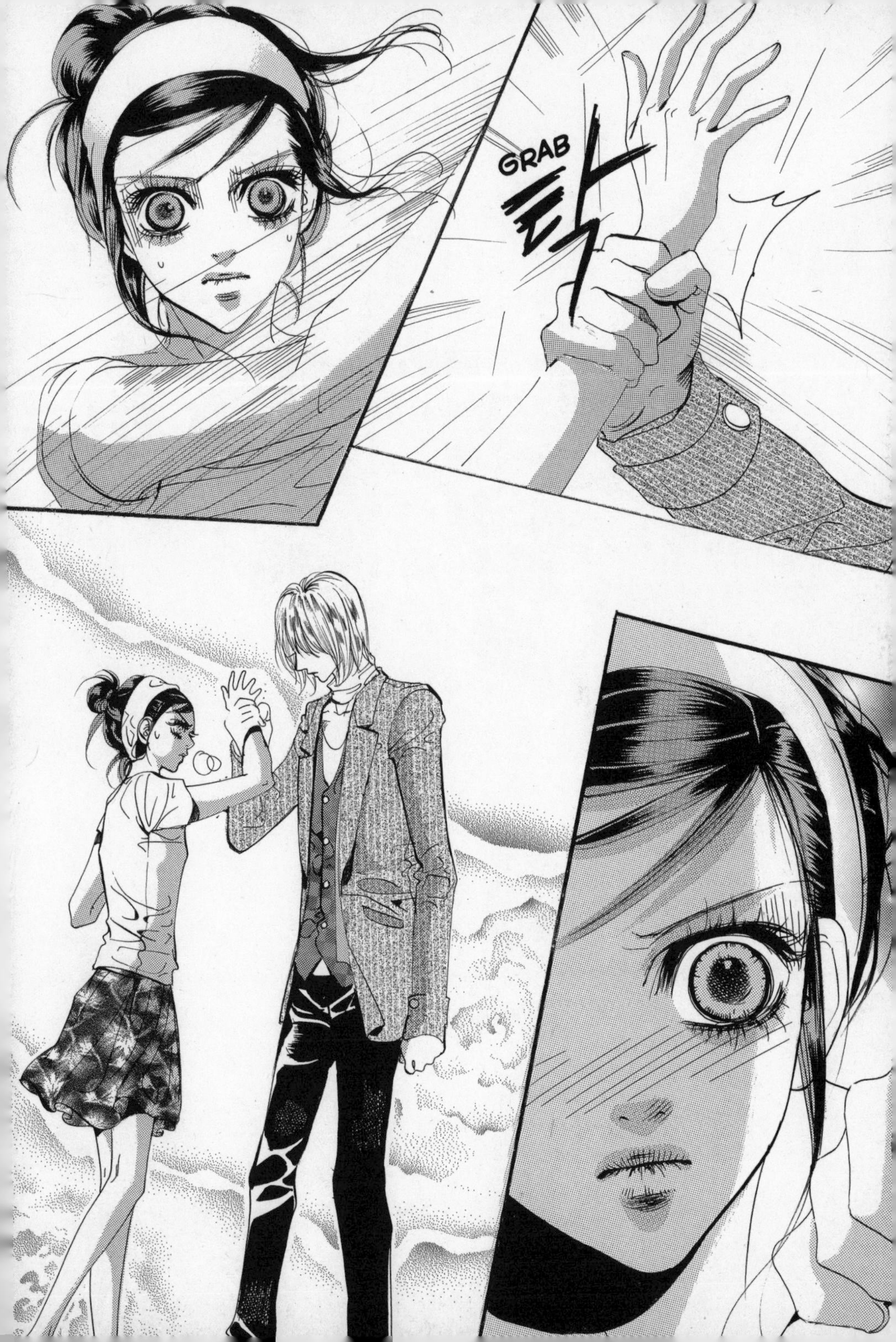
GRAB

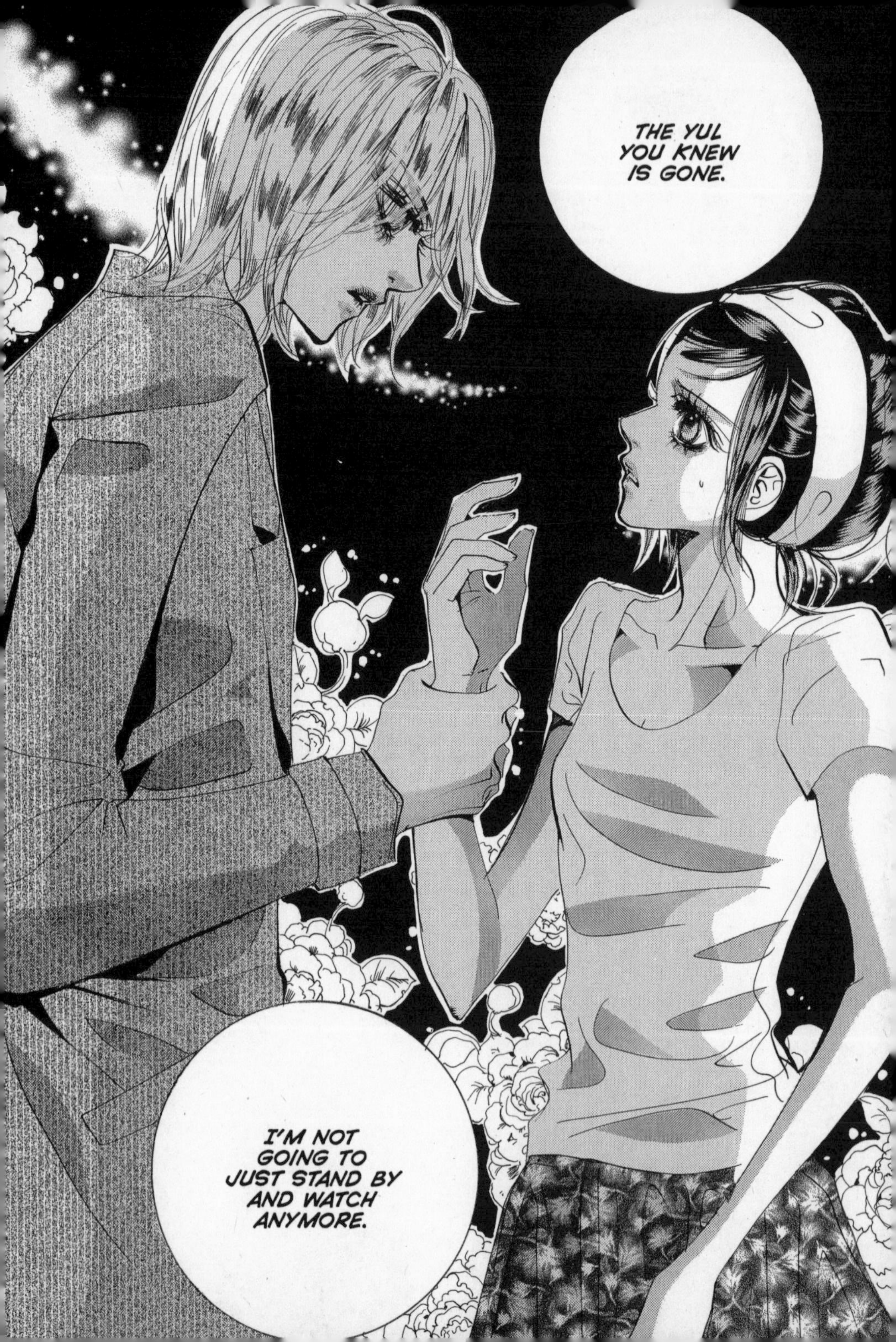
THE YUL YOU KNEW IS GONE.
I'M NOT GOING TO JUST STAND BY AND WATCH ANYMORE.

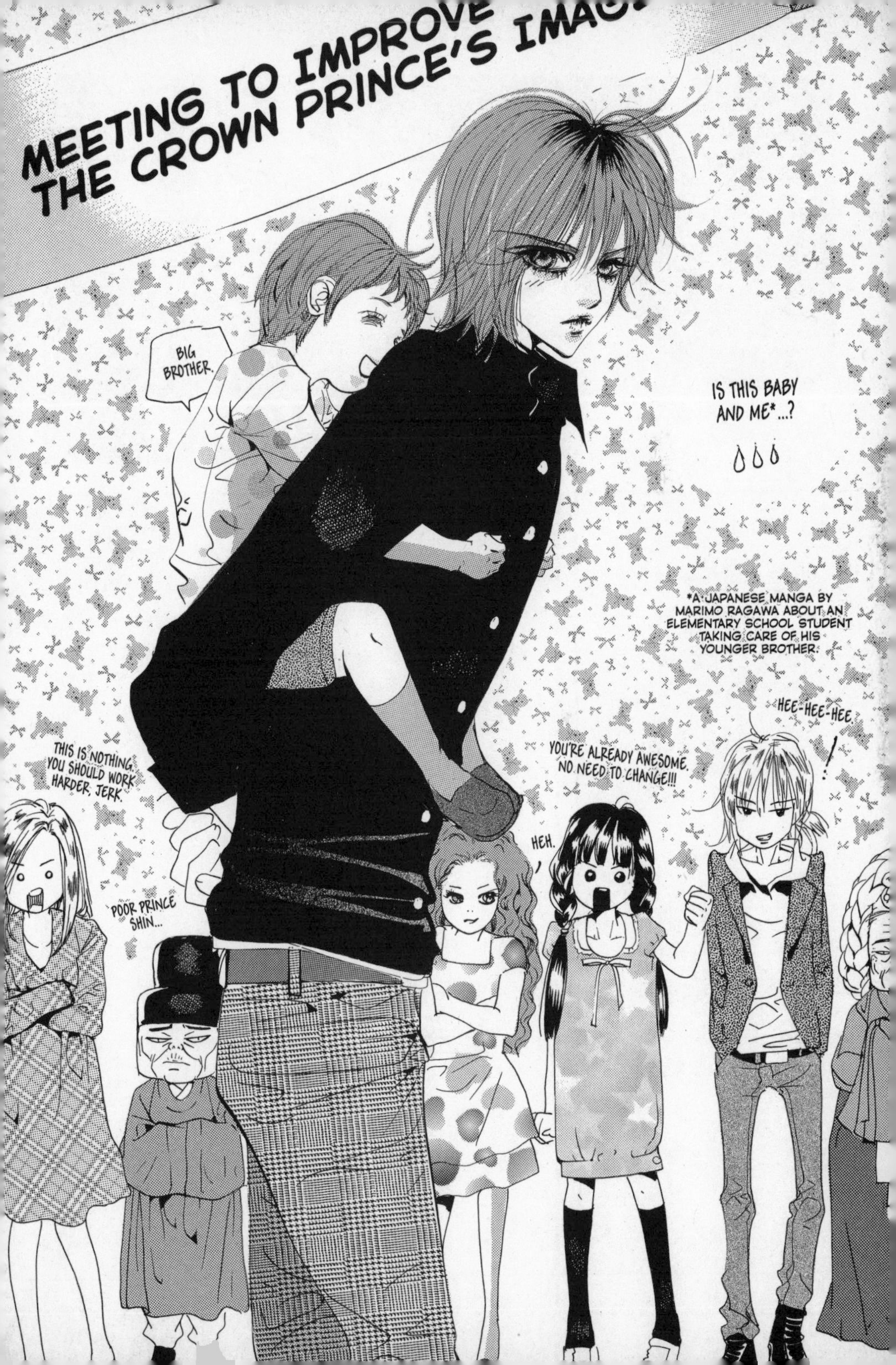

MEETING TO IMPROVE THE CROWN PRINCE'S IMA
BIG BROTHER.
IS THIS BABY AND ME*...?
*A JAPANESE MANGA BY MARIMO RAGAWA ABOUT AN ELEMENTARY SCHOOL STUDENT TAKING CARE OF HIS YOUNGER BROTHER.
THIS IS NOTHING. YOU SHOULD WORK HARDER, JERK.
POOR PRINCE SHIN...
HEH.
YOU'RE ALREADY AWESOME. NO NEED TO CHANGE!!!
HEE-HEE-HEE.

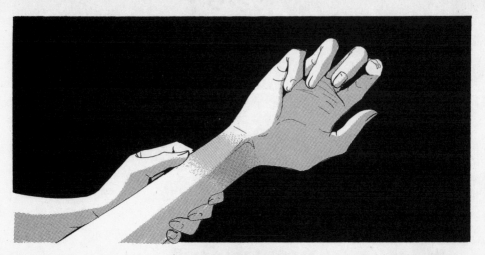

IT WOULDN'T BE ENOUGH FOR YUL TO BEG ON HIS KNEES FOR FORGIVENESS IN FRONT OF EVERYONE...

...BUT NOW HE'S ACTUALLY THREATENING ME —?!

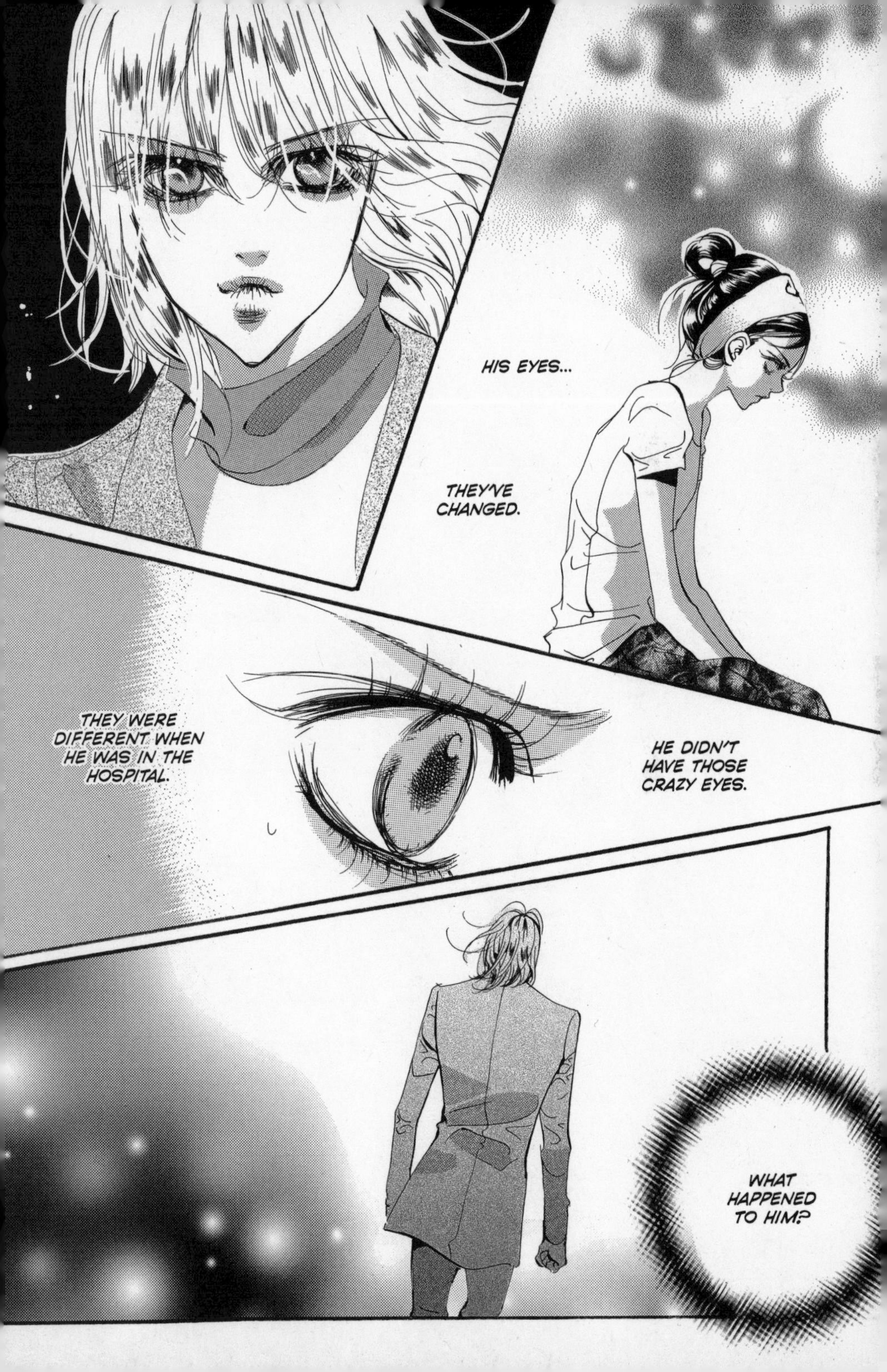
HIS EYES...
THEY'VE CHANGED.
THEY WERE DIFFERENT WHEN HE WAS IN THE HOSPITAL.
HE DIDN'T HAVE THOSE CRAZY EYES.
WHAT HAPPENED TO HIM?

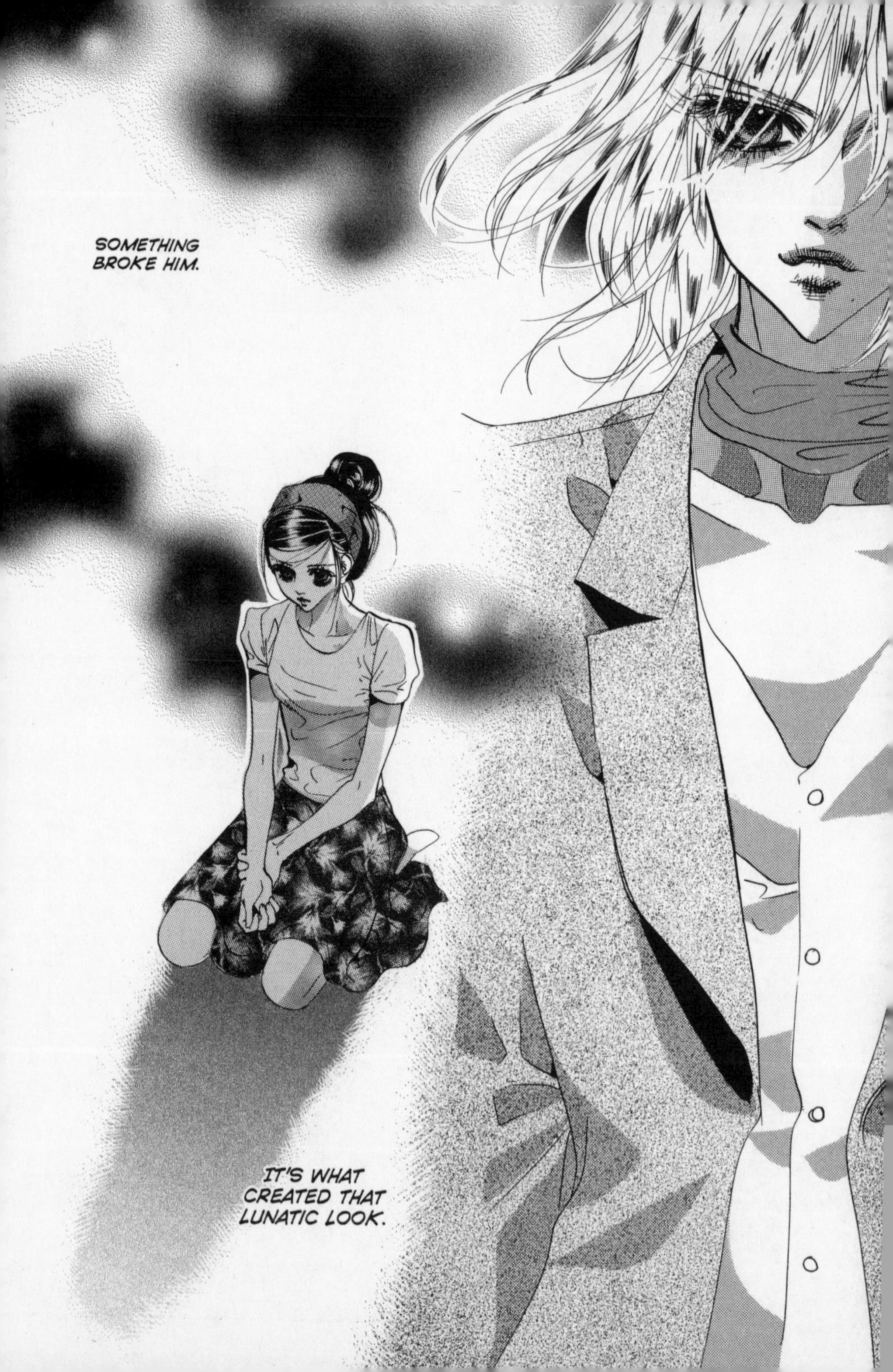
SOMETHING BROKE HIM.
IT'S WHAT CREATED THAT LUNATIC LOOK.

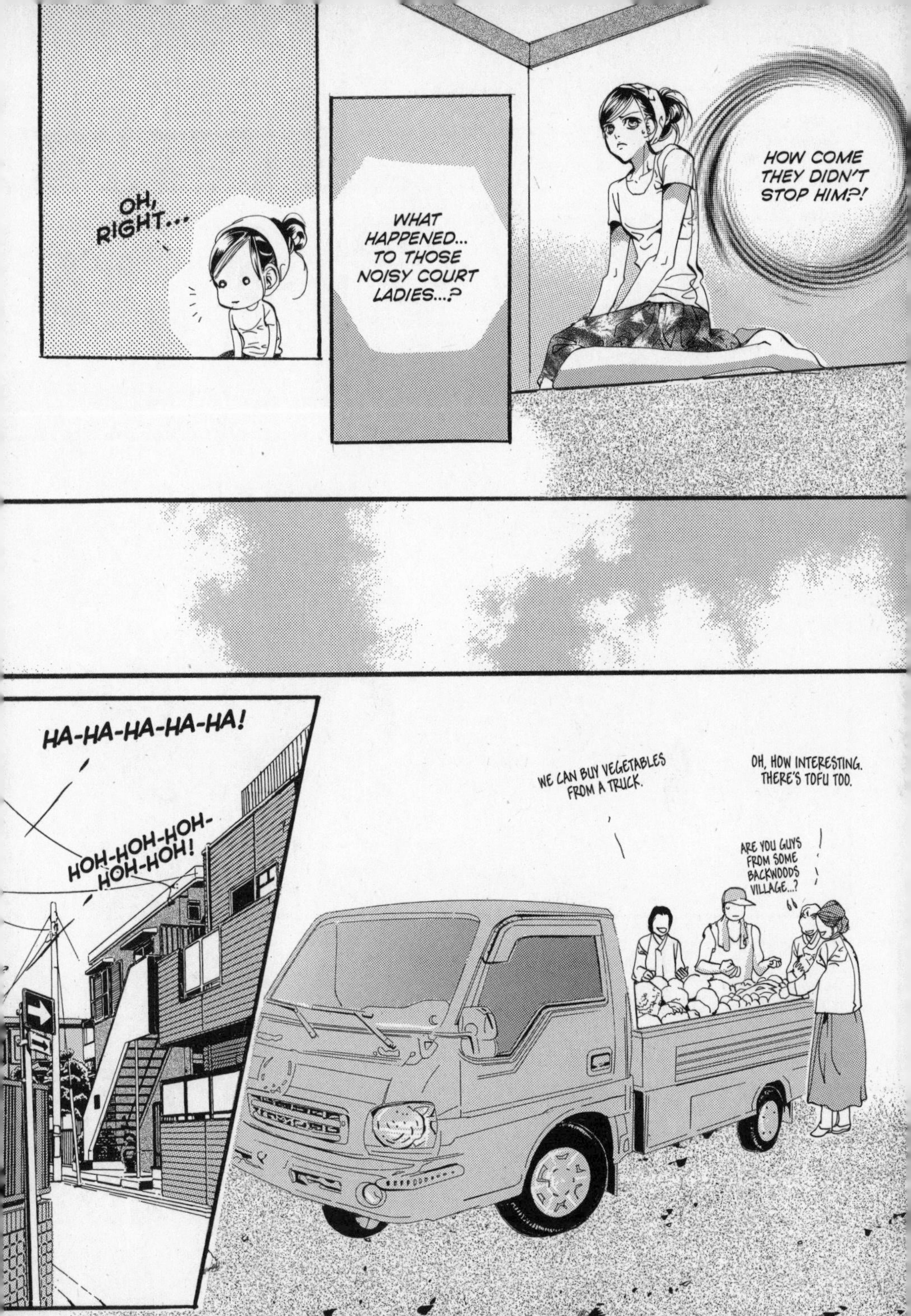

OH, RIGHT...
WHAT HAPPENED... TO THOSE NOISY COURT LADIES...?
HOW COME THEY DIDN'T STOP HIM?!
HA-HA-HA-HA-HA!
HOH-HOH-HOH-HOH-HOH!
WE CAN BUY VEGETABLES FROM A TRUCK.
OH, HOW INTERESTING. THERE'S TOFU TOO.
ARE YOU GUYS FROM SOME BACKWOODS VILLAGE...?

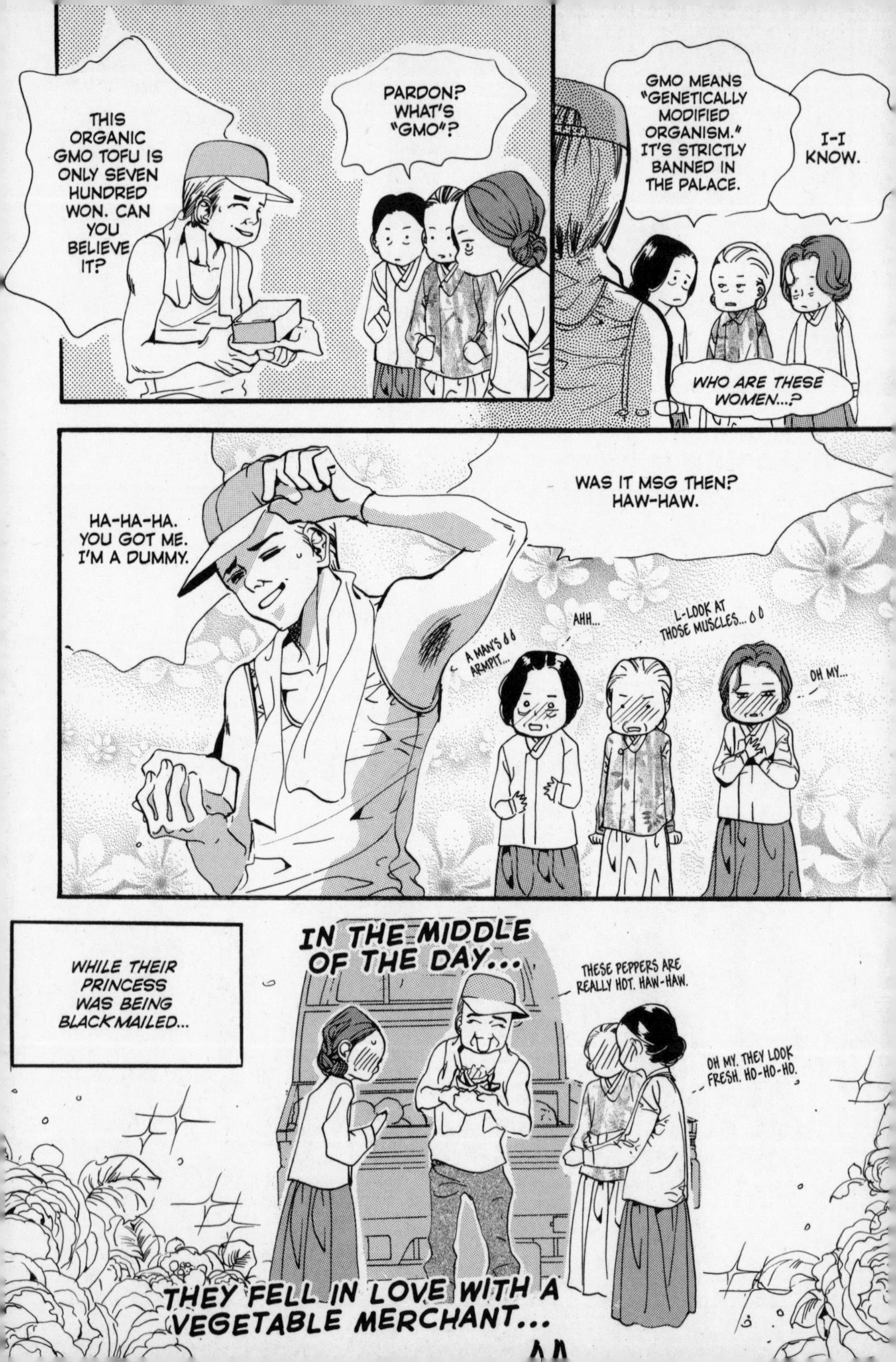
THIS ORGANIC GMO TOFU IS ONLY SEVEN HUNDRED WON. CAN YOU BELIEVE IT?
PARDON? WHAT'S "GMO"?
GMO MEANS "GENETICALLY MODIFIED ORGANISM." IT'S STRICTLY BANNED IN THE PALACE.
I-I KNOW.
WHO ARE THESE WOMEN...?
HA-HA-HA. YOU GOT ME. I'M A DUMMY.
WAS IT MSG THEN? HAW-HAW.
A MAN'S ARMPIT...
AHH...
L-LOOK AT THOSE MUSCLES...
OH MY...
WHILE THEIR PRINCESS WAS BEING BLACKMAILED...
IN THE MIDDLE OF THE DAY...
THESE PEPPERS ARE REALLY HOT. HAW-HAW.
OH MY. THEY LOOK FRESH. HO-HO-HO.
THEY FELL IN LOVE WITH A VEGETABLE MERCHANT...

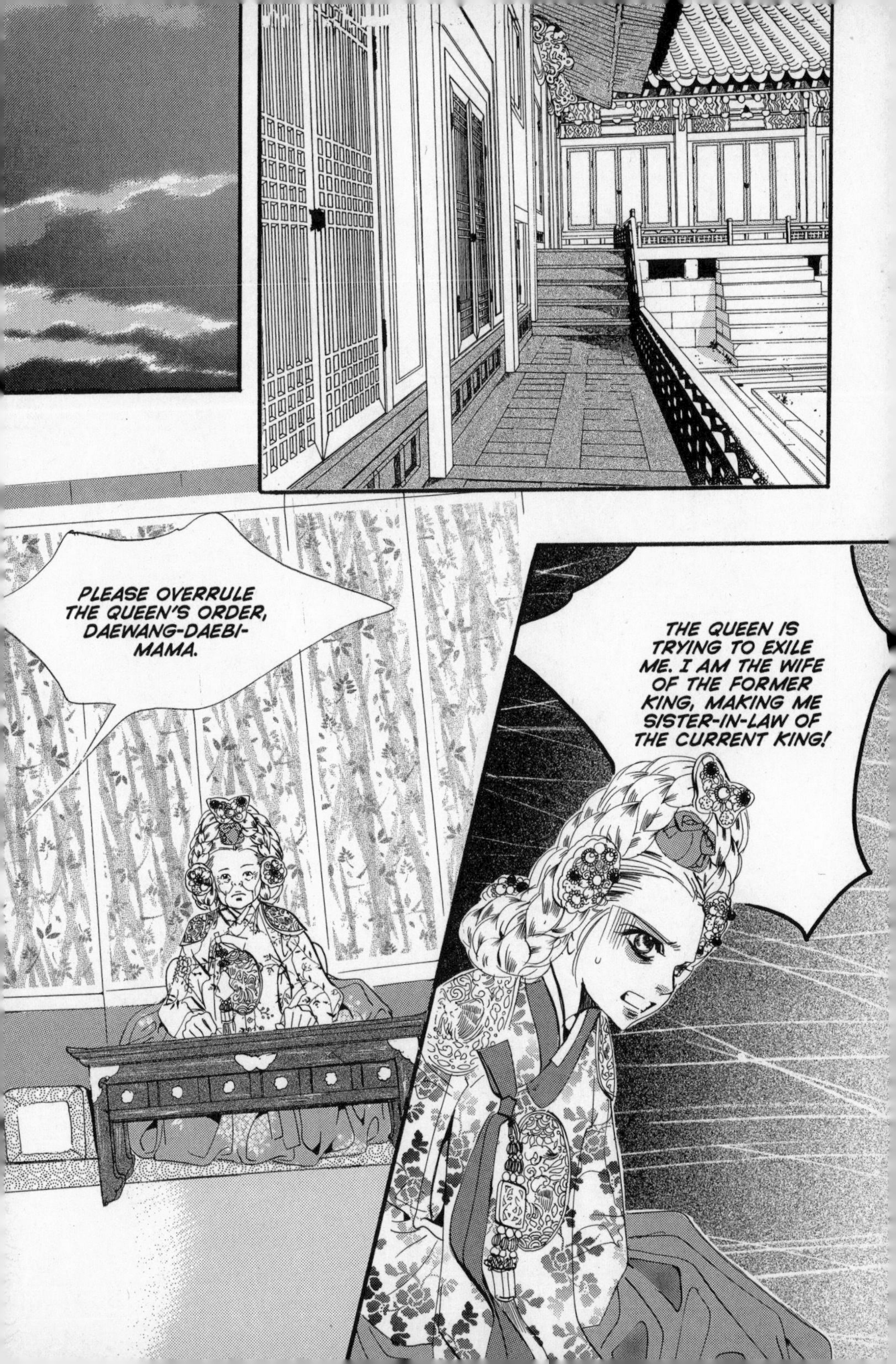
PLEASE OVERRULE THE QUEEN'S ORDER, DAEWANG-DAEBI-MAMA.
THE QUEEN IS TRYING TO EXILE ME. I AM THE WIFE OF THE FORMER KING, MAKING ME SISTER-IN-LAW OF THE CURRENT KING!

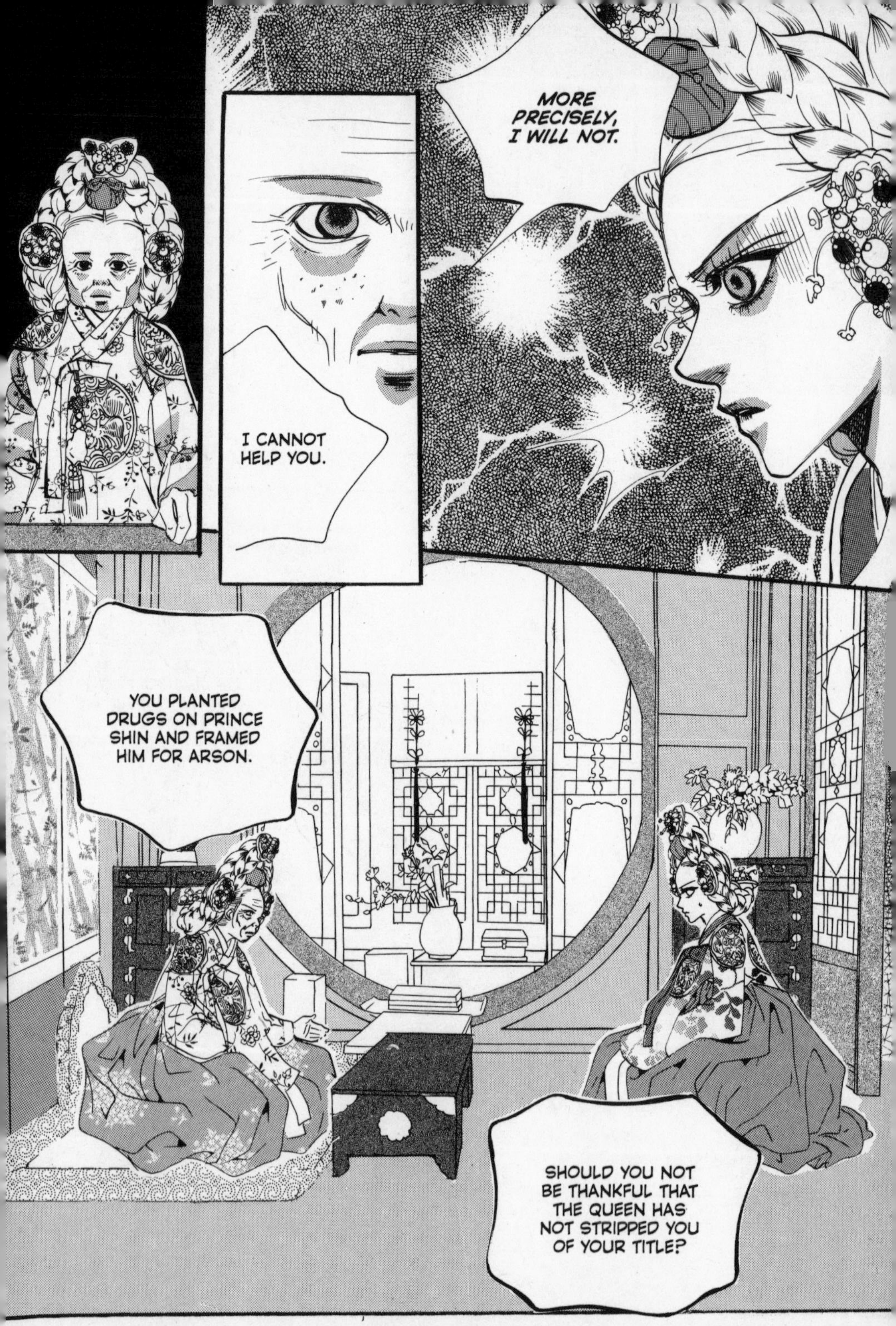
MORE PRECISELY, I WILL NOT.
I CANNOT HELP YOU.
YOU PLANTED DRUGS ON PRINCE SHIN AND FRAMED HIM FOR ARSON.
SHOULD YOU NOT BE THANKFUL THAT THE QUEEN HAS NOT STRIPPED YOU OF YOUR TITLE?

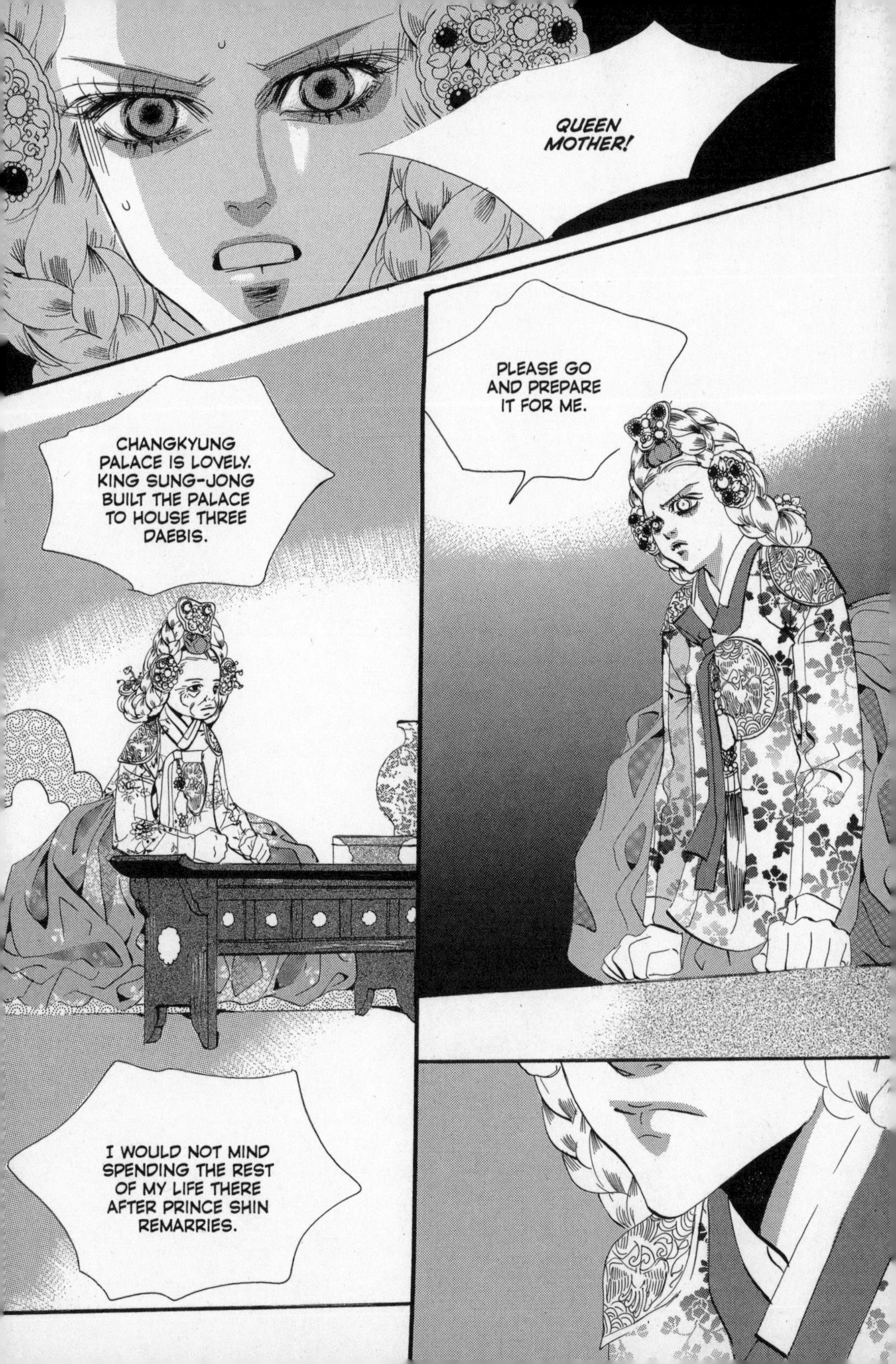
QUEEN MOTHER!
CHANGKYUNG PALACE IS LOVELY. KING SUNG-JONG BUILT THE PALACE TO HOUSE THREE DAEBIS.
I WOULD NOT MIND SPENDING THE REST OF MY LIFE THERE AFTER PRINCE SHIN REMARRIES.
PLEASE GO AND PREPARE IT FOR ME.

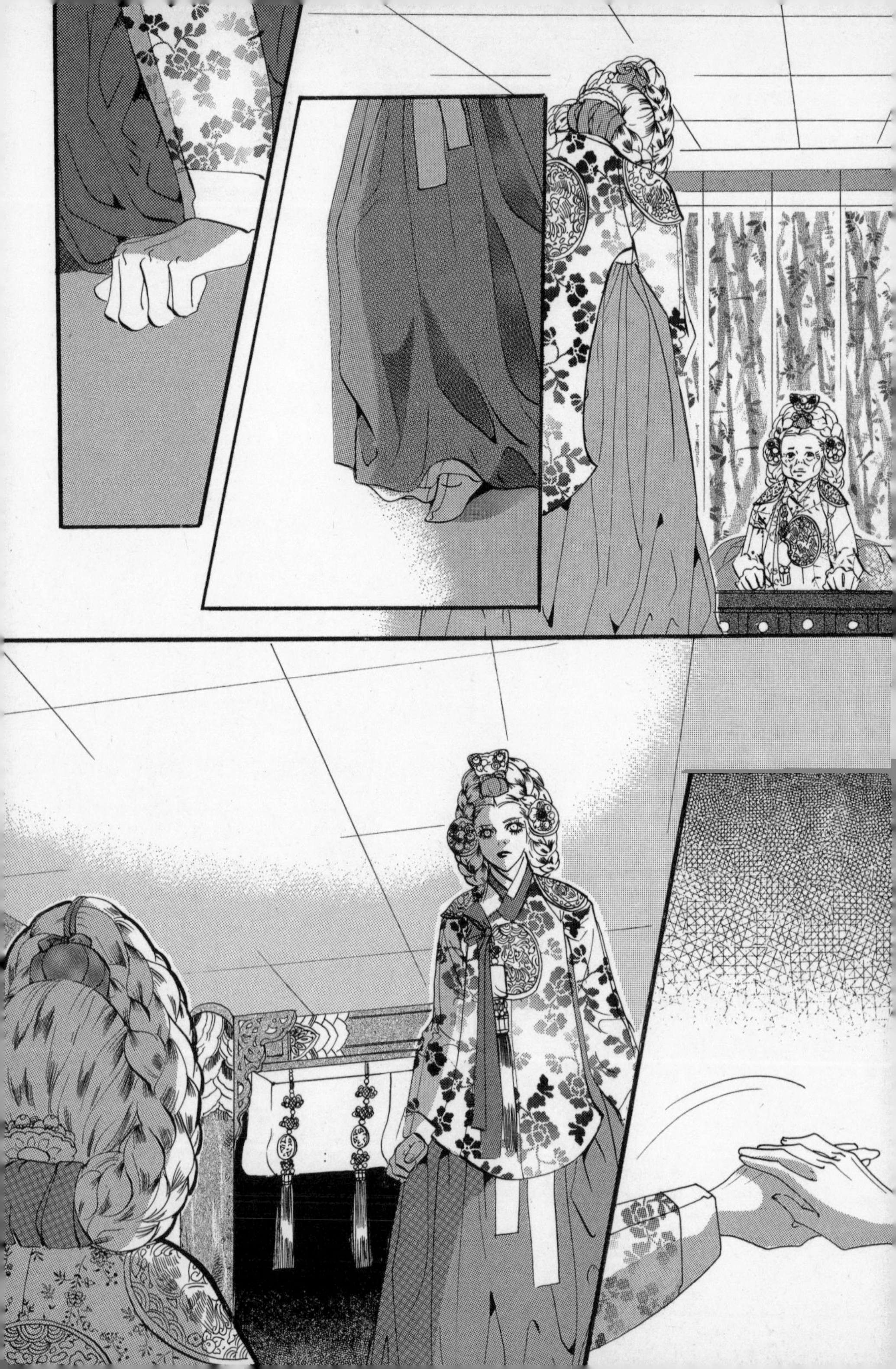

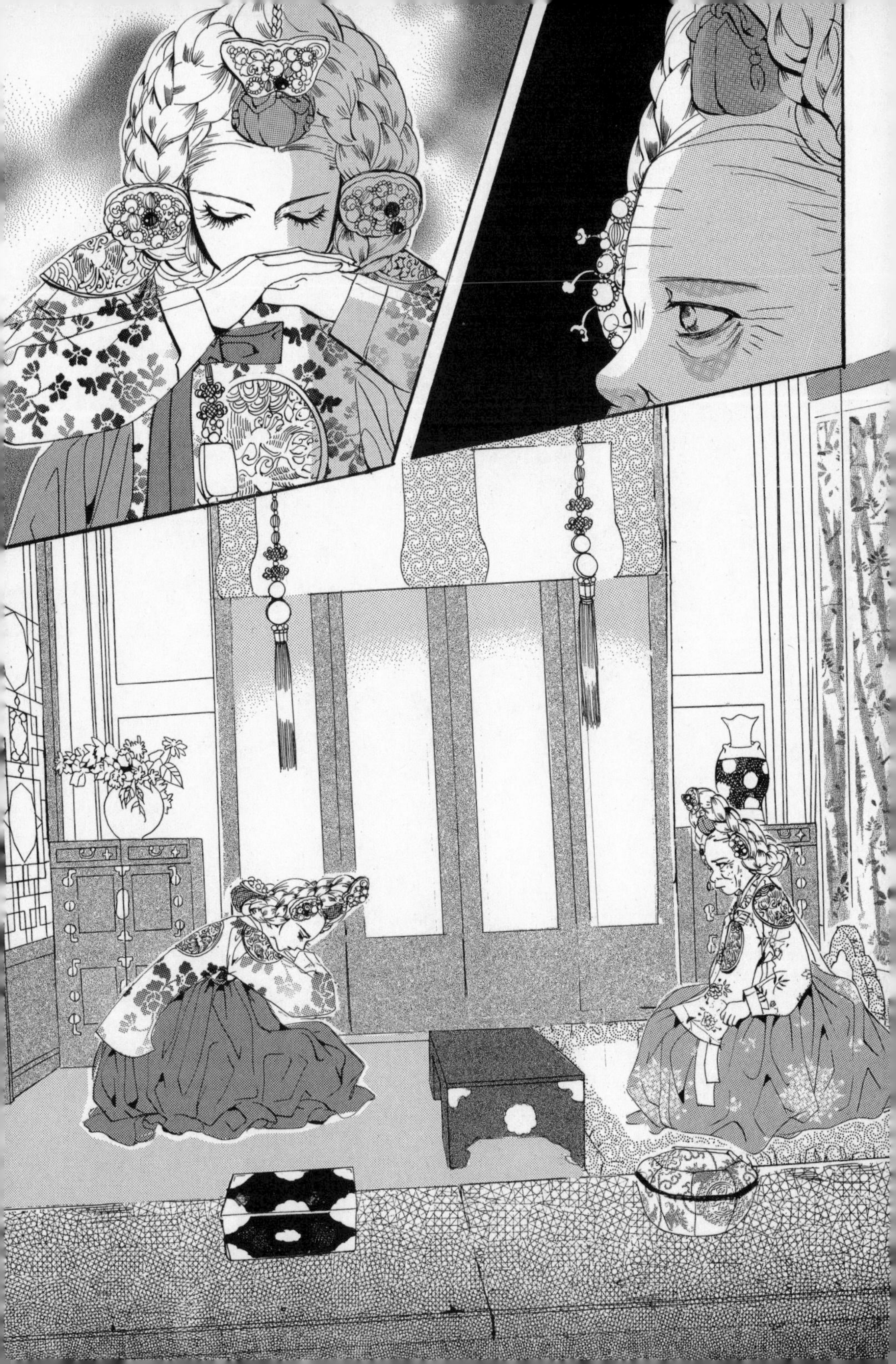

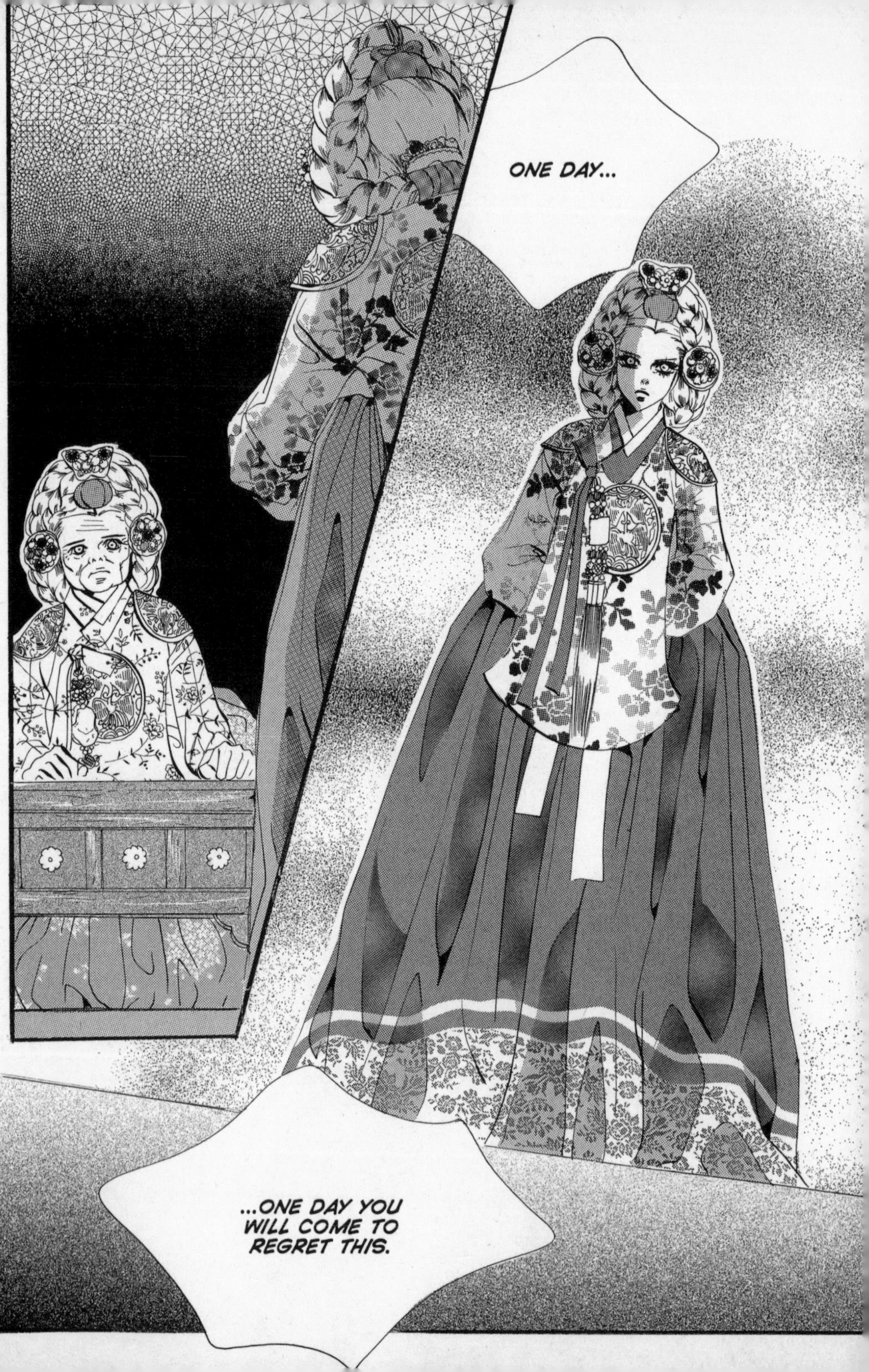
ONE DAY...
...ONE DAY YOU WILL COME TO REGRET THIS.

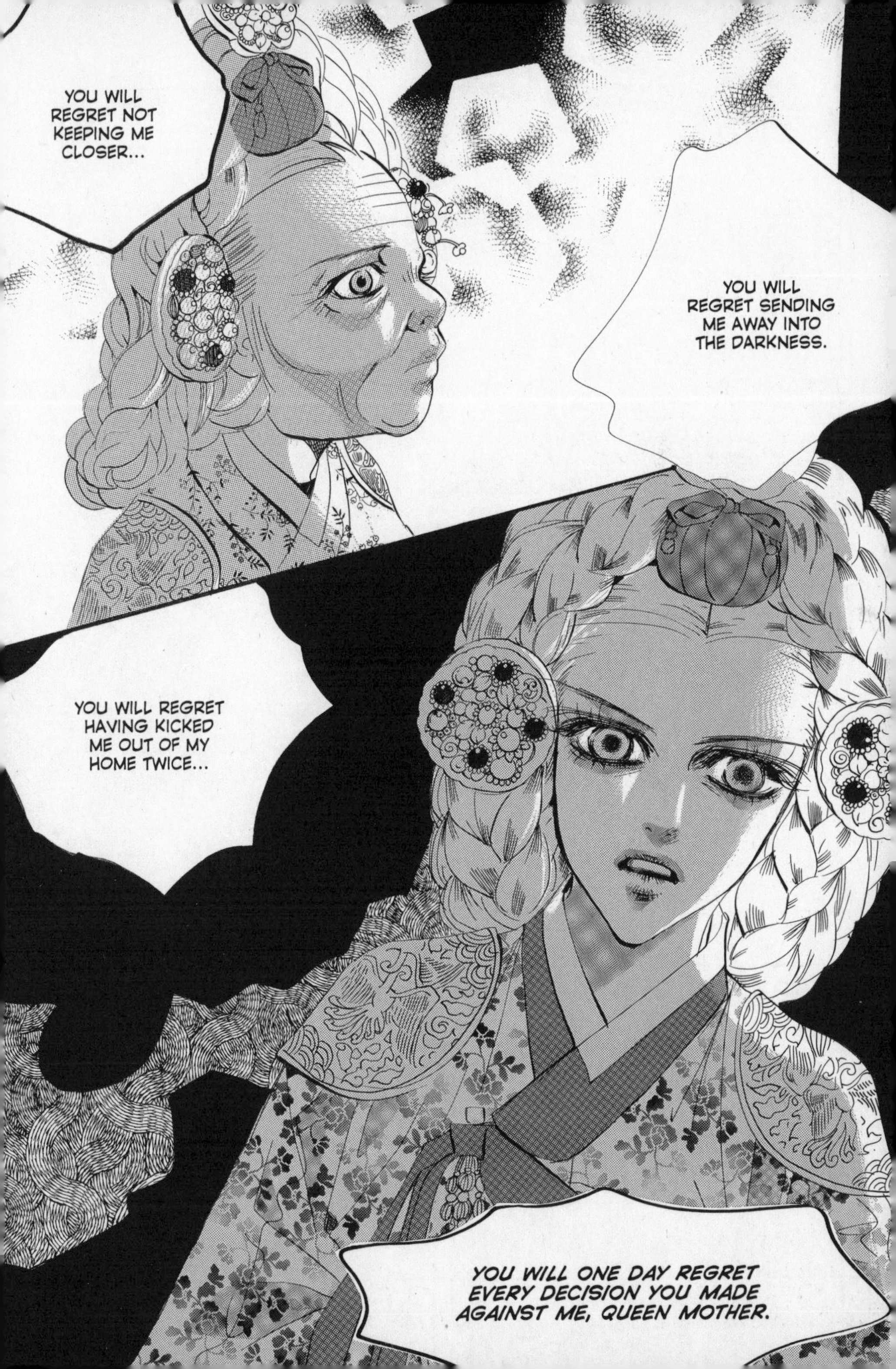
YOU WILL REGRET NOT KEEPING ME CLOSER...
YOU WILL REGRET SENDING ME AWAY INTO THE DARKNESS.
YOU WILL REGRET HAVING KICKED ME OUT OF MY HOME TWICE...
YOU WILL ONE DAY REGRET EVERY DECISION YOU MADE AGAINST ME, QUEEN MOTHER.

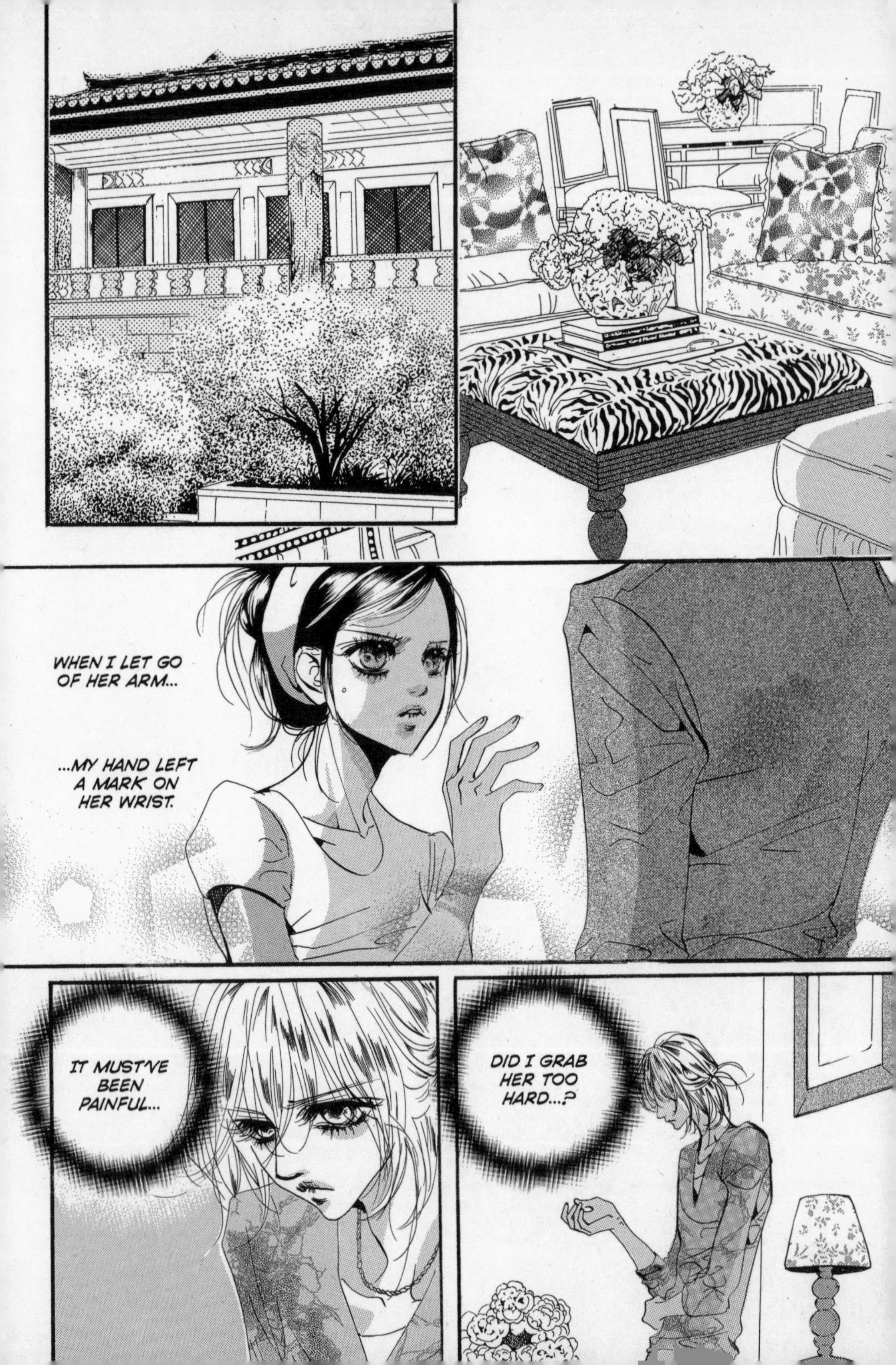
WHEN I LET GO OF HER ARM...
...MY HAND LEFT A MARK ON HER WRIST.
IT MUST'VE BEEN PAINFUL...
DID I GRAB HER TOO HARD...?

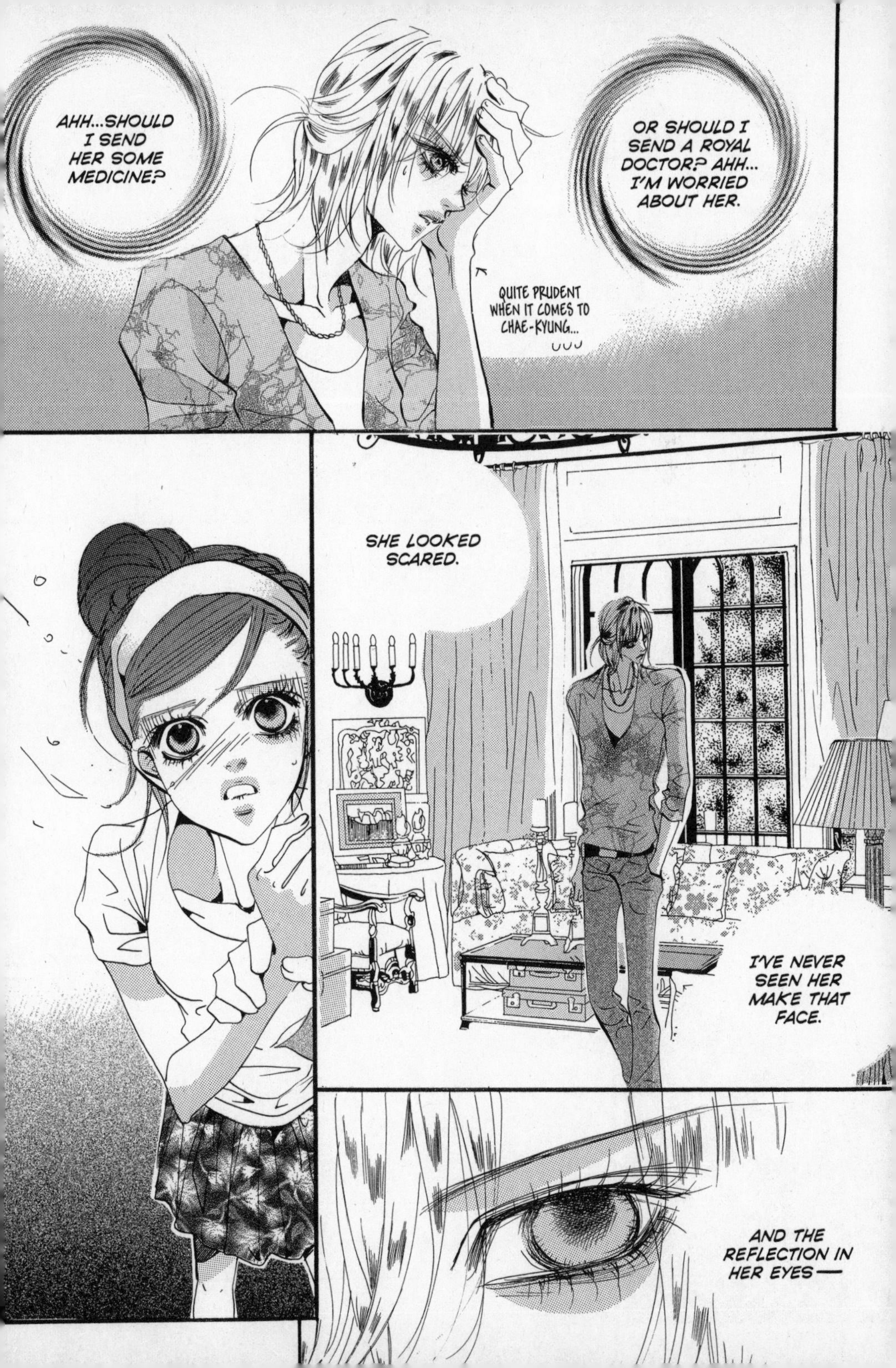
AHH...SHOULD I SEND HER SOME MEDICINE?
OR SHOULD I SEND A ROYAL DOCTOR? AHH... I'M WORRIED ABOUT HER.
QUITE PRUDENT WHEN IT COMES TO CHAE-KYUNG...
SHE LOOKED SCARED.
I'VE NEVER SEEN HER MAKE THAT FACE.
AND THE REFLECTION IN HER EYES—

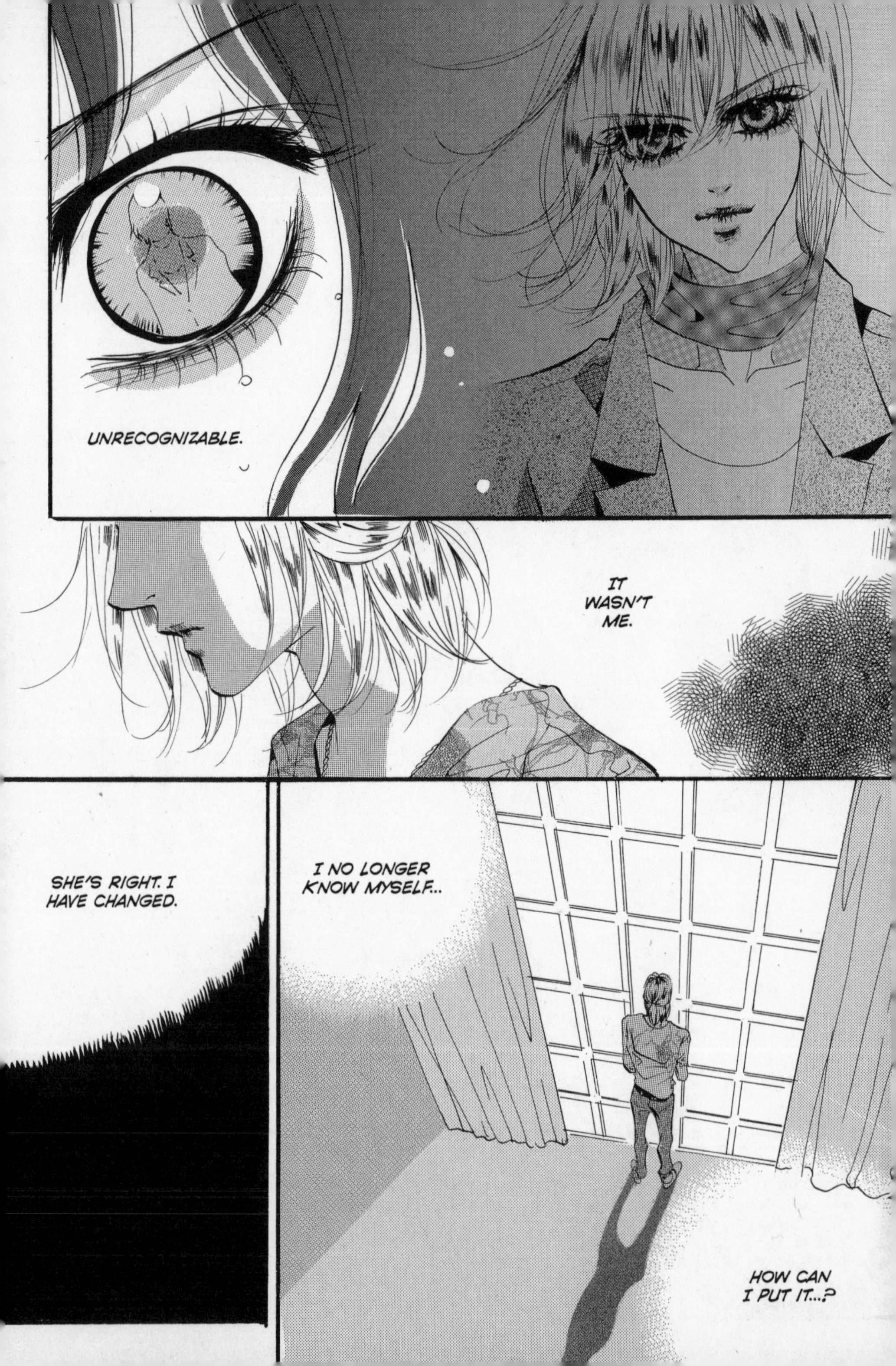
UNRECOGNIZABLE.
IT WASN'T ME.
SHE'S RIGHT. I HAVE CHANGED.
I NO LONGER KNOW MYSELF...
HOW CAN I PUT IT...?

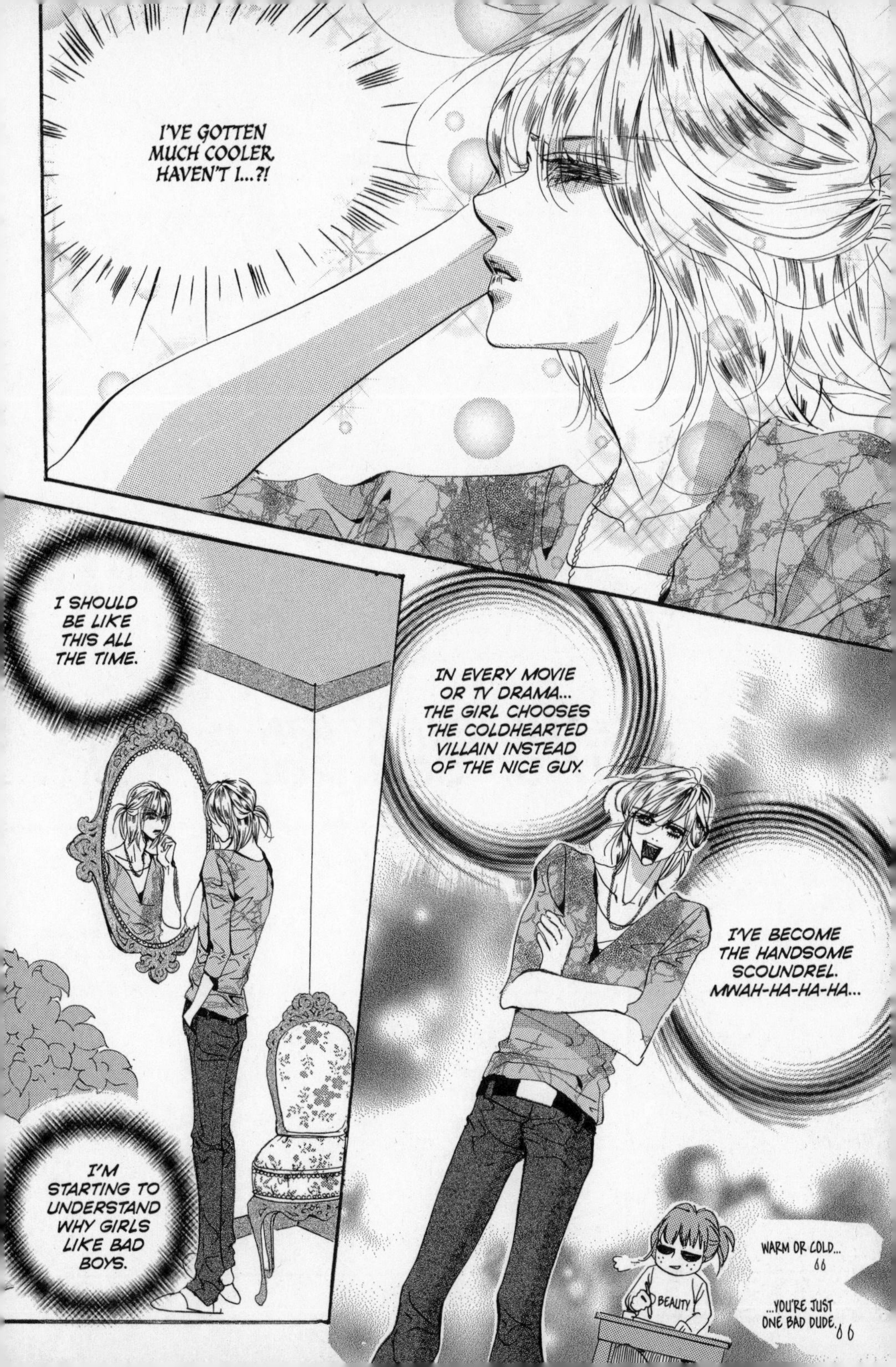
I'VE GOTTEN MUCH COOLER HAVEN'T I...?!
I SHOULD BE LIKE THIS ALL THE TIME.
I'M STARTING TO UNDERSTAND WHY GIRLS LIKE BAD BOYS.
IN EVERY MOVIE OR TV DRAMA... THE GIRL CHOOSES THE COLDHEARTED VILLAIN INSTEAD OF THE NICE GUY.
I'VE BECOME THE HANDSOME SCOUNDREL. MWAH-HA-HA-HA...
BEAUTY
WARM OR COLD...
...YOU'RE JUST ONE BAD DUDE.

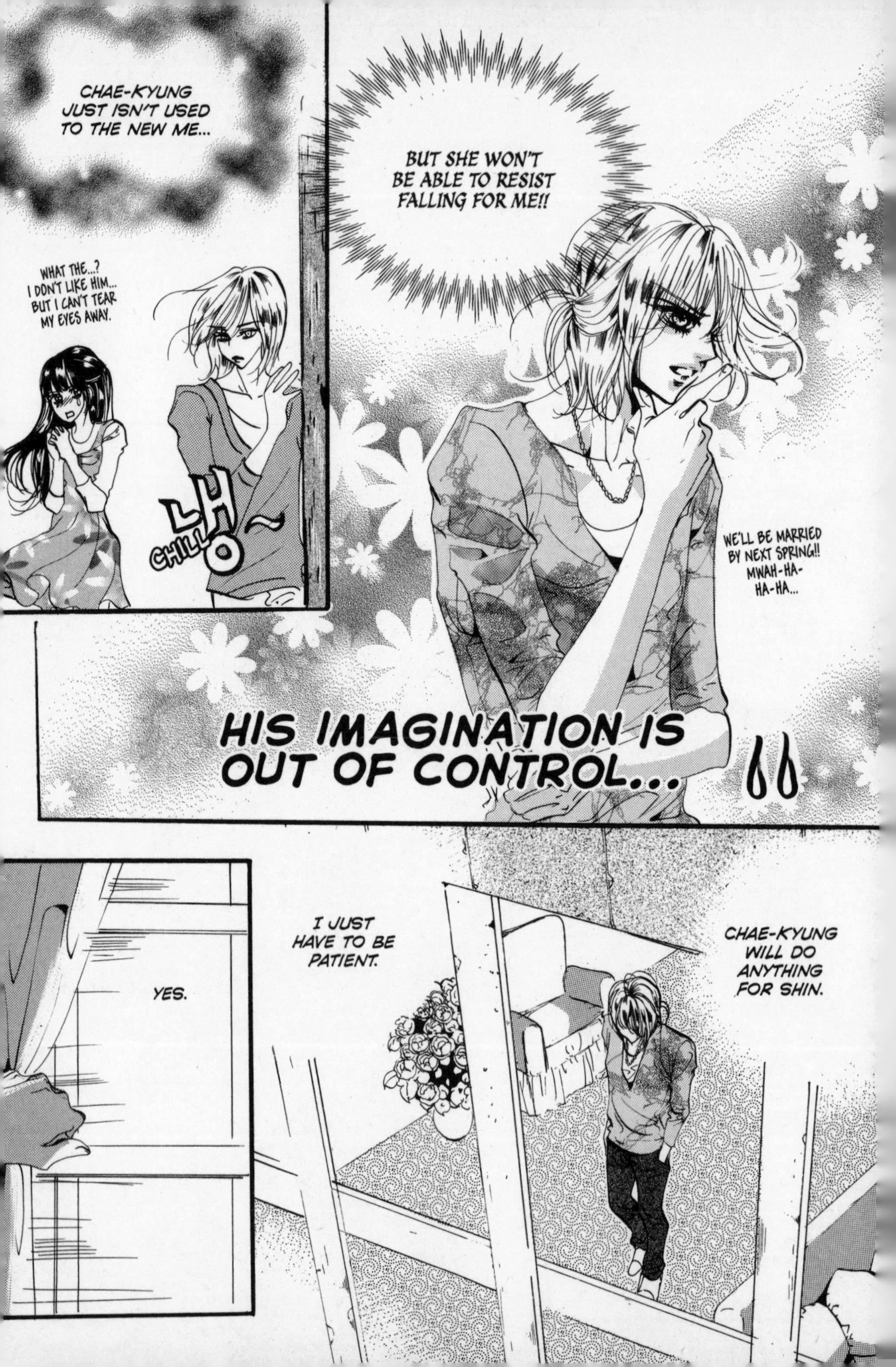
CHAE-KYUNG JUST ISN'T USED TO THE NEW ME...
WHAT THE...? I DON'T LIKE HIM... BUT I CAN'T TEAR MY EYES AWAY.
냉~
CHILL
BUT SHE WON'T BE ABLE TO RESIST FALLING FOR ME!!
WE'LL BE MARRIED BY NEXT SPRING!! MWAH-HA-HA-HA...
HIS IMAGINATION IS OUT OF CONTROL...
YES.
I JUST HAVE TO BE PATIENT.
CHAE-KYUNG WILL DO ANYTHING FOR SHIN.

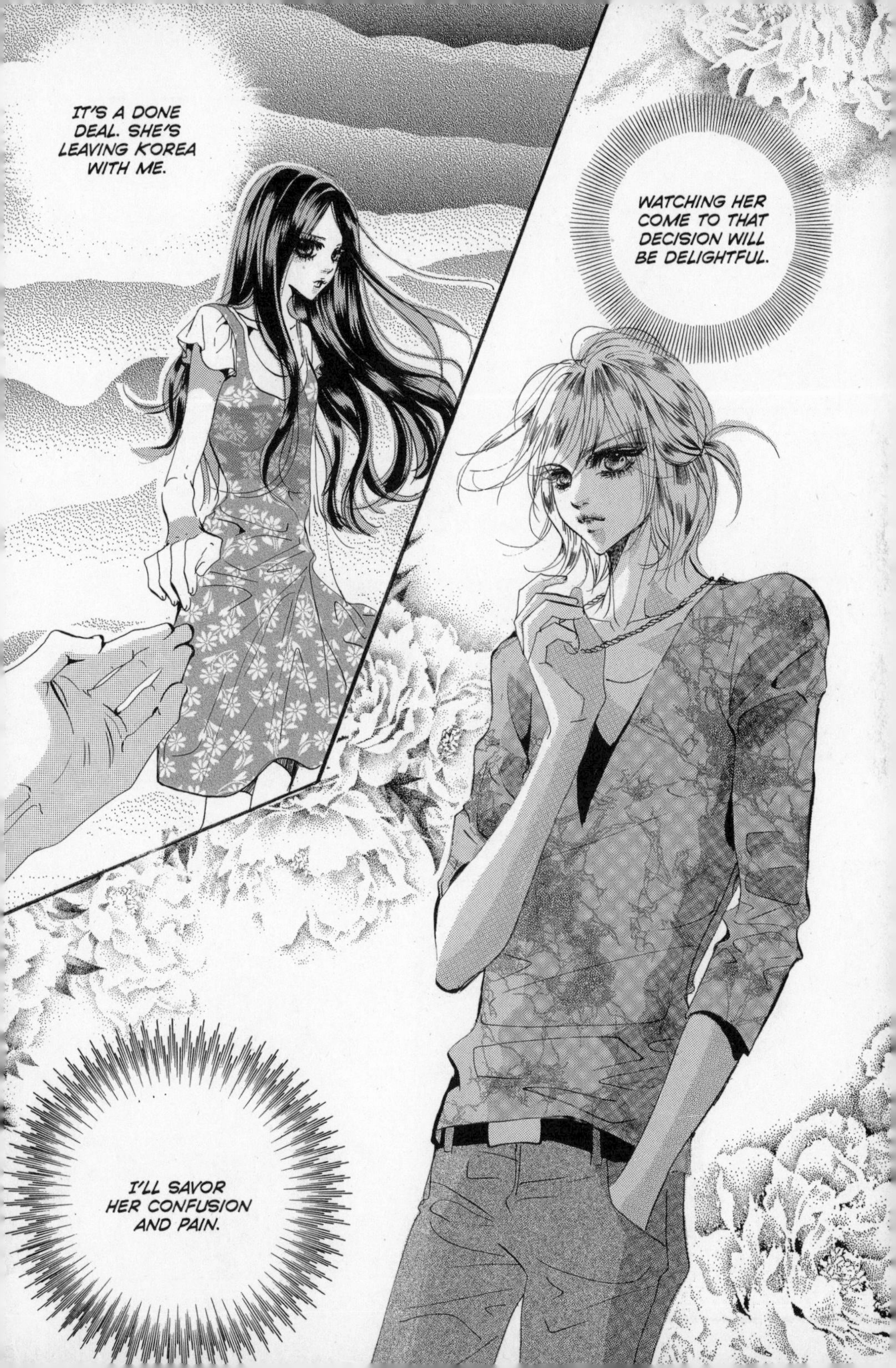
IT'S A DONE DEAL. SHE'S LEAVING KOREA WITH ME.
WATCHING HER COME TO THAT DECISION WILL BE DELIGHTFUL.
I'LL SAVOR HER CONFUSION AND PAIN.

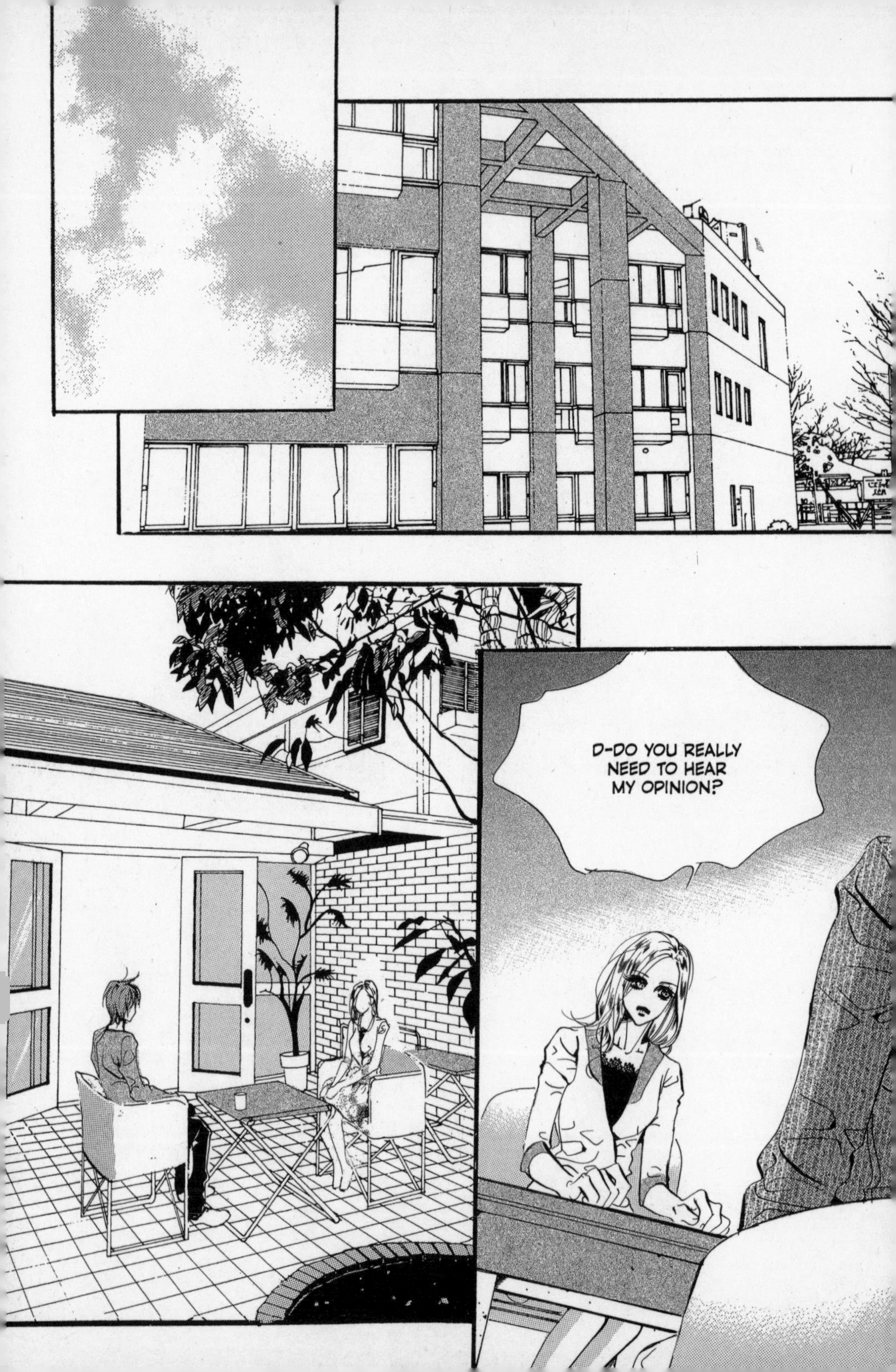
D-DO YOU REALLY NEED TO HEAR MY OPINION?

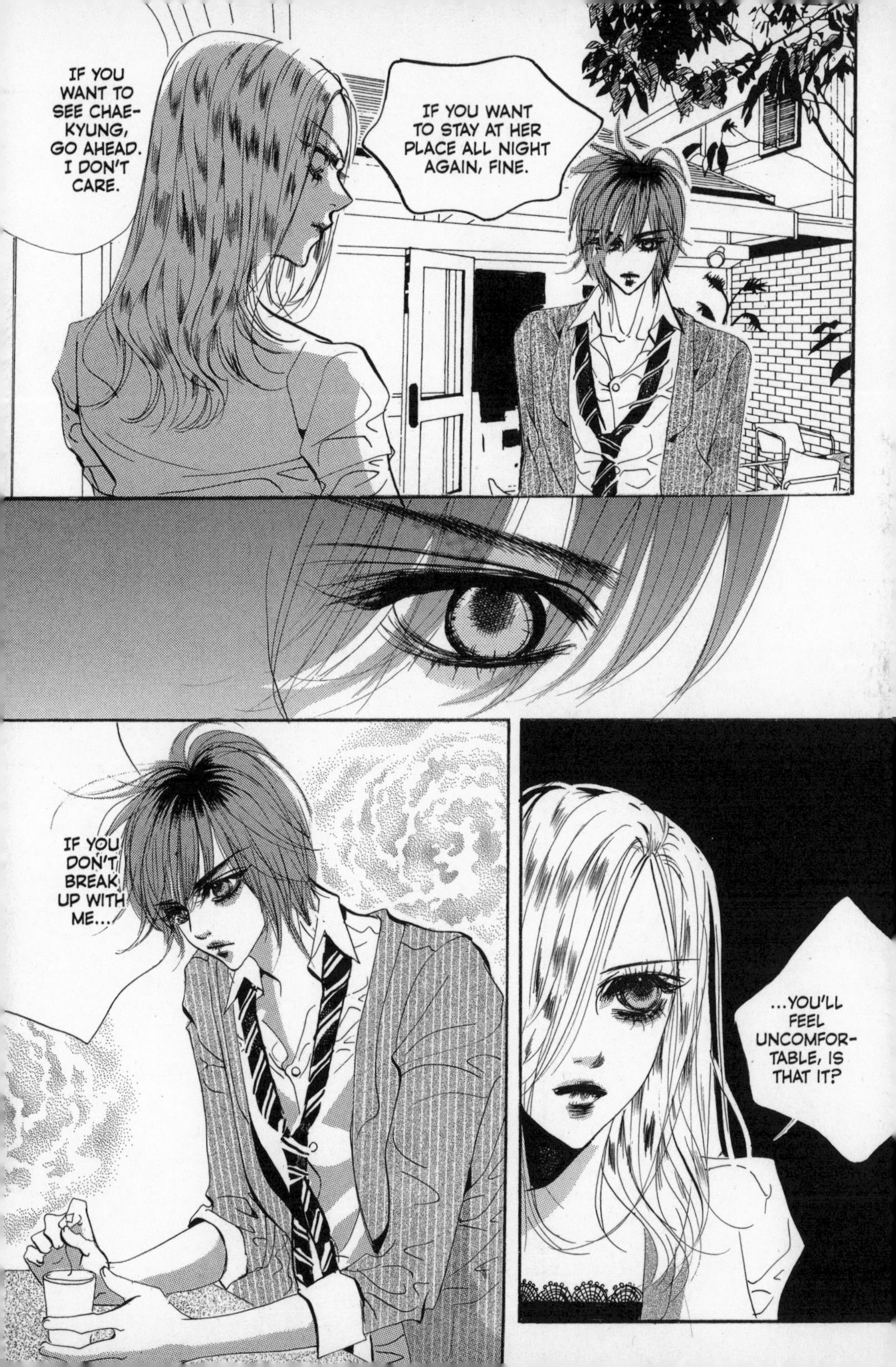
IF YOU WANT TO SEE CHAE-KYUNG, GO AHEAD. I DON'T CARE.
IF YOU WANT TO STAY AT HER PLACE ALL NIGHT AGAIN, FINE.
IF YOU DON'T BREAK UP WITH ME...
...YOU'LL FEEL UNCOMFOR-TABLE, IS THAT IT?

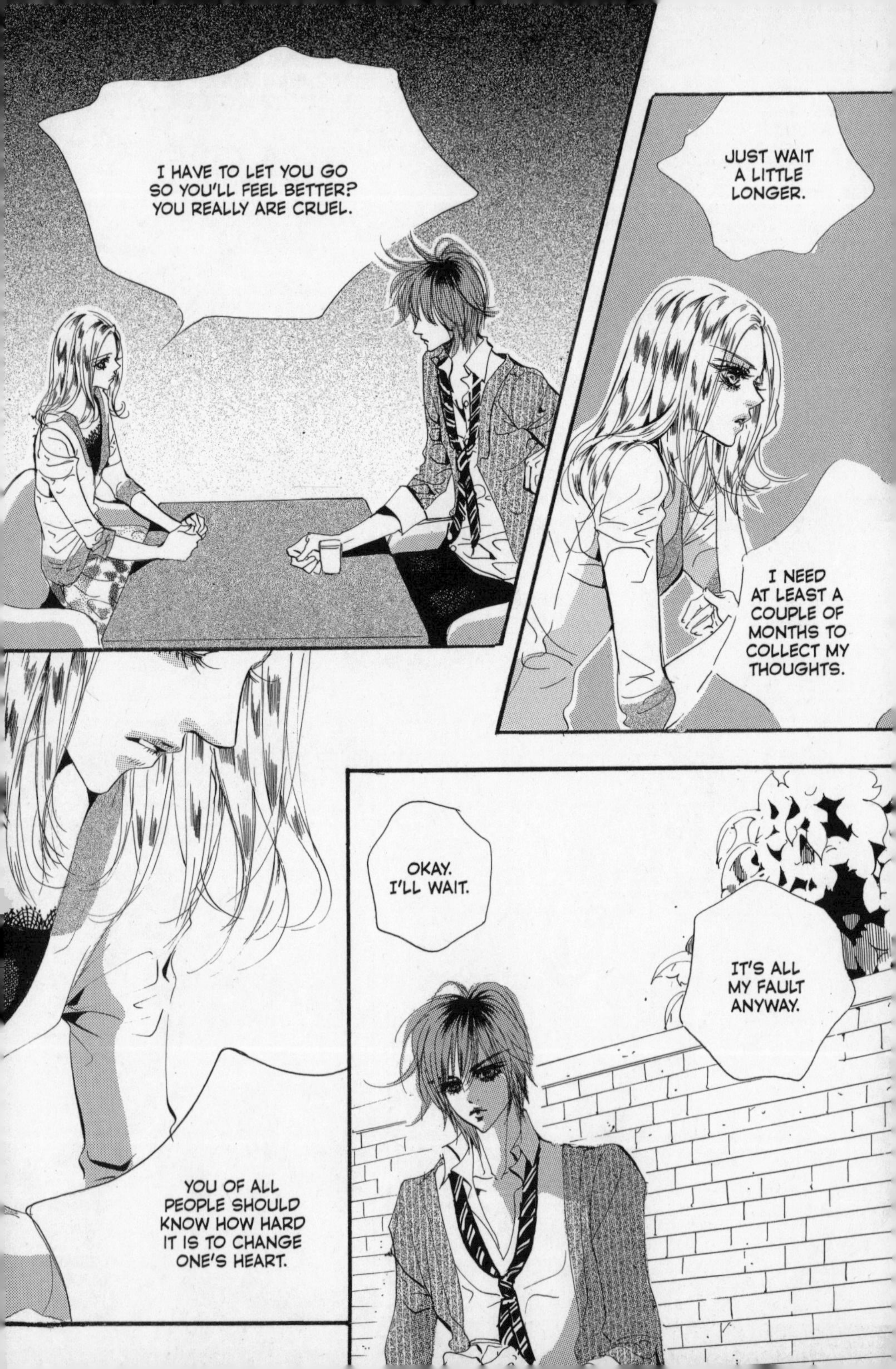
I HAVE TO LET YOU GO SO YOU'LL FEEL BETTER? YOU REALLY ARE CRUEL.
JUST WAIT A LITTLE LONGER.
I NEED AT LEAST A COUPLE OF MONTHS TO COLLECT MY THOUGHTS.
YOU OF ALL PEOPLE SHOULD KNOW HOW HARD IT IS TO CHANGE ONE'S HEART.
OKAY. I'LL WAIT.
IT'S ALL MY FAULT ANYWAY.

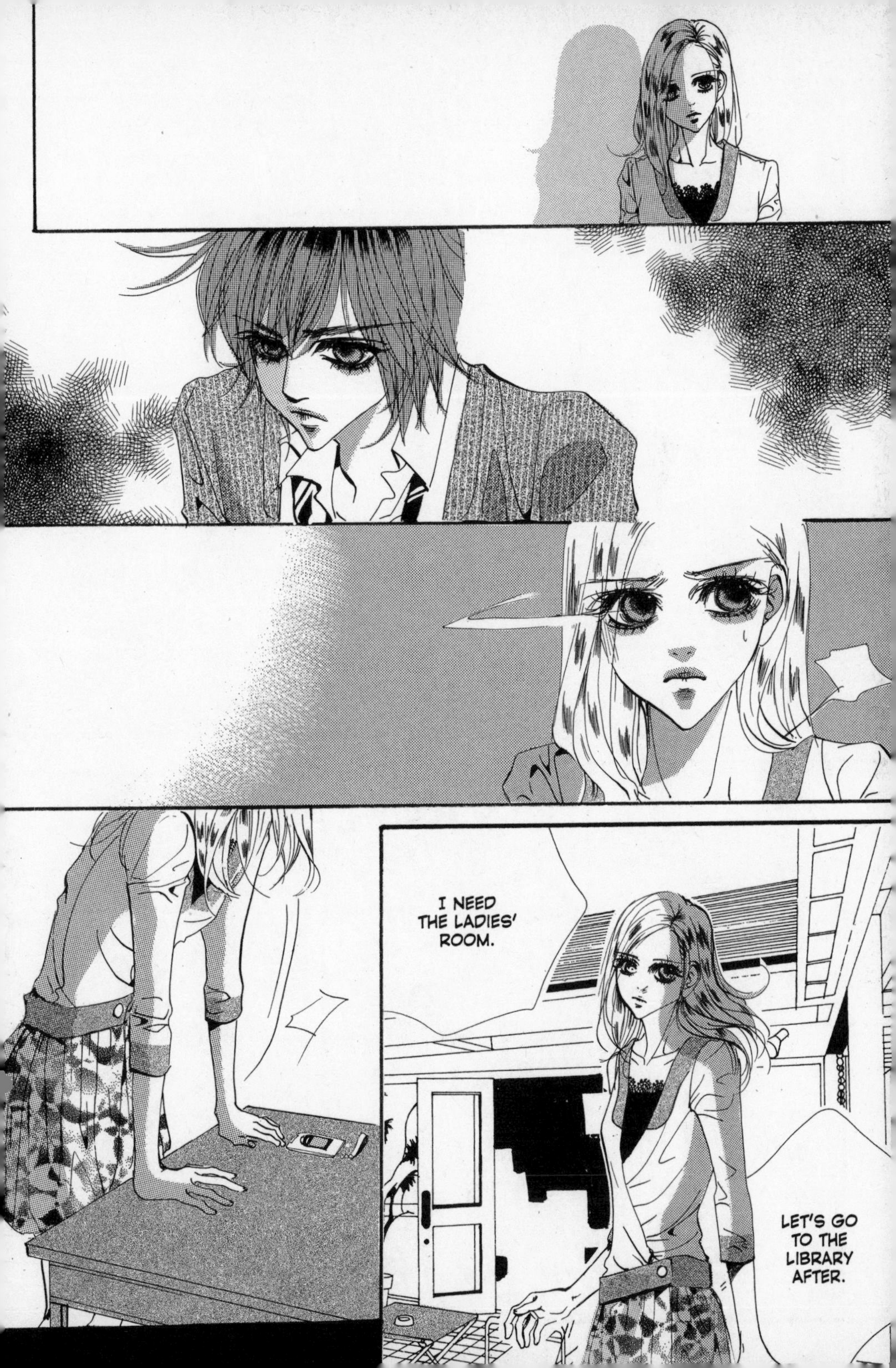
I NEED THE LADIES' ROOM.
LET'S GO TO THE LIBRARY AFTER.

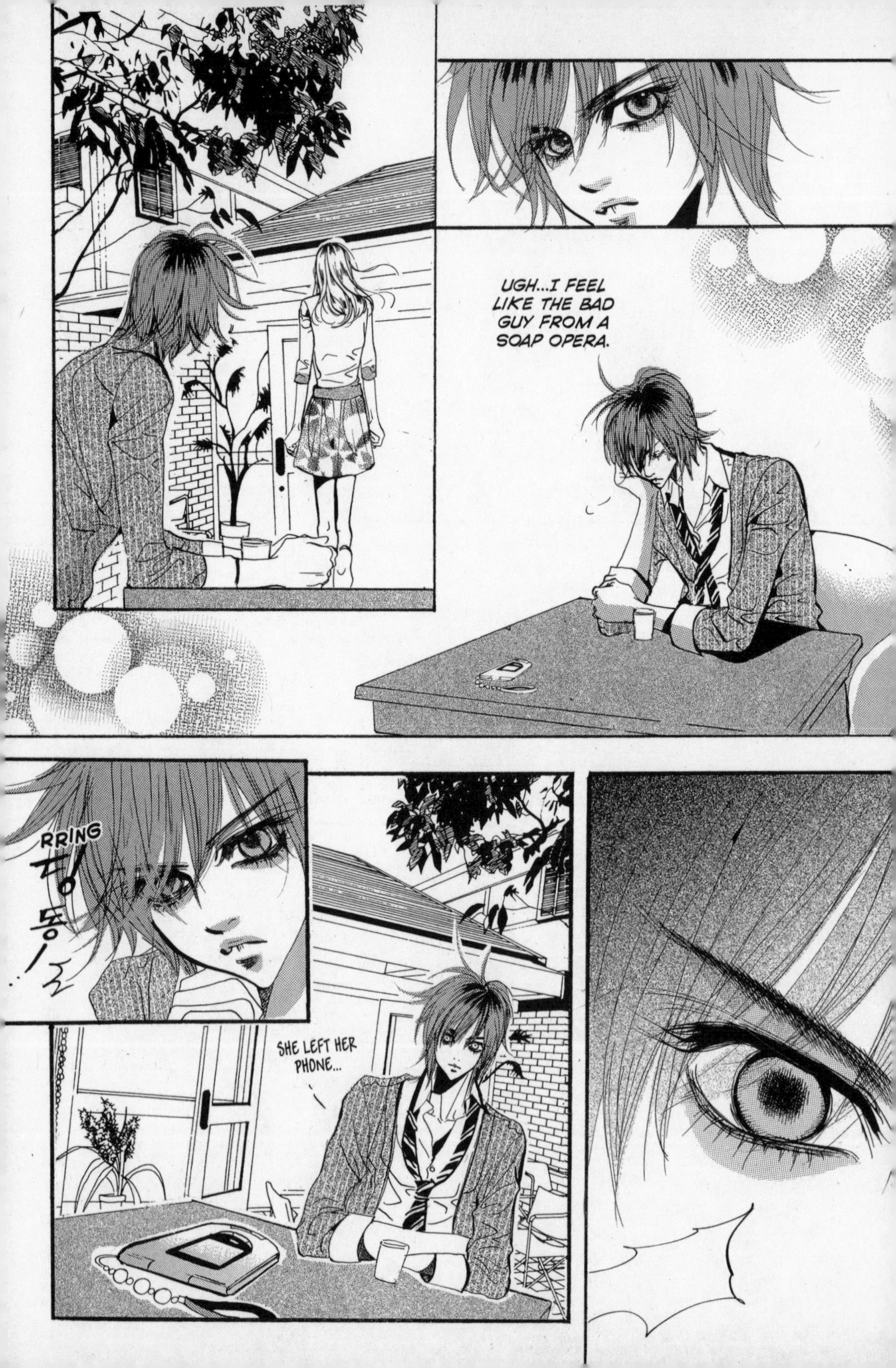
UGH...I FEEL LIKE THE BAD GUY FROM A SOAP OPERA.
RRING
SHE LEFT HER PHONE...

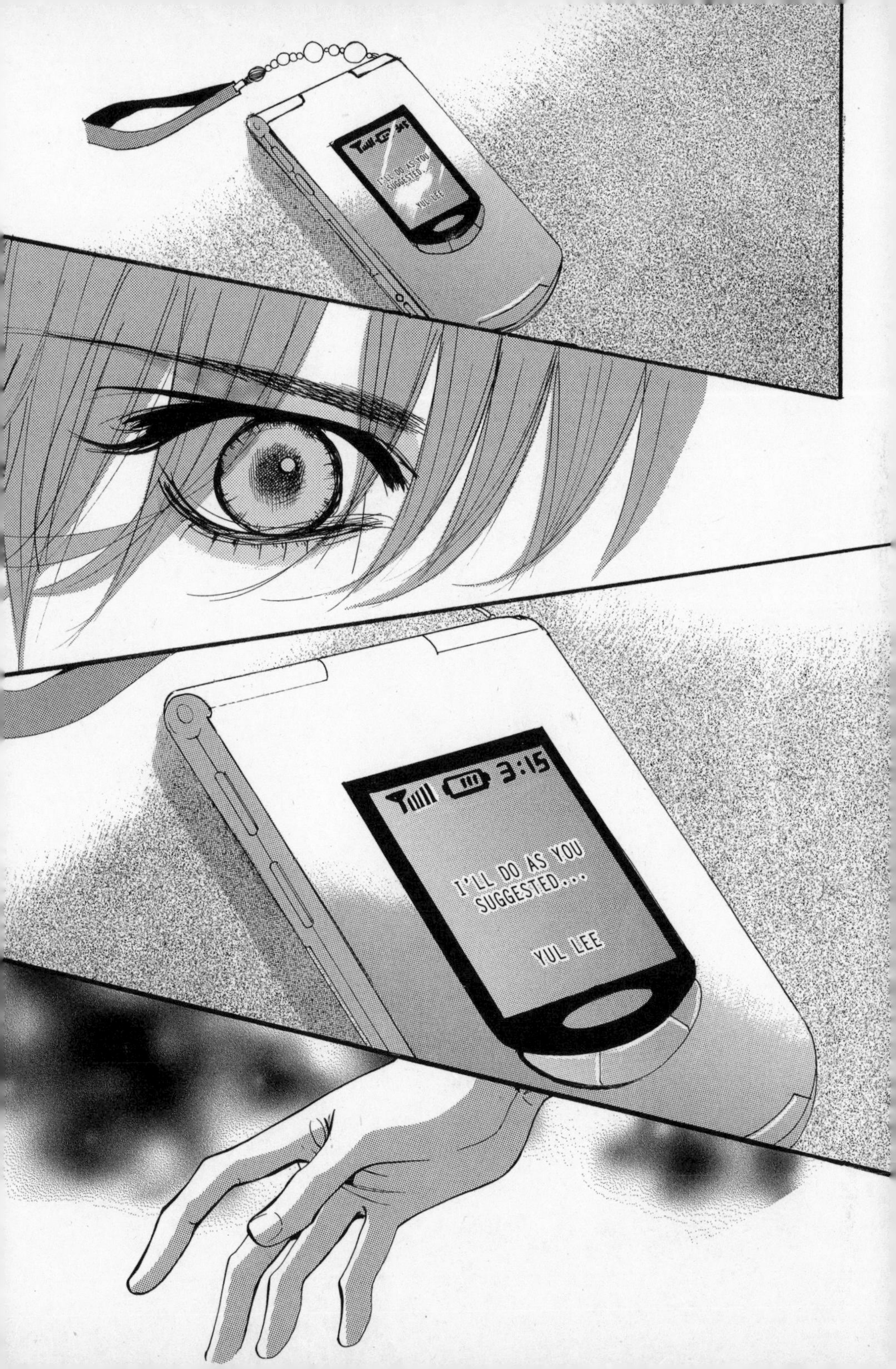
I'LL DO AS YOU SUGGESTED...
YUL LEE
3:15
I'LL DO AS YOU SUGGESTED...
YUL LEE

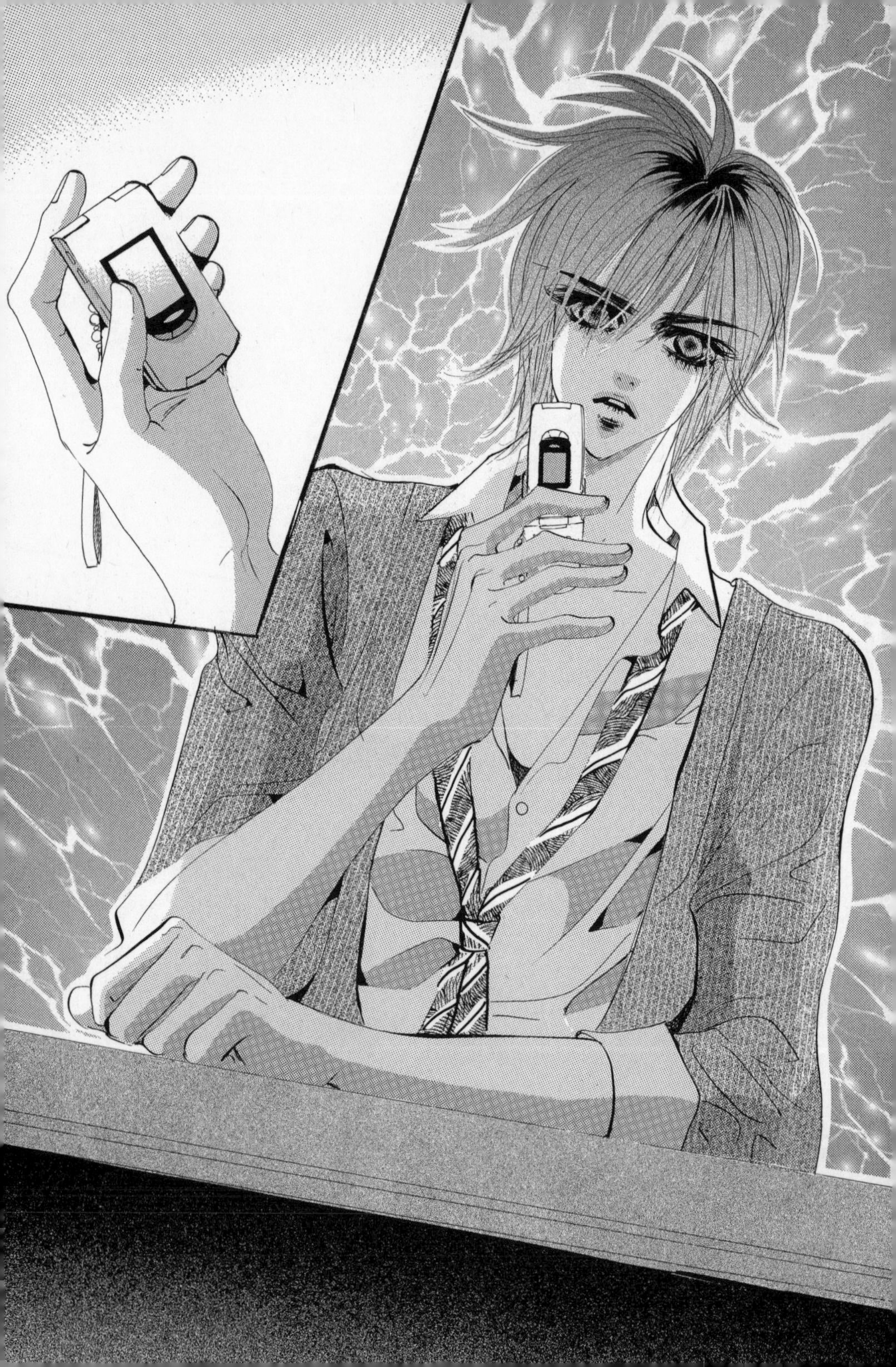

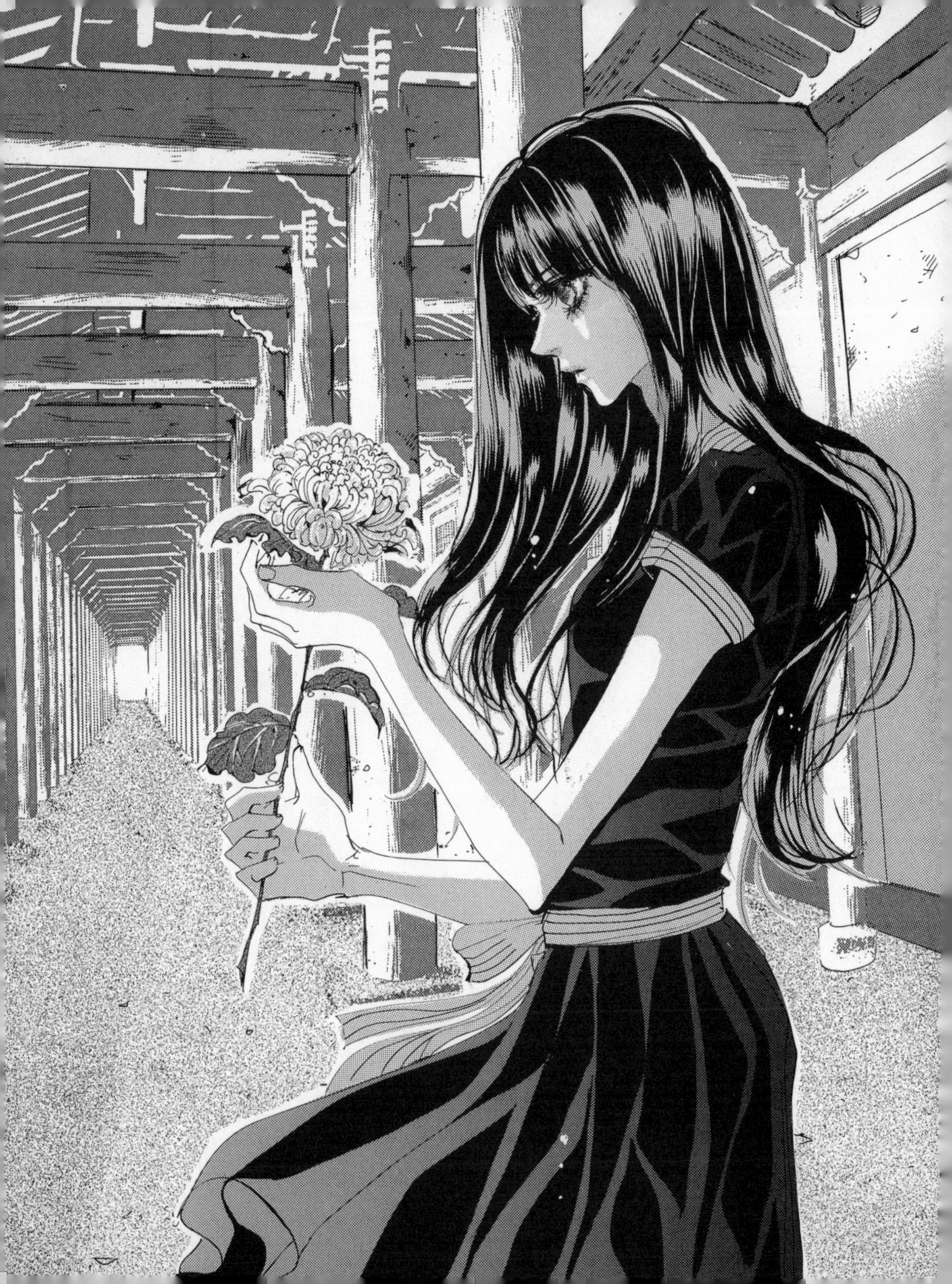

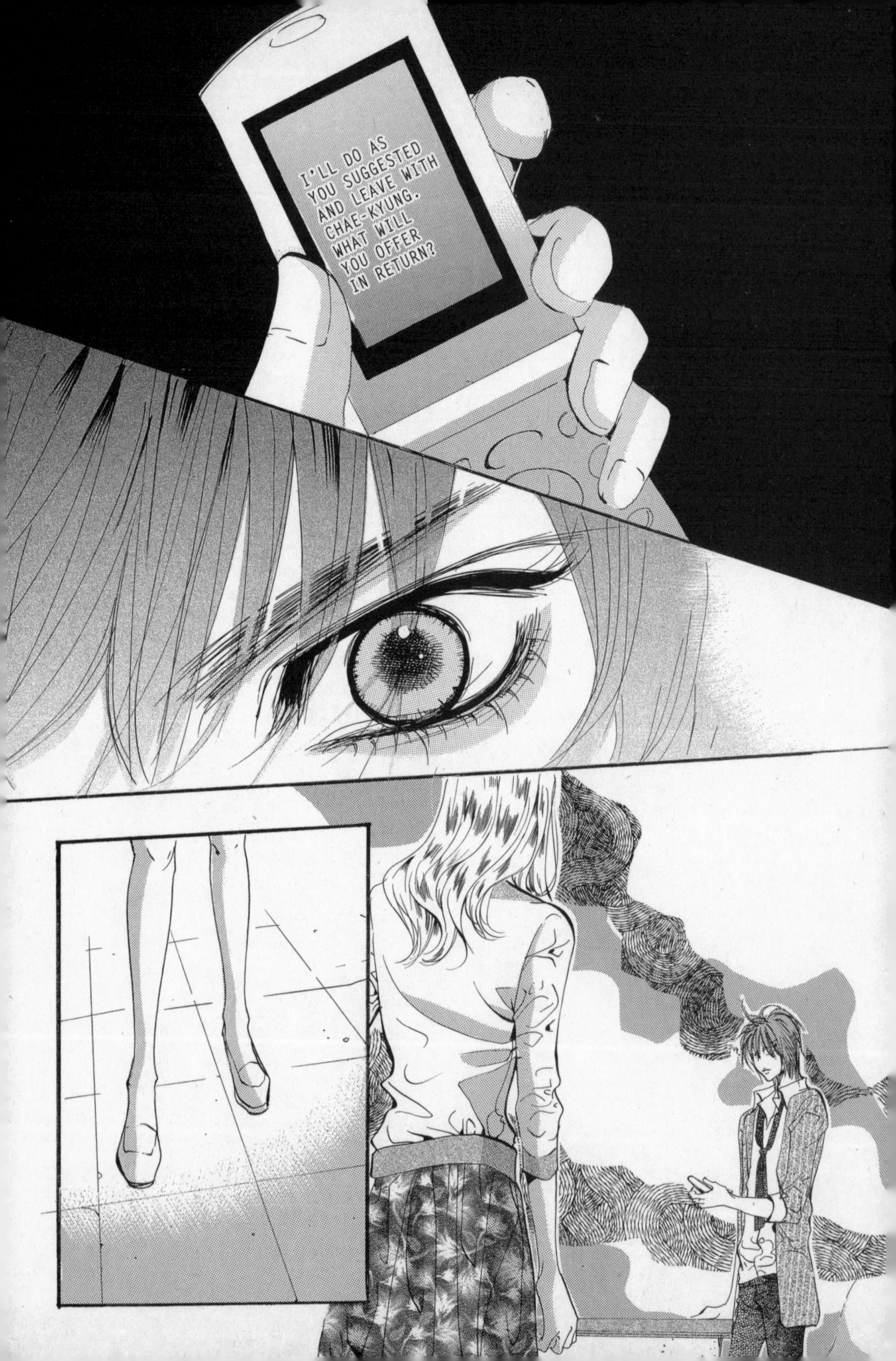
I'LL DO AS YOU SUGGESTED AND LEAVE WITH CHAE-KYUNG. WHAT WILL YOU OFFER IN RETURN?

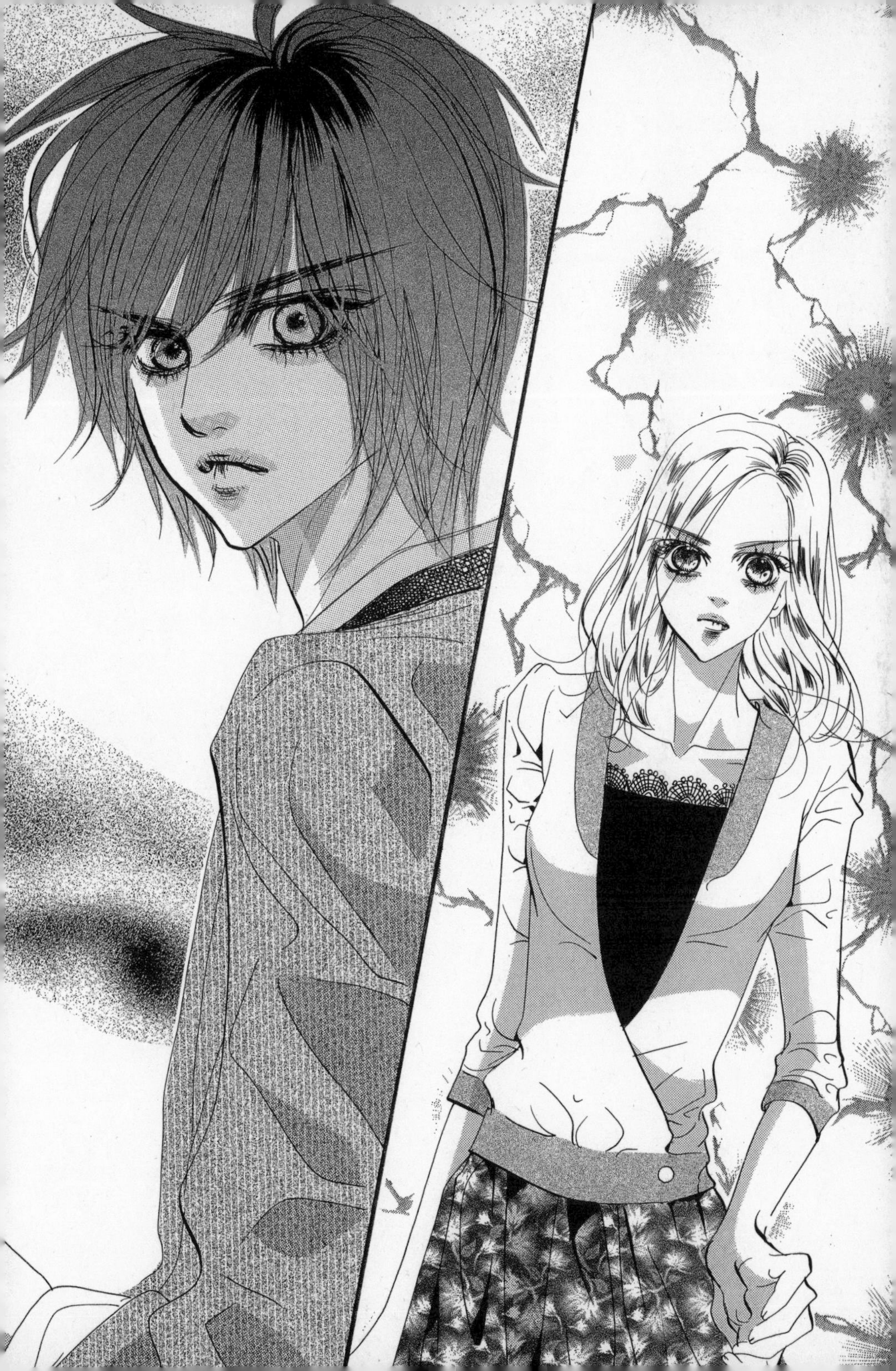

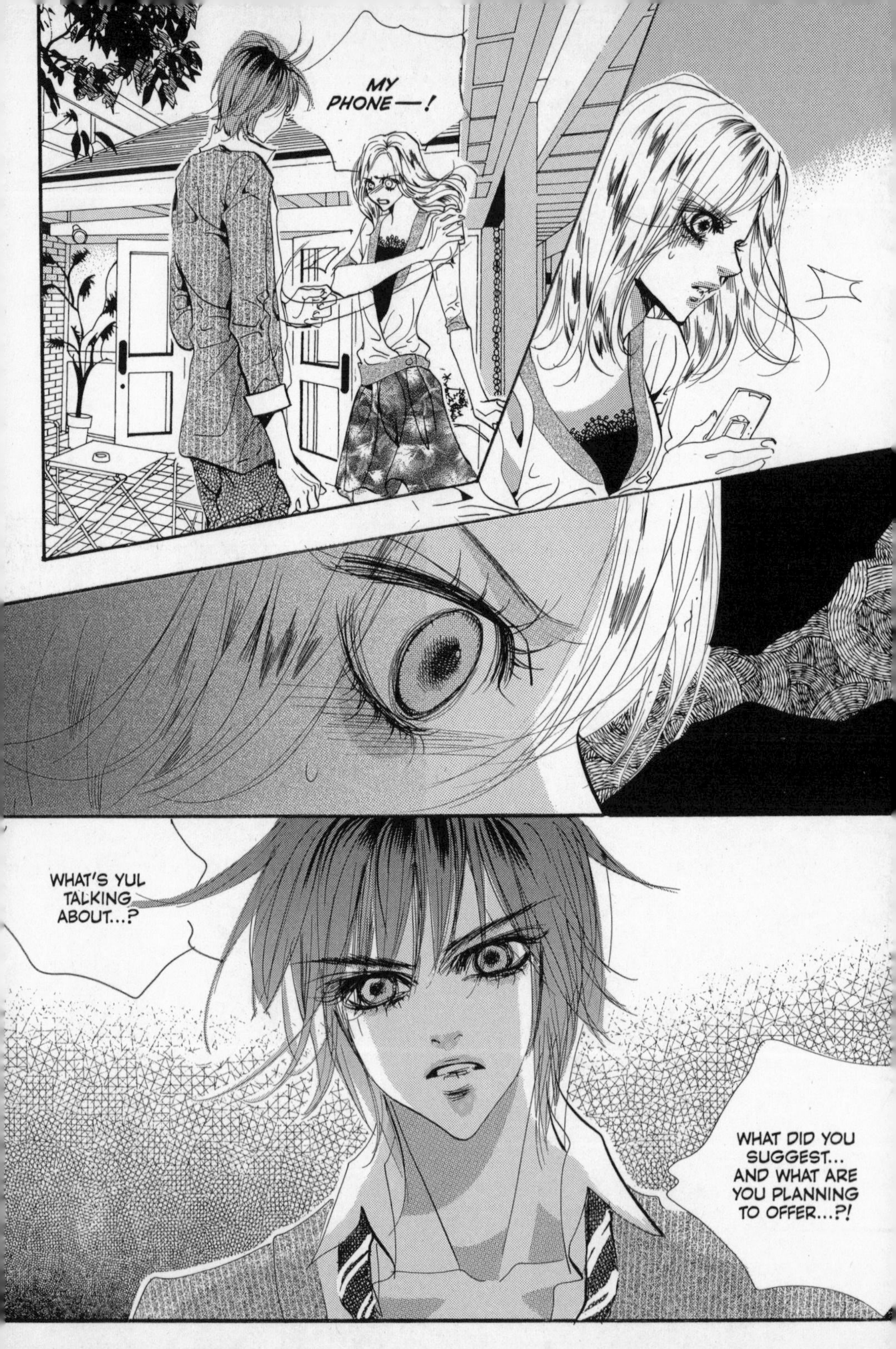
MY PHONE—!
WHAT'S YUL TALKING ABOUT...?
WHAT DID YOU SUGGEST... AND WHAT ARE YOU PLANNING TO OFFER...?!

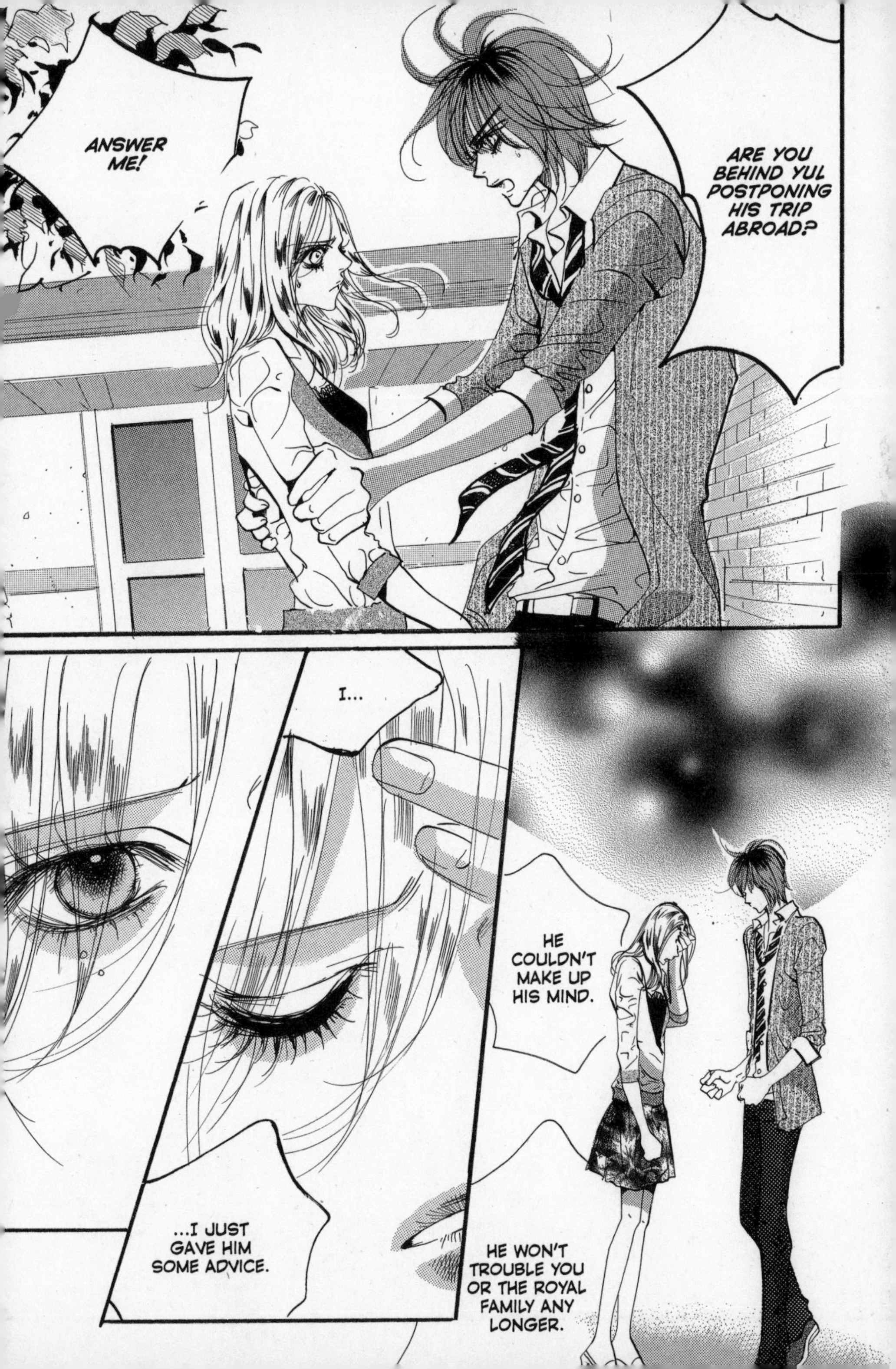
ANSWER ME!
ARE YOU BEHIND YUL POSTPONING HIS TRIP ABROAD?
I...
...I JUST GAVE HIM SOME ADVICE.
HE COULDN'T MAKE UP HIS MIND.
HE WON'T TROUBLE YOU OR THE ROYAL FAMILY ANY LONGER.

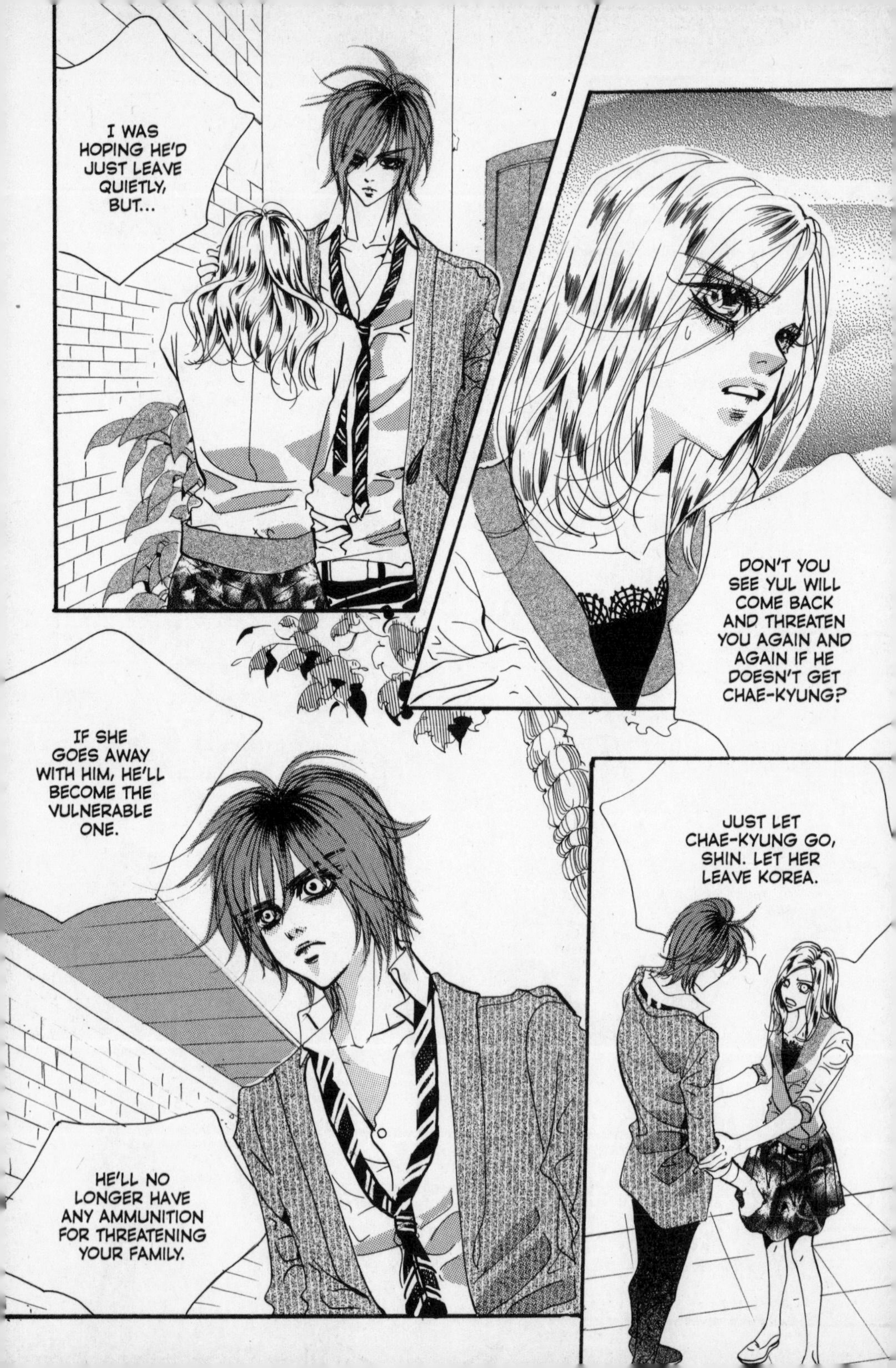
I WAS HOPING HE'D JUST LEAVE QUIETLY, BUT...
DON'T YOU SEE YUL WILL COME BACK AND THREATEN YOU AGAIN AND AGAIN IF HE DOESN'T GET CHAE-KYUNG?
IF SHE GOES AWAY WITH HIM, HE'LL BECOME THE VULNERABLE ONE.
HE'LL NO LONGER HAVE ANY AMMUNITION FOR THREATENING YOUR FAMILY.
JUST LET CHAE-KYUNG GO, SHIN. LET HER LEAVE KOREA.

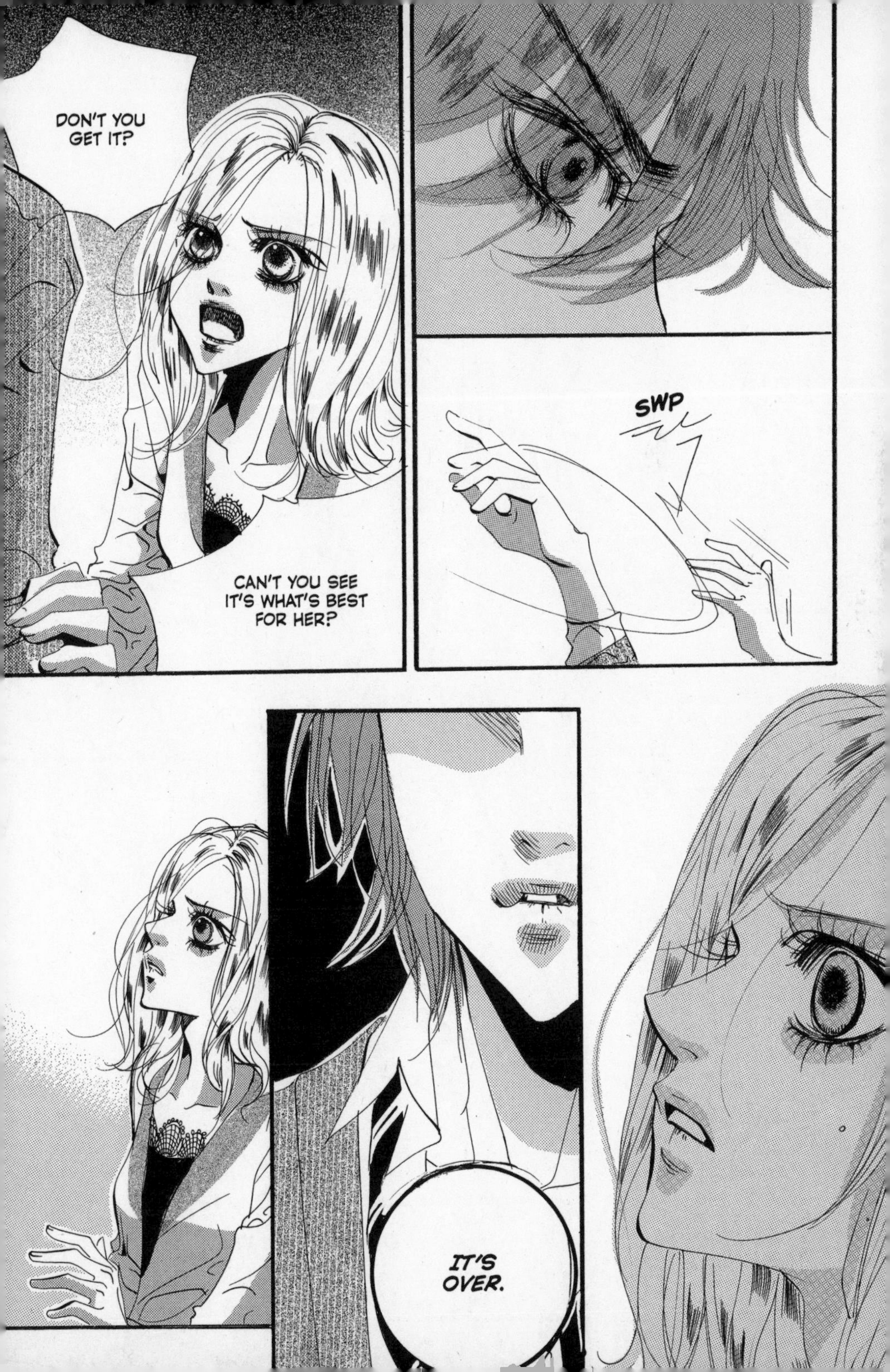
DON'T YOU GET IT?
CAN'T YOU SEE IT'S WHAT'S BEST FOR HER?
SWP
IT'S OVER.

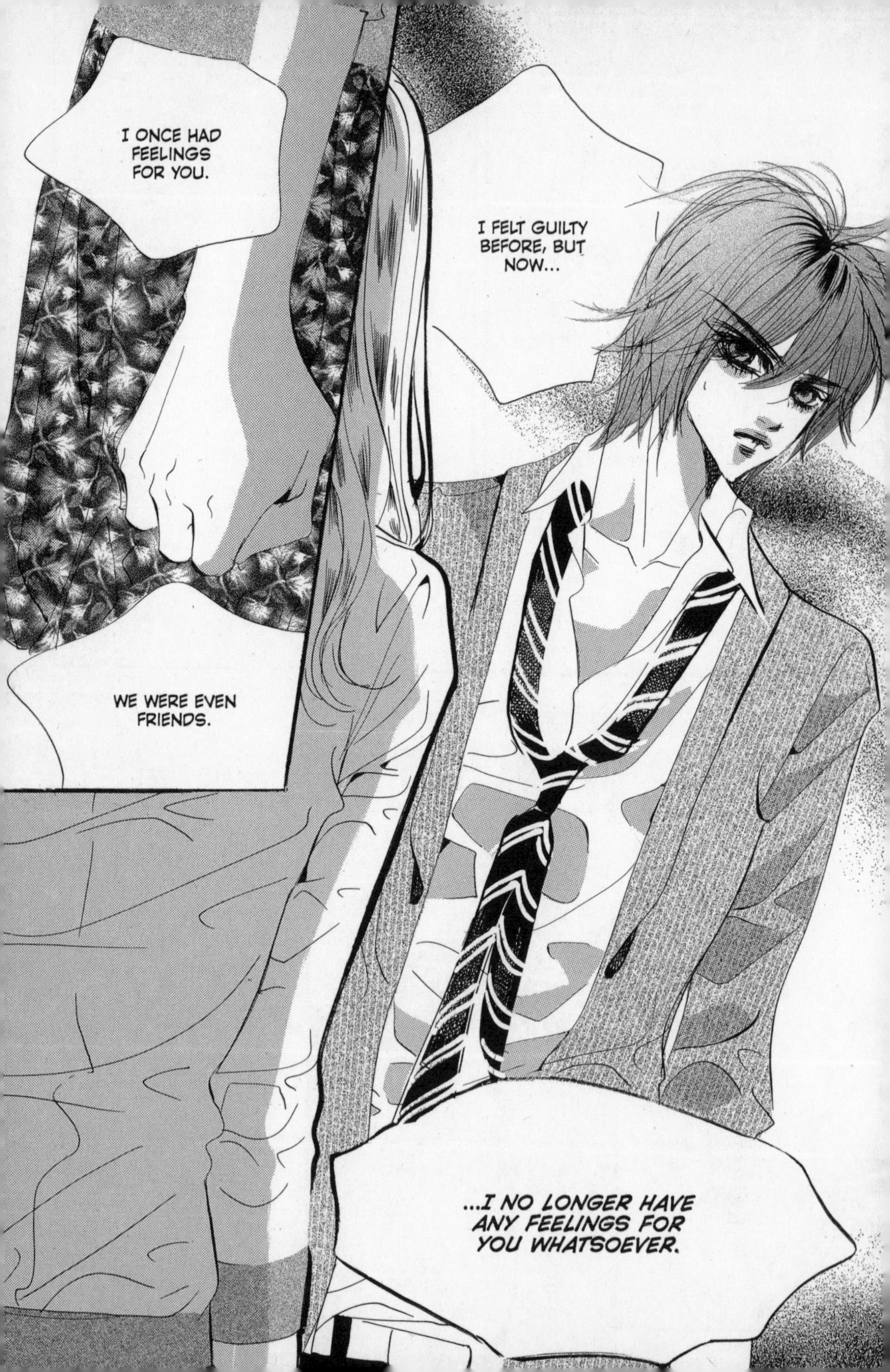
I ONCE HAD FEELINGS FOR YOU.
WE WERE EVEN FRIENDS.
I FELT GUILTY BEFORE, BUT NOW...
...I NO LONGER HAVE ANY FEELINGS FOR YOU WHATSOEVER.

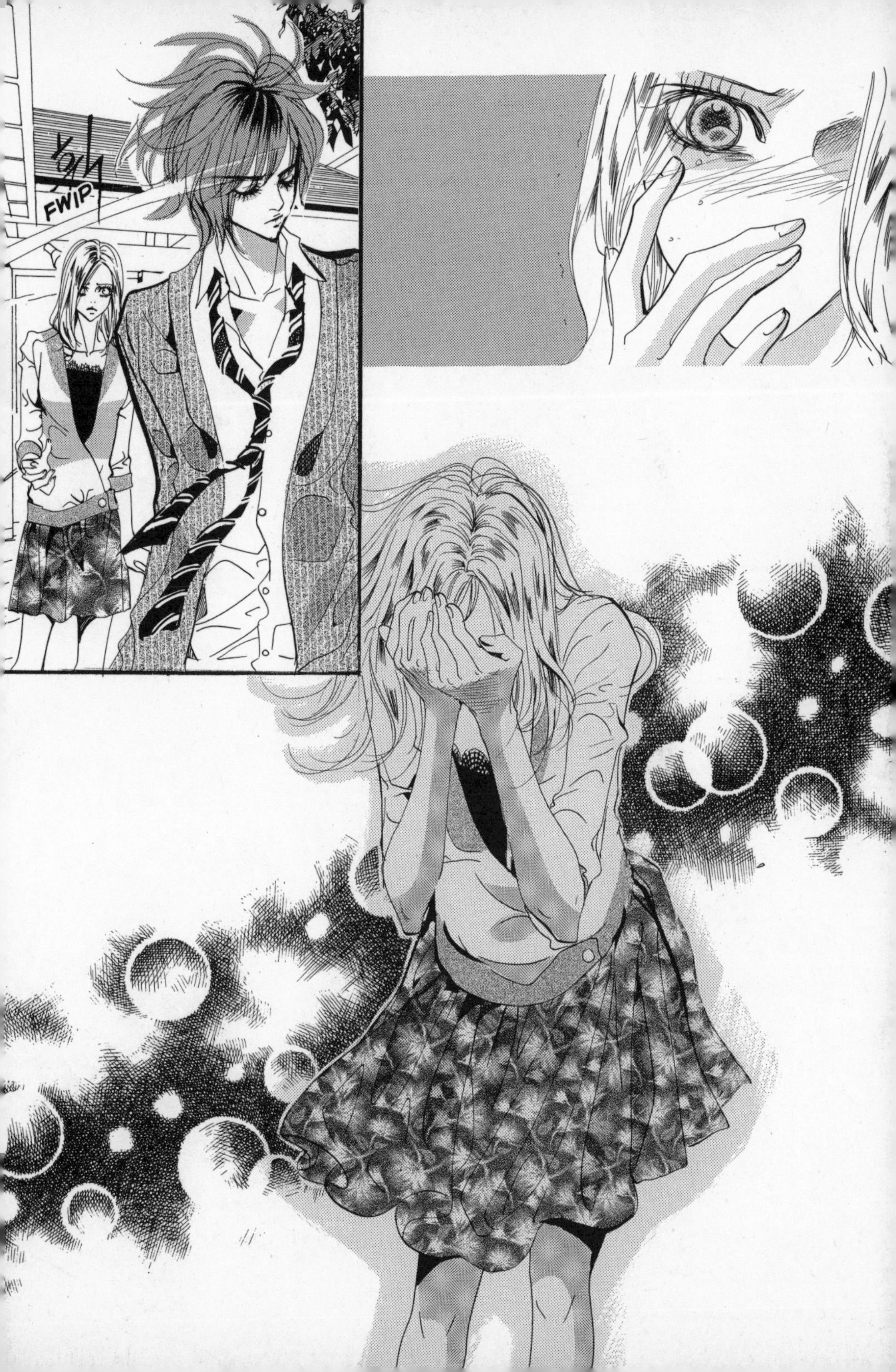
FWIP

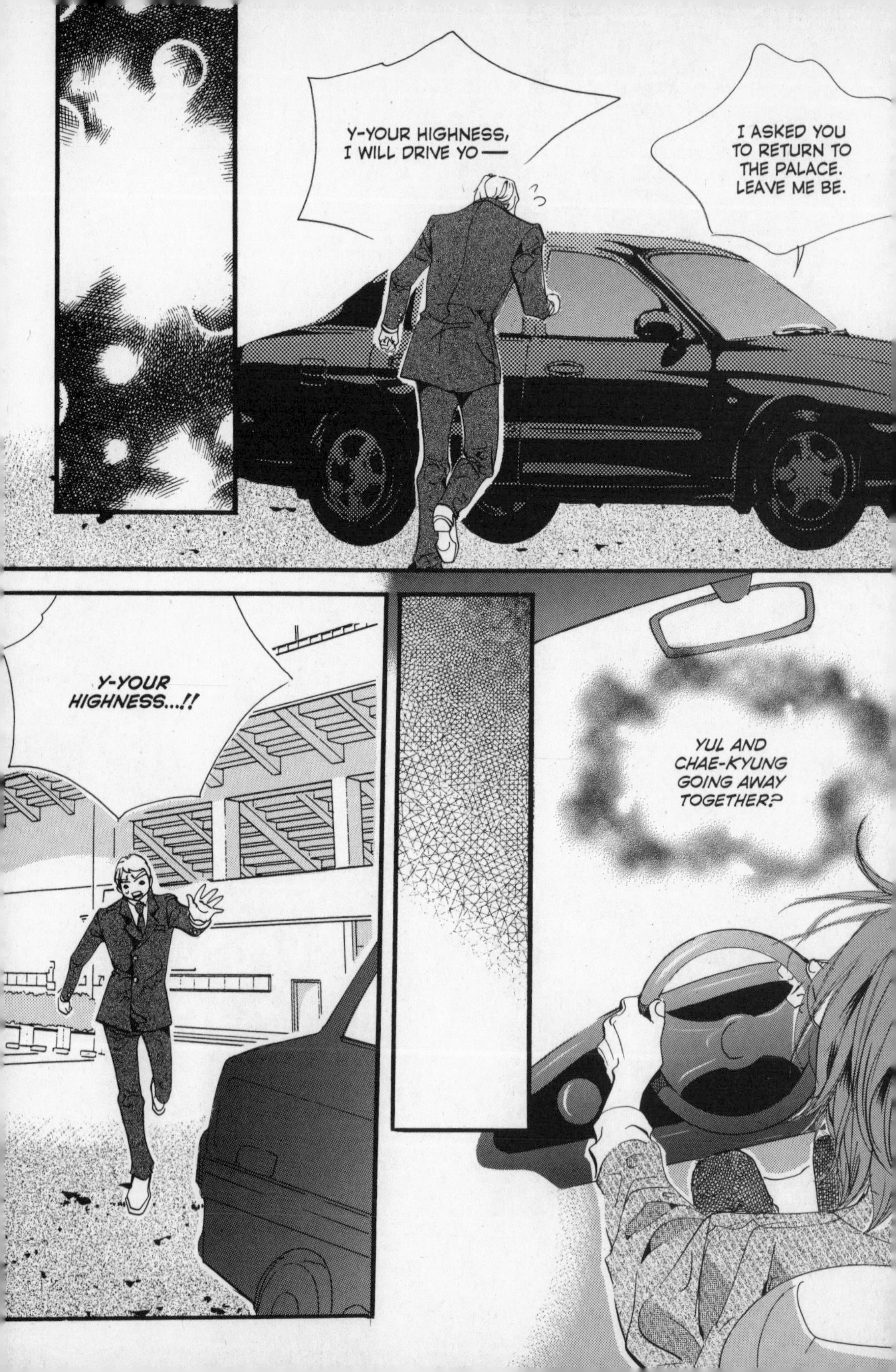
Y-YOUR HIGHNESS, I WILL DRIVE YO—
I ASKED YOU TO RETURN TO THE PALACE. LEAVE ME BE.
Y-YOUR HIGHNESS...!!
YUL AND CHAE-KYUNG GOING AWAY TOGETHER?

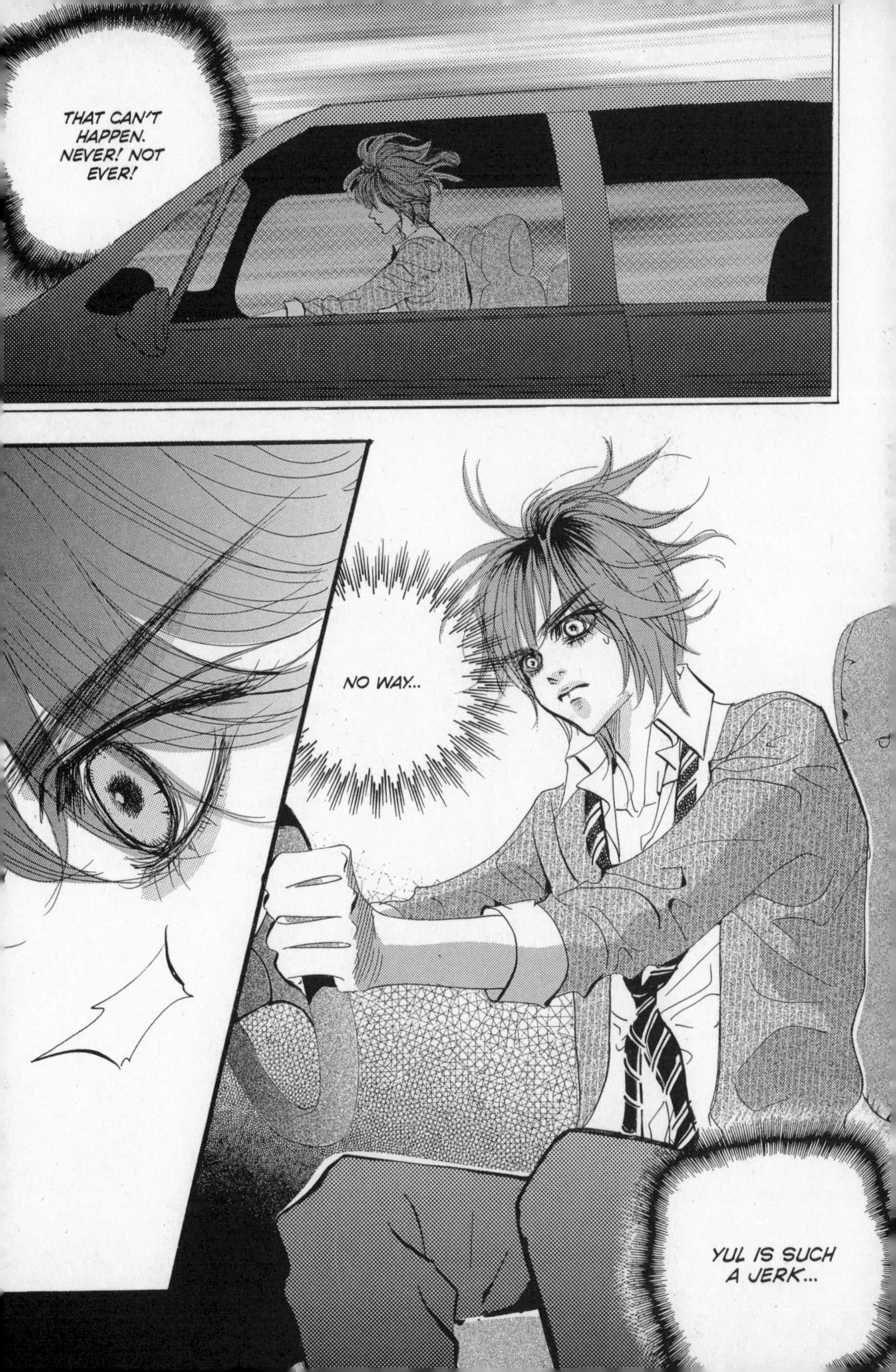
THAT CAN'T HAPPEN. NEVER! NOT EVER!
NO WAY...
YUL IS SUCH A JERK...

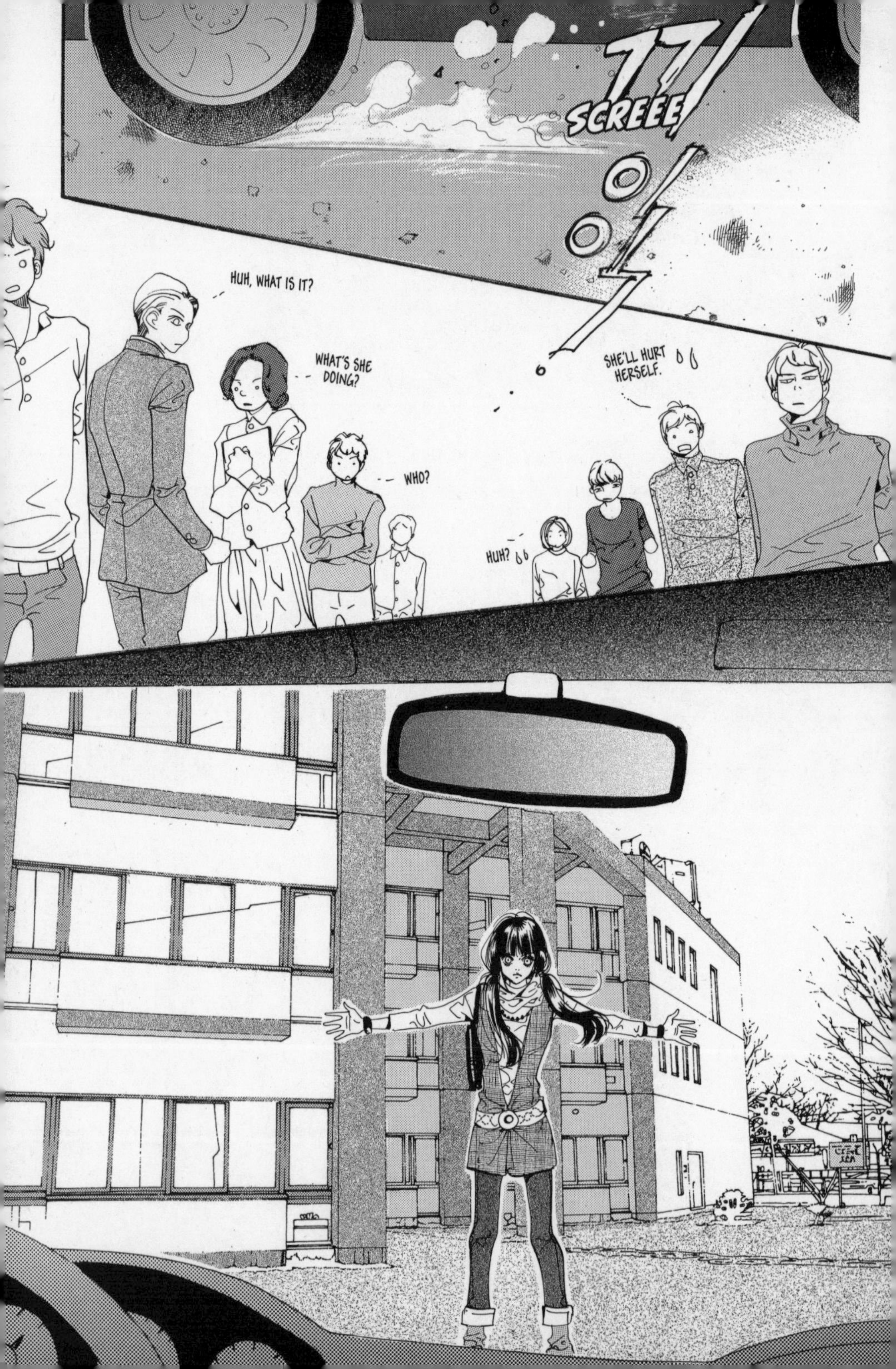
SCREEEE
HUH, WHAT IS IT?
WHAT'S SHE DOING?
WHO?
HUH?
SHE'LL HURT HERSELF.

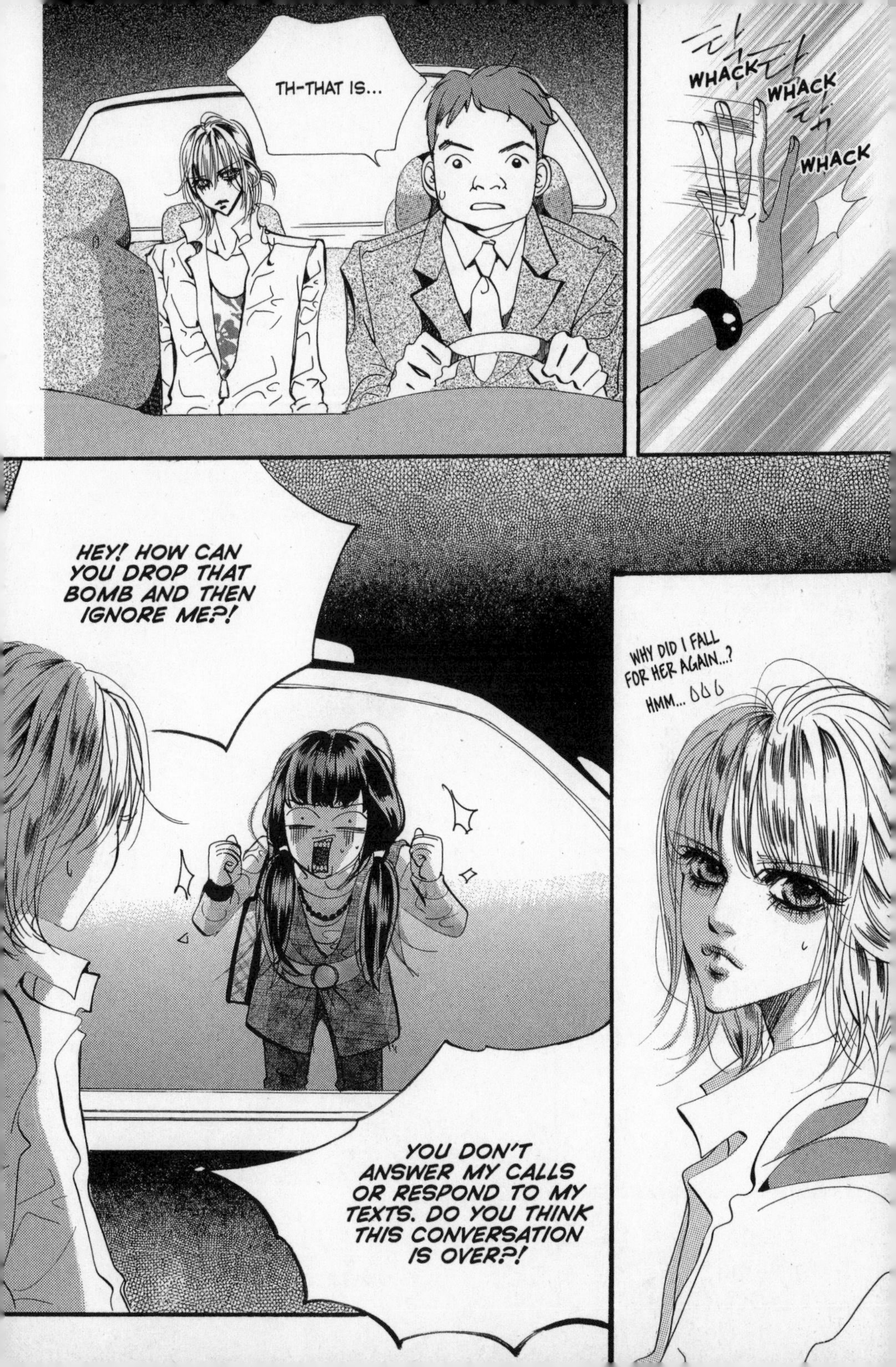

TH-THAT IS...
WHACK
WHACK
WHACK
HEY! HOW CAN YOU DROP THAT BOMB AND THEN IGNORE ME?!
YOU DON'T ANSWER MY CALLS OR RESPOND TO MY TEXTS. DO YOU THINK THIS CONVERSATION IS OVER?!
WHY DID I FALL FOR HER AGAIN...?
HMM...

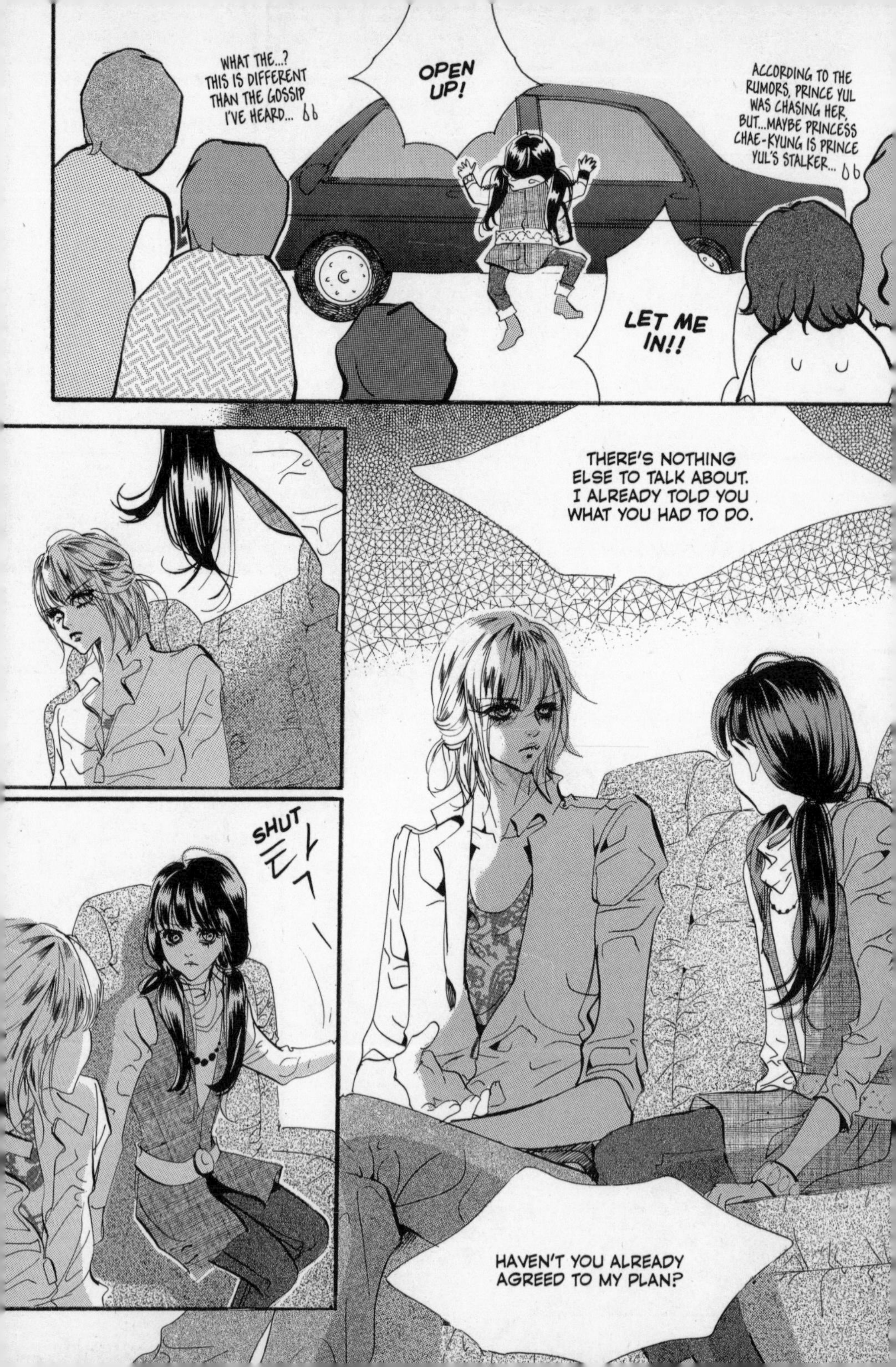
WHAT THE...? THIS IS DIFFERENT THAN THE GOSSIP I'VE HEARD...
OPEN UP!
ACCORDING TO THE RUMORS, PRINCE YUL WAS CHASING HER, BUT...MAYBE PRINCESS CHAE-KYUNG IS PRINCE YUL'S STALKER...
LET ME IN!!
SHUT
탁
THERE'S NOTHING ELSE TO TALK ABOUT. I ALREADY TOLD YOU WHAT YOU HAD TO DO.
HAVEN'T YOU ALREADY AGREED TO MY PLAN?

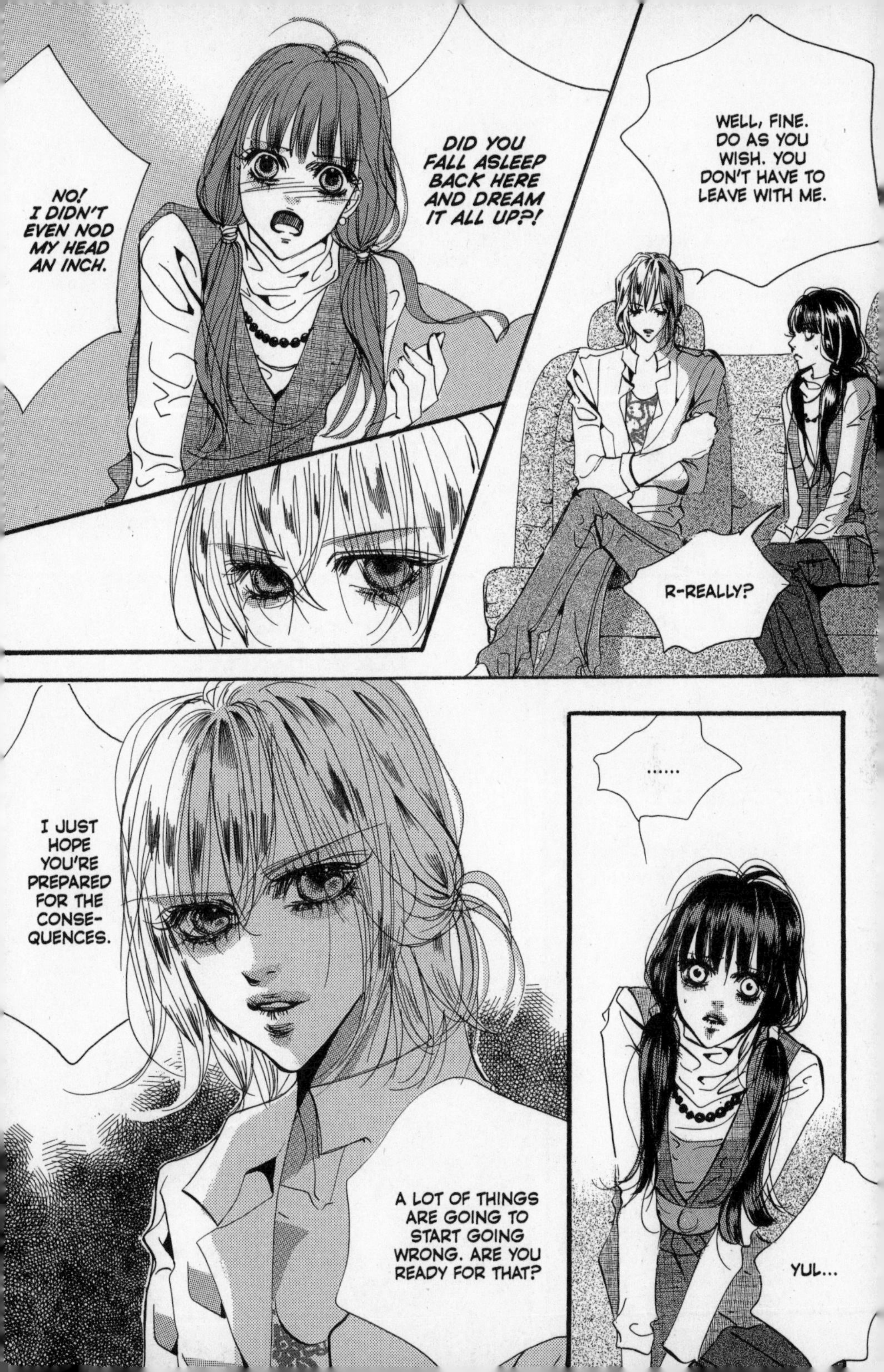

NO! I DIDN'T EVEN NOD MY HEAD AN INCH.
DID YOU FALL ASLEEP BACK HERE AND DREAM IT ALL UP?!
WELL, FINE. DO AS YOU WISH. YOU DON'T HAVE TO LEAVE WITH ME.
R-REALLY?
I JUST HOPE YOU'RE PREPARED FOR THE CONSE-QUENCES.
A LOT OF THINGS ARE GOING TO START GOING WRONG. ARE YOU READY FOR THAT?
......
YUL...

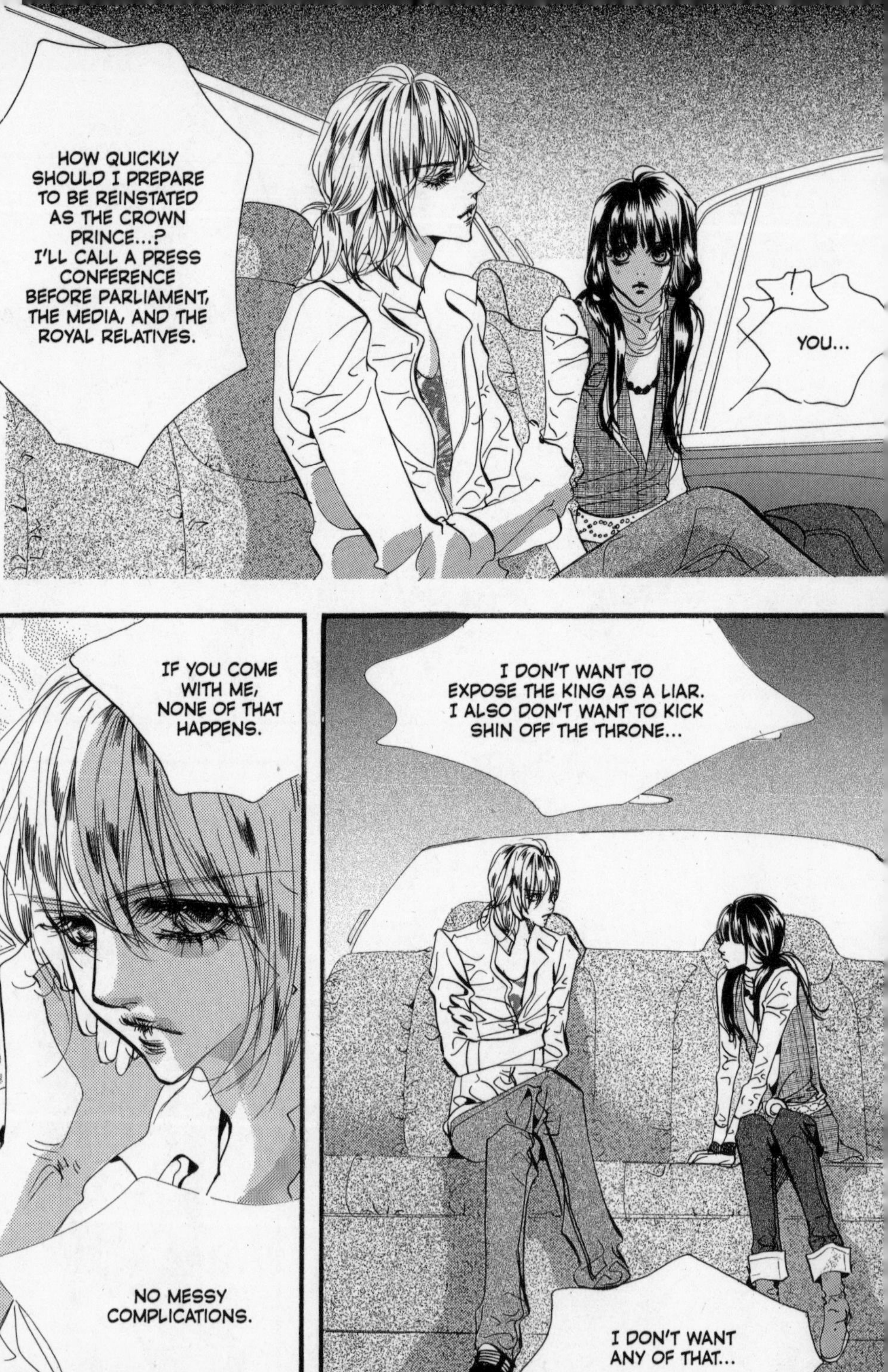
HOW QUICKLY SHOULD I PREPARE TO BE REINSTATED AS THE CROWN PRINCE...? I'LL CALL A PRESS CONFERENCE BEFORE PARLIAMENT, THE MEDIA, AND THE ROYAL RELATIVES.
!
YOU...
IF YOU COME WITH ME, NONE OF THAT HAPPENS.
NO MESSY COMPLICATIONS.
I DON'T WANT TO EXPOSE THE KING AS A LIAR. I ALSO DON'T WANT TO KICK SHIN OFF THE THRONE...
I DON'T WANT ANY OF THAT...

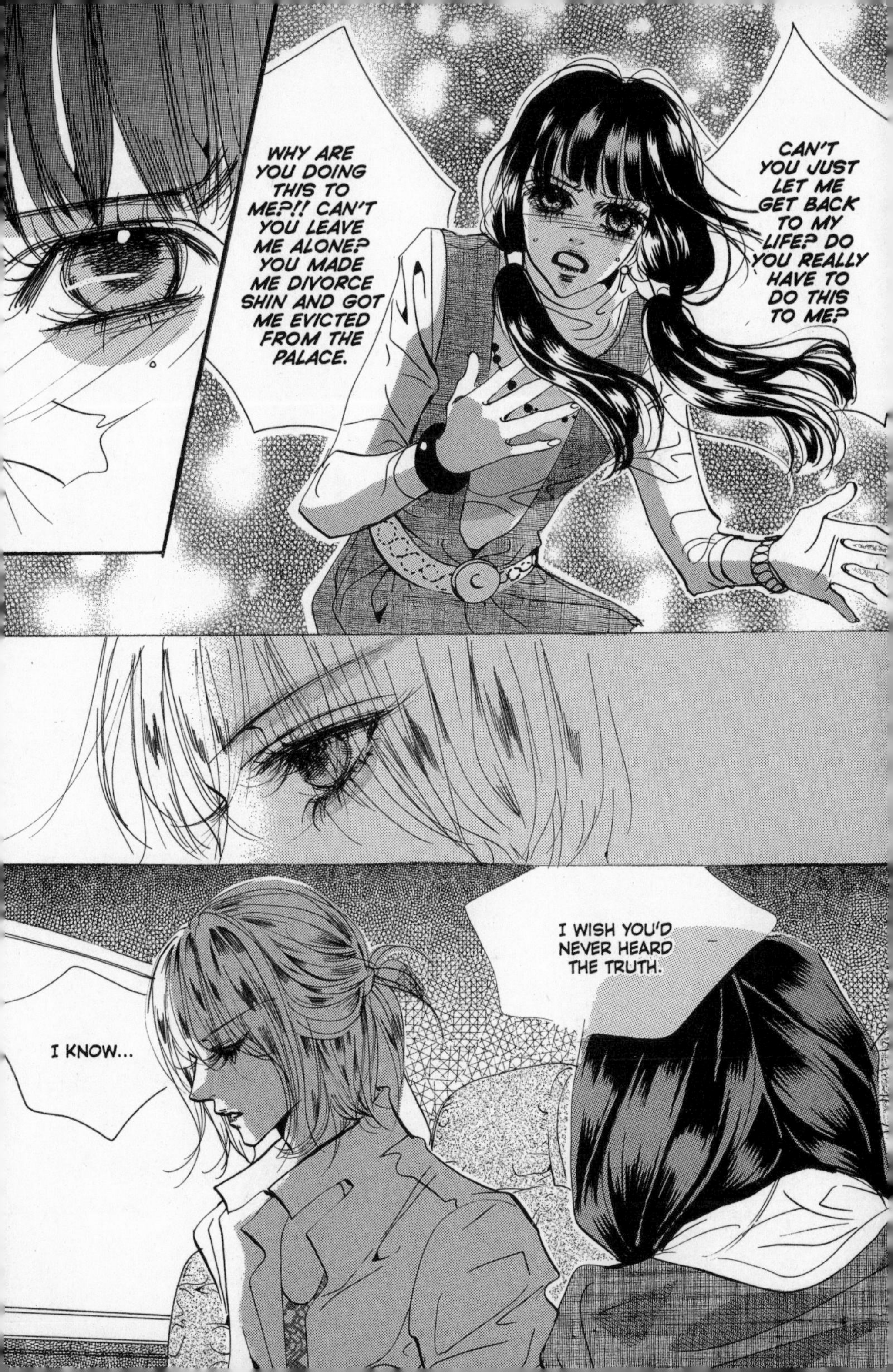
WHY ARE YOU DOING THIS TO ME?!! CAN'T YOU LEAVE ME ALONE? YOU MADE ME DIVORCE SHIN AND GOT ME EVICTED FROM THE PALACE.
CAN'T YOU JUST LET ME GET BACK TO MY LIFE? DO YOU REALLY HAVE TO DO THIS TO ME?
I KNOW...
I WISH YOU'D NEVER HEARD THE TRUTH.

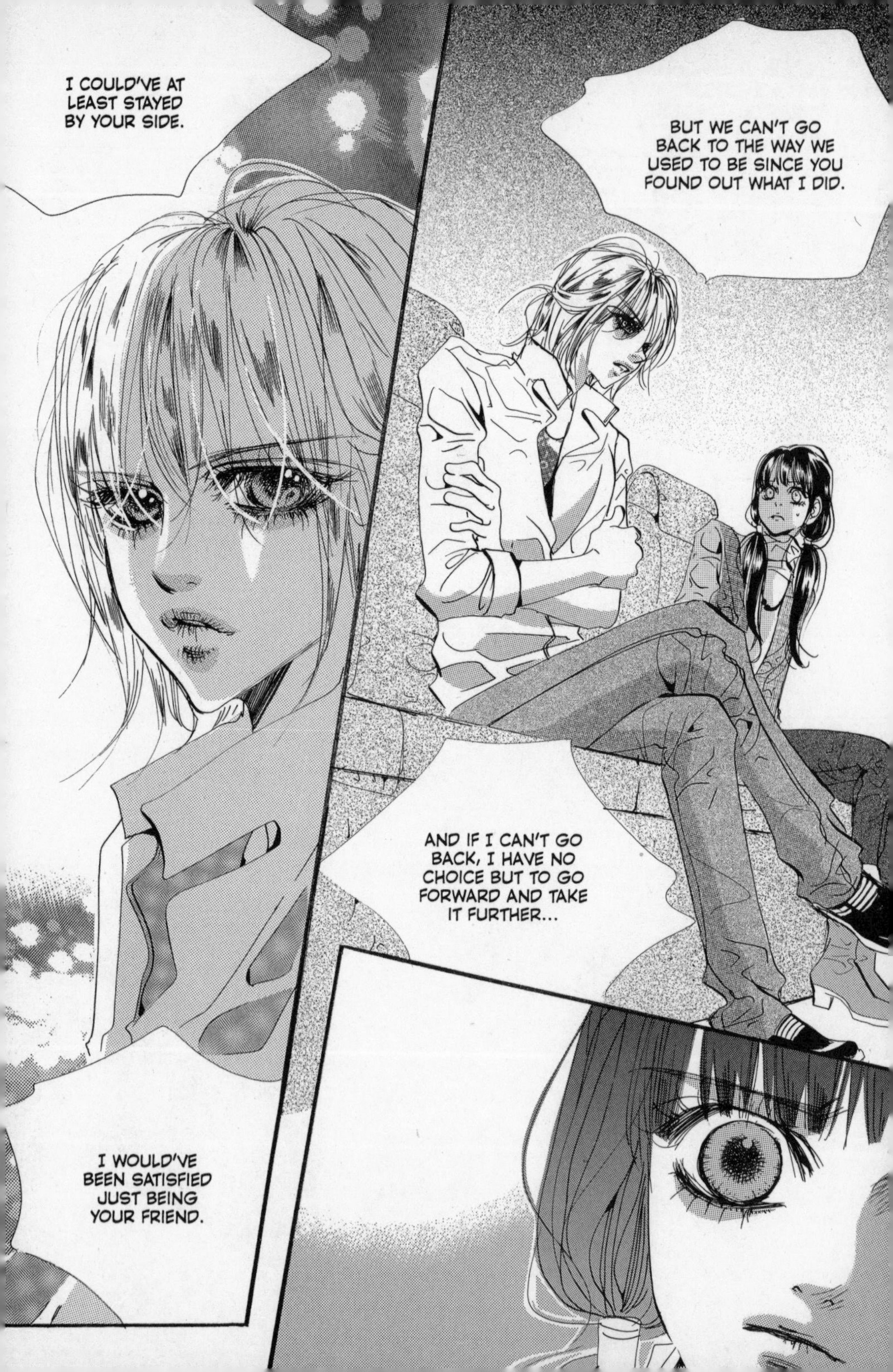
I COULD'VE AT LEAST STAYED BY YOUR SIDE.
I WOULD'VE BEEN SATISFIED JUST BEING YOUR FRIEND.
BUT WE CAN'T GO BACK TO THE WAY WE USED TO BE SINCE YOU FOUND OUT WHAT I DID.
AND IF I CAN'T GO BACK, I HAVE NO CHOICE BUT TO GO FORWARD AND TAKE IT FURTHER...

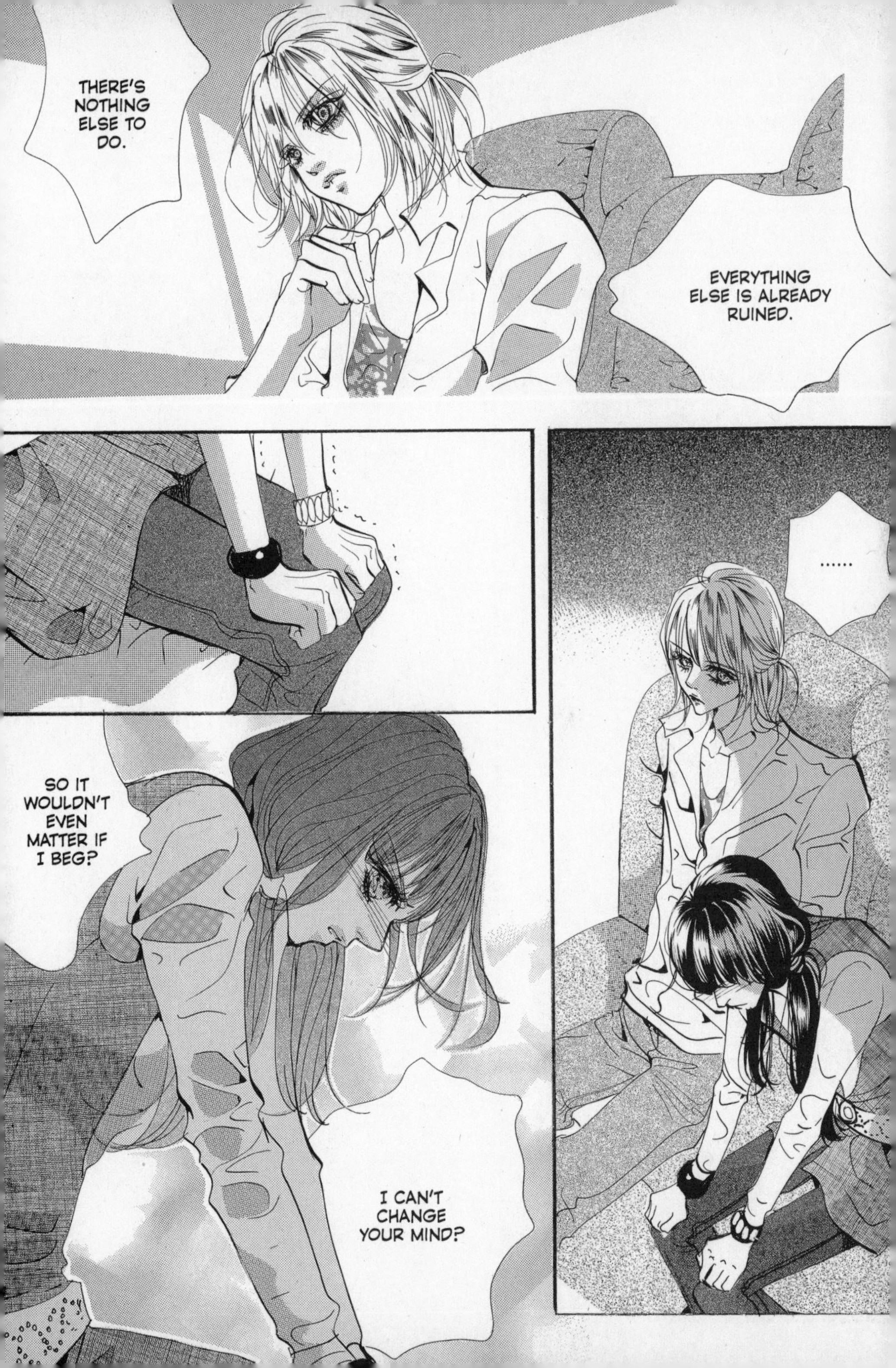
THERE'S NOTHING ELSE TO DO.
EVERYTHING ELSE IS ALREADY RUINED.
SO IT WOULDN'T EVEN MATTER IF I BEG?
I CAN'T CHANGE YOUR MIND?
......

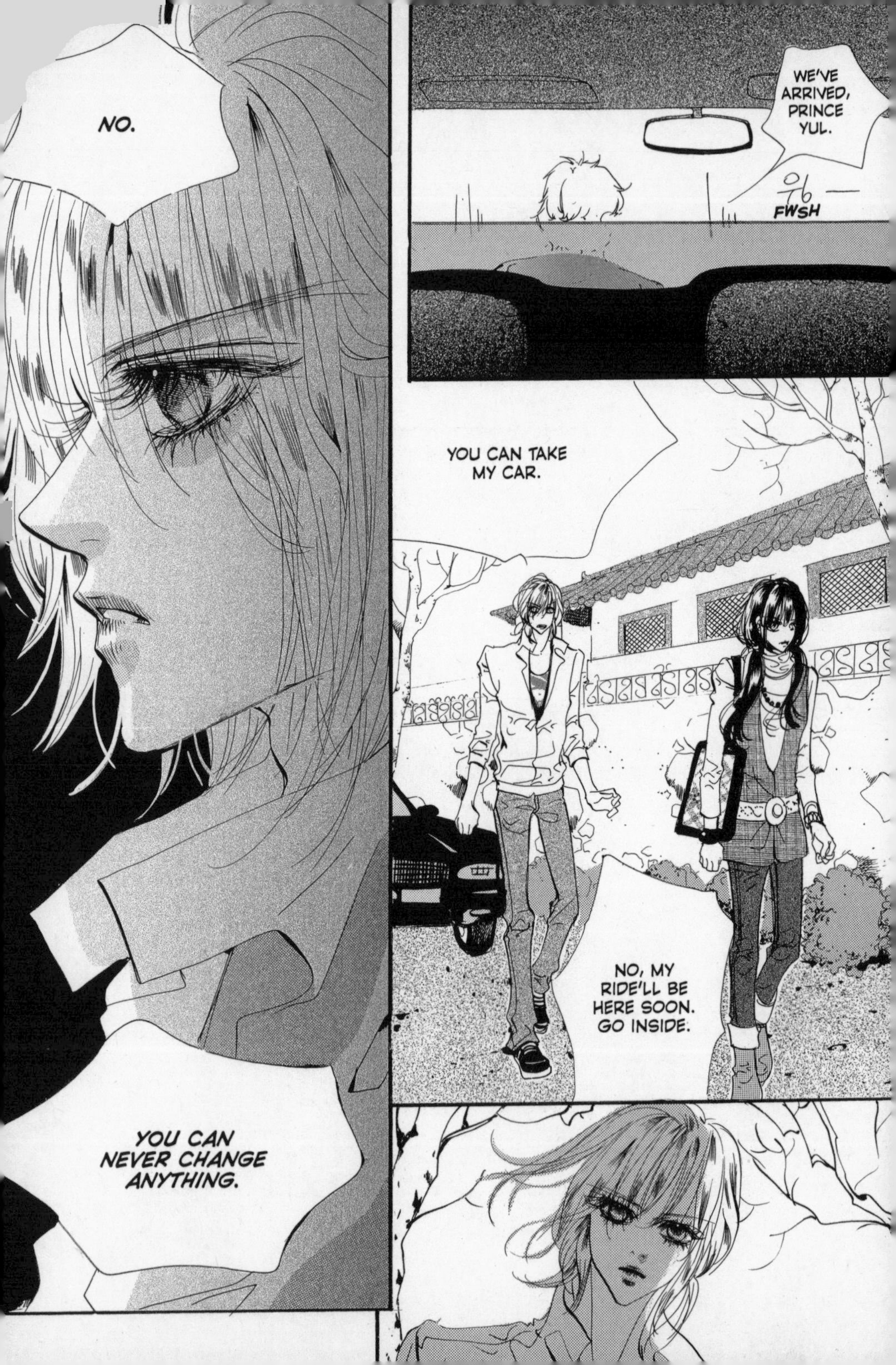
NO.
YOU CAN NEVER CHANGE ANYTHING.
WE'VE ARRIVED, PRINCE YUL.
FWSH
YOU CAN TAKE MY CAR.
NO, MY RIDE'LL BE HERE SOON. GO INSIDE.

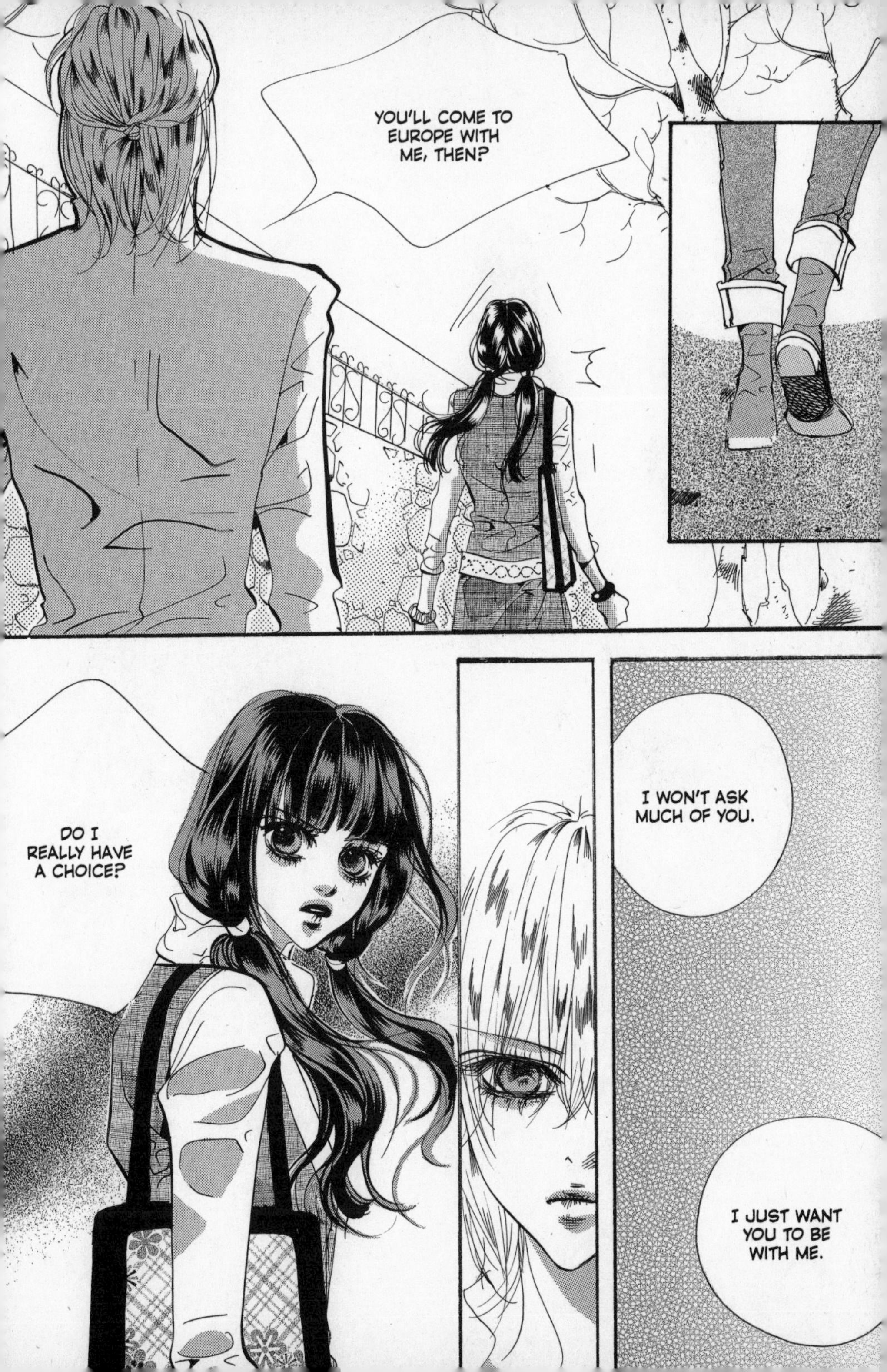
YOU'LL COME TO EUROPE WITH ME, THEN?
DO I REALLY HAVE A CHOICE?
I WON'T ASK MUCH OF YOU.
I JUST WANT YOU TO BE WITH ME.

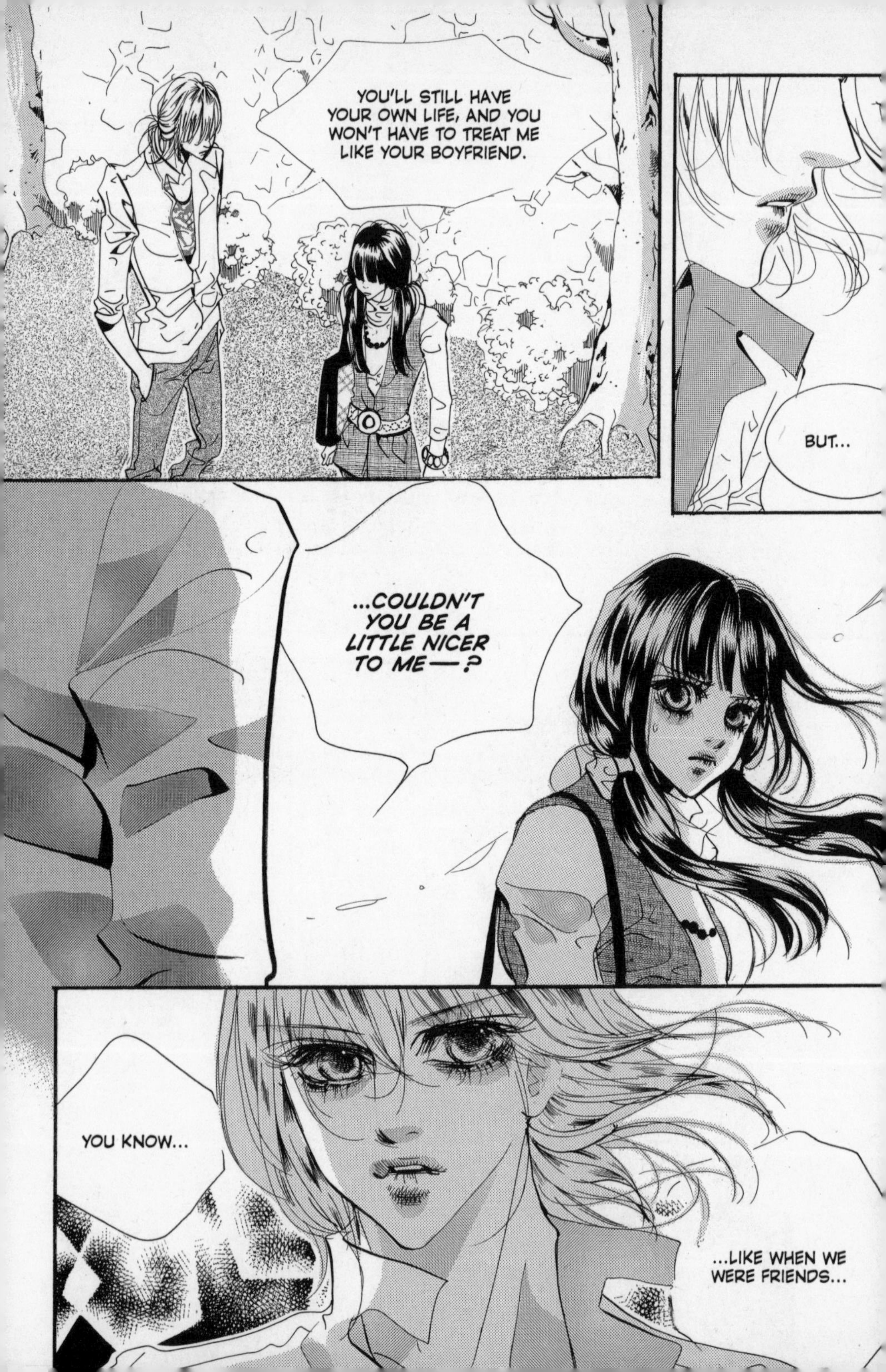
YOU'LL STILL HAVE YOUR OWN LIFE, AND YOU WON'T HAVE TO TREAT ME LIKE YOUR BOYFRIEND.
BUT...
...COULDN'T YOU BE A LITTLE NICER TO ME—?
YOU KNOW...
...LIKE WHEN WE WERE FRIENDS...

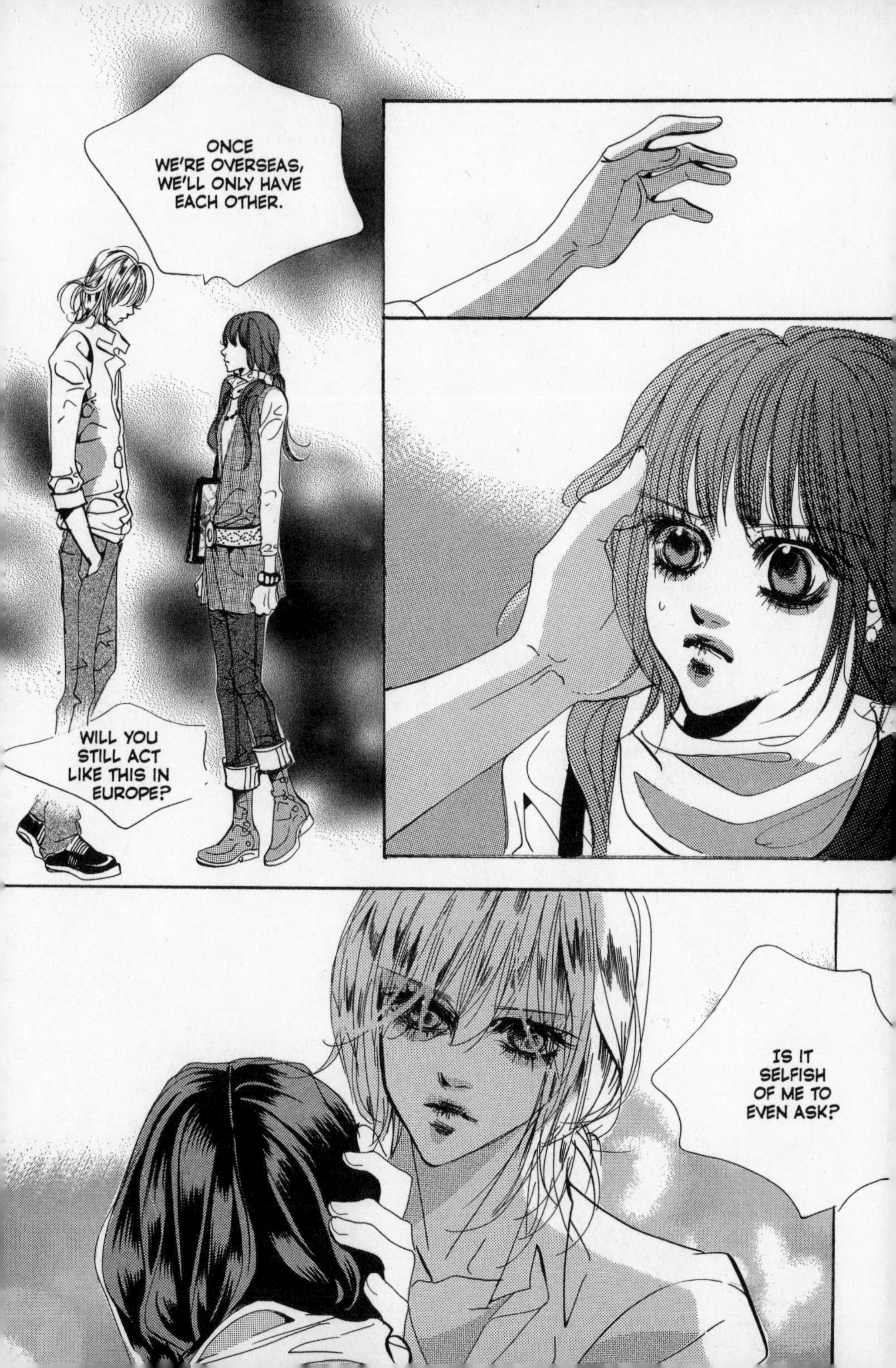
ONCE WE'RE OVERSEAS, WE'LL ONLY HAVE EACH OTHER.
WILL YOU STILL ACT LIKE THIS IN EUROPE?
IS IT SELFISH OF ME TO EVEN ASK?

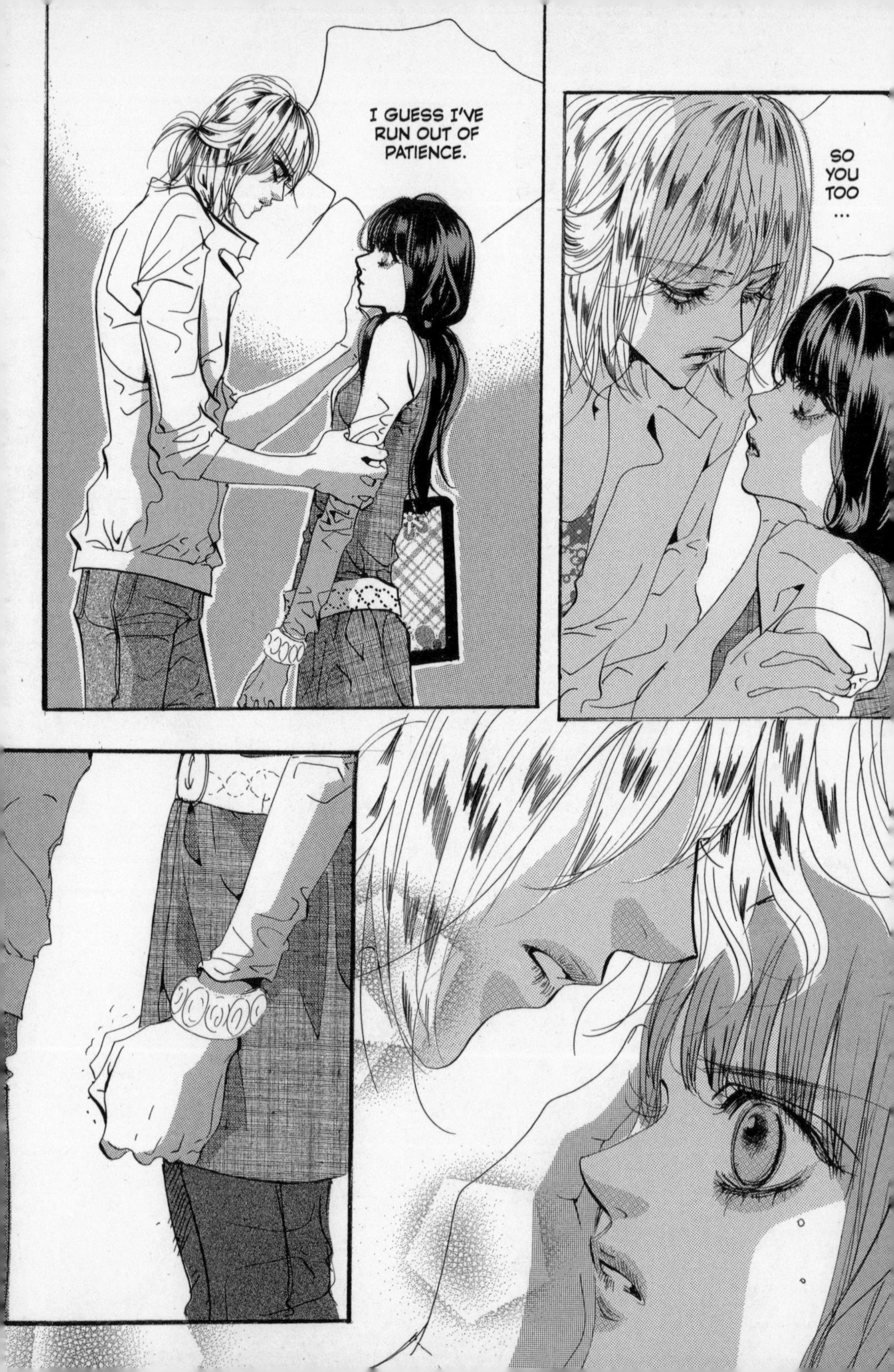
I GUESS I'VE RUN OUT OF PATIENCE.
SO YOU TOO ...

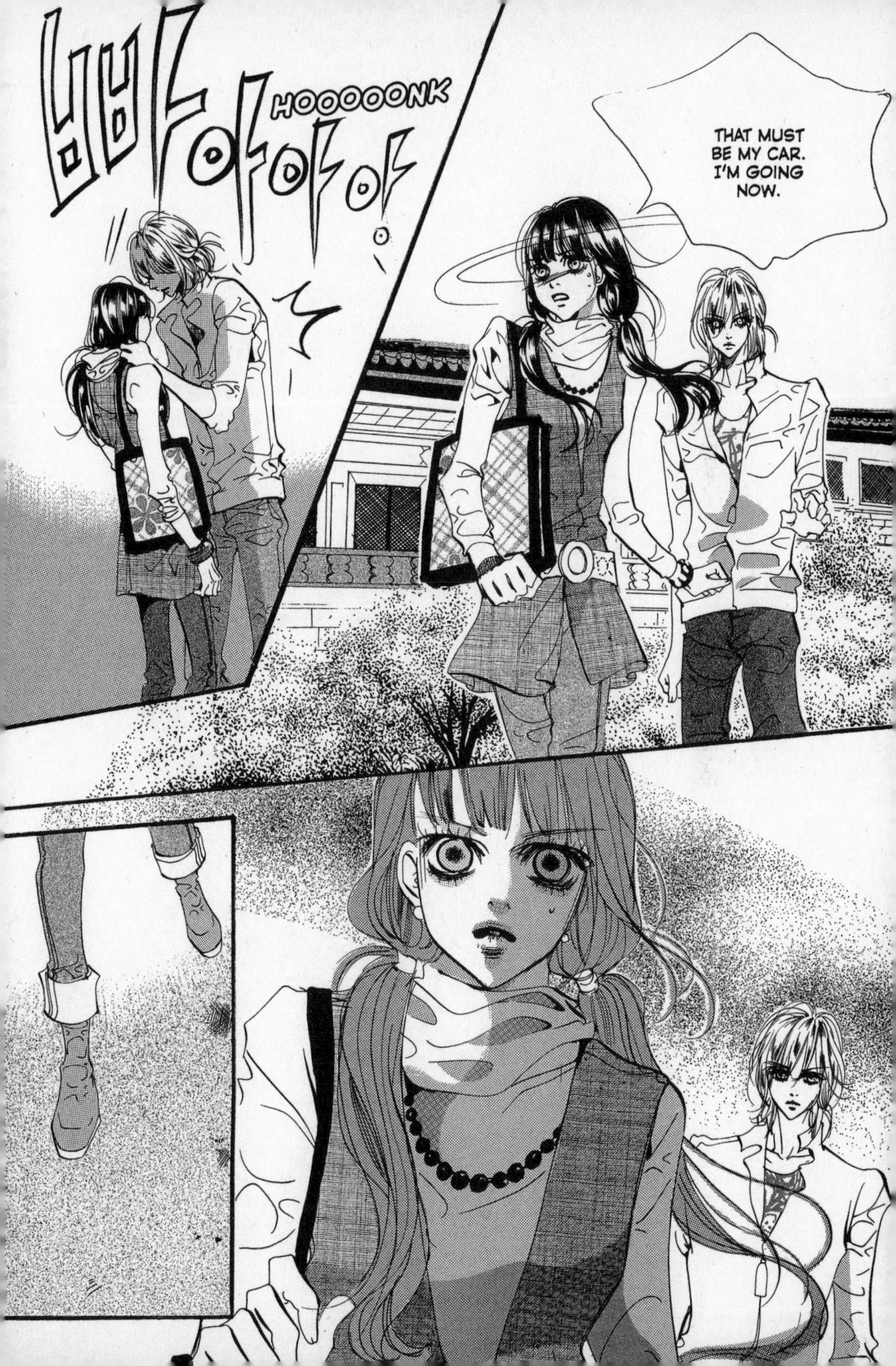
HOOOOONK
THAT MUST BE MY CAR. I'M GOING NOW.

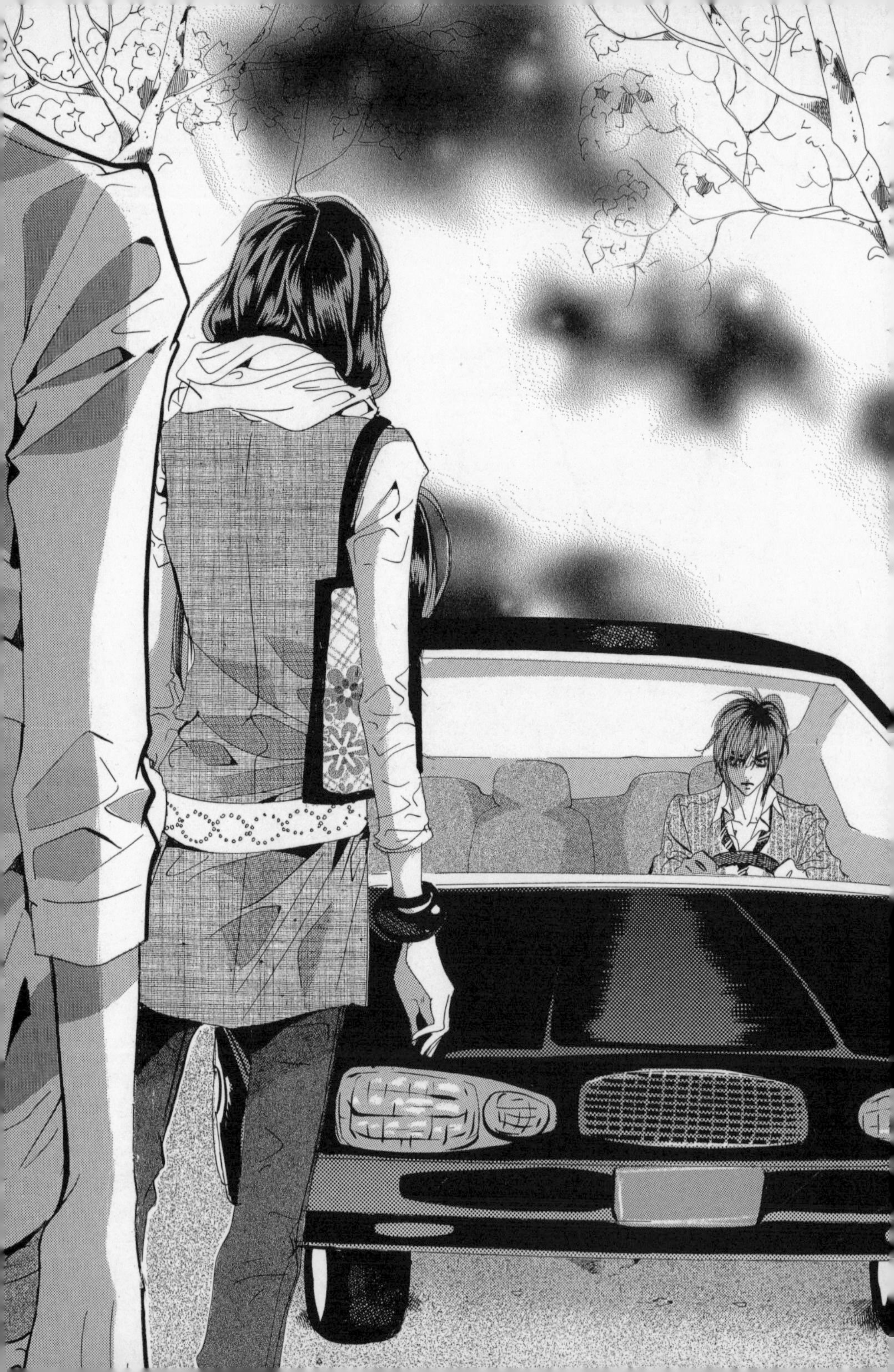

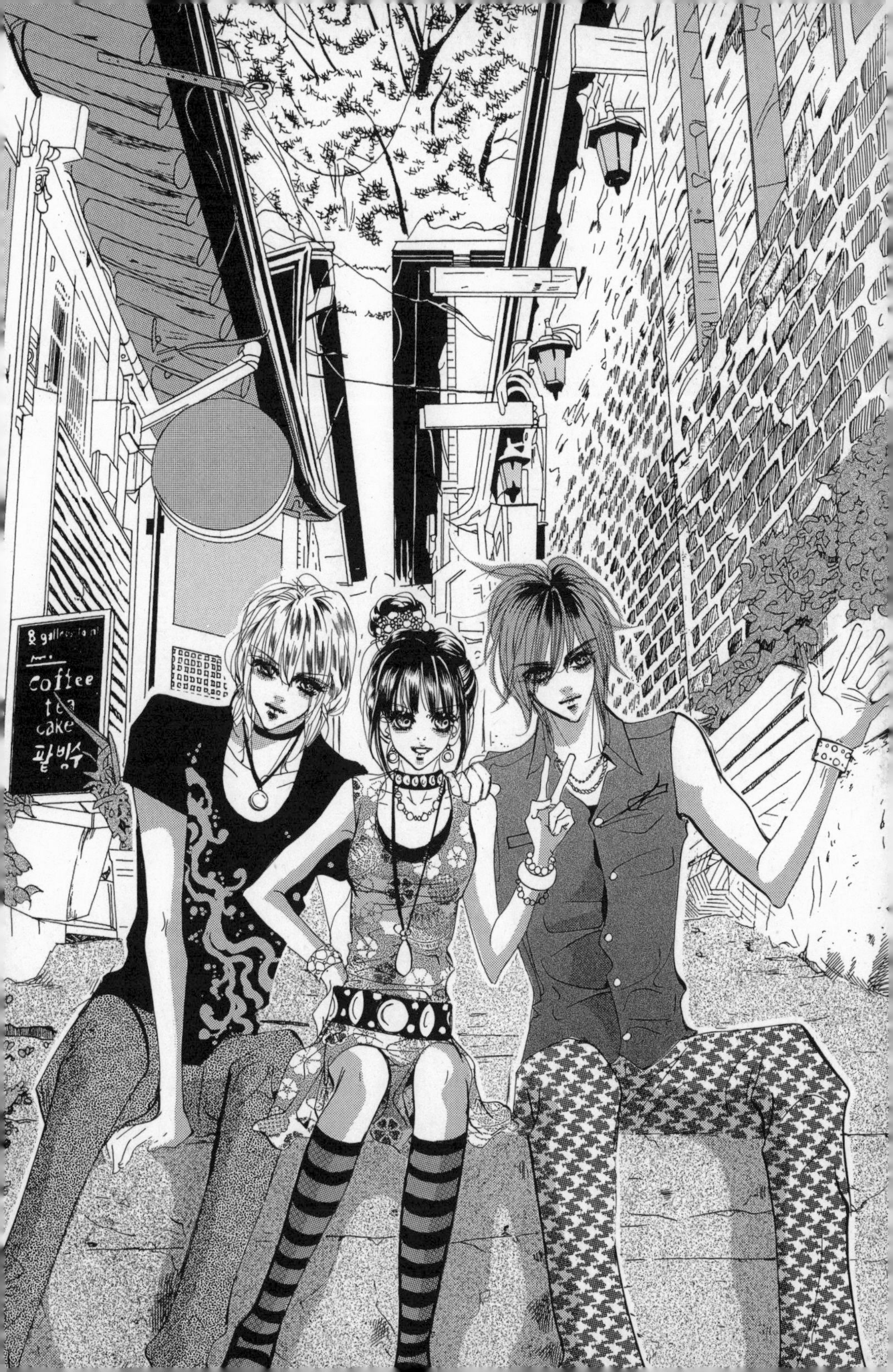
coffee
tea
cake
팥빙수

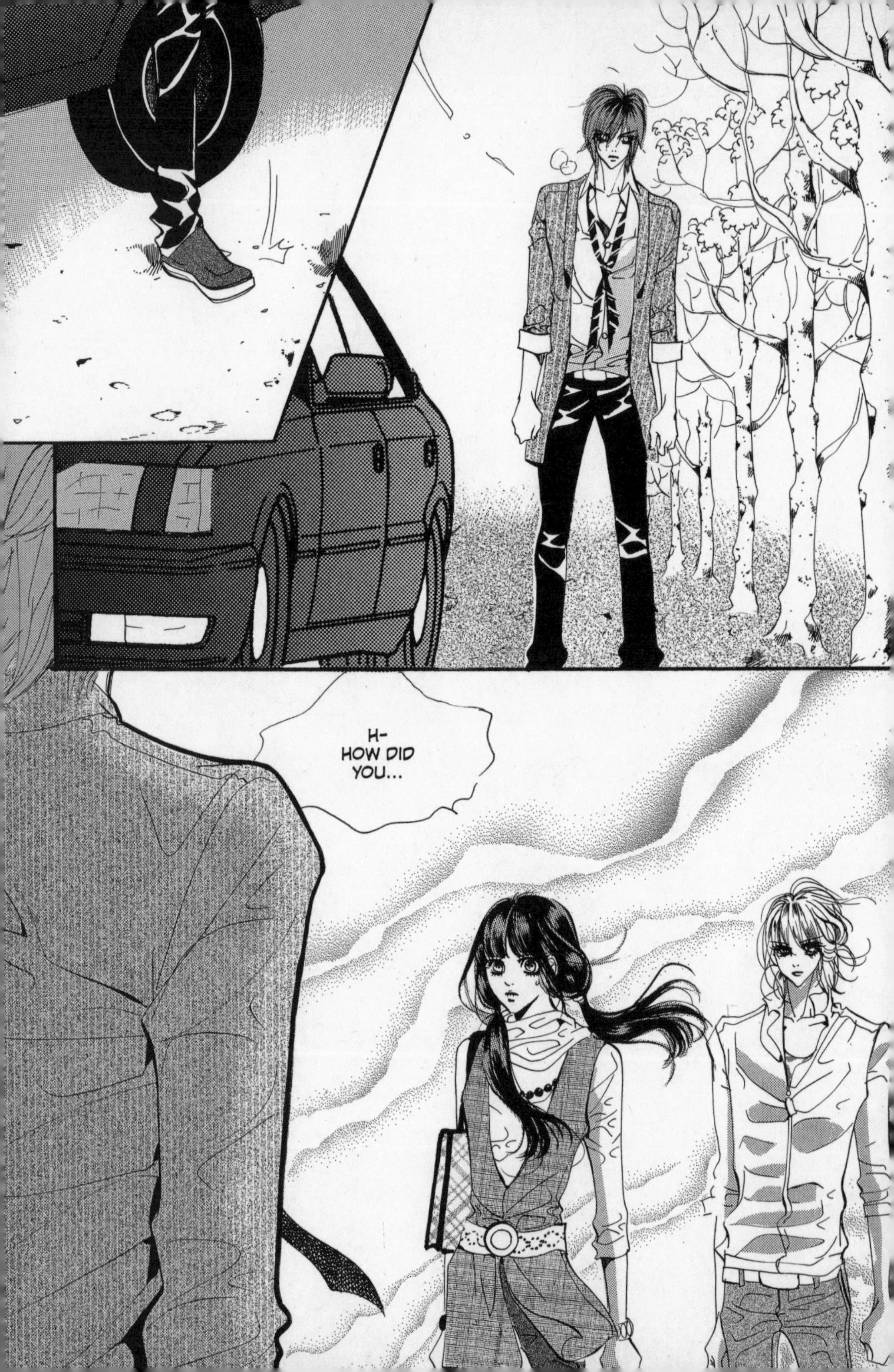
H- HOW DID YOU...

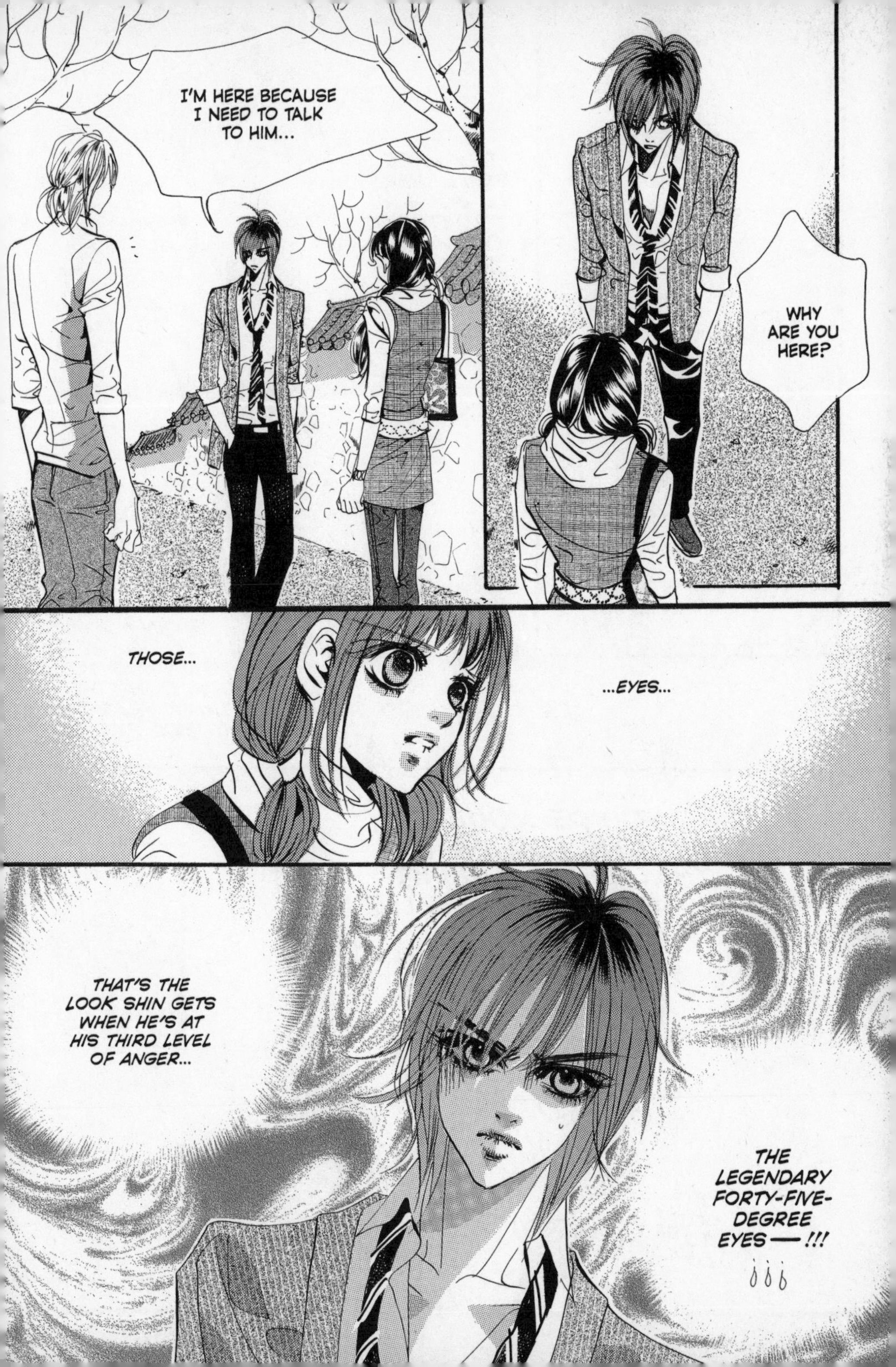
I'M HERE BECAUSE I NEED TO TALK TO HIM...
WHY ARE YOU HERE?
THOSE...
...EYES...
THAT'S THE LOOK SHIN GETS WHEN HE'S AT HIS THIRD LEVEL OF ANGER...
THE LEGENDARY FORTY-FIVE-DEGREE EYES—!!!

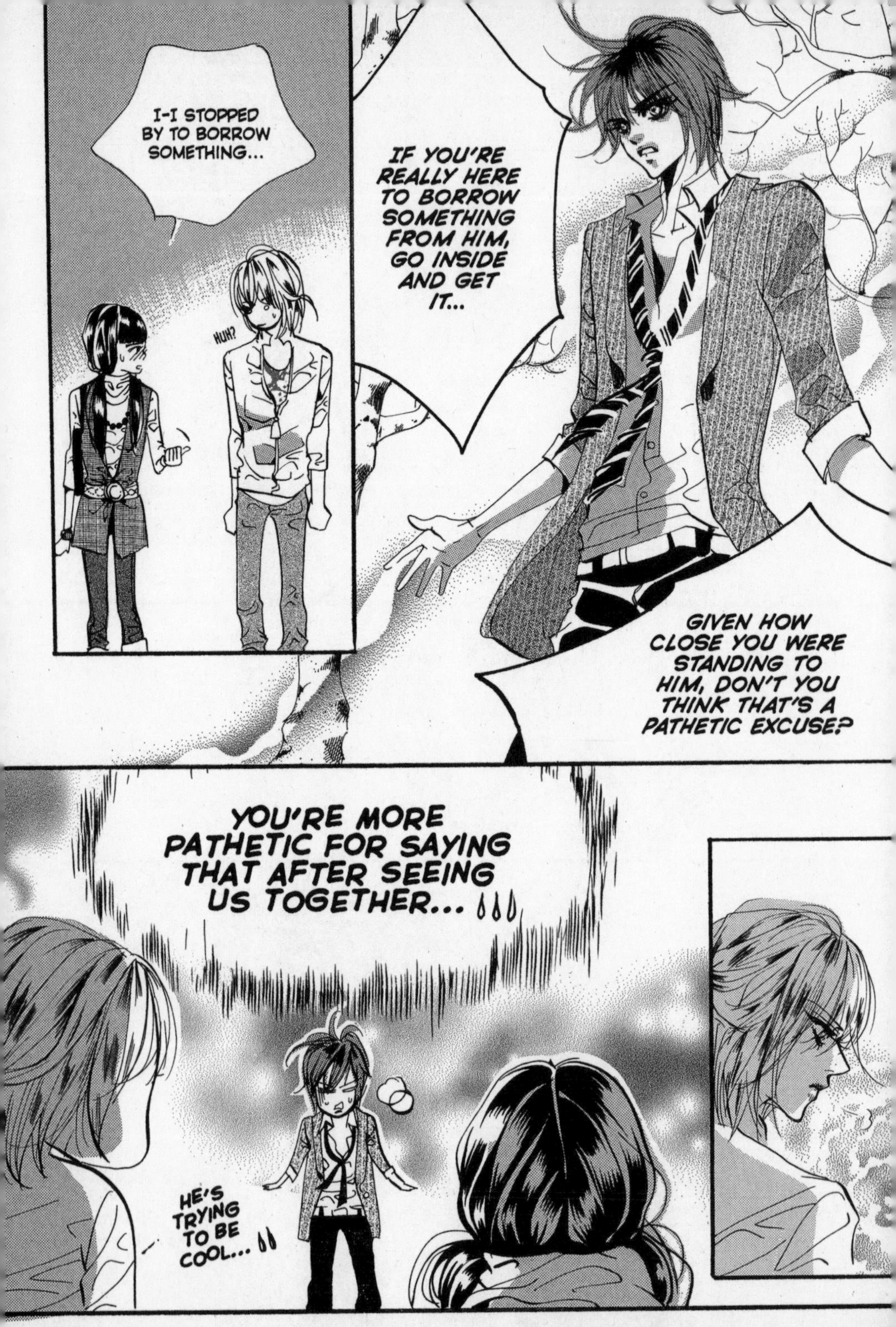
I-I STOPPED BY TO BORROW SOMETHING...
HUH?
IF YOU'RE REALLY HERE TO BORROW SOMETHING FROM HIM, GO INSIDE AND GET IT...
GIVEN HOW CLOSE YOU WERE STANDING TO HIM, DON'T YOU THINK THAT'S A PATHETIC EXCUSE?
YOU'RE MORE PATHETIC FOR SAYING THAT AFTER SEEING US TOGETHER...
HE'S TRYING TO BE COOL...

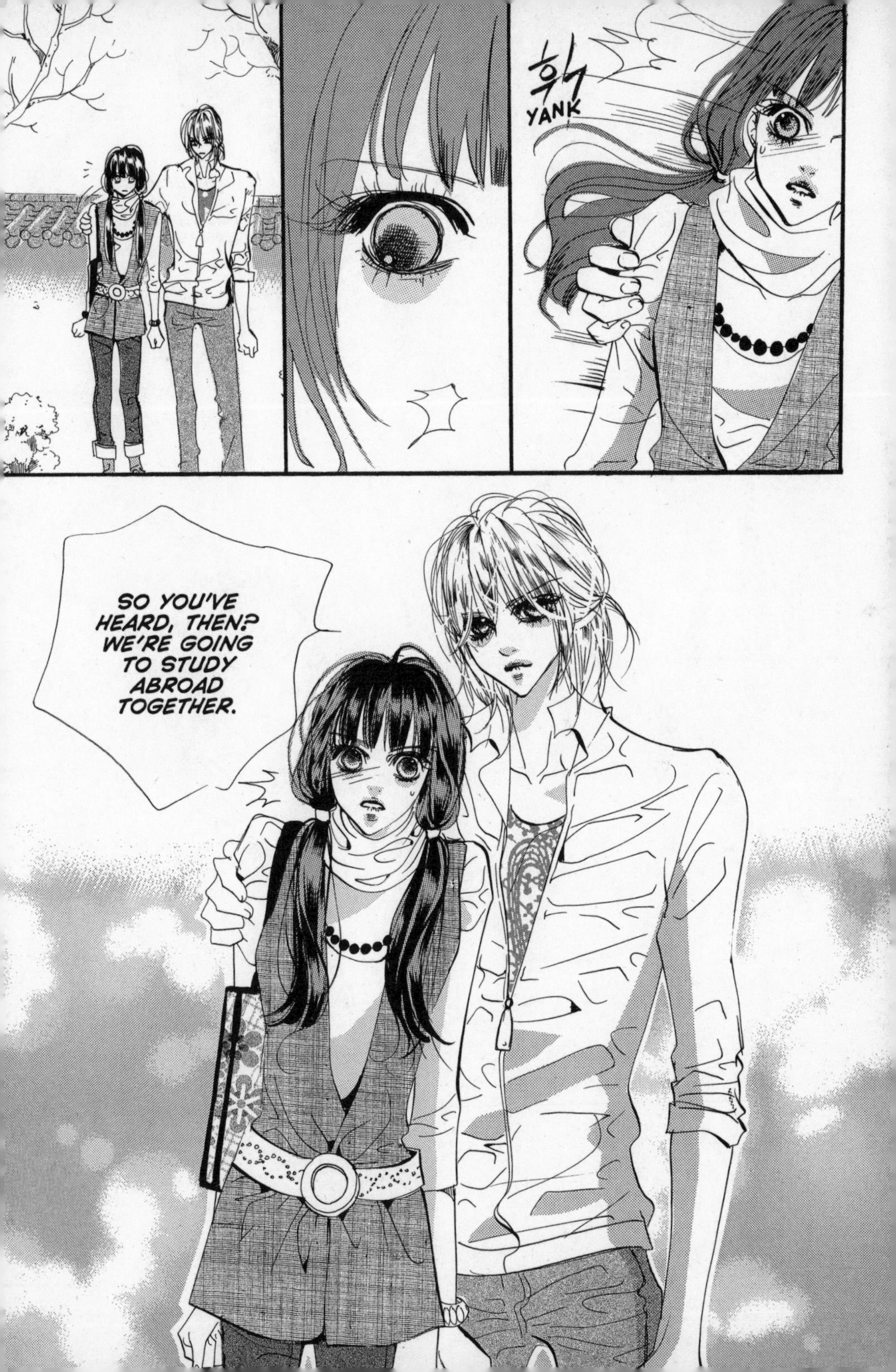
훅
YANK
SO YOU'VE HEARD, THEN? WE'RE GOING TO STUDY ABROAD TOGETHER.

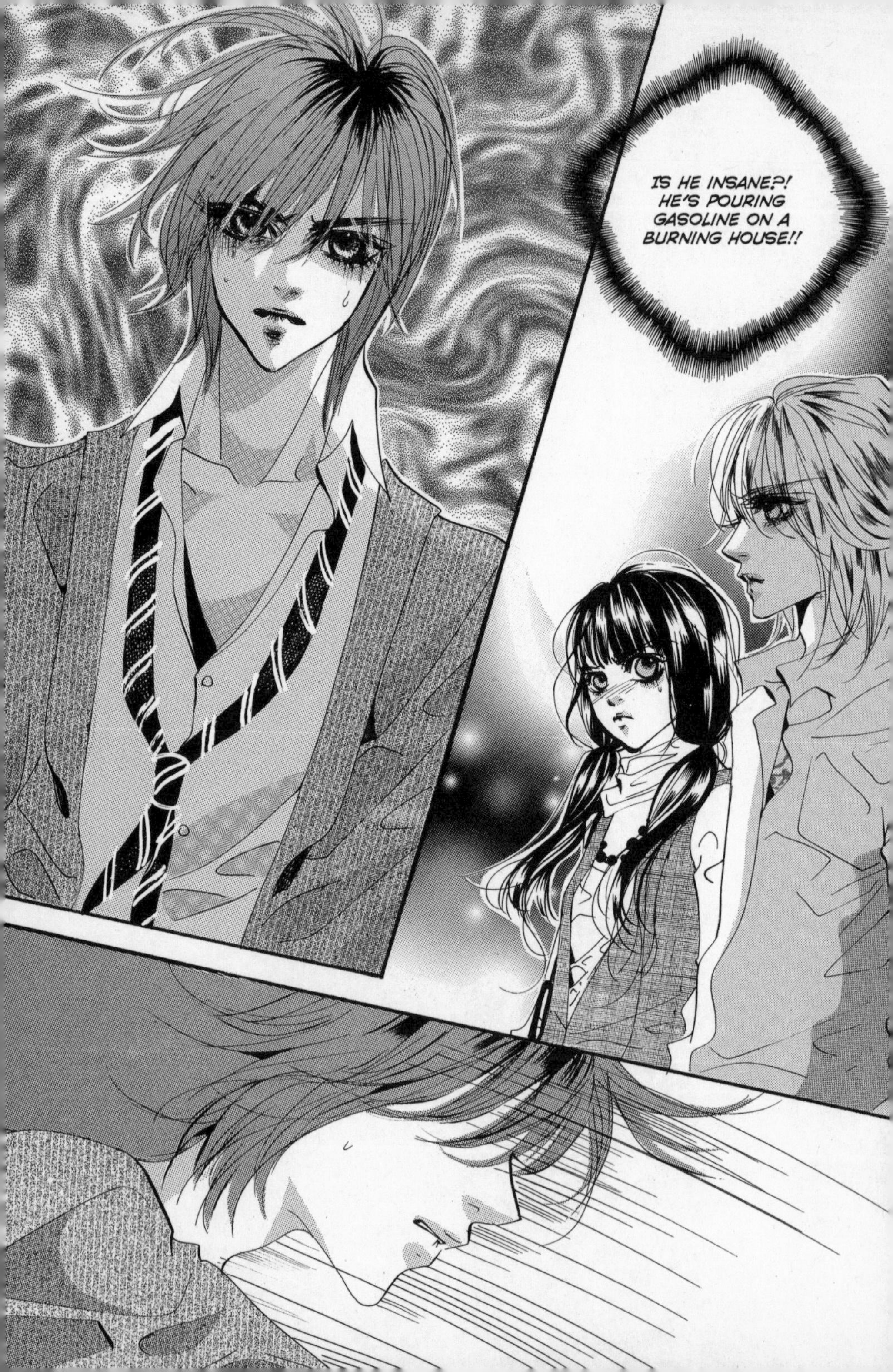
IS HE INSANE?! HE'S POURING GASOLINE ON A BURNING HOUSE!!

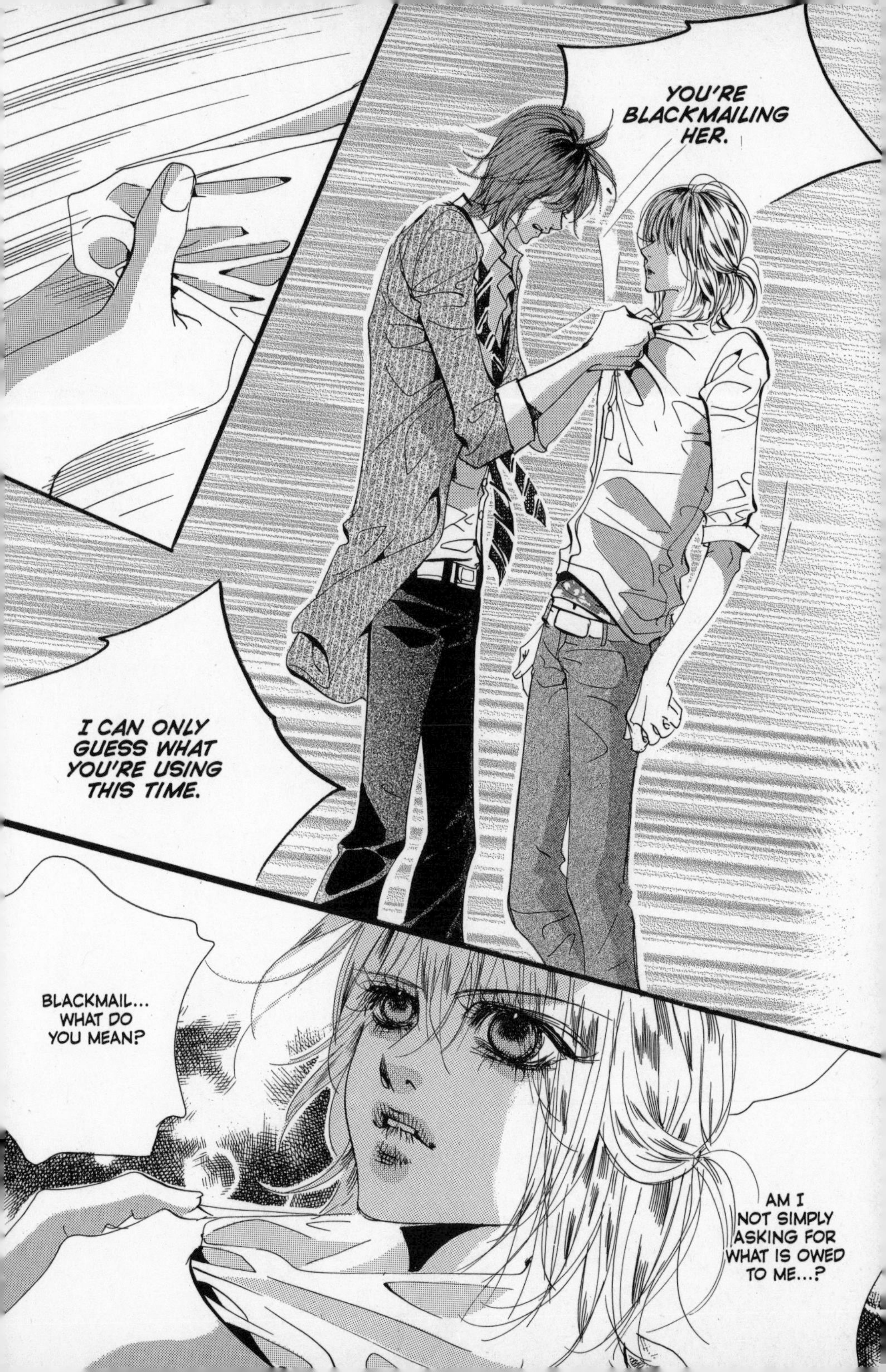
YOU'RE BLACKMAILING HER.
I CAN ONLY GUESS WHAT YOU'RE USING THIS TIME.
BLACKMAIL... WHAT DO YOU MEAN?
AM I NOT SIMPLY ASKING FOR WHAT IS OWED TO ME...?

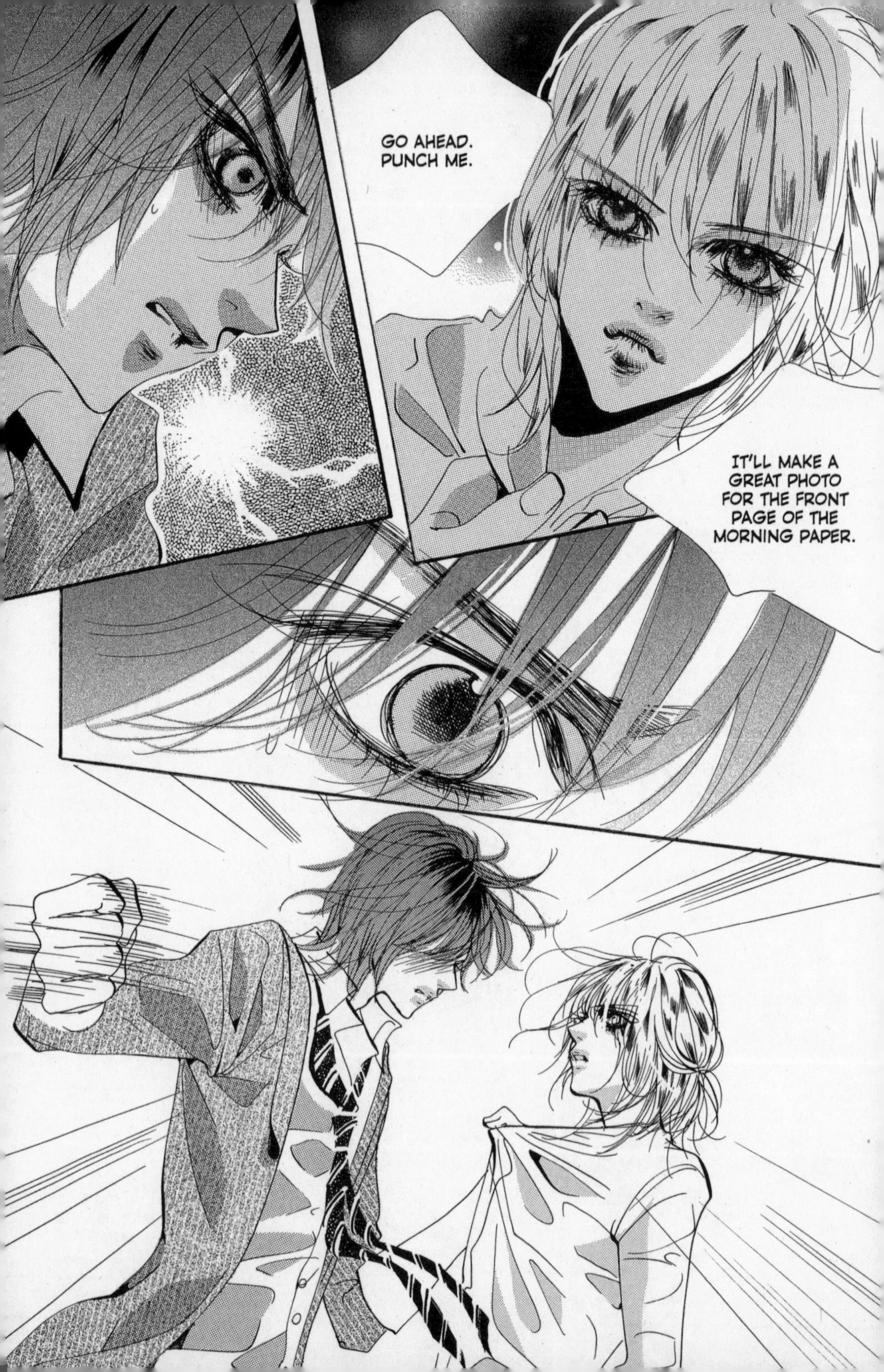
GO AHEAD. PUNCH ME.
IT'LL MAKE A GREAT PHOTO FOR THE FRONT PAGE OF THE MORNING PAPER.

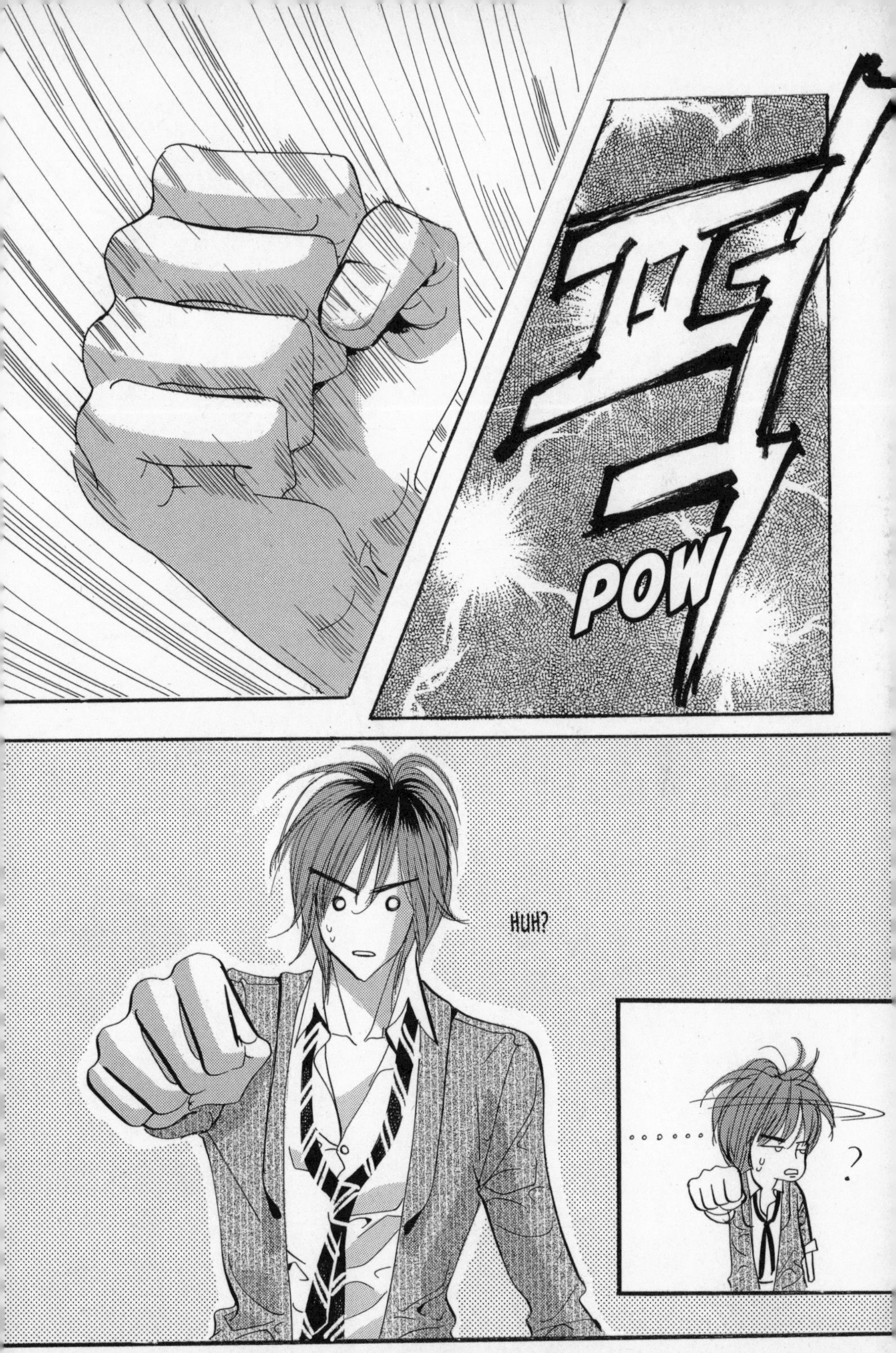
POW
HUH?
......
?

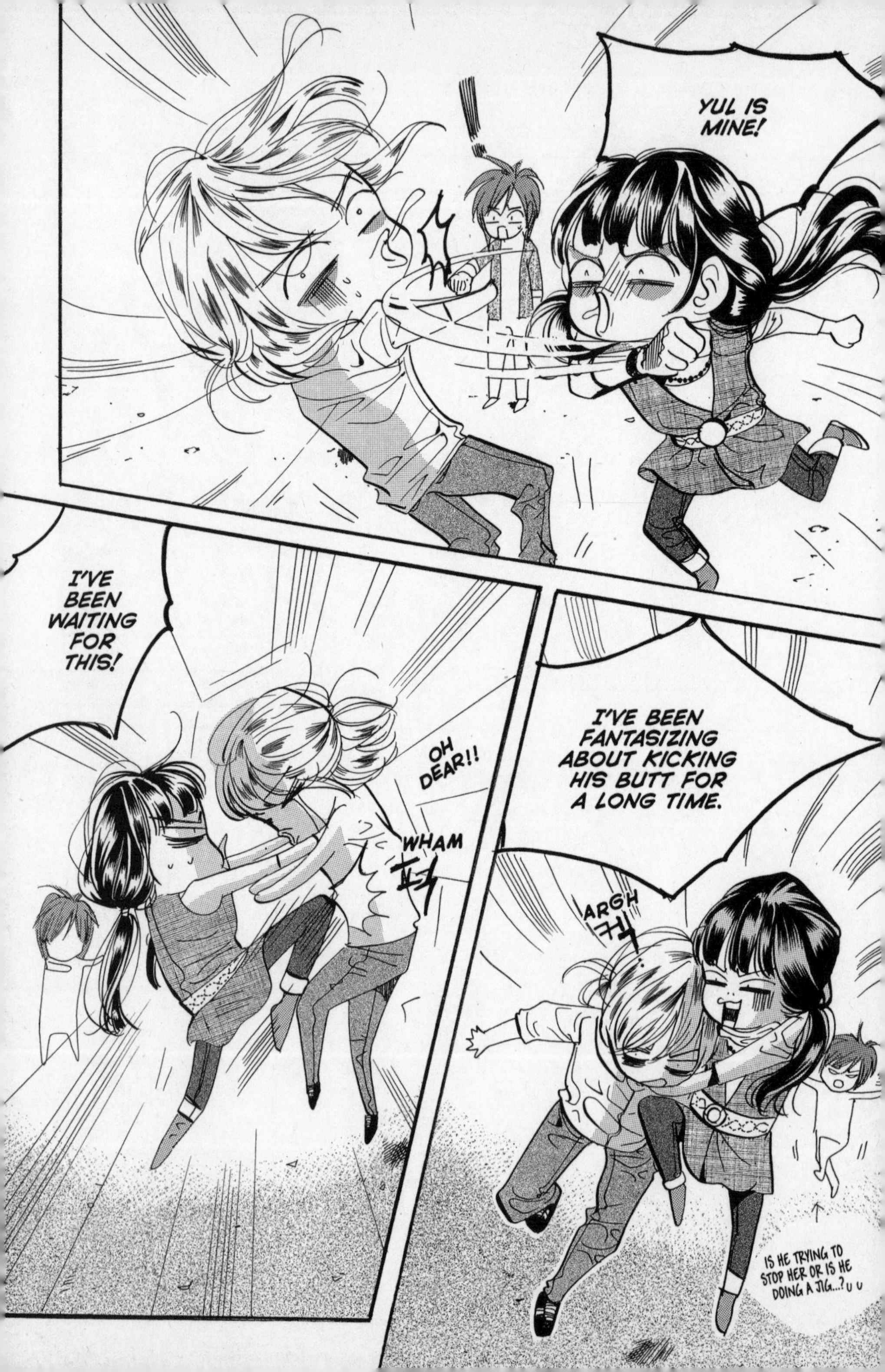
!
YUL IS MINE!
I'VE BEEN WAITING FOR THIS!
OH DEAR!!
WHAM
I'VE BEEN FANTASIZING ABOUT KICKING HIS BUTT FOR A LONG TIME.
ARGH
IS HE TRYING TO STOP HER OR IS HE DOING A JIG...?

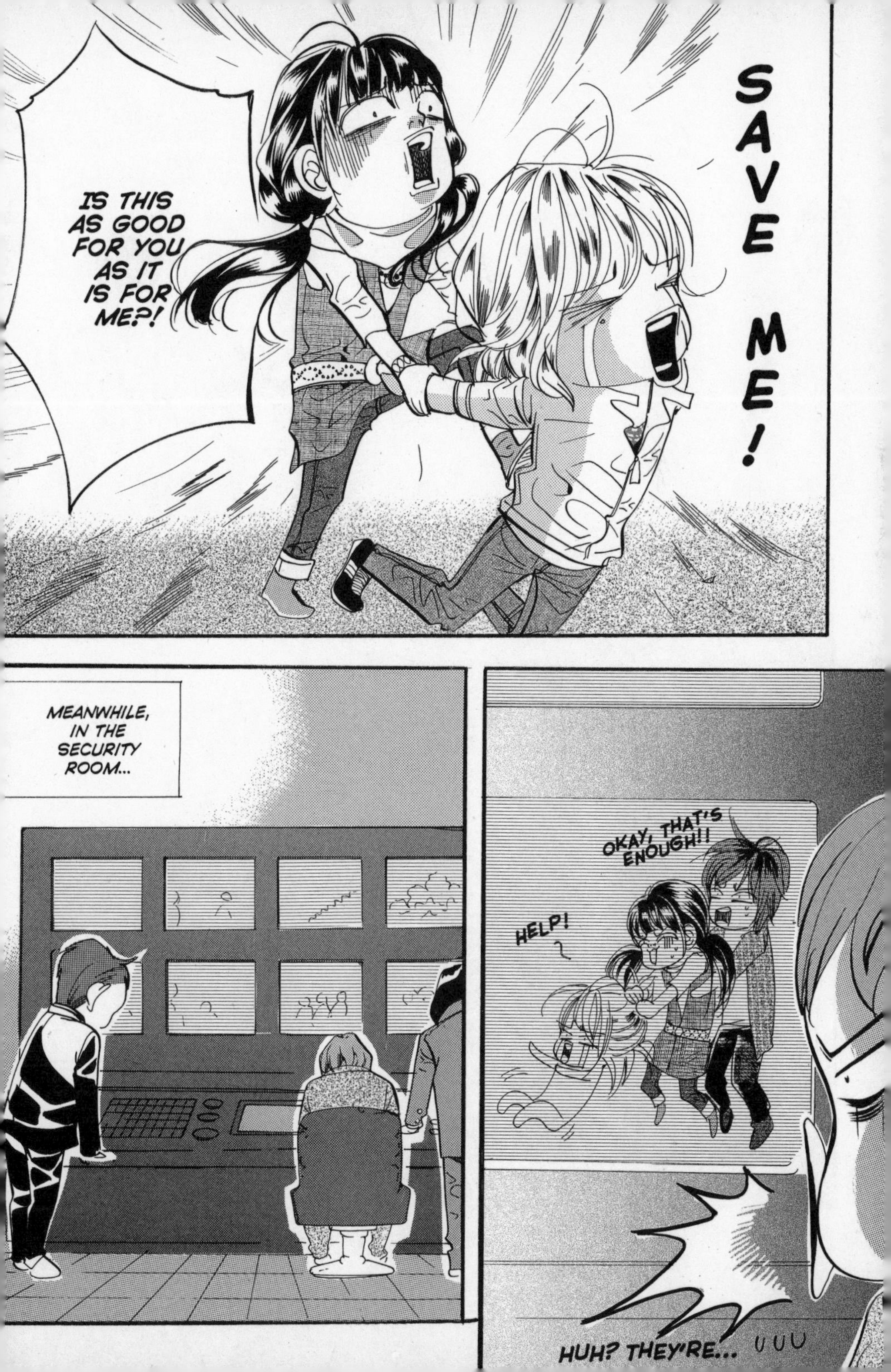
IS THIS AS GOOD FOR YOU AS IT IS FOR ME?!
SAVE ME!
MEANWHILE, IN THE SECURITY ROOM...
OKAY, THAT'S ENOUGH!!
HELP!
HUH? THEY'RE...
UUU

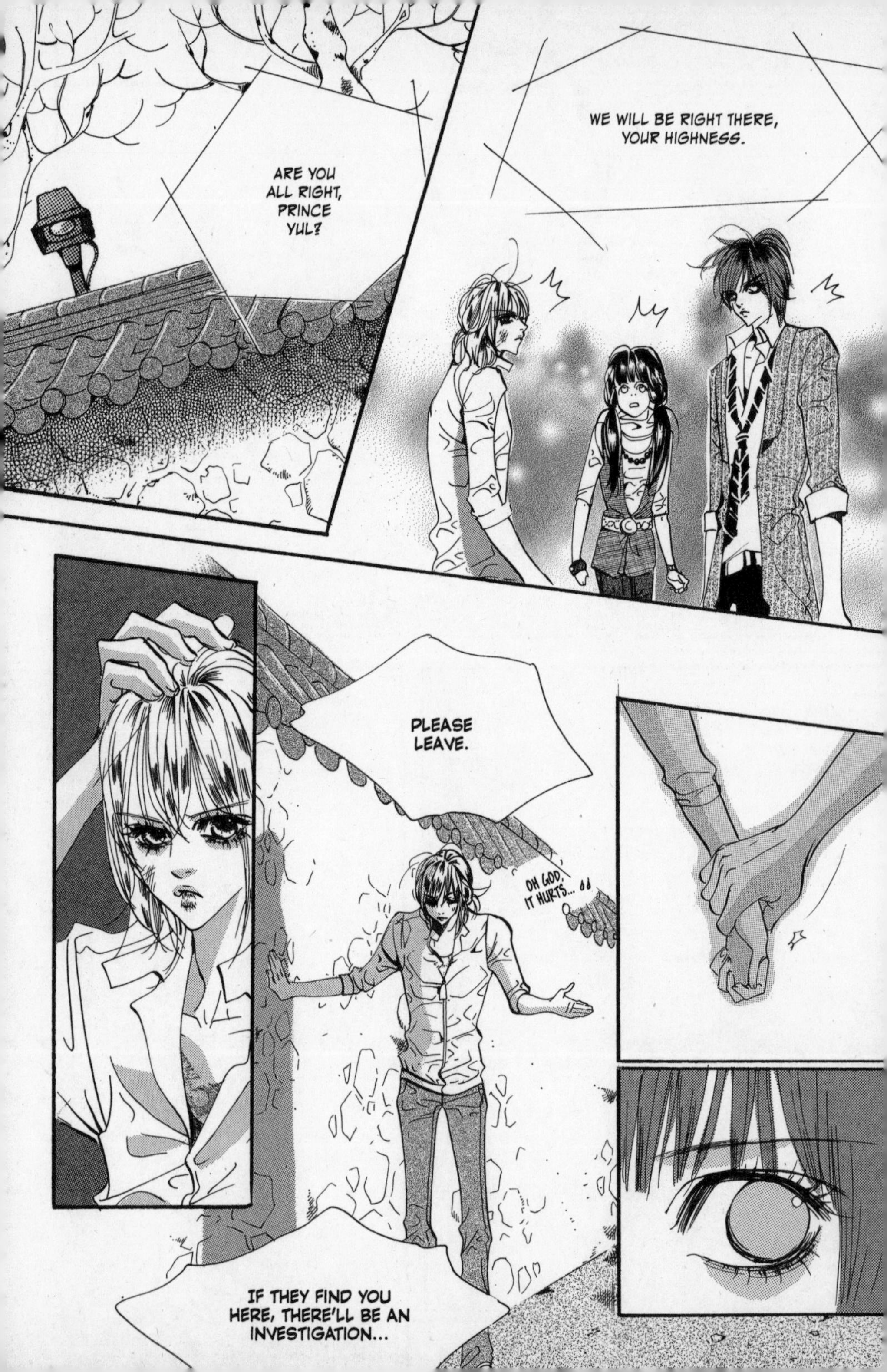
ARE YOU ALL RIGHT, PRINCE YUL?
WE WILL BE RIGHT THERE, YOUR HIGHNESS.
PLEASE LEAVE.
OH GOD, IT HURTS...
IF THEY FIND YOU HERE, THERE'LL BE AN INVESTIGATION...

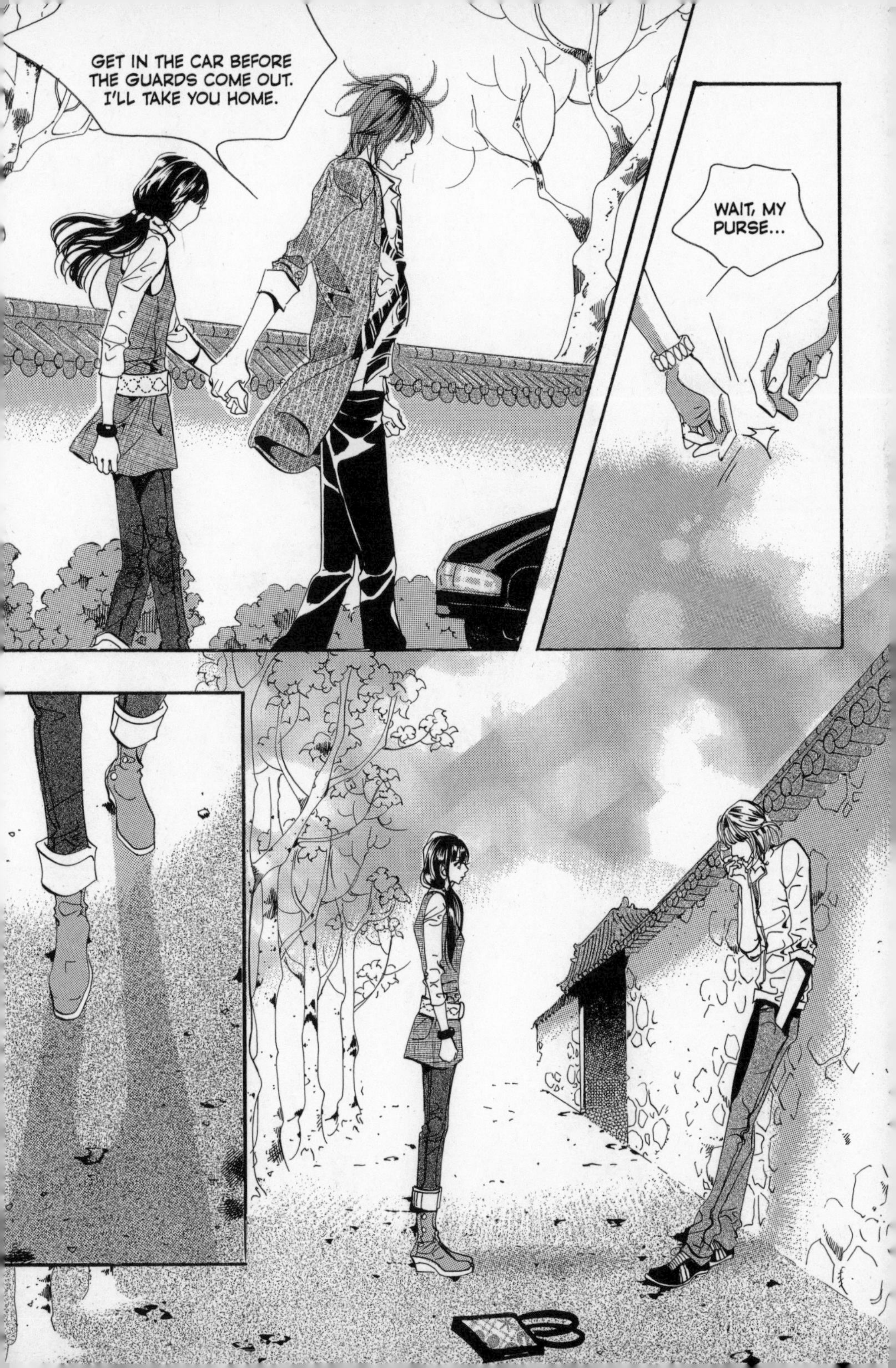
GET IN THE CAR BEFORE THE GUARDS COME OUT. I'LL TAKE YOU HOME.
WAIT, MY PURSE...

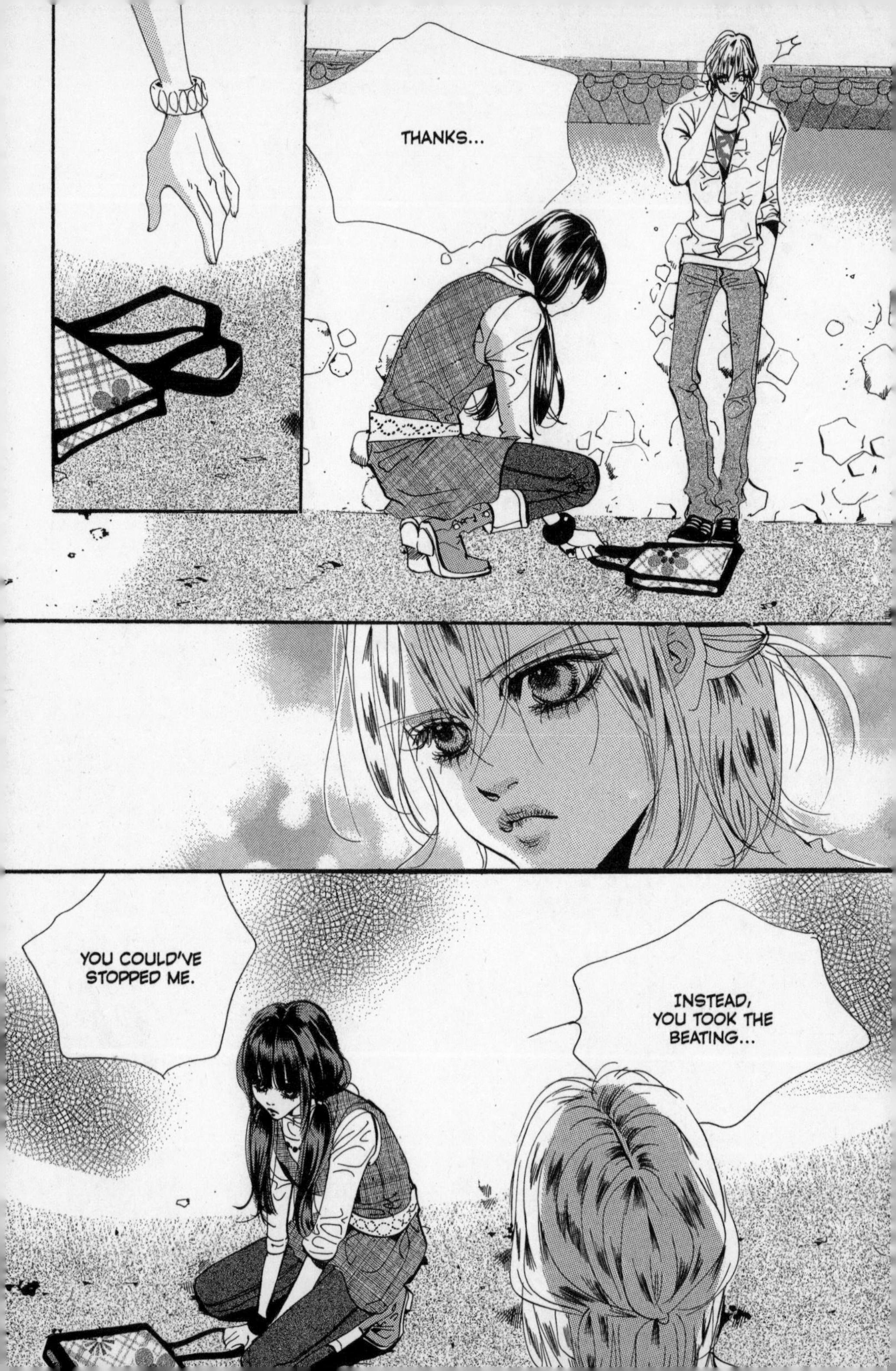
THANKS...
YOU COULD'VE STOPPED ME.
INSTEAD, YOU TOOK THE BEATING...

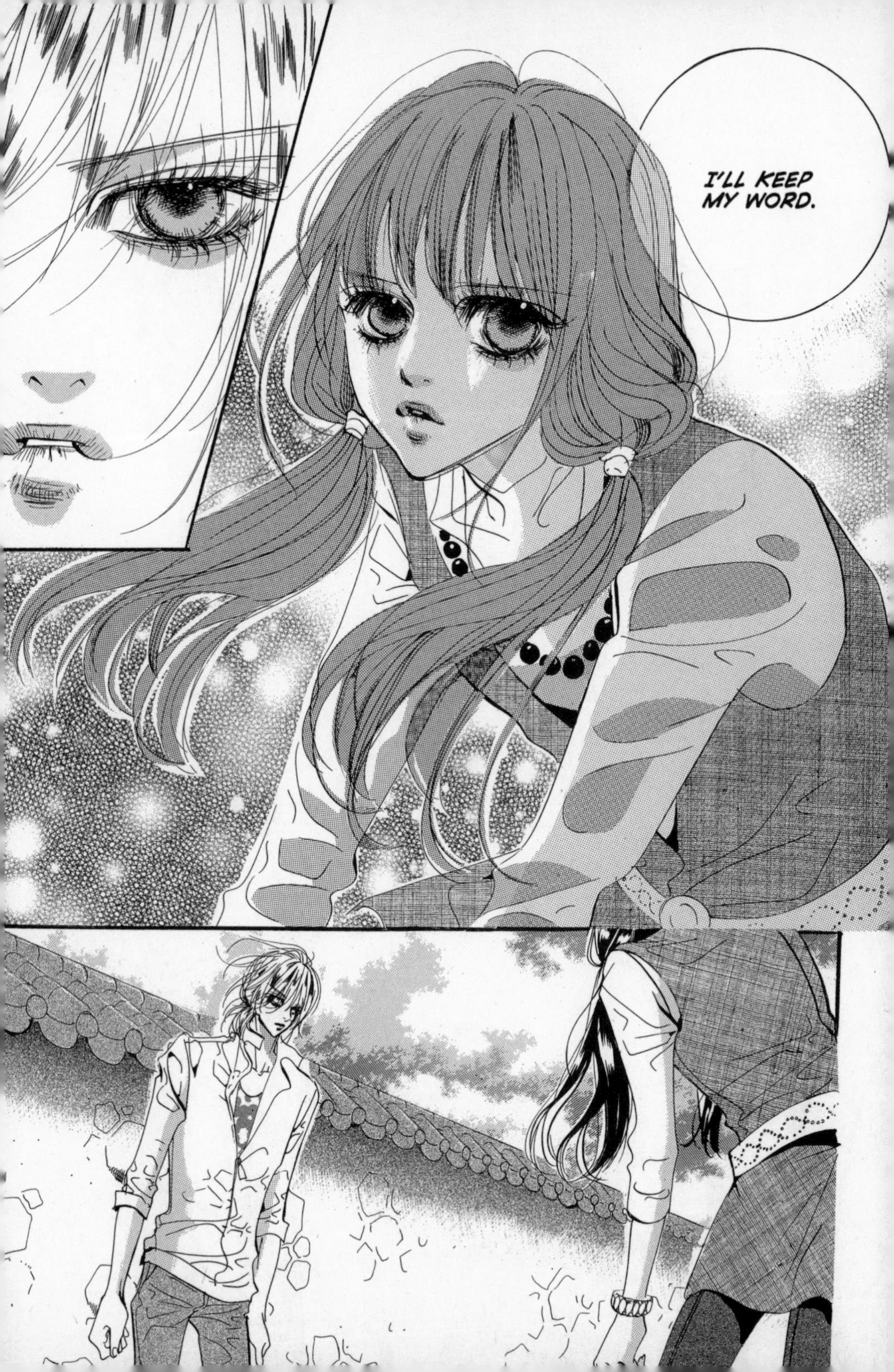
I'LL KEEP MY WORD.

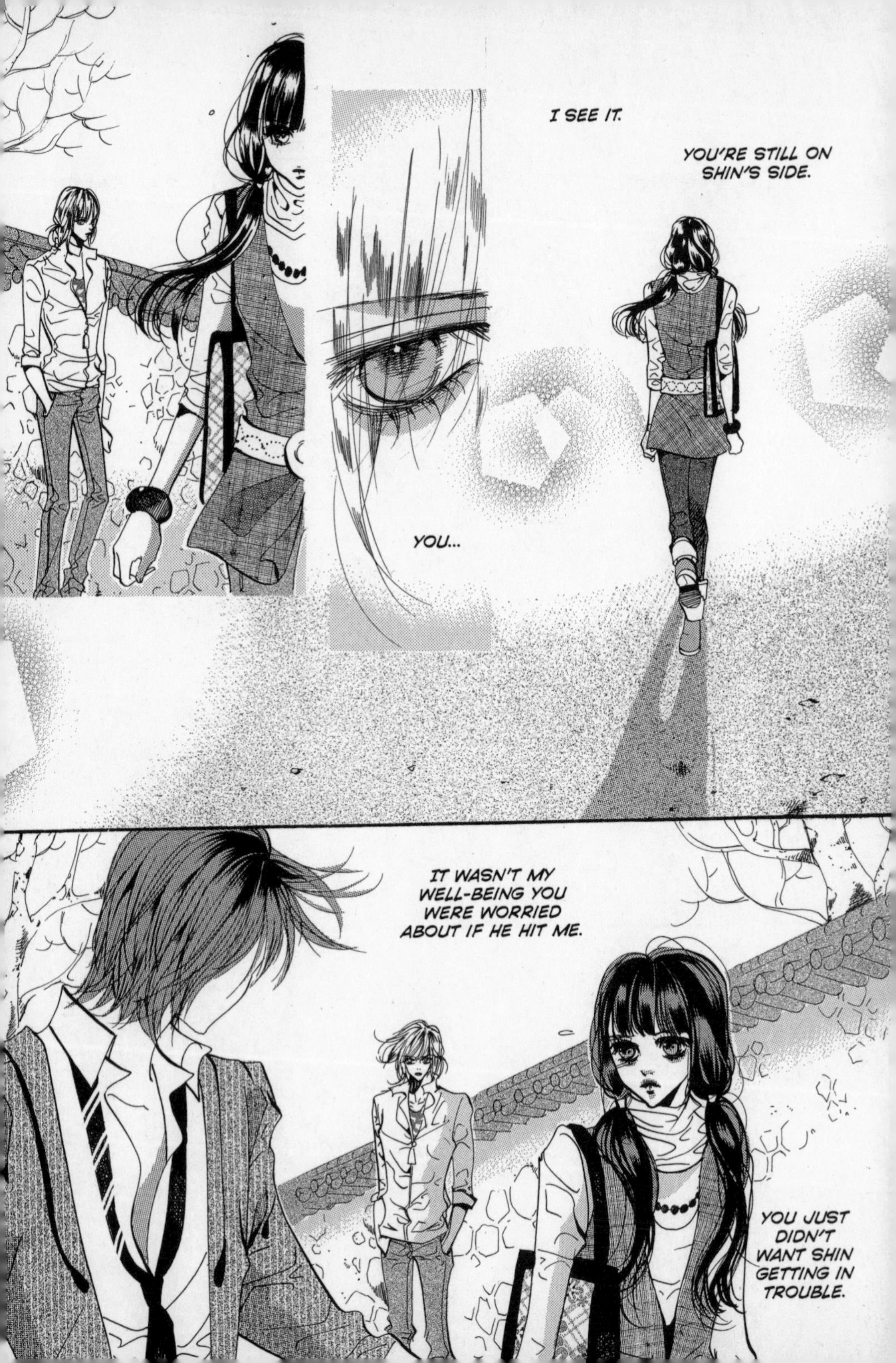
I SEE IT.
YOU'RE STILL ON SHIN'S SIDE.
YOU...
IT WASN'T MY WELL-BEING YOU WERE WORRIED ABOUT IF HE HIT ME.
YOU JUST DIDN'T WANT SHIN GETTING IN TROUBLE.

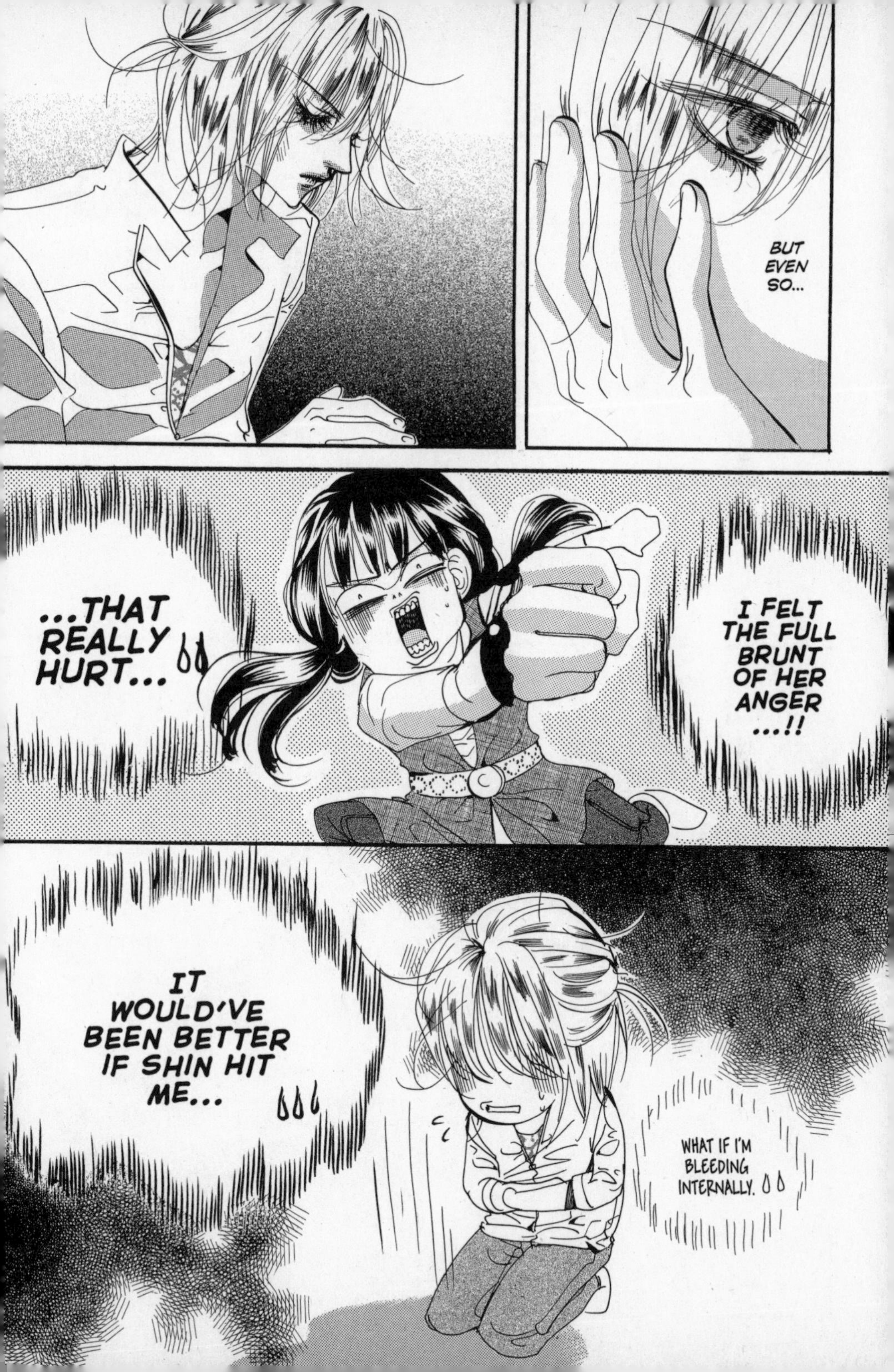
BUT EVEN SO...
...THAT REALLY HURT...
I FELT THE FULL BRUNT OF HER ANGER ...!!
IT WOULD'VE BEEN BETTER IF SHIN HIT ME...
WHAT IF I'M BLEEDING INTERNALLY.

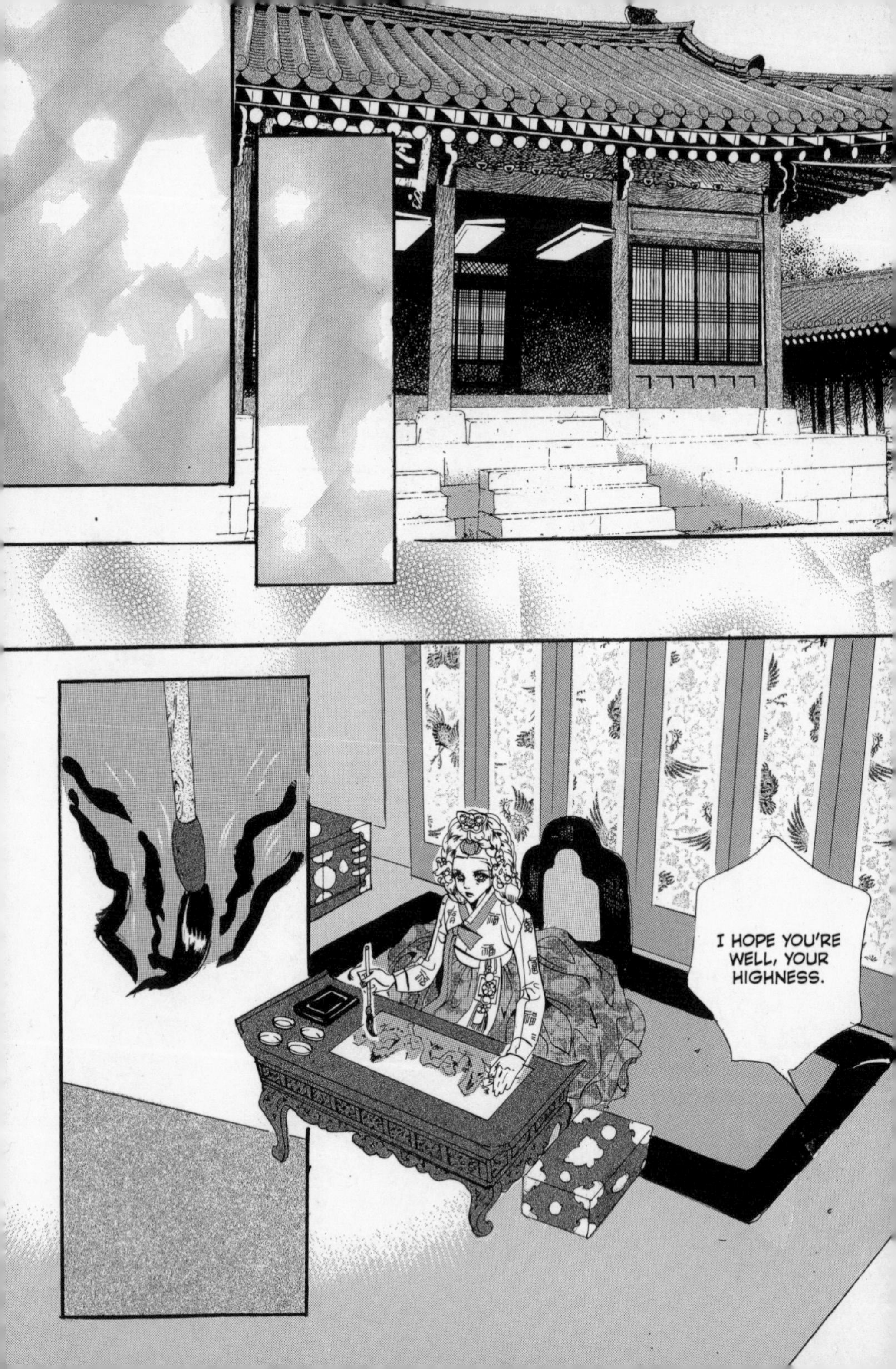
I HOPE YOU'RE WELL, YOUR HIGHNESS.

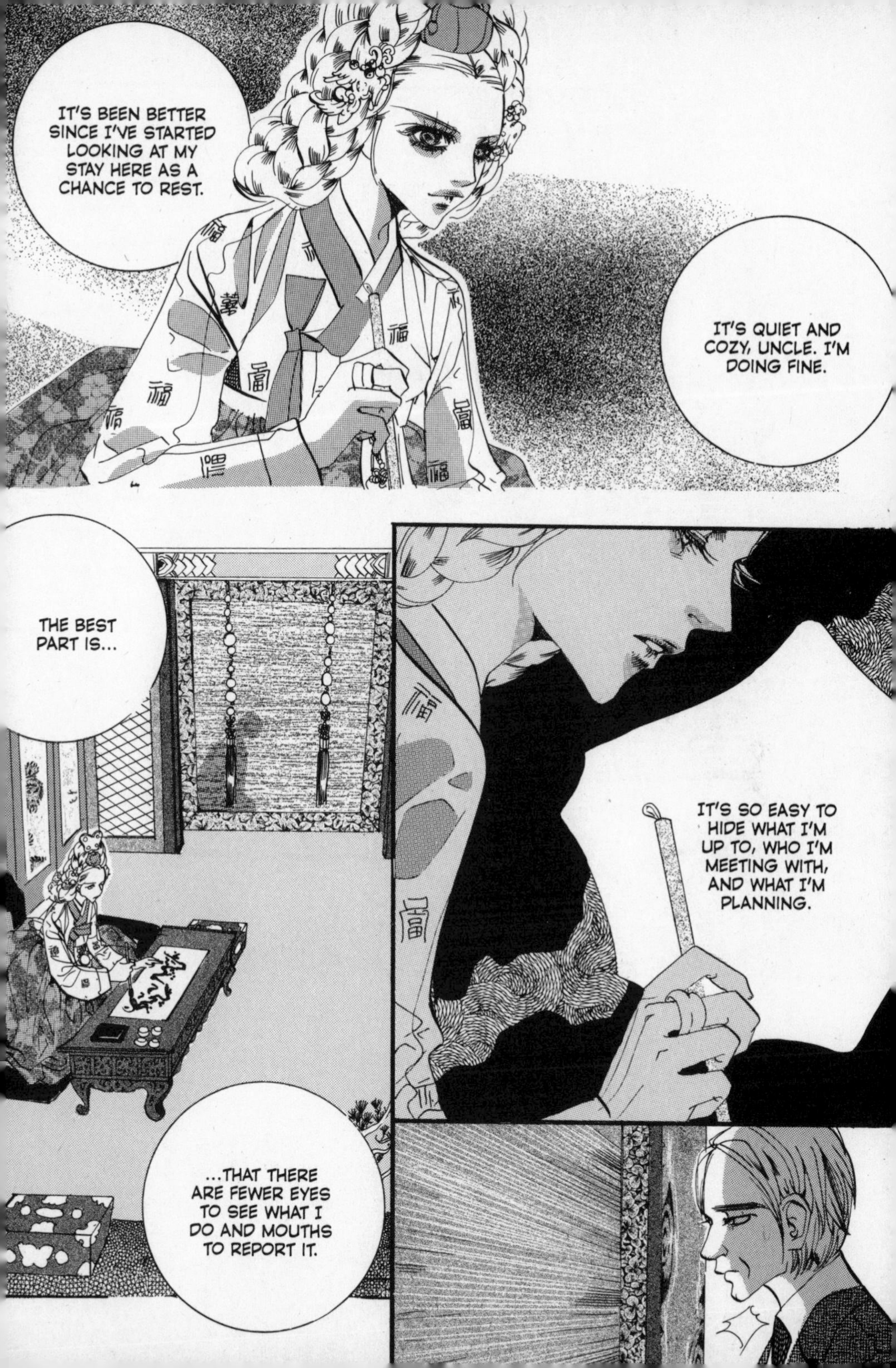
IT'S BEEN BETTER SINCE I'VE STARTED LOOKING AT MY STAY HERE AS A CHANCE TO REST.
IT'S QUIET AND COZY, UNCLE. I'M DOING FINE.
THE BEST PART IS...
...THAT THERE ARE FEWER EYES TO SEE WHAT I DO AND MOUTHS TO REPORT IT.
IT'S SO EASY TO HIDE WHAT I'M UP TO, WHO I'M MEETING WITH, AND WHAT I'M PLANNING.

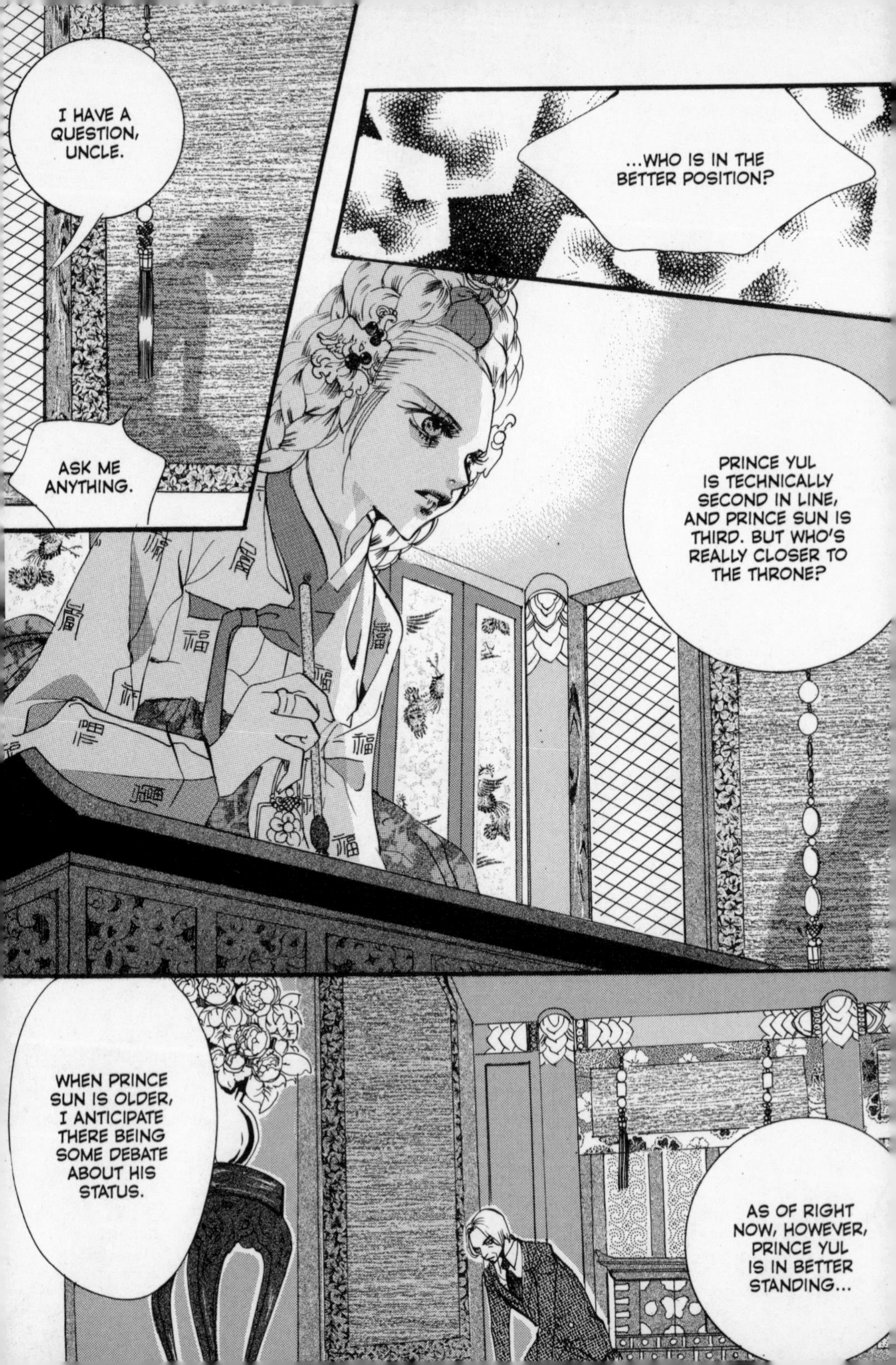
I HAVE A QUESTION, UNCLE.
ASK ME ANYTHING.
...WHO IS IN THE BETTER POSITION?
PRINCE YUL IS TECHNICALLY SECOND IN LINE, AND PRINCE SUN IS THIRD. BUT WHO'S REALLY CLOSER TO THE THRONE?
WHEN PRINCE SUN IS OLDER, I ANTICIPATE THERE BEING SOME DEBATE ABOUT HIS STATUS.
AS OF RIGHT NOW, HOWEVER, PRINCE YUL IS IN BETTER STANDING...

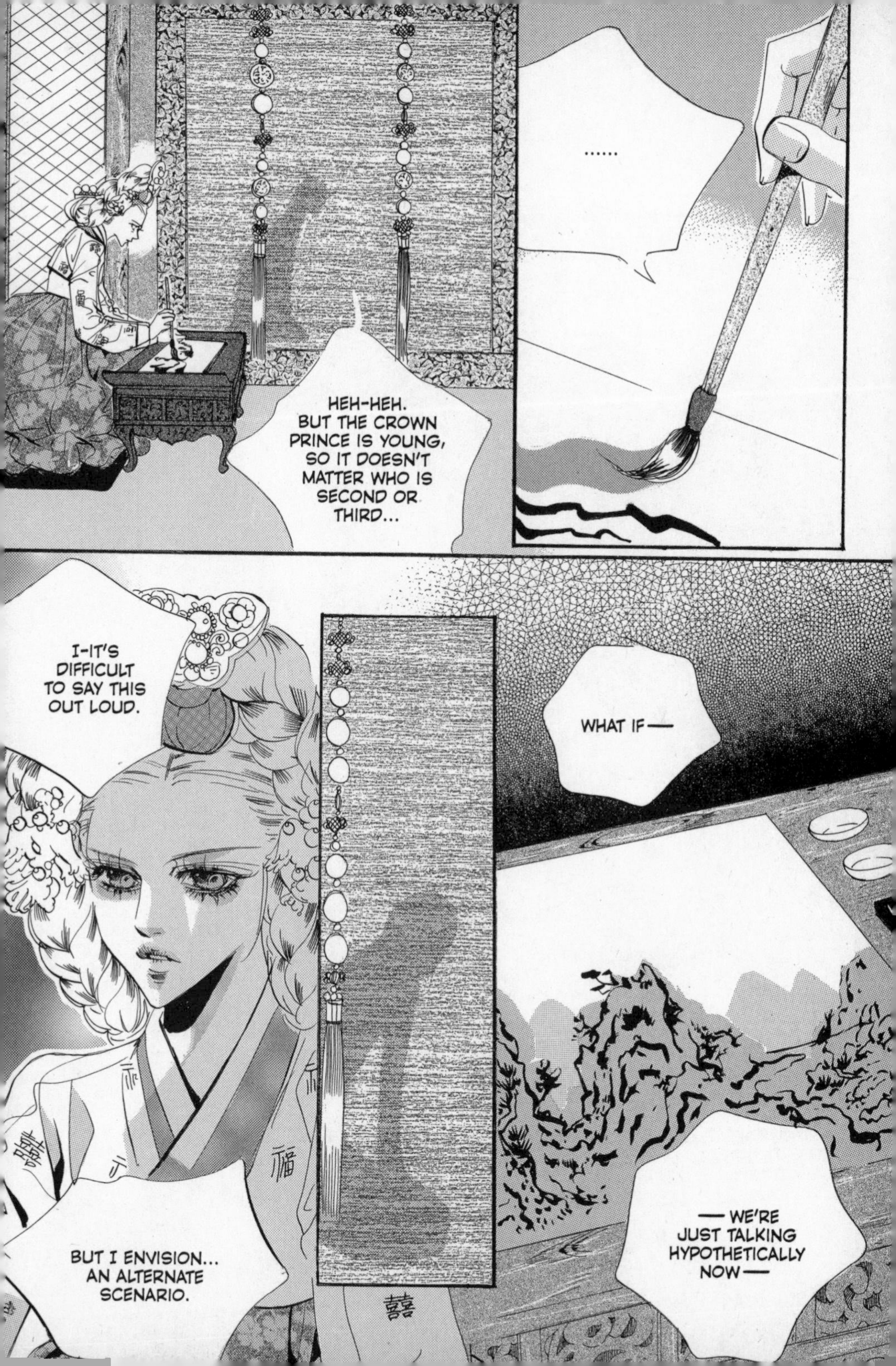
HEH-HEH. BUT THE CROWN PRINCE IS YOUNG, SO IT DOESN'T MATTER WHO IS SECOND OR THIRD...
......
I-IT'S DIFFICULT TO SAY THIS OUT LOUD.
BUT I ENVISION... AN ALTERNATE SCENARIO.
WHAT IF—
—WE'RE JUST TALKING HYPOTHETICALLY NOW—

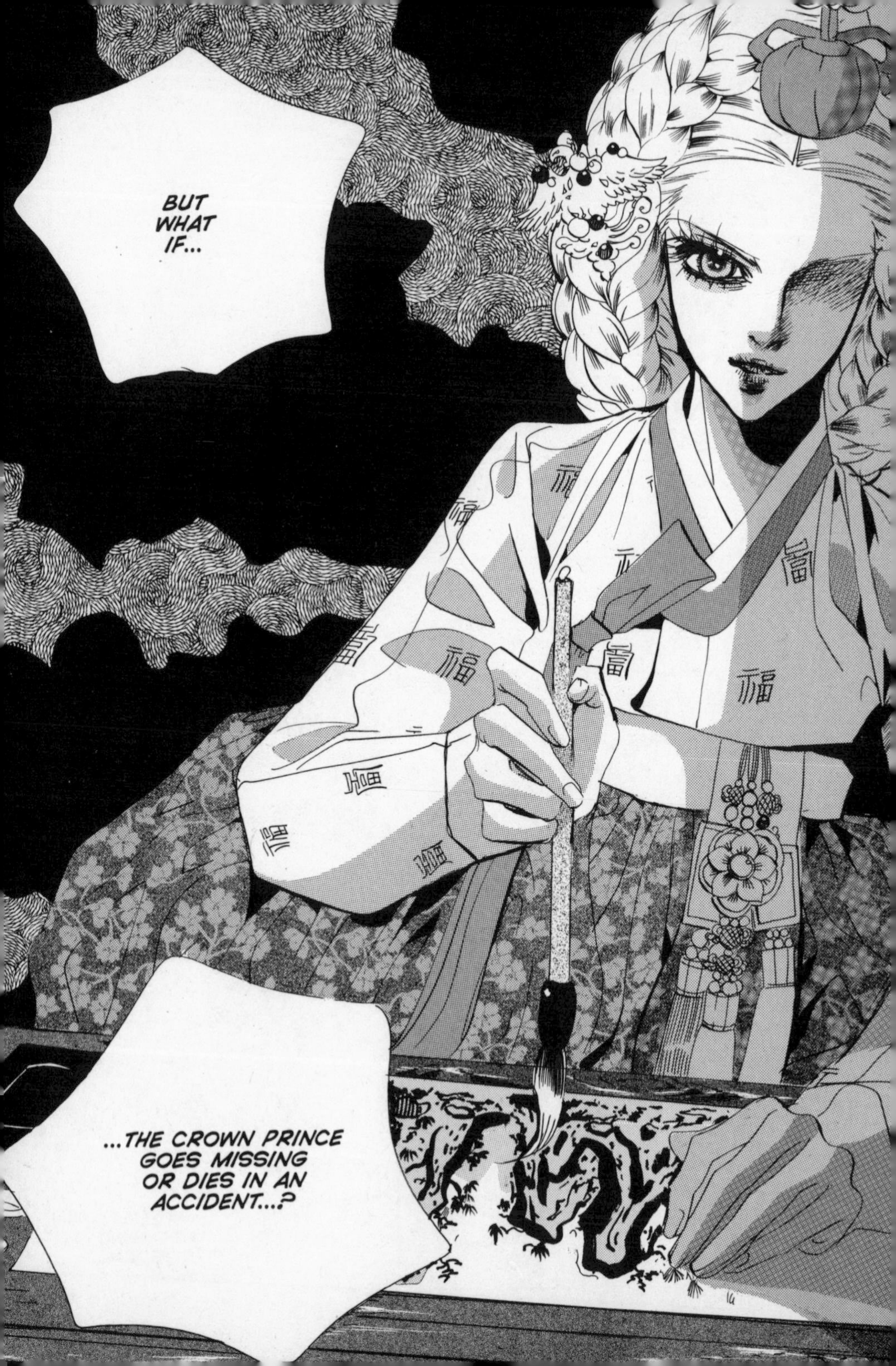
BUT WHAT IF...
...THE CROWN PRINCE GOES MISSING OR DIES IN AN ACCIDENT...?

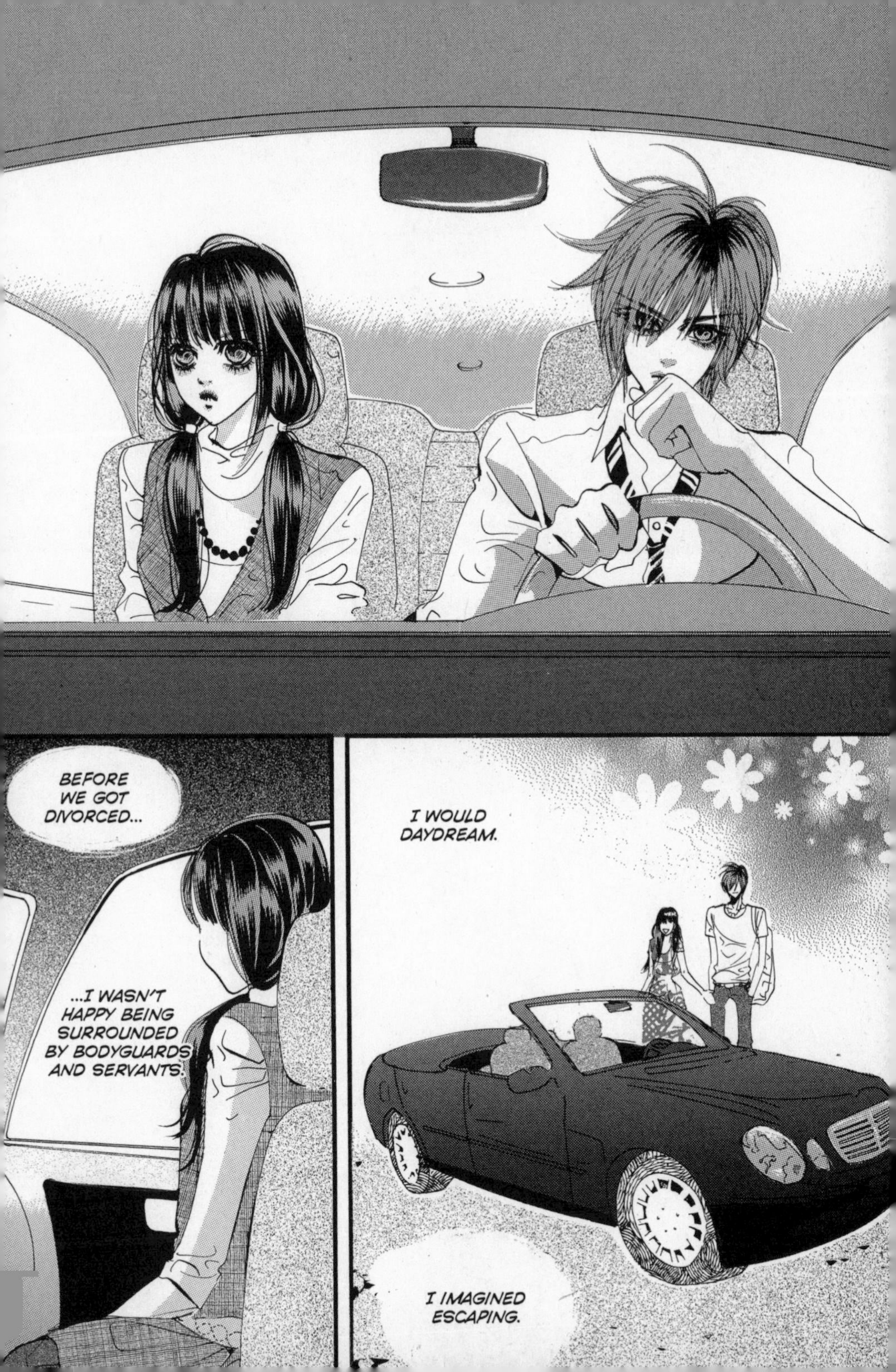
BEFORE WE GOT DIVORCED...
...I WASN'T HAPPY BEING SURROUNDED BY BODYGUARDS AND SERVANTS.
I WOULD DAYDREAM.
I IMAGINED ESCAPING.

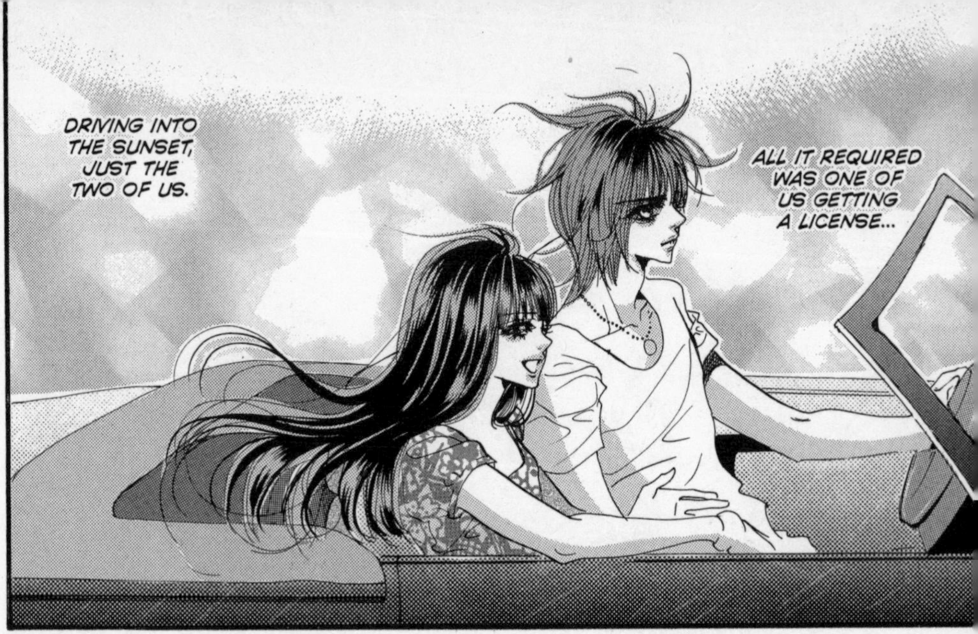
DRIVING INTO THE SUNSET, JUST THE TWO OF US.
ALL IT REQUIRED WAS ONE OF US GETTING A LICENSE...

BUT...

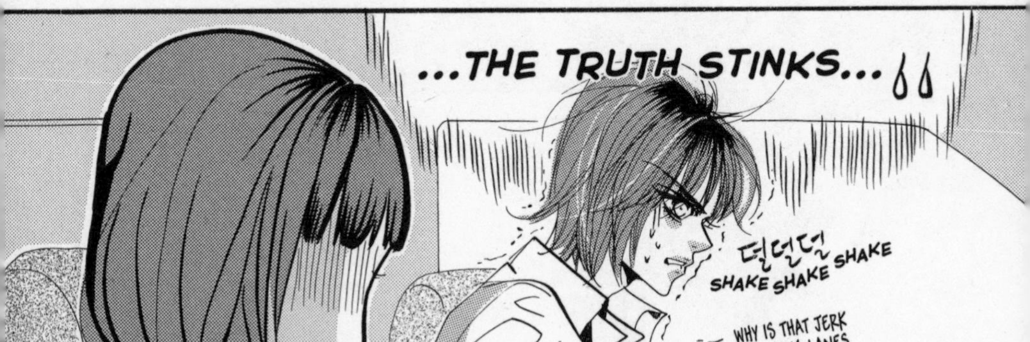
...THE TRUTH STINKS...
덜덜덜
SHAKE SHAKE SHAKE
WHY IS THAT JERK CHANGING LANES WITHOUT SIGNALING?!!!

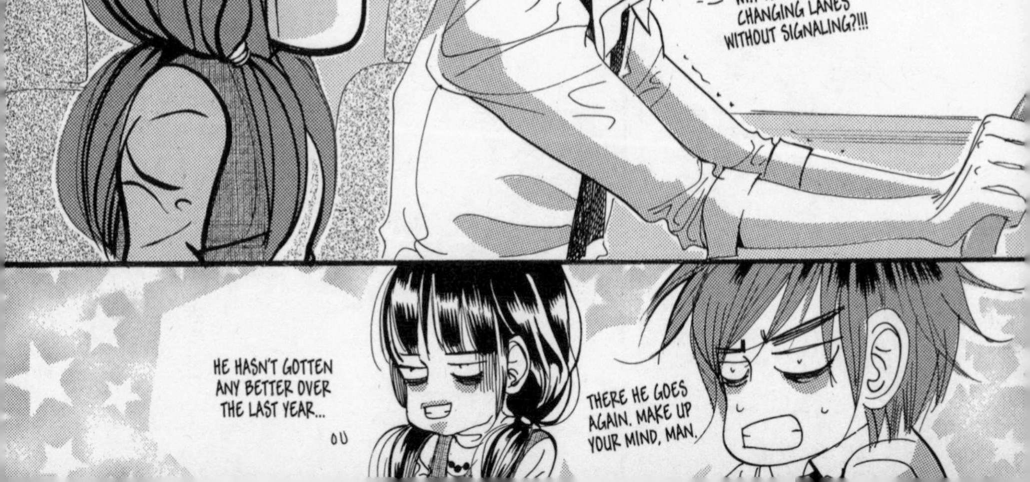
HE HASN'T GOTTEN ANY BETTER OVER THE LAST YEAR...
THERE HE GOES AGAIN. MAKE UP YOUR MIND, MAN.

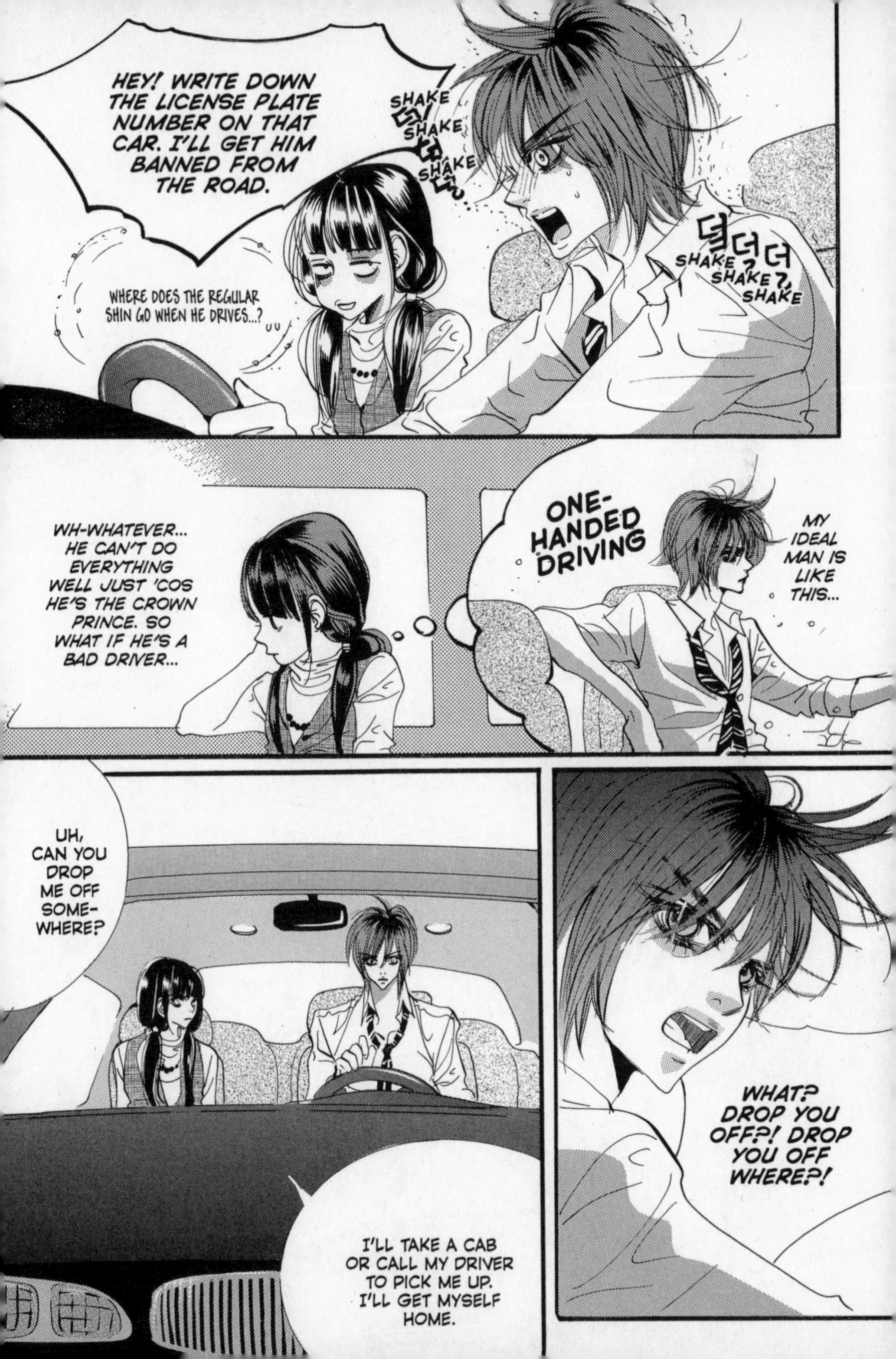
HEY! WRITE DOWN THE LICENSE PLATE NUMBER ON THAT CAR. I'LL GET HIM BANNED FROM THE ROAD.
SHAKE 덜 SHAKE 덜 SHAKE 덜
WHERE DOES THE REGULAR SHIN GO WHEN HE DRIVES...?
덜더더 SHAKE SHAKE SHAKE
WH-WHATEVER... HE CAN'T DO EVERYTHING WELL JUST 'COS HE'S THE CROWN PRINCE. SO WHAT IF HE'S A BAD DRIVER...
ONE-HANDED DRIVING
MY IDEAL MAN IS LIKE THIS...
UH, CAN YOU DROP ME OFF SOME-WHERE?
I'LL TAKE A CAB OR CALL MY DRIVER TO PICK ME UP. I'LL GET MYSELF HOME.
WHAT? DROP YOU OFF?! DROP YOU OFF WHERE?!

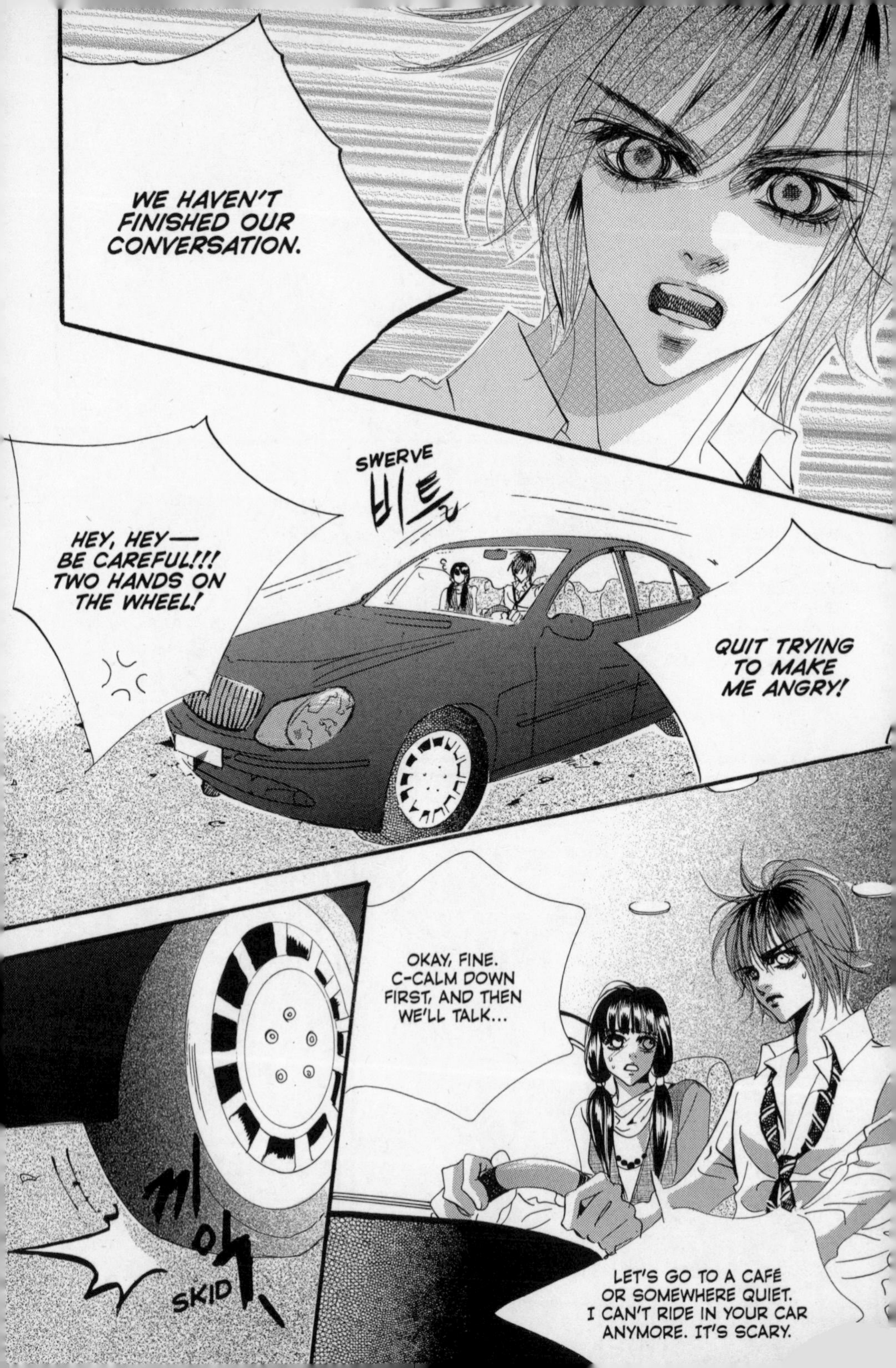
WE HAVEN'T FINISHED OUR CONVERSATION.
HEY, HEY— BE CAREFUL!!! TWO HANDS ON THE WHEEL!
SWERVE
비틀
QUIT TRYING TO MAKE ME ANGRY!
끼익
SKID
OKAY, FINE. C-CALM DOWN FIRST, AND THEN WE'LL TALK...
LET'S GO TO A CAFÉ OR SOMEWHERE QUIET. I CAN'T RIDE IN YOUR CAR ANYMORE. IT'S SCARY.

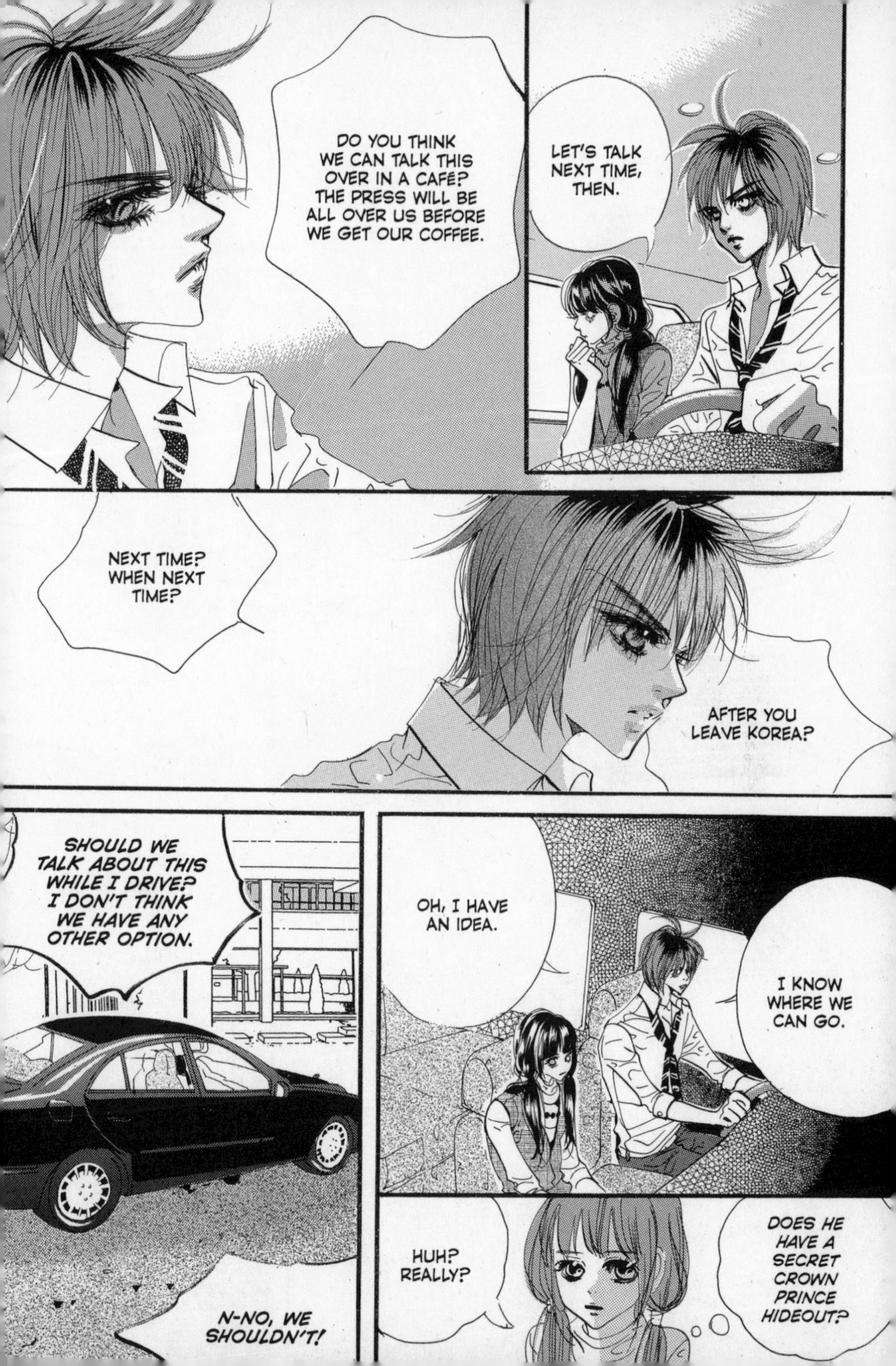
DO YOU THINK WE CAN TALK THIS OVER IN A CAFÉ? THE PRESS WILL BE ALL OVER US BEFORE WE GET OUR COFFEE.
LET'S TALK NEXT TIME, THEN.
NEXT TIME? WHEN NEXT TIME?
AFTER YOU LEAVE KOREA?
SHOULD WE TALK ABOUT THIS WHILE I DRIVE? I DON'T THINK WE HAVE ANY OTHER OPTION.
N-NO, WE SHOULDN'T!
OH, I HAVE AN IDEA.
I KNOW WHERE WE CAN GO.
HUH? REALLY?
DOES HE HAVE A SECRET CROWN PRINCE HIDEOUT?

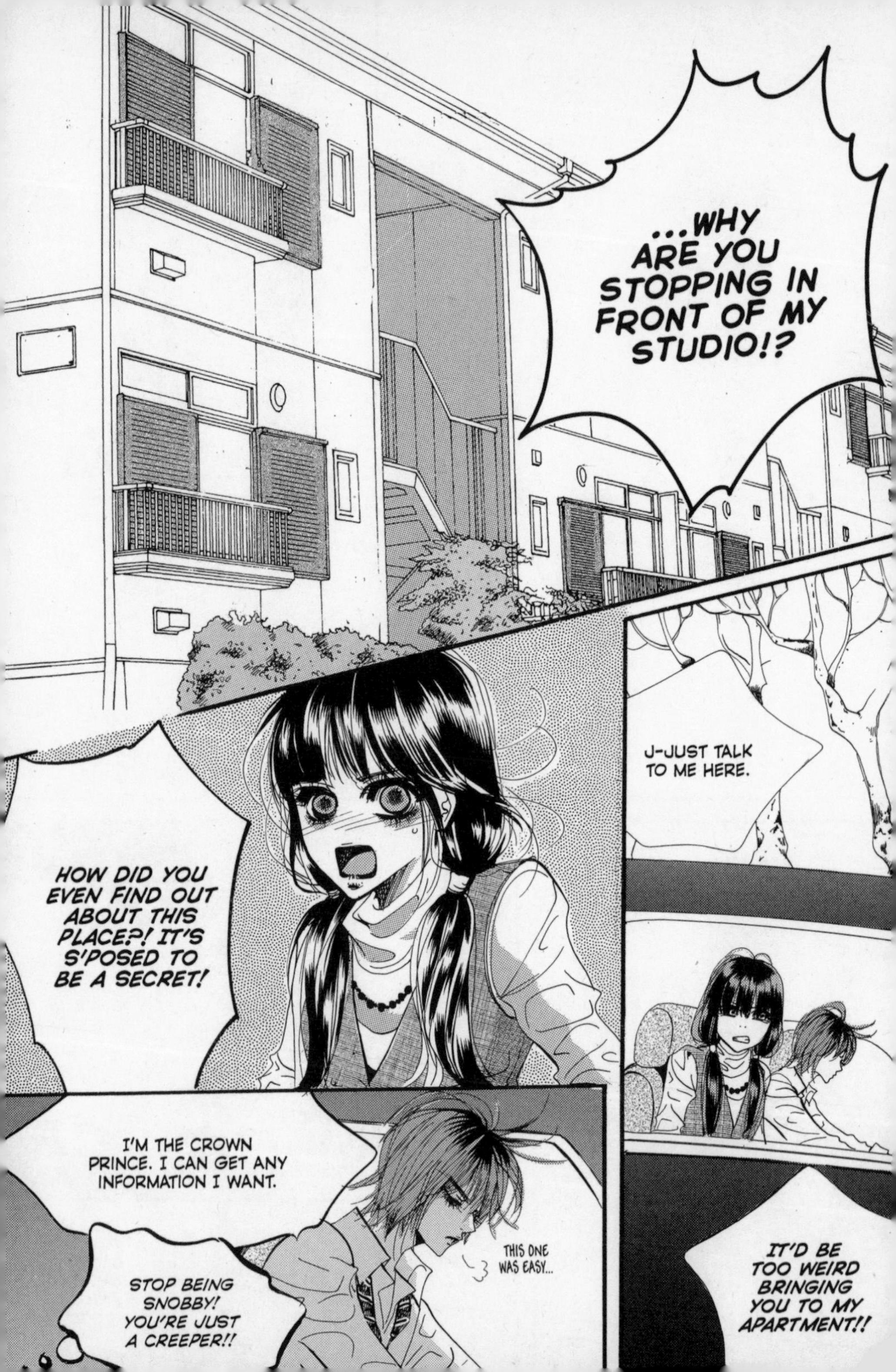
...WHY ARE YOU STOPPING IN FRONT OF MY STUDIO!?
HOW DID YOU EVEN FIND OUT ABOUT THIS PLACE?! IT'S S'POSED TO BE A SECRET!
J-JUST TALK TO ME HERE.
I'M THE CROWN PRINCE. I CAN GET ANY INFORMATION I WANT.
STOP BEING SNOBBY! YOU'RE JUST A CREEPER!!
THIS ONE WAS EASY...
IT'D BE TOO WEIRD BRINGING YOU TO MY APARTMENT!!

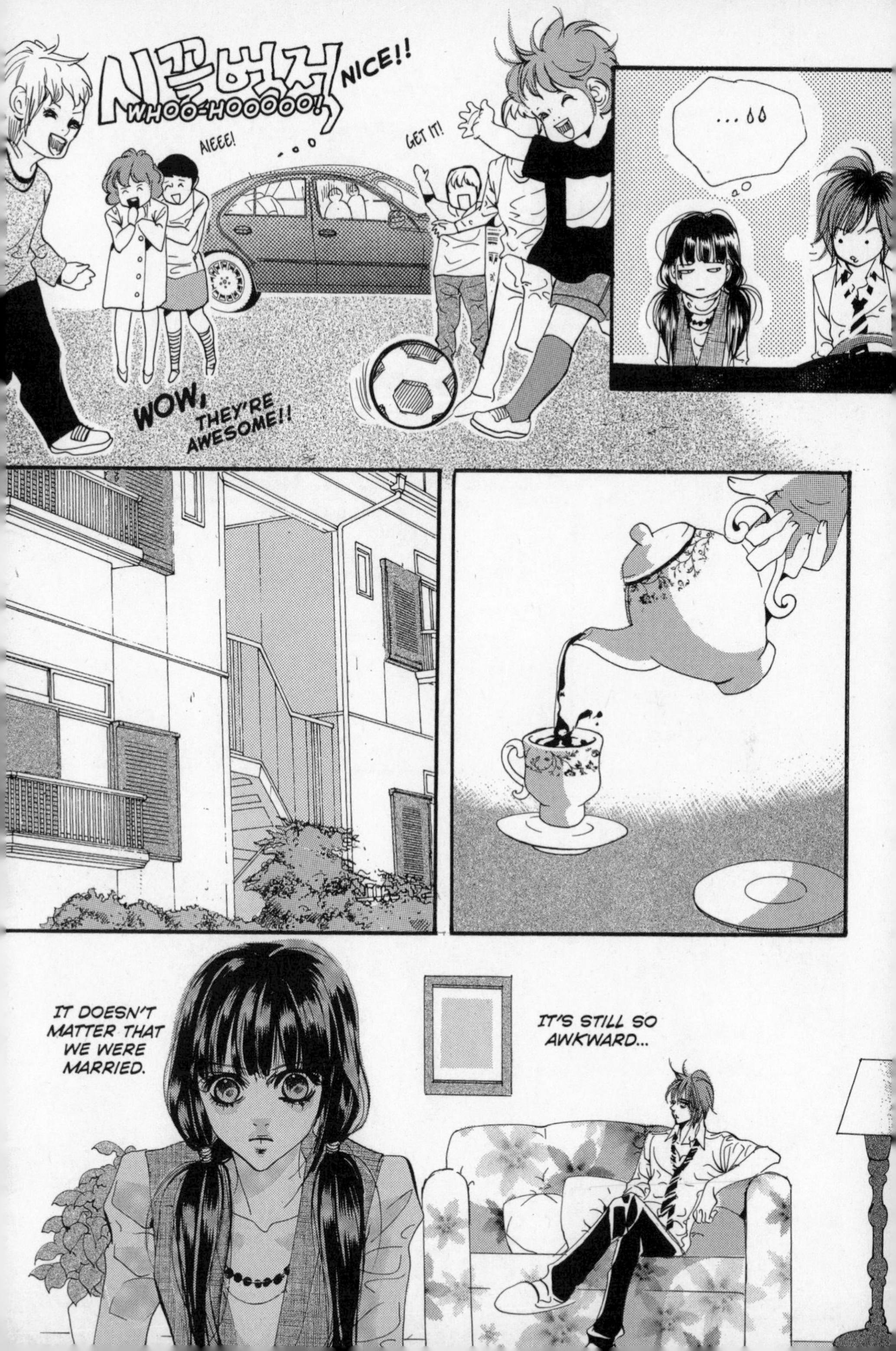
시끌벅적
WHOO-HOOOOO!
NICE!!
AIEEE!
...
GET IT!
WOW, THEY'RE AWESOME!!
...
IT DOESN'T MATTER THAT WE WERE MARRIED.
IT'S STILL SO AWKWARD...

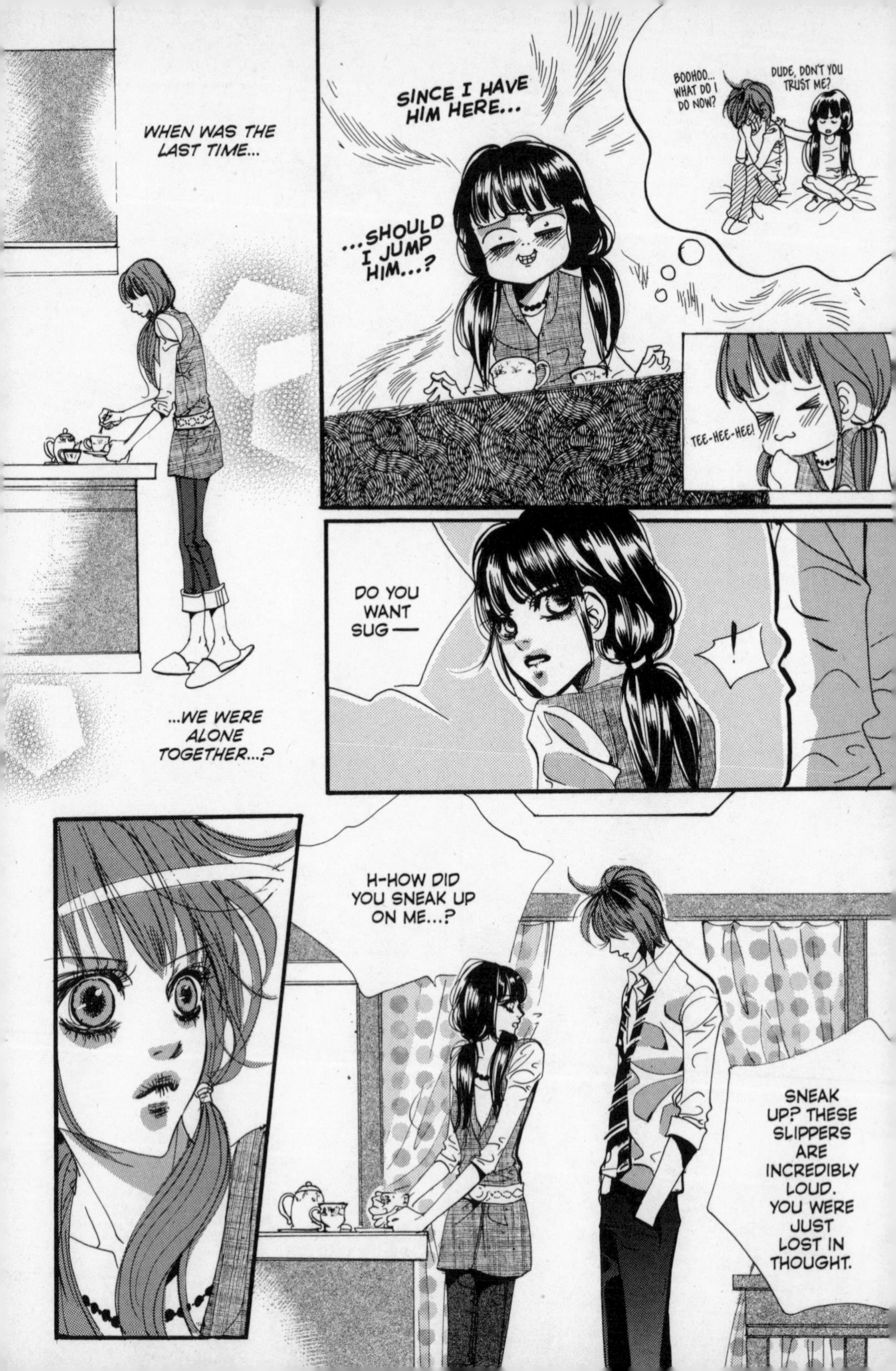
WHEN WAS THE LAST TIME...
...WE WERE ALONE TOGETHER...?
SINCE I HAVE HIM HERE...
...SHOULD I JUMP HIM...?
BOOHOO... WHAT DO I DO NOW?
DUDE, DON'T YOU TRUST ME?
TEE-HEE-HEE!
DO YOU WANT SUG—
!
H-HOW DID YOU SNEAK UP ON ME...?
SNEAK UP? THESE SLIPPERS ARE INCREDIBLY LOUD. YOU WERE JUST LOST IN THOUGHT.

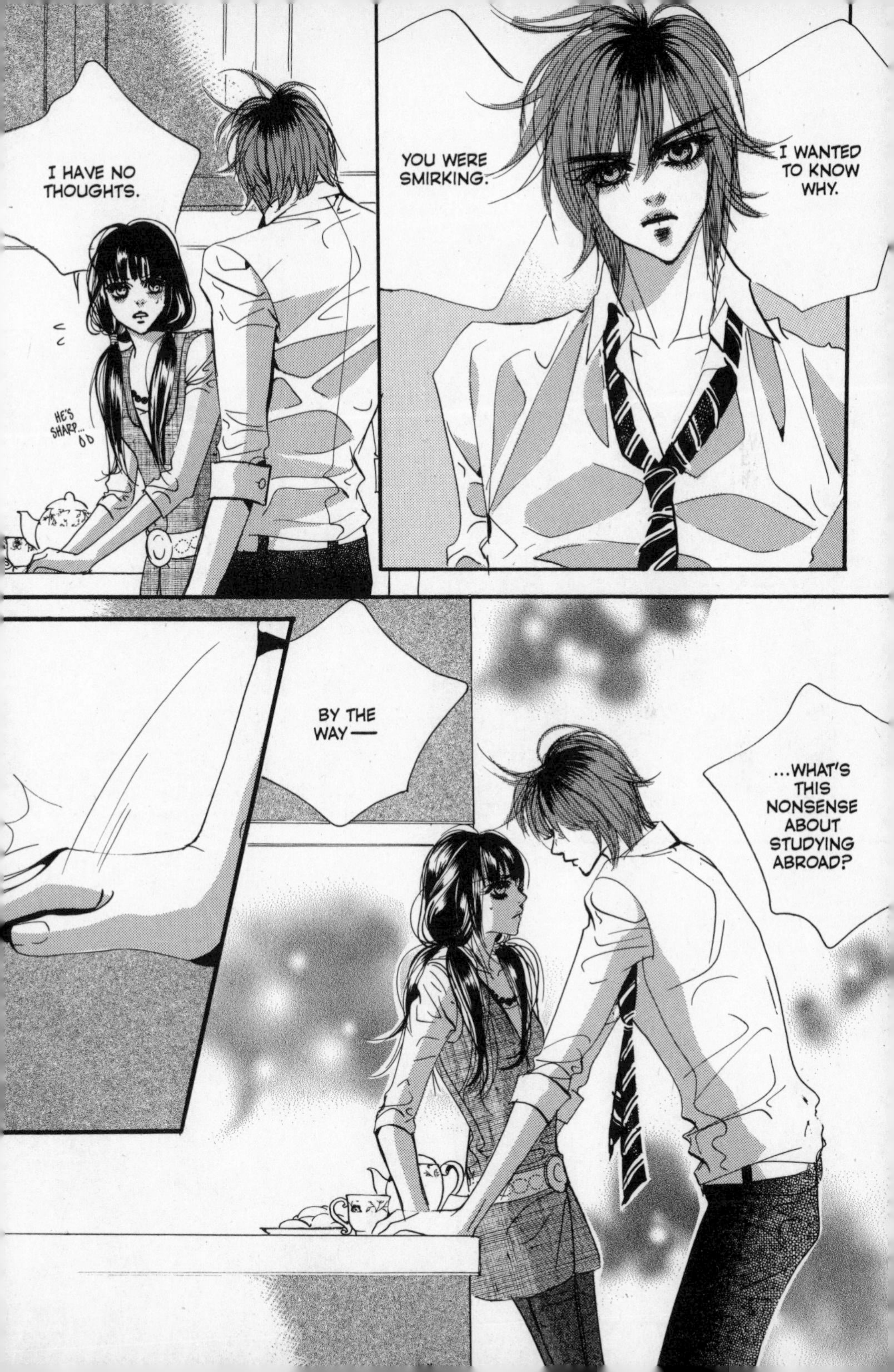
I HAVE NO THOUGHTS.
HE'S SHARP...
YOU WERE SMIRKING.
I WANTED TO KNOW WHY.
BY THE WAY—
...WHAT'S THIS NONSENSE ABOUT STUDYING ABROAD?

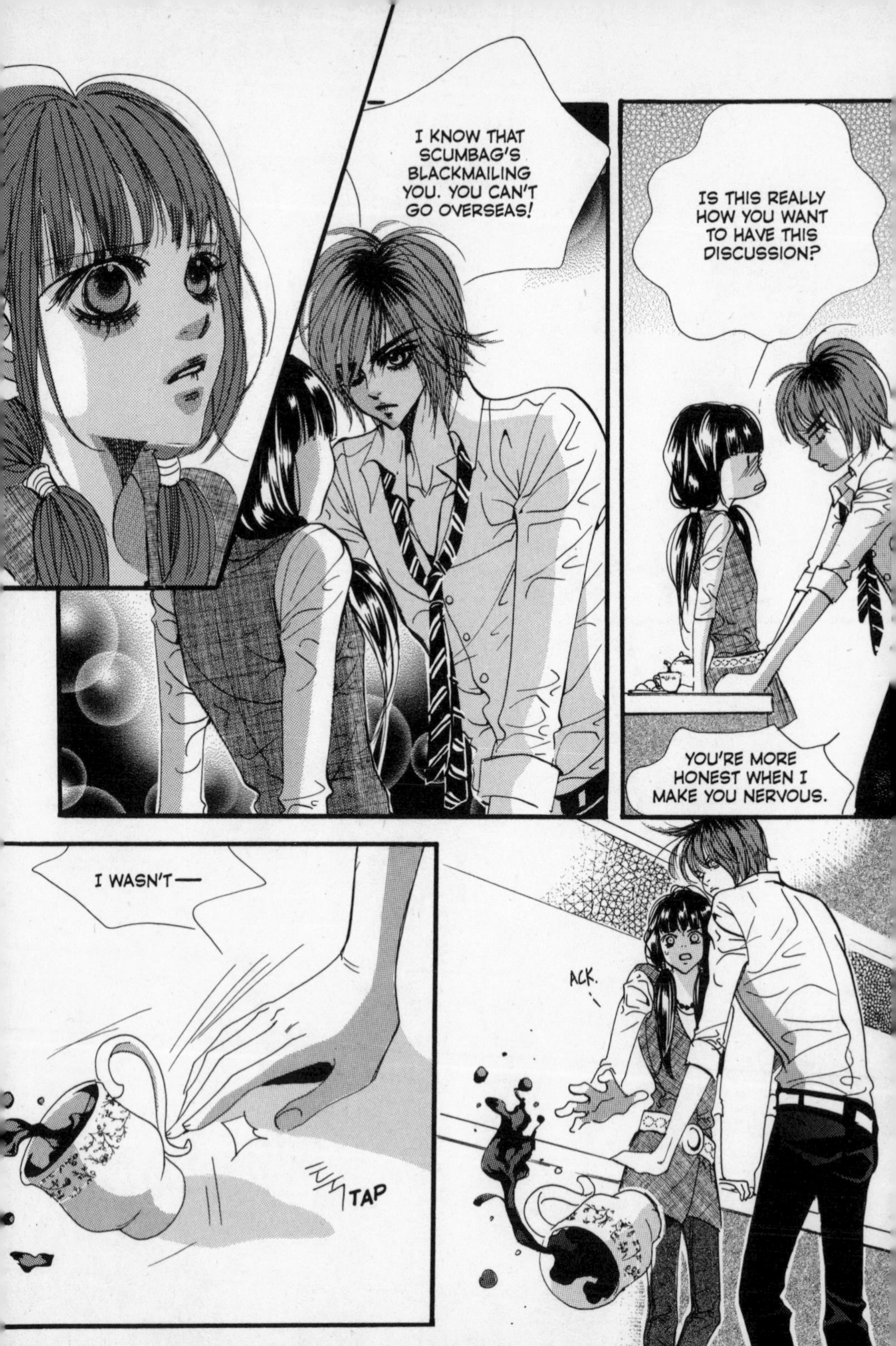
I KNOW THAT SCUMBAG'S BLACKMAILING YOU. YOU CAN'T GO OVERSEAS!
IS THIS REALLY HOW YOU WANT TO HAVE THIS DISCUSSION?
YOU'RE MORE HONEST WHEN I MAKE YOU NERVOUS.
I WASN'T—
TAP
ACK.

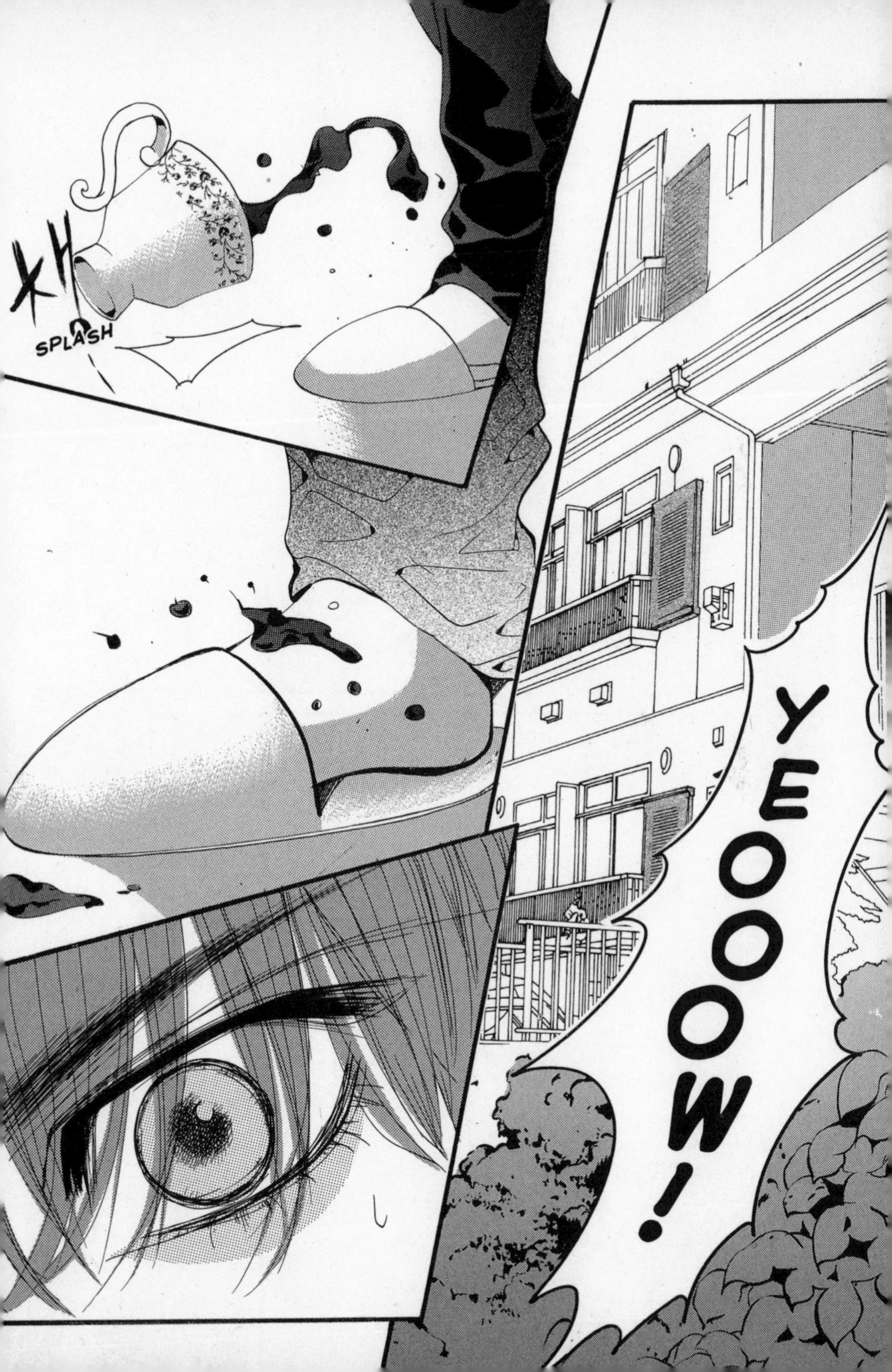

KH
SPLASH
YEOOOOW!

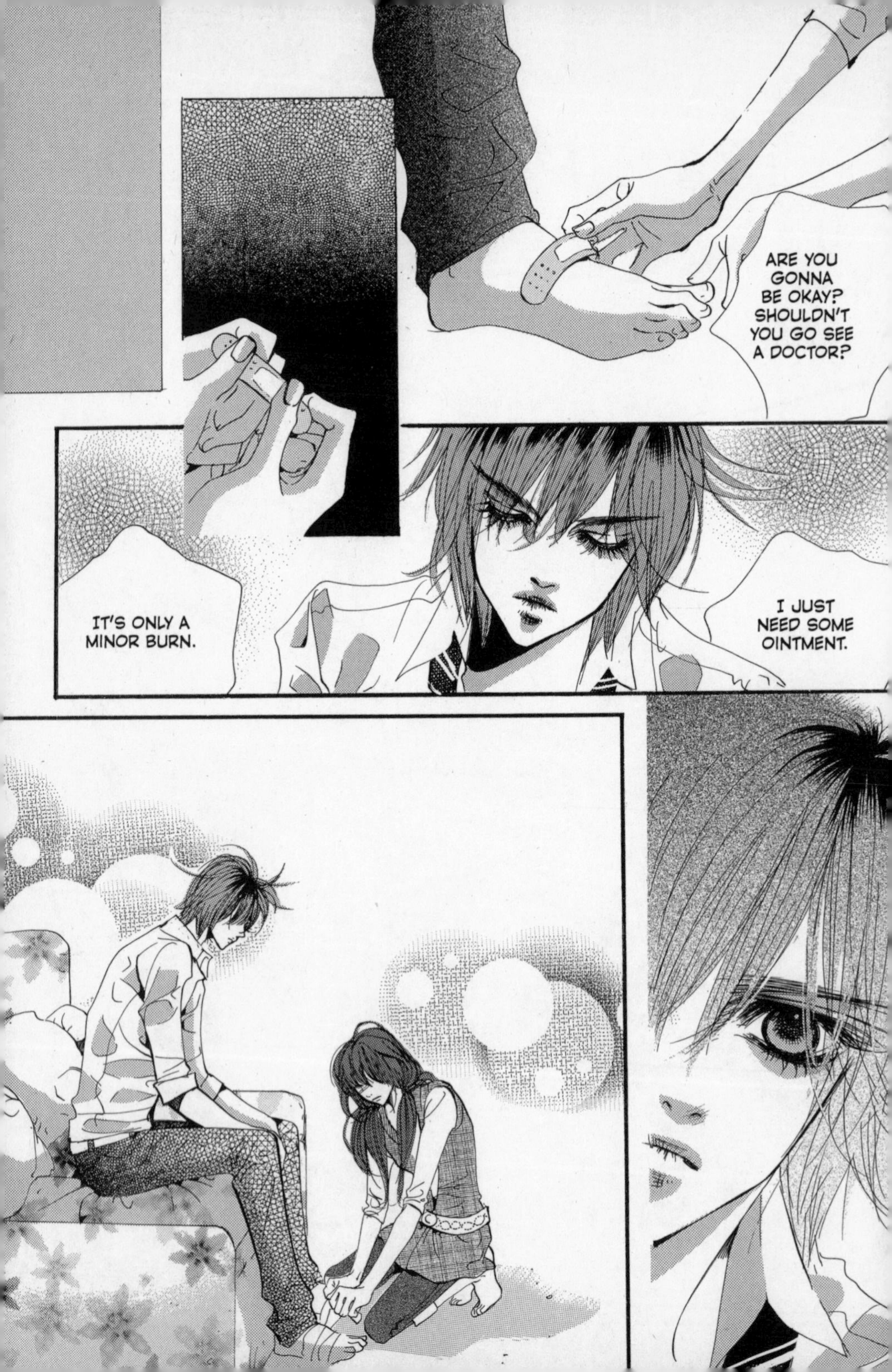
ARE YOU GONNA BE OKAY? SHOULDN'T YOU GO SEE A DOCTOR?
IT'S ONLY A MINOR BURN.
I JUST NEED SOME OINTMENT.

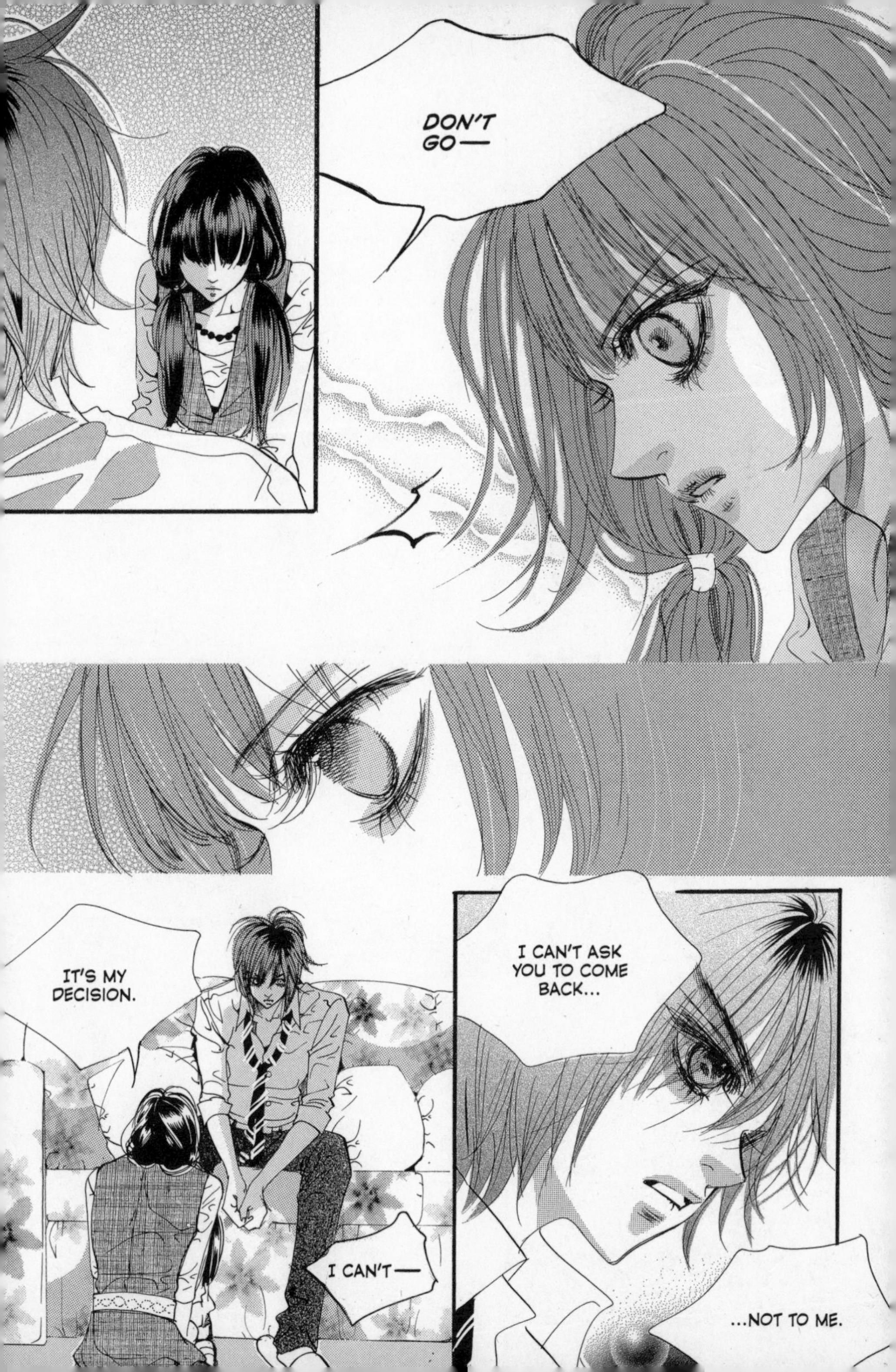
DON'T GO—
IT'S MY DECISION.
I CAN'T—
I CAN'T ASK YOU TO COME BACK...
...NOT TO ME.

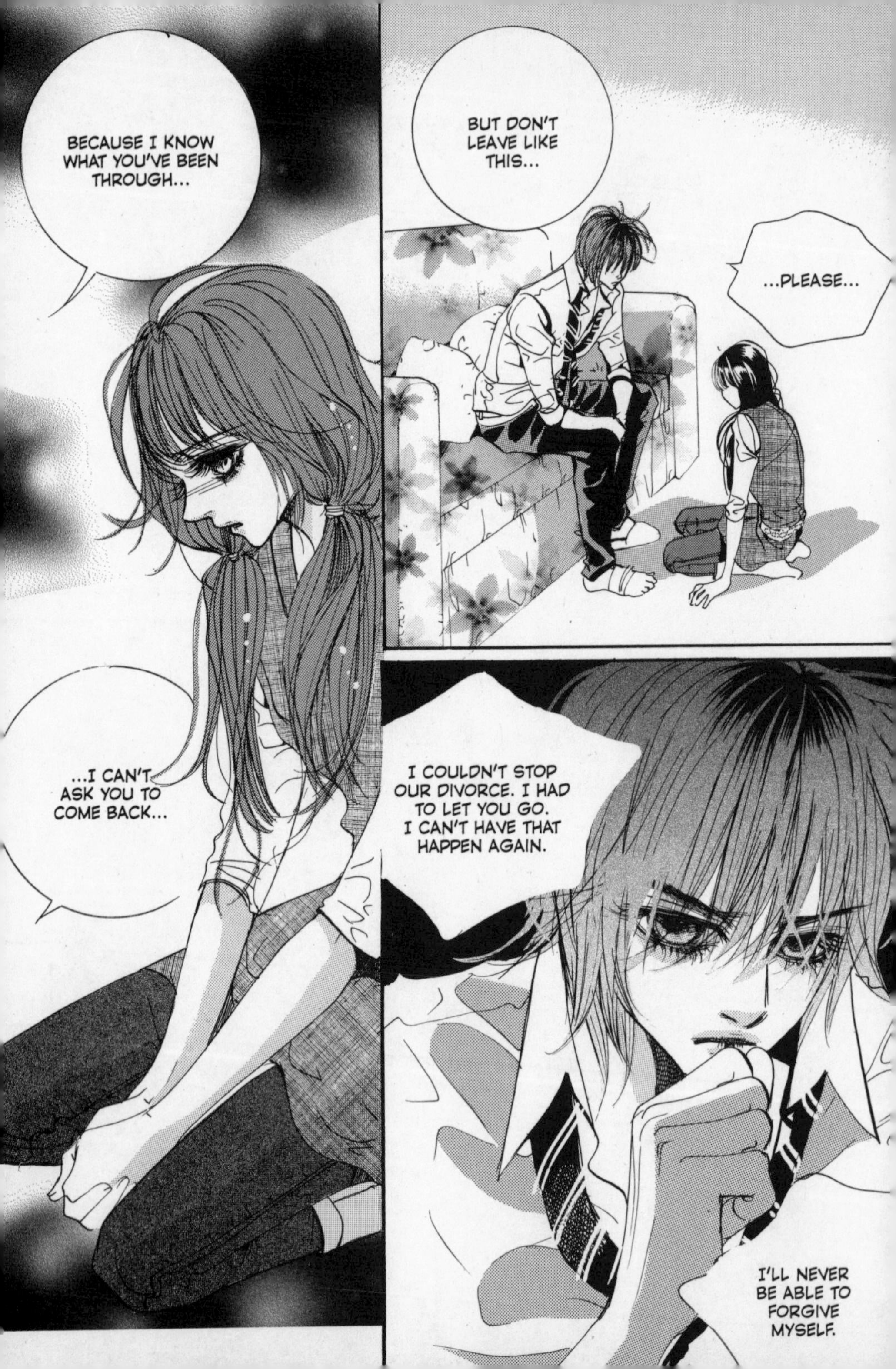
BECAUSE I KNOW WHAT YOU'VE BEEN THROUGH...
...I CAN'T ASK YOU TO COME BACK...
BUT DON'T LEAVE LIKE THIS...
...PLEASE...
I COULDN'T STOP OUR DIVORCE. I HAD TO LET YOU GO. I CAN'T HAVE THAT HAPPEN AGAIN.
I'LL NEVER BE ABLE TO FORGIVE MYSELF.

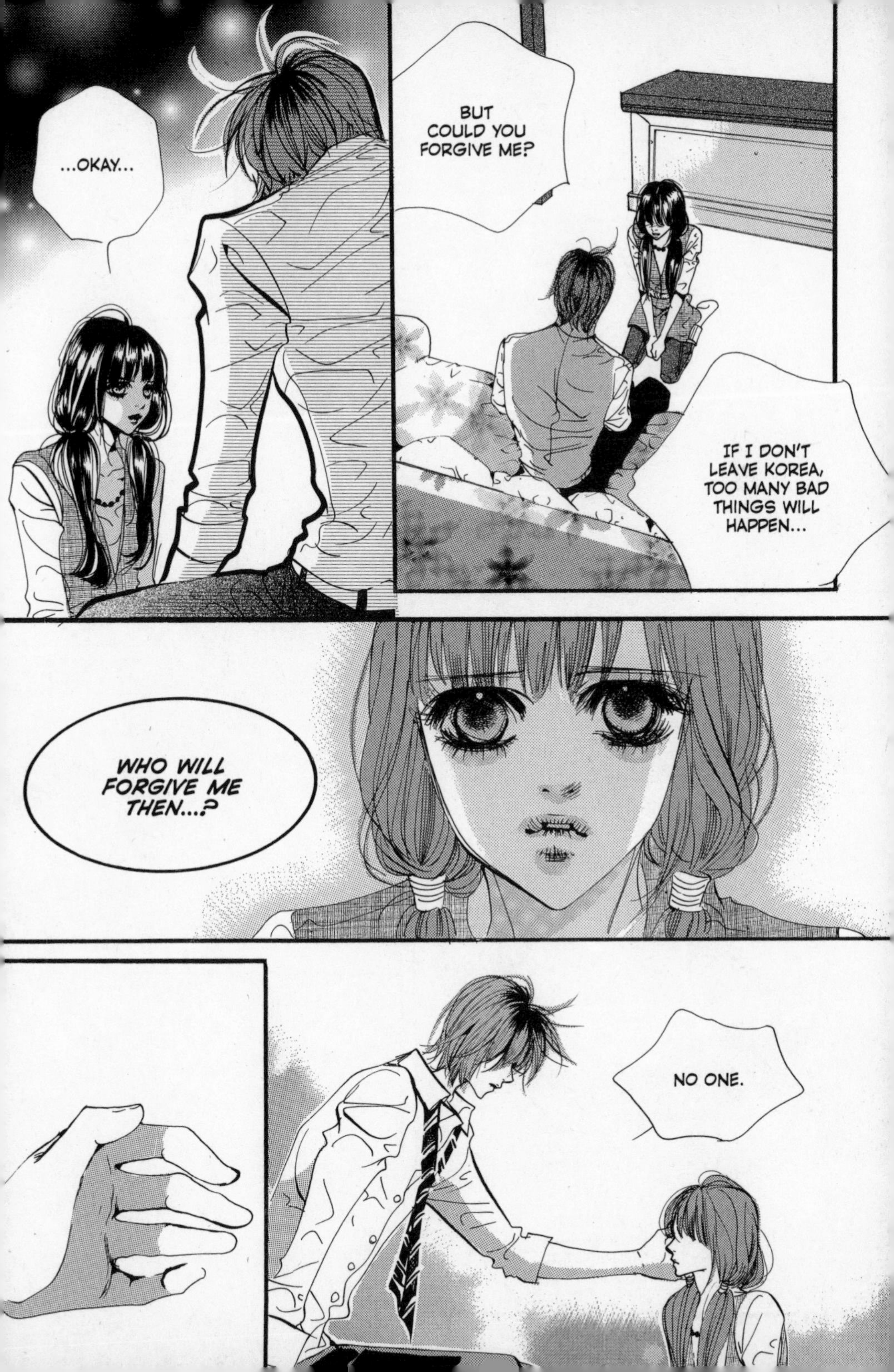
...OKAY...
BUT COULD YOU FORGIVE ME?
IF I DON'T LEAVE KOREA, TOO MANY BAD THINGS WILL HAPPEN...
WHO WILL FORGIVE ME THEN...?
NO ONE.

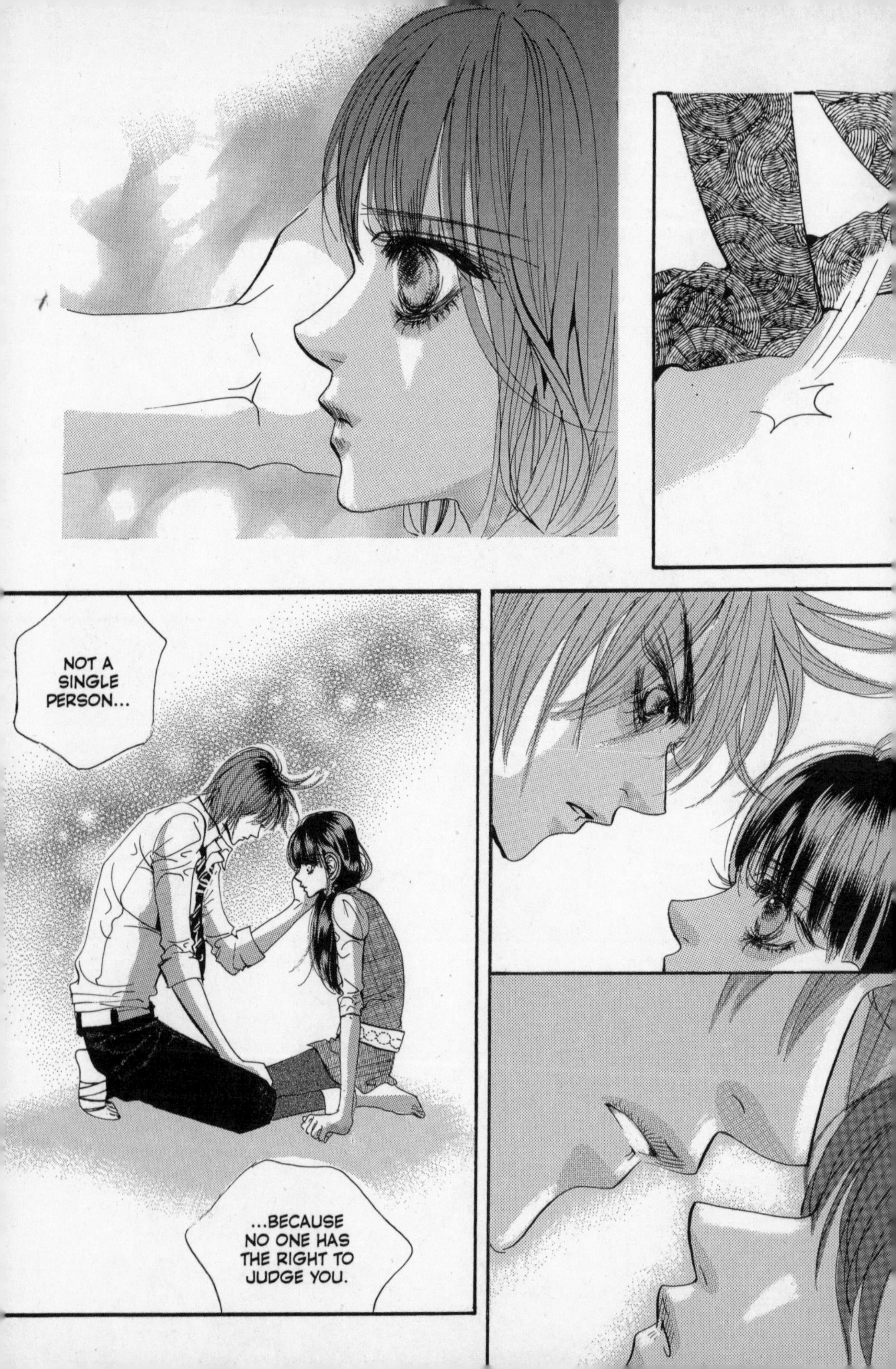
NOT A SINGLE PERSON...
...BECAUSE NO ONE HAS THE RIGHT TO JUDGE YOU.

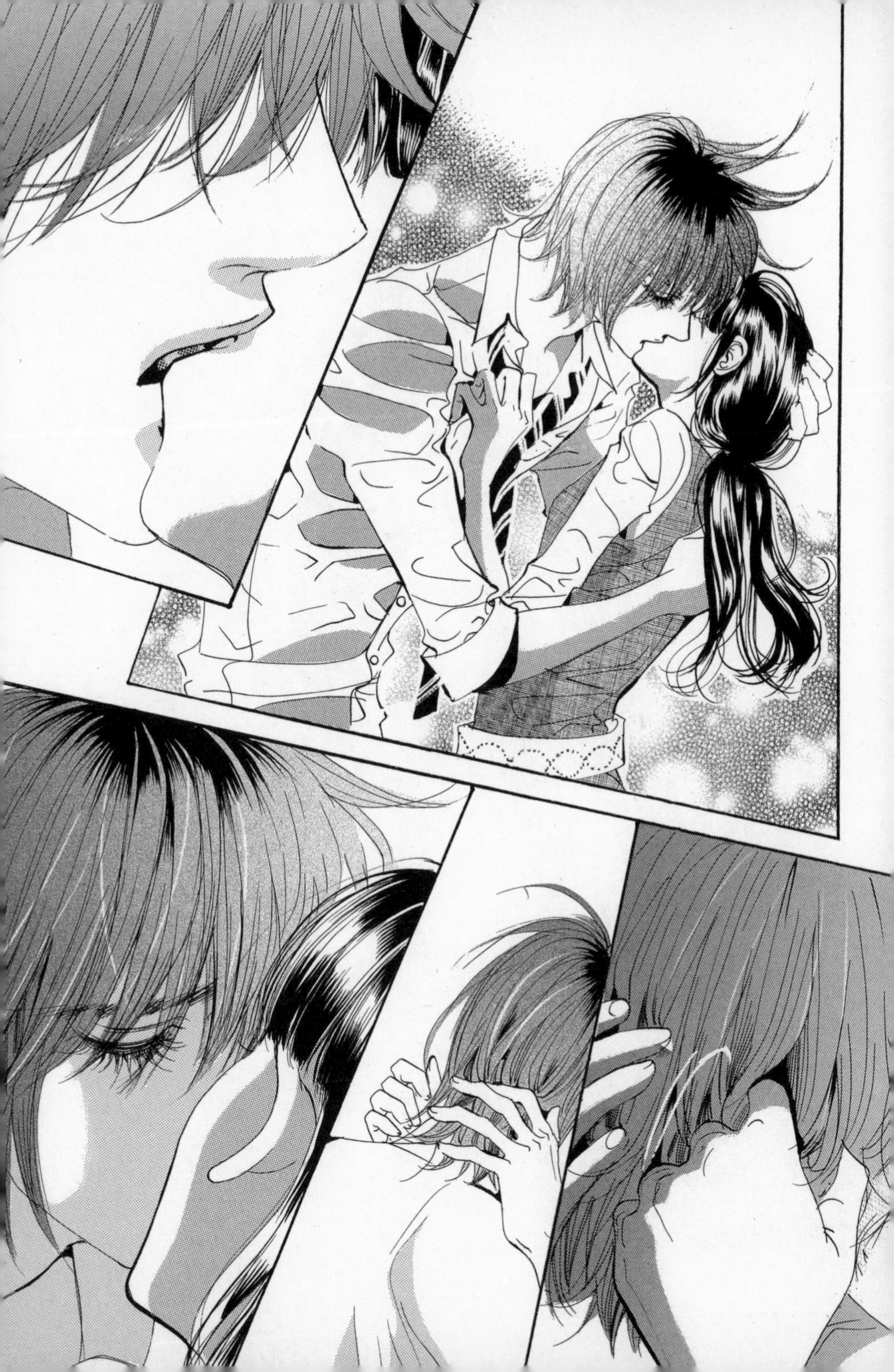

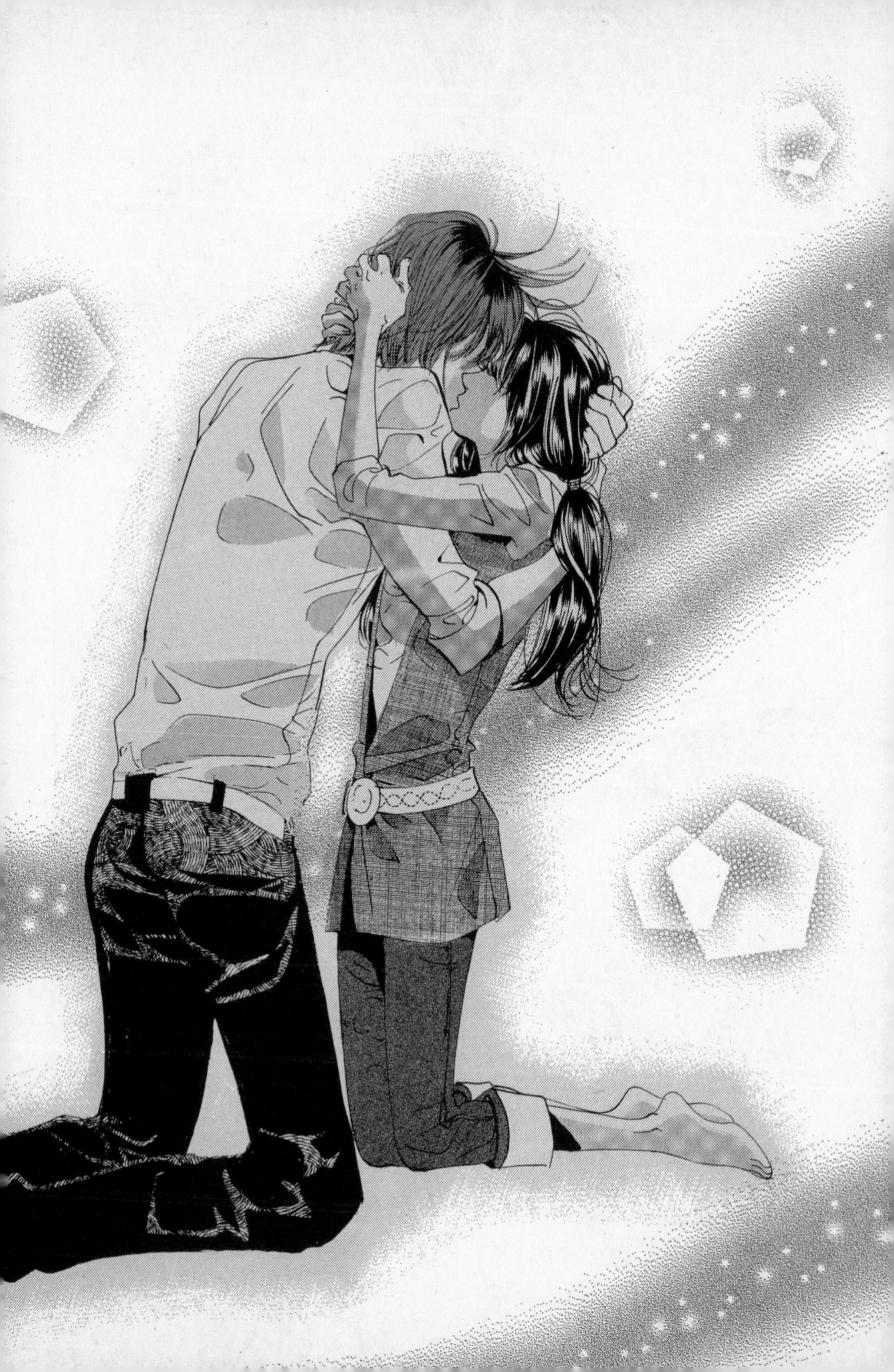

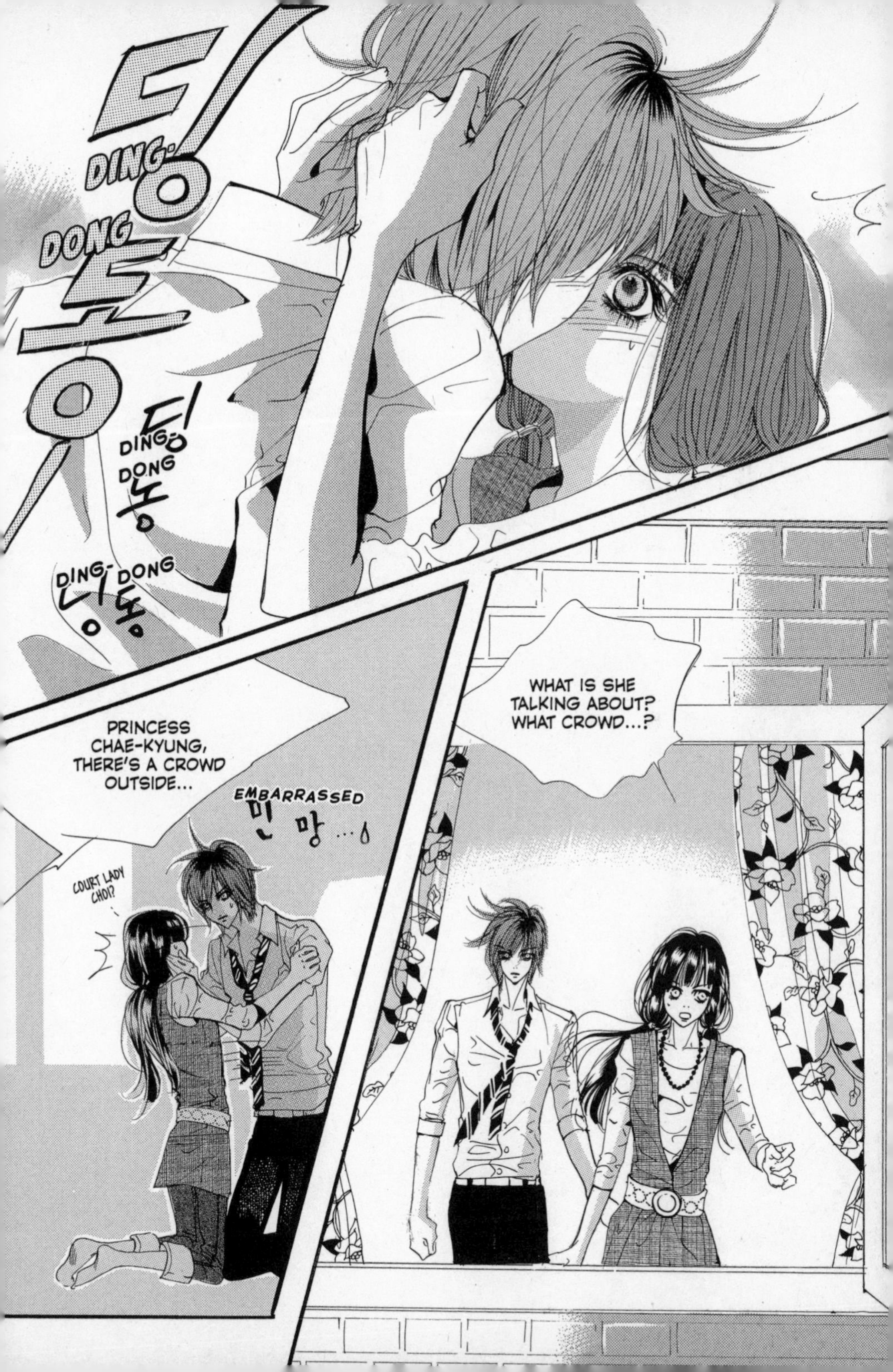

딩동
DING-DONG
딩동
DING-DONG
딩동
DING-DONG
PRINCESS CHAE-KYUNG, THERE'S A CROWD OUTSIDE...
EMBARRASSED
민망...
COURT LADY CHOI?
WHAT IS SHE TALKING ABOUT? WHAT CROWD...?

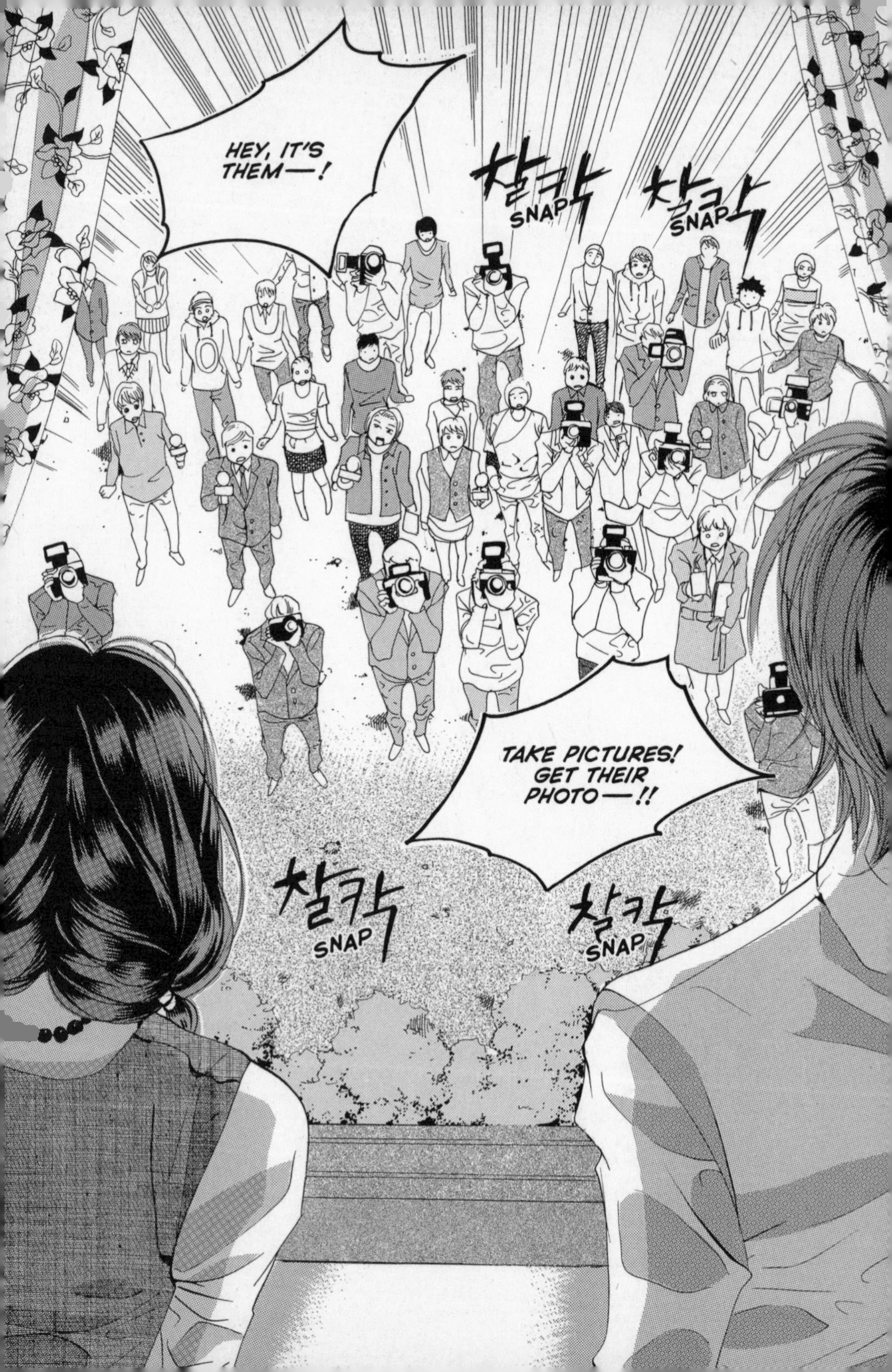

HEY, IT'S THEM—!
찰칵 SNAP
찰칵 SNAP
TAKE PICTURES! GET THEIR PHOTO—!!
찰칵 SNAP
찰칵 SNAP

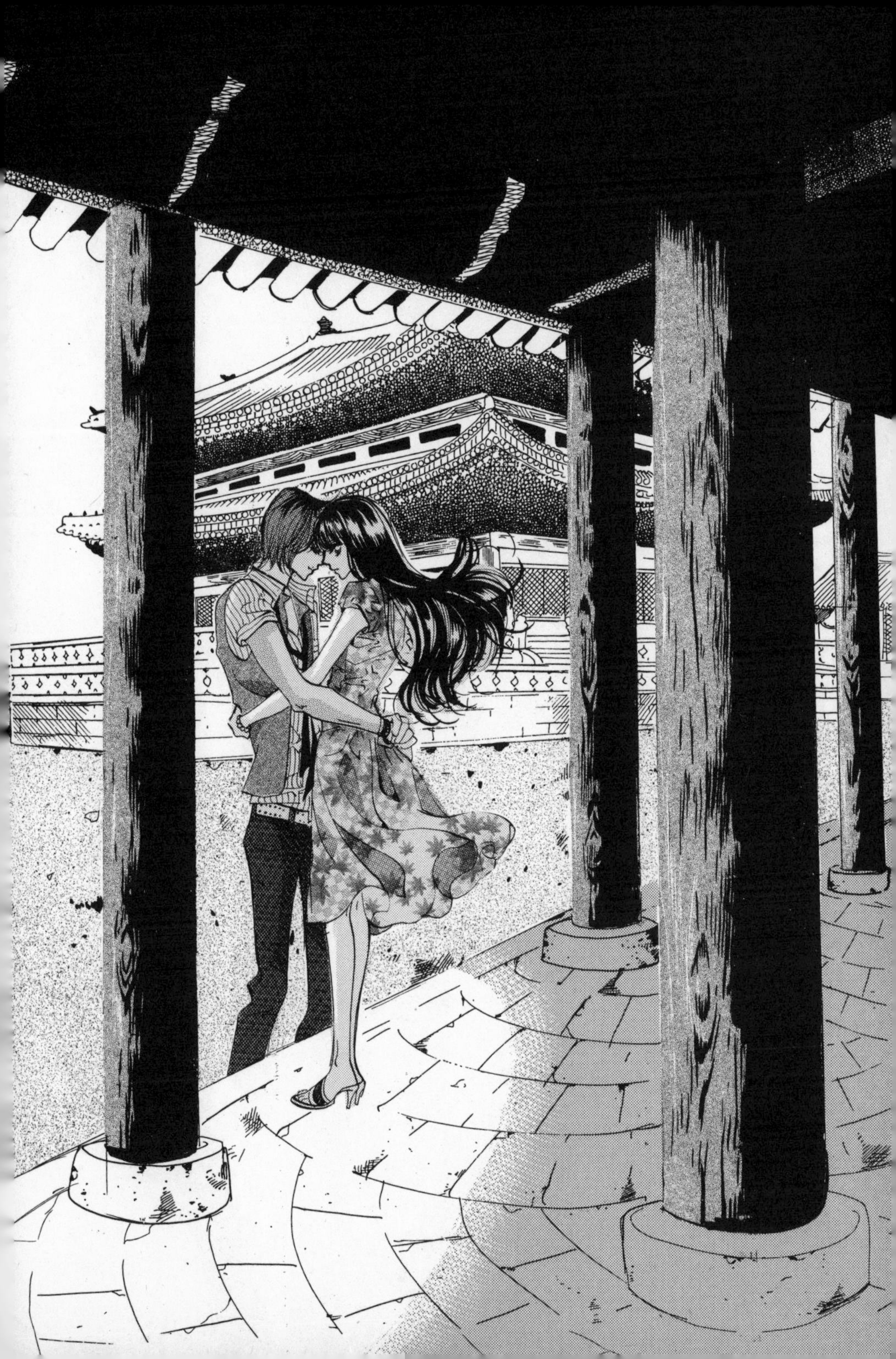

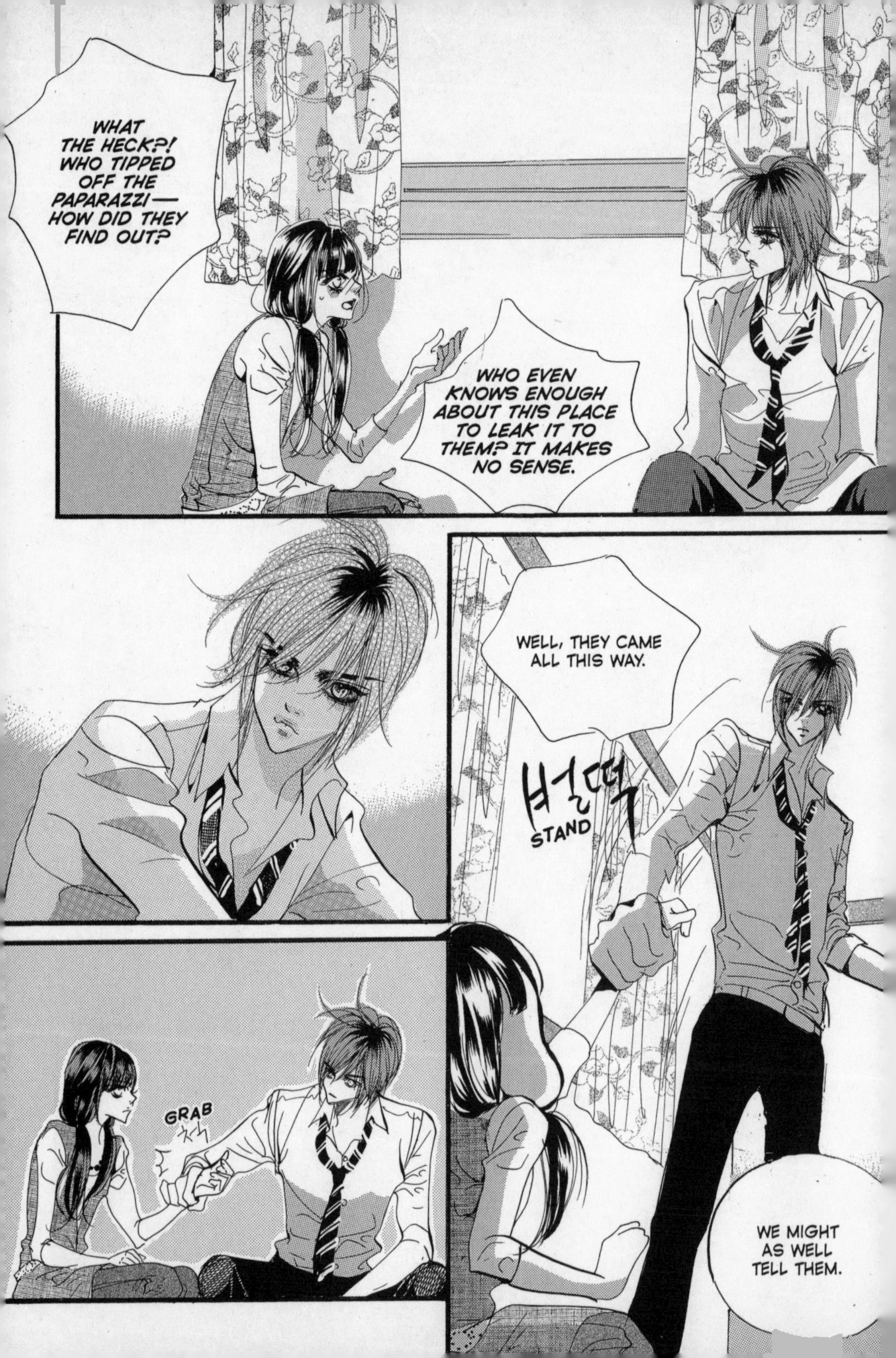
WHAT THE HECK?! WHO TIPPED OFF THE PAPARAZZI— HOW DID THEY FIND OUT?
WHO EVEN KNOWS ENOUGH ABOUT THIS PLACE TO LEAK IT TO THEM? IT MAKES NO SENSE.
GRAB
WELL, THEY CAME ALL THIS WAY.
벌떡
STAND
WE MIGHT AS WELL TELL THEM.

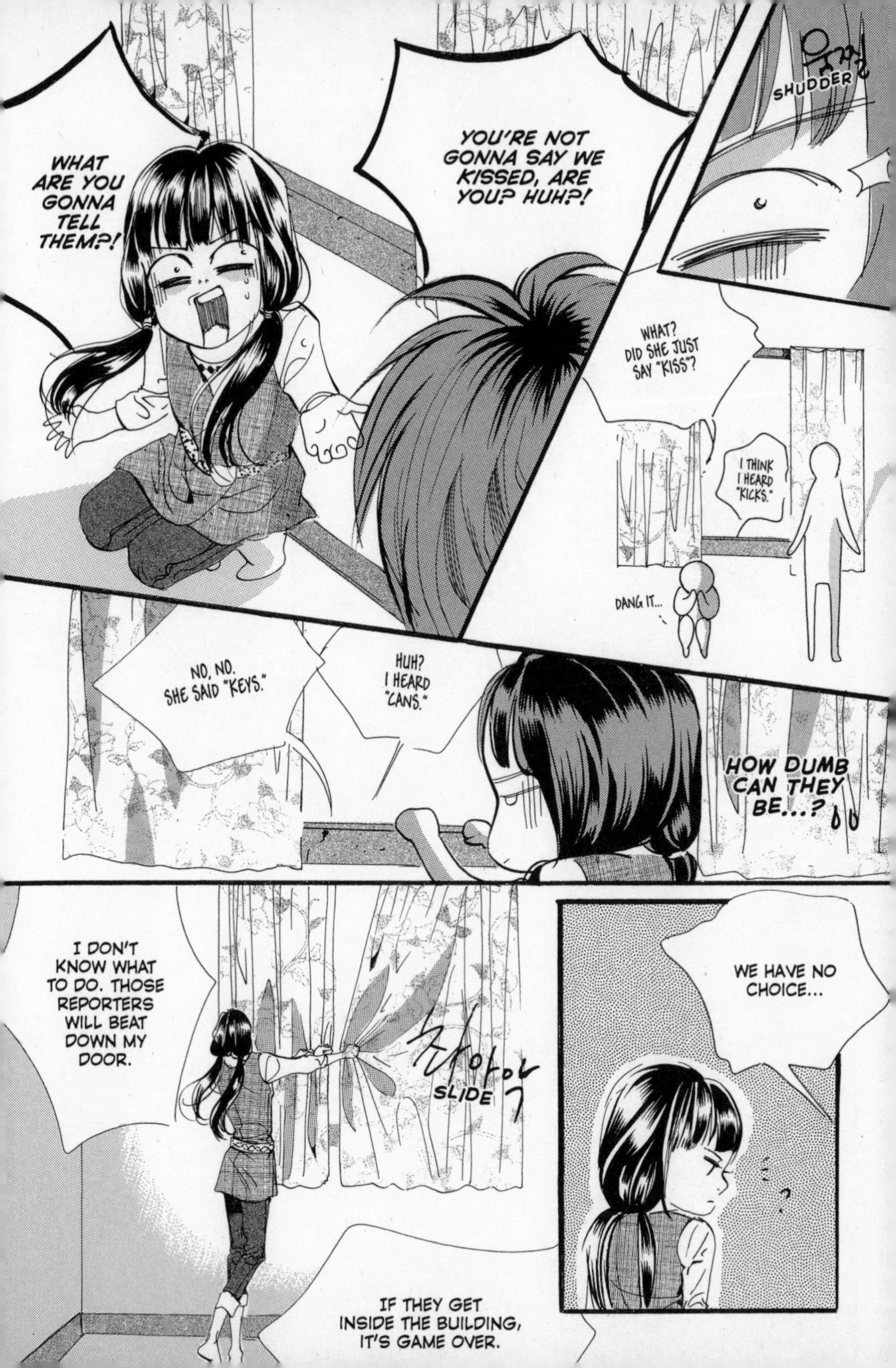
WHAT ARE YOU GONNA TELL THEM?!
YOU'RE NOT GONNA SAY WE KISSED, ARE YOU? HUH?!
SHUDDER
WHAT? DID SHE JUST SAY "KISS"?
I THINK I HEARD "KICKS."
DANG IT...
NO, NO. SHE SAID "KEYS."
HUH? I HEARD "CANS."
HOW DUMB CAN THEY BE...?
I DON'T KNOW WHAT TO DO. THOSE REPORTERS WILL BEAT DOWN MY DOOR.
SLIDE
IF THEY GET INSIDE THE BUILDING, IT'S GAME OVER.
WE HAVE NO CHOICE...

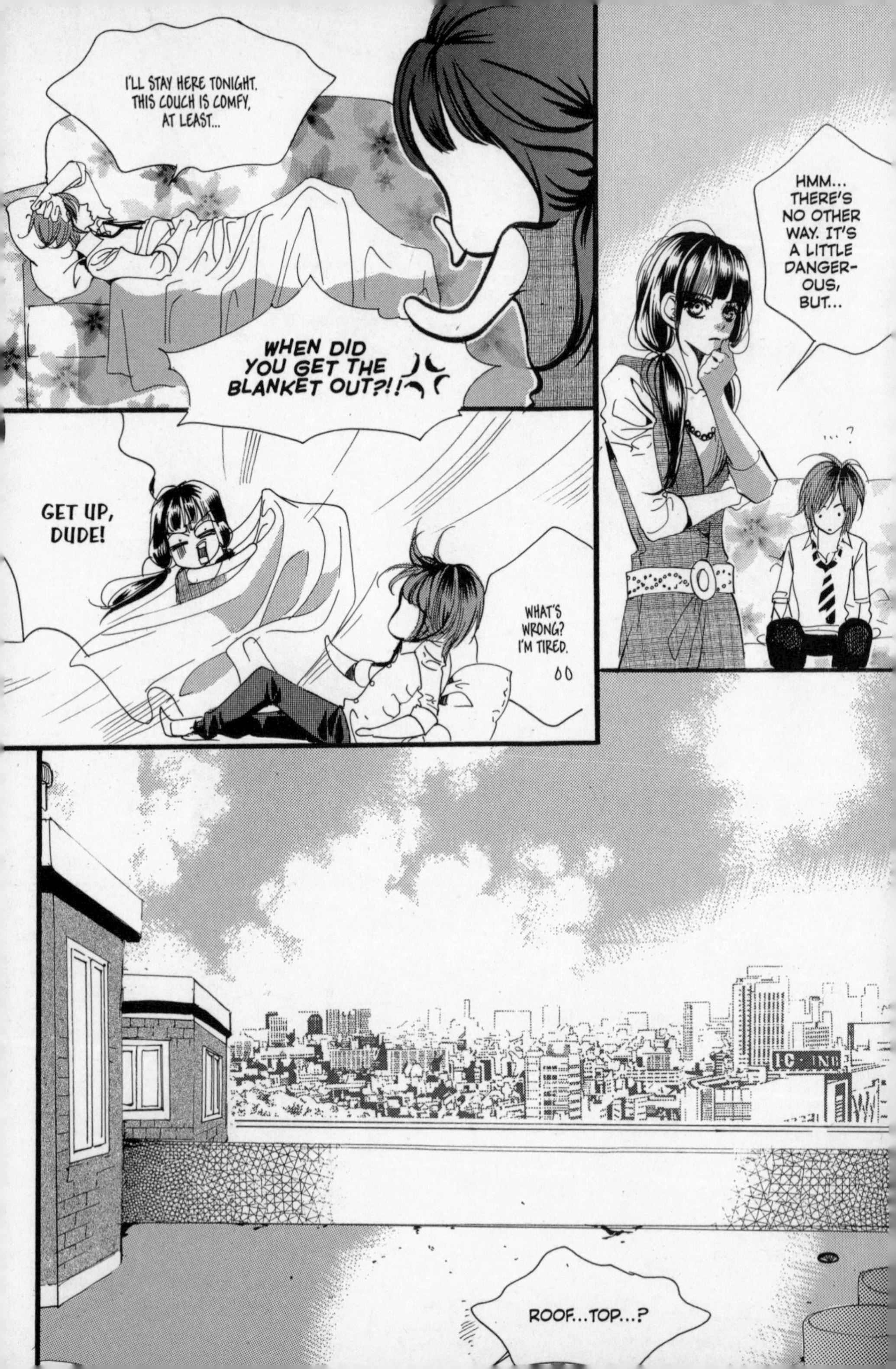
I'LL STAY HERE TONIGHT. THIS COUCH IS COMFY, AT LEAST...
WHEN DID YOU GET THE BLANKET OUT?!!
HMM... THERE'S NO OTHER WAY. IT'S A LITTLE DANGER-OUS, BUT...
...?
GET UP, DUDE!
WHAT'S WRONG? I'M TIRED.
ROOF...TOP...?

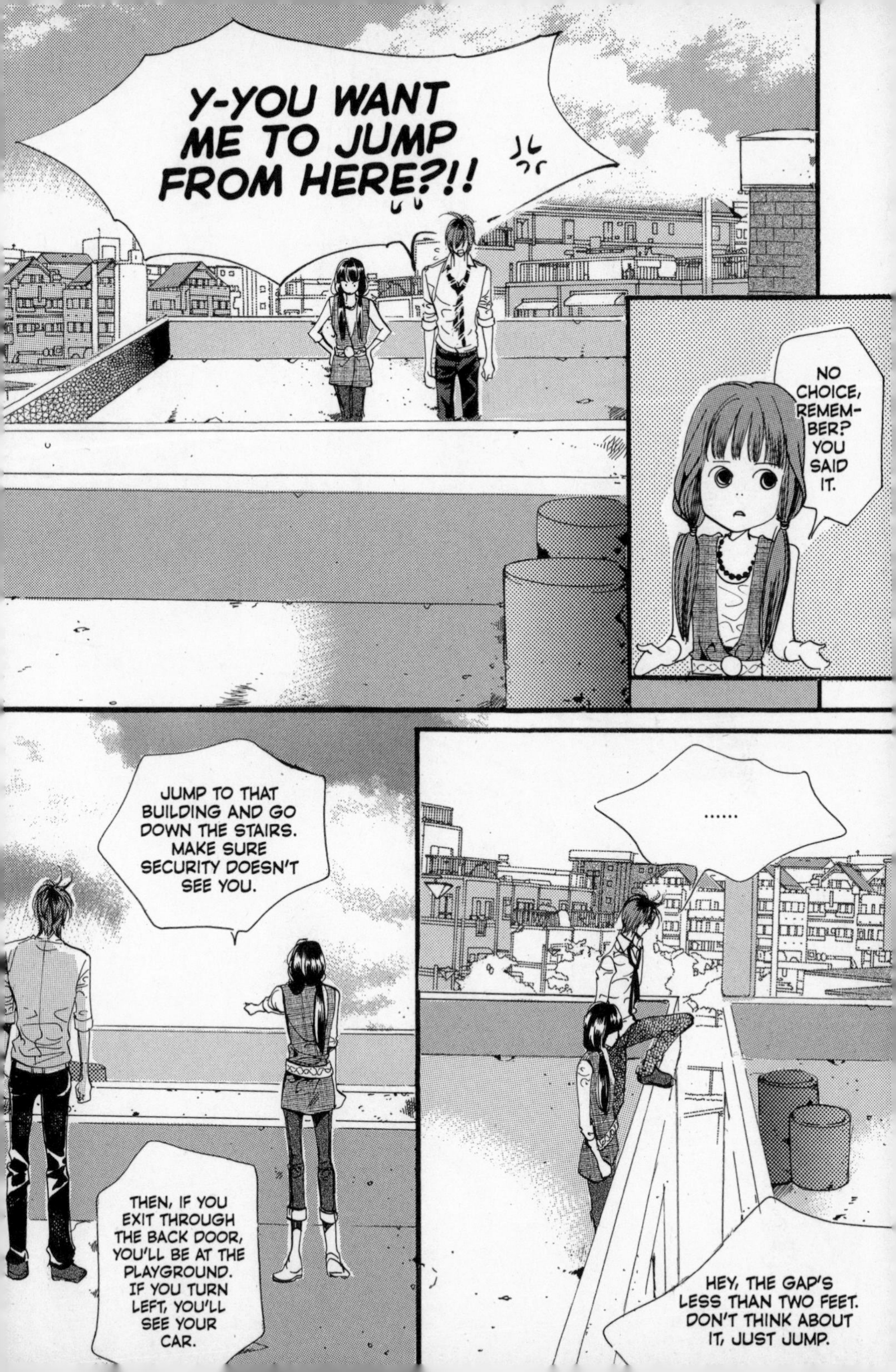
Y-YOU WANT ME TO JUMP FROM HERE?!!
NO CHOICE, REMEMBER? YOU SAID IT.
JUMP TO THAT BUILDING AND GO DOWN THE STAIRS. MAKE SURE SECURITY DOESN'T SEE YOU.
THEN, IF YOU EXIT THROUGH THE BACK DOOR, YOU'LL BE AT THE PLAYGROUND. IF YOU TURN LEFT, YOU'LL SEE YOUR CAR.
......
HEY, THE GAP'S LESS THAN TWO FEET. DON'T THINK ABOUT IT, JUST JUMP.

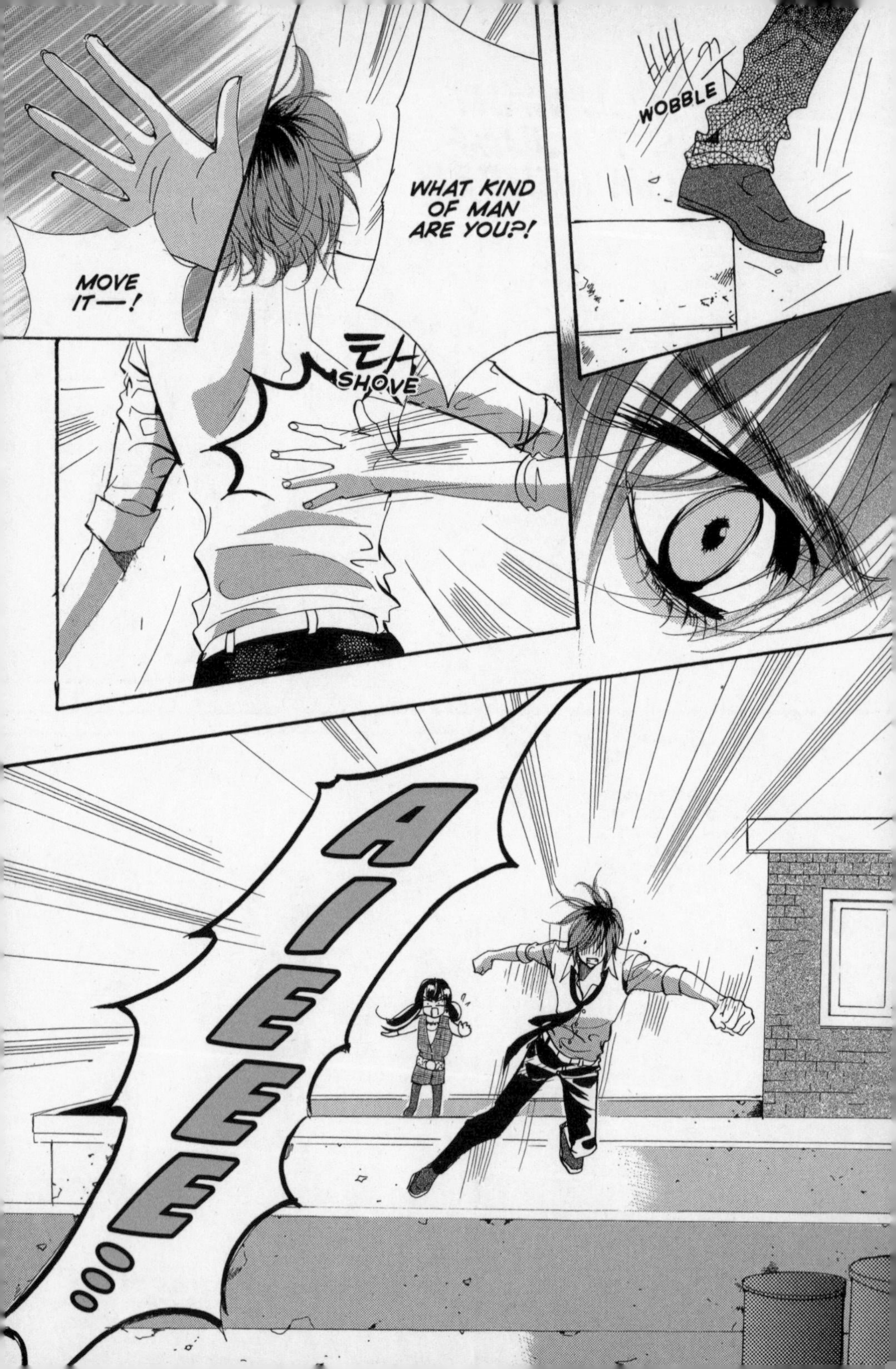
MOVE IT—!
WHAT KIND OF MAN ARE YOU?!
WOBBLE
SHOVE
AIEEEEE...

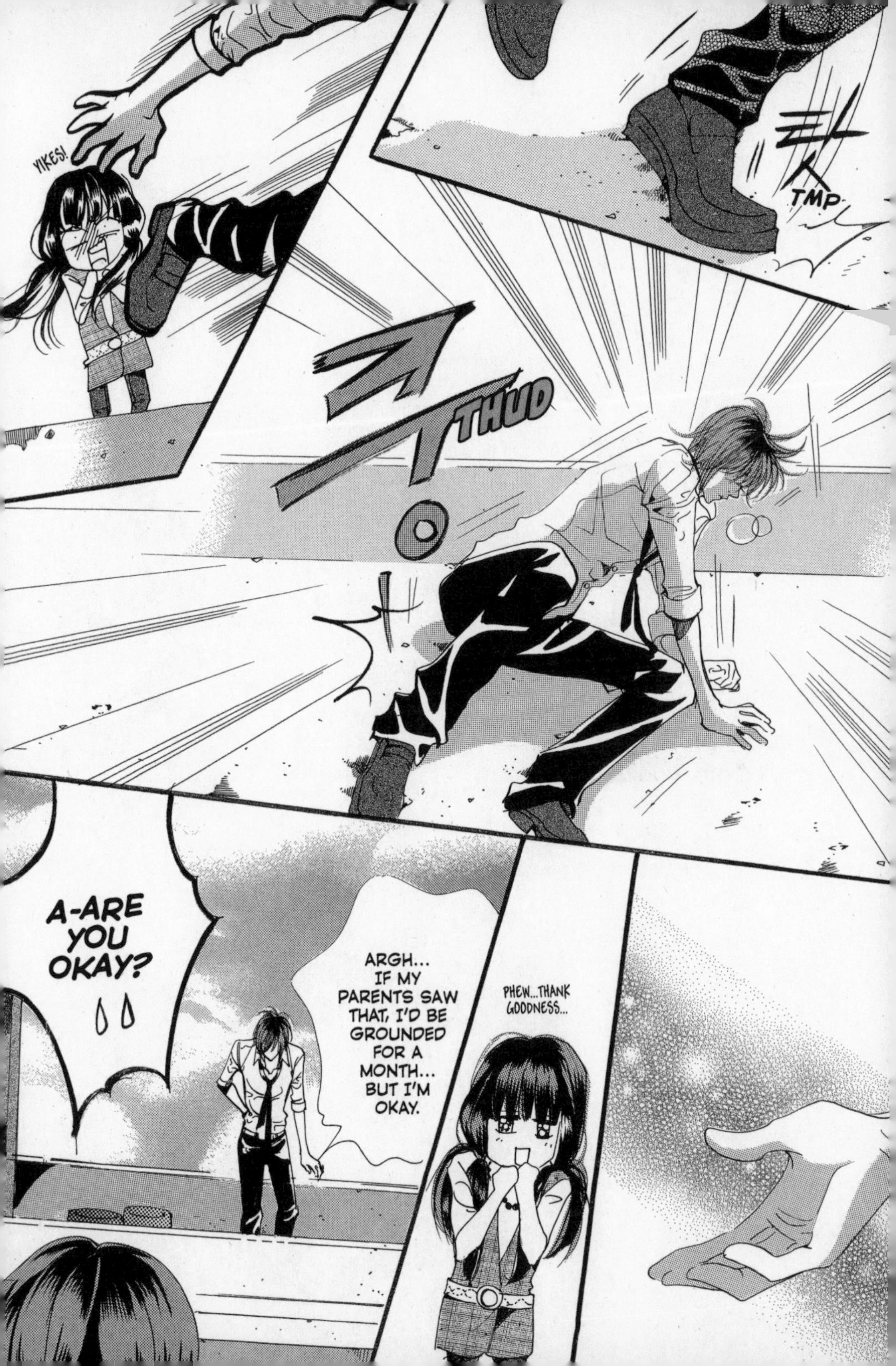
YIKES!
TMP
THUD
A-ARE YOU OKAY?
ARGH... IF MY PARENTS SAW THAT, I'D BE GROUNDED FOR A MONTH... BUT I'M OKAY.
PHEW...THANK GOODNESS...

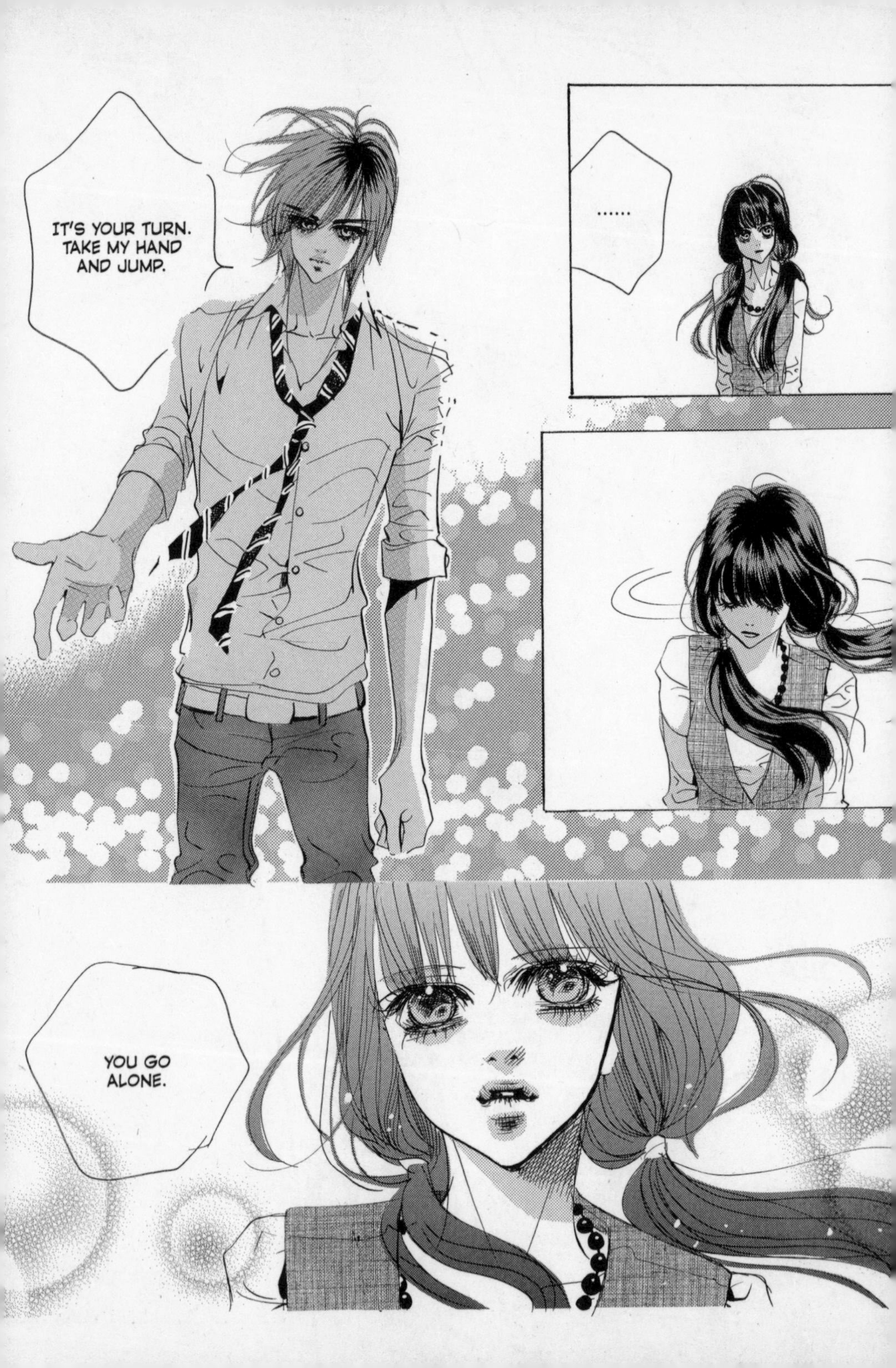
IT'S YOUR TURN. TAKE MY HAND AND JUMP.
......
YOU GO ALONE.

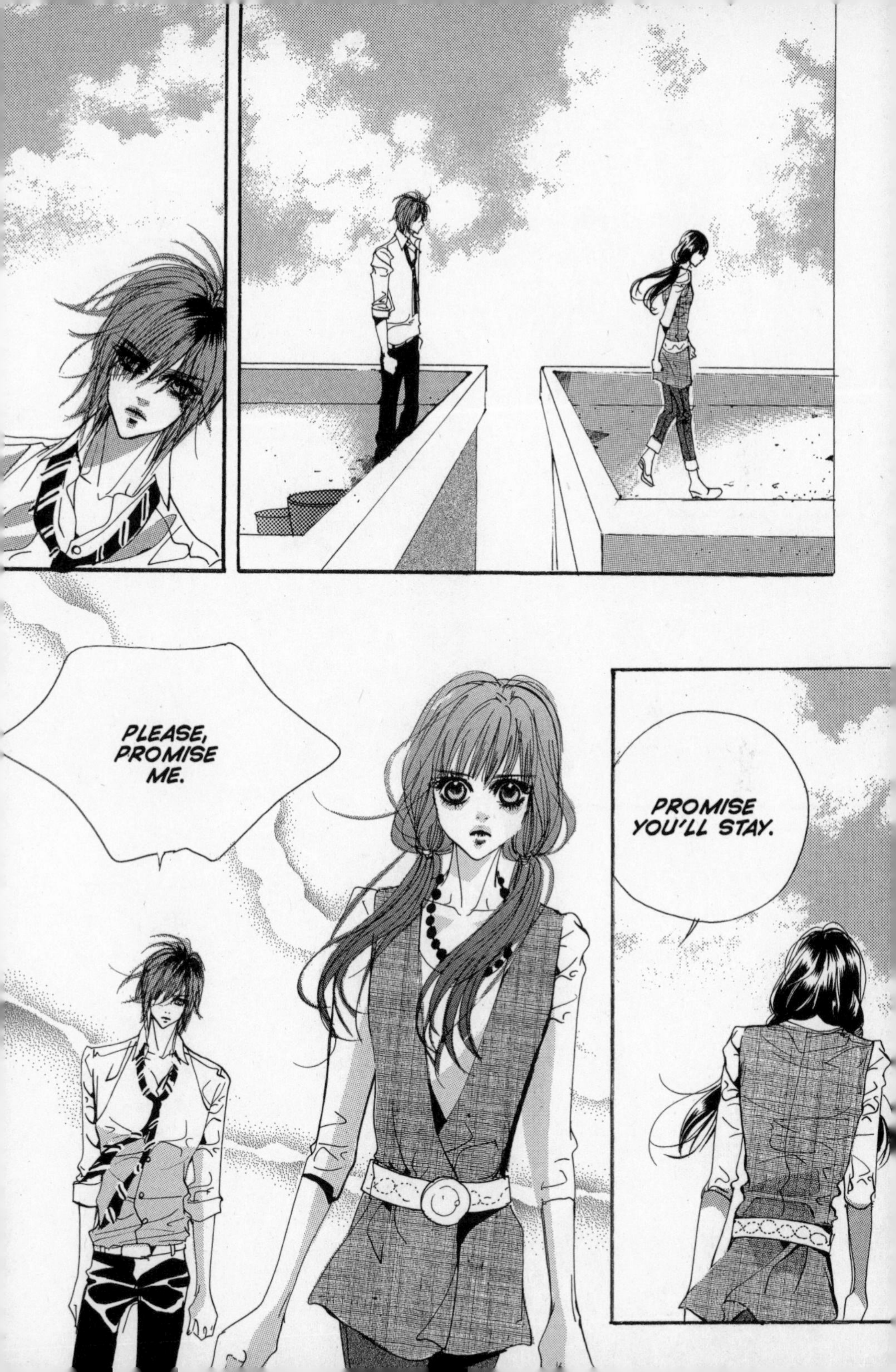
PLEASE, PROMISE ME.
PROMISE YOU'LL STAY.

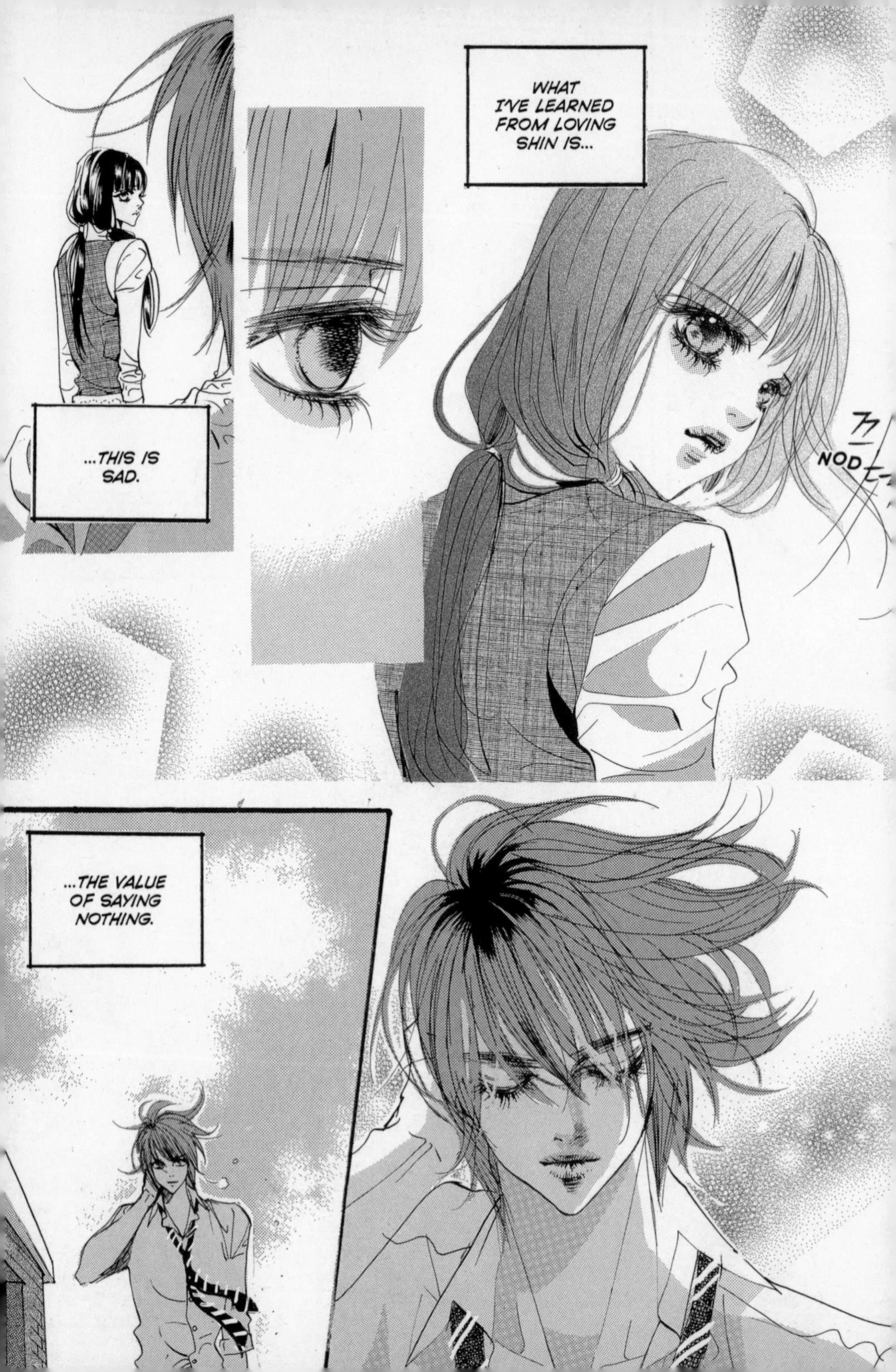
...THIS IS SAD.
WHAT I'VE LEARNED FROM LOVING SHIN IS...
NOD
...THE VALUE OF SAYING NOTHING.

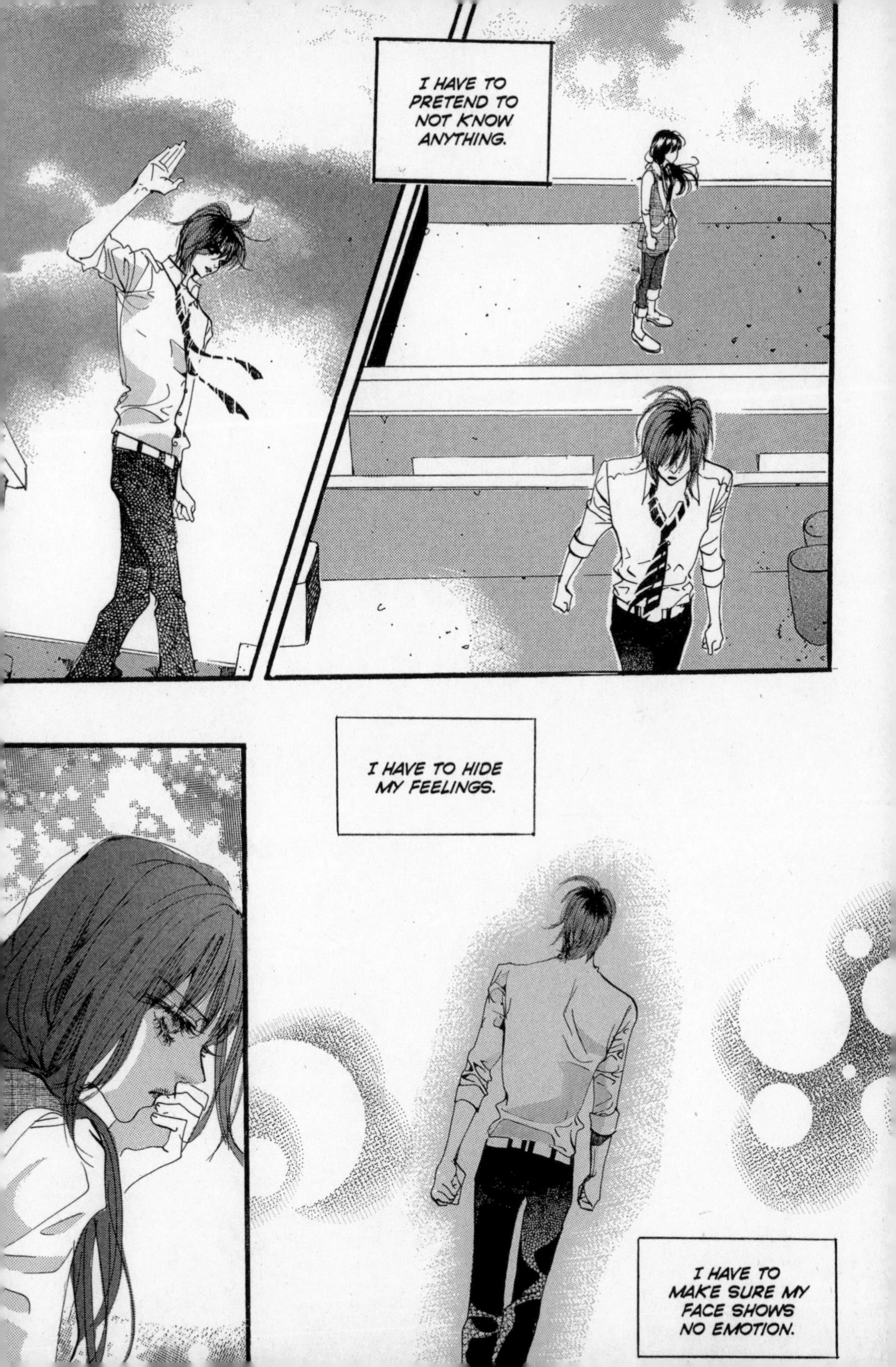
I HAVE TO PRETEND TO NOT KNOW ANYTHING.
I HAVE TO HIDE MY FEELINGS.
I HAVE TO MAKE SURE MY FACE SHOWS NO EMOTION.

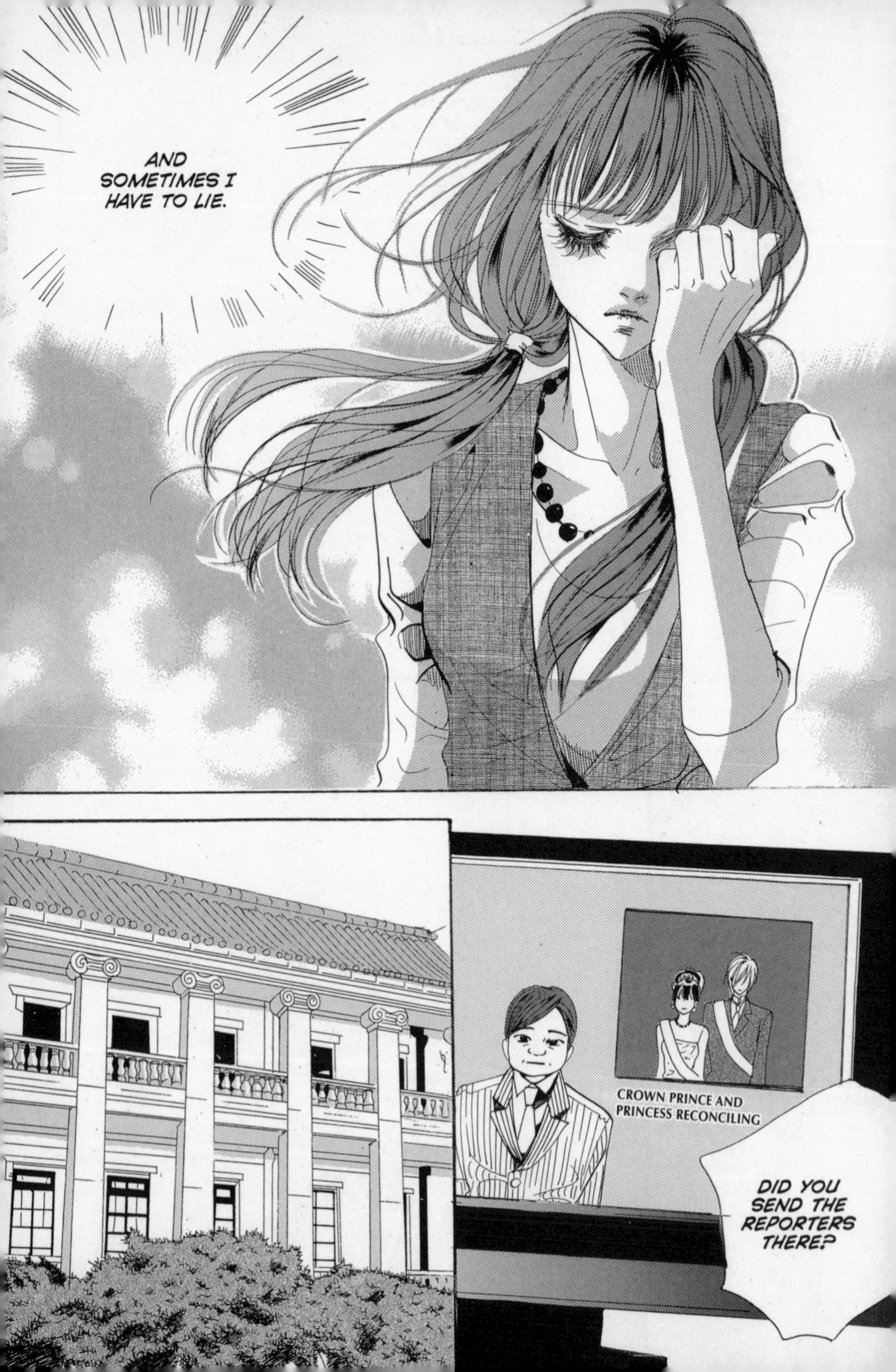
AND SOMETIMES I HAVE TO LIE.
CROWN PRINCE AND PRINCESS RECONCILING
DID YOU SEND THE REPORTERS THERE?

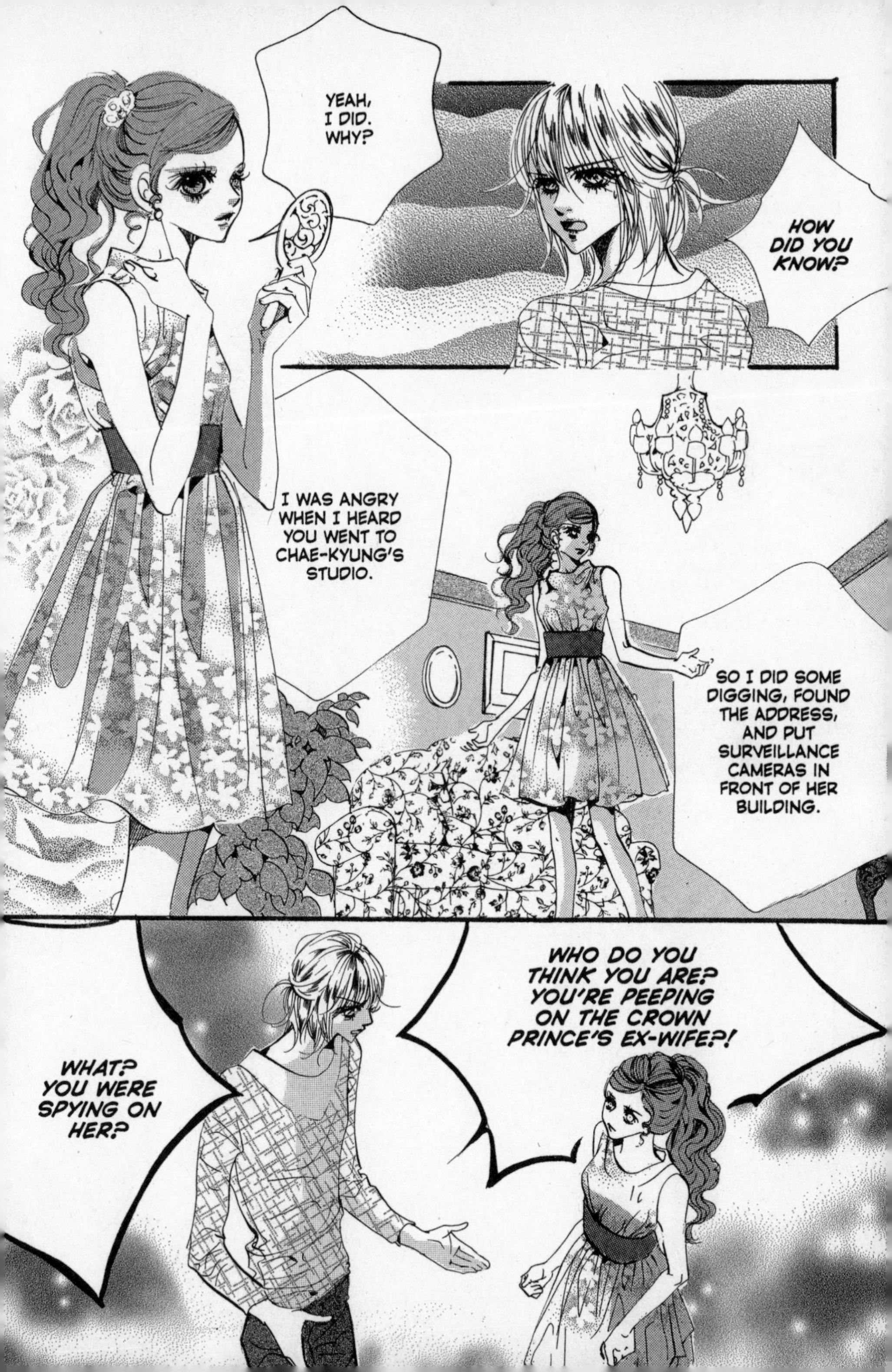
YEAH, I DID. WHY?
HOW DID YOU KNOW?
I WAS ANGRY WHEN I HEARD YOU WENT TO CHAE-KYUNG'S STUDIO.
SO I DID SOME DIGGING, FOUND THE ADDRESS, AND PUT SURVEILLANCE CAMERAS IN FRONT OF HER BUILDING.
WHAT? YOU WERE SPYING ON HER?
WHO DO YOU THINK YOU ARE? YOU'RE PEEPING ON THE CROWN PRINCE'S EX-WIFE?!

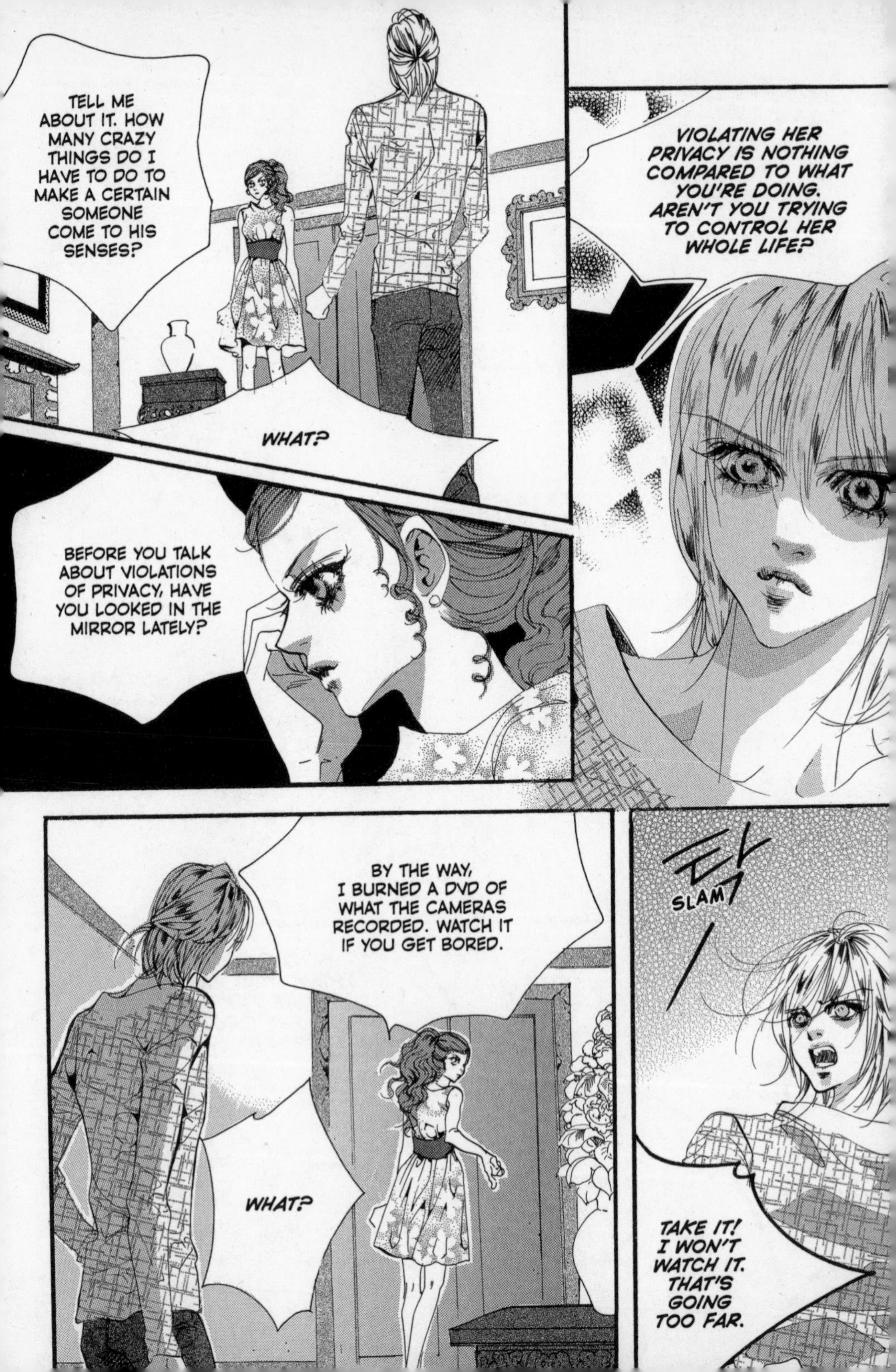
TELL ME ABOUT IT. HOW MANY CRAZY THINGS DO I HAVE TO DO TO MAKE A CERTAIN SOMEONE COME TO HIS SENSES?
WHAT?
BEFORE YOU TALK ABOUT VIOLATIONS OF PRIVACY, HAVE YOU LOOKED IN THE MIRROR LATELY?
VIOLATING HER PRIVACY IS NOTHING COMPARED TO WHAT YOU'RE DOING. AREN'T YOU TRYING TO CONTROL HER WHOLE LIFE?
BY THE WAY, I BURNED A DVD OF WHAT THE CAMERAS RECORDED. WATCH IT IF YOU GET BORED.
WHAT?
SLAM
TAKE IT! I WON'T WATCH IT. THAT'S GOING TOO FAR.

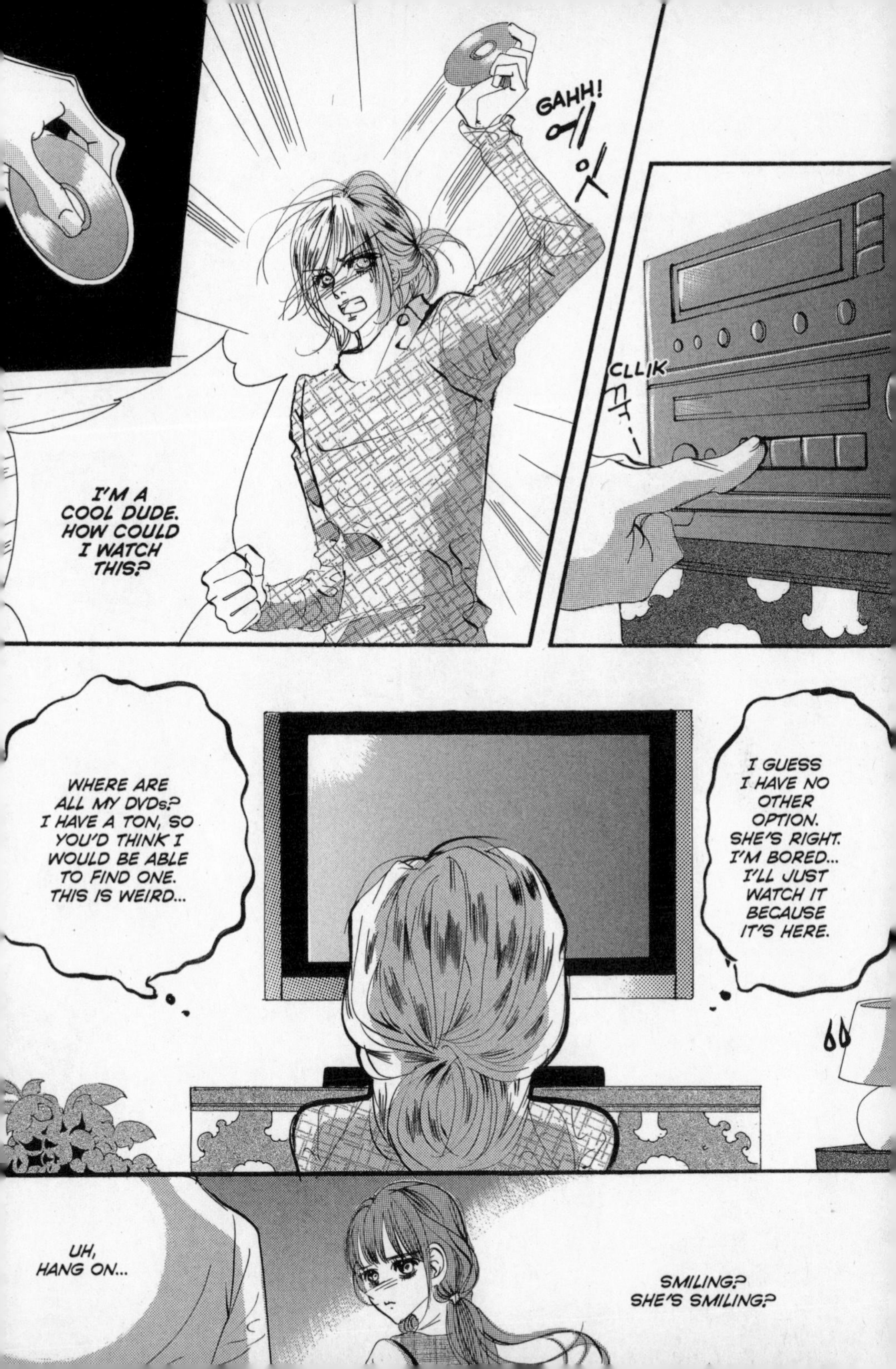
GAHH!
에잇
I'M A COOL DUDE. HOW COULD I WATCH THIS?
CLLIK
WHERE ARE ALL MY DVDs? I HAVE A TON, SO YOU'D THINK I WOULD BE ABLE TO FIND ONE. THIS IS WEIRD...
I GUESS I HAVE NO OTHER OPTION. SHE'S RIGHT. I'M BORED... I'LL JUST WATCH IT BECAUSE IT'S HERE.
UH, HANG ON...
SMILING? SHE'S SMILING?

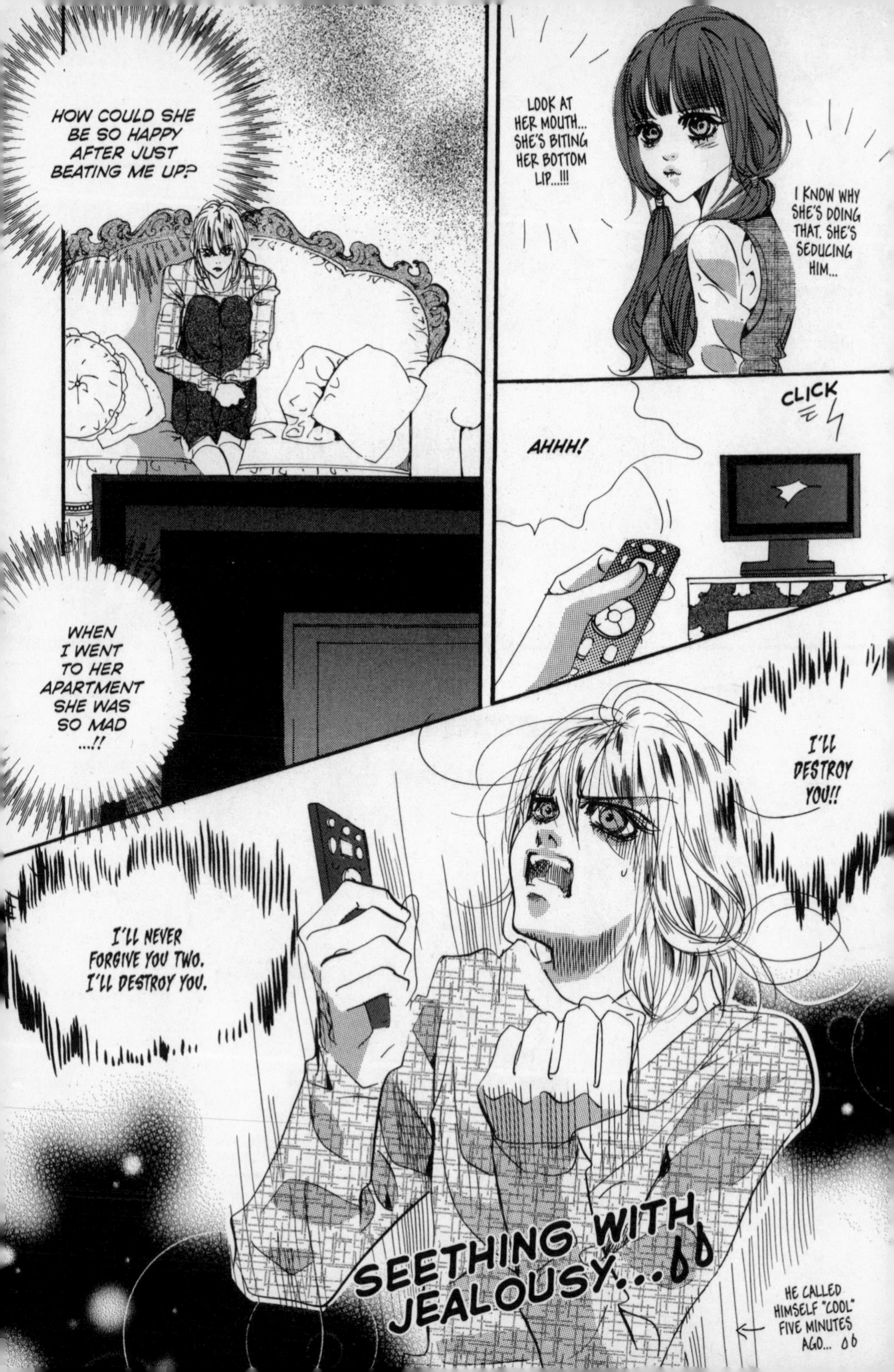

HOW COULD SHE BE SO HAPPY AFTER JUST BEATING ME UP?
WHEN I WENT TO HER APARTMENT SHE WAS SO MAD ...!!
LOOK AT HER MOUTH... SHE'S BITING HER BOTTOM LIP...!!!
I KNOW WHY SHE'S DOING THAT. SHE'S SEDUCING HIM...
AHHH!
CLICK
I'LL NEVER FORGIVE YOU TWO. I'LL DESTROY YOU.
I'LL DESTROY YOU!!
SEETHING WITH JEALOUSY...
HE CALLED HIMSELF "COOL" FIVE MINUTES AGO...

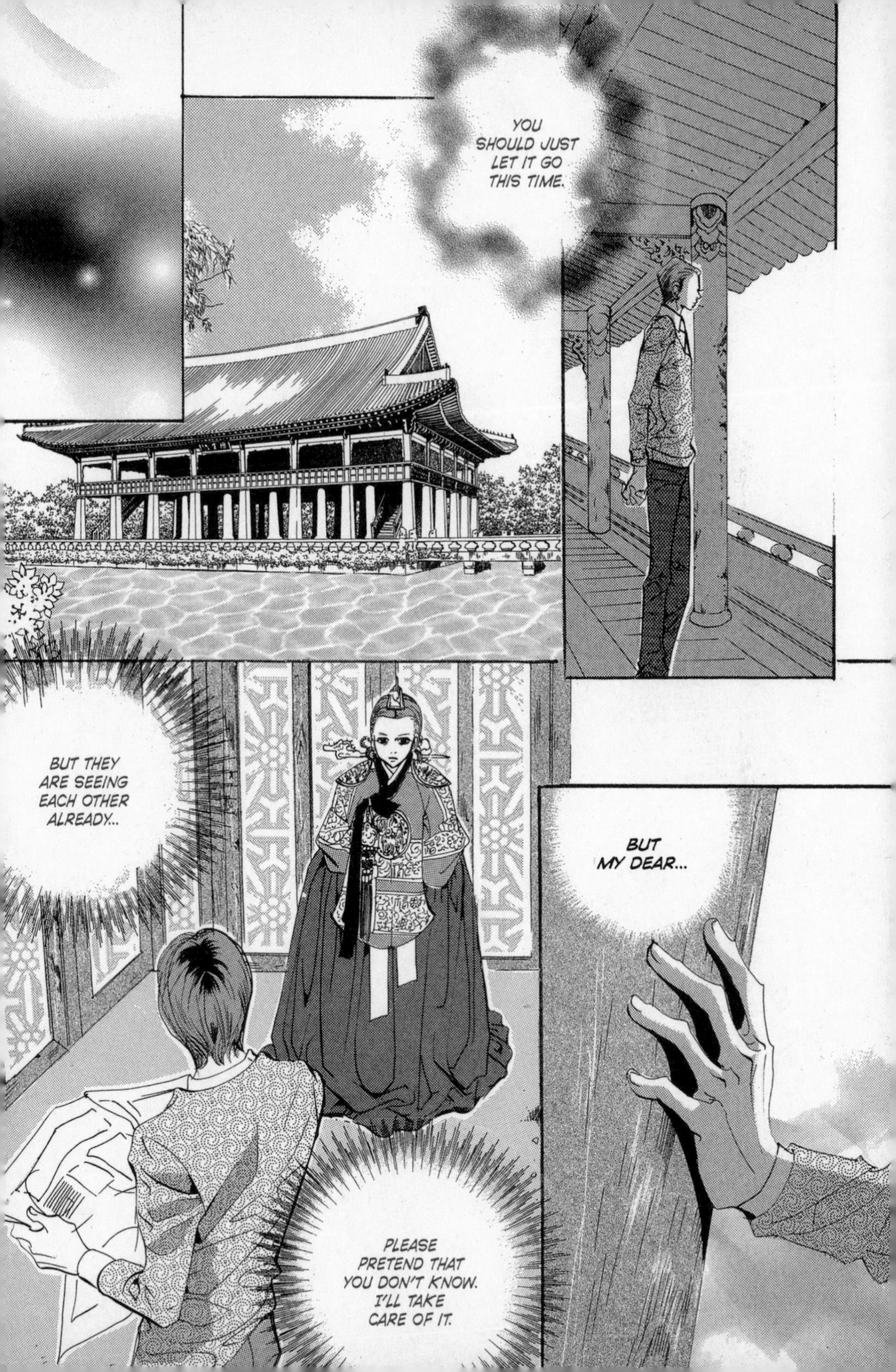
YOU SHOULD JUST LET IT GO THIS TIME.
BUT THEY ARE SEEING EACH OTHER ALREADY...
PLEASE PRETEND THAT YOU DON'T KNOW. I'LL TAKE CARE OF IT.
BUT MY DEAR...

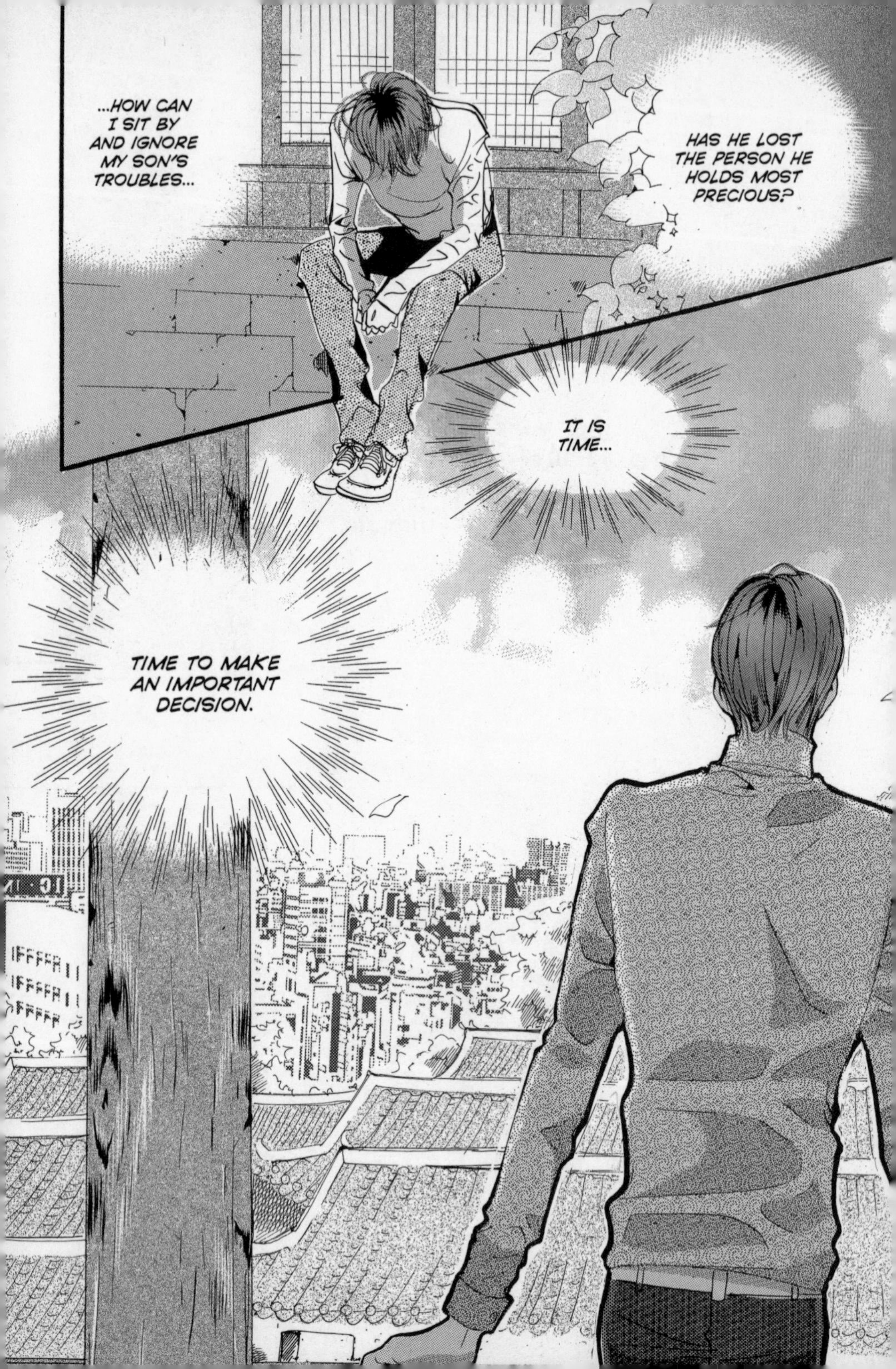
...HOW CAN I SIT BY AND IGNORE MY SON'S TROUBLES...
HAS HE LOST THE PERSON HE HOLDS MOST PRECIOUS?
IT IS TIME...
TIME TO MAKE AN IMPORTANT DECISION.

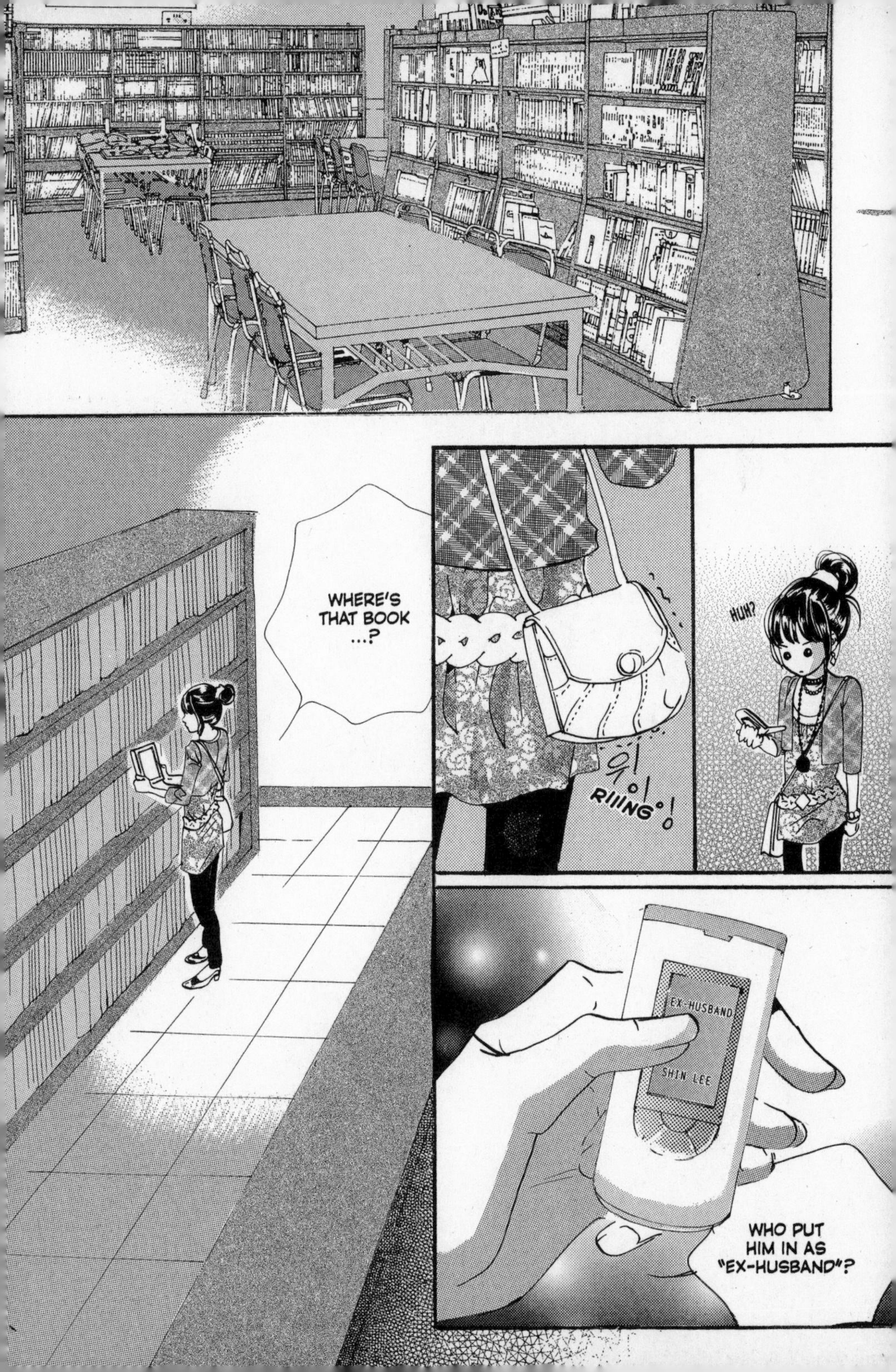

WHERE'S THAT BOOK ...?
RIIING
HUH?
EX-HUSBAND
SHIN LEE
WHO PUT HIM IN AS "EX-HUSBAND"?

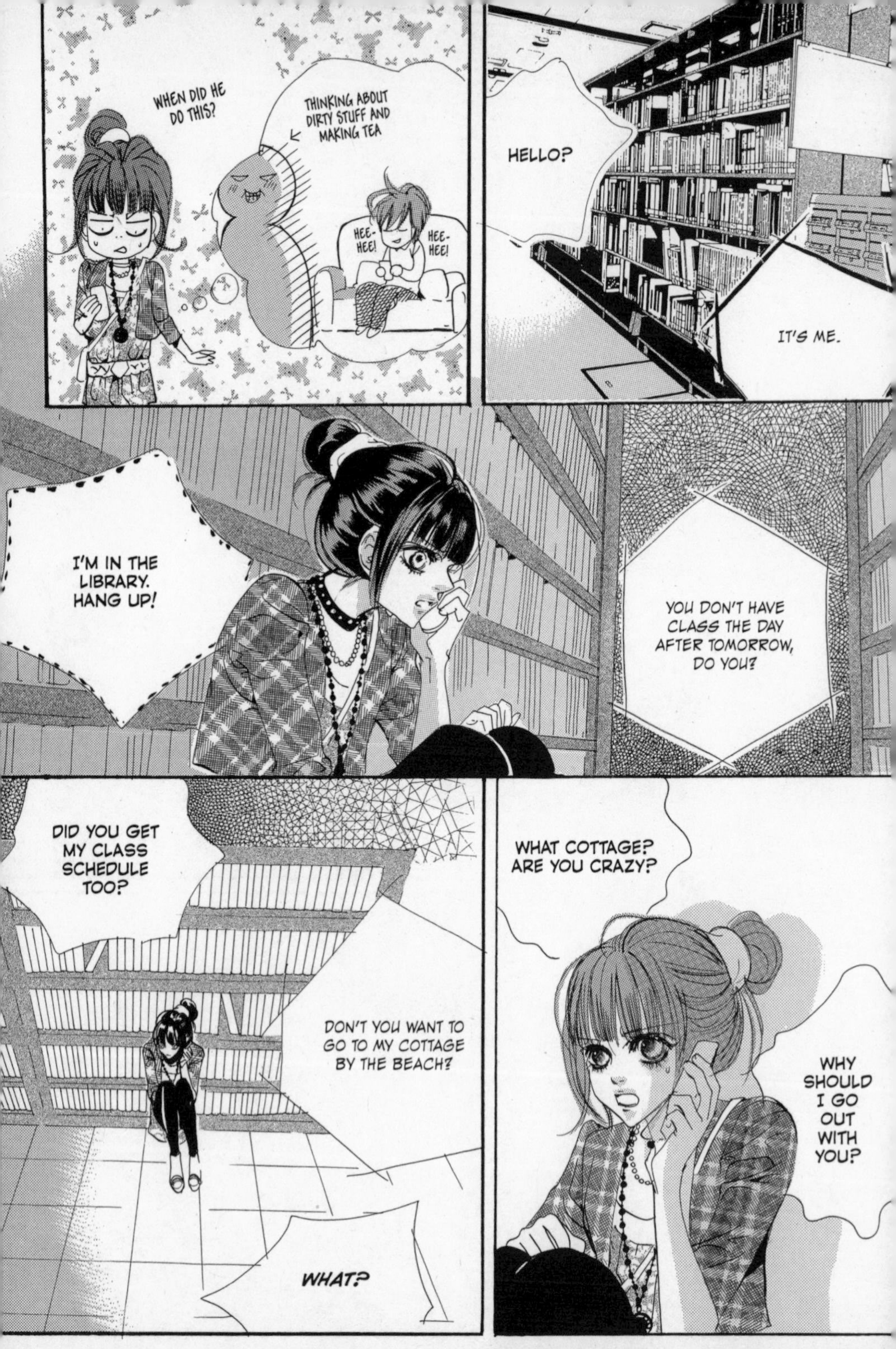
WHEN DID HE DO THIS?
THINKING ABOUT DIRTY STUFF AND MAKING TEA
HEE-HEE!
HEE-HEE!
HELLO?
IT'S ME.
I'M IN THE LIBRARY. HANG UP!
YOU DON'T HAVE CLASS THE DAY AFTER TOMORROW, DO YOU?
DID YOU GET MY CLASS SCHEDULE TOO?
DON'T YOU WANT TO GO TO MY COTTAGE BY THE BEACH?
WHAT?
WHAT COTTAGE? ARE YOU CRAZY?
WHY SHOULD I GO OUT WITH YOU?

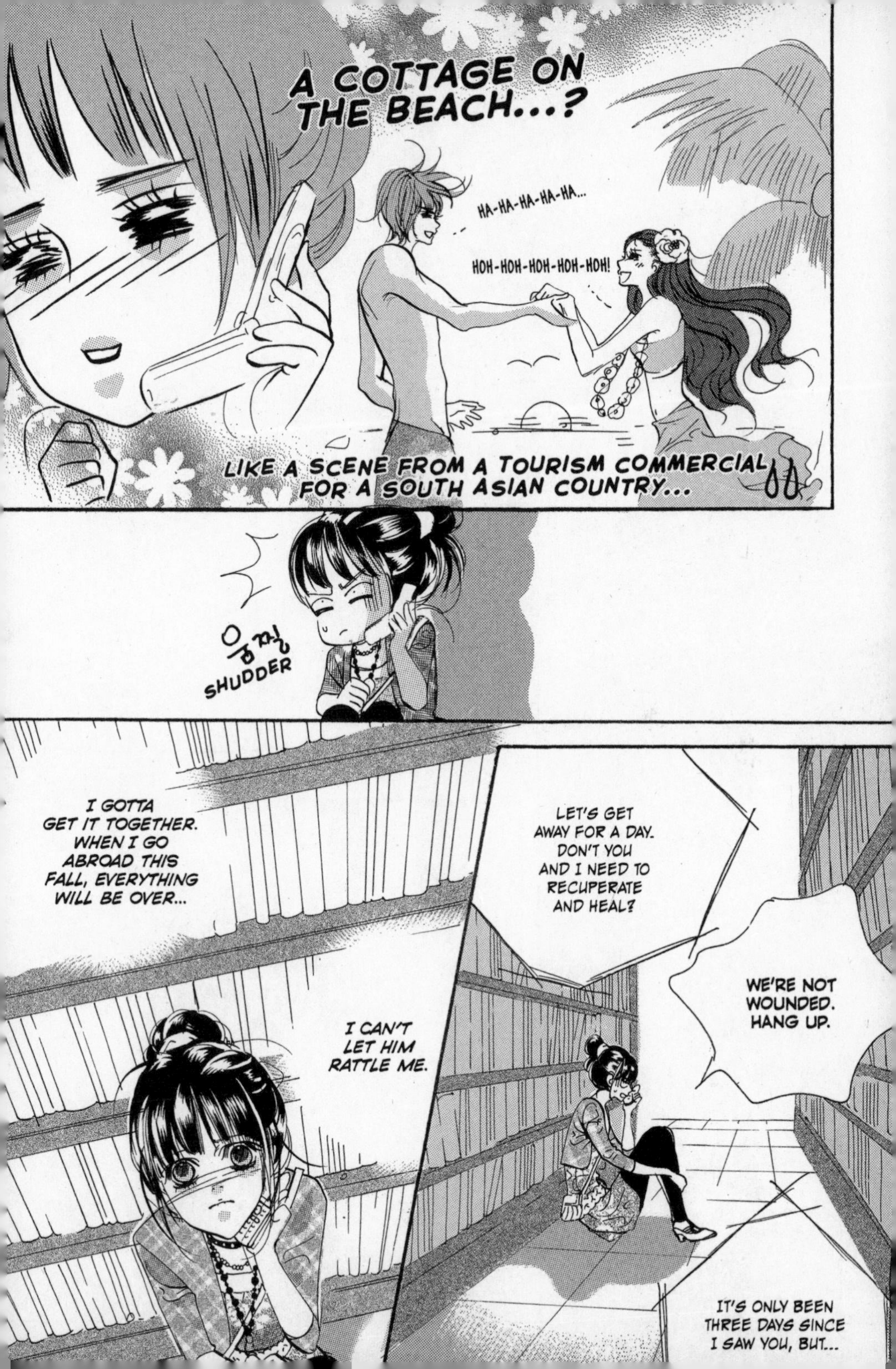
A COTTAGE ON THE BEACH...?
HA-HA-HA-HA-HA...
HOH-HOH-HOH-HOH-HOH!
LIKE A SCENE FROM A TOURISM COMMERCIAL FOR A SOUTH ASIAN COUNTRY...
움찔
SHUDDER
I GOTTA GET IT TOGETHER. WHEN I GO ABROAD THIS FALL, EVERYTHING WILL BE OVER...
I CAN'T LET HIM RATTLE ME.
LET'S GET AWAY FOR A DAY. DON'T YOU AND I NEED TO RECUPERATE AND HEAL?
WE'RE NOT WOUNDED. HANG UP.
IT'S ONLY BEEN THREE DAYS SINCE I SAW YOU, BUT...

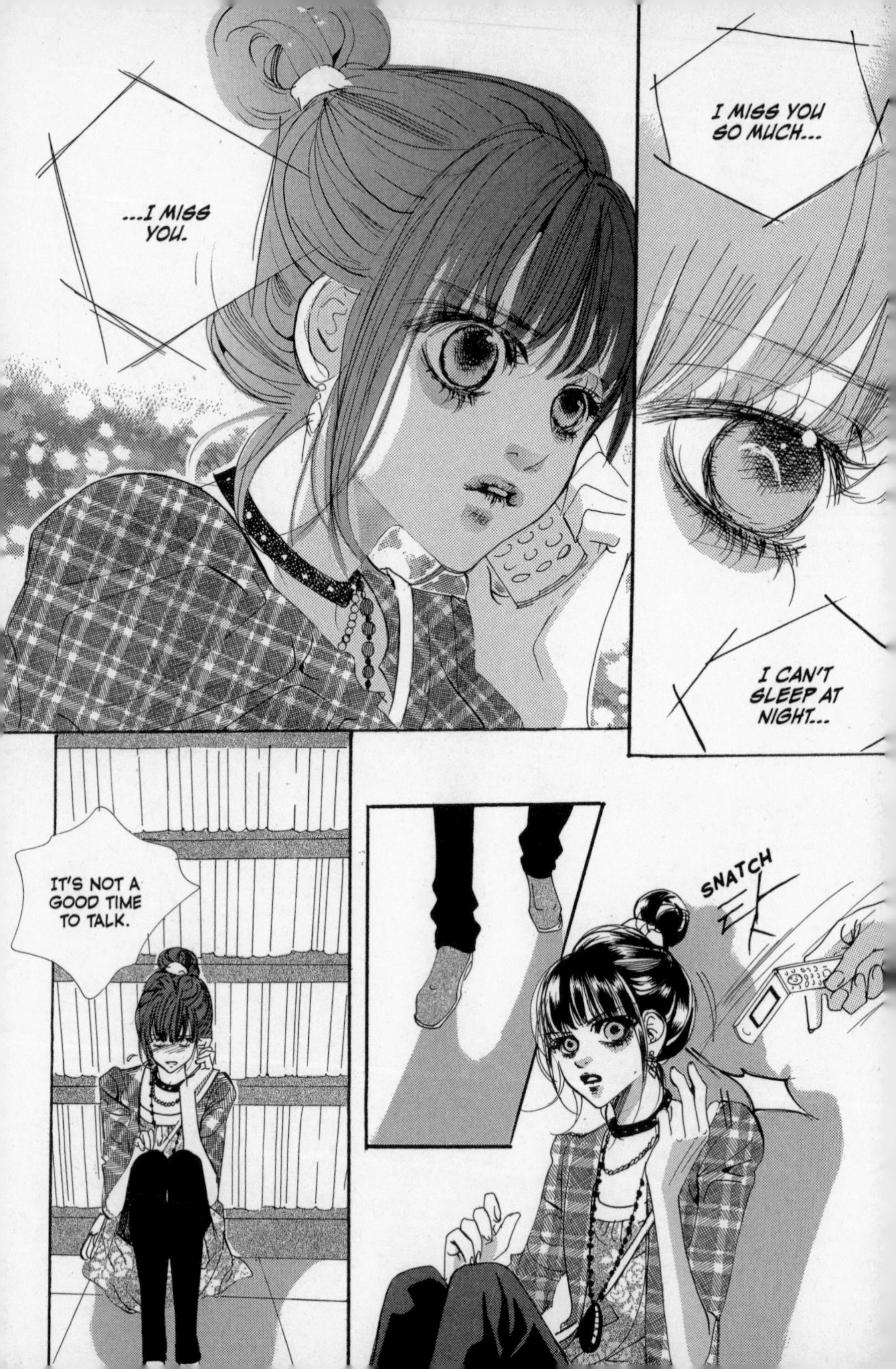
...I MISS YOU.
I MISS YOU SO MUCH...
I CAN'T SLEEP AT NIGHT...
IT'S NOT A GOOD TIME TO TALK.
SNATCH

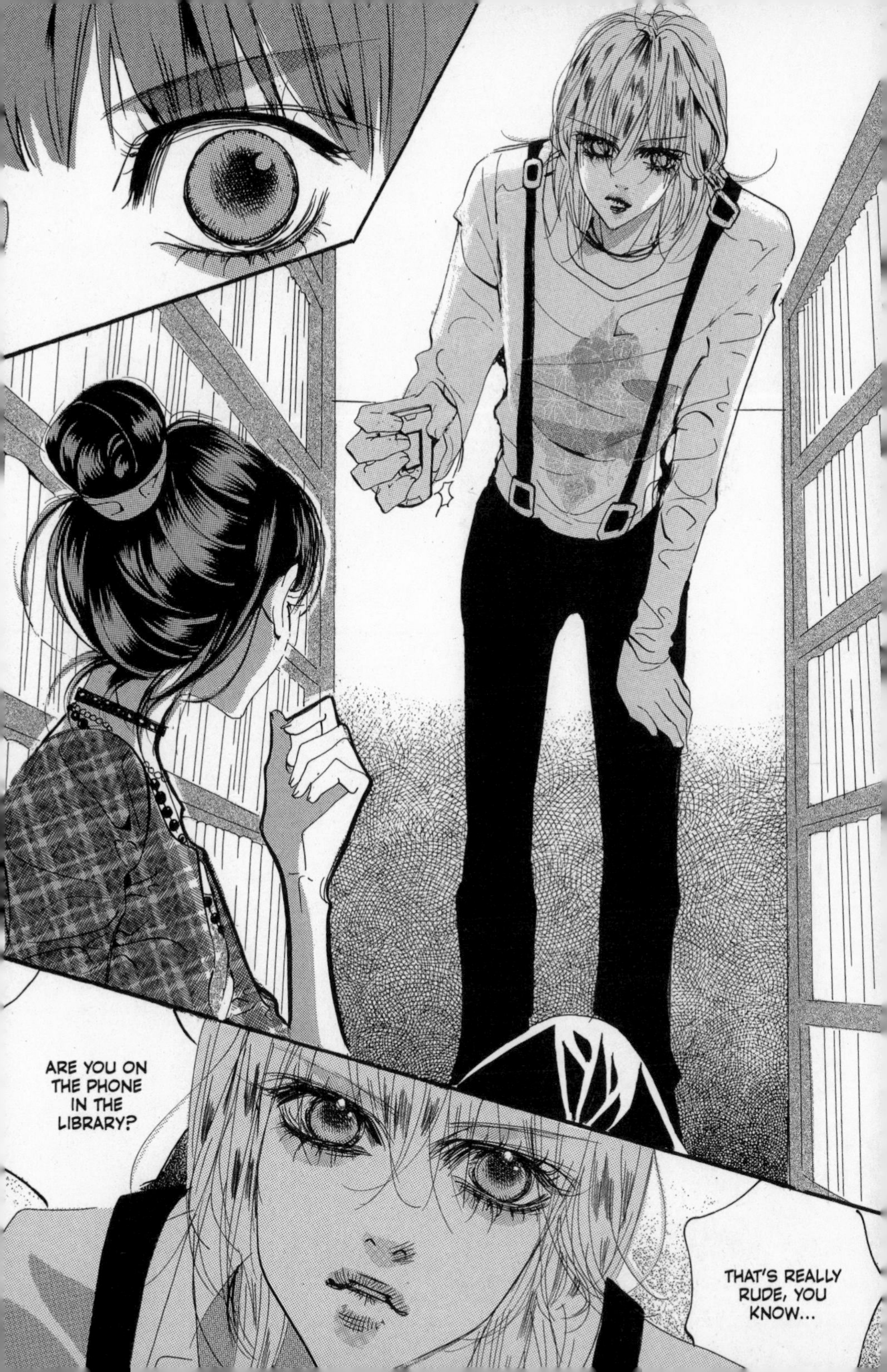
ARE YOU ON THE PHONE IN THE LIBRARY?
THAT'S REALLY RUDE, YOU KNOW...

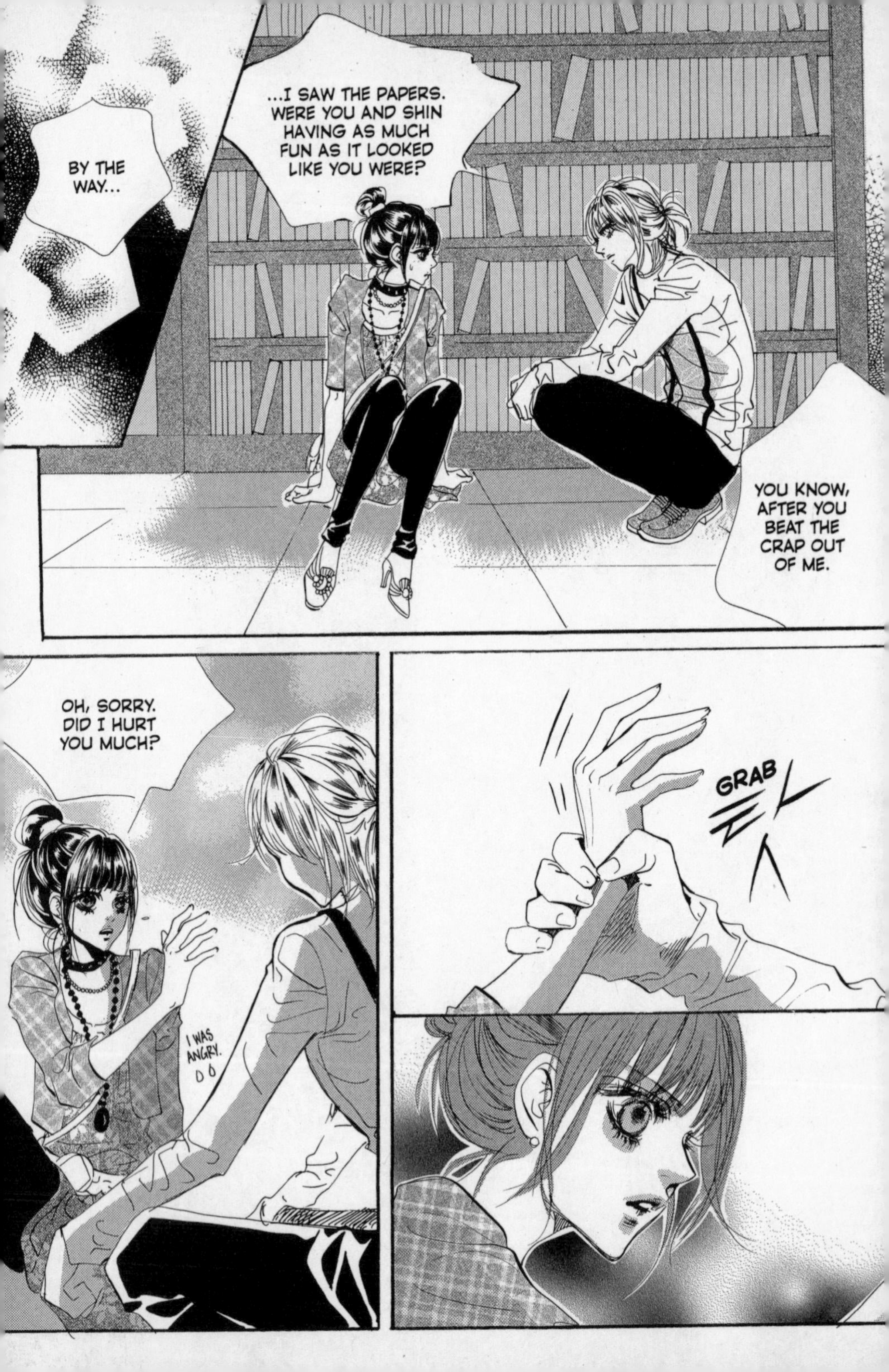
BY THE WAY...
...I SAW THE PAPERS. WERE YOU AND SHIN HAVING AS MUCH FUN AS IT LOOKED LIKE YOU WERE?
YOU KNOW, AFTER YOU BEAT THE CRAP OUT OF ME.
OH, SORRY. DID I HURT YOU MUCH?
I WAS ANGRY.
GRAB

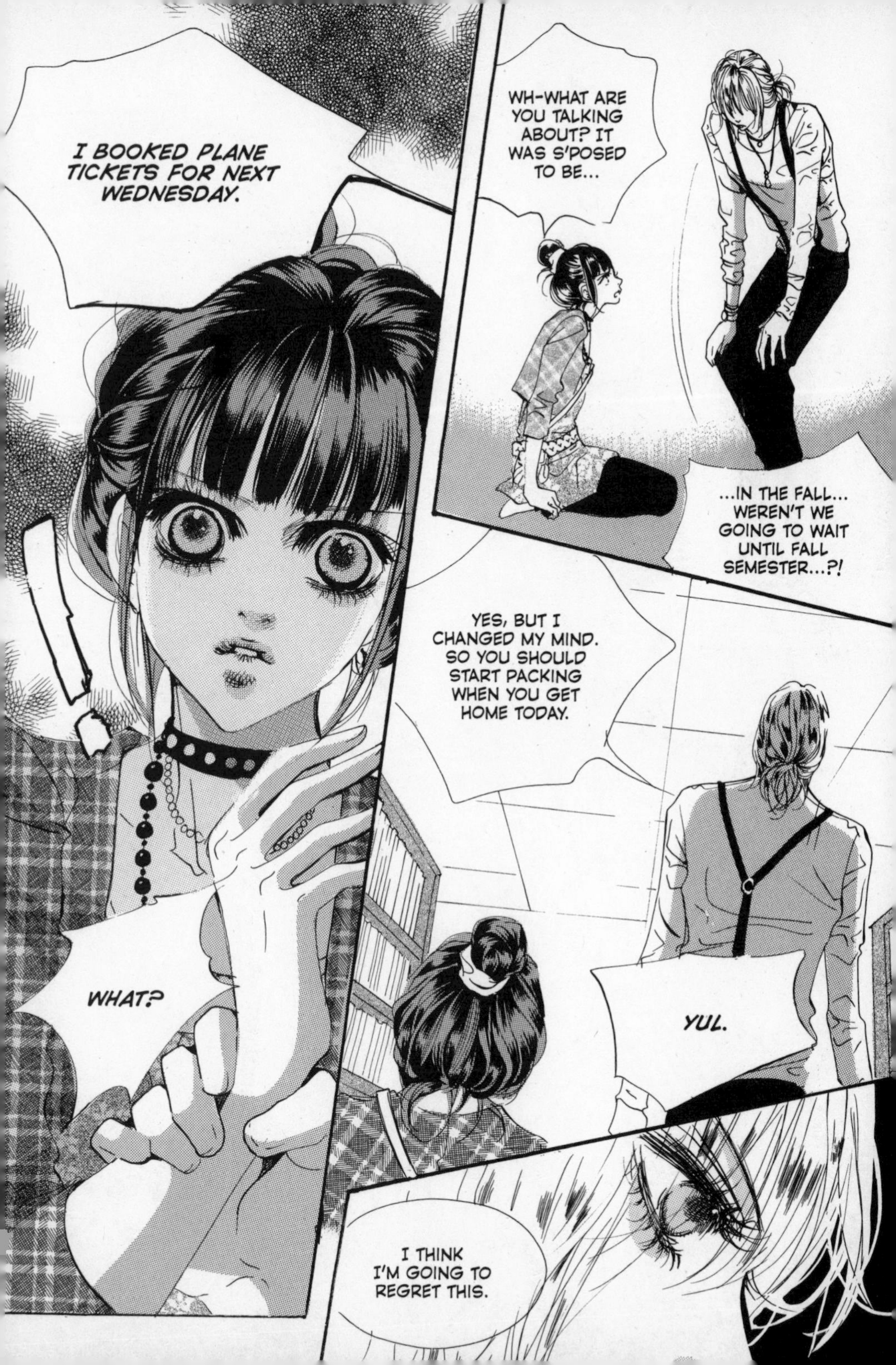
I BOOKED PLANE TICKETS FOR NEXT WEDNESDAY.
WHAT?
WH-WHAT ARE YOU TALKING ABOUT? IT WAS S'POSED TO BE...
...IN THE FALL... WEREN'T WE GOING TO WAIT UNTIL FALL SEMESTER...?!
YES, BUT I CHANGED MY MIND. SO YOU SHOULD START PACKING WHEN YOU GET HOME TODAY.
YUL.
I THINK I'M GOING TO REGRET THIS.

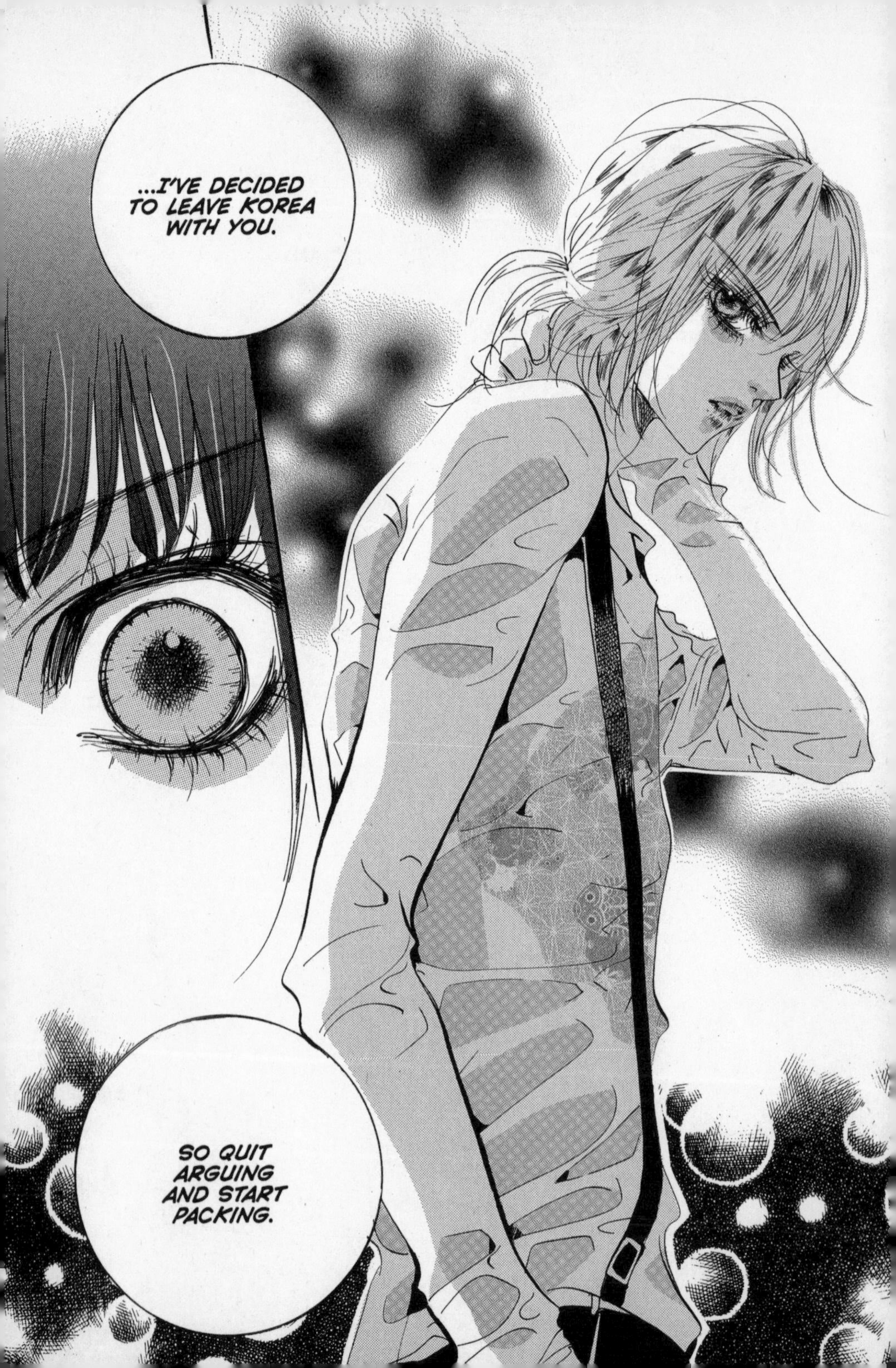
...I'VE DECIDED TO LEAVE KOREA WITH YOU.
SO QUIT ARGUING AND START PACKING.

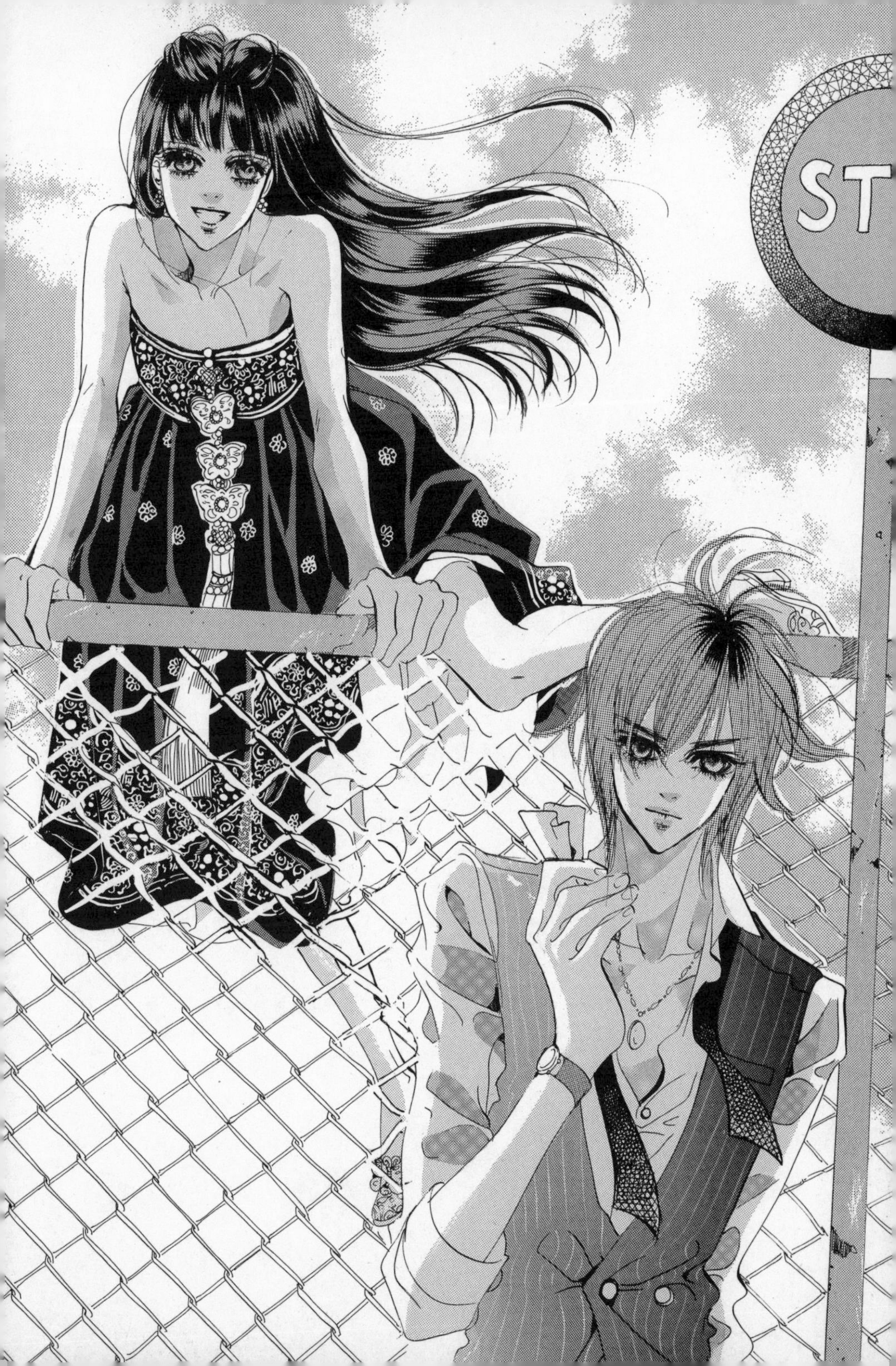
ST

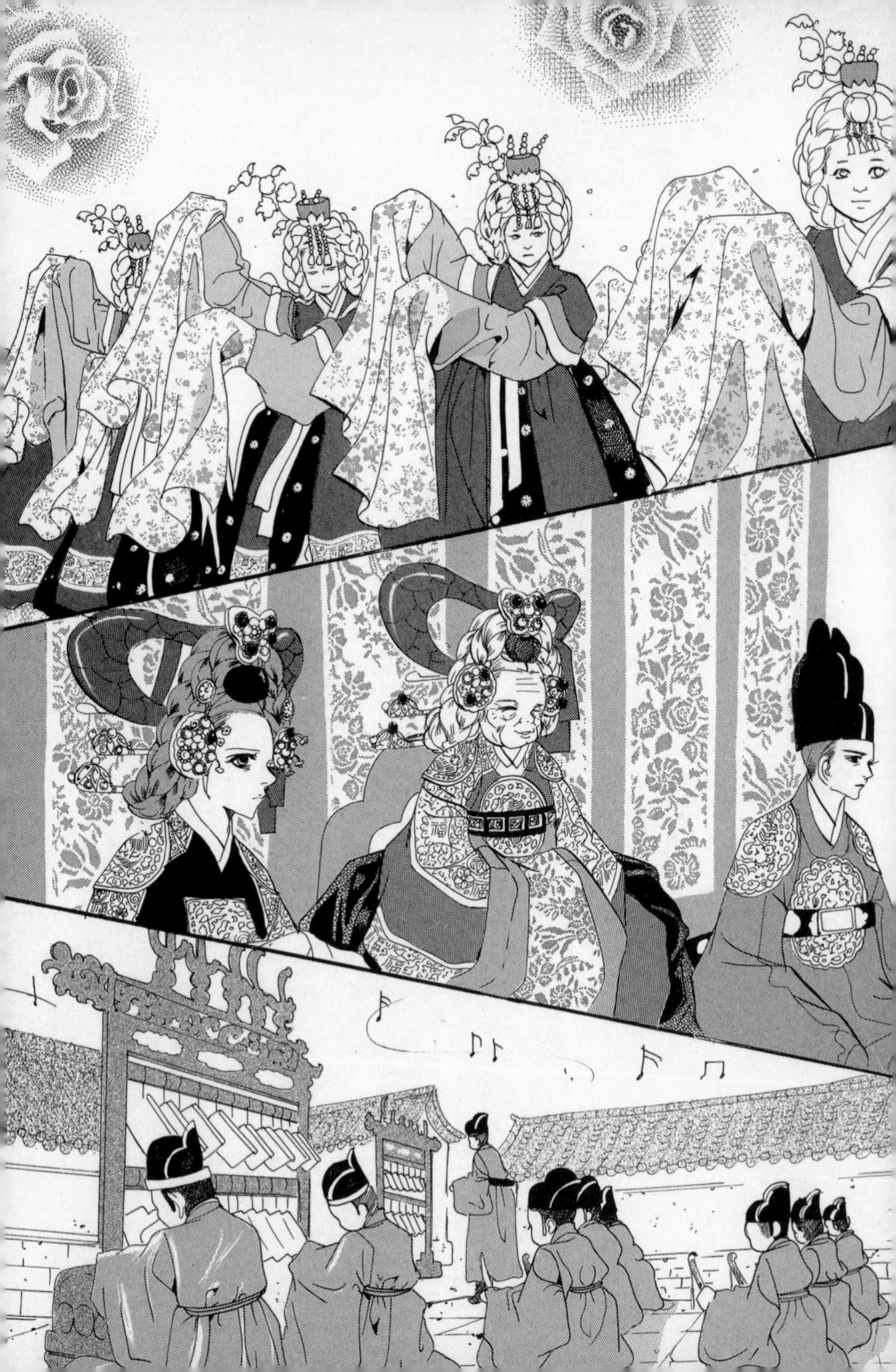

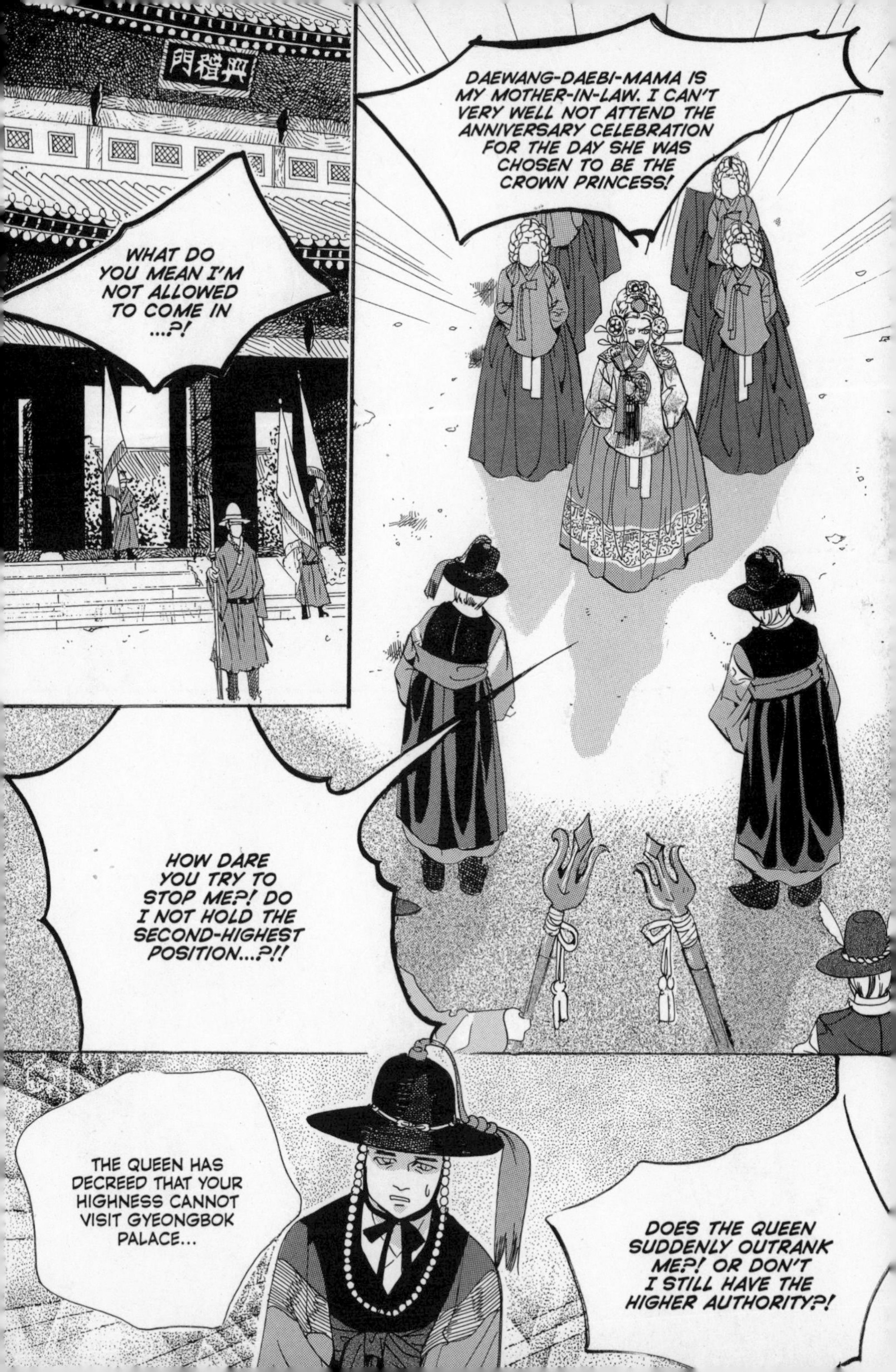
興禮門
WHAT DO YOU MEAN I'M NOT ALLOWED TO COME IN ...?!
DAEWANG-DAEBI-MAMA IS MY MOTHER-IN-LAW. I CAN'T VERY WELL NOT ATTEND THE ANNIVERSARY CELEBRATION FOR THE DAY SHE WAS CHOSEN TO BE THE CROWN PRINCESS!
HOW DARE YOU TRY TO STOP ME?! DO I NOT HOLD THE SECOND-HIGHEST POSITION...?!!
THE QUEEN HAS DECREED THAT YOUR HIGHNESS CANNOT VISIT GYEONGBOK PALACE...
DOES THE QUEEN SUDDENLY OUTRANK ME?! OR DON'T I STILL HAVE THE HIGHER AUTHORITY?!

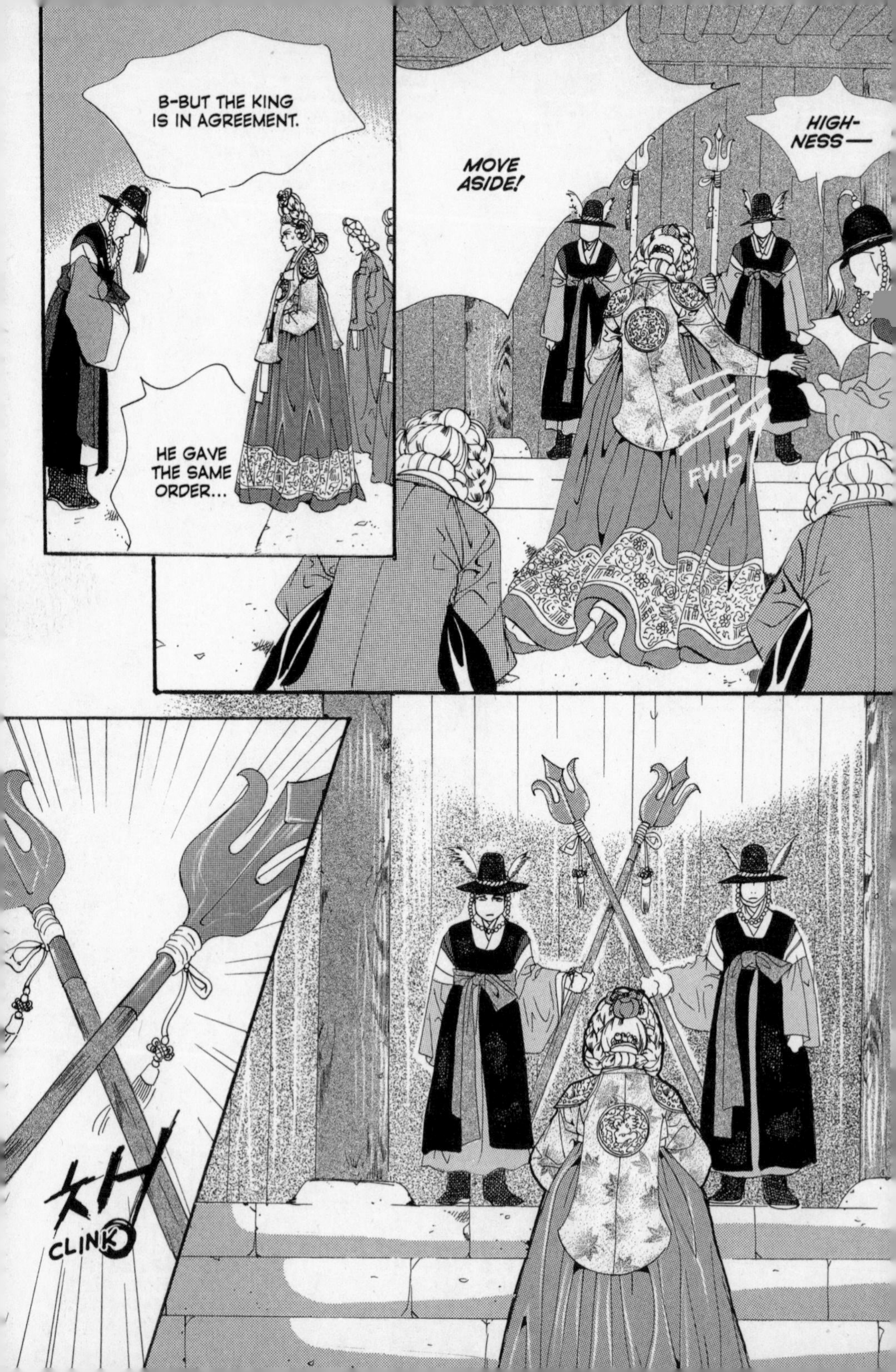
B-BUT THE KING IS IN AGREEMENT.
HE GAVE THE SAME ORDER...
MOVE ASIDE!
HIGH-NESS—
FWIP
CLINK

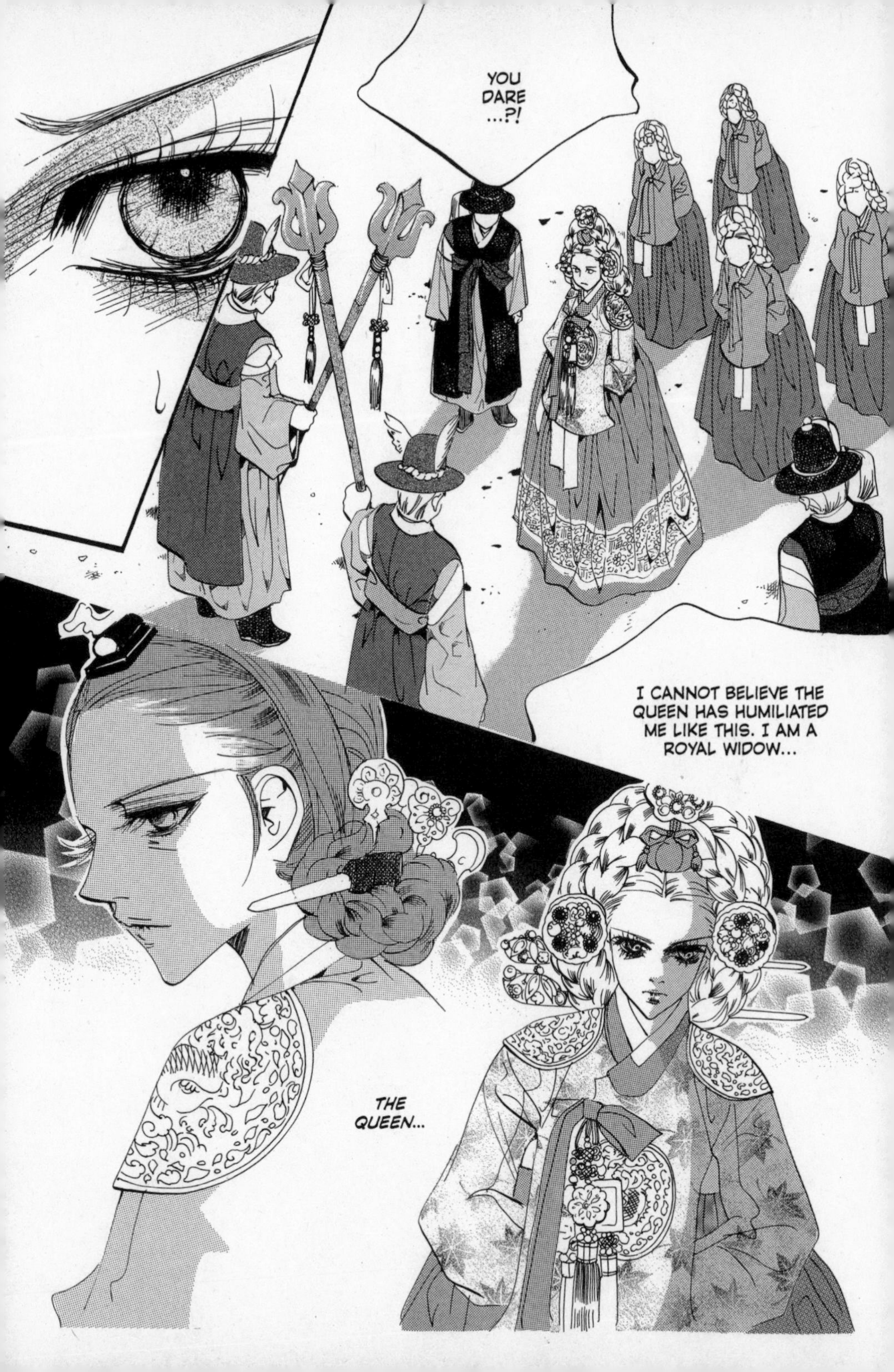
YOU DARE ...?!
I CANNOT BELIEVE THE QUEEN HAS HUMILIATED ME LIKE THIS. I AM A ROYAL WIDOW...
THE QUEEN...

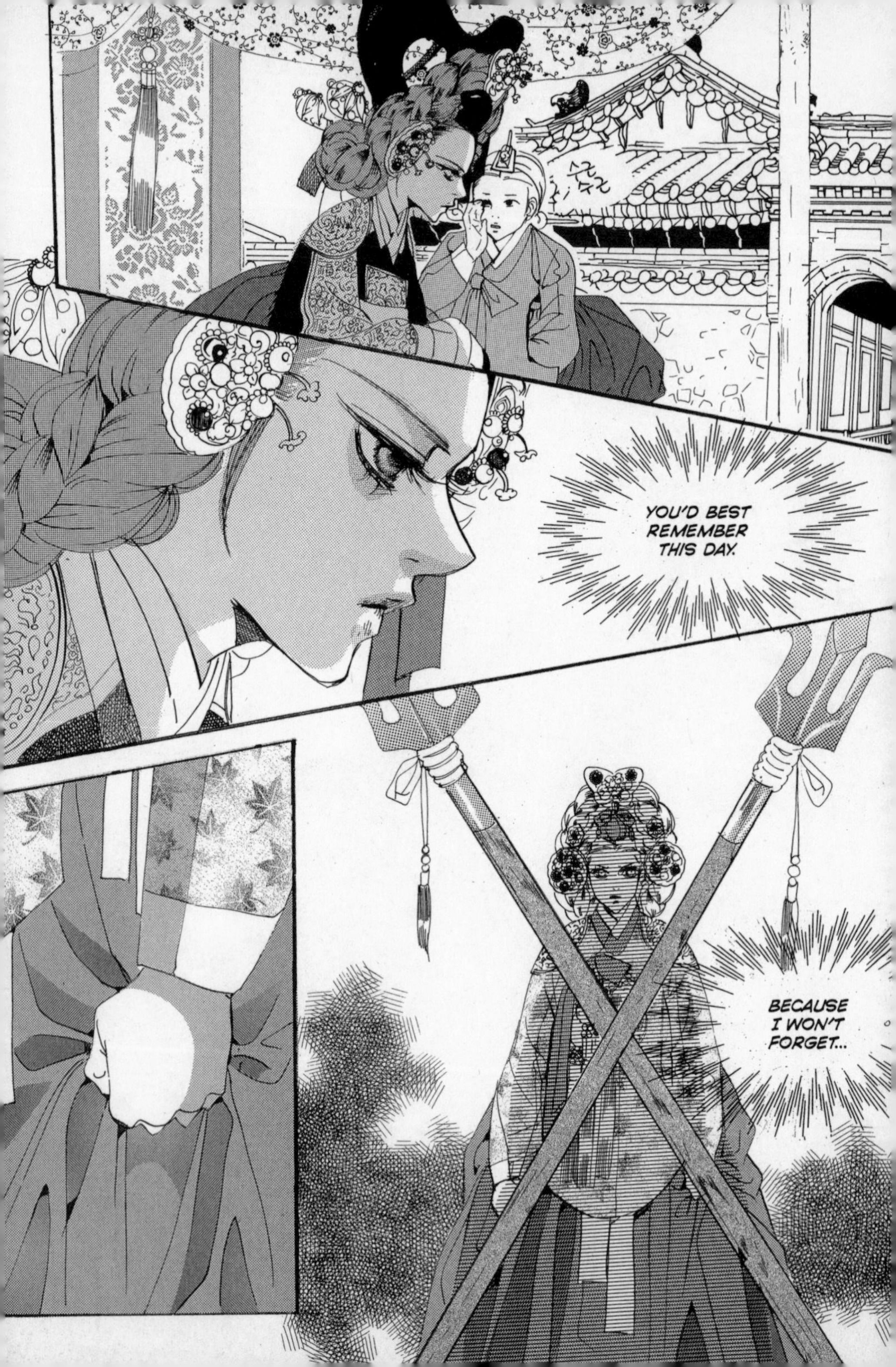
YOU'D BEST REMEMBER THIS DAY.
BECAUSE I WON'T FORGET...

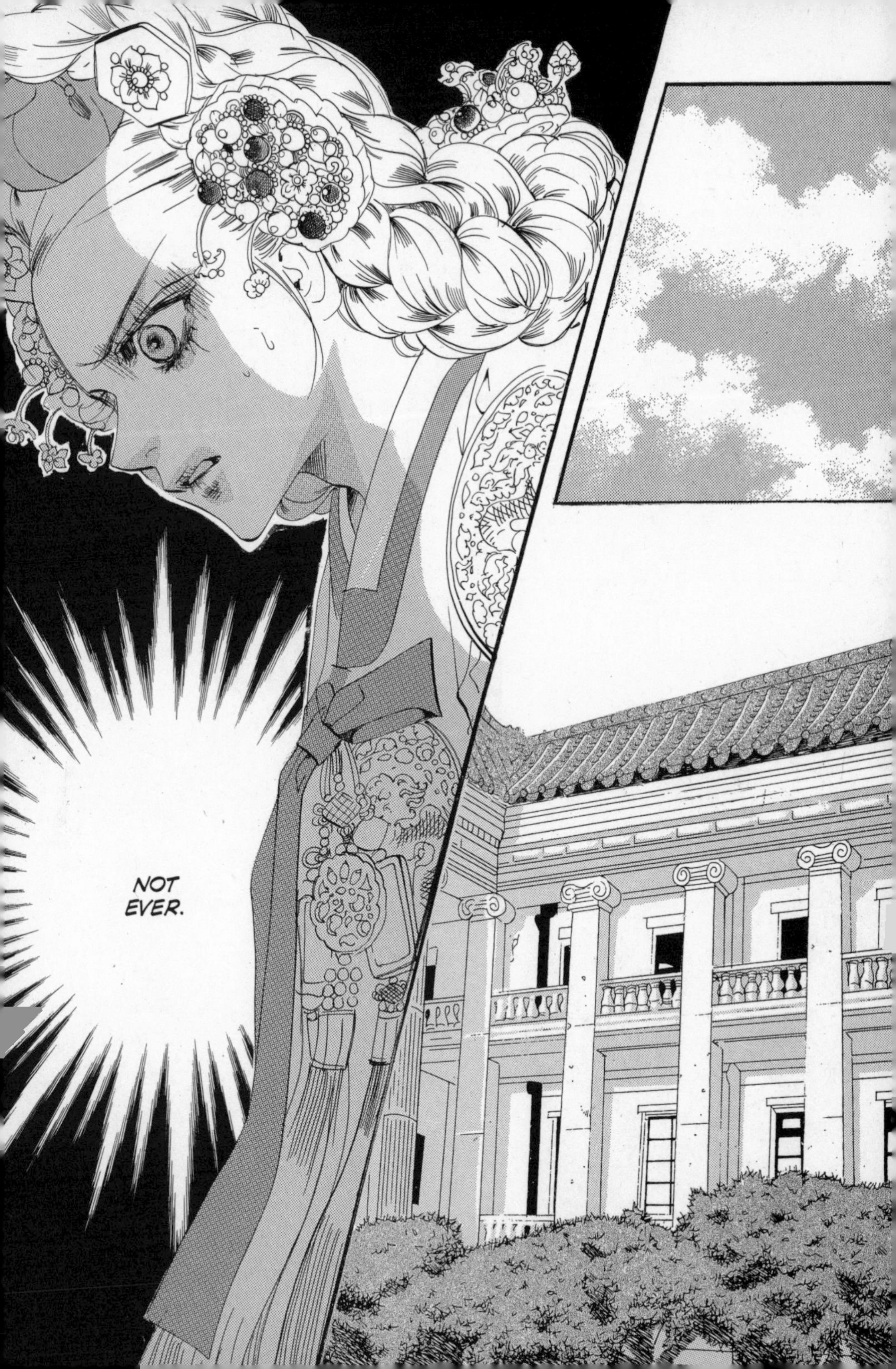
NOT
EVER.

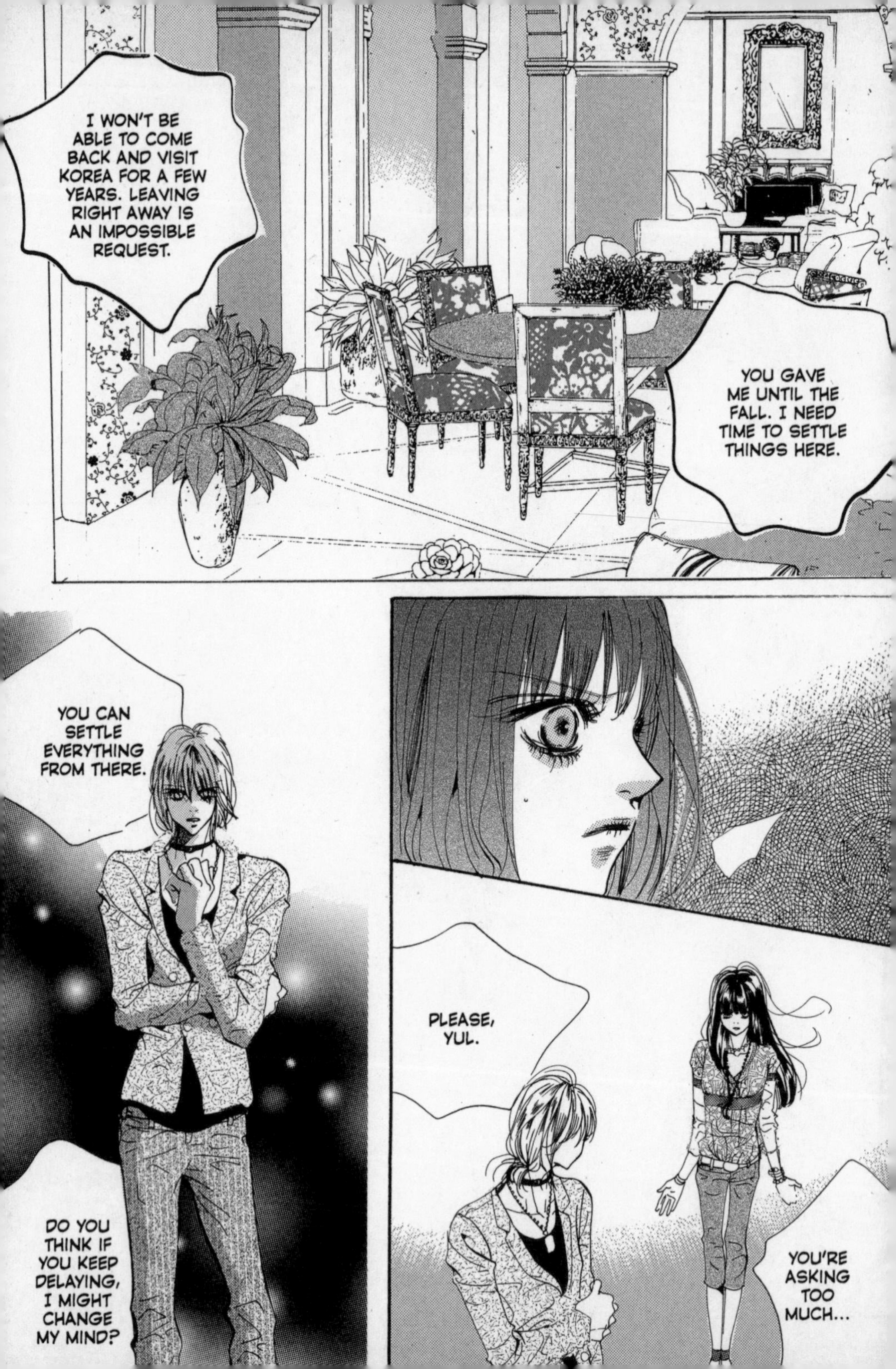
I WON'T BE ABLE TO COME BACK AND VISIT KOREA FOR A FEW YEARS. LEAVING RIGHT AWAY IS AN IMPOSSIBLE REQUEST.
YOU GAVE ME UNTIL THE FALL. I NEED TIME TO SETTLE THINGS HERE.
YOU CAN SETTLE EVERYTHING FROM THERE.
DO YOU THINK IF YOU KEEP DELAYING, I MIGHT CHANGE MY MIND?
PLEASE, YUL.
YOU'RE ASKING TOO MUCH...

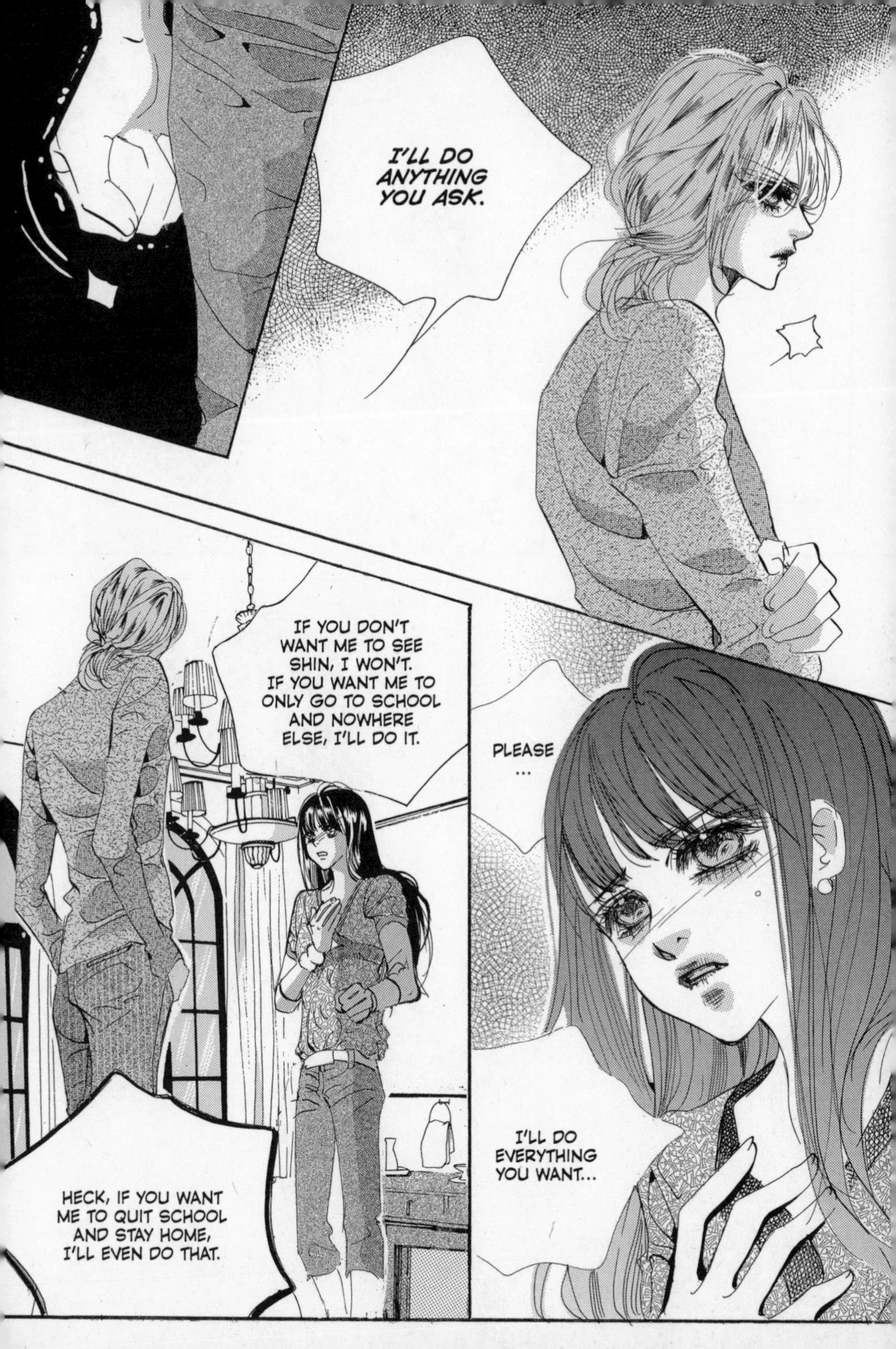
I'LL DO ANYTHING YOU ASK.
IF YOU DON'T WANT ME TO SEE SHIN, I WON'T. IF YOU WANT ME TO ONLY GO TO SCHOOL AND NOWHERE ELSE, I'LL DO IT.
HECK, IF YOU WANT ME TO QUIT SCHOOL AND STAY HOME, I'LL EVEN DO THAT.
PLEASE ...
I'LL DO EVERYTHING YOU WANT...

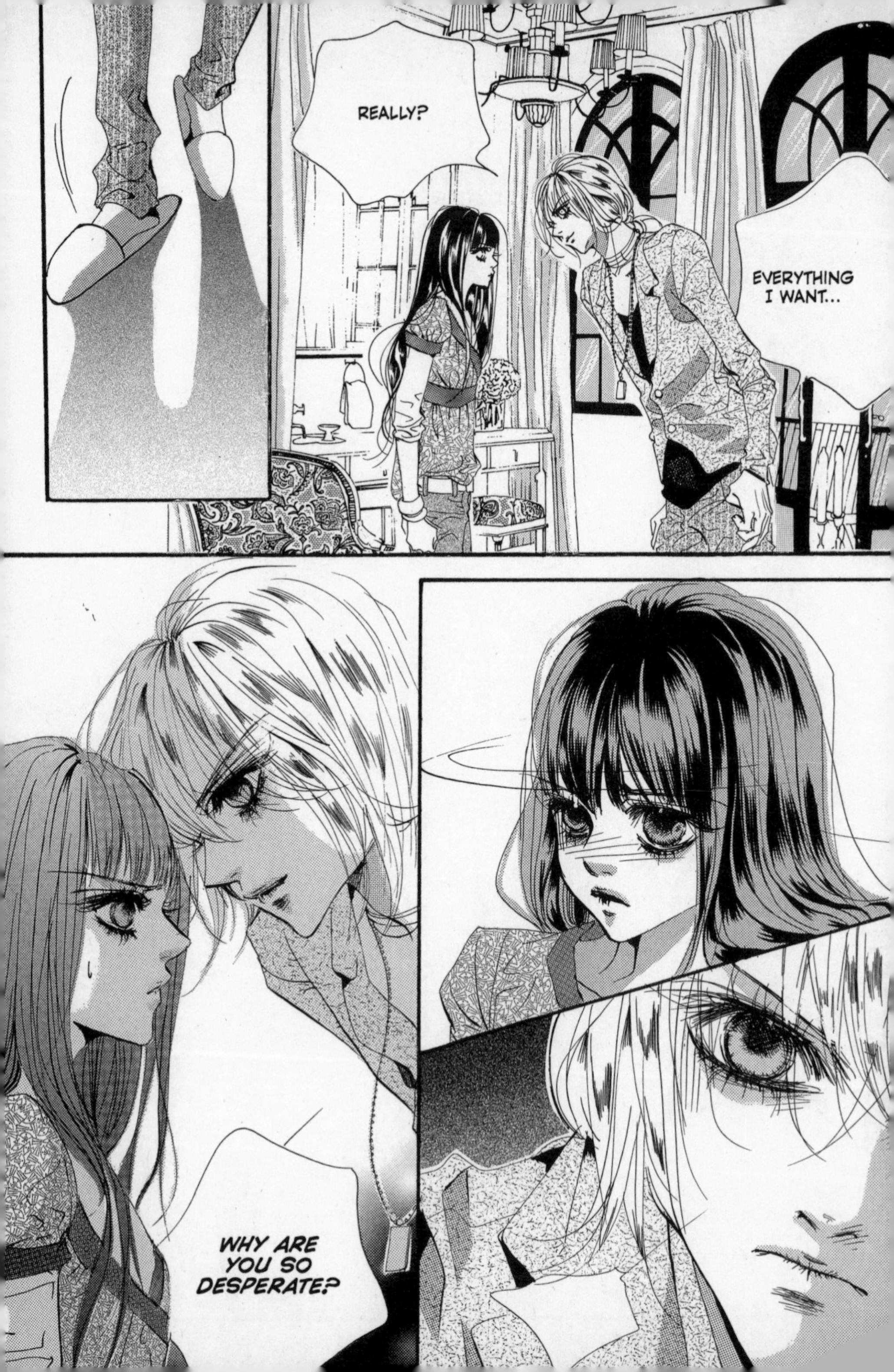
REALLY?
EVERYTHING I WANT...
WHY ARE YOU SO DESPERATE?

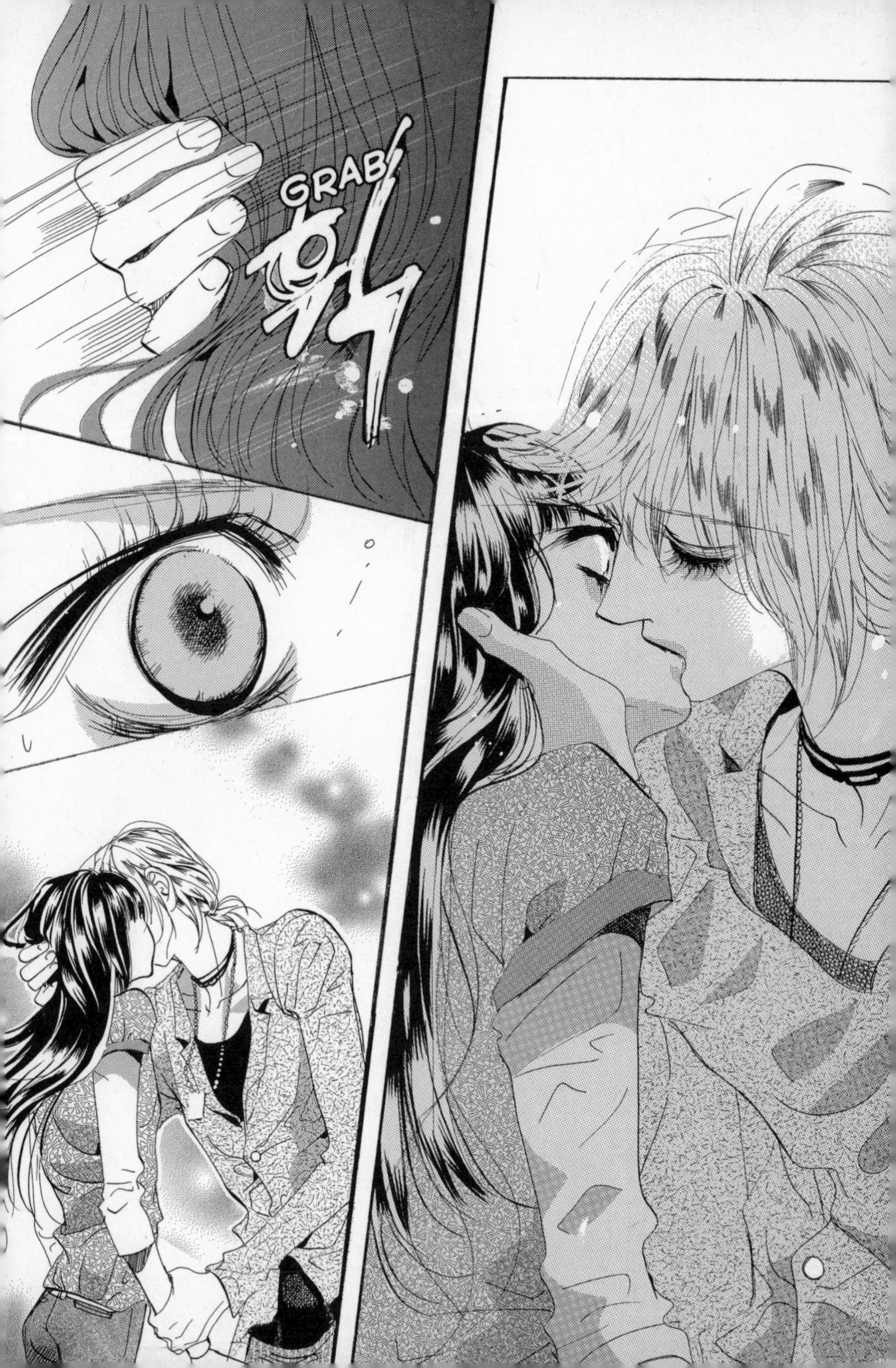
GRAB
휙

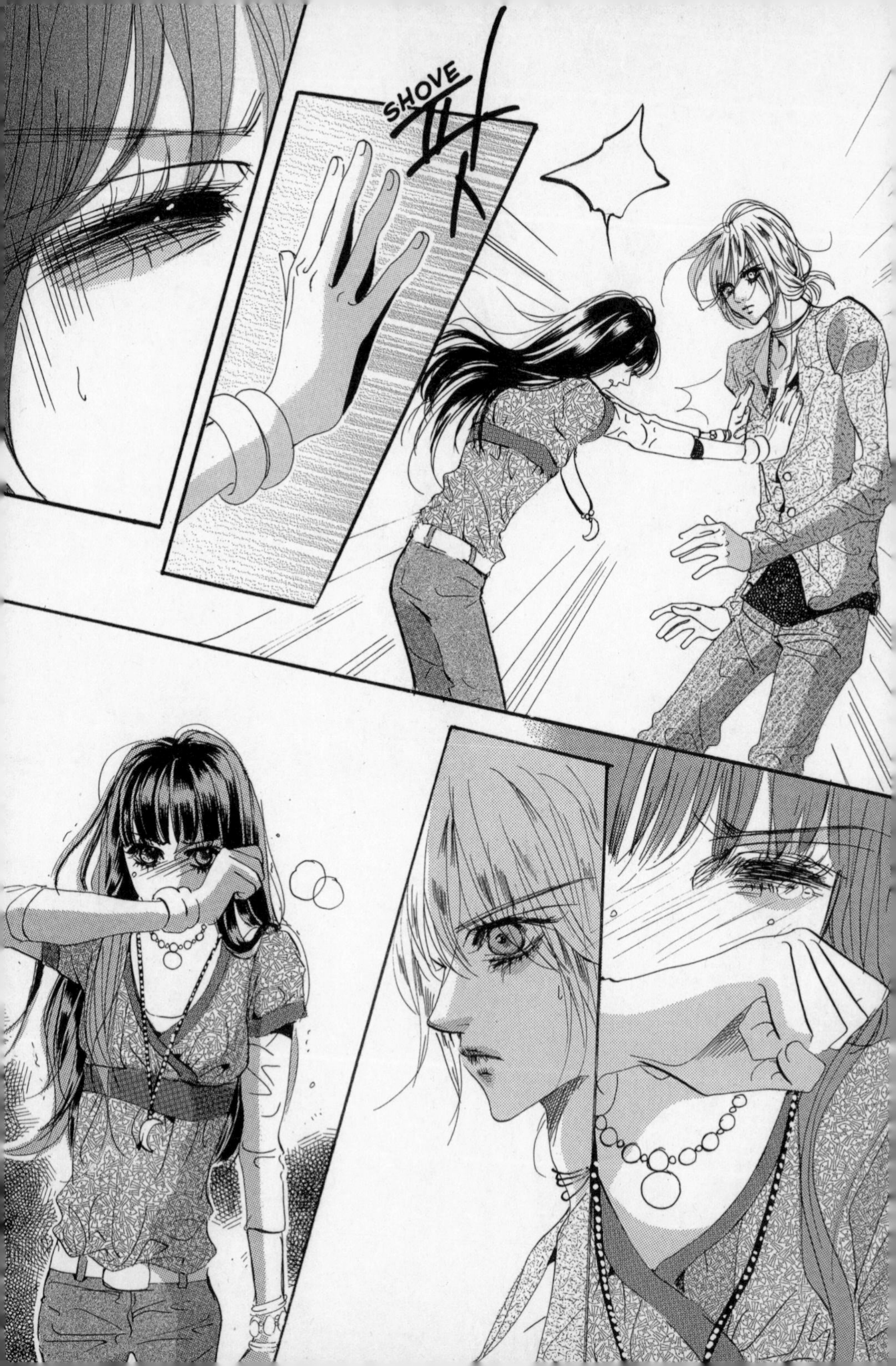
SHOVE

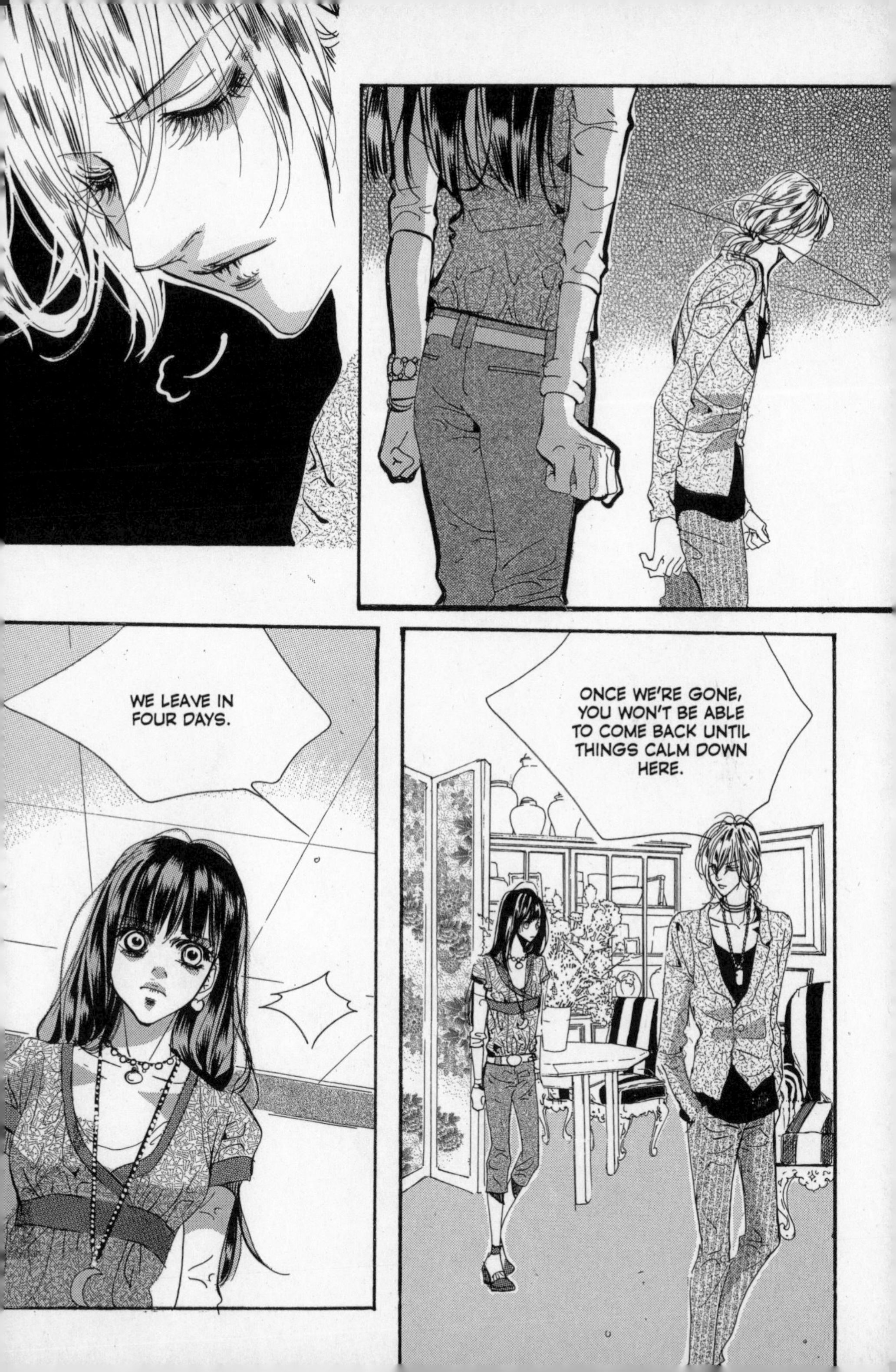
WE LEAVE IN FOUR DAYS.
ONCE WE'RE GONE, YOU WON'T BE ABLE TO COME BACK UNTIL THINGS CALM DOWN HERE.

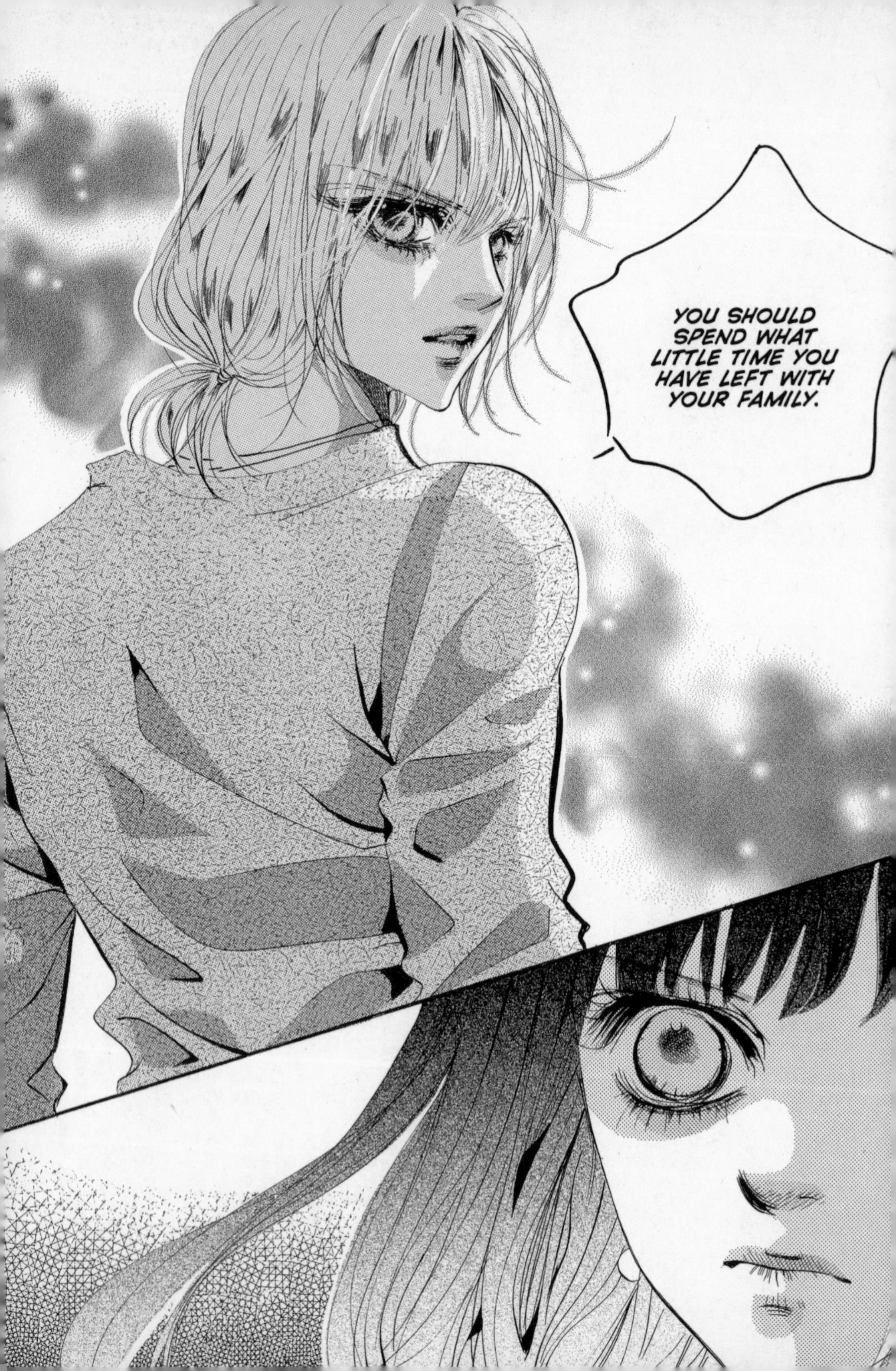
YOU SHOULD SPEND WHAT LITTLE TIME YOU HAVE LEFT WITH YOUR FAMILY.

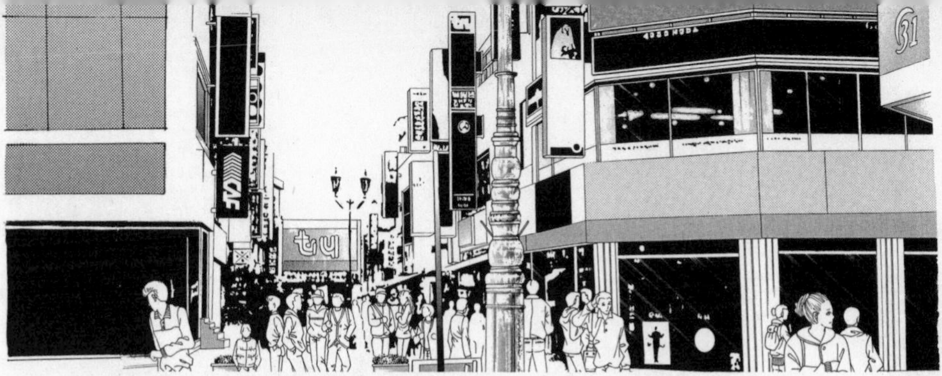
tu
31

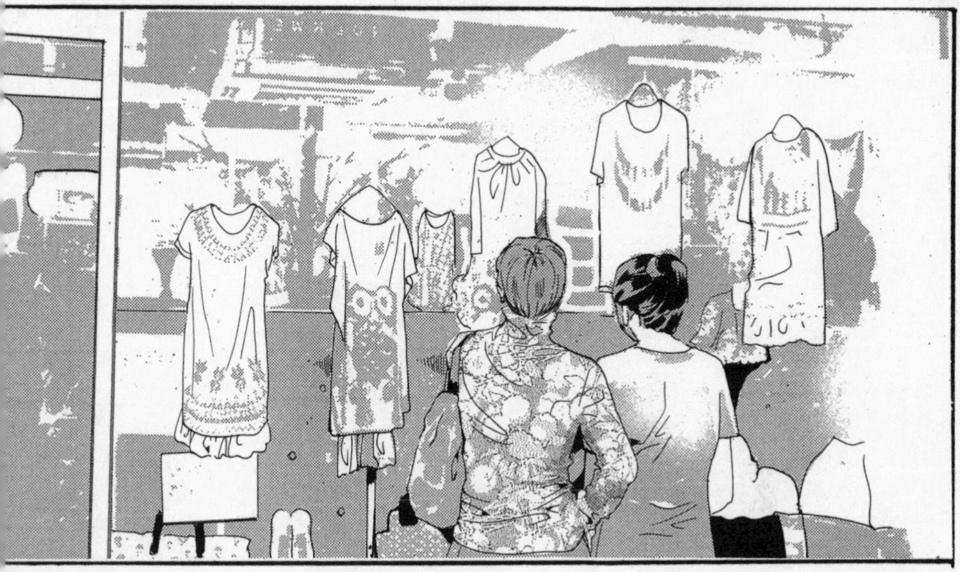

SIGN: SHINPO MANDOO PLACE

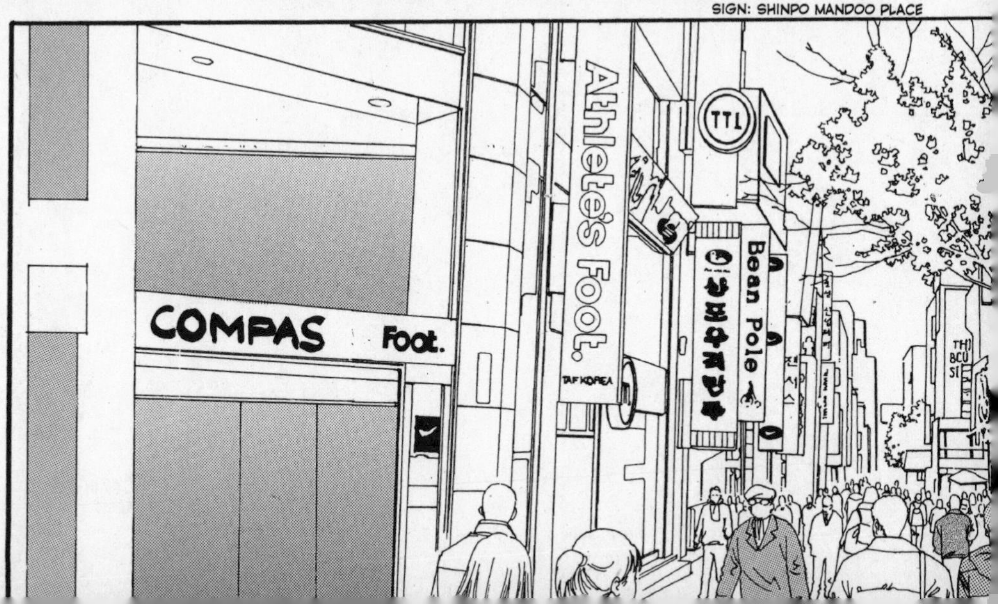
COMPAS
Foot.
Athlete's Foot.
TAF KOREA
TTL
Bean Pole

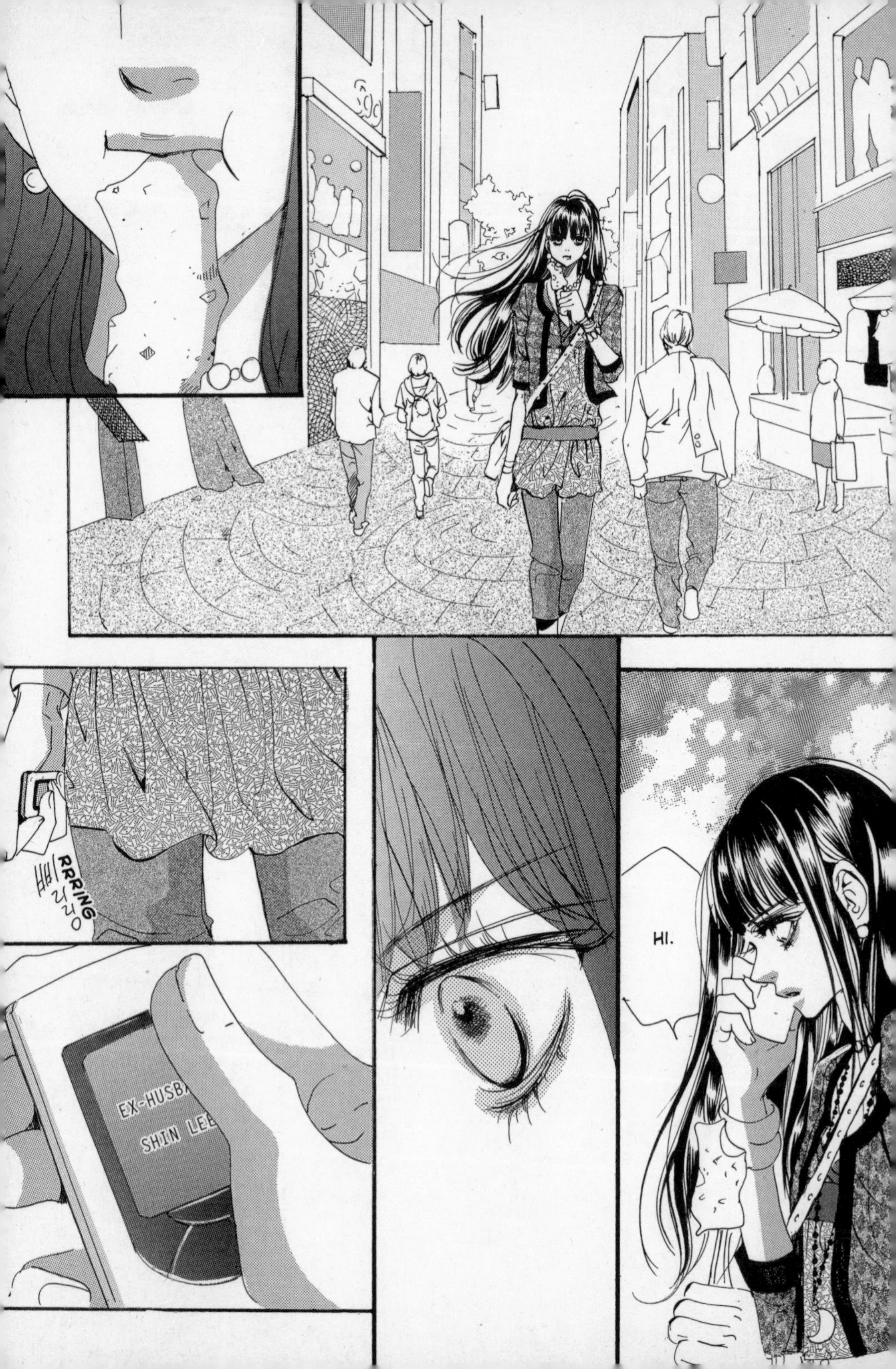
RRRING
띠리링
EX-HUSBA
SHIN LEE
HI.

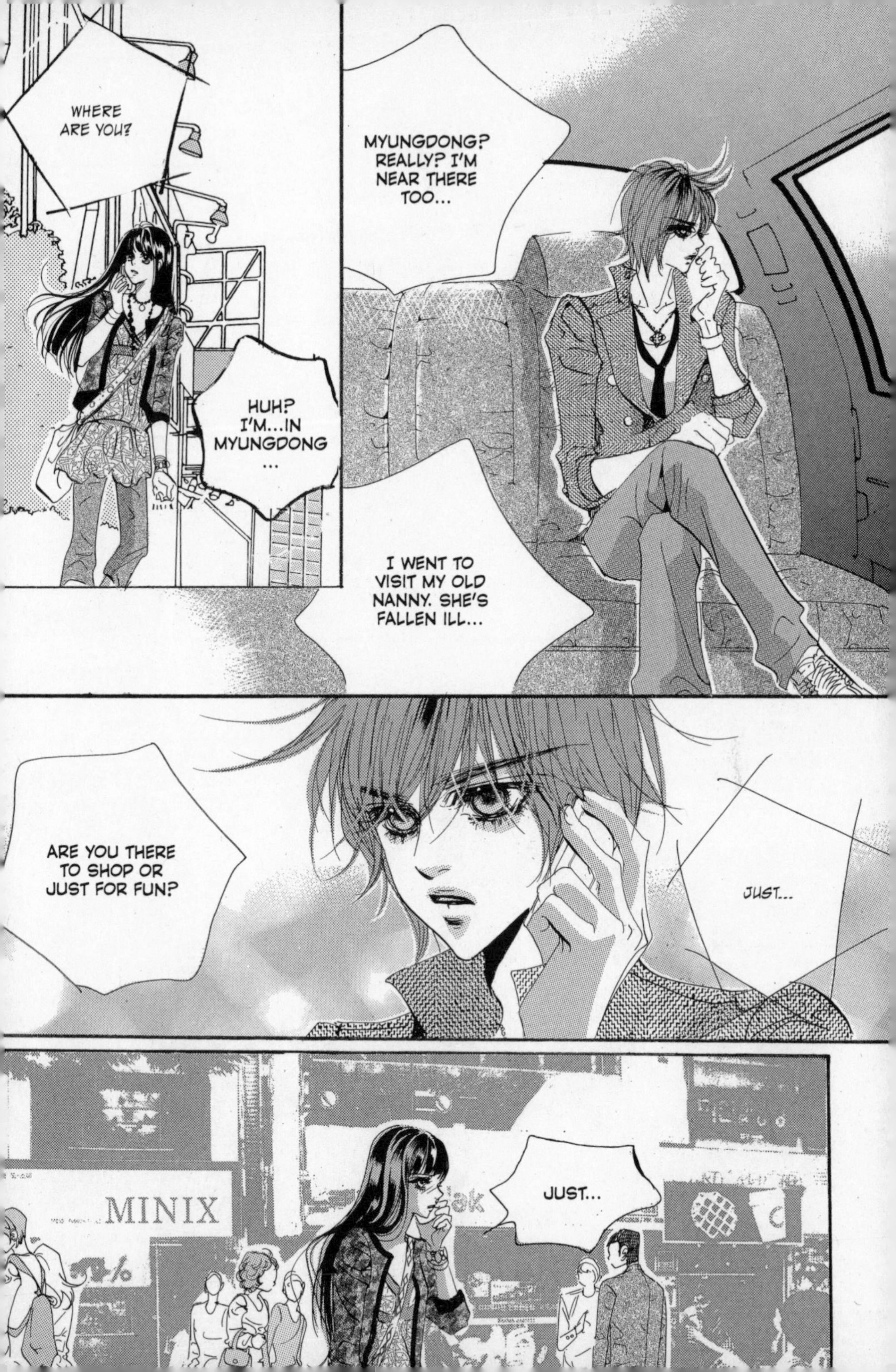
WHERE ARE YOU?
HUH? I'M...IN MYUNGDONG ...
MYUNGDONG? REALLY? I'M NEAR THERE TOO...
I WENT TO VISIT MY OLD NANNY. SHE'S FALLEN ILL...
ARE YOU THERE TO SHOP OR JUST FOR FUN?
JUST...
JUST...
MINIX

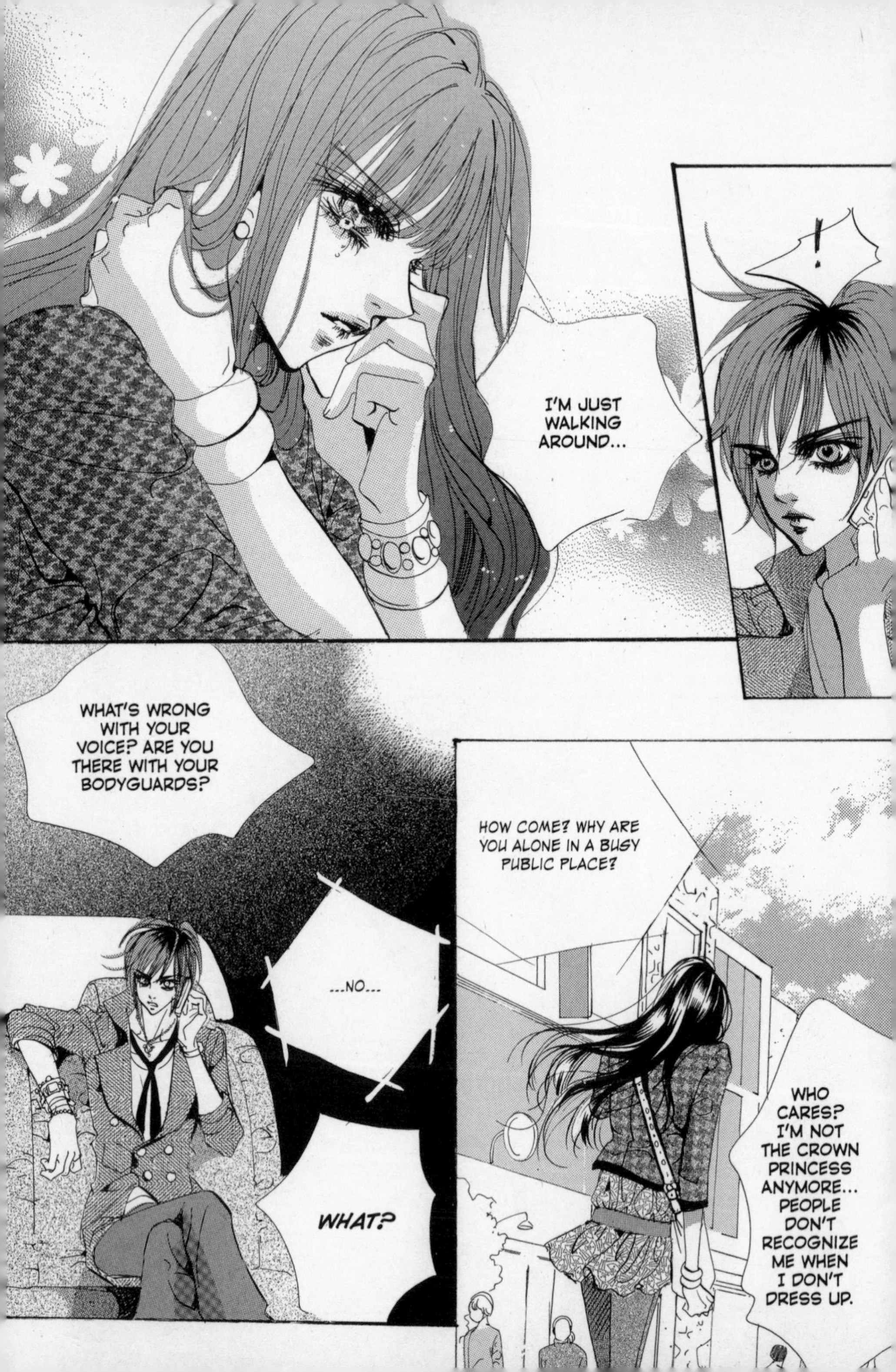
I'M JUST WALKING AROUND...
!
WHAT'S WRONG WITH YOUR VOICE? ARE YOU THERE WITH YOUR BODYGUARDS?
...NO...
WHAT?
HOW COME? WHY ARE YOU ALONE IN A BUSY PUBLIC PLACE?
WHO CARES? I'M NOT THE CROWN PRINCESS ANYMORE... PEOPLE DON'T RECOGNIZE ME WHEN I DON'T DRESS UP.

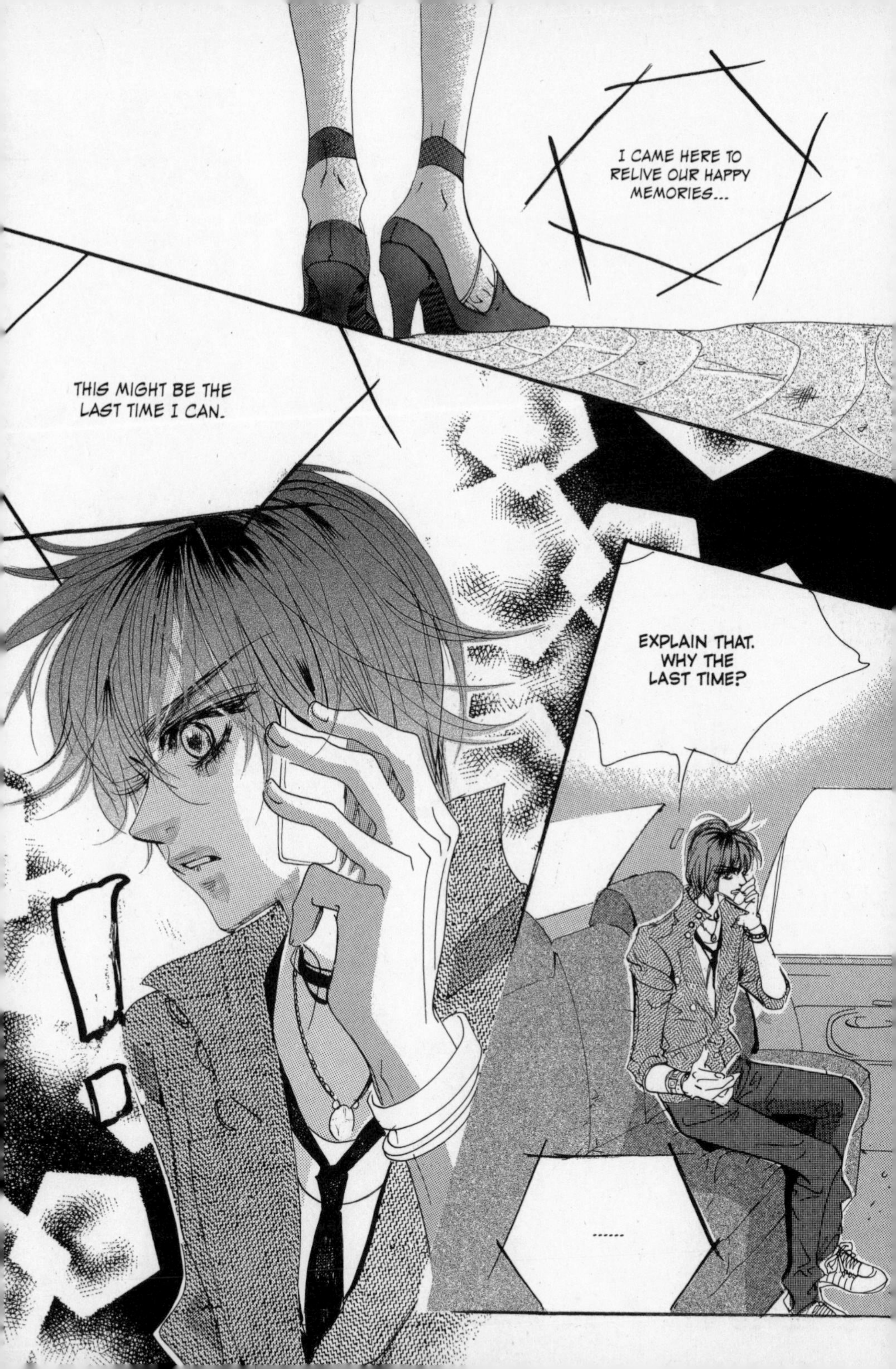

I CAME HERE TO RELIVE OUR HAPPY MEMORIES...
THIS MIGHT BE THE LAST TIME I CAN.
!
EXPLAIN THAT. WHY THE LAST TIME?
......

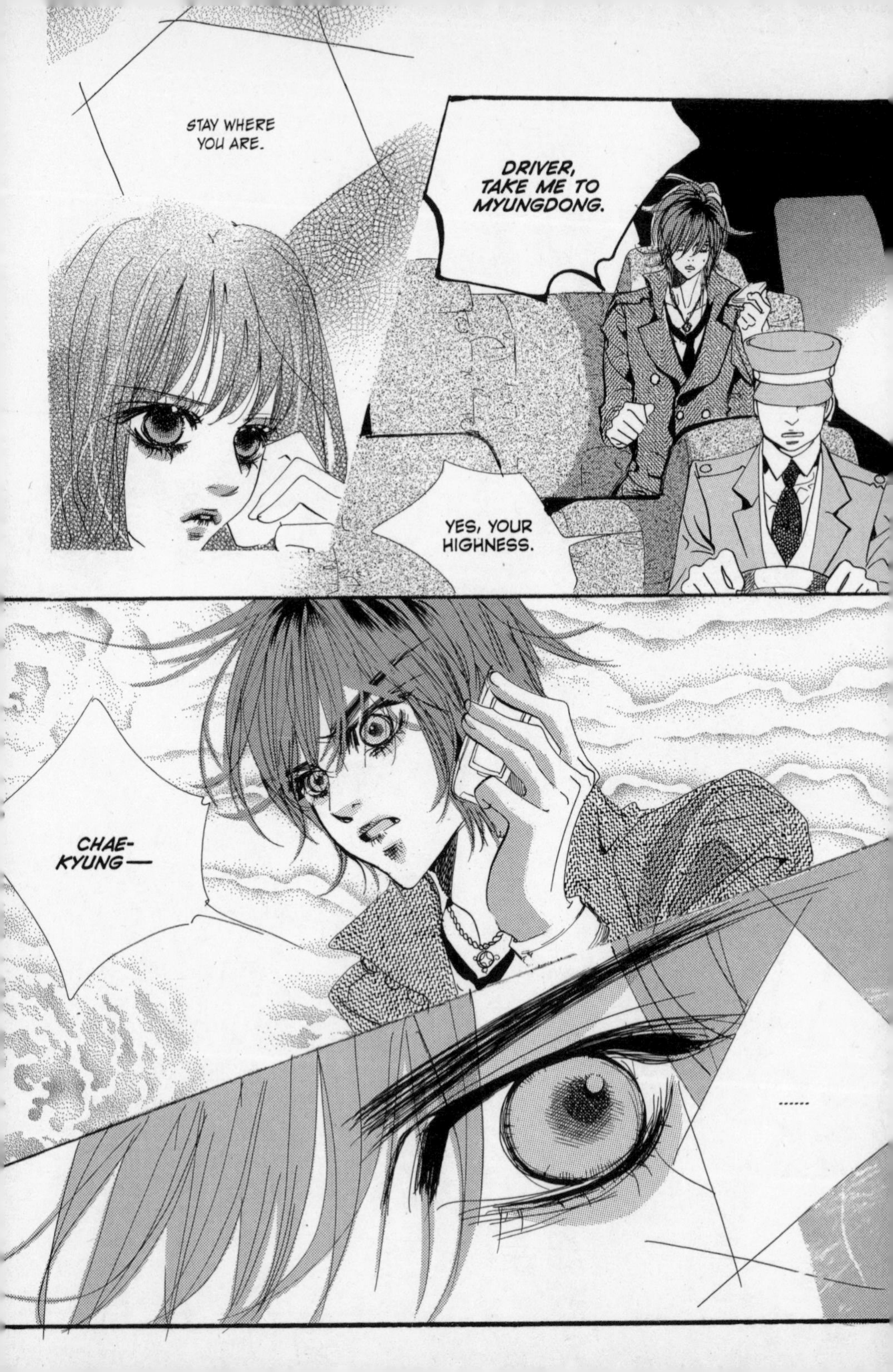
STAY WHERE YOU ARE.
DRIVER, TAKE ME TO MYUNGDONG.
YES, YOUR HIGHNESS.
CHAE-KYUNG—
......

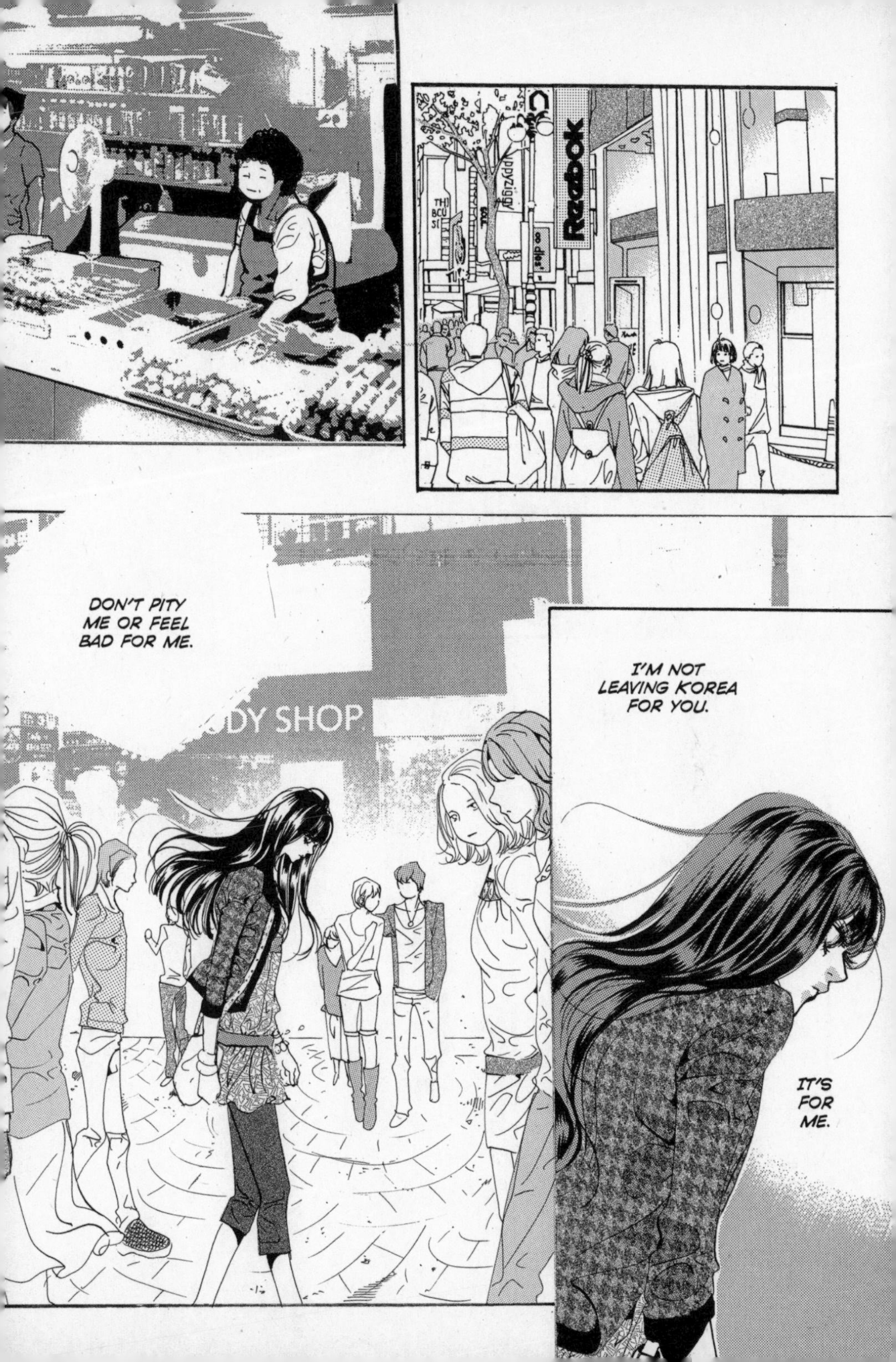
DON'T PITY ME OR FEEL BAD FOR ME.
I'M NOT LEAVING KOREA FOR YOU.
IT'S FOR ME.

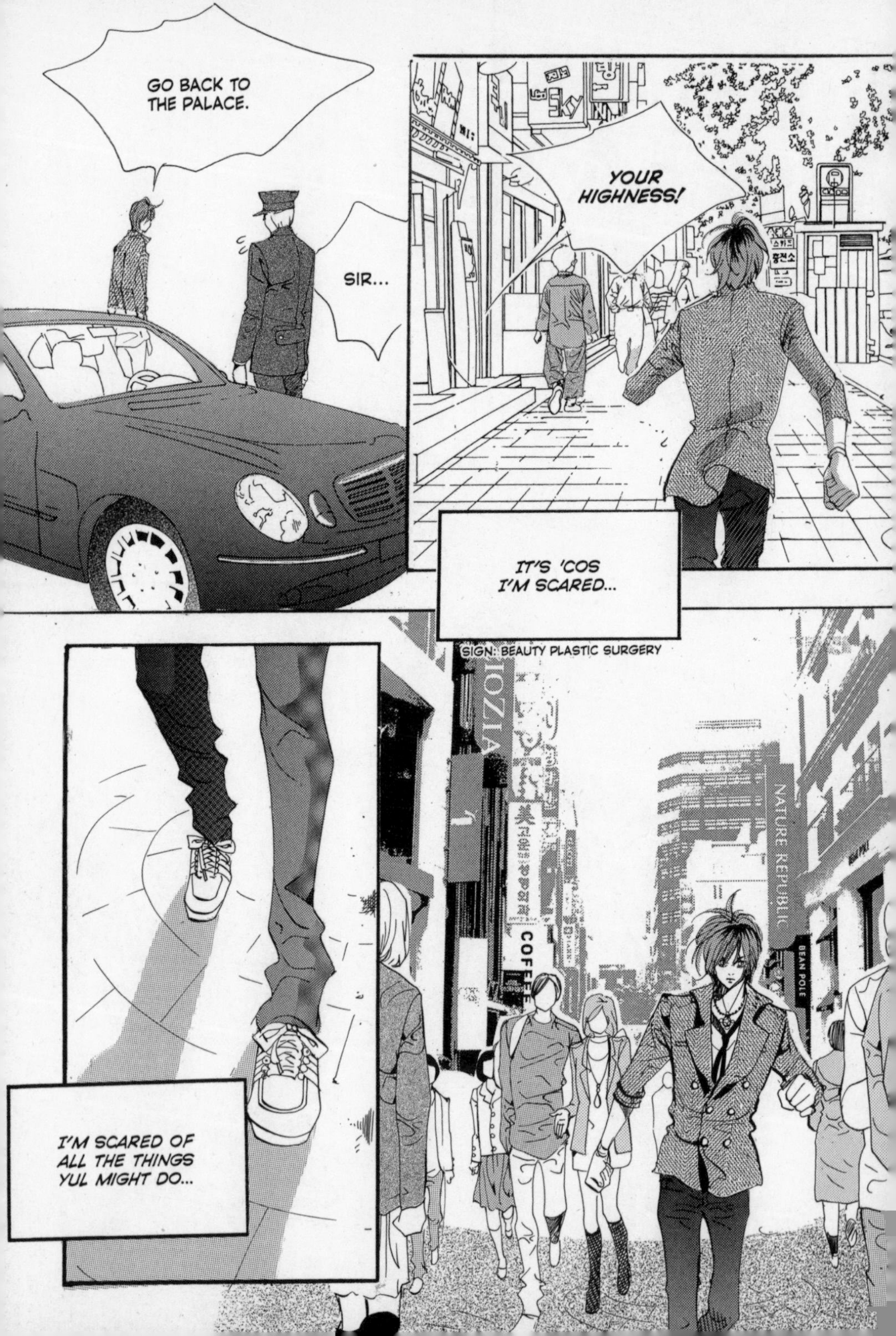
GO BACK TO THE PALACE.
SIR...
YOUR HIGHNESS!
IT'S 'COS I'M SCARED...
SIGN: BEAUTY PLASTIC SURGERY
I'M SCARED OF ALL THE THINGS YUL MIGHT DO...
COFFEE
NATURE REPUBLIC
BEAN POLE

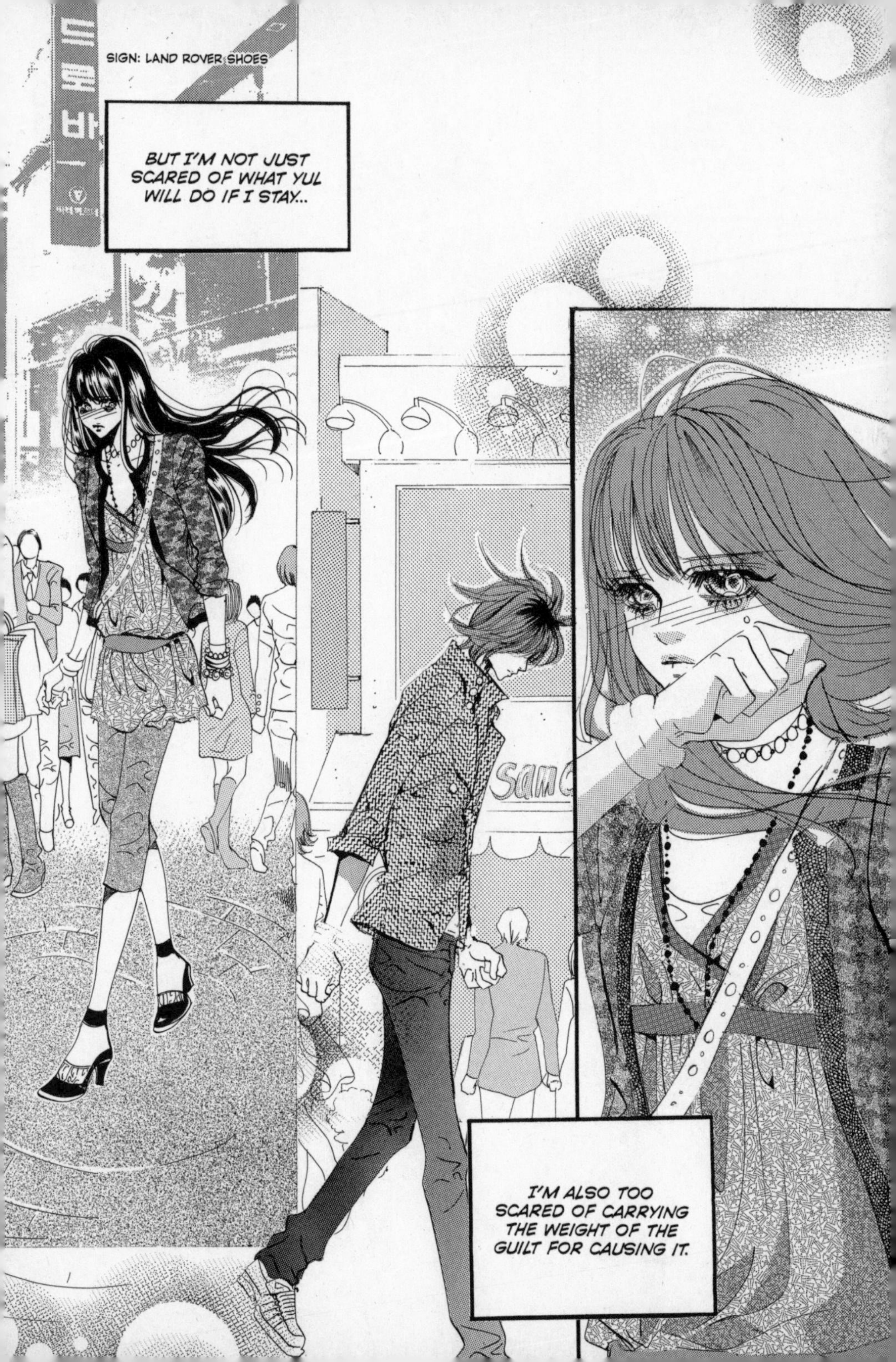
SIGN: LAND ROVER SHOES
BUT I'M NOT JUST SCARED OF WHAT YUL WILL DO IF I STAY...
I'M ALSO TOO SCARED OF CARRYING THE WEIGHT OF THE GUILT FOR CAUSING IT.

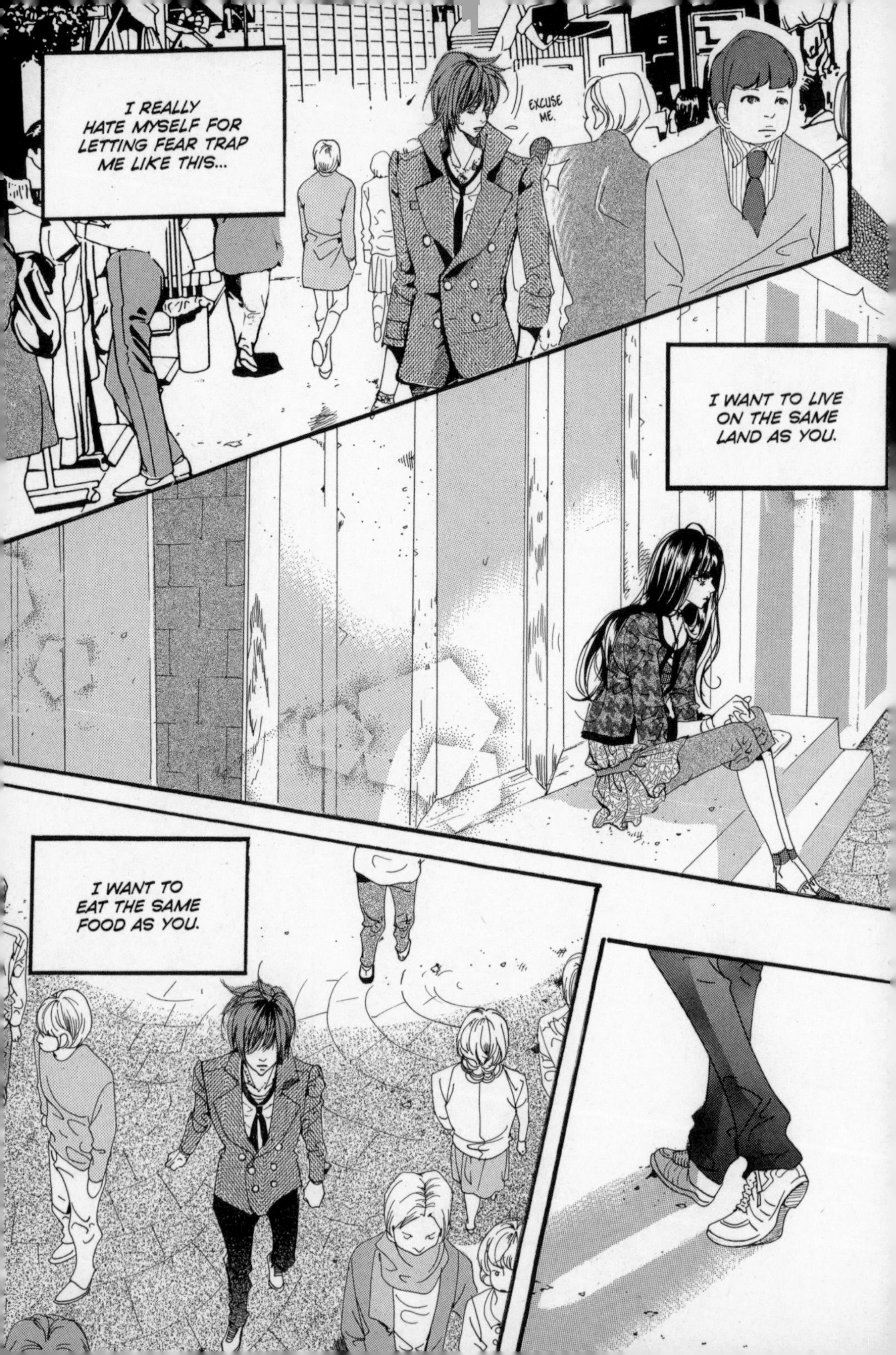
I REALLY HATE MYSELF FOR LETTING FEAR TRAP ME LIKE THIS...
EXCUSE ME.
I WANT TO LIVE ON THE SAME LAND AS YOU.
I WANT TO EAT THE SAME FOOD AS YOU.

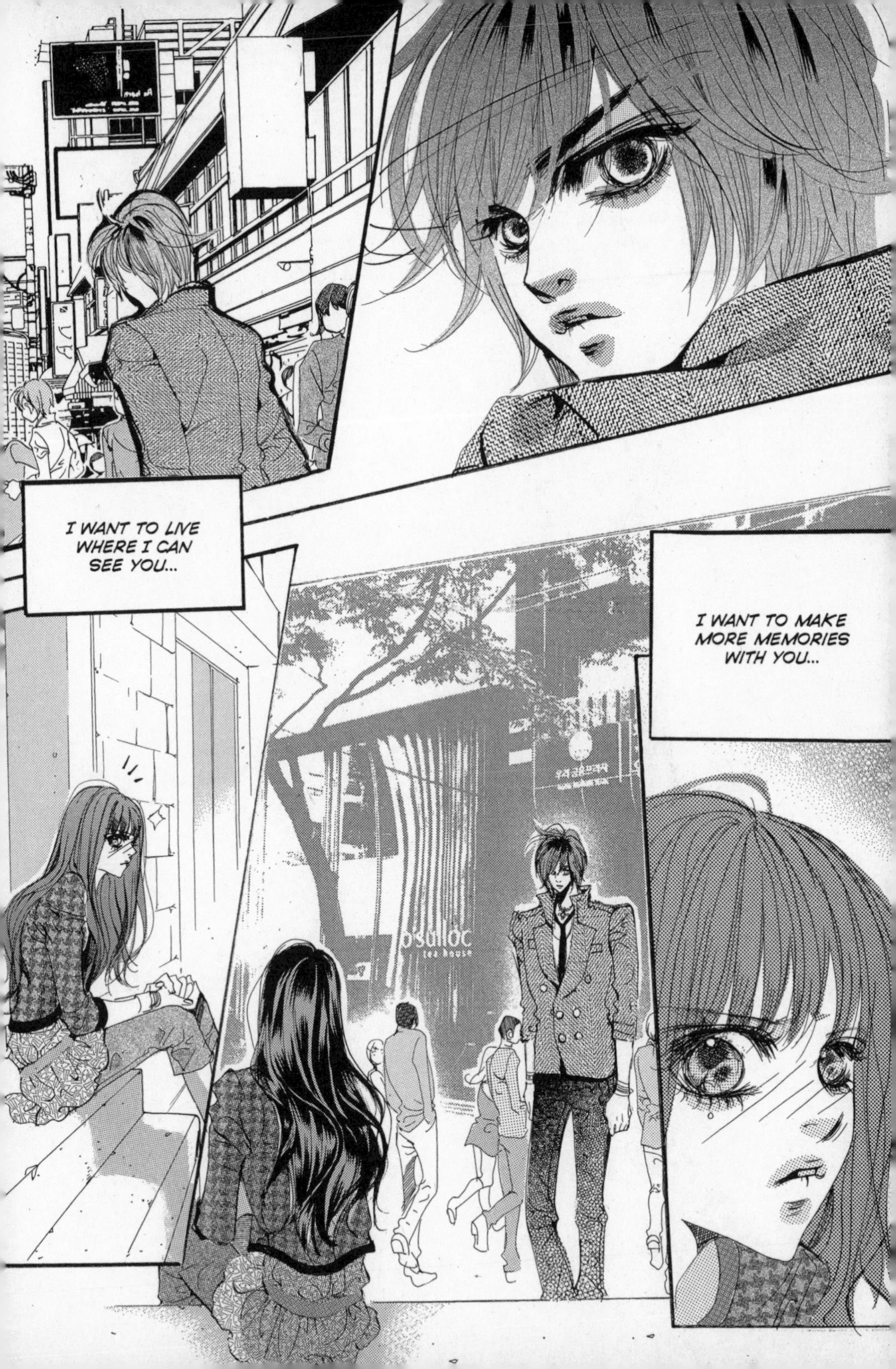
I WANT TO LIVE WHERE I CAN SEE YOU...
I WANT TO MAKE MORE MEMORIES WITH YOU...

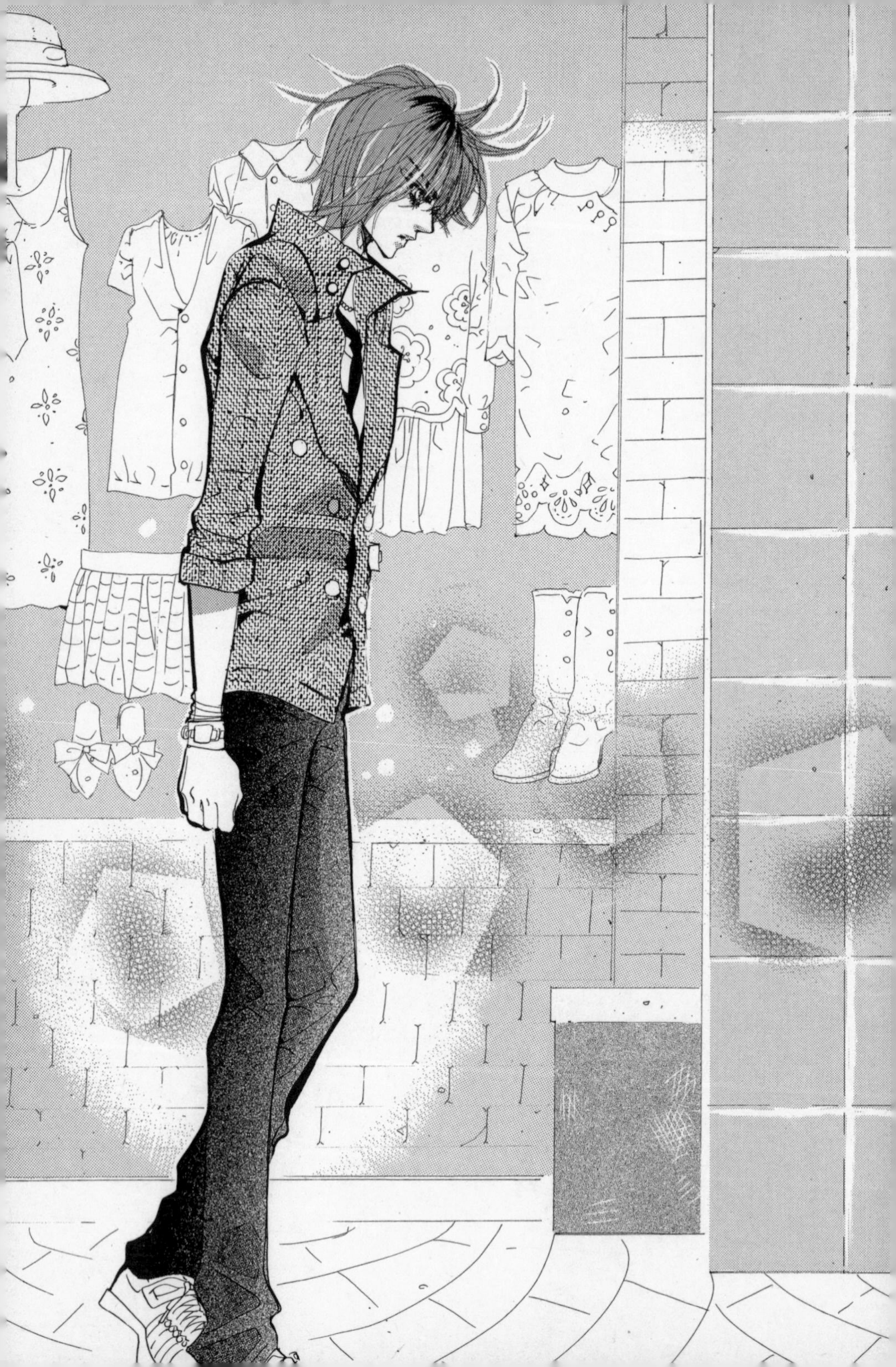

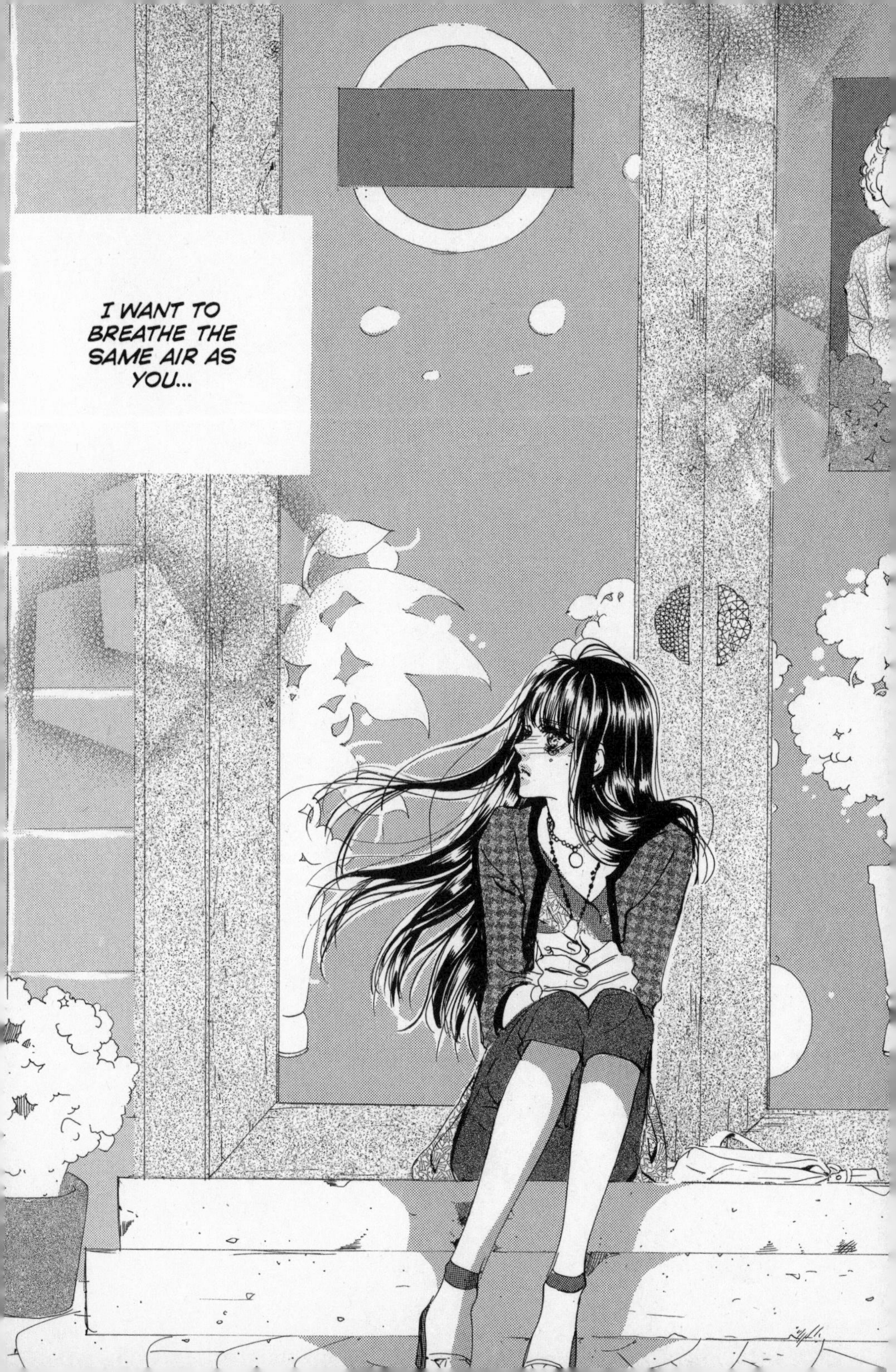
I WANT TO BREATHE THE SAME AIR AS YOU...

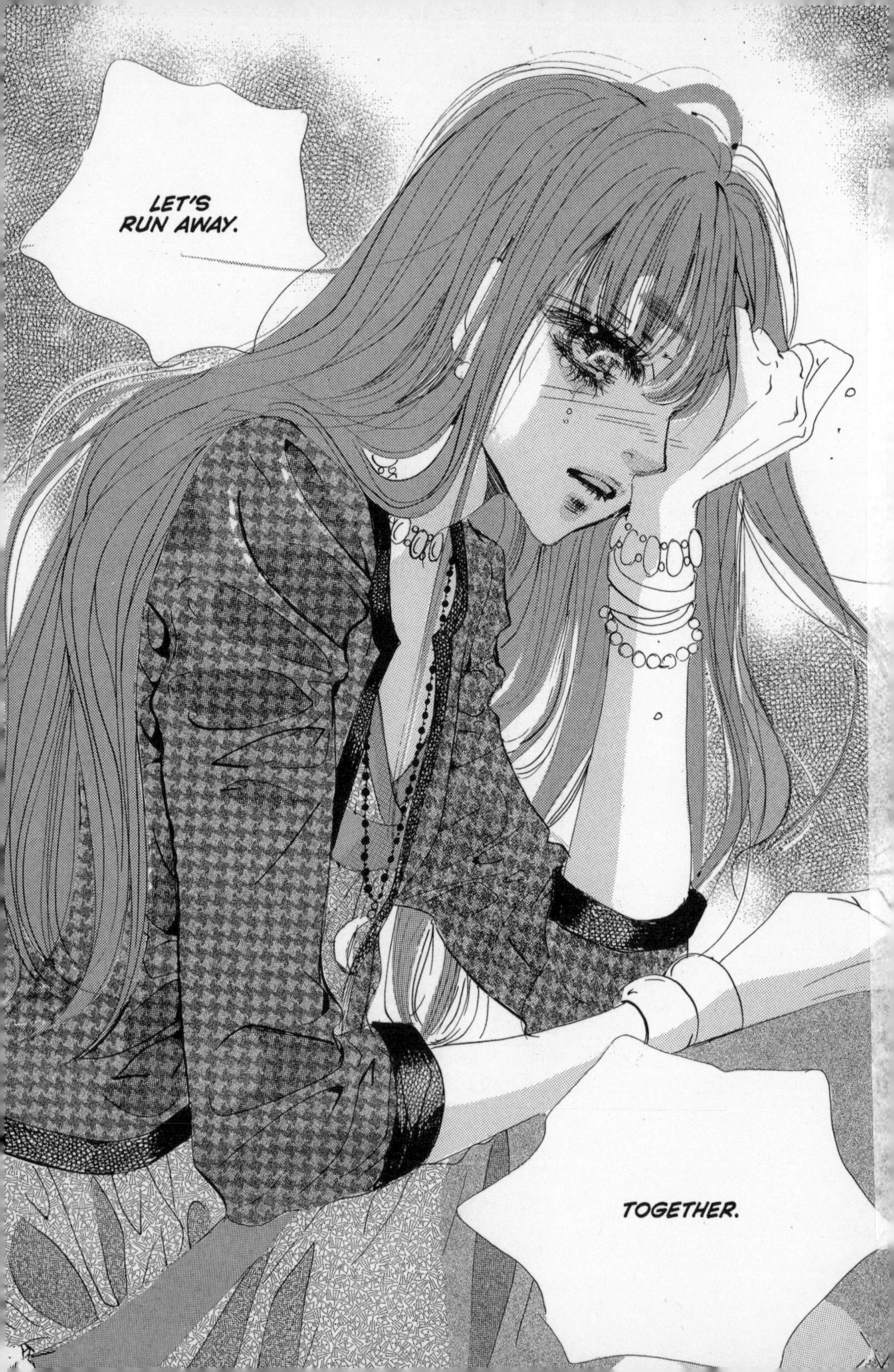
LET'S RUN AWAY.
TOGETHER.

The Royal Palace

Goong

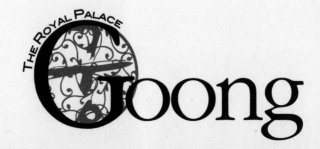

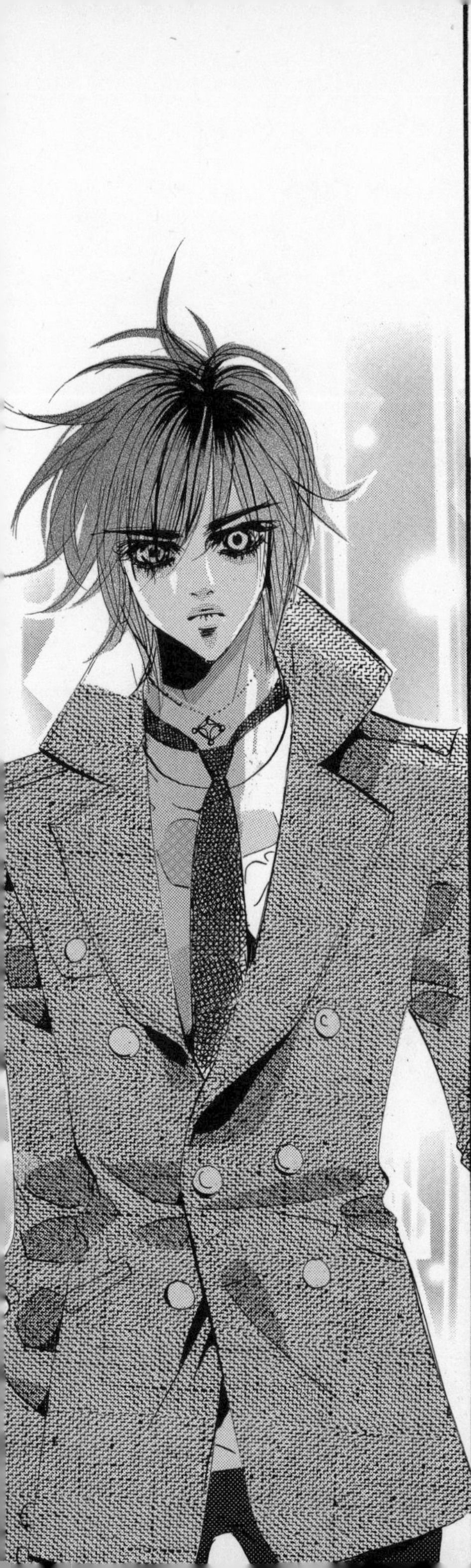

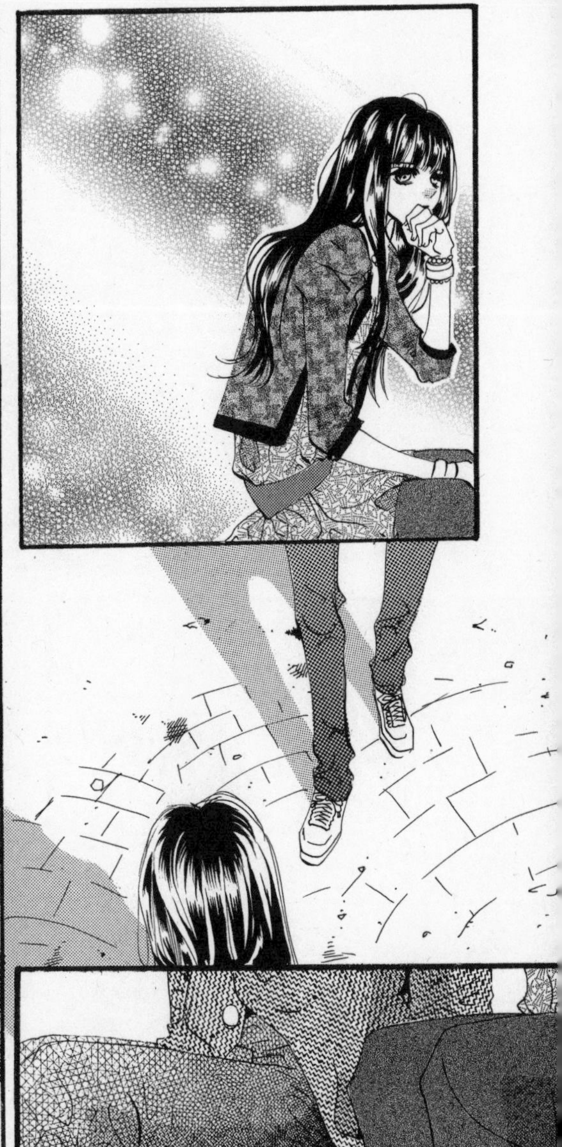

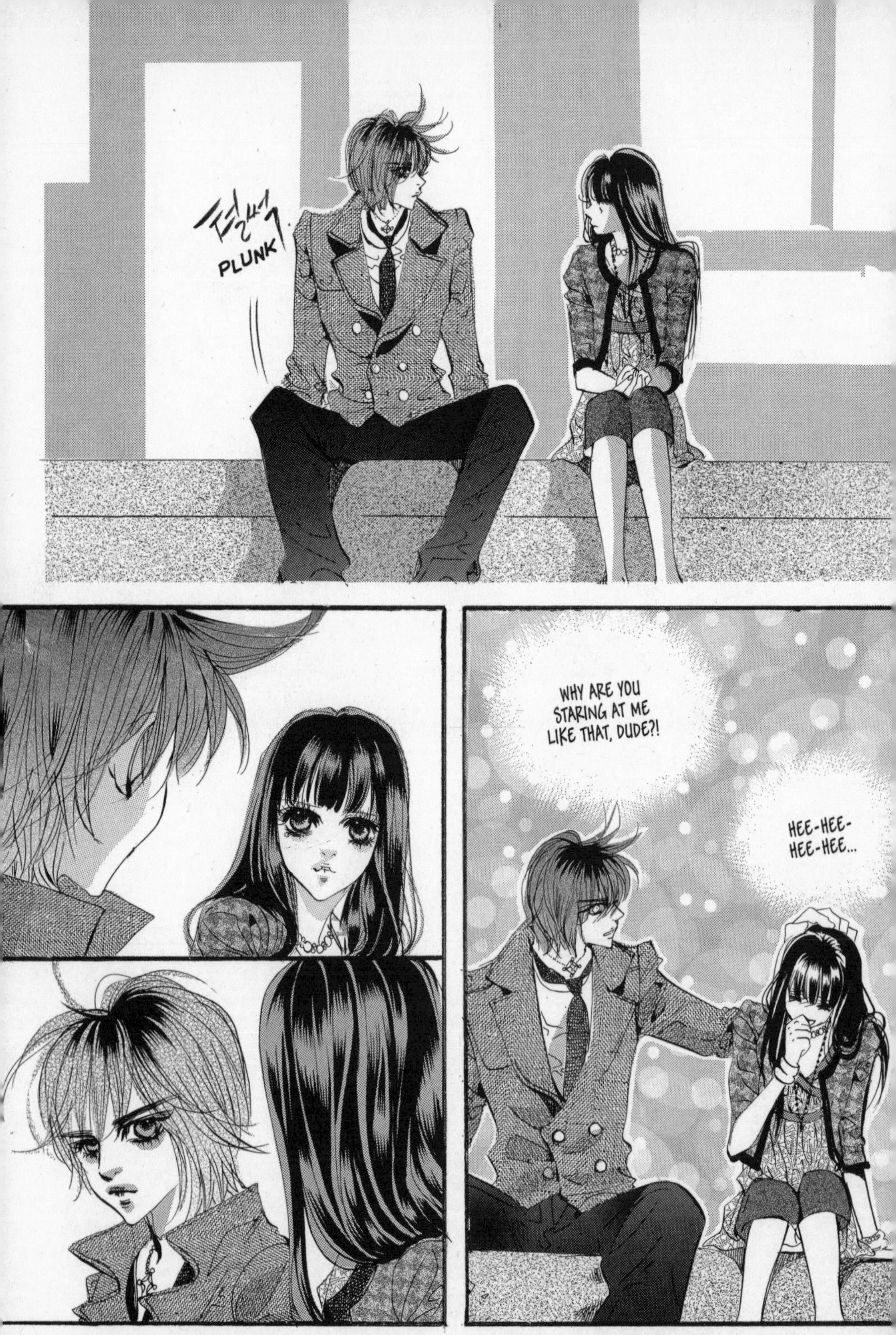
털썩
PLUNK
WHY ARE YOU STARING AT ME LIKE THAT, DUDE?!
HEE-HEE-HEE-HEE...

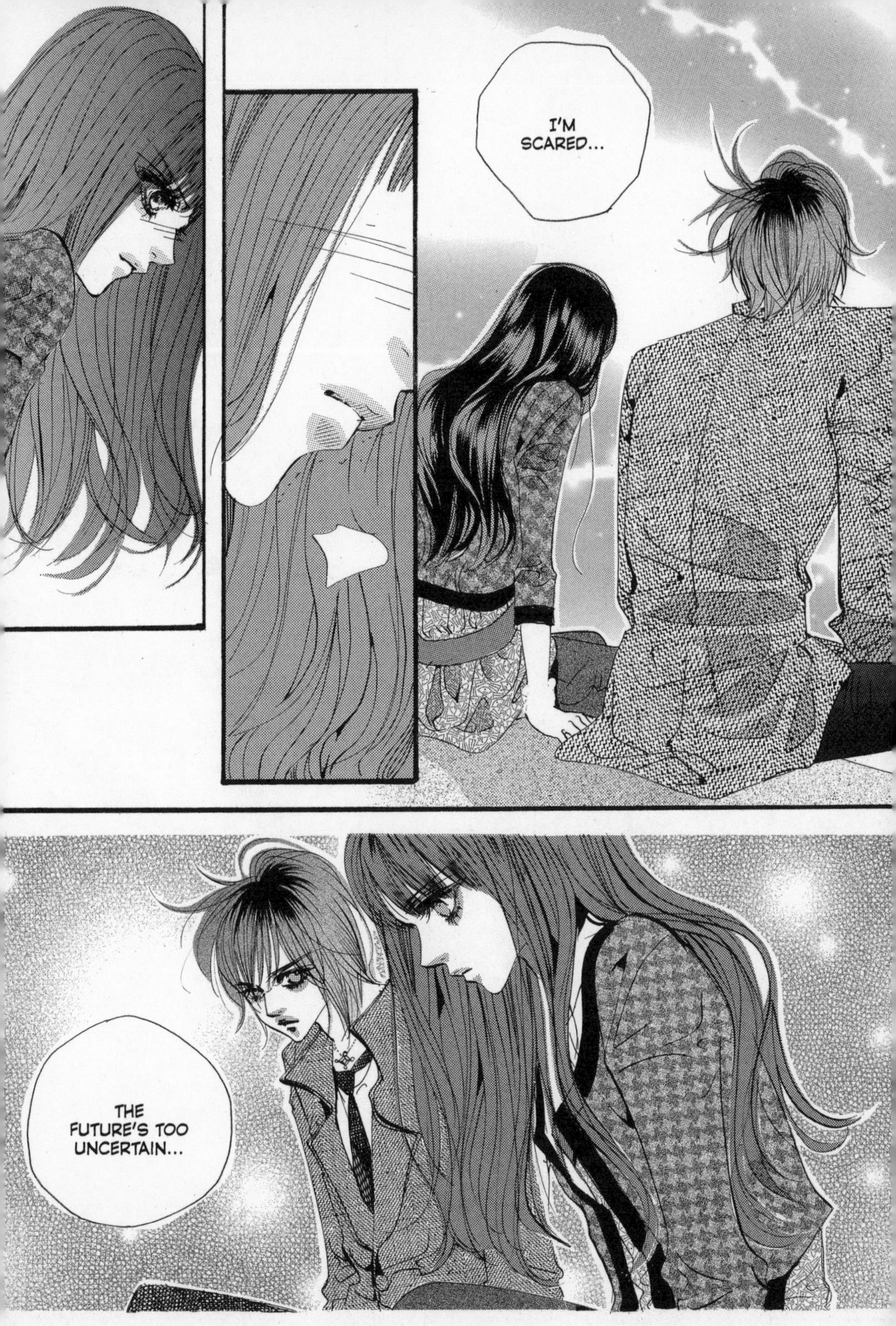
I'M SCARED...
THE FUTURE'S TOO UNCERTAIN...

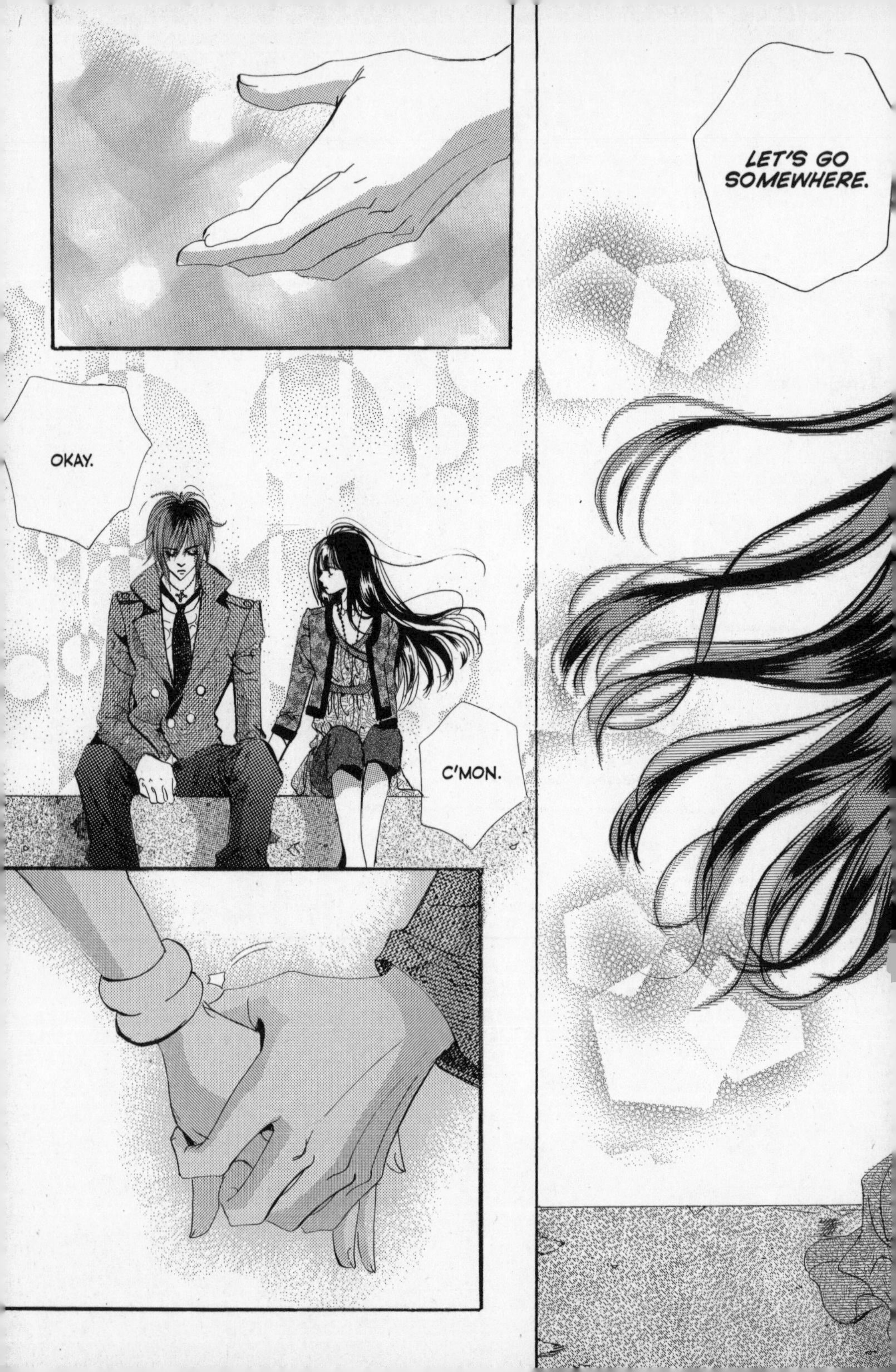
OKAY.
C'MON.
LET'S GO SOMEWHERE.

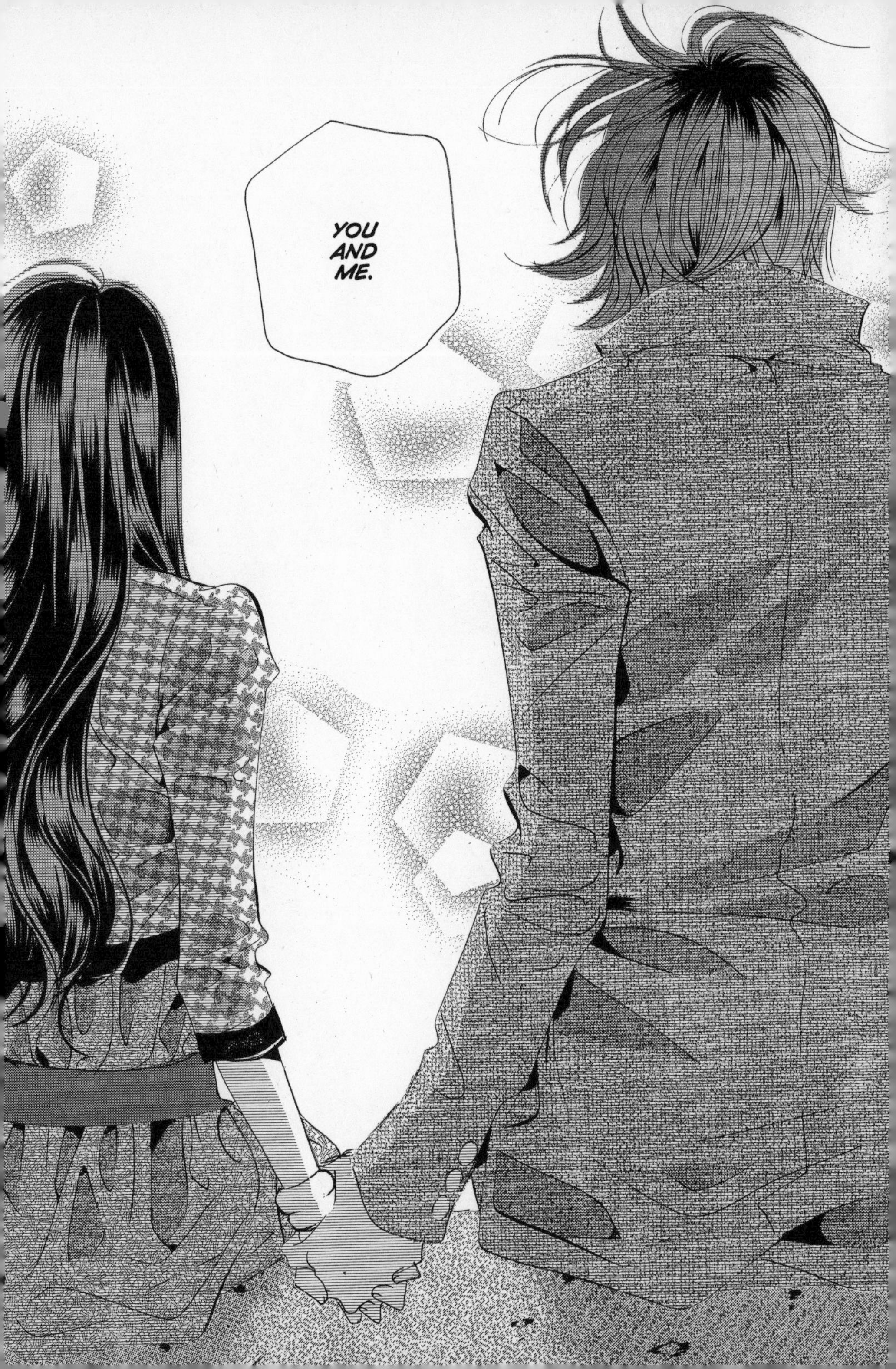
YOU AND ME.

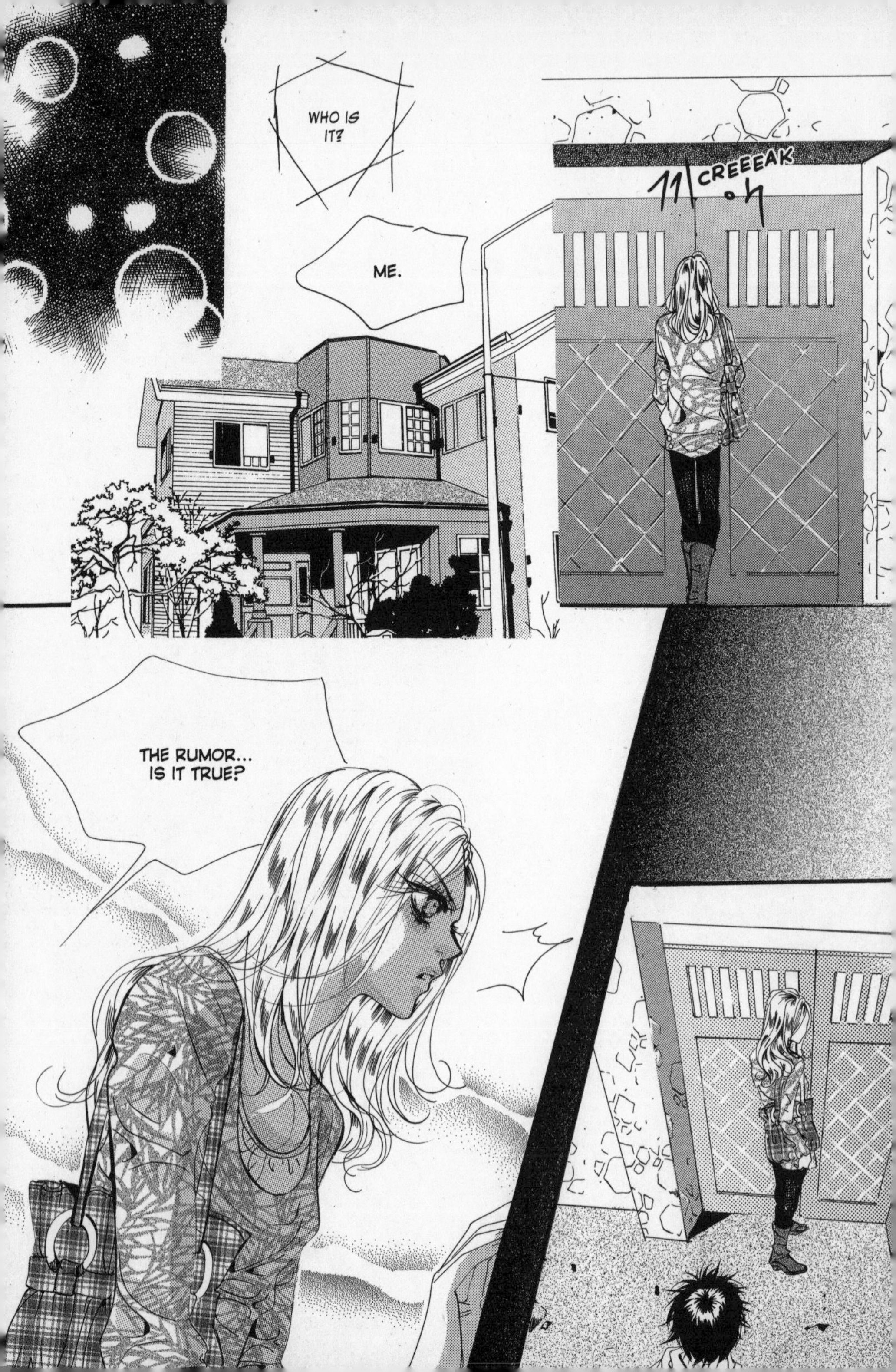
WHO IS IT?
ME.
CREEEAK
THE RUMOR... IS IT TRUE?

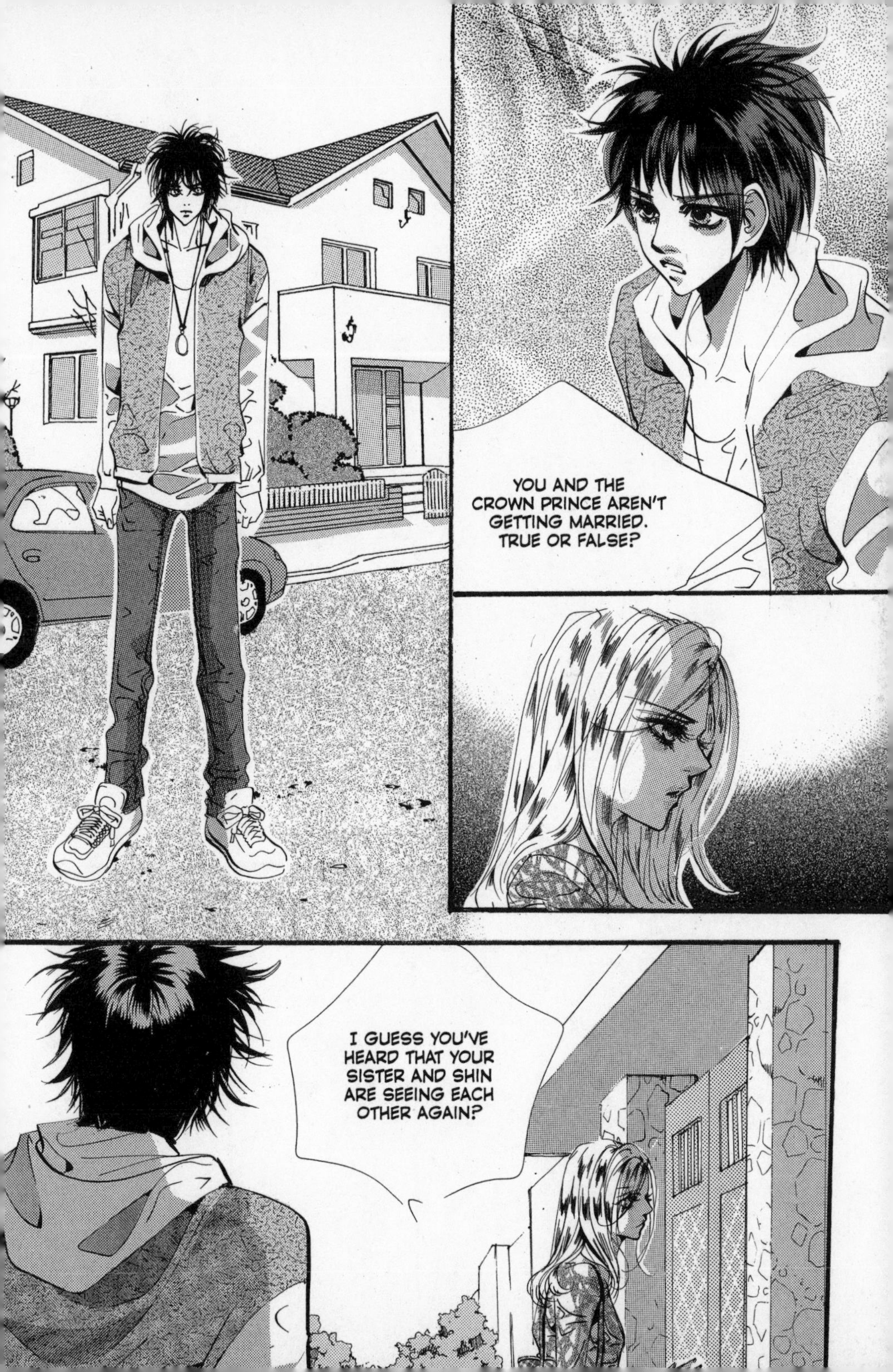
YOU AND THE CROWN PRINCE AREN'T GETTING MARRIED. TRUE OR FALSE?
I GUESS YOU'VE HEARD THAT YOUR SISTER AND SHIN ARE SEEING EACH OTHER AGAIN?

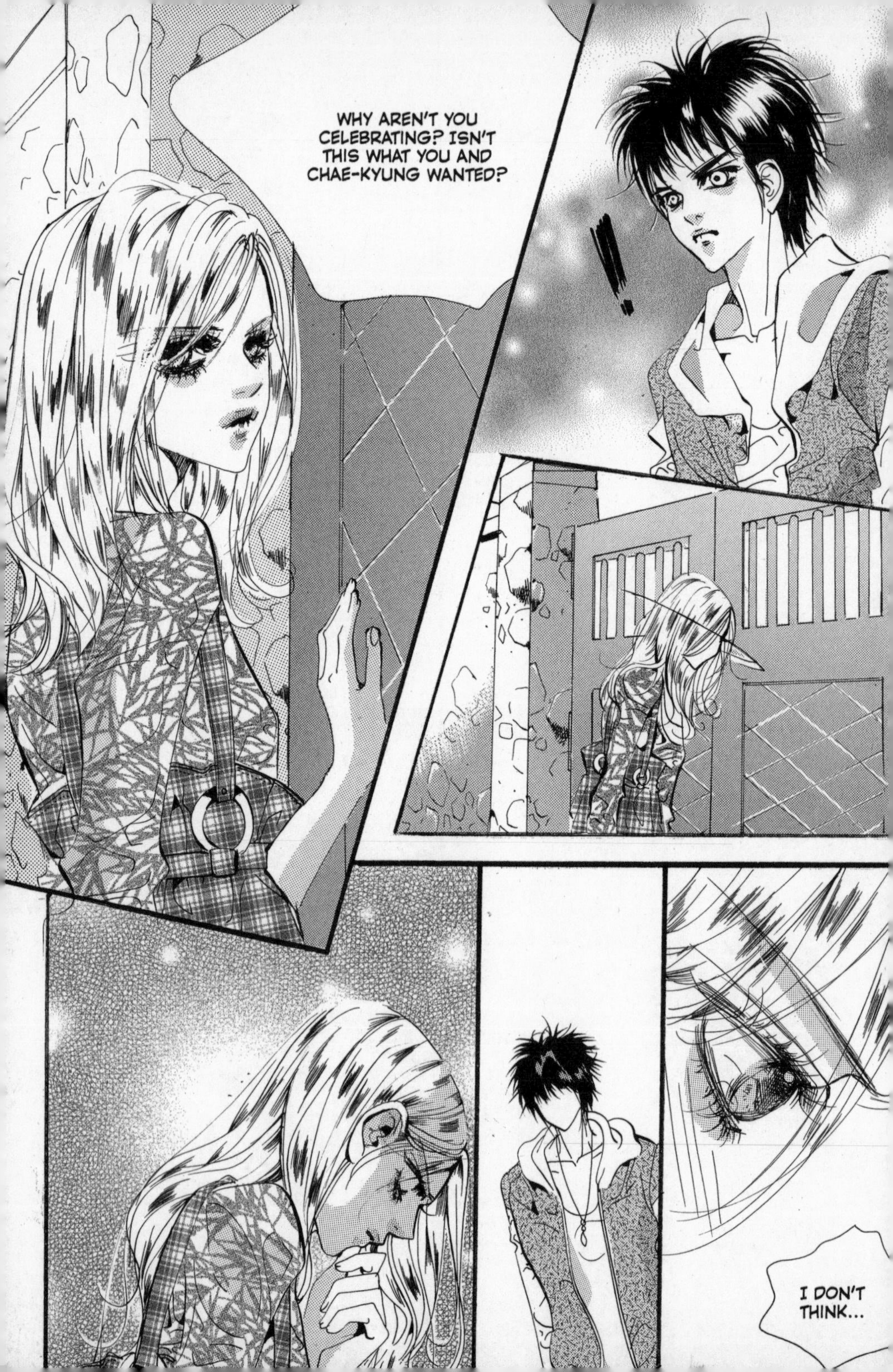
WHY AREN'T YOU CELEBRATING? ISN'T THIS WHAT YOU AND CHAE-KYUNG WANTED?
!
I DON'T THINK...

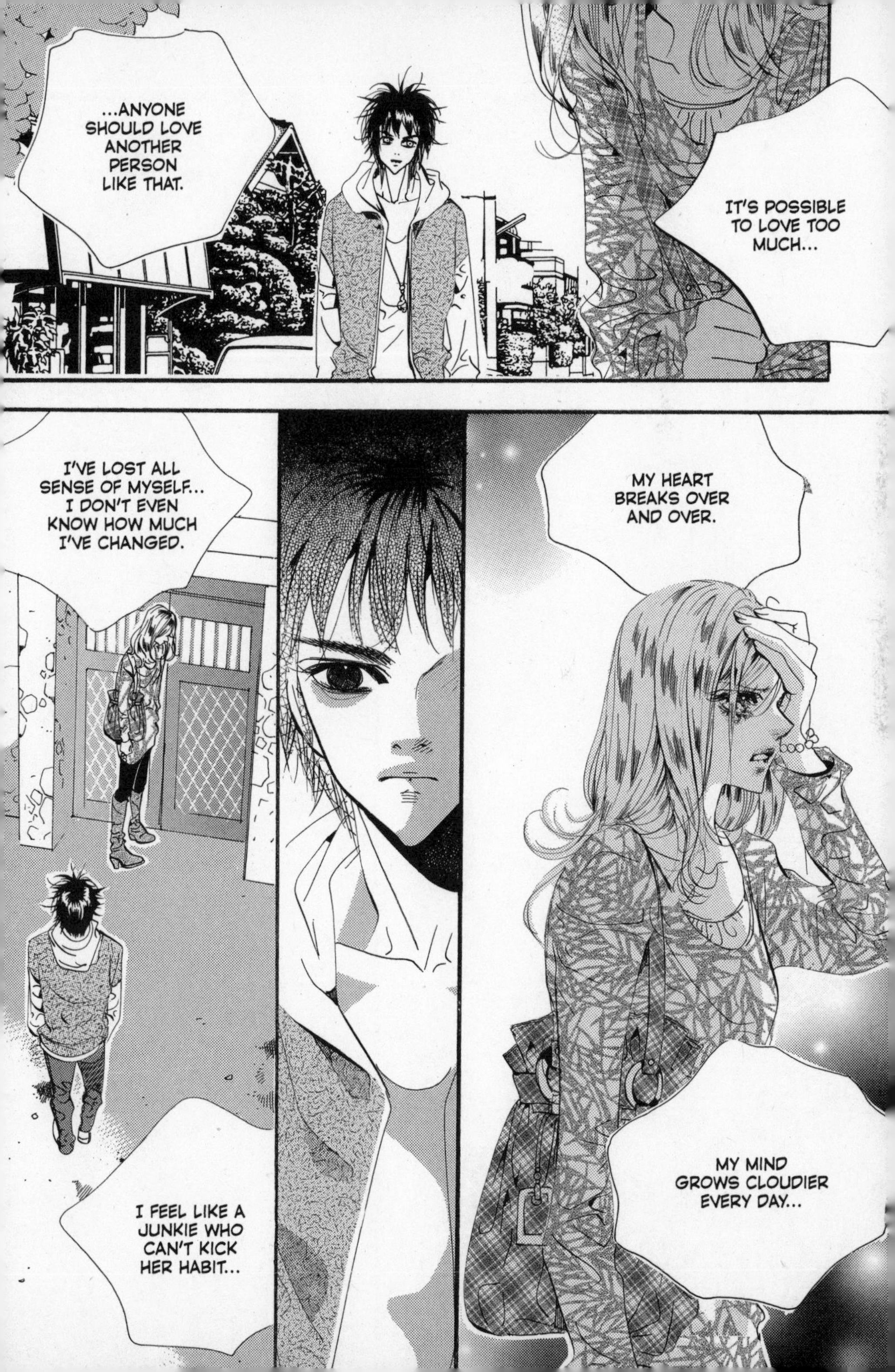
...ANYONE SHOULD LOVE ANOTHER PERSON LIKE THAT.
IT'S POSSIBLE TO LOVE TOO MUCH...
I'VE LOST ALL SENSE OF MYSELF... I DON'T EVEN KNOW HOW MUCH I'VE CHANGED.
I FEEL LIKE A JUNKIE WHO CAN'T KICK HER HABIT...
MY HEART BREAKS OVER AND OVER.
MY MIND GROWS CLOUDIER EVERY DAY...

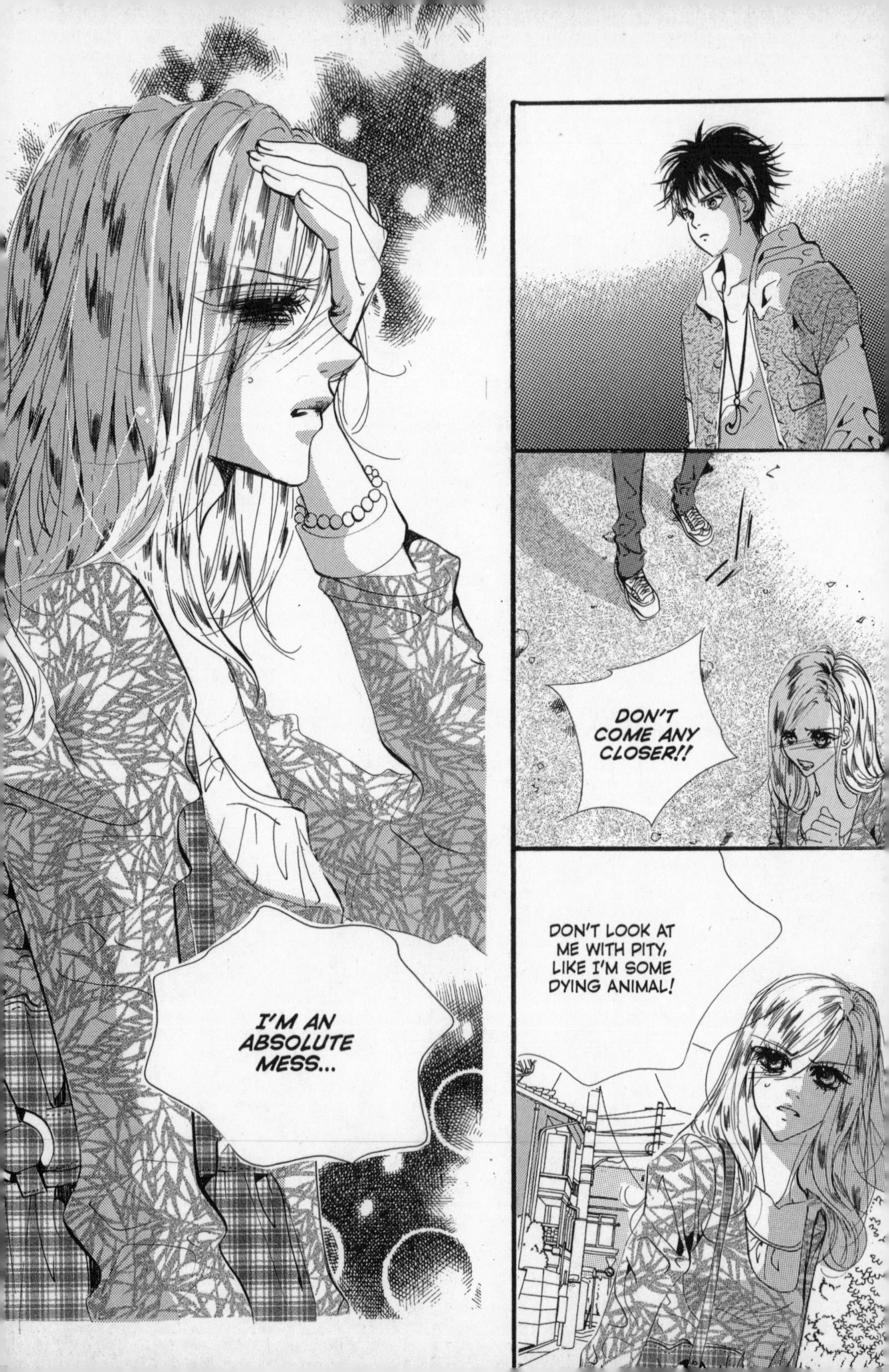
I'M AN ABSOLUTE MESS...
DON'T COME ANY CLOSER!!
DON'T LOOK AT ME WITH PITY, LIKE I'M SOME DYING ANIMAL!

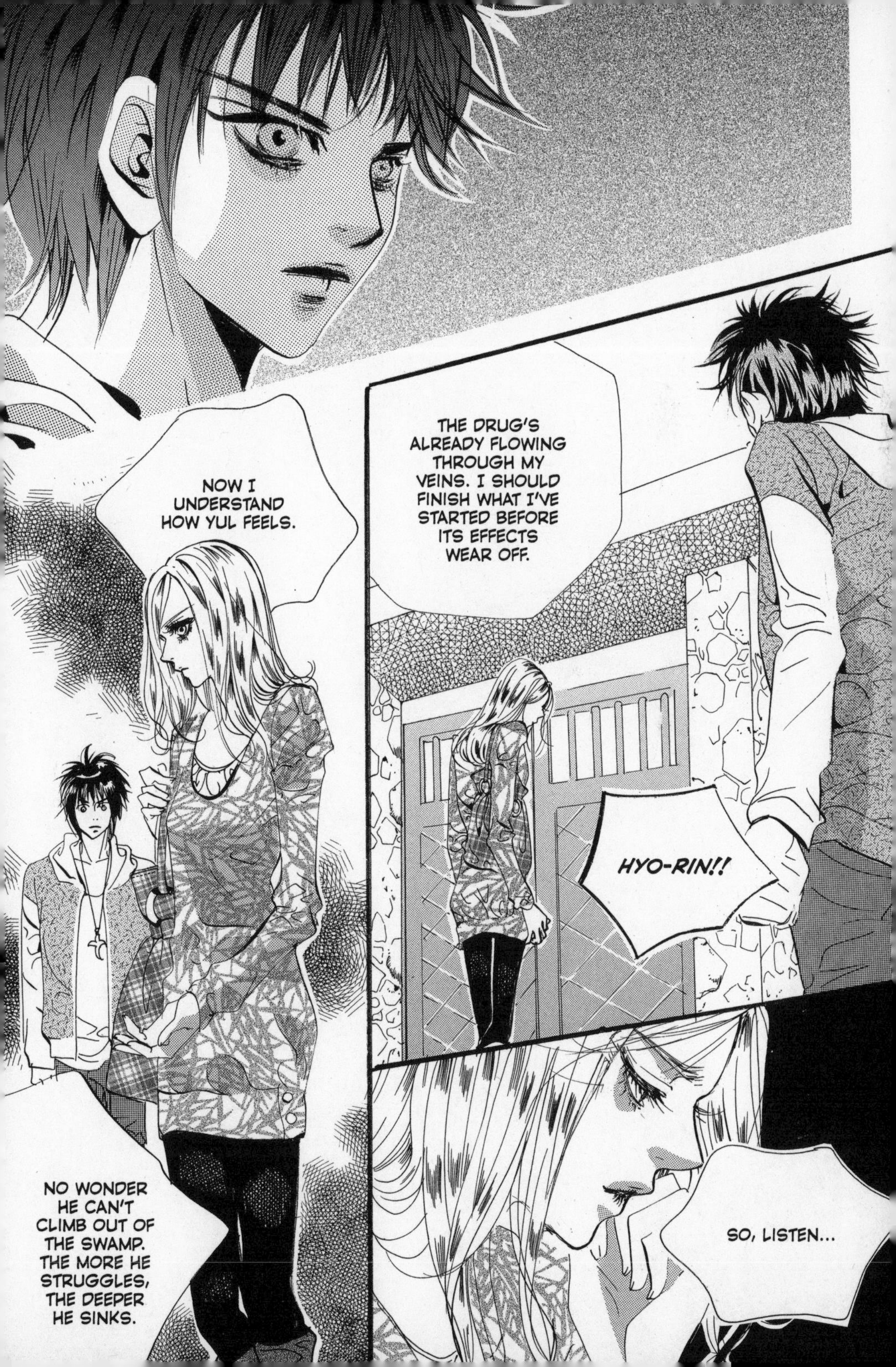
NOW I UNDERSTAND HOW YUL FEELS.
NO WONDER HE CAN'T CLIMB OUT OF THE SWAMP. THE MORE HE STRUGGLES, THE DEEPER HE SINKS.
THE DRUG'S ALREADY FLOWING THROUGH MY VEINS. I SHOULD FINISH WHAT I'VE STARTED BEFORE ITS EFFECTS WEAR OFF.
HYO-RIN!!
SO, LISTEN...

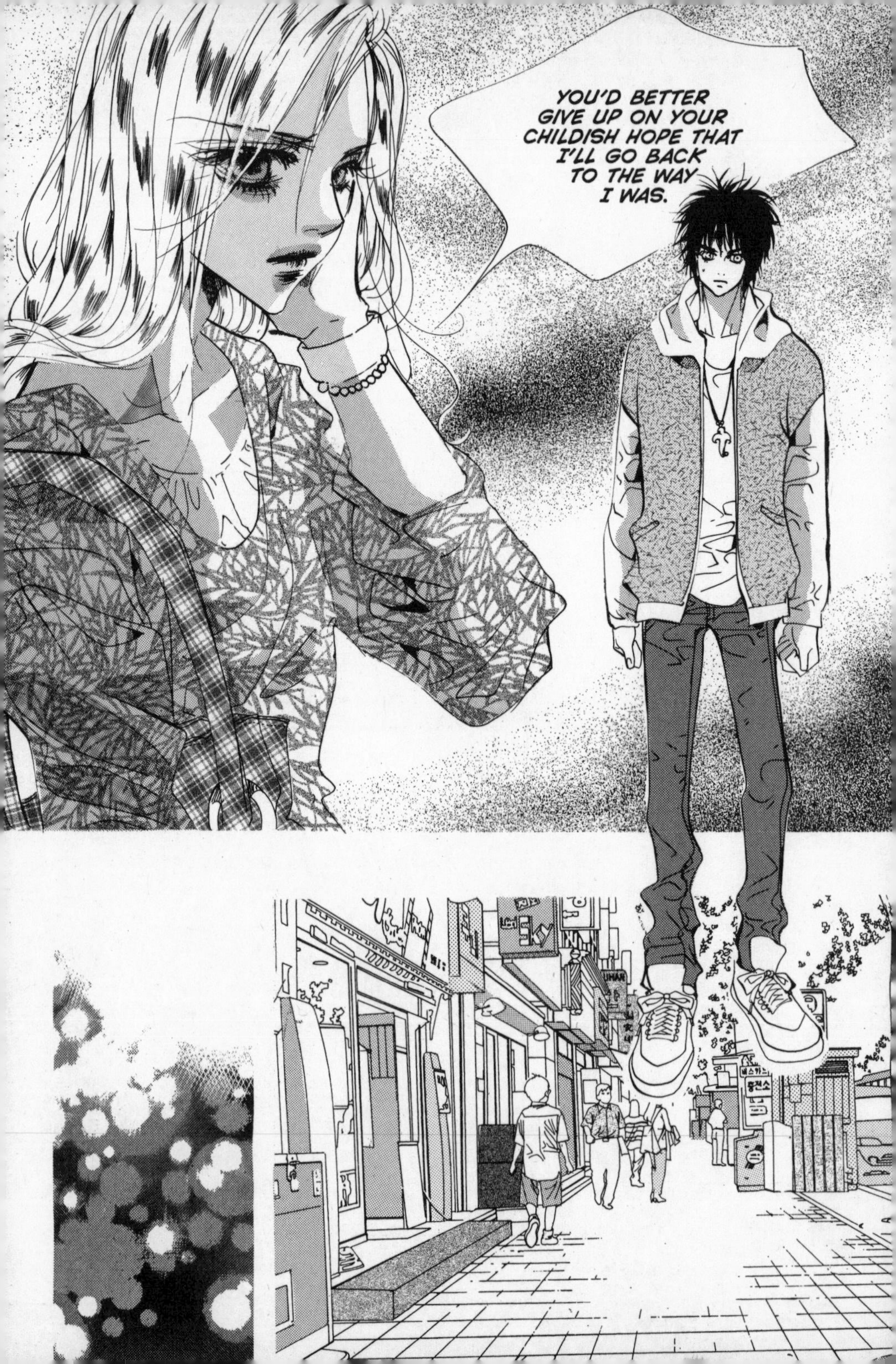
YOU'D BETTER GIVE UP ON YOUR CHILDISH HOPE THAT I'LL GO BACK TO THE WAY I WAS.

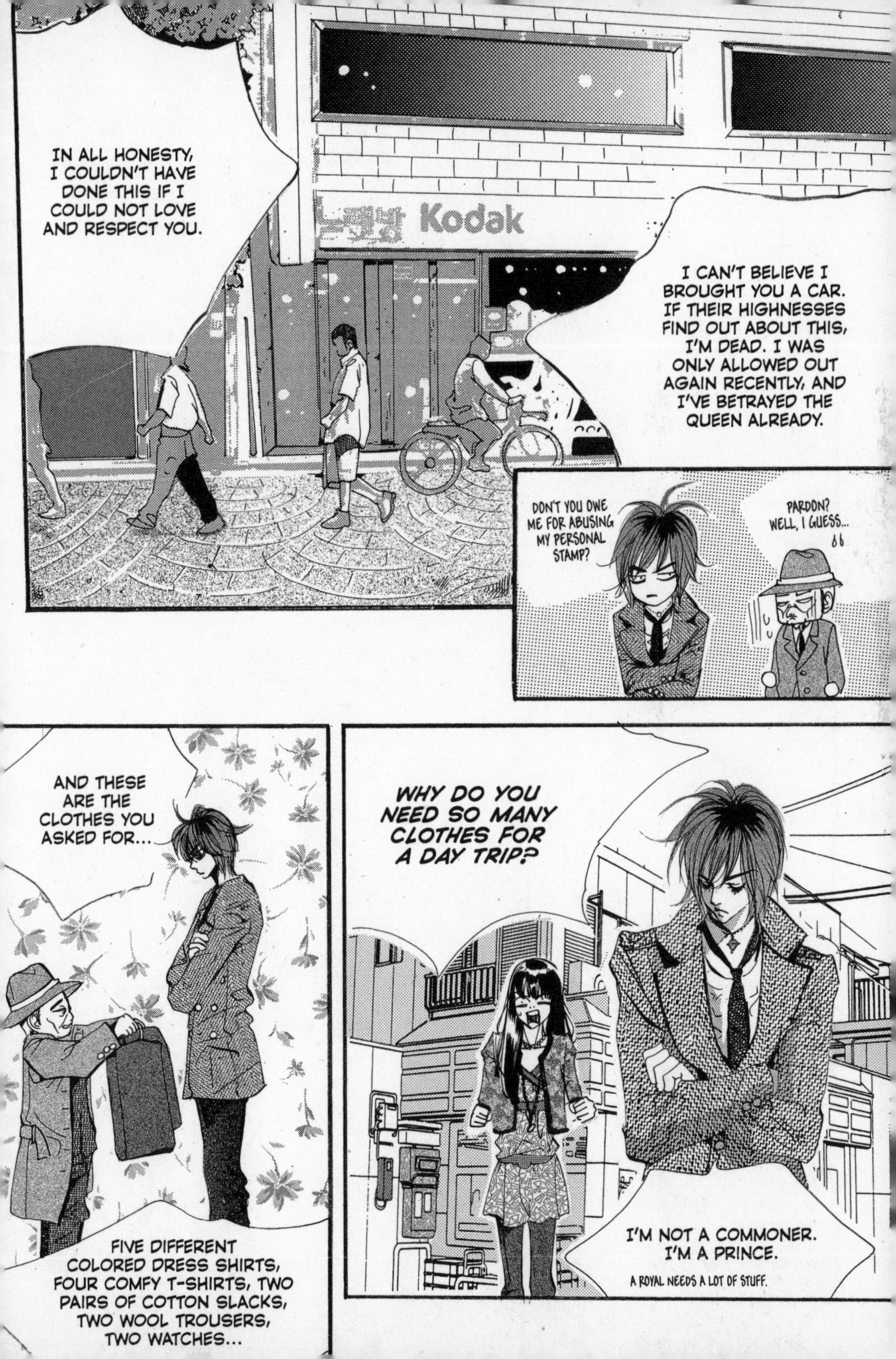
IN ALL HONESTY, I COULDN'T HAVE DONE THIS IF I COULD NOT LOVE AND RESPECT YOU.
Kodak
I CAN'T BELIEVE I BROUGHT YOU A CAR. IF THEIR HIGHNESSES FIND OUT ABOUT THIS, I'M DEAD. I WAS ONLY ALLOWED OUT AGAIN RECENTLY, AND I'VE BETRAYED THE QUEEN ALREADY.
DON'T YOU OWE ME FOR ABUSING MY PERSONAL STAMP?
PARDON? WELL, I GUESS...
AND THESE ARE THE CLOTHES YOU ASKED FOR...
FIVE DIFFERENT COLORED DRESS SHIRTS, FOUR COMFY T-SHIRTS, TWO PAIRS OF COTTON SLACKS, TWO WOOL TROUSERS, TWO WATCHES...
WHY DO YOU NEED SO MANY CLOTHES FOR A DAY TRIP?
I'M NOT A COMMONER. I'M A PRINCE.
A ROYAL NEEDS A LOT OF STUFF.

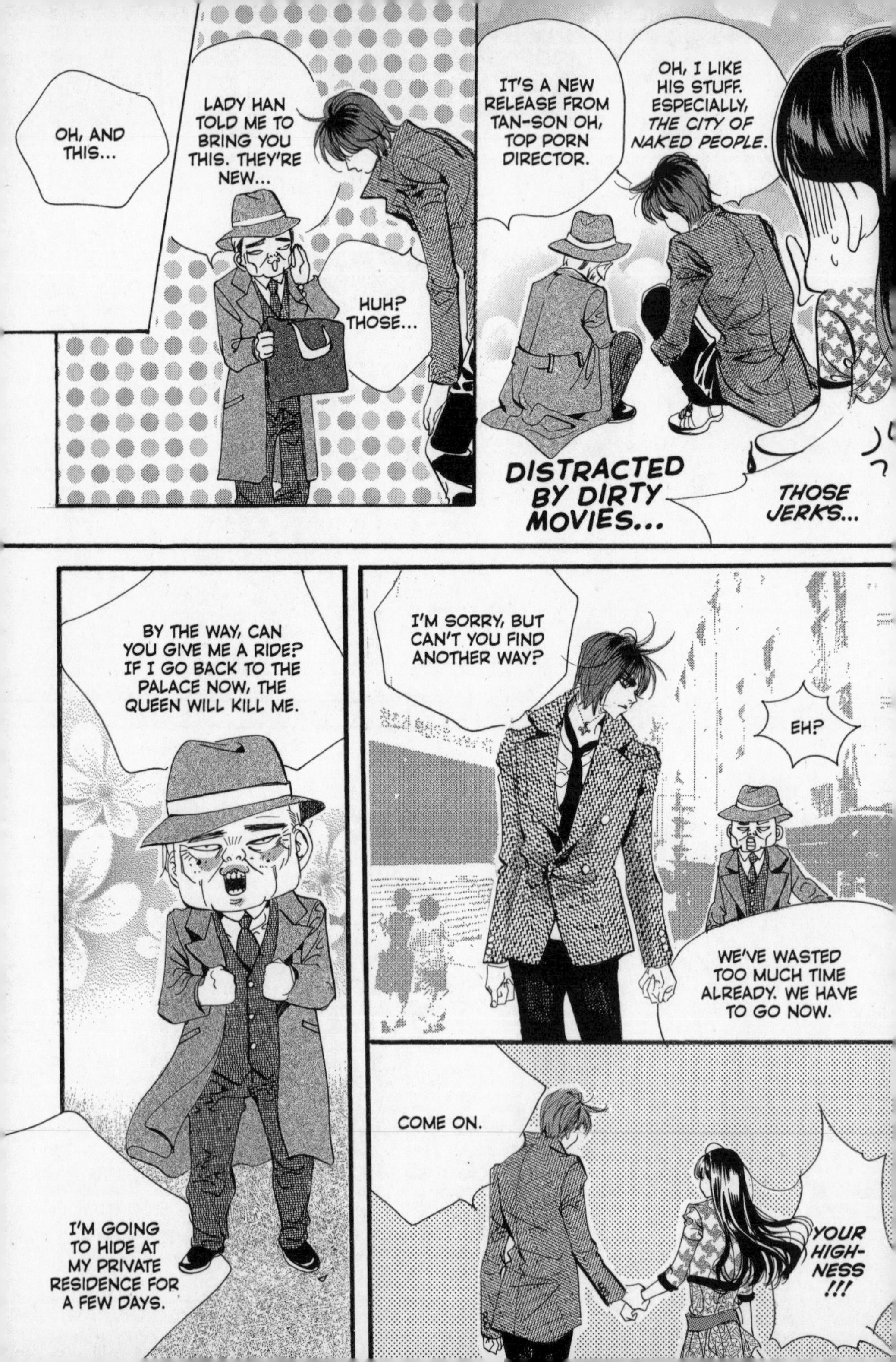
OH, AND THIS...
LADY HAN TOLD ME TO BRING YOU THIS. THEY'RE NEW...
HUH? THOSE...
IT'S A NEW RELEASE FROM TAN-SON OH, TOP PORN DIRECTOR.
OH, I LIKE HIS STUFF. ESPECIALLY, *THE CITY OF NAKED PEOPLE.*
DISTRACTED BY DIRTY MOVIES...
THOSE JERKS...
BY THE WAY, CAN YOU GIVE ME A RIDE? IF I GO BACK TO THE PALACE NOW, THE QUEEN WILL KILL ME.
I'M GOING TO HIDE AT MY PRIVATE RESIDENCE FOR A FEW DAYS.
I'M SORRY, BUT CAN'T YOU FIND ANOTHER WAY?
EH?
WE'VE WASTED TOO MUCH TIME ALREADY. WE HAVE TO GO NOW.
COME ON.
YOUR HIGH-NESS!!!

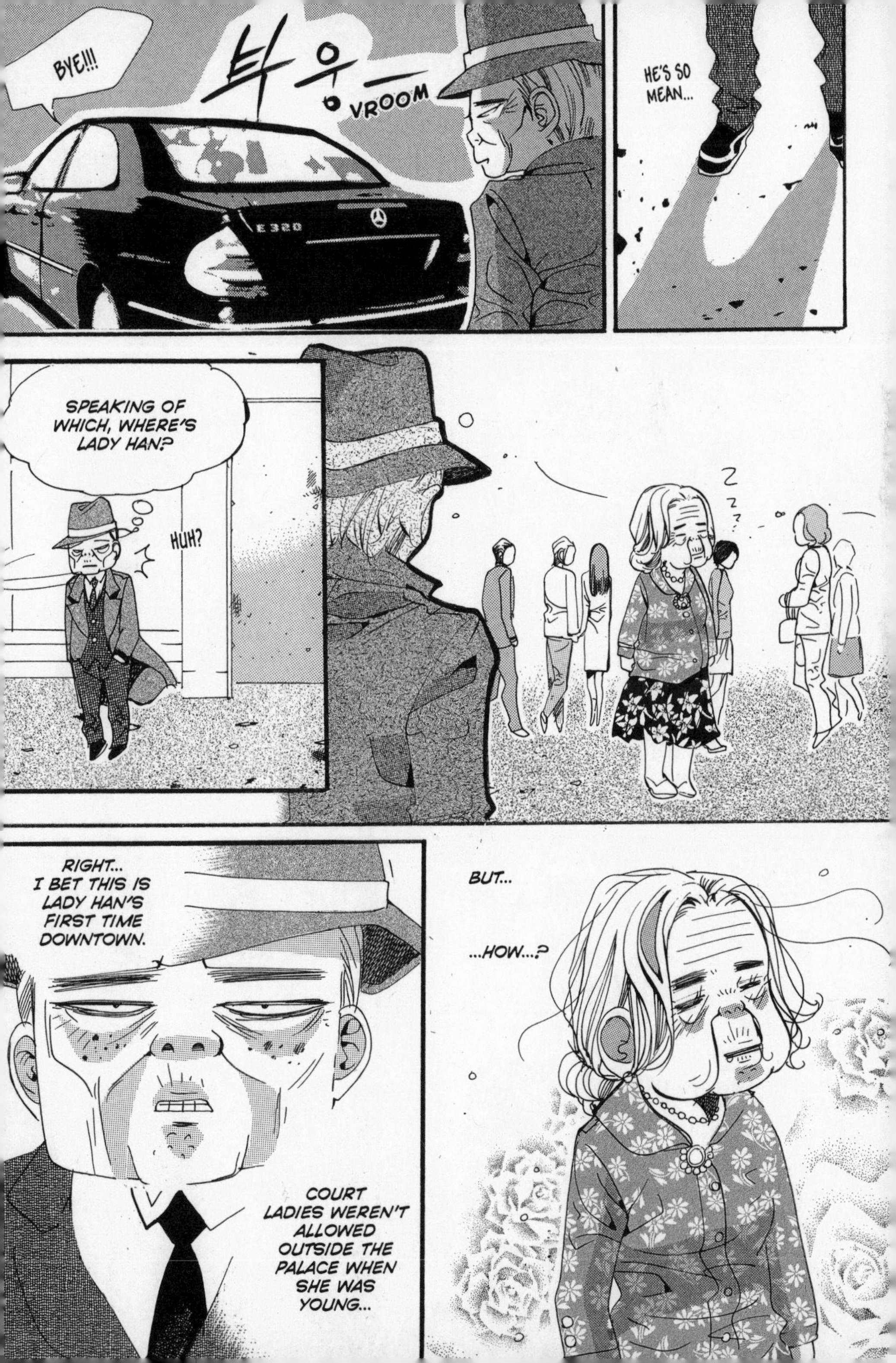
BYE!!!
부웅—
VROOM
HE'S SO MEAN...
SPEAKING OF WHICH, WHERE'S LADY HAN?
HUH?
RIGHT... I BET THIS IS LADY HAN'S FIRST TIME DOWNTOWN.
COURT LADIES WEREN'T ALLOWED OUTSIDE THE PALACE WHEN SHE WAS YOUNG...
BUT...
...HOW...?

HOW IS SHE SOOO CUTE...? ♡

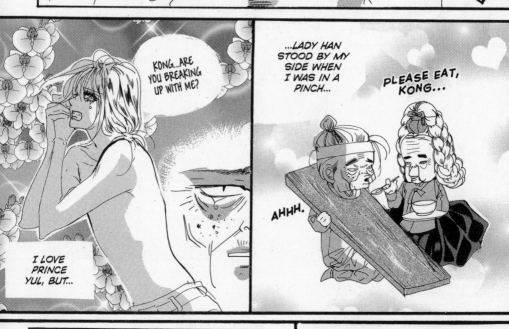

KONG...ARE YOU BREAKING UP WITH ME?

I LOVE PRINCE YUL, BUT...

...LADY HAN STOOD BY MY SIDE WHEN I WAS IN A PINCH...

PLEASE EAT, KONG...

AHHH.

AND OUT OF NOWHERE...

GO OR STOP?

I LOVE YOU, KONG...

I SAID, GO OR STOP?

WHAT'S WRONG WITH YOU...?

LADY HAN...

...SHE TOLD ME THAT SHE LOVED ME...

RIGHT...
I THINK I NEED
A WOMAN...
I CAN LEAN ON
IN MY OLD AGE.

LADY HAN...

KONG...

SHALL WE...
GET MARRIED
...?

BGM
"PERHAPS LOVE"*
—J & HOWL

♪ I DON'T REMEMBER
WHEN IT WAS~ ♪♪

♪ I GOT DIZZY
BECAUSE
OF YOU~ ♪♪

**"PERHAPS LOVE" WAS THE THEME SONG FOR THE 2006 GOONG TV SHOW

LET'S LOVE
EACH OTHER,
CLEAN THE DIRT
FROM BETWEEN
EACH OTHER'S
TOES, THE FOOD
FROM EACH
OTHER'S
TEETH...

KONG...

...LET'S TAKE
CARE OF EACH
OTHER AND
LIVE HAPPILY
EVER AFTER...

LADY HAN...

IS THIS LOVE? IF YOU
FEEL THE SAME, HAS
OUR LOVE BEGUN? ♪

KONG...

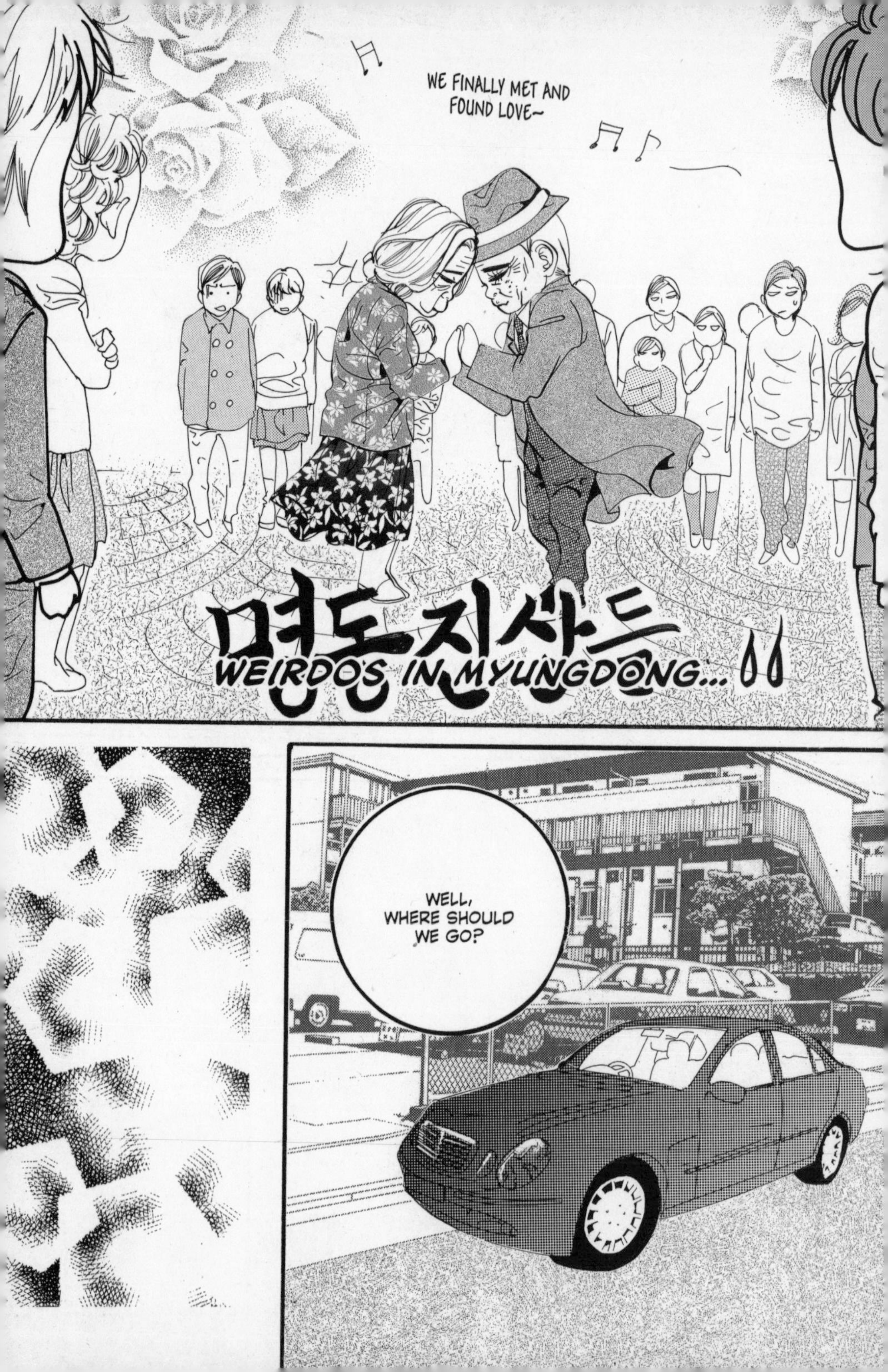
WE FINALLY MET AND FOUND LOVE~
명동지샤드
WEIRDOS IN MYUNGDONG...
WELL, WHERE SHOULD WE GO?

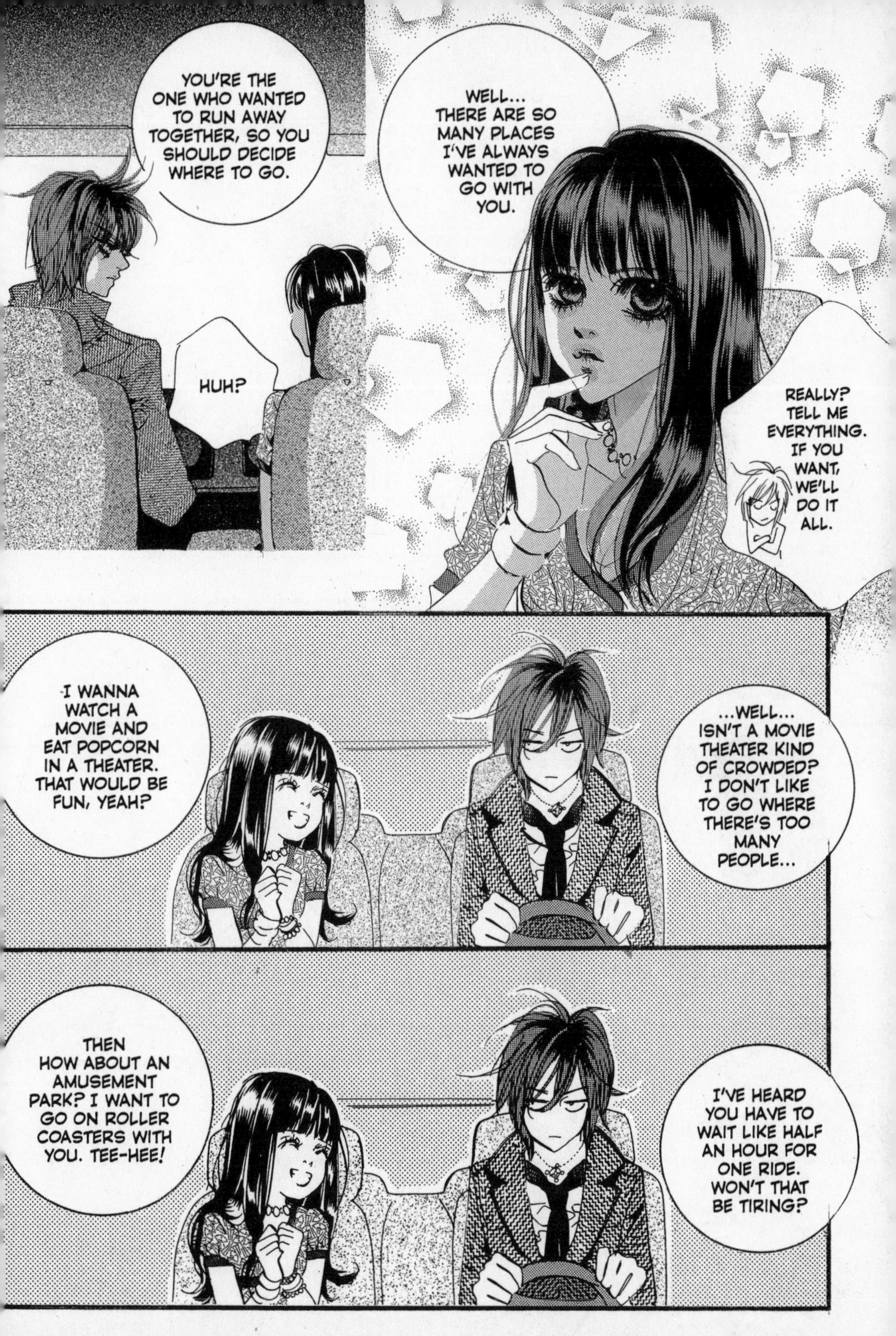
YOU'RE THE ONE WHO WANTED TO RUN AWAY TOGETHER, SO YOU SHOULD DECIDE WHERE TO GO.
HUH?
WELL... THERE ARE SO MANY PLACES I'VE ALWAYS WANTED TO GO WITH YOU.
REALLY? TELL ME EVERYTHING. IF YOU WANT, WE'LL DO IT ALL.
I WANNA WATCH A MOVIE AND EAT POPCORN IN A THEATER. THAT WOULD BE FUN, YEAH?
...WELL... ISN'T A MOVIE THEATER KIND OF CROWDED? I DON'T LIKE TO GO WHERE THERE'S TOO MANY PEOPLE...
THEN HOW ABOUT AN AMUSEMENT PARK? I WANT TO GO ON ROLLER COASTERS WITH YOU. TEE-HEE!
I'VE HEARD YOU HAVE TO WAIT LIKE HALF AN HOUR FOR ONE RIDE. WON'T THAT BE TIRING?

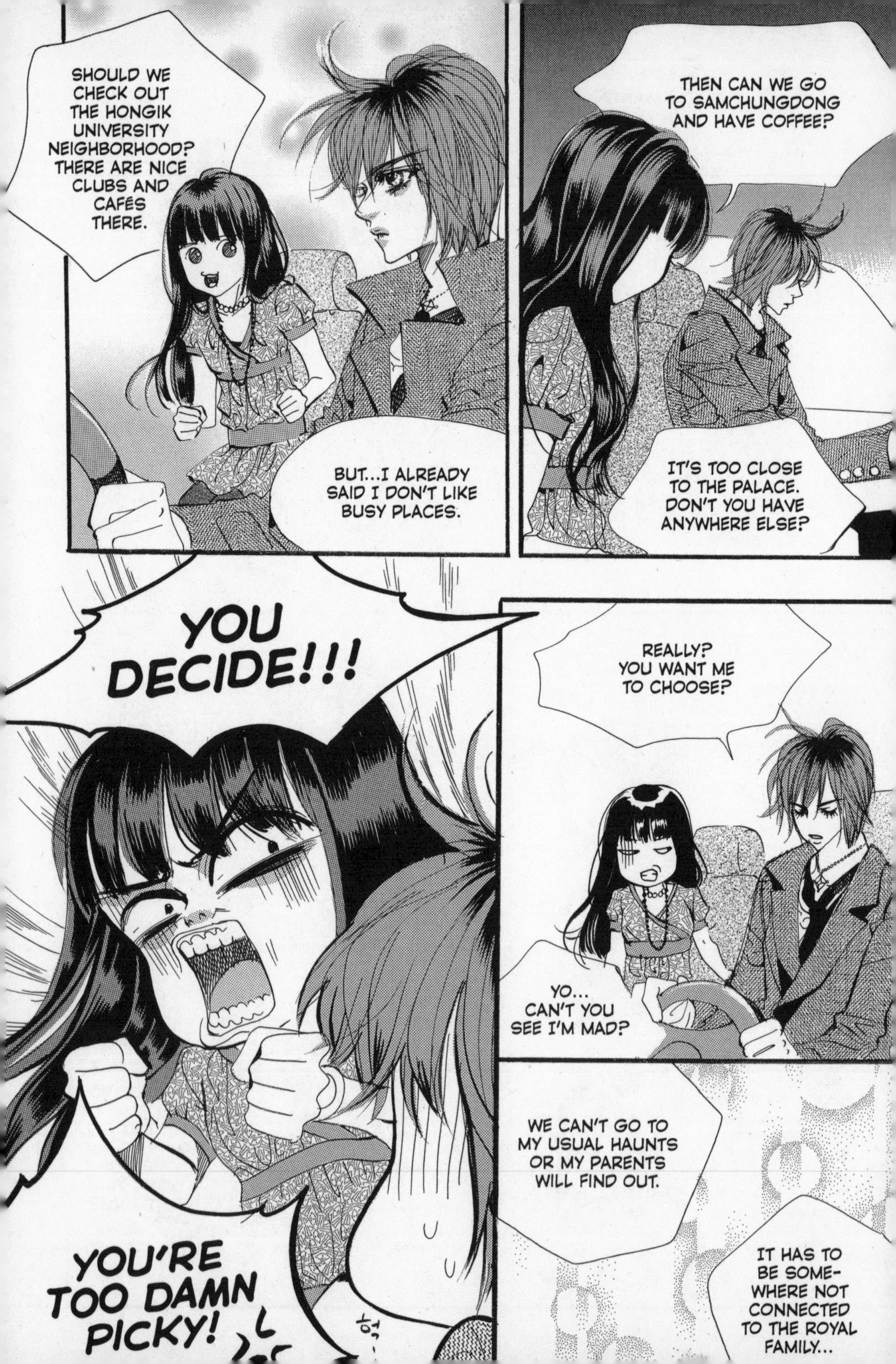
SHOULD WE CHECK OUT THE HONGIK UNIVERSITY NEIGHBORHOOD? THERE ARE NICE CLUBS AND CAFÉS THERE.
BUT...I ALREADY SAID I DON'T LIKE BUSY PLACES.
THEN CAN WE GO TO SAMCHUNGDONG AND HAVE COFFEE?
IT'S TOO CLOSE TO THE PALACE. DON'T YOU HAVE ANYWHERE ELSE?
YOU DECIDE!!!
YOU'RE TOO DAMN PICKY!
REALLY? YOU WANT ME TO CHOOSE?
YO... CAN'T YOU SEE I'M MAD?
WE CAN'T GO TO MY USUAL HAUNTS OR MY PARENTS WILL FIND OUT.
IT HAS TO BE SOME-WHERE NOT CONNECTED TO THE ROYAL FAMILY...

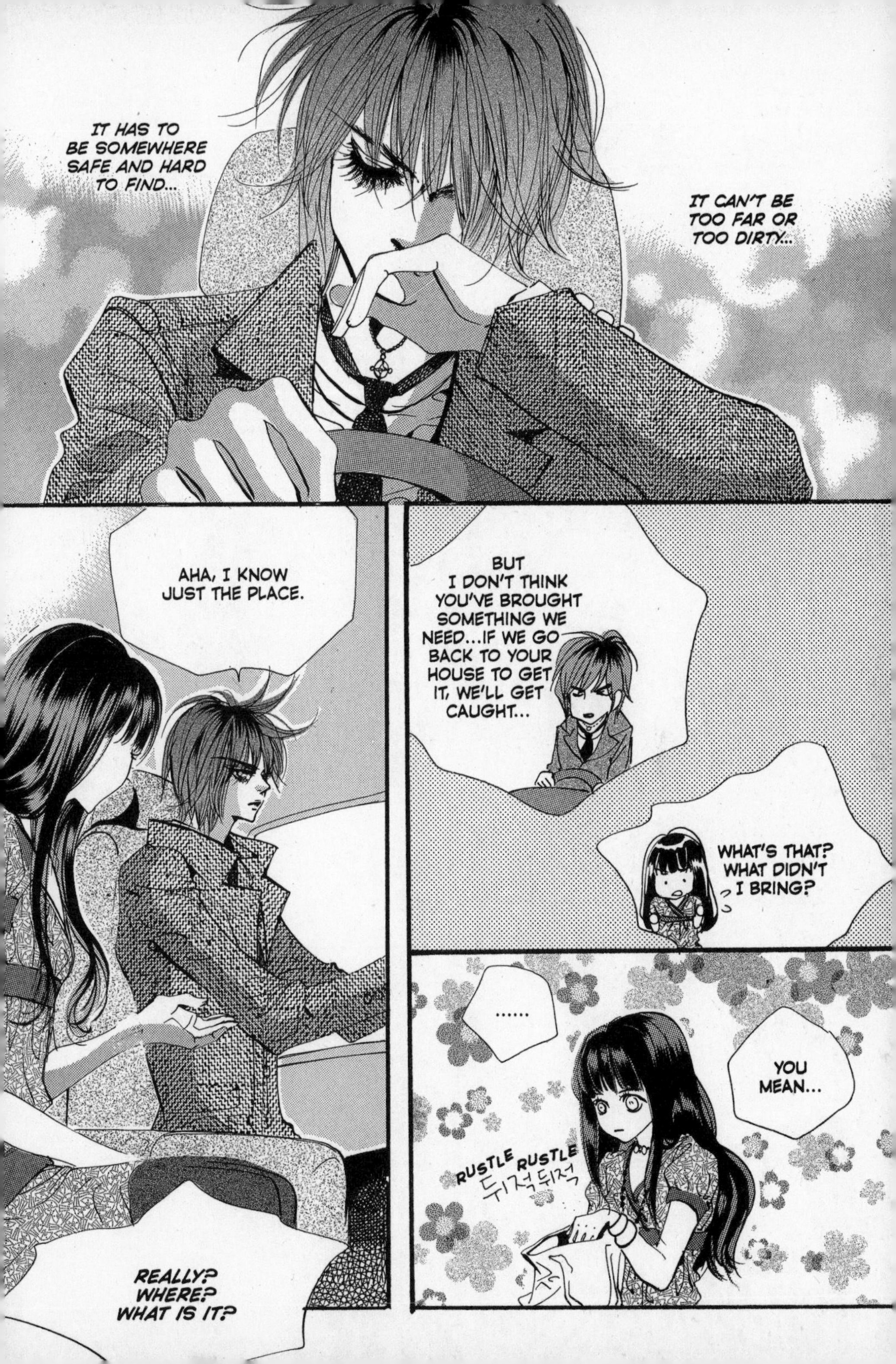
IT HAS TO BE SOMEWHERE SAFE AND HARD TO FIND...
IT CAN'T BE TOO FAR OR TOO DIRTY...
AHA, I KNOW JUST THE PLACE.
REALLY? WHERE? WHAT IS IT?
BUT I DON'T THINK YOU'VE BROUGHT SOMETHING WE NEED...IF WE GO BACK TO YOUR HOUSE TO GET IT, WE'LL GET CAUGHT...
WHAT'S THAT? WHAT DIDN'T I BRING?
......
YOU MEAN...
RUSTLE RUSTLE
뒤적뒤적

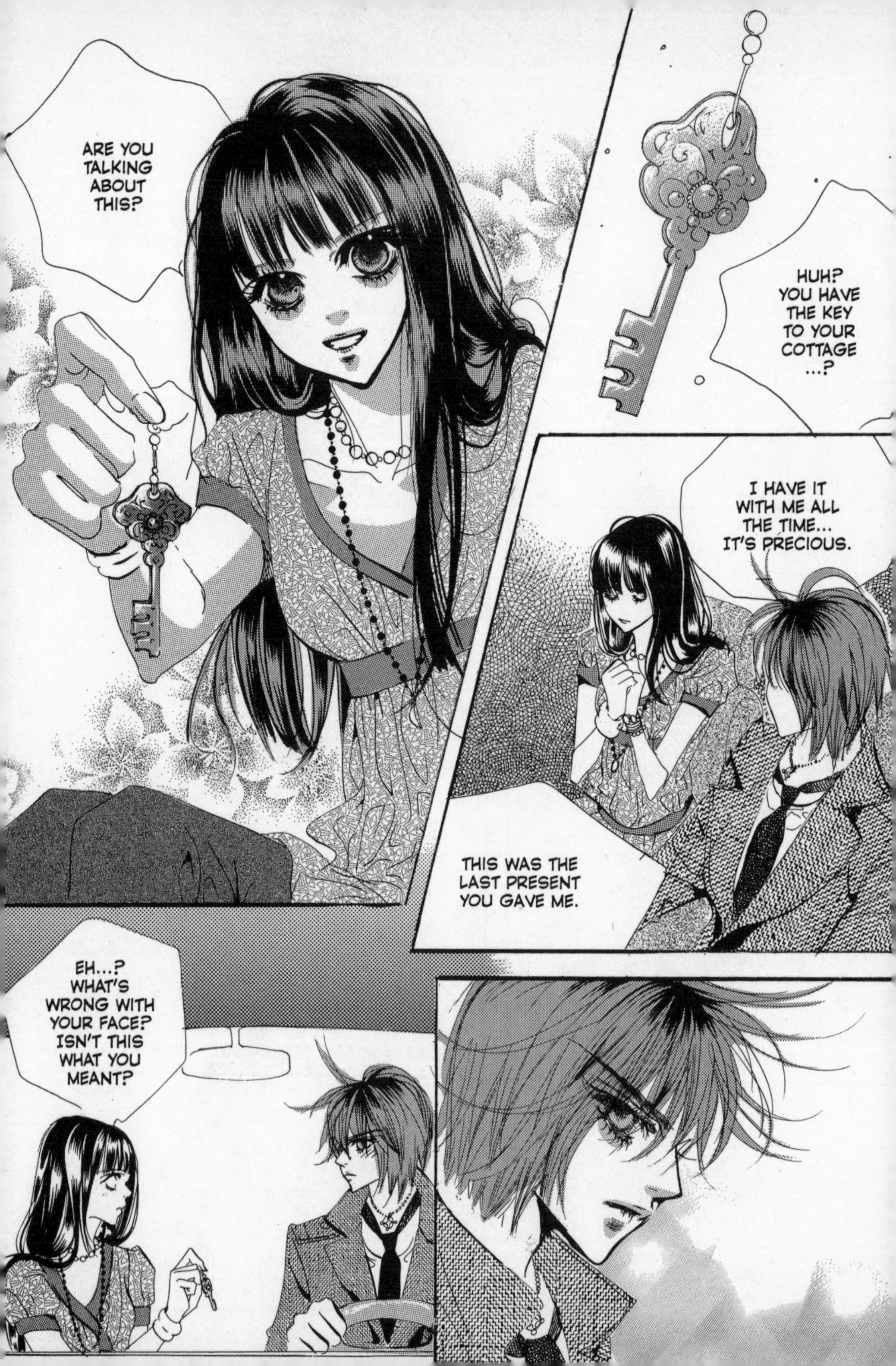
ARE YOU TALKING ABOUT THIS?
HUH? YOU HAVE THE KEY TO YOUR COTTAGE ...?
I HAVE IT WITH ME ALL THE TIME... IT'S PRECIOUS.
THIS WAS THE LAST PRESENT YOU GAVE ME.
EH...? WHAT'S WRONG WITH YOUR FACE? ISN'T THIS WHAT YOU MEANT?

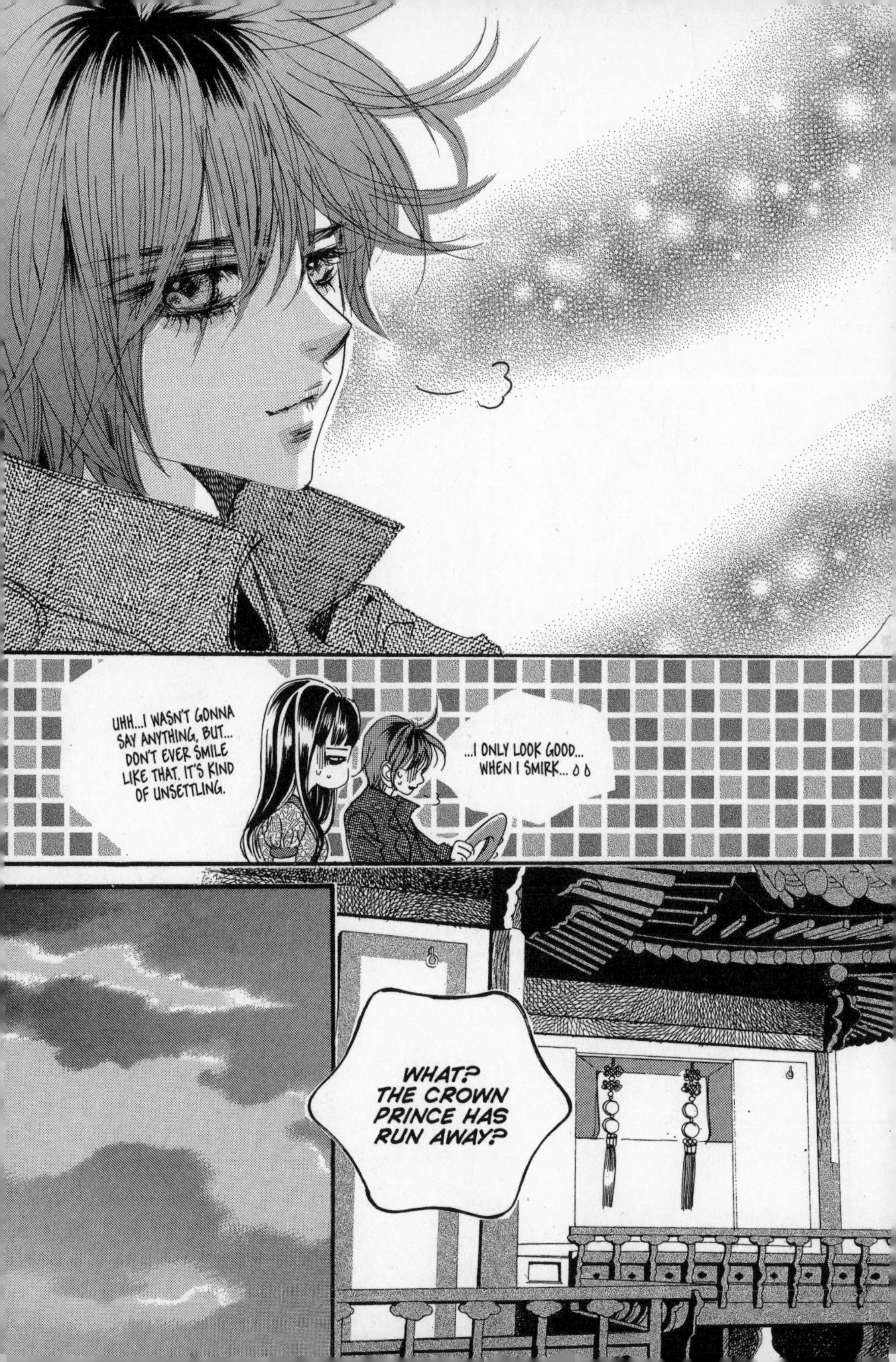
UHH...I WASN'T GONNA SAY ANYTHING, BUT... DON'T EVER SMILE LIKE THAT. IT'S KIND OF UNSETTLING.
...I ONLY LOOK GOOD... WHEN I SMIRK...
WHAT? THE CROWN PRINCE HAS RUN AWAY?

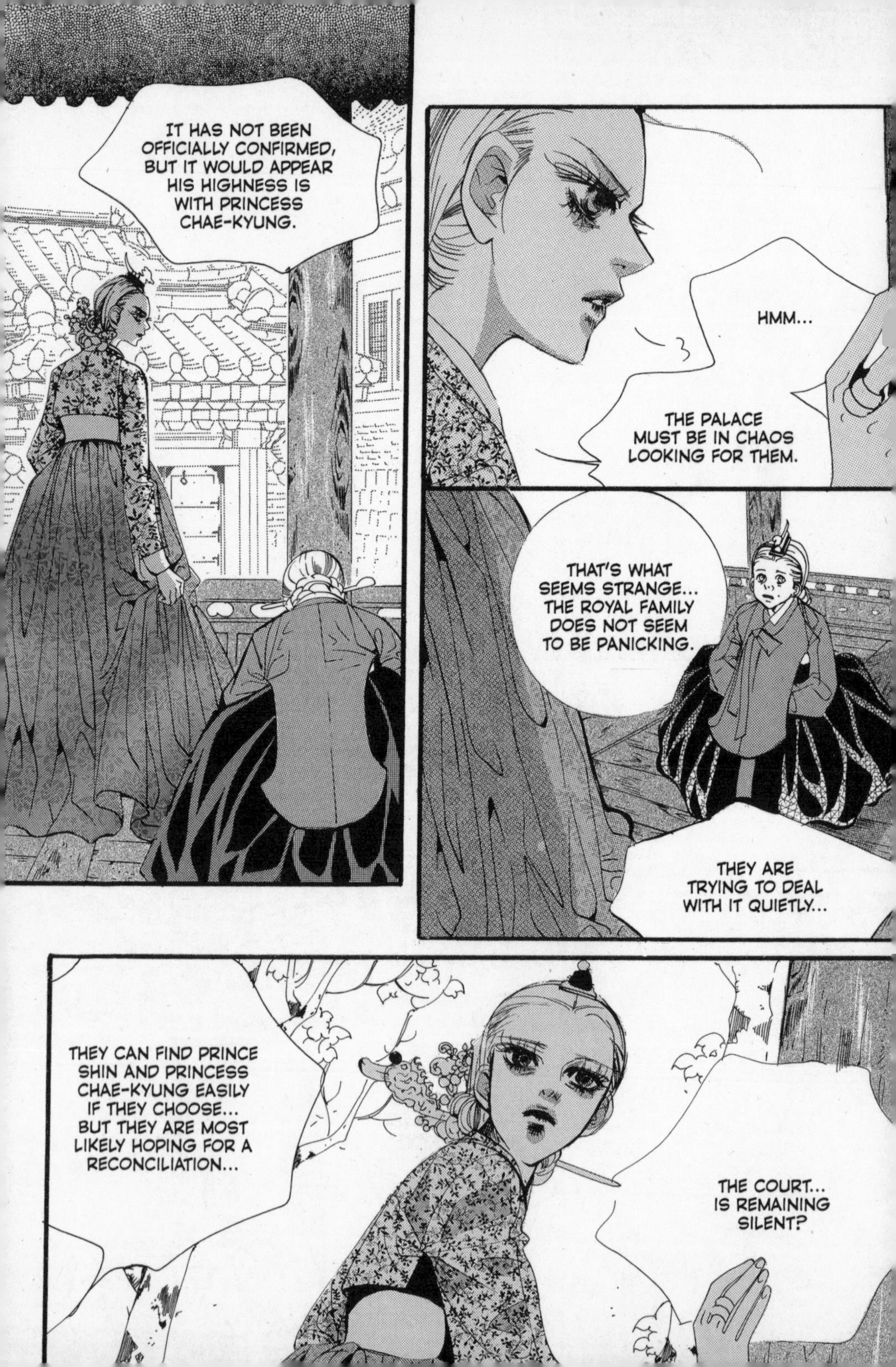
IT HAS NOT BEEN OFFICIALLY CONFIRMED, BUT IT WOULD APPEAR HIS HIGHNESS IS WITH PRINCESS CHAE-KYUNG.
HMM...
THE PALACE MUST BE IN CHAOS LOOKING FOR THEM.
THAT'S WHAT SEEMS STRANGE... THE ROYAL FAMILY DOES NOT SEEM TO BE PANICKING.
THEY ARE TRYING TO DEAL WITH IT QUIETLY...
THEY CAN FIND PRINCE SHIN AND PRINCESS CHAE-KYUNG EASILY IF THEY CHOOSE... BUT THEY ARE MOST LIKELY HOPING FOR A RECONCILIATION...
THE COURT... IS REMAINING SILENT?

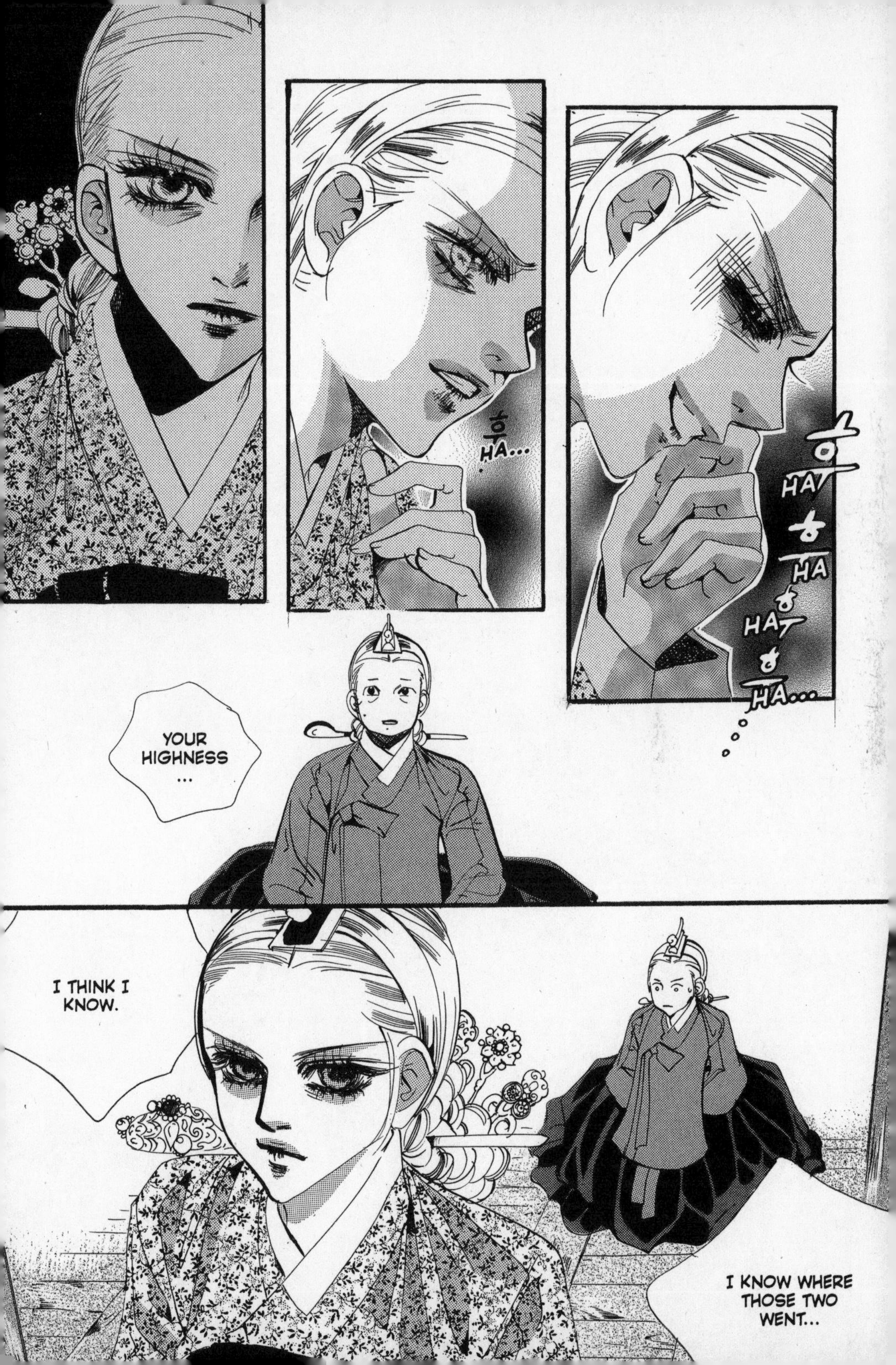
HA...
HA HA HA HA...
YOUR HIGHNESS ...
I THINK I KNOW.
I KNOW WHERE THOSE TWO WENT...

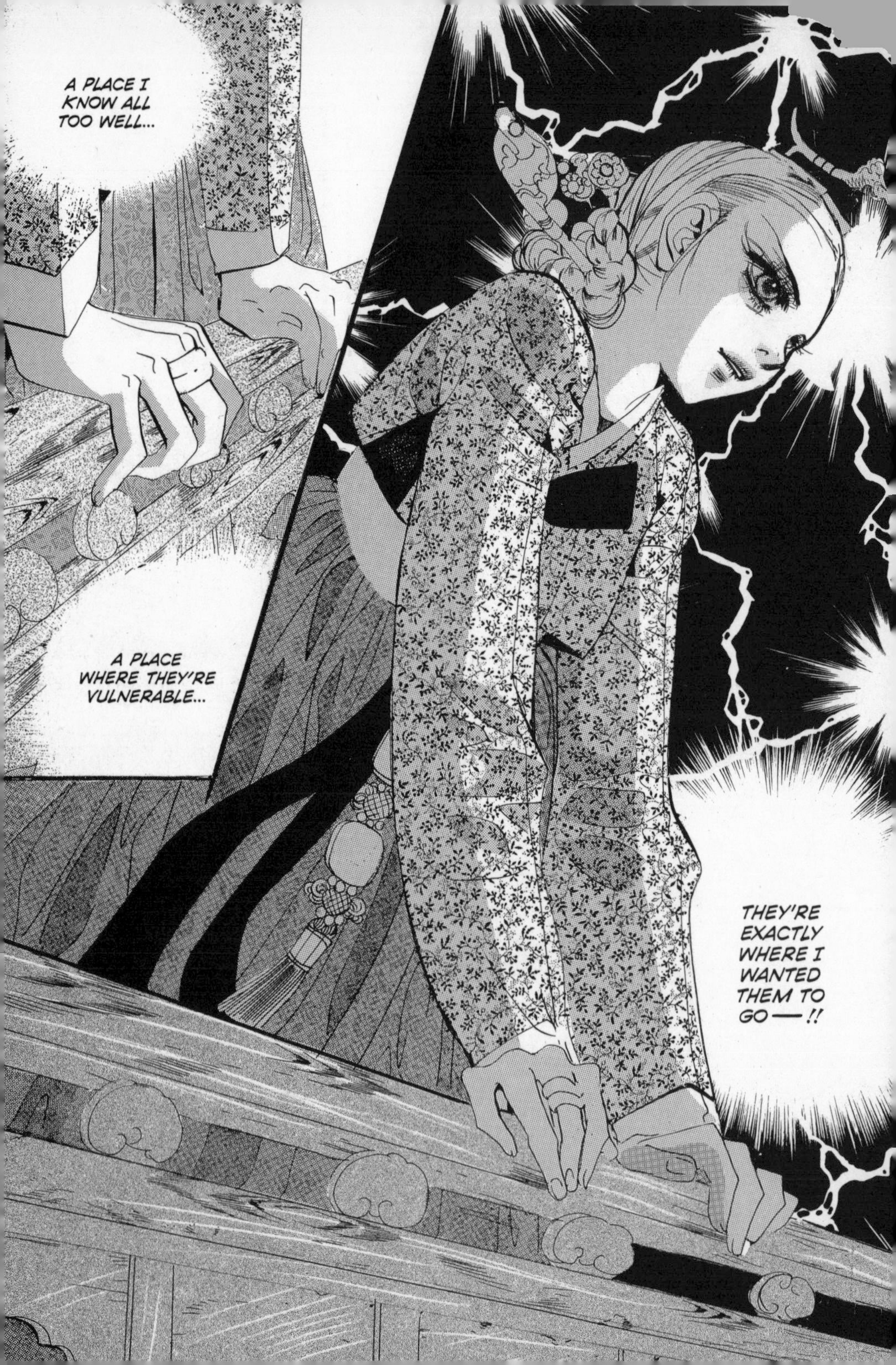
A PLACE I KNOW ALL TOO WELL...
A PLACE WHERE THEY'RE VULNERABLE...
THEY'RE EXACTLY WHERE I WANTED THEM TO GO—!!

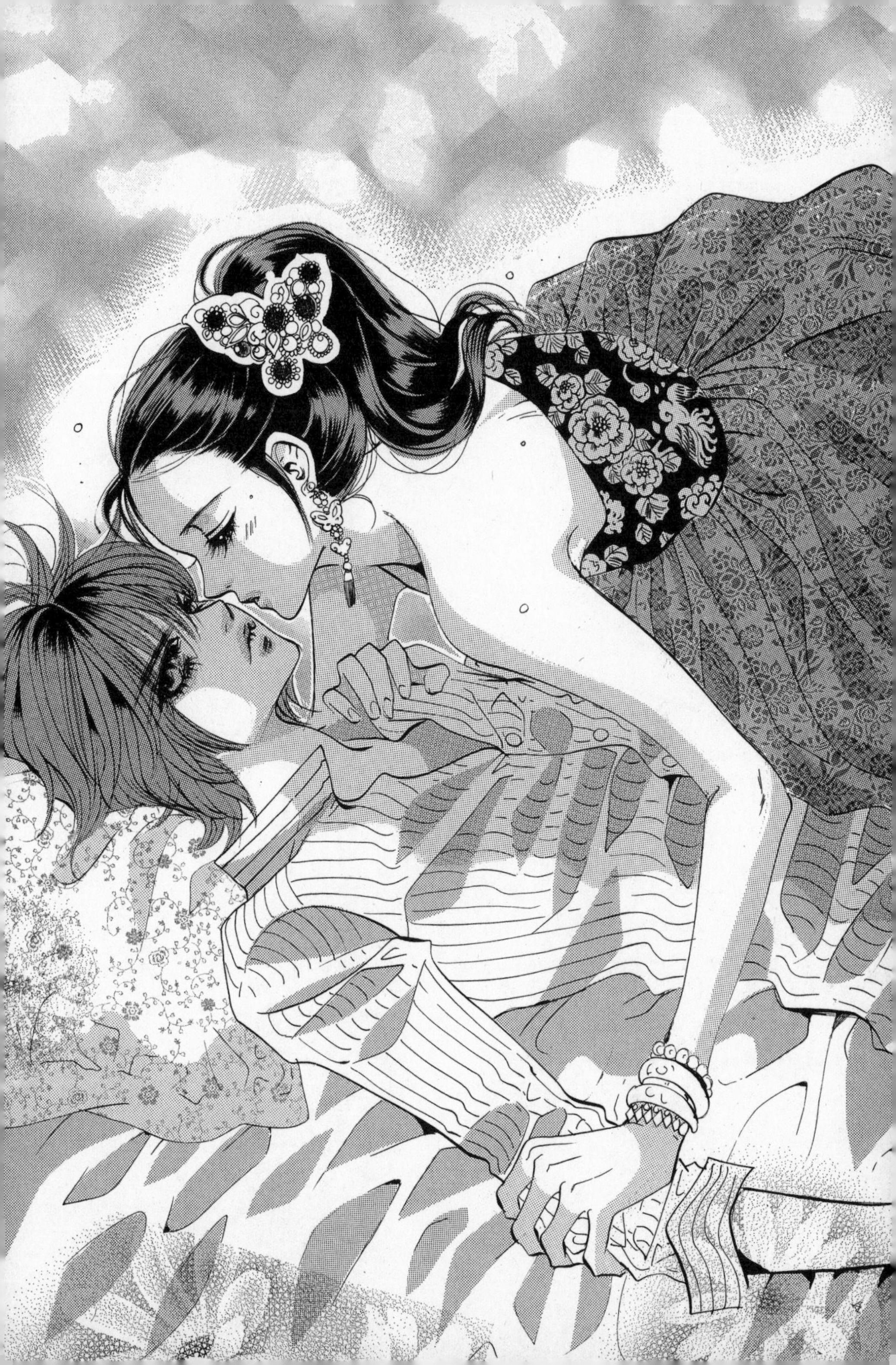

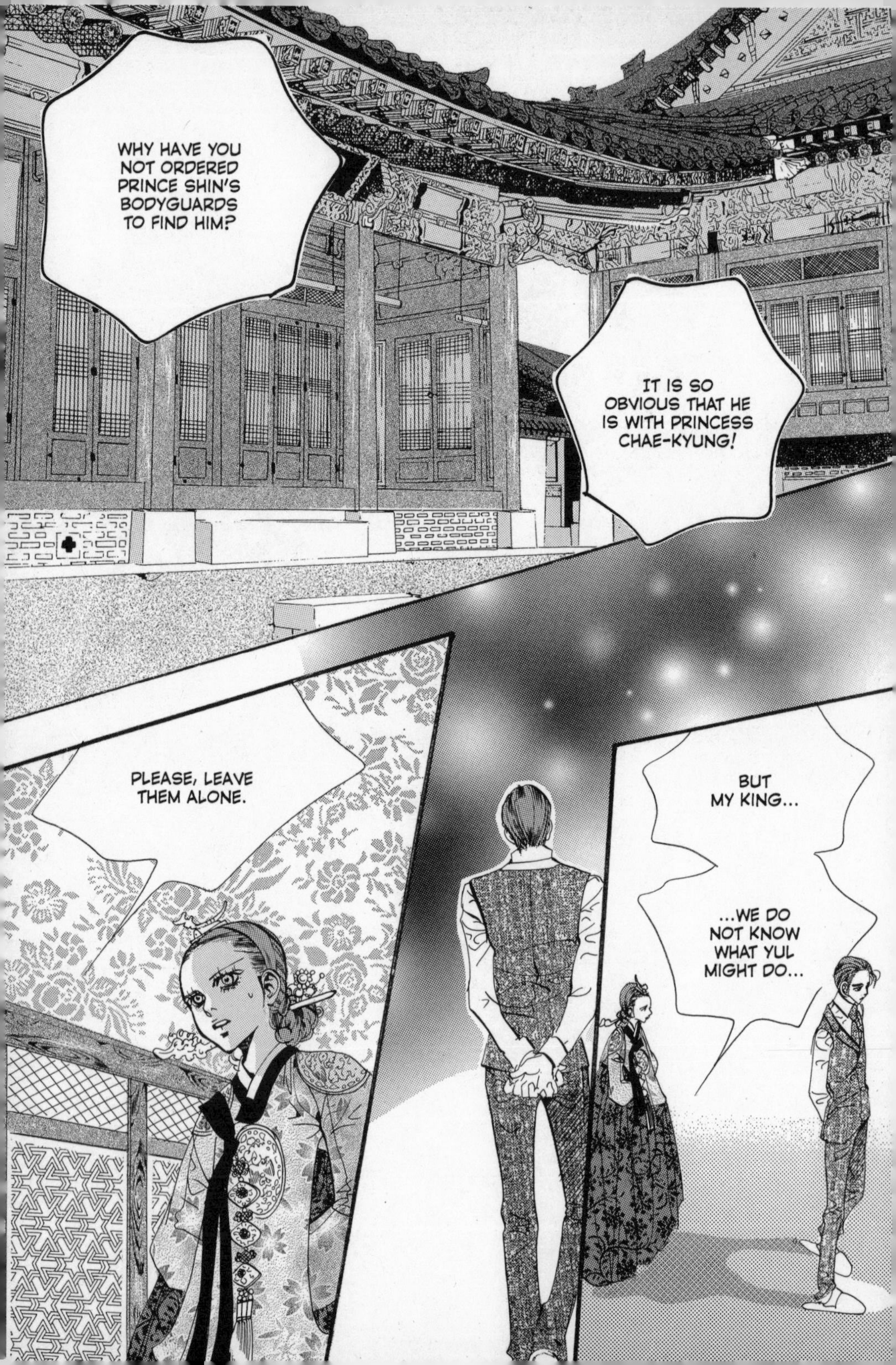
WHY HAVE YOU NOT ORDERED PRINCE SHIN'S BODYGUARDS TO FIND HIM?
IT IS SO OBVIOUS THAT HE IS WITH PRINCESS CHAE-KYUNG!
PLEASE, LEAVE THEM ALONE.
BUT MY KING...
...WE DO NOT KNOW WHAT YUL MIGHT DO...

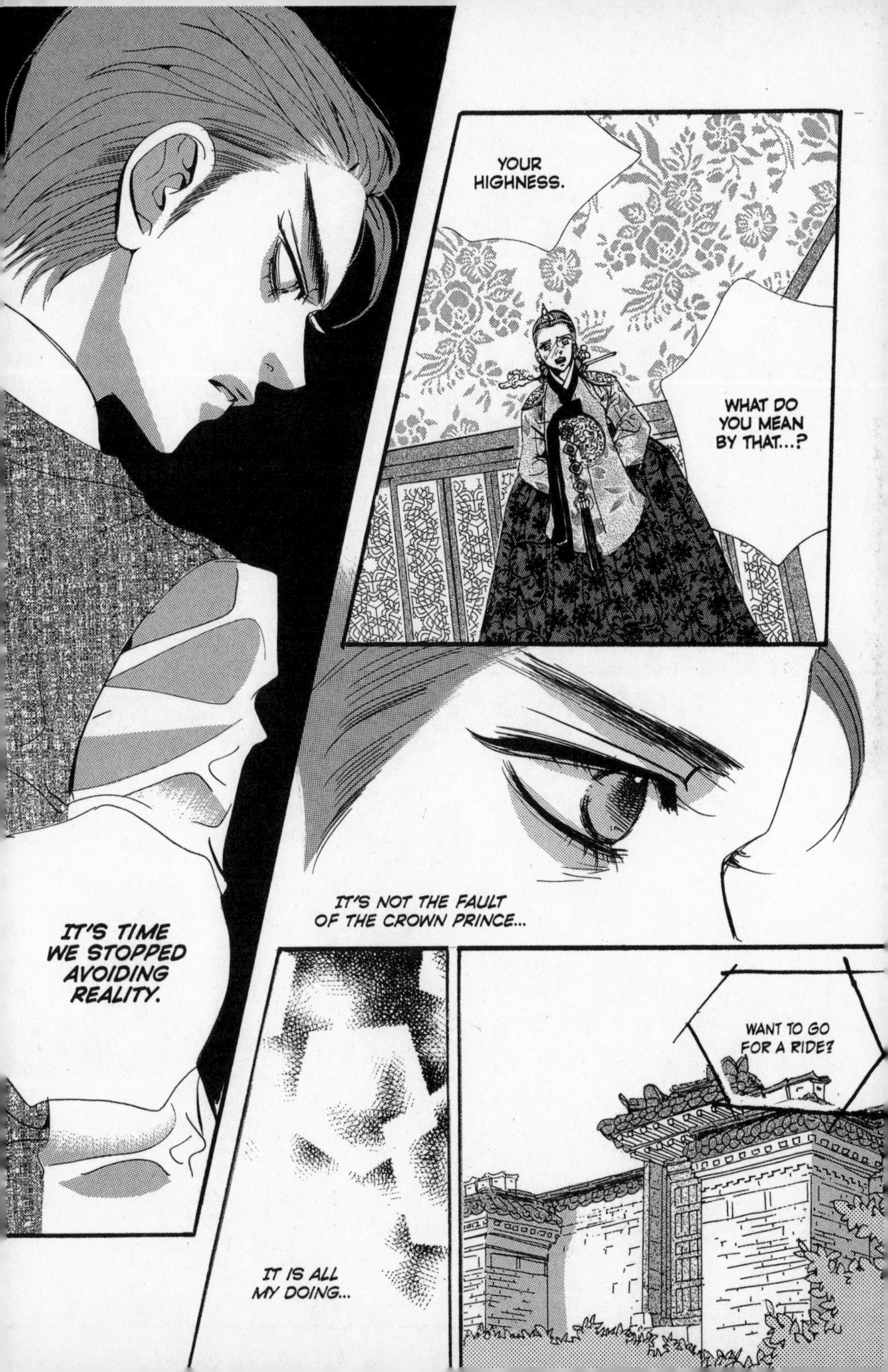
IT'S TIME WE STOPPED AVOIDING REALITY.
YOUR HIGHNESS.
WHAT DO YOU MEAN BY THAT...?
IT'S NOT THE FAULT OF THE CROWN PRINCE...
IT IS ALL MY DOING...
WANT TO GO FOR A RIDE?

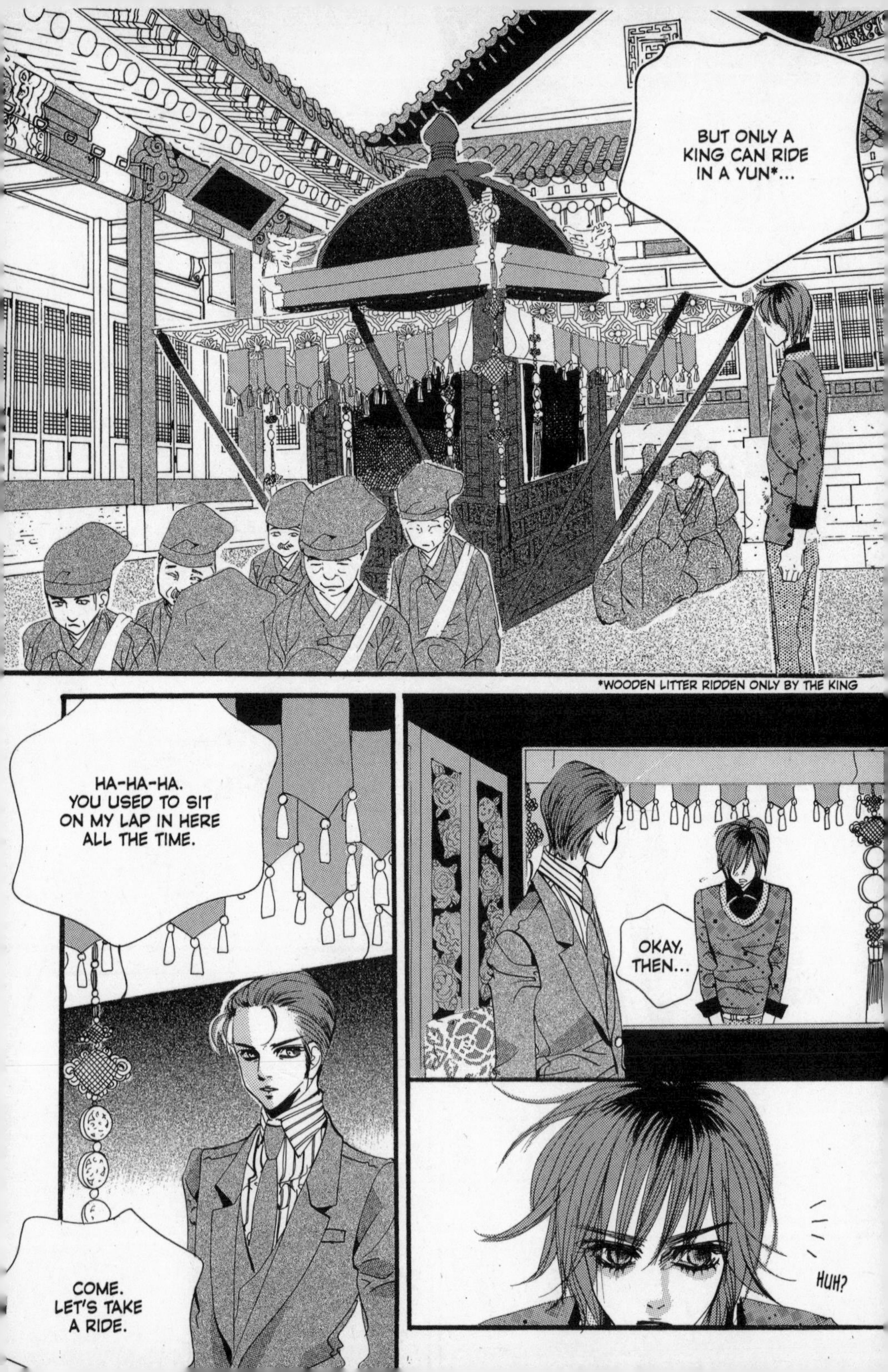
BUT ONLY A KING CAN RIDE IN A YUN*...
*WOODEN LITTER RIDDEN ONLY BY THE KING
HA-HA-HA. YOU USED TO SIT ON MY LAP IN HERE ALL THE TIME.
OKAY, THEN...
COME. LET'S TAKE A RIDE.
HUH?

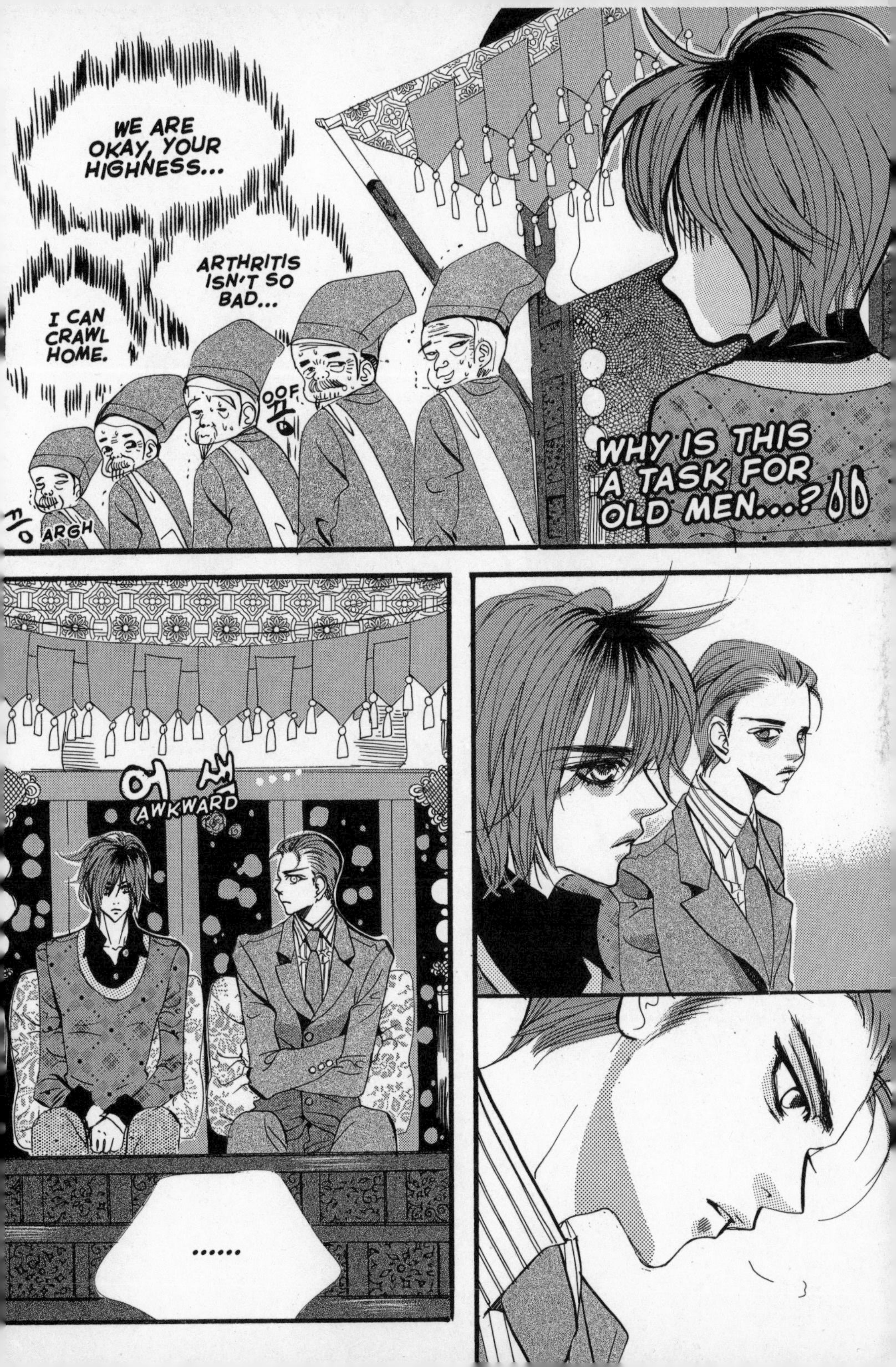
WE ARE OKAY, YOUR HIGHNESS...
ARTHRITIS ISN'T SO BAD...
I CAN CRAWL HOME.
OOF
ARGH
WHY IS THIS A TASK FOR OLD MEN...?
어색
AWKWARD
......

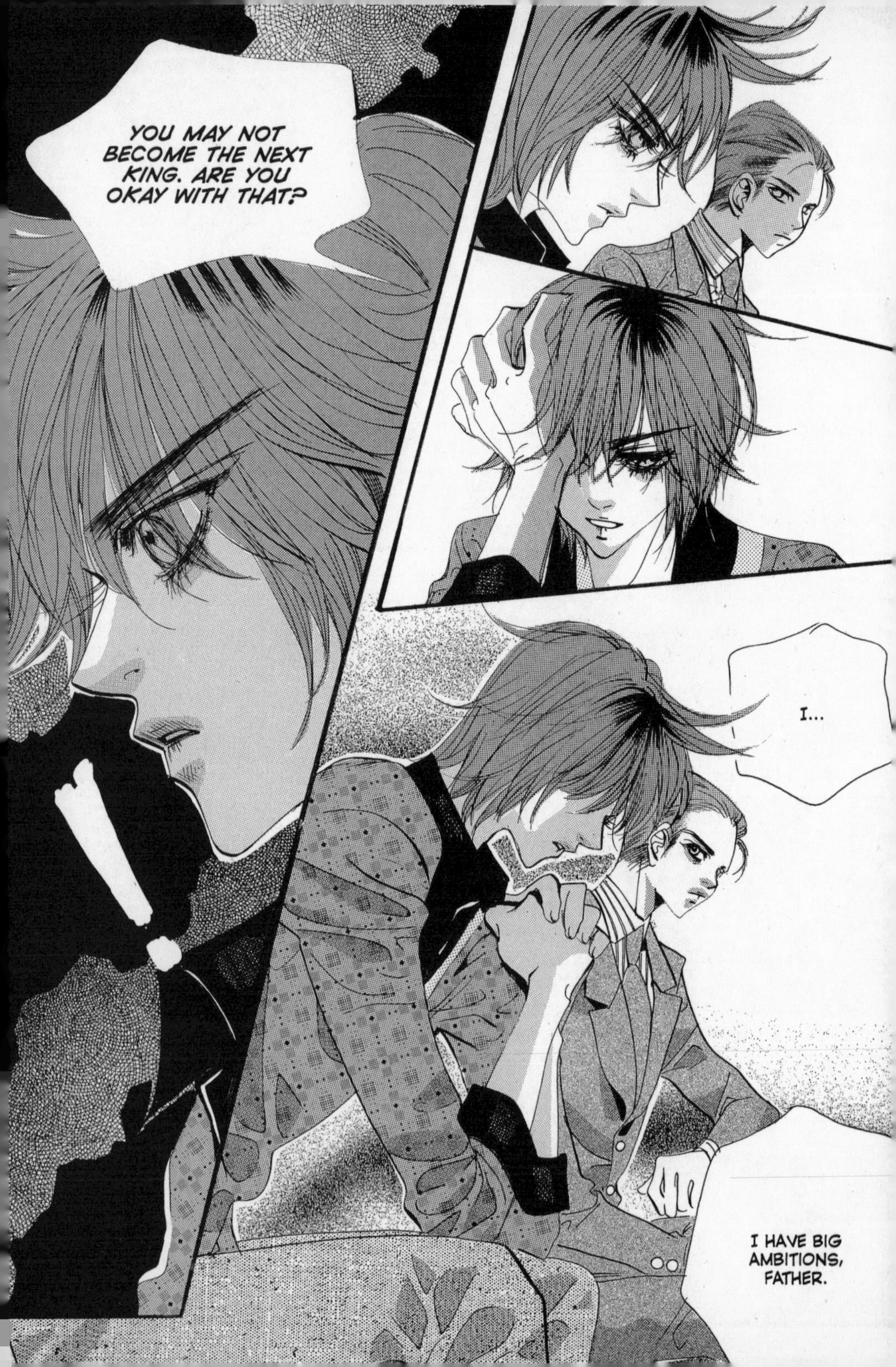
YOU MAY NOT BECOME THE NEXT KING. ARE YOU OKAY WITH THAT?
I...
I HAVE BIG AMBITIONS, FATHER.

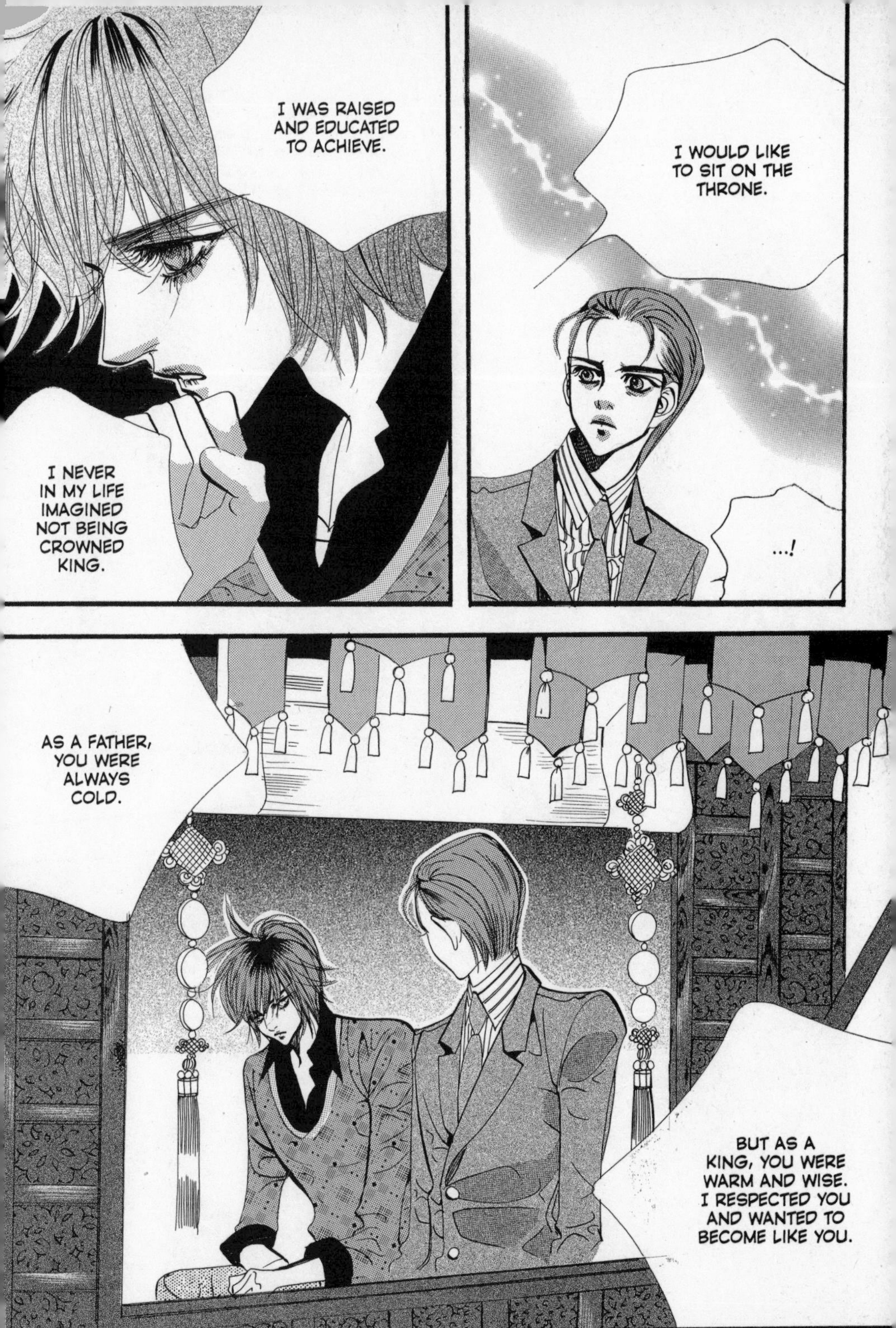
I WAS RAISED AND EDUCATED TO ACHIEVE.
I NEVER IN MY LIFE IMAGINED NOT BEING CROWNED KING.
I WOULD LIKE TO SIT ON THE THRONE.
...!
AS A FATHER, YOU WERE ALWAYS COLD.
BUT AS A KING, YOU WERE WARM AND WISE. I RESPECTED YOU AND WANTED TO BECOME LIKE YOU.

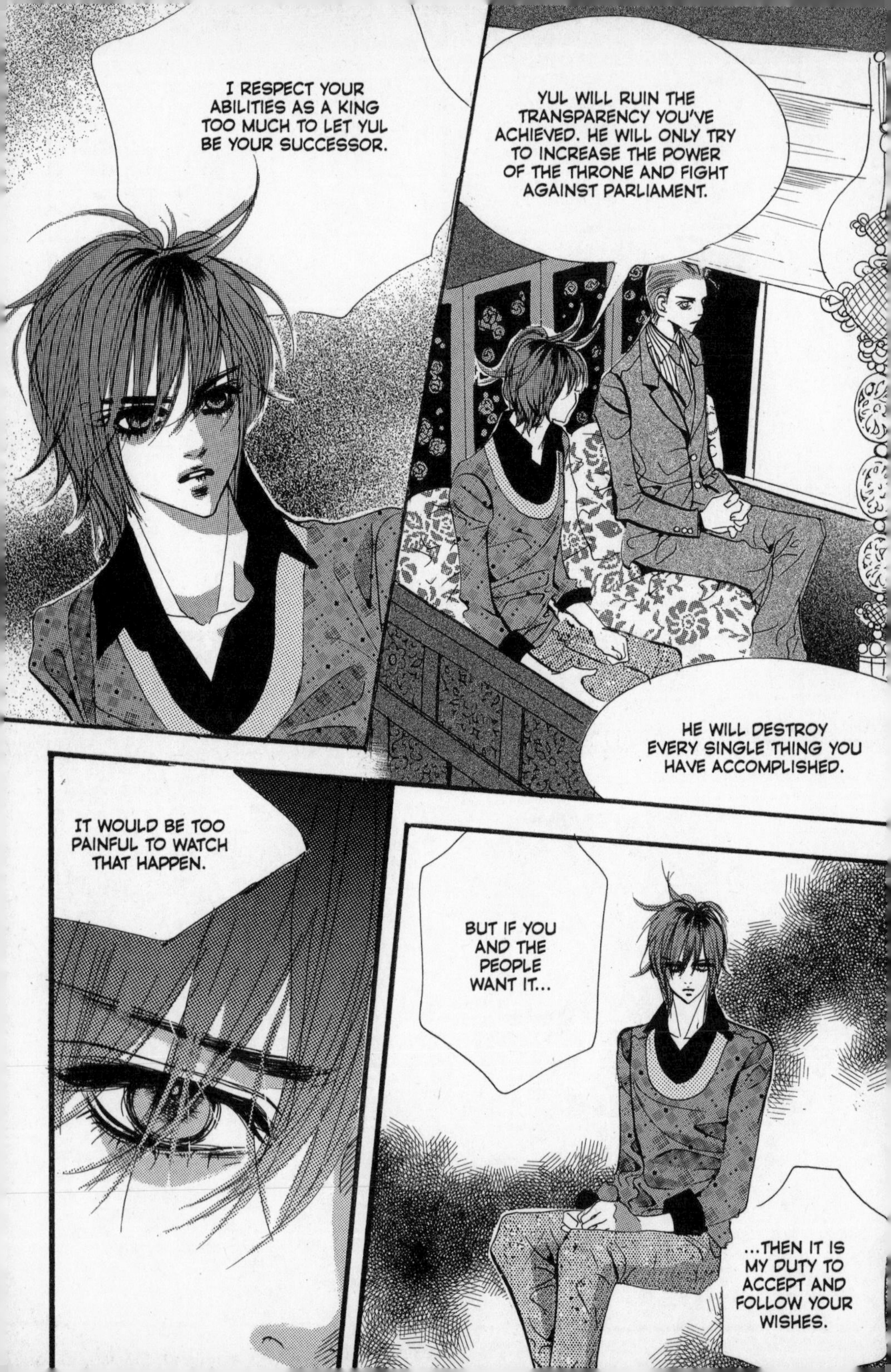

I RESPECT YOUR ABILITIES AS A KING TOO MUCH TO LET YUL BE YOUR SUCCESSOR.
YUL WILL RUIN THE TRANSPARENCY YOU'VE ACHIEVED. HE WILL ONLY TRY TO INCREASE THE POWER OF THE THRONE AND FIGHT AGAINST PARLIAMENT.
HE WILL DESTROY EVERY SINGLE THING YOU HAVE ACCOMPLISHED.
IT WOULD BE TOO PAINFUL TO WATCH THAT HAPPEN.
BUT IF YOU AND THE PEOPLE WANT IT...
...THEN IT IS MY DUTY TO ACCEPT AND FOLLOW YOUR WISHES.

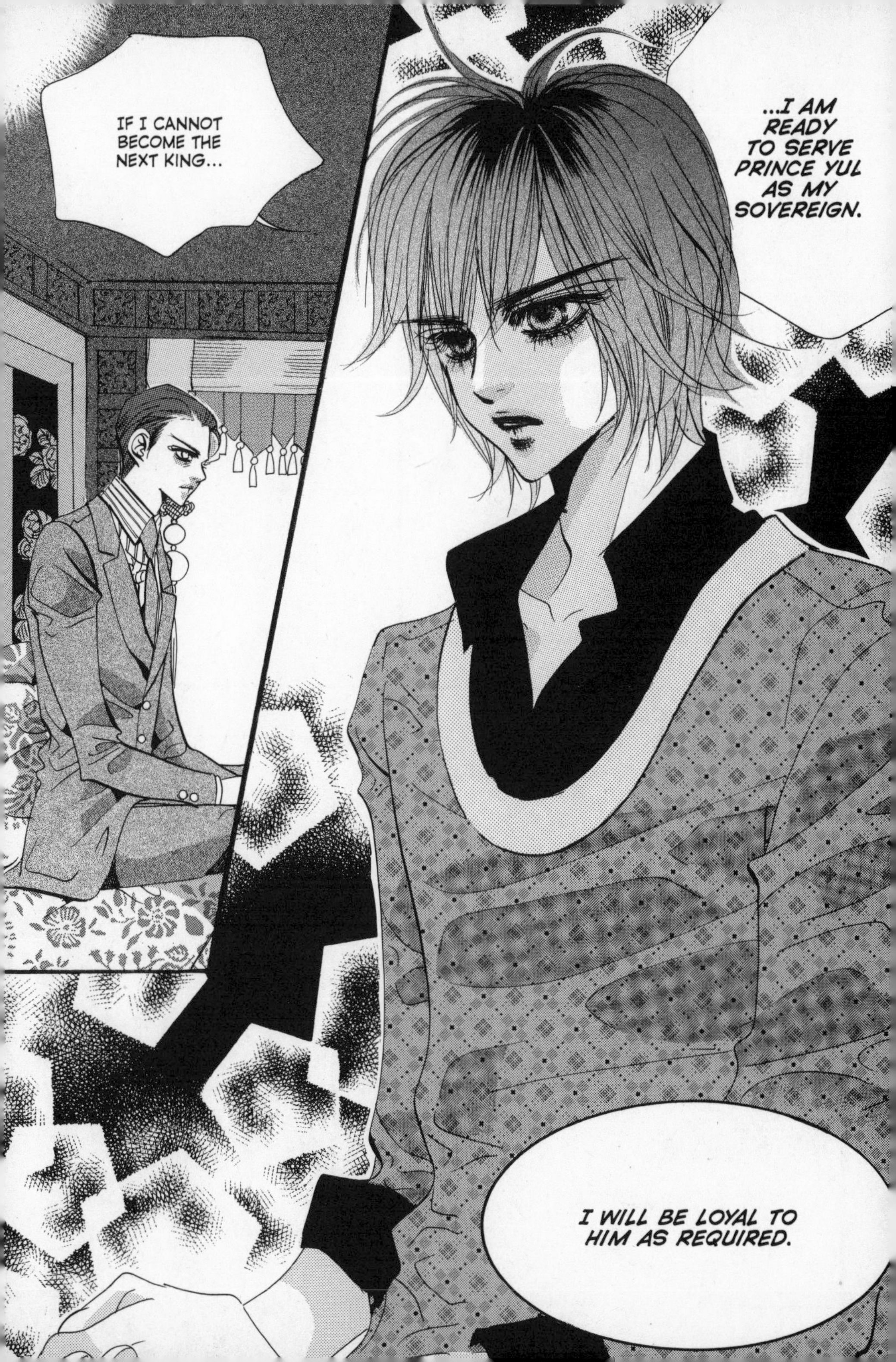
IF I CANNOT BECOME THE NEXT KING...
...I AM READY TO SERVE PRINCE YUL AS MY SOVEREIGN.
I WILL BE LOYAL TO HIM AS REQUIRED.

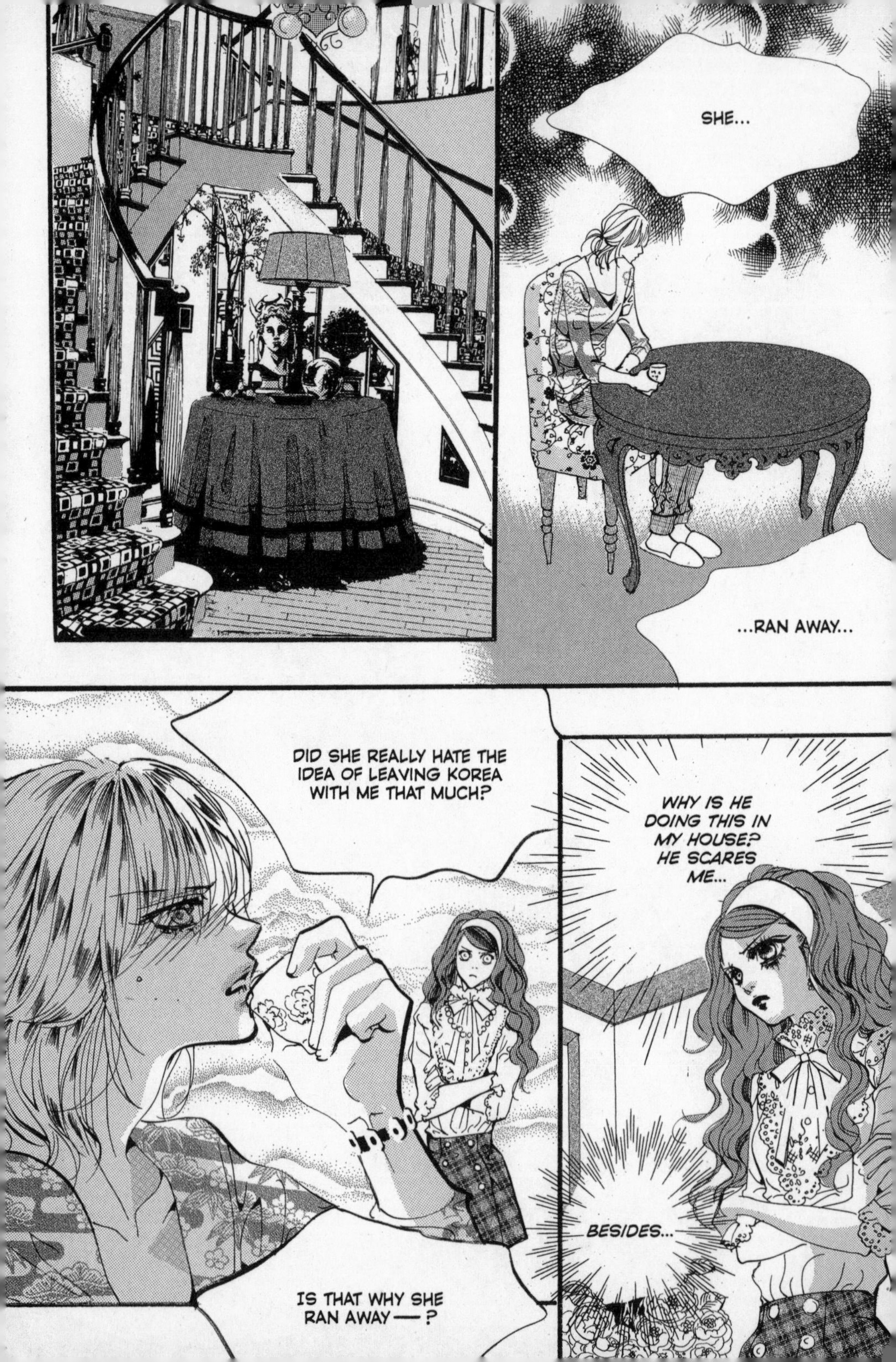
SHE...
...RAN AWAY...
DID SHE REALLY HATE THE IDEA OF LEAVING KOREA WITH ME THAT MUCH?
IS THAT WHY SHE RAN AWAY—?
WHY IS HE DOING THIS IN MY HOUSE? HE SCARES ME...
BESIDES...

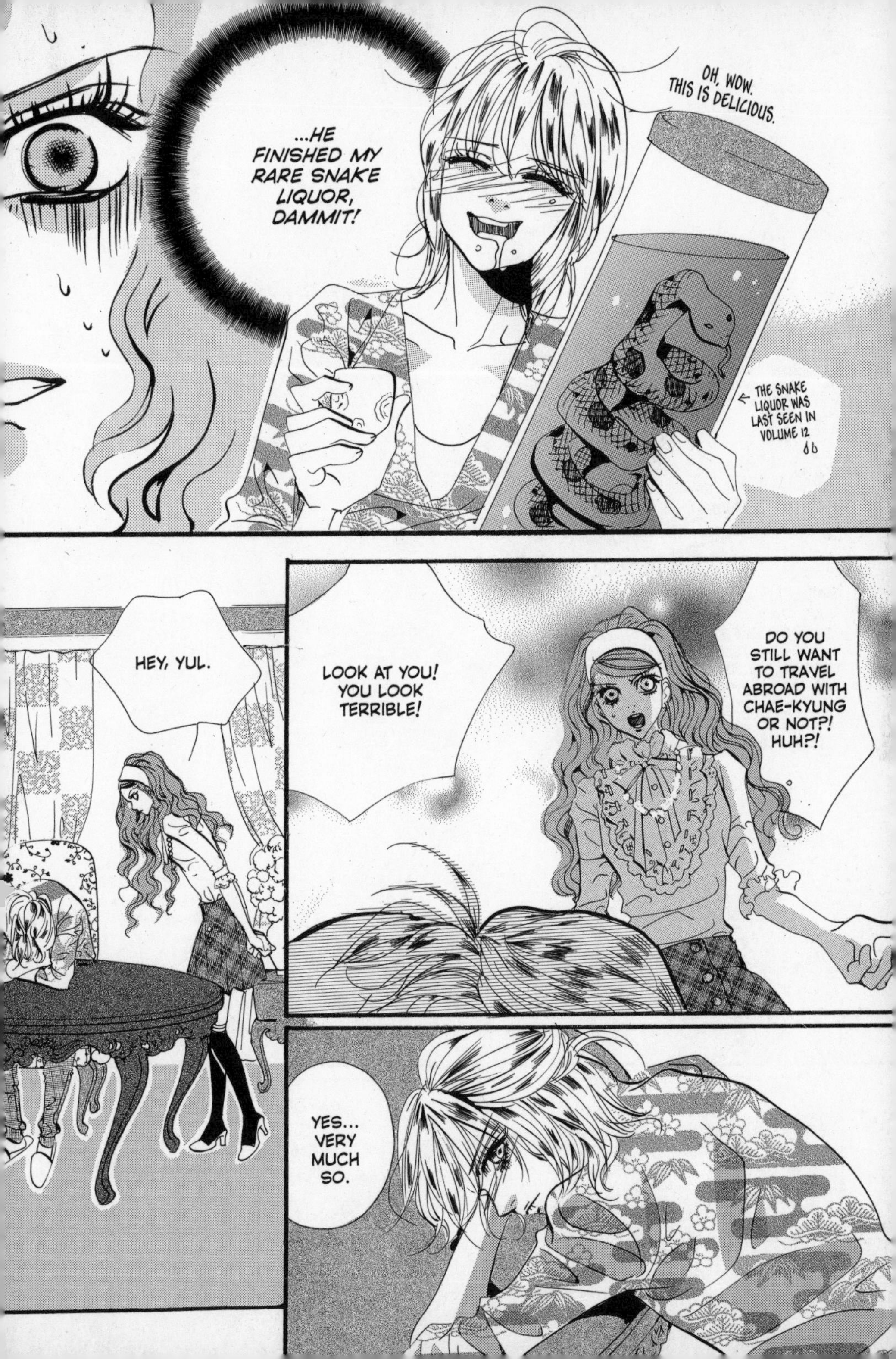
...HE FINISHED MY RARE SNAKE LIQUOR, DAMMIT!
OH, WOW. THIS IS DELICIOUS.
THE SNAKE LIQUOR WAS LAST SEEN IN VOLUME 12
HEY, YUL.
LOOK AT YOU! YOU LOOK TERRIBLE!
DO YOU STILL WANT TO TRAVEL ABROAD WITH CHAE-KYUNG OR NOT?! HUH?!
YES... VERY MUCH SO.

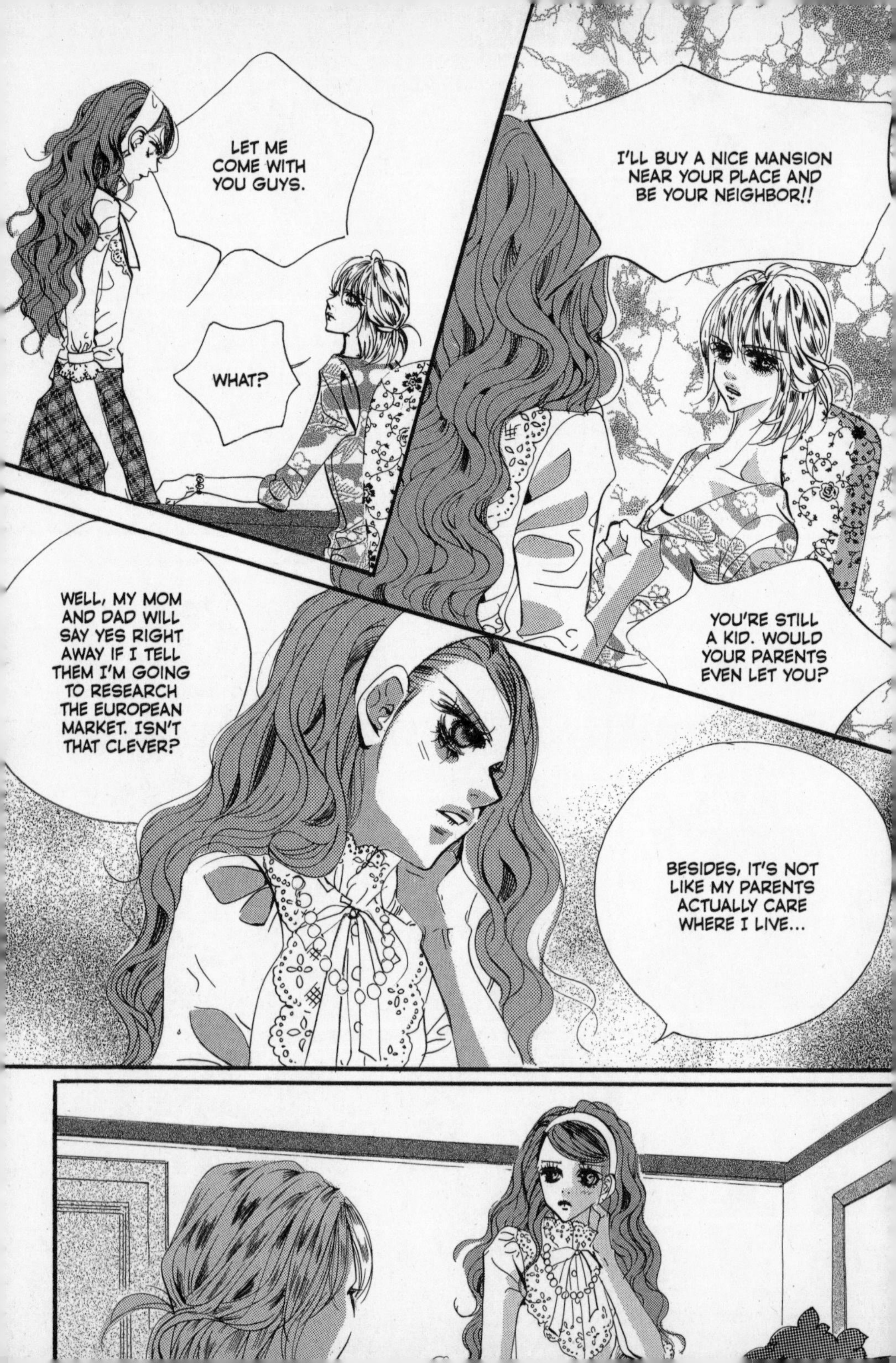
LET ME COME WITH YOU GUYS.
WHAT?
I'LL BUY A NICE MANSION NEAR YOUR PLACE AND BE YOUR NEIGHBOR!!
YOU'RE STILL A KID. WOULD YOUR PARENTS EVEN LET YOU?
WELL, MY MOM AND DAD WILL SAY YES RIGHT AWAY IF I TELL THEM I'M GOING TO RESEARCH THE EUROPEAN MARKET. ISN'T THAT CLEVER?
BESIDES, IT'S NOT LIKE MY PARENTS ACTUALLY CARE WHERE I LIVE...

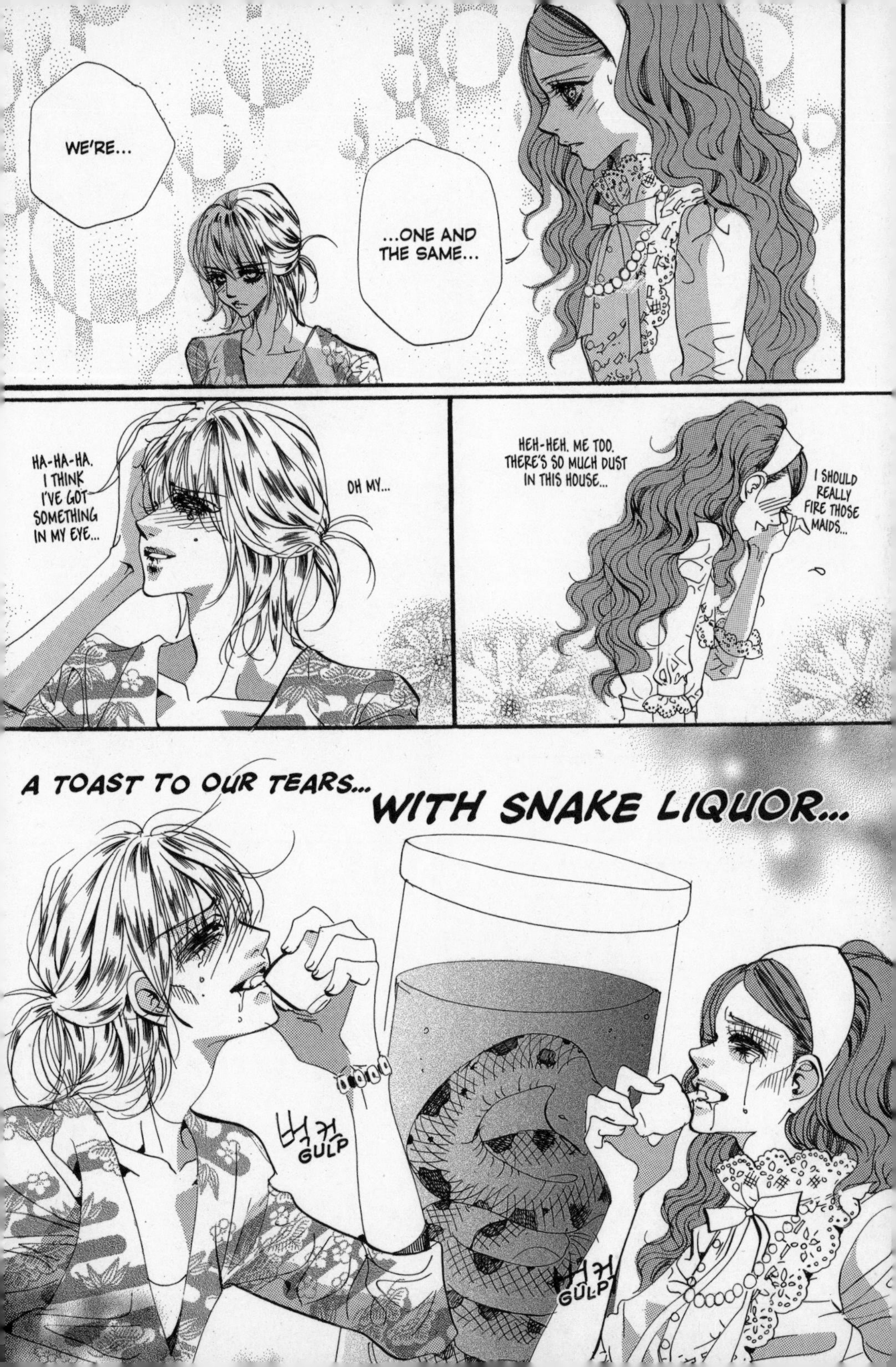
WE'RE...
...ONE AND THE SAME...
HA-HA-HA. I THINK I'VE GOT SOMETHING IN MY EYE...
OH MY...
HEH-HEH. ME TOO. THERE'S SO MUCH DUST IN THIS HOUSE...
I SHOULD REALLY FIRE THOSE MAIDS...
A TOAST TO OUR TEARS... WITH SNAKE LIQUOR...
벌컥
GULP
벌컥
GULP

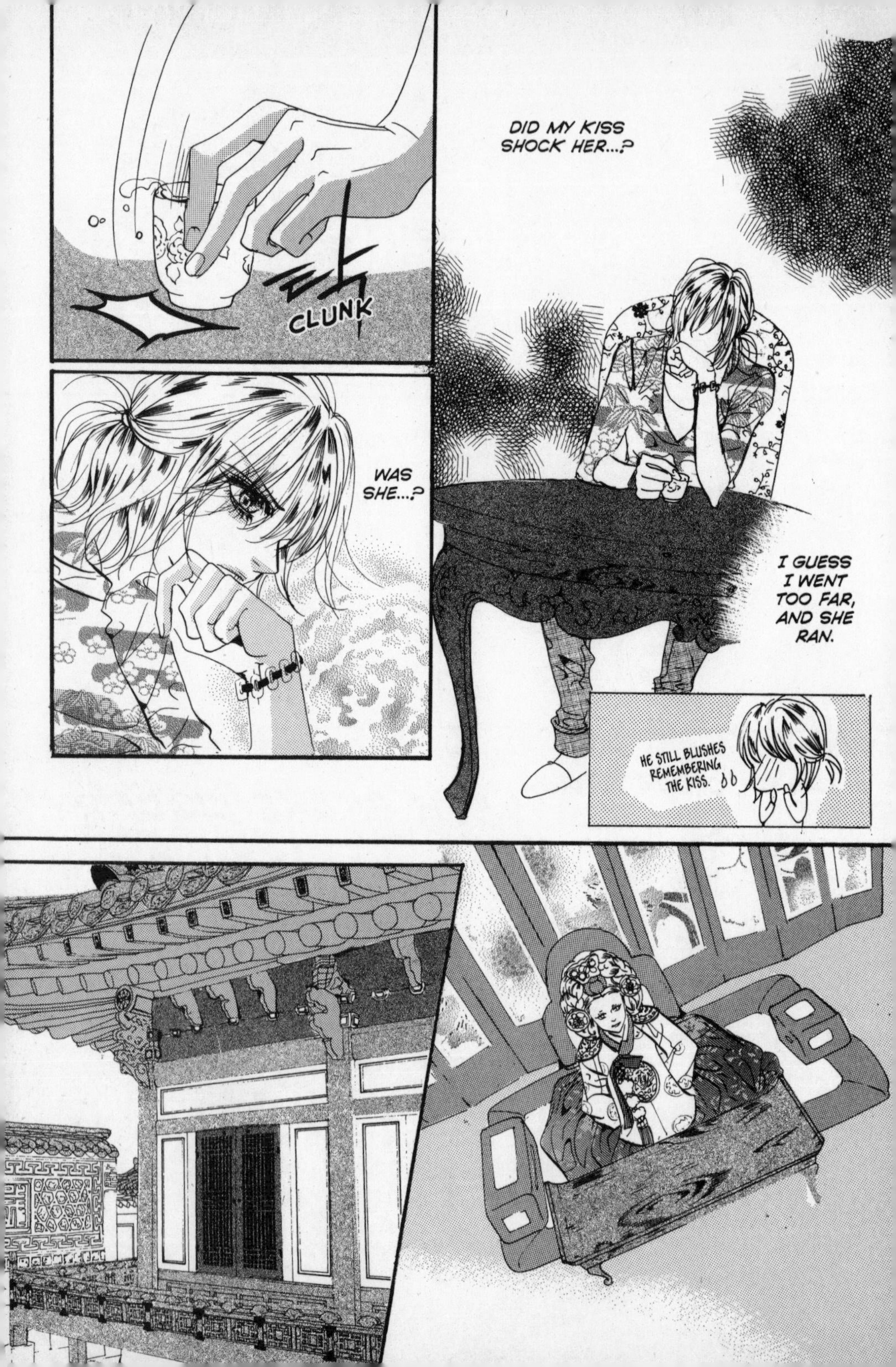
CLUNK
WAS SHE...?
DID MY KISS SHOCK HER...?
I GUESS I WENT TOO FAR, AND SHE RAN.
HE STILL BLUSHES REMEMBERING THE KISS.

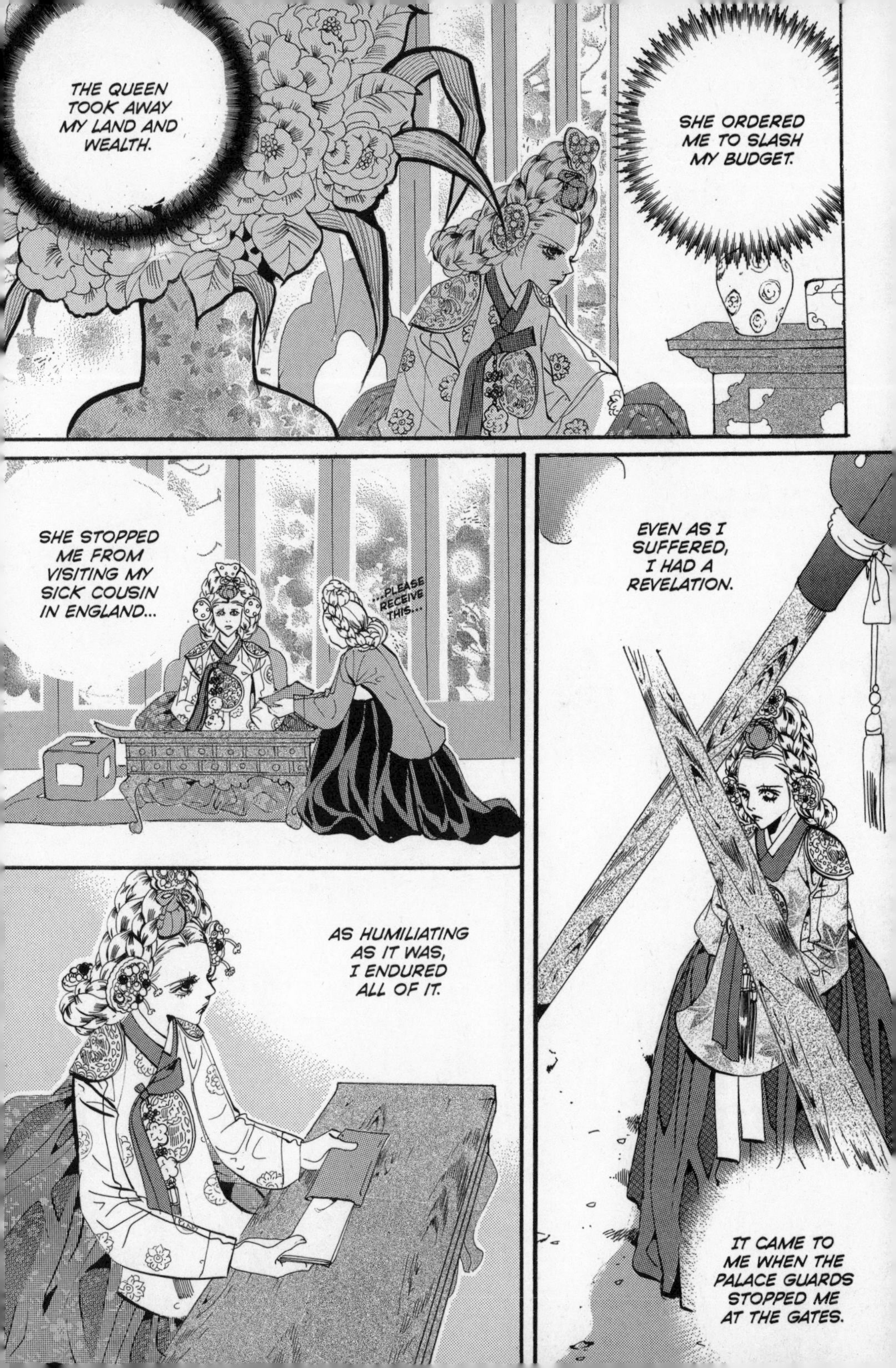
THE QUEEN TOOK AWAY MY LAND AND WEALTH.
SHE ORDERED ME TO SLASH MY BUDGET.
SHE STOPPED ME FROM VISITING MY SICK COUSIN IN ENGLAND...
...PLEASE RECEIVE THIS...
AS HUMILIATING AS IT WAS, I ENDURED ALL OF IT.
EVEN AS I SUFFERED, I HAD A REVELATION.
IT CAME TO ME WHEN THE PALACE GUARDS STOPPED ME AT THE GATES.

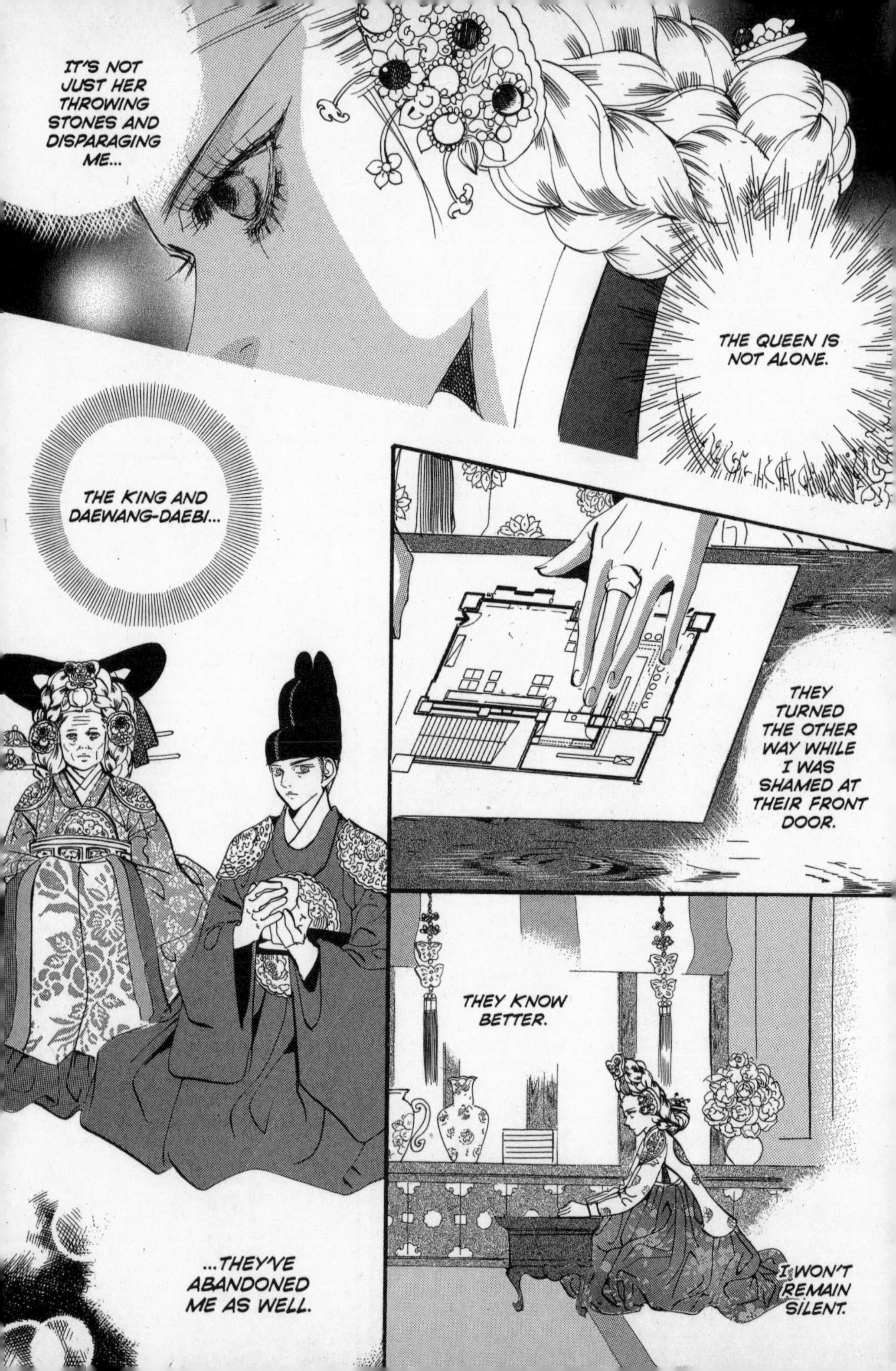
IT'S NOT JUST HER THROWING STONES AND DISPARAGING ME...
THE QUEEN IS NOT ALONE.
THE KING AND DAEWANG-DAEBI...
...THEY'VE ABANDONED ME AS WELL.
THEY TURNED THE OTHER WAY WHILE I WAS SHAMED AT THEIR FRONT DOOR.
THEY KNOW BETTER.
I WON'T REMAIN SILENT.

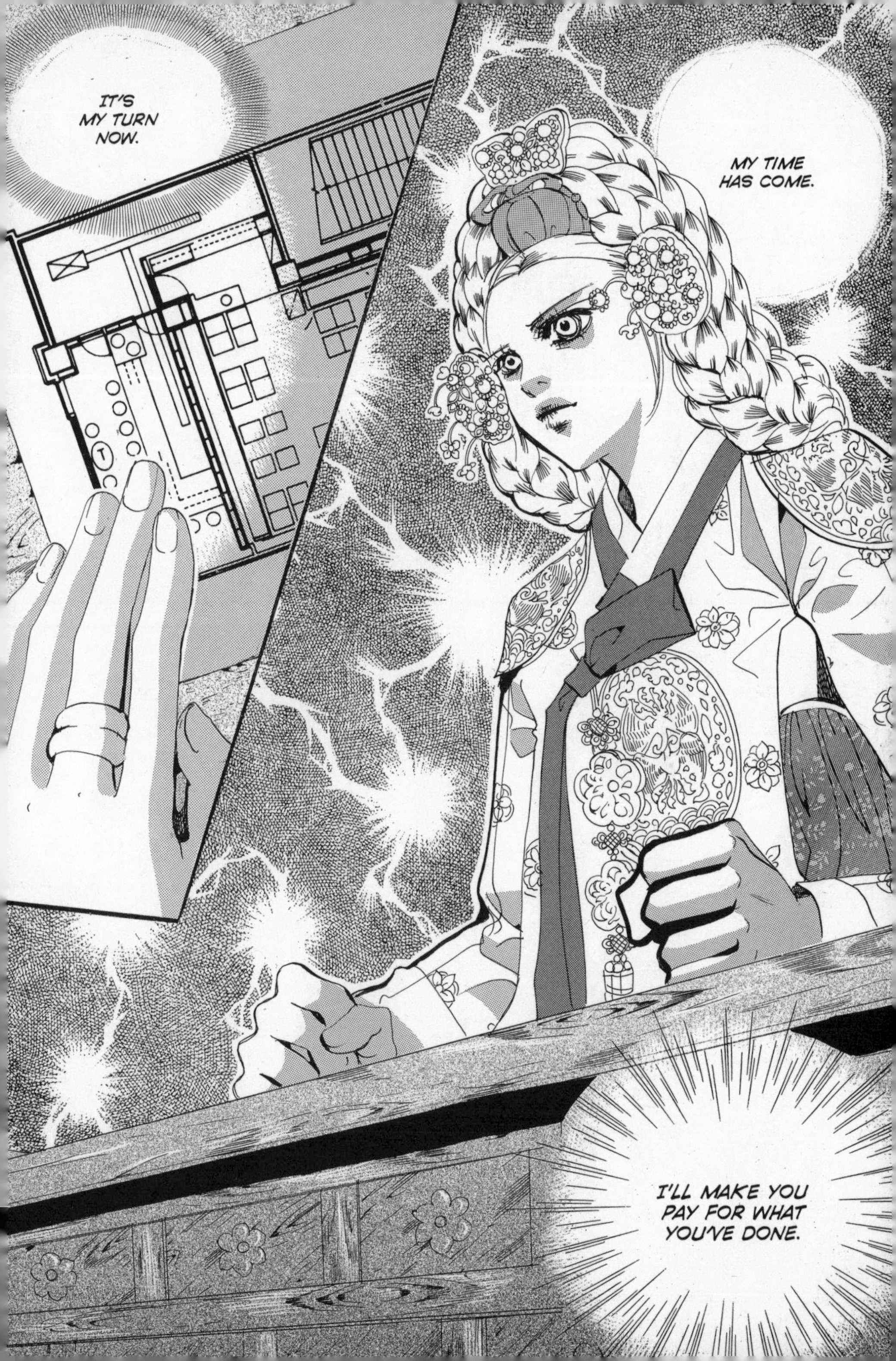
IT'S MY TURN NOW.
MY TIME HAS COME.
I'LL MAKE YOU PAY FOR WHAT YOU'VE DONE.

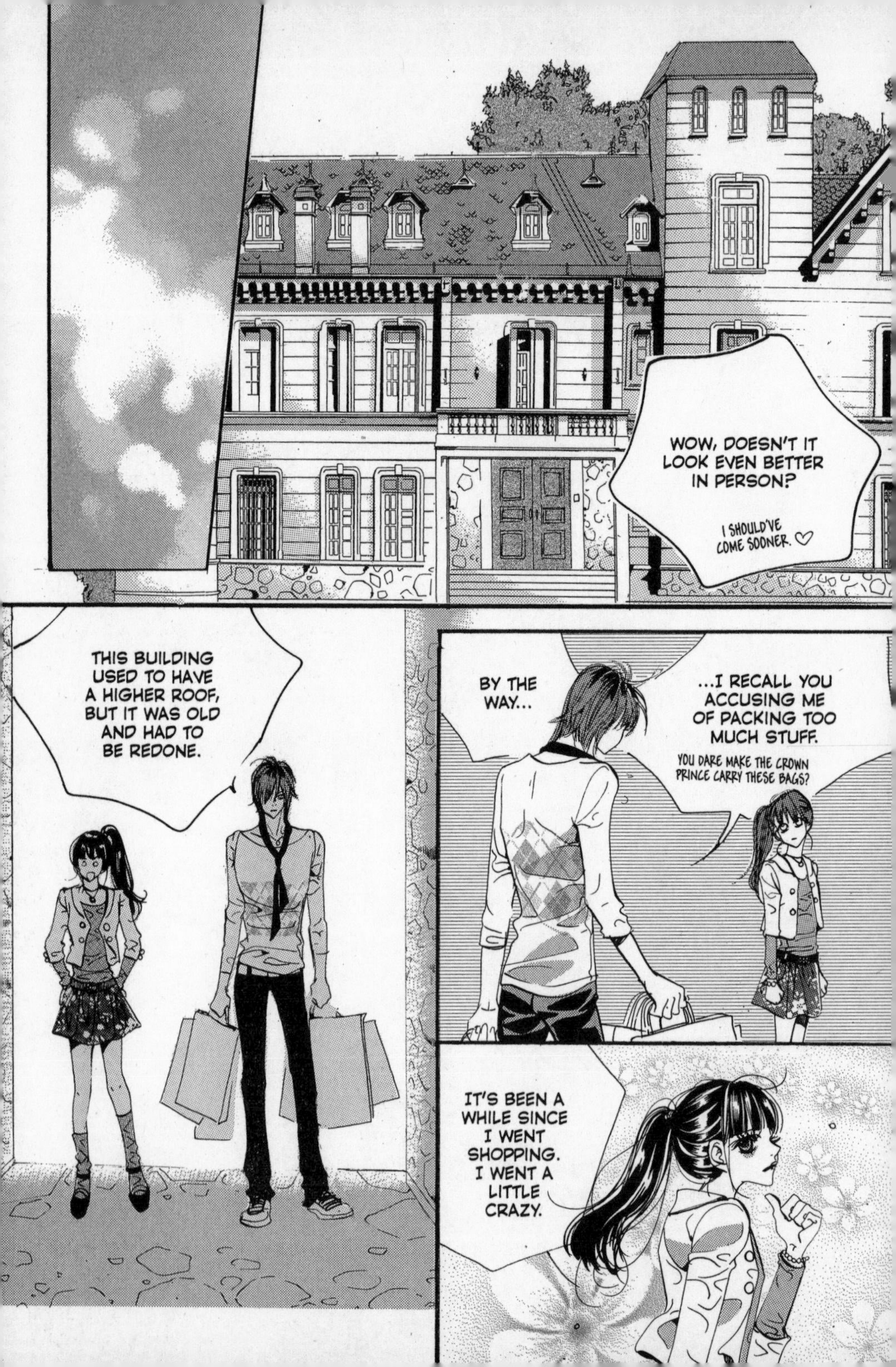
WOW, DOESN'T IT LOOK EVEN BETTER IN PERSON?
I SHOULD'VE COME SOONER. ♡
THIS BUILDING USED TO HAVE A HIGHER ROOF, BUT IT WAS OLD AND HAD TO BE REDONE.
BY THE WAY...
...I RECALL YOU ACCUSING ME OF PACKING TOO MUCH STUFF.
YOU DARE MAKE THE CROWN PRINCE CARRY THESE BAGS?
IT'S BEEN A WHILE SINCE I WENT SHOPPING. I WENT A LITTLE CRAZY.

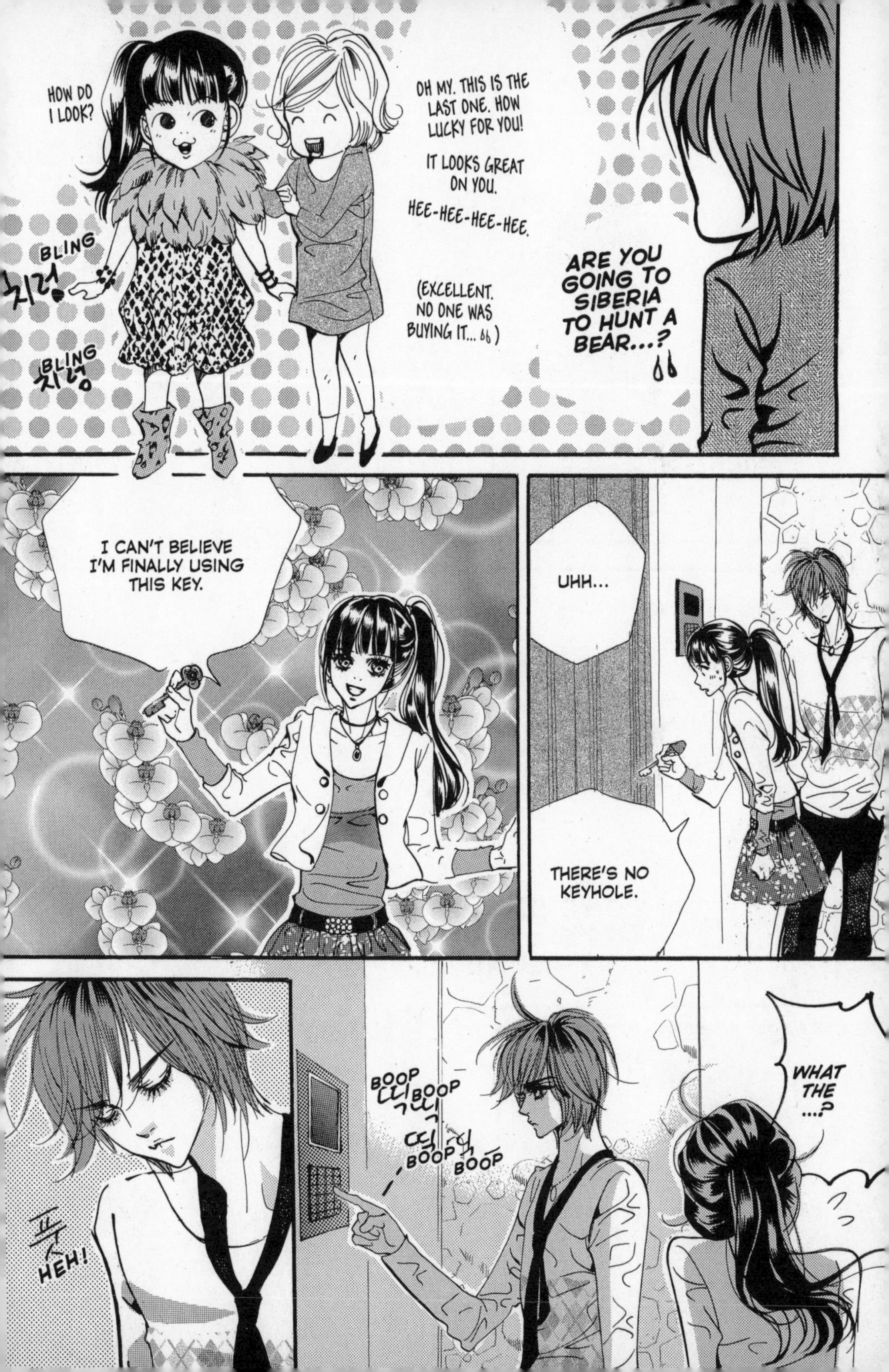
HOW DO I LOOK?
BLING
BLING
OH MY. THIS IS THE LAST ONE. HOW LUCKY FOR YOU!
IT LOOKS GREAT ON YOU.
HEE-HEE-HEE-HEE.
(EXCELLENT. NO ONE WAS BUYING IT...)
ARE YOU GOING TO SIBERIA TO HUNT A BEAR...?
I CAN'T BELIEVE I'M FINALLY USING THIS KEY.
UHH...
THERE'S NO KEYHOLE.
HEH!
BOOP BOOP
BOOP BOOP
WHAT THE ...?

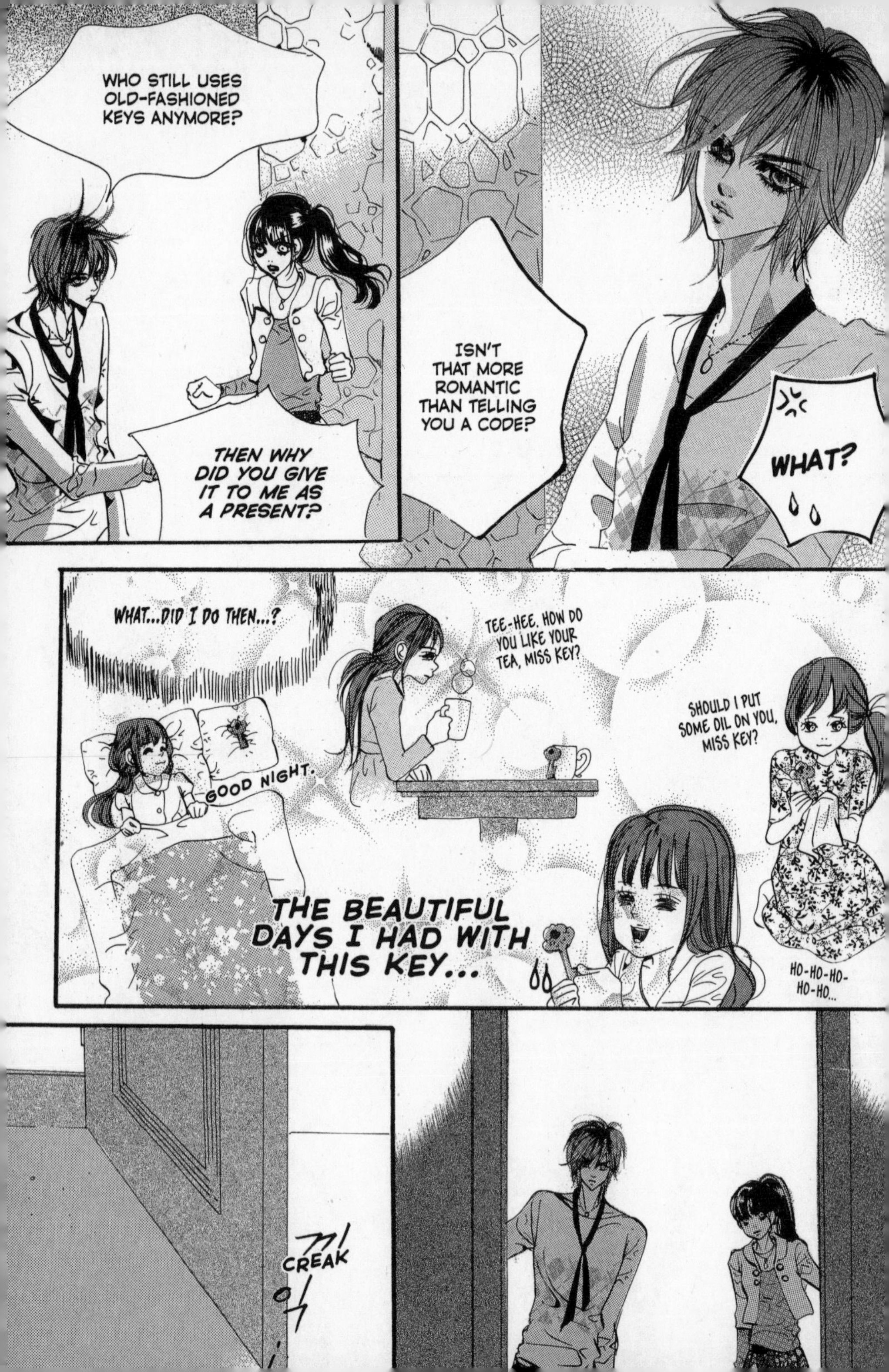
WHO STILL USES OLD-FASHIONED KEYS ANYMORE?
THEN WHY DID YOU GIVE IT TO ME AS A PRESENT?
ISN'T THAT MORE ROMANTIC THAN TELLING YOU A CODE?
WHAT?
WHAT...DID I DO THEN...?
GOOD NIGHT.
TEE-HEE. HOW DO YOU LIKE YOUR TEA, MISS KEY?
SHOULD I PUT SOME OIL ON YOU, MISS KEY?
THE BEAUTIFUL DAYS I HAD WITH THIS KEY...
HO-HO-HO-HO-HO...
끼
CREAK
익

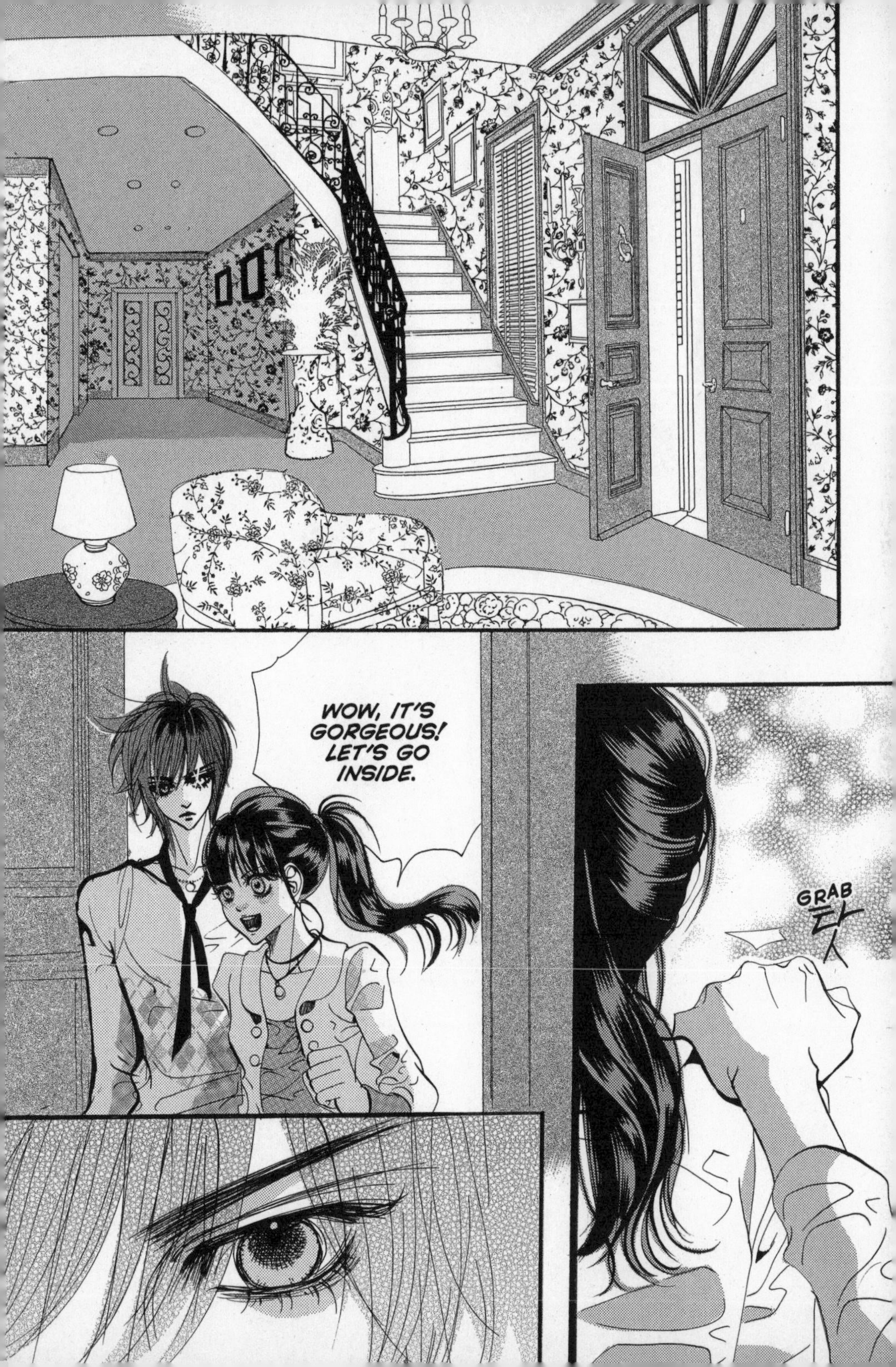
WOW, IT'S GORGEOUS! LET'S GO INSIDE.
GRAB
탁

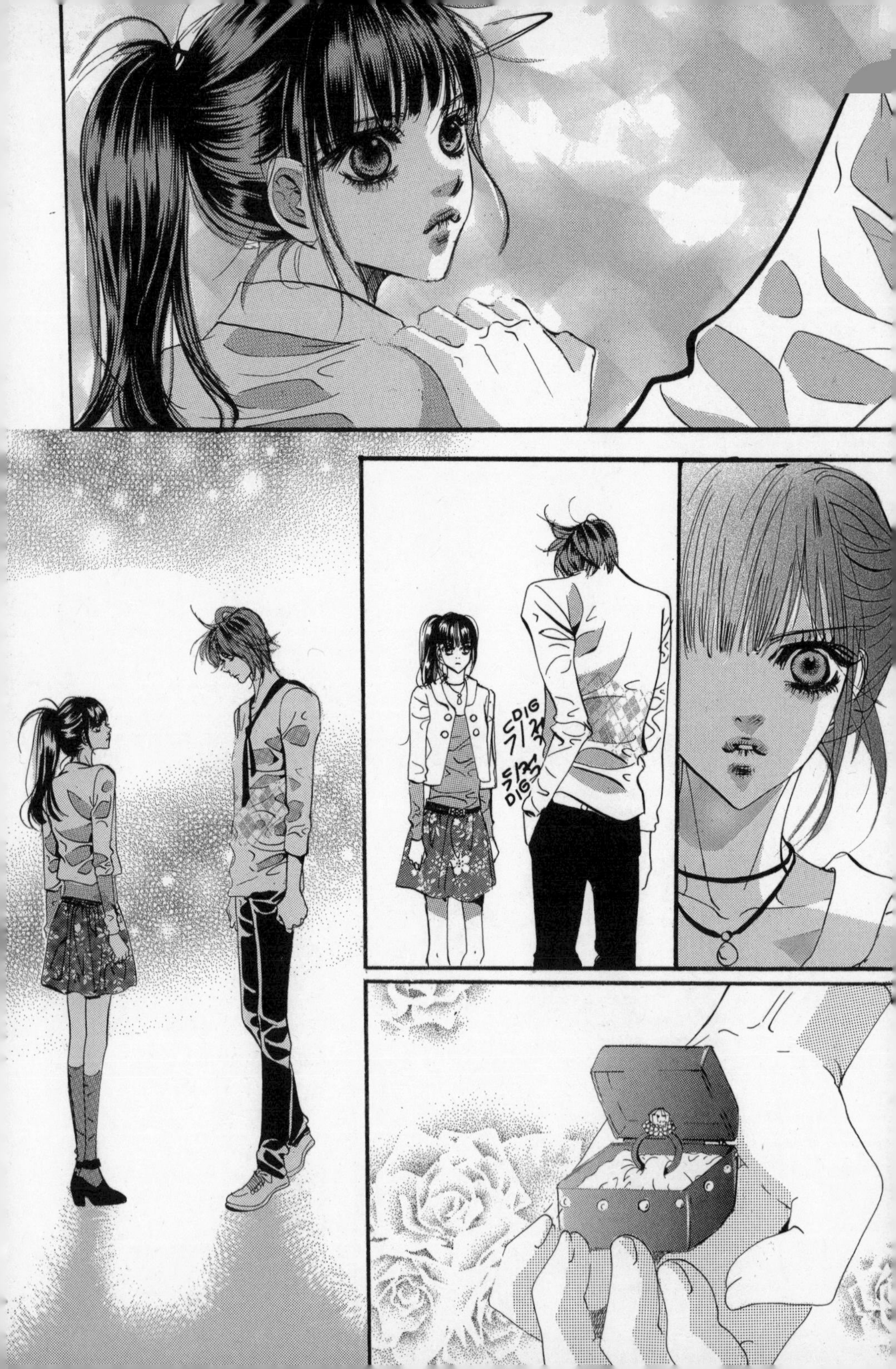
DIG
DIG

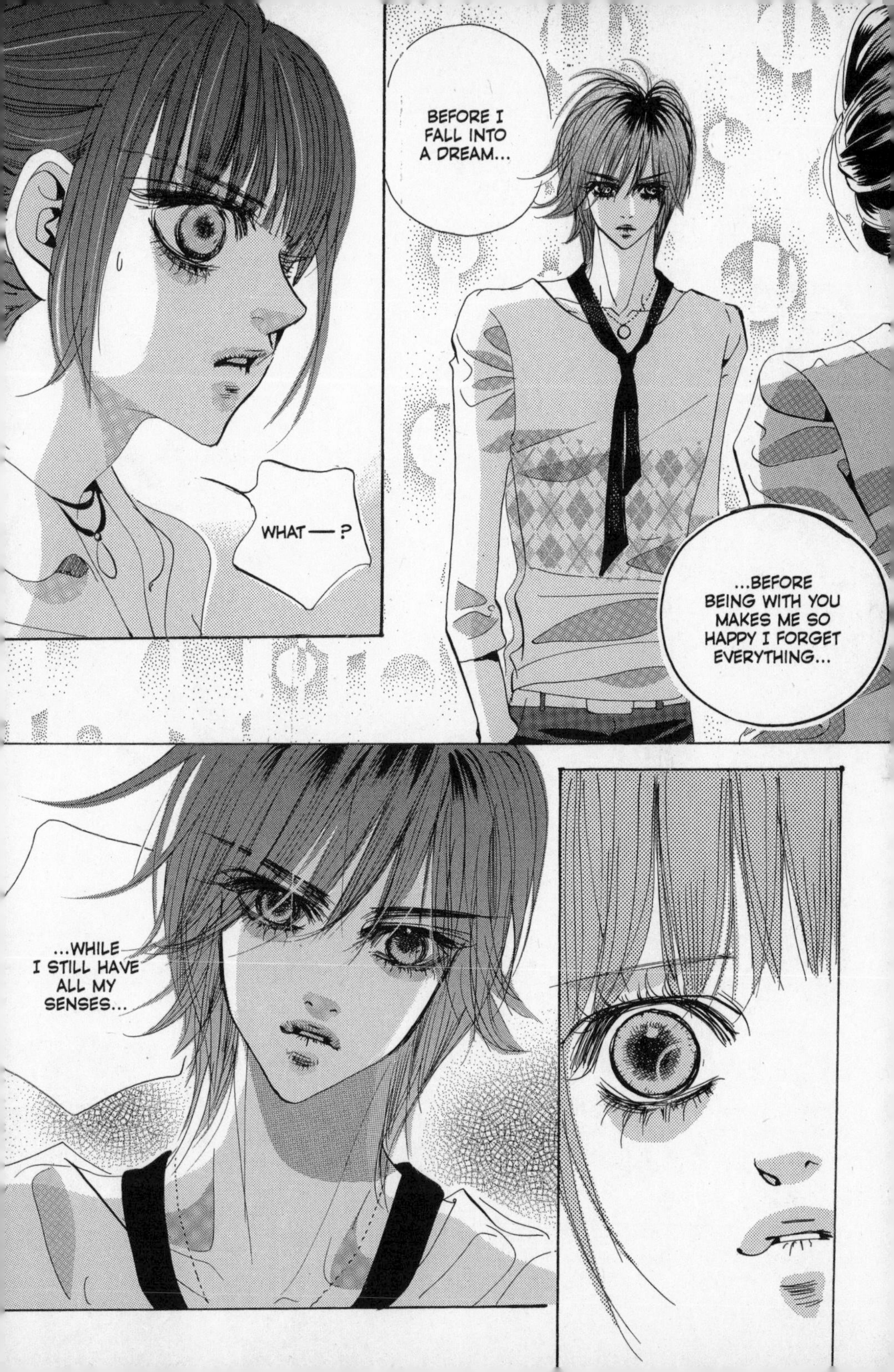
WHAT — ?
BEFORE I FALL INTO A DREAM...
...BEFORE BEING WITH YOU MAKES ME SO HAPPY I FORGET EVERYTHING...
...WHILE I STILL HAVE ALL MY SENSES...

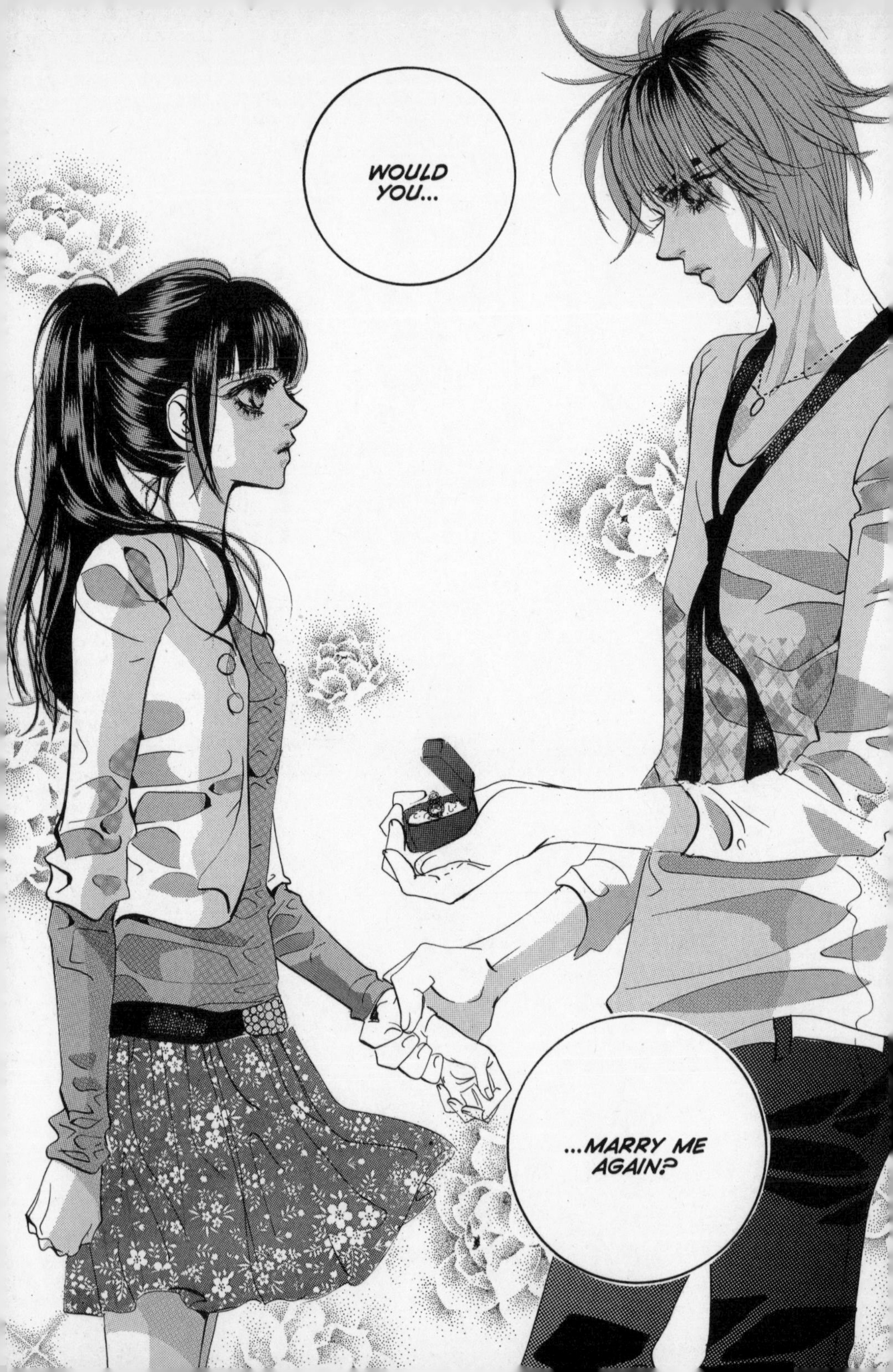
WOULD YOU...
...MARRY ME AGAIN?

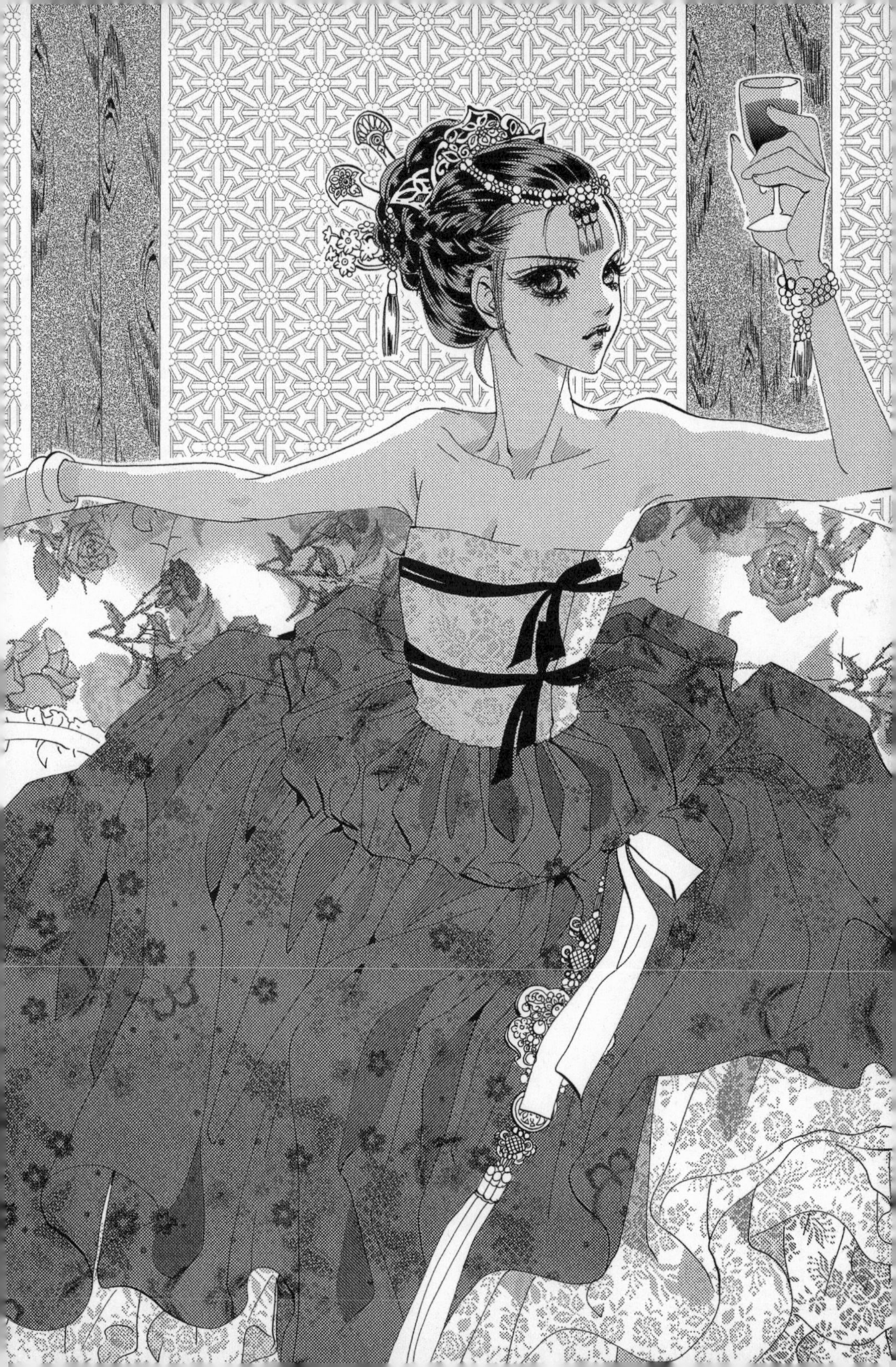

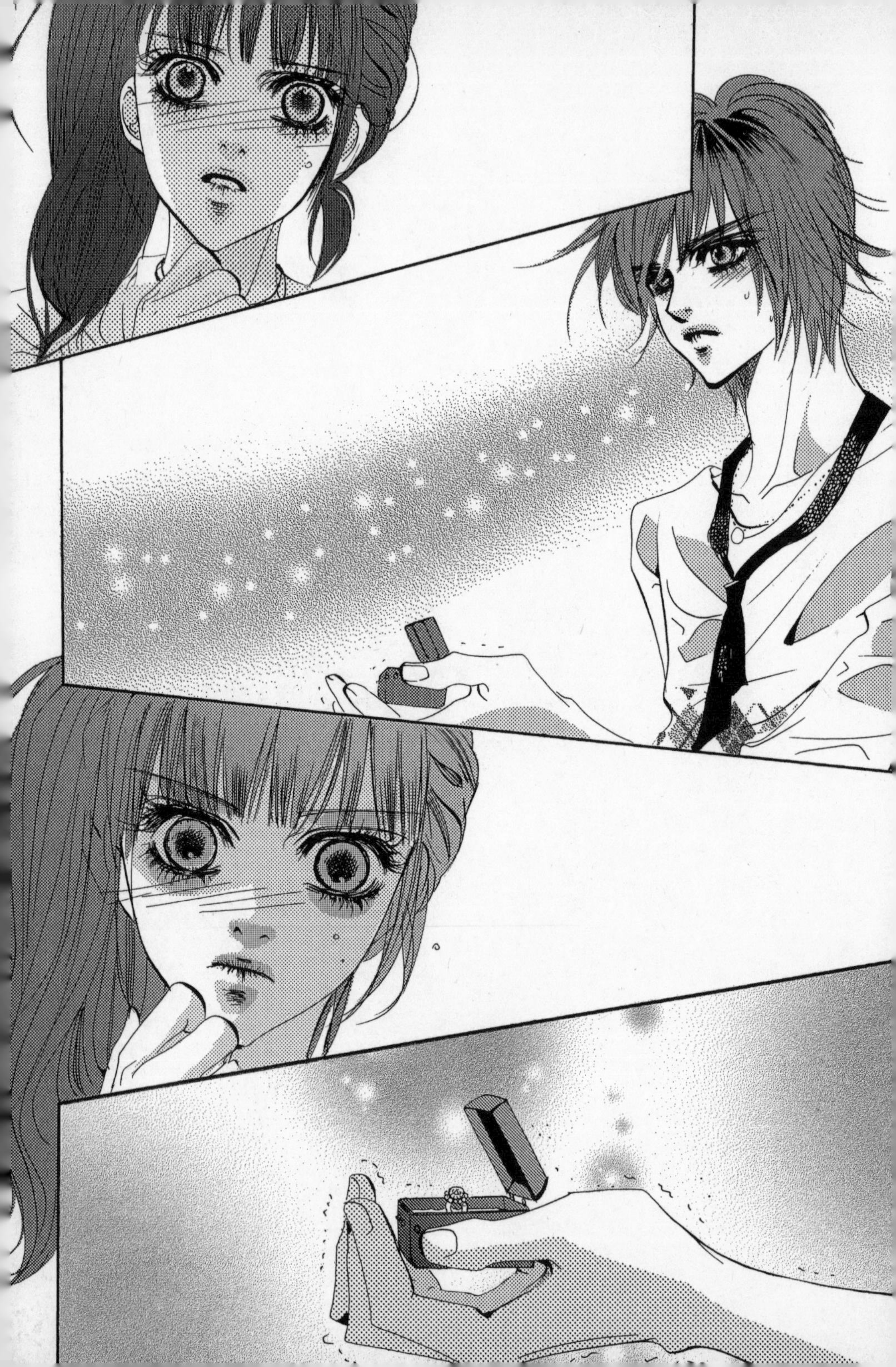

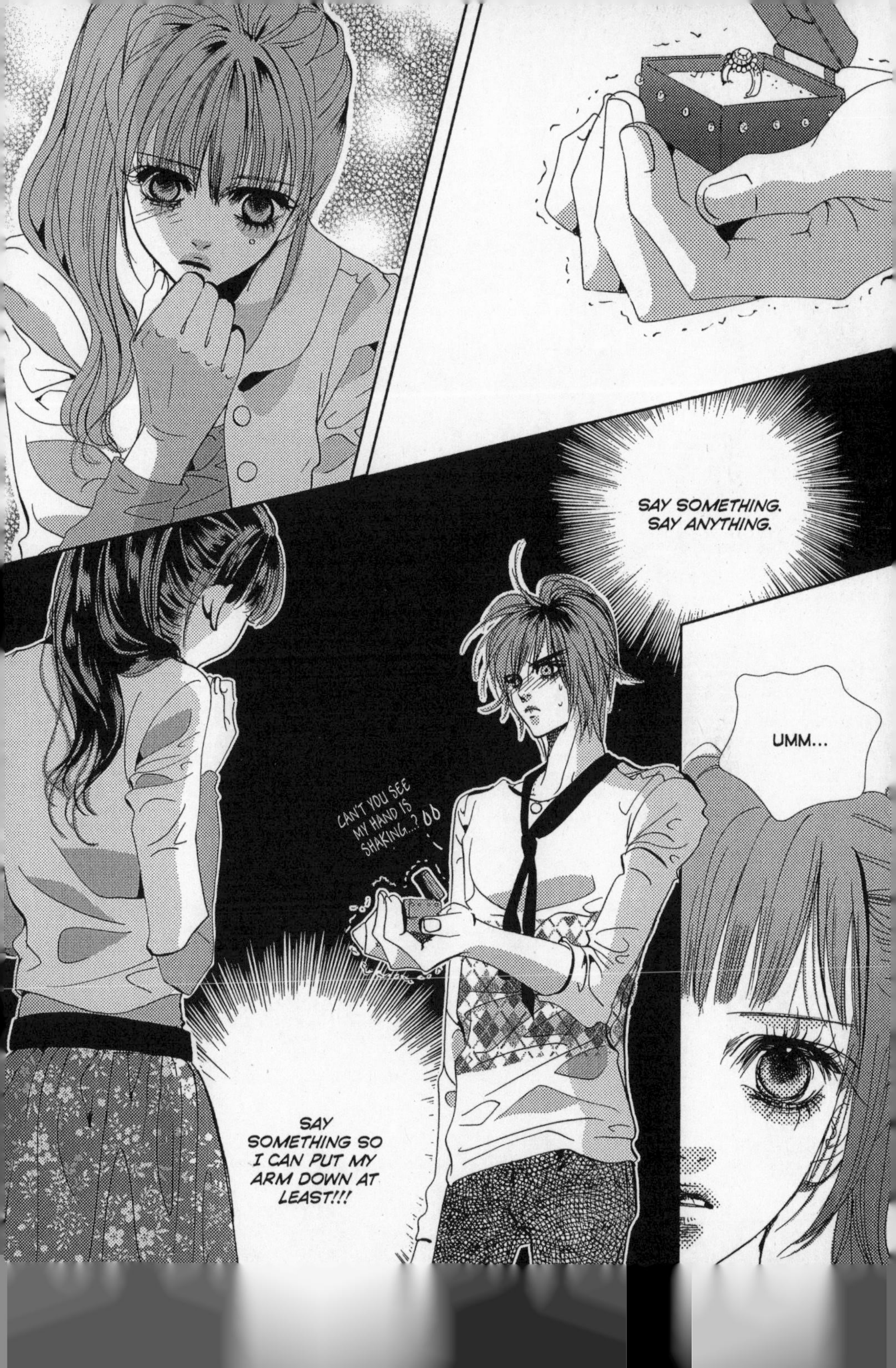
SAY SOMETHING.
SAY ANYTHING.
CAN'T YOU SEE MY HAND IS SHAKING...?
SAY SOMETHING SO I CAN PUT MY ARM DOWN AT LEAST!!!
UMM...

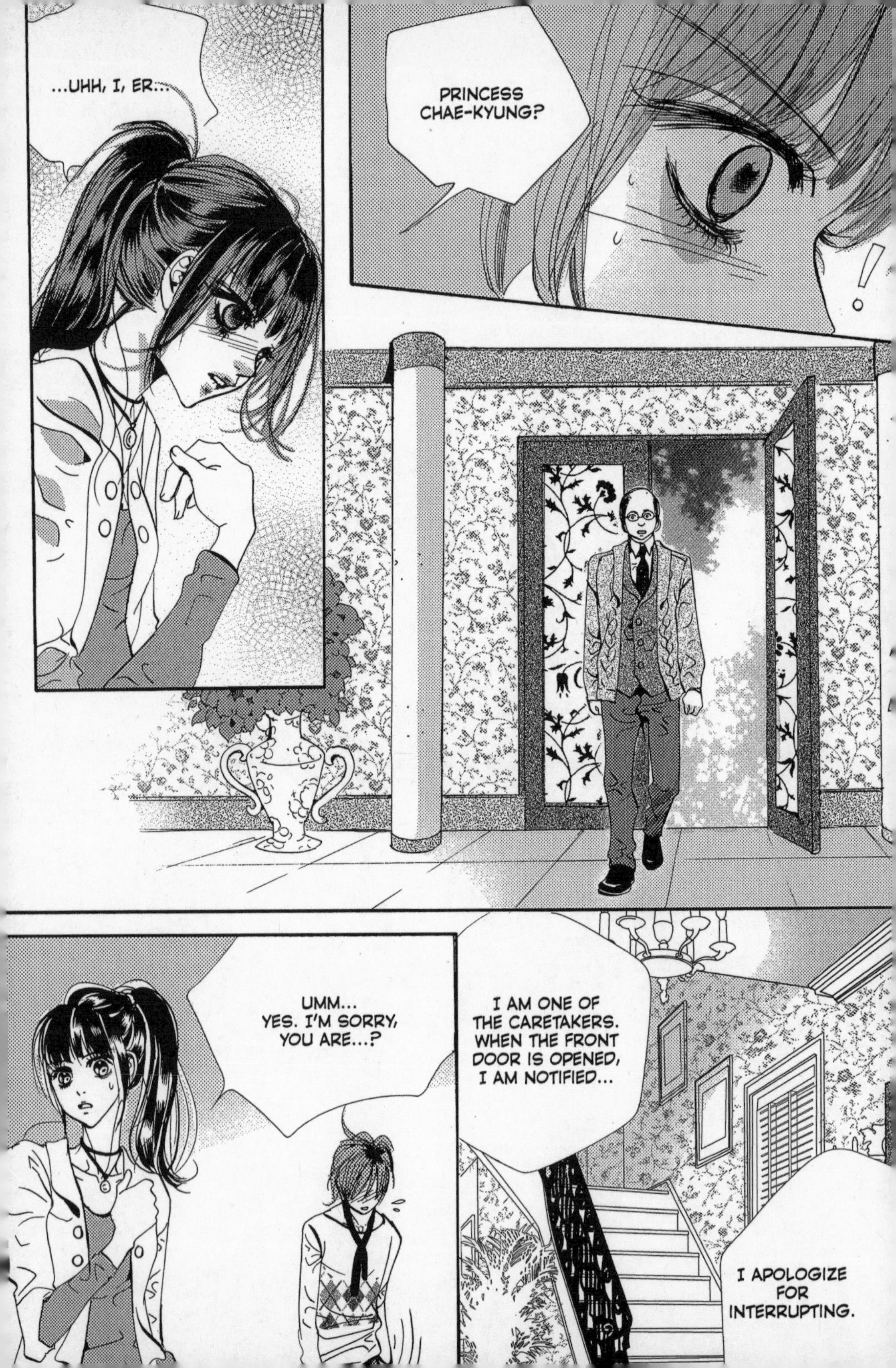
...UHH, I, ER...
PRINCESS CHAE-KYUNG?
!
UMM... YES. I'M SORRY, YOU ARE...?
I AM ONE OF THE CARETAKERS. WHEN THE FRONT DOOR IS OPENED, I AM NOTIFIED...
I APOLOGIZE FOR INTERRUPTING.

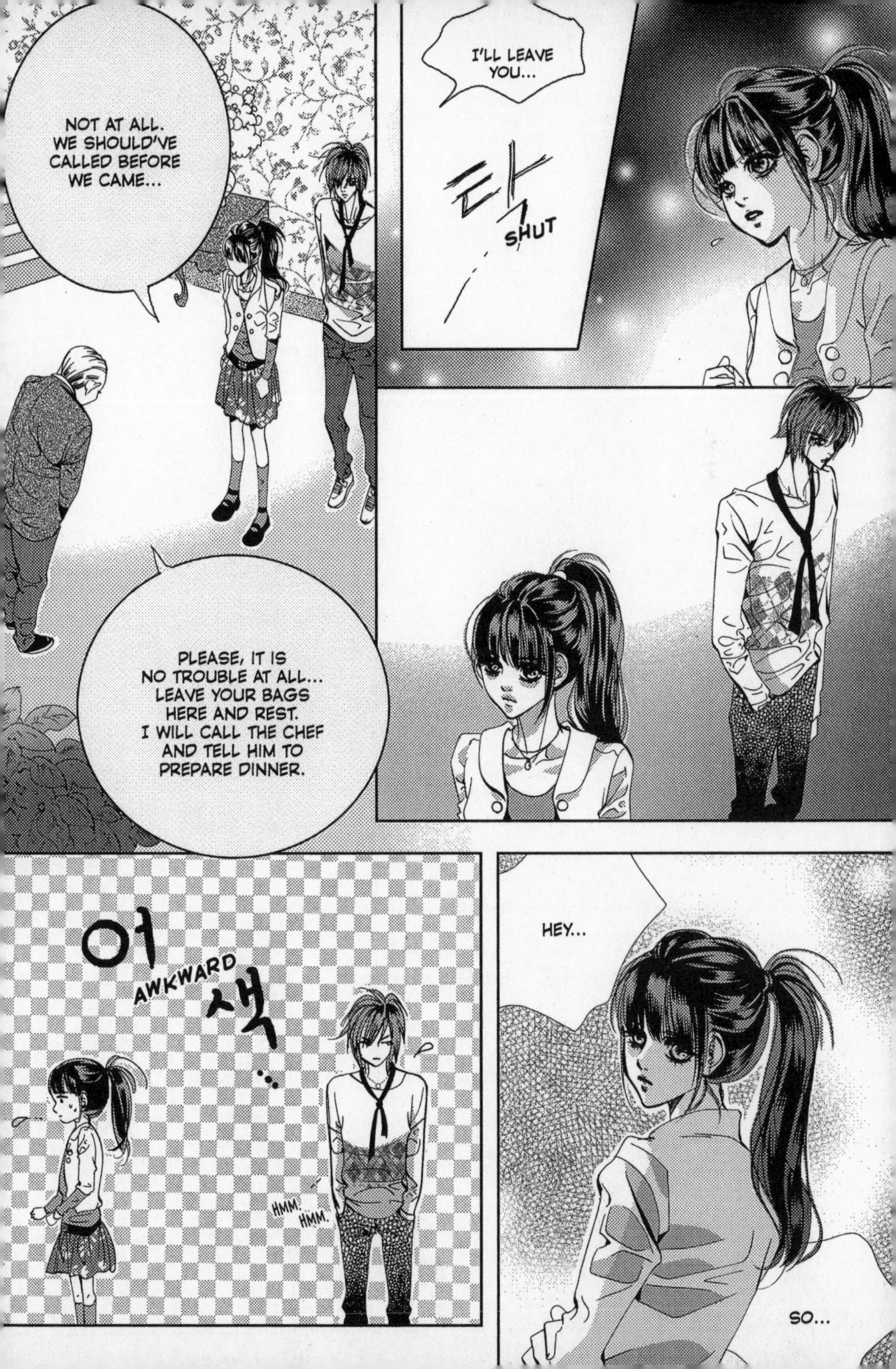
NOT AT ALL. WE SHOULD'VE CALLED BEFORE WE CAME...
PLEASE, IT IS NO TROUBLE AT ALL... LEAVE YOUR BAGS HERE AND REST. I WILL CALL THE CHEF AND TELL HIM TO PREPARE DINNER.
I'LL LEAVE YOU...
탁
SHUT
어색
AWKWARD
HMM. HMM.
HEY...
SO...

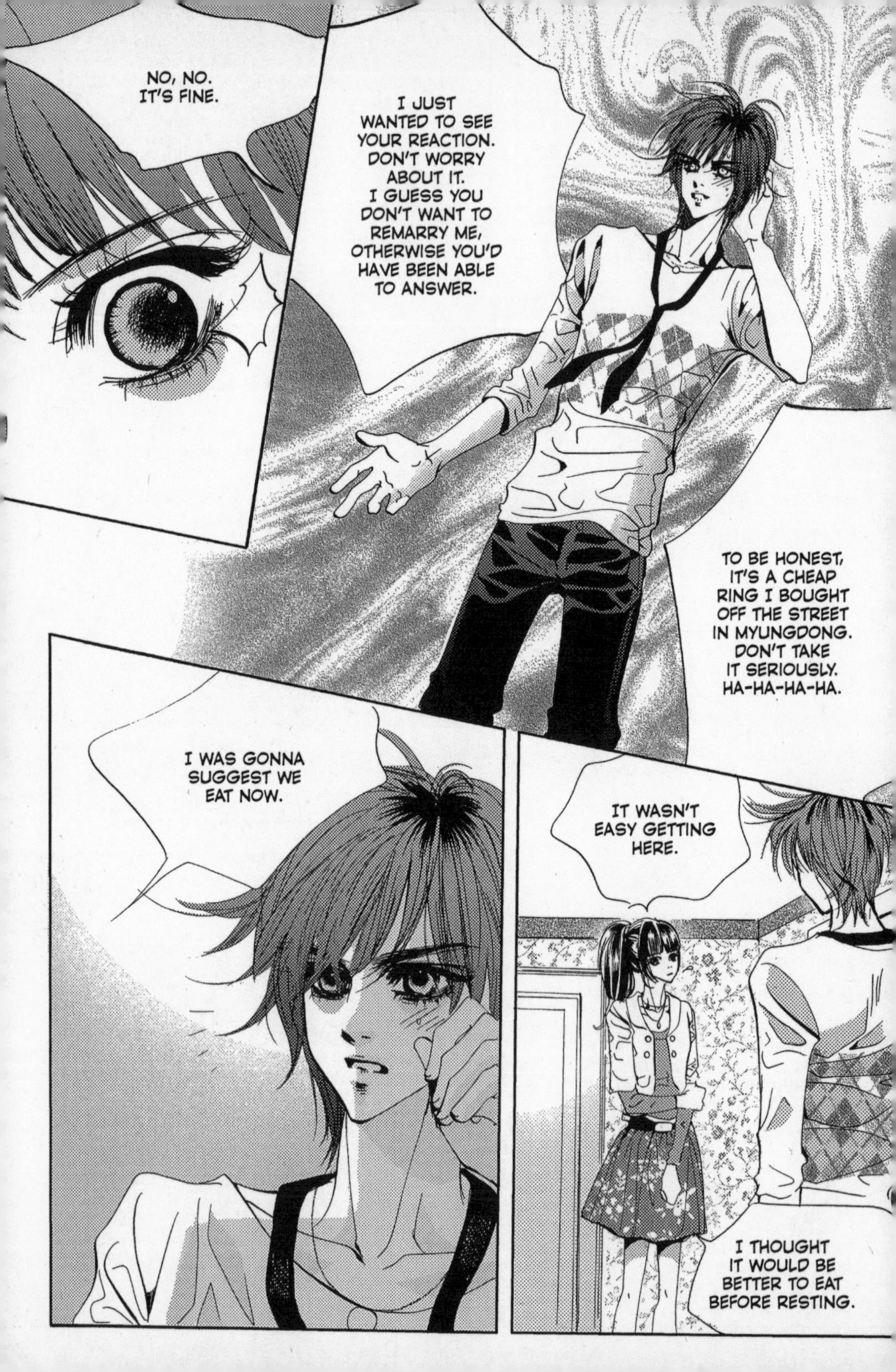
NO, NO. IT'S FINE.
I JUST WANTED TO SEE YOUR REACTION. DON'T WORRY ABOUT IT. I GUESS YOU DON'T WANT TO REMARRY ME, OTHERWISE YOU'D HAVE BEEN ABLE TO ANSWER.
TO BE HONEST, IT'S A CHEAP RING I BOUGHT OFF THE STREET IN MYUNGDONG. DON'T TAKE IT SERIOUSLY. HA-HA-HA-HA.
I WAS GONNA SUGGEST WE EAT NOW.
IT WASN'T EASY GETTING HERE.
I THOUGHT IT WOULD BE BETTER TO EAT BEFORE RESTING.

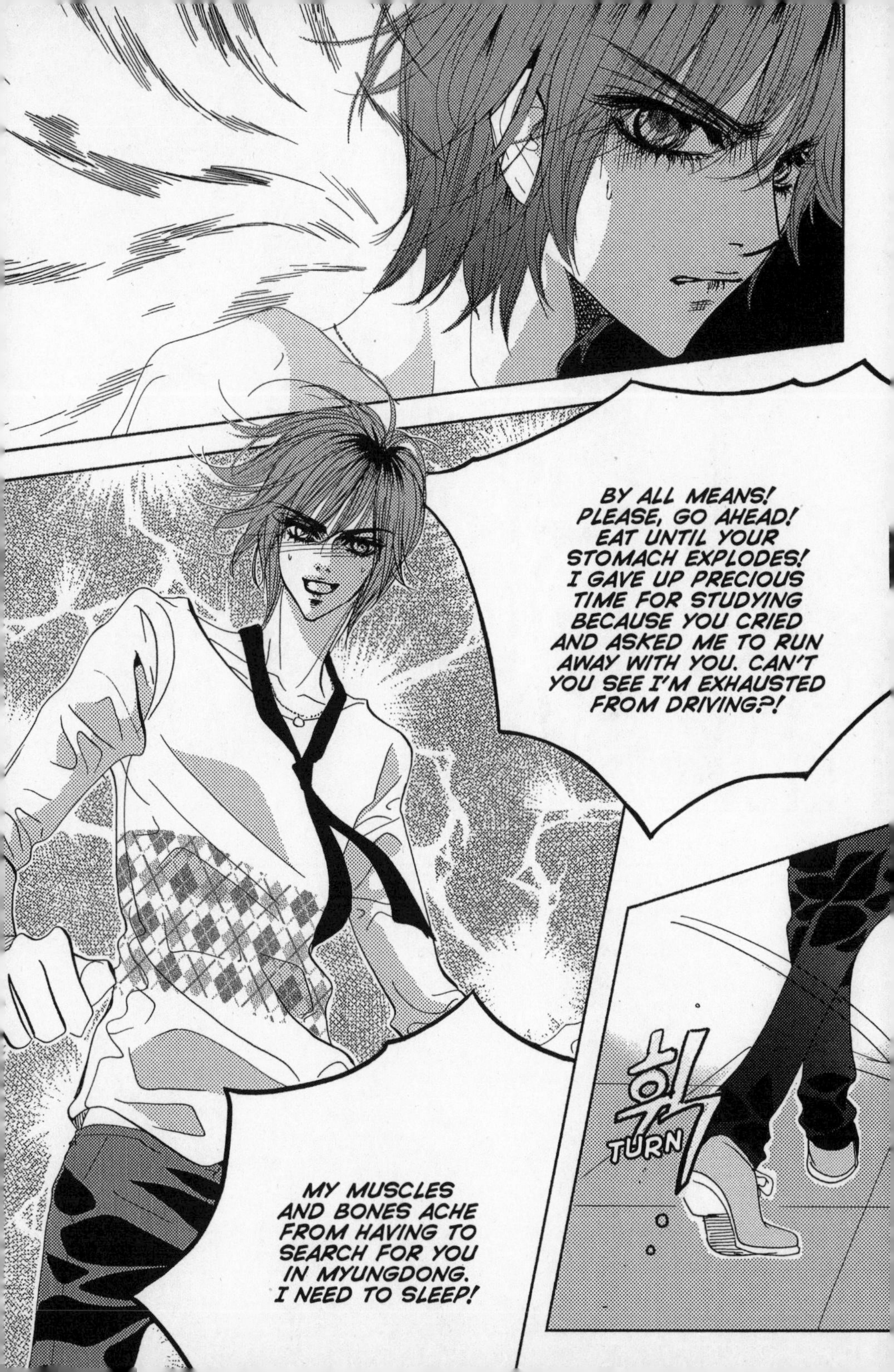

BY ALL MEANS! PLEASE, GO AHEAD! EAT UNTIL YOUR STOMACH EXPLODES! I GAVE UP PRECIOUS TIME FOR STUDYING BECAUSE YOU CRIED AND ASKED ME TO RUN AWAY WITH YOU. CAN'T YOU SEE I'M EXHAUSTED FROM DRIVING?!
MY MUSCLES AND BONES ACHE FROM HAVING TO SEARCH FOR YOU IN MYUNGDONG. I NEED TO SLEEP!
휙
TURN

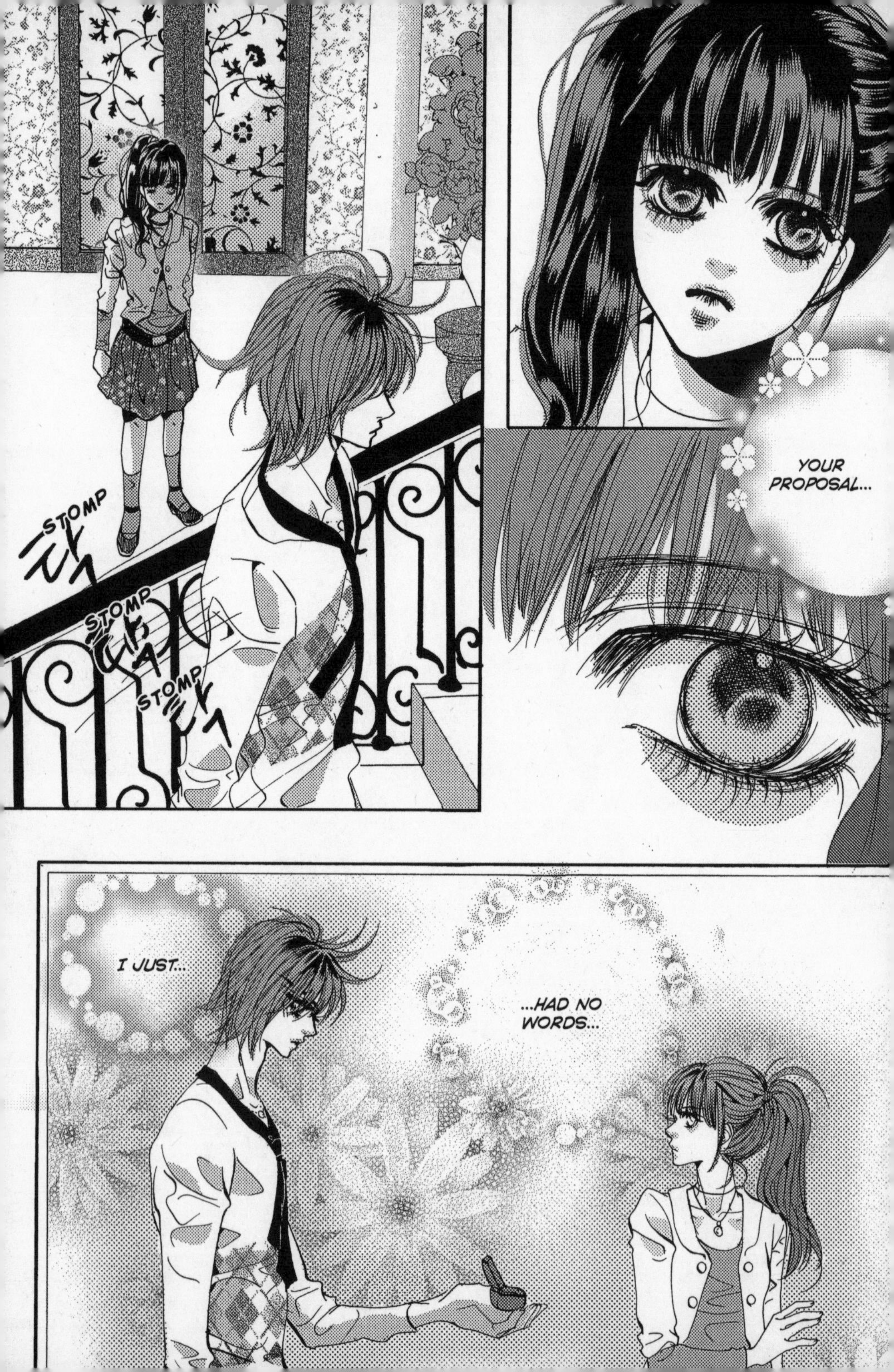
STOMP
STOMP
STOMP
YOUR PROPOSAL...
I JUST...
...HAD NO WORDS...

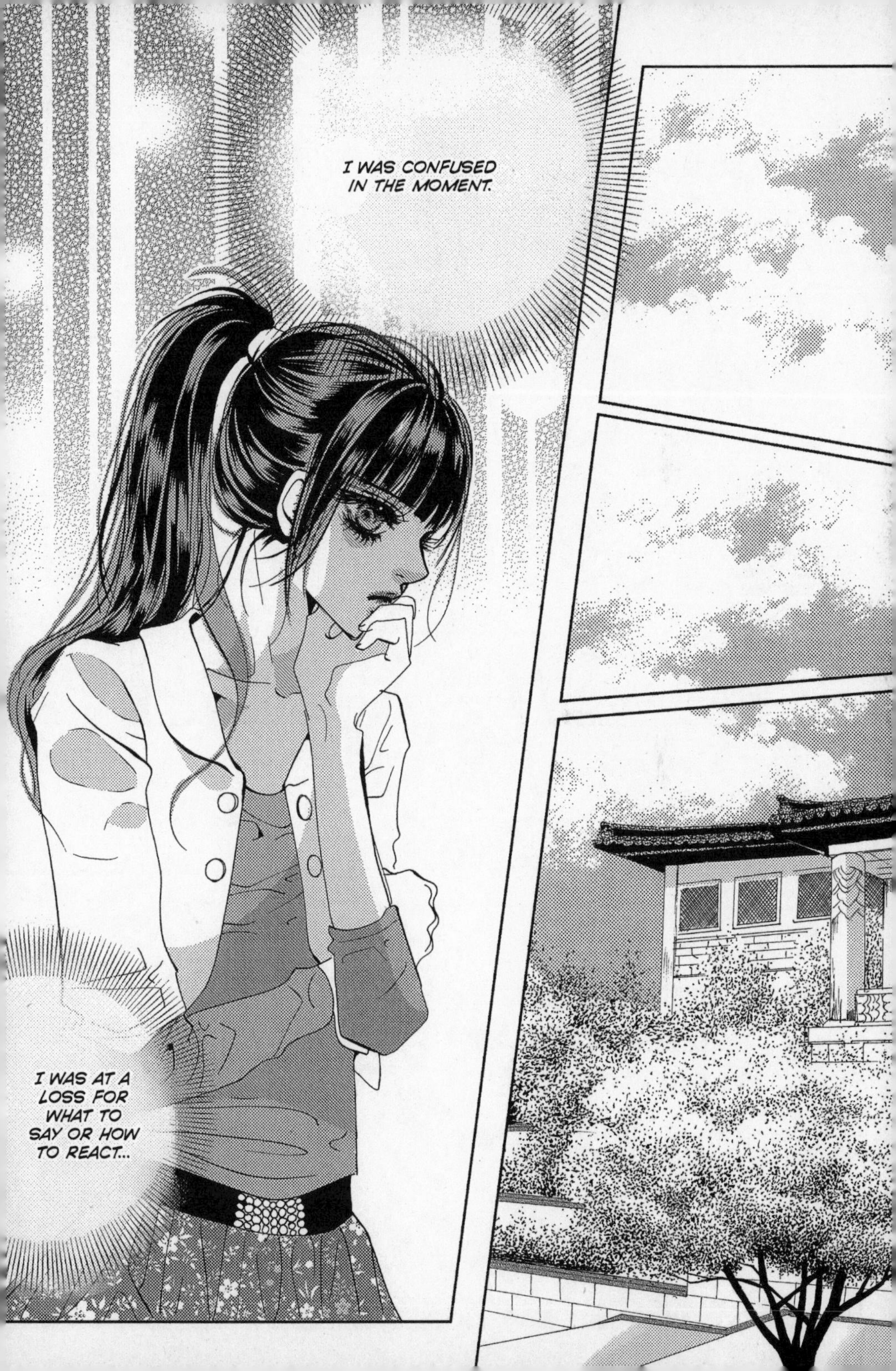
I WAS CONFUSED IN THE MOMENT.
I WAS AT A LOSS FOR WHAT TO SAY OR HOW TO REACT...

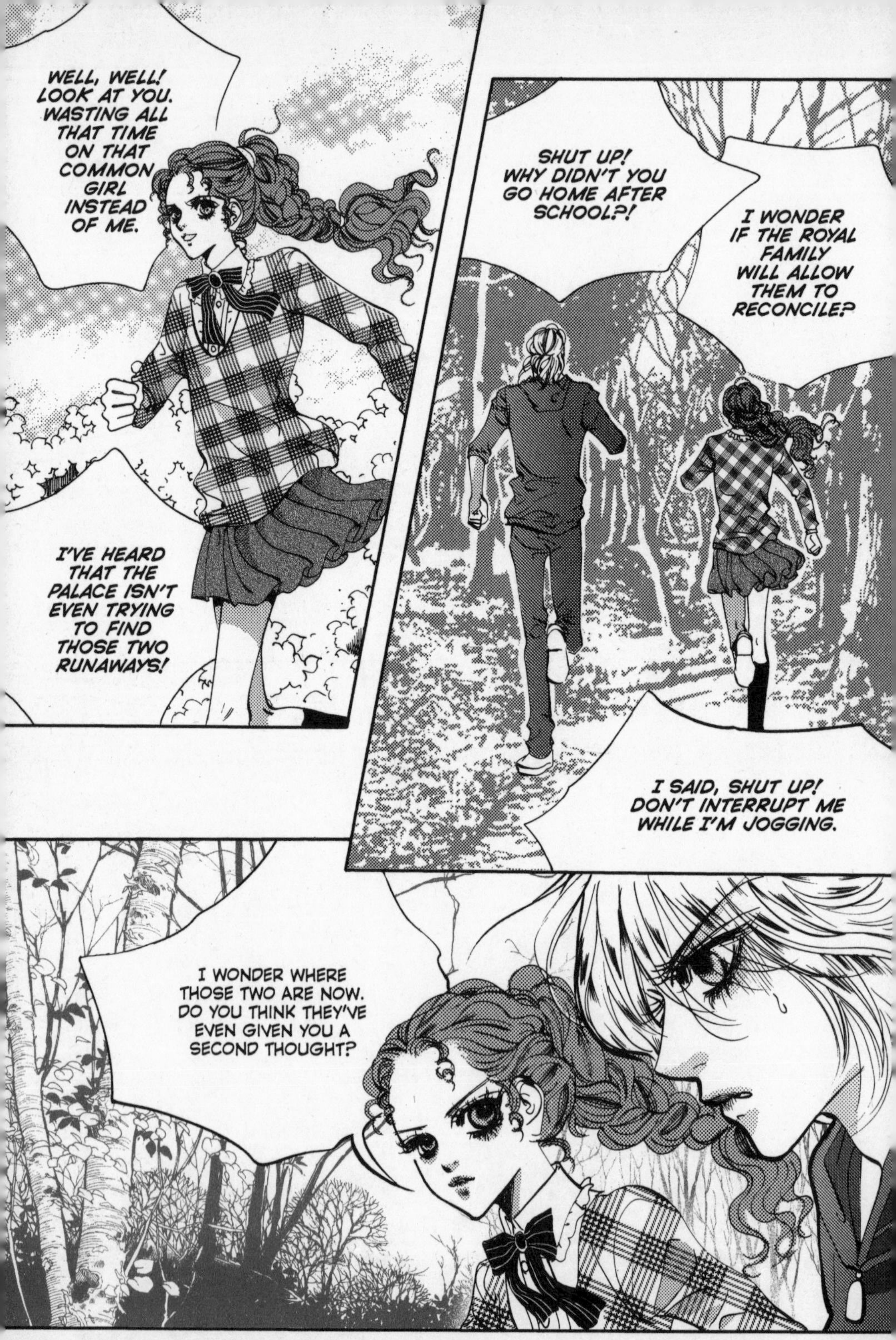
WELL, WELL! LOOK AT YOU. WASTING ALL THAT TIME ON THAT COMMON GIRL INSTEAD OF ME.
I'VE HEARD THAT THE PALACE ISN'T EVEN TRYING TO FIND THOSE TWO RUNAWAYS!
SHUT UP! WHY DIDN'T YOU GO HOME AFTER SCHOOL?!
I WONDER IF THE ROYAL FAMILY WILL ALLOW THEM TO RECONCILE?
I SAID, SHUT UP! DON'T INTERRUPT ME WHILE I'M JOGGING.
I WONDER WHERE THOSE TWO ARE NOW. DO YOU THINK THEY'VE EVEN GIVEN YOU A SECOND THOUGHT?

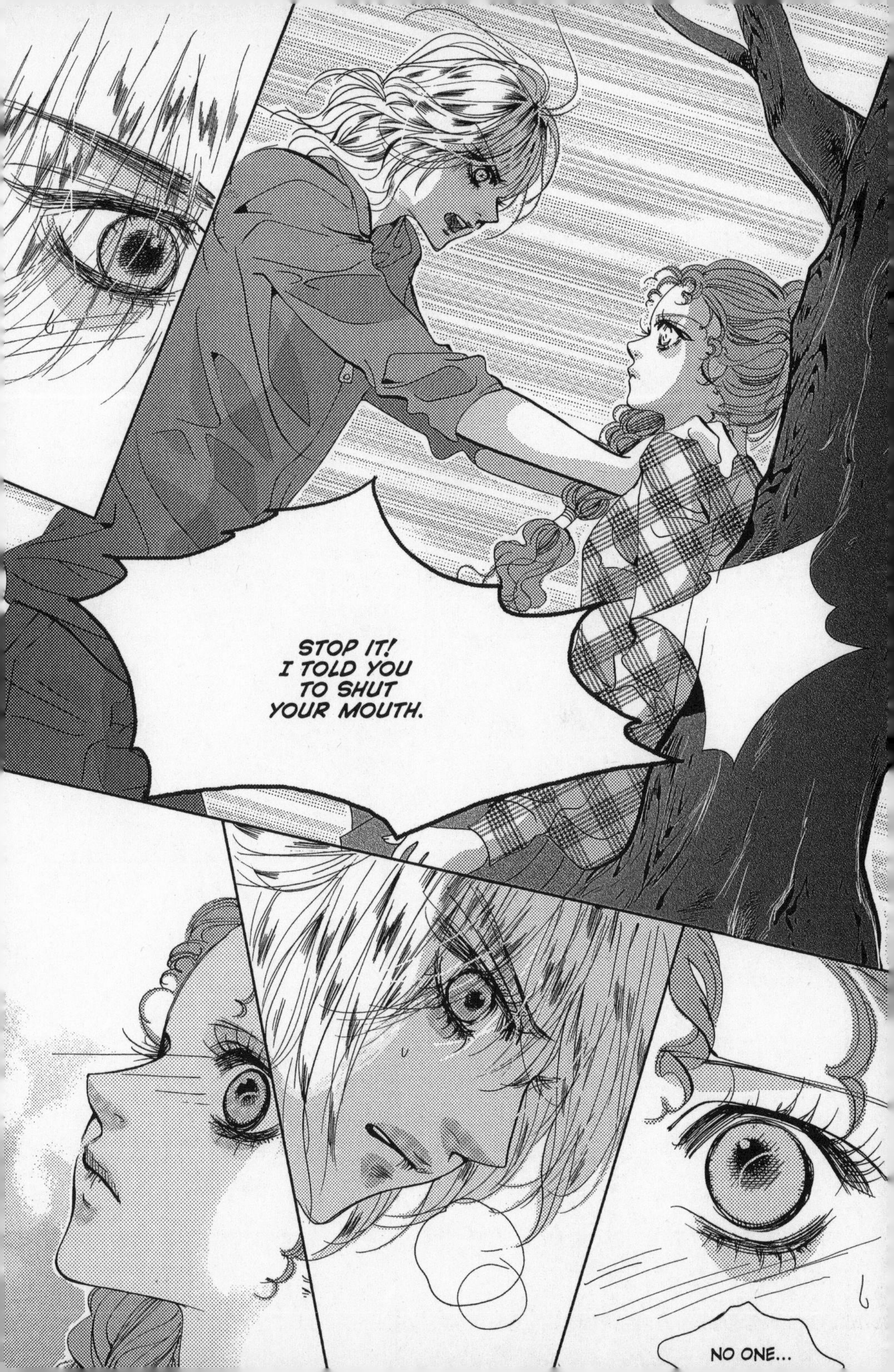
STOP IT! I TOLD YOU TO SHUT YOUR MOUTH.
NO ONE...

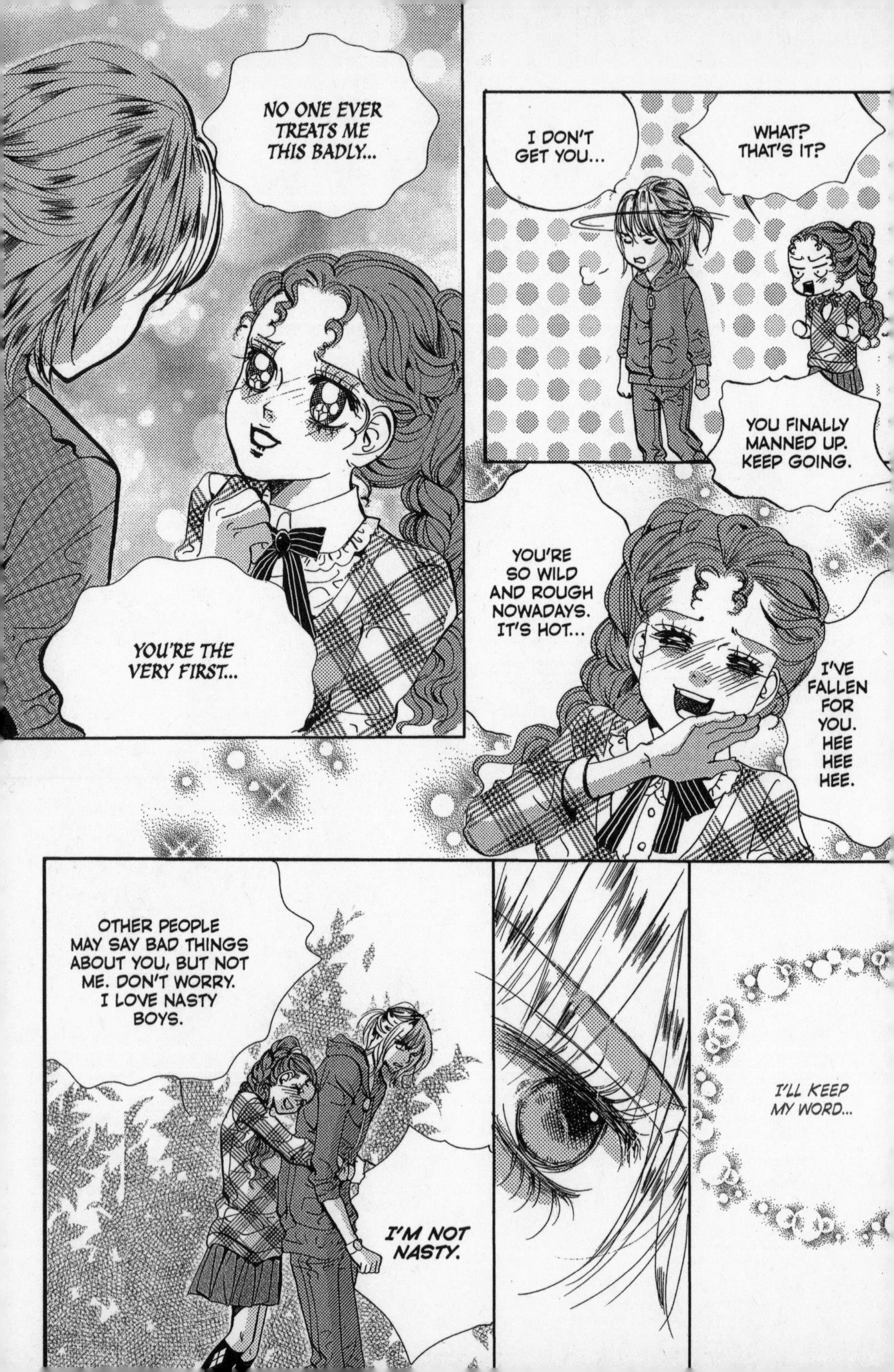
NO ONE EVER TREATS ME THIS BADLY...
YOU'RE THE VERY FIRST...
I DON'T GET YOU...
WHAT? THAT'S IT?
YOU FINALLY MANNED UP. KEEP GOING.
YOU'RE SO WILD AND ROUGH NOWADAYS. IT'S HOT...
I'VE FALLEN FOR YOU. HEE HEE HEE.
OTHER PEOPLE MAY SAY BAD THINGS ABOUT YOU, BUT NOT ME. DON'T WORRY. I LOVE NASTY BOYS.
I'M NOT NASTY.
I'LL KEEP MY WORD...

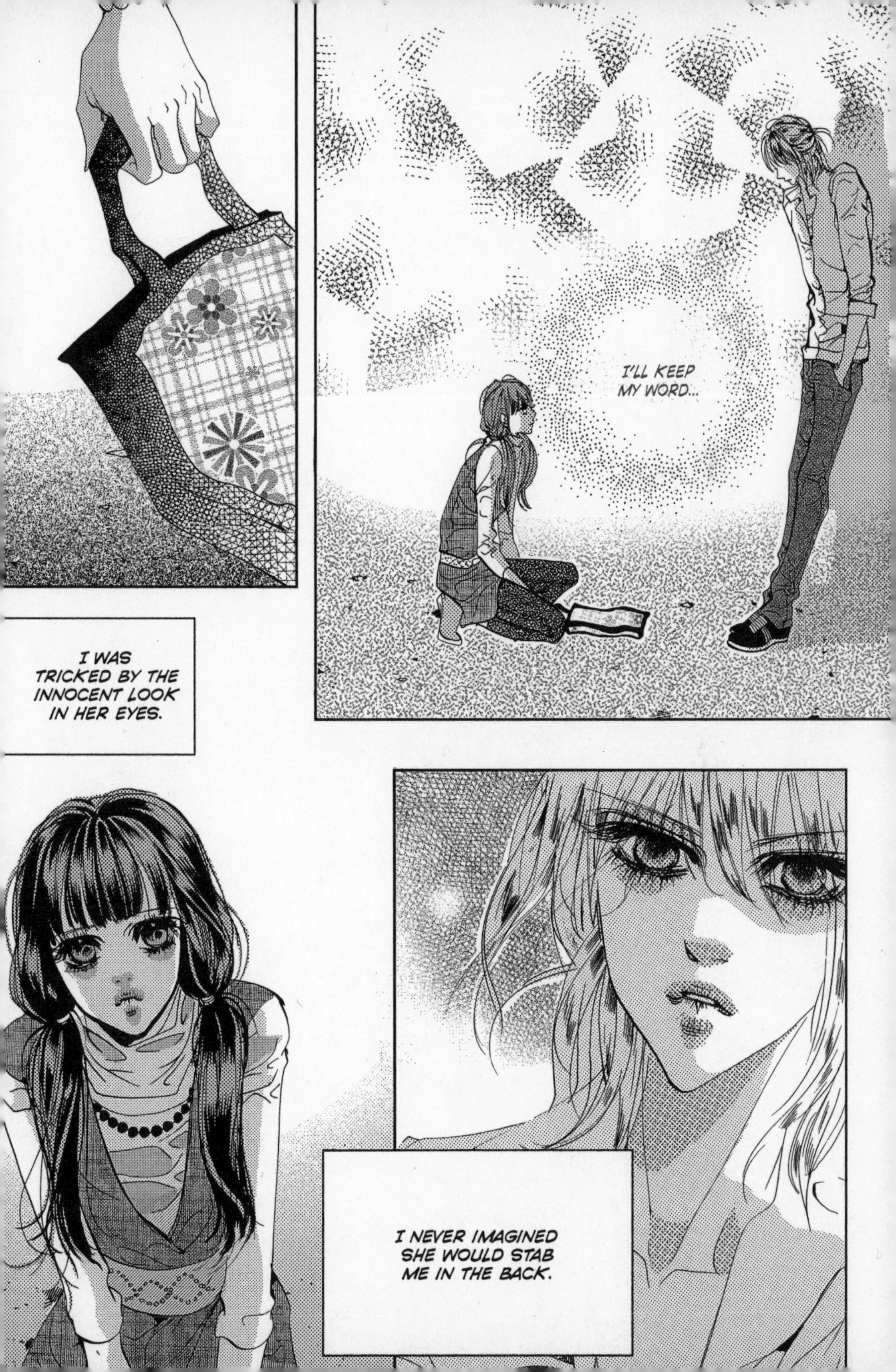
I'LL KEEP MY WORD...
I WAS TRICKED BY THE INNOCENT LOOK IN HER EYES.
I NEVER IMAGINED SHE WOULD STAB ME IN THE BACK.

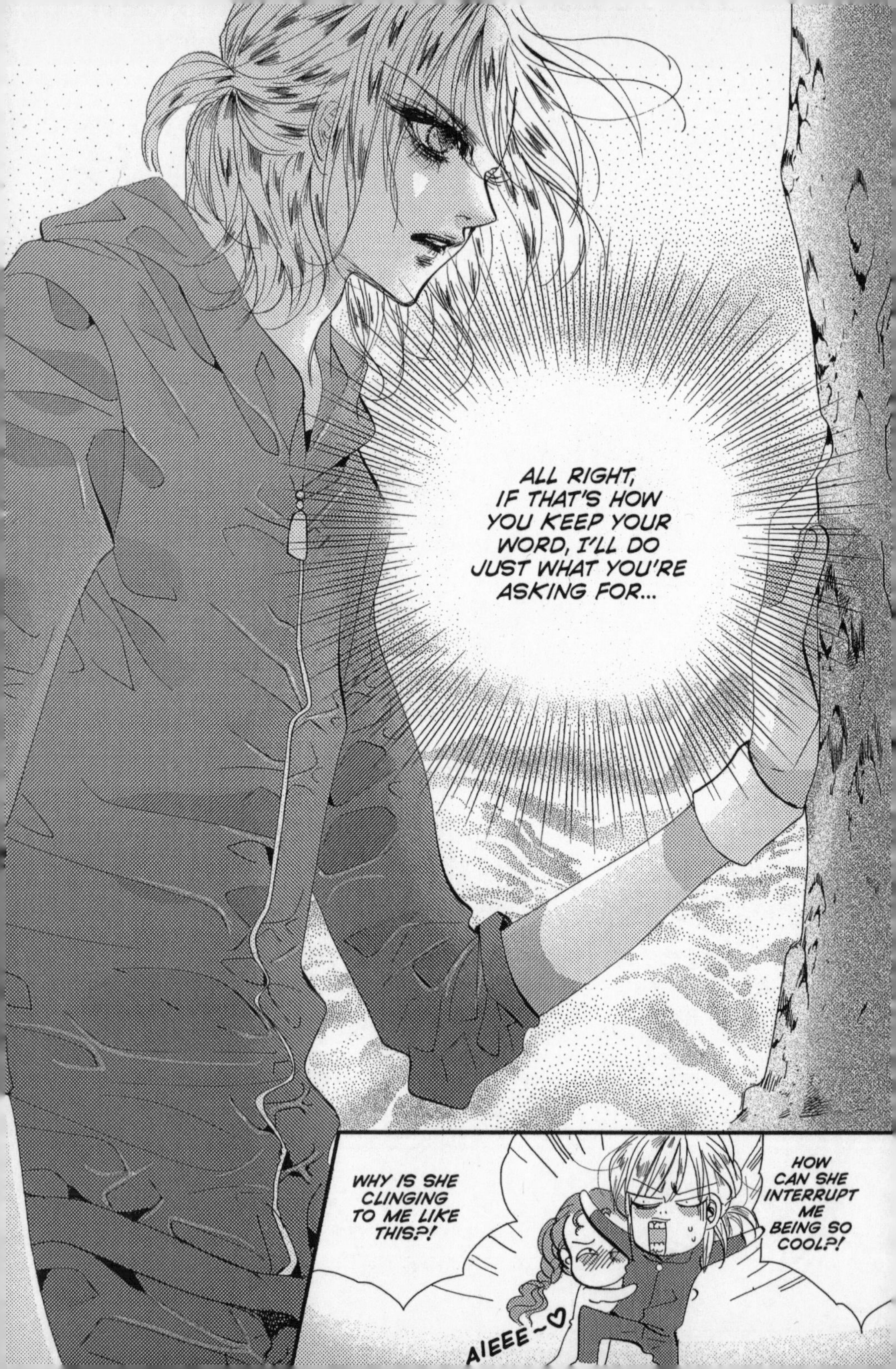
ALL RIGHT, IF THAT'S HOW YOU KEEP YOUR WORD, I'LL DO JUST WHAT YOU'RE ASKING FOR...
WHY IS SHE CLINGING TO ME LIKE THIS?!
HOW CAN SHE INTERRUPT ME BEING SO COOL?!
AIEEE~♡

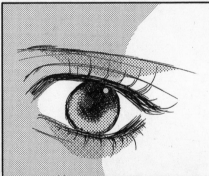

AUNTIE.

I MEAN, YOUR HIGHNESS...

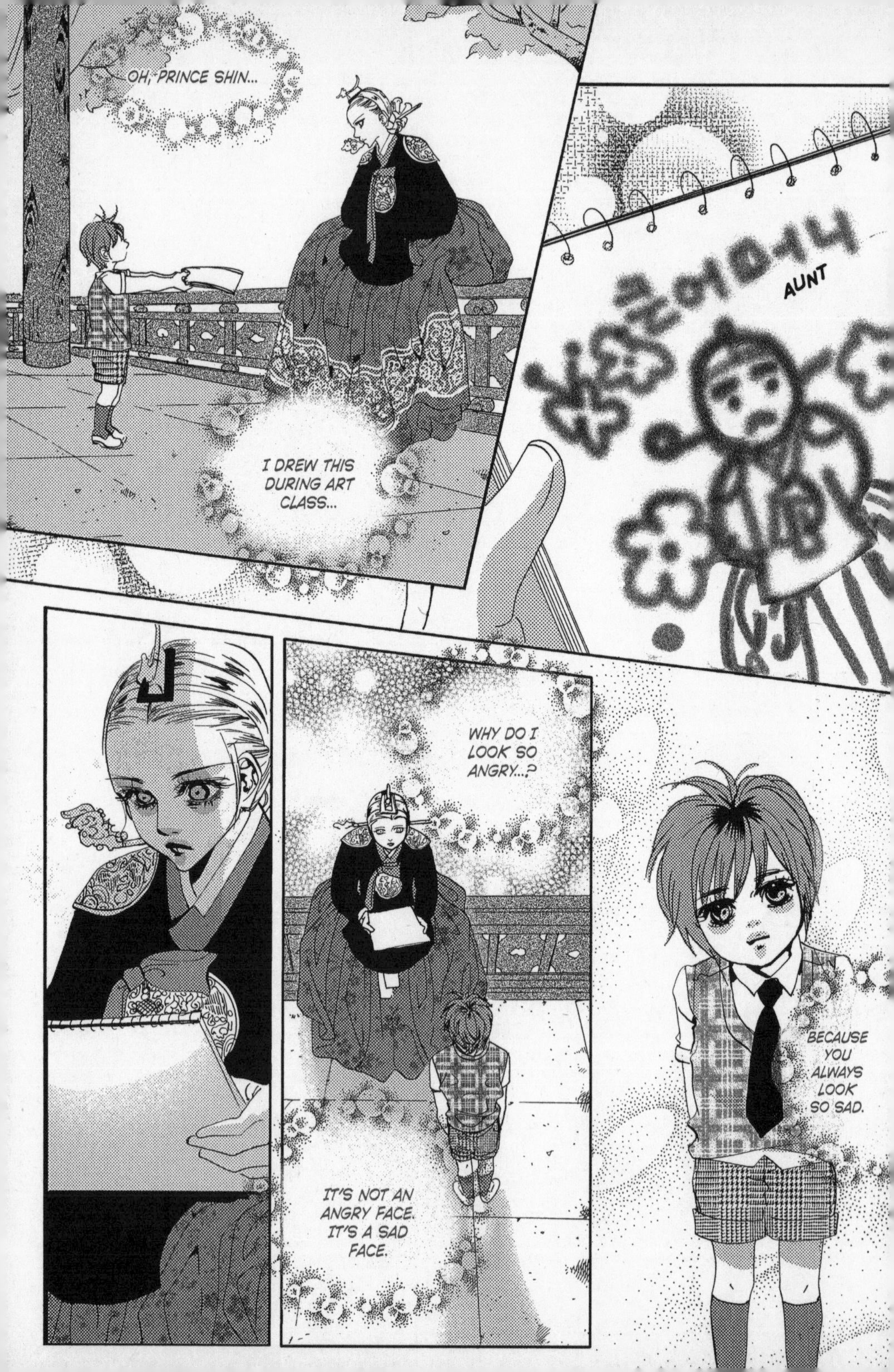
OH, PRINCE SHIN...
I DREW THIS DURING ART CLASS...
AUNT
WHY DO I LOOK SO ANGRY...?
IT'S NOT AN ANGRY FACE. IT'S A SAD FACE.
BECAUSE YOU ALWAYS LOOK SO SAD.

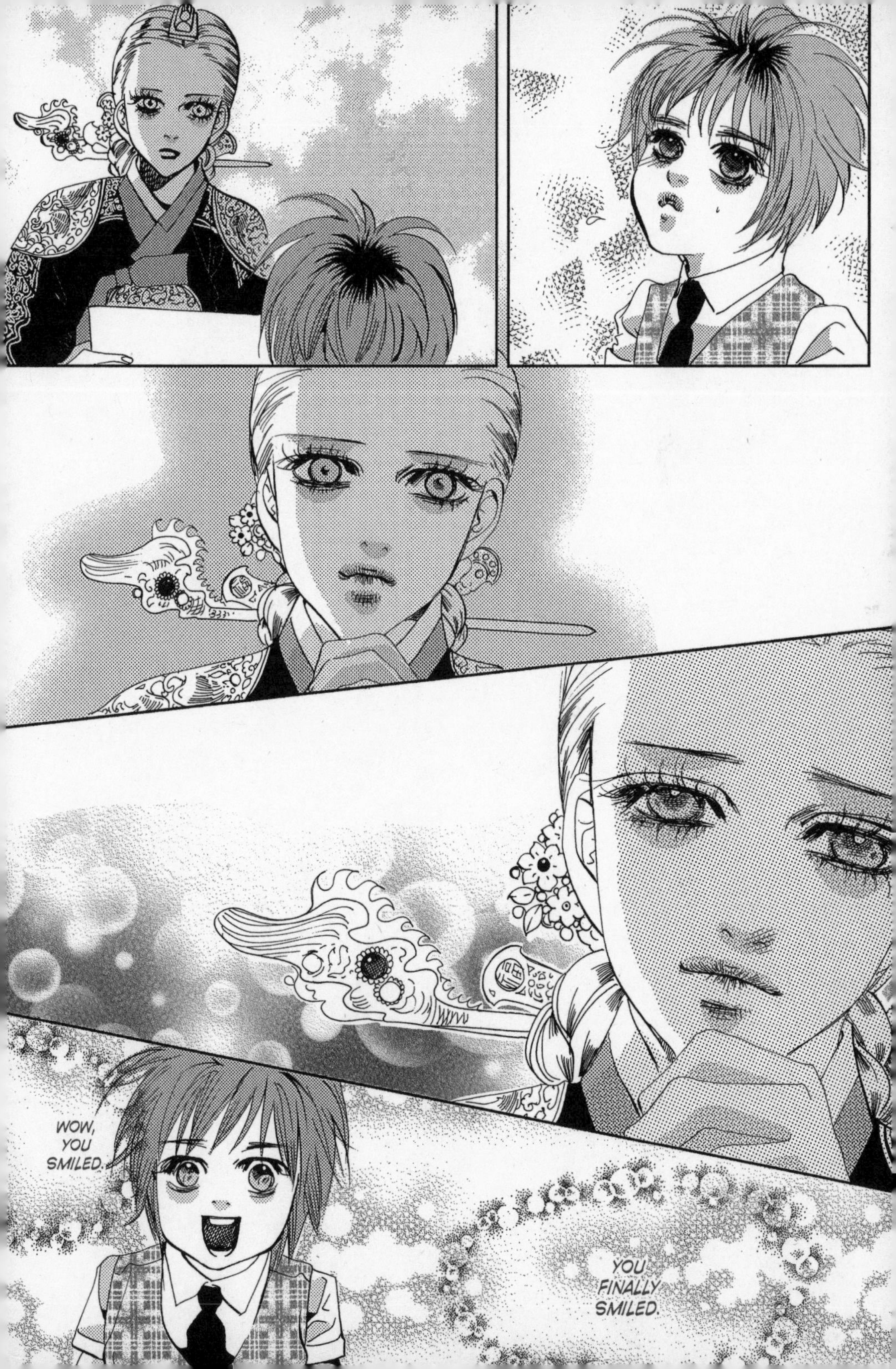
WOW, YOU SMILED.
YOU FINALLY SMILED.

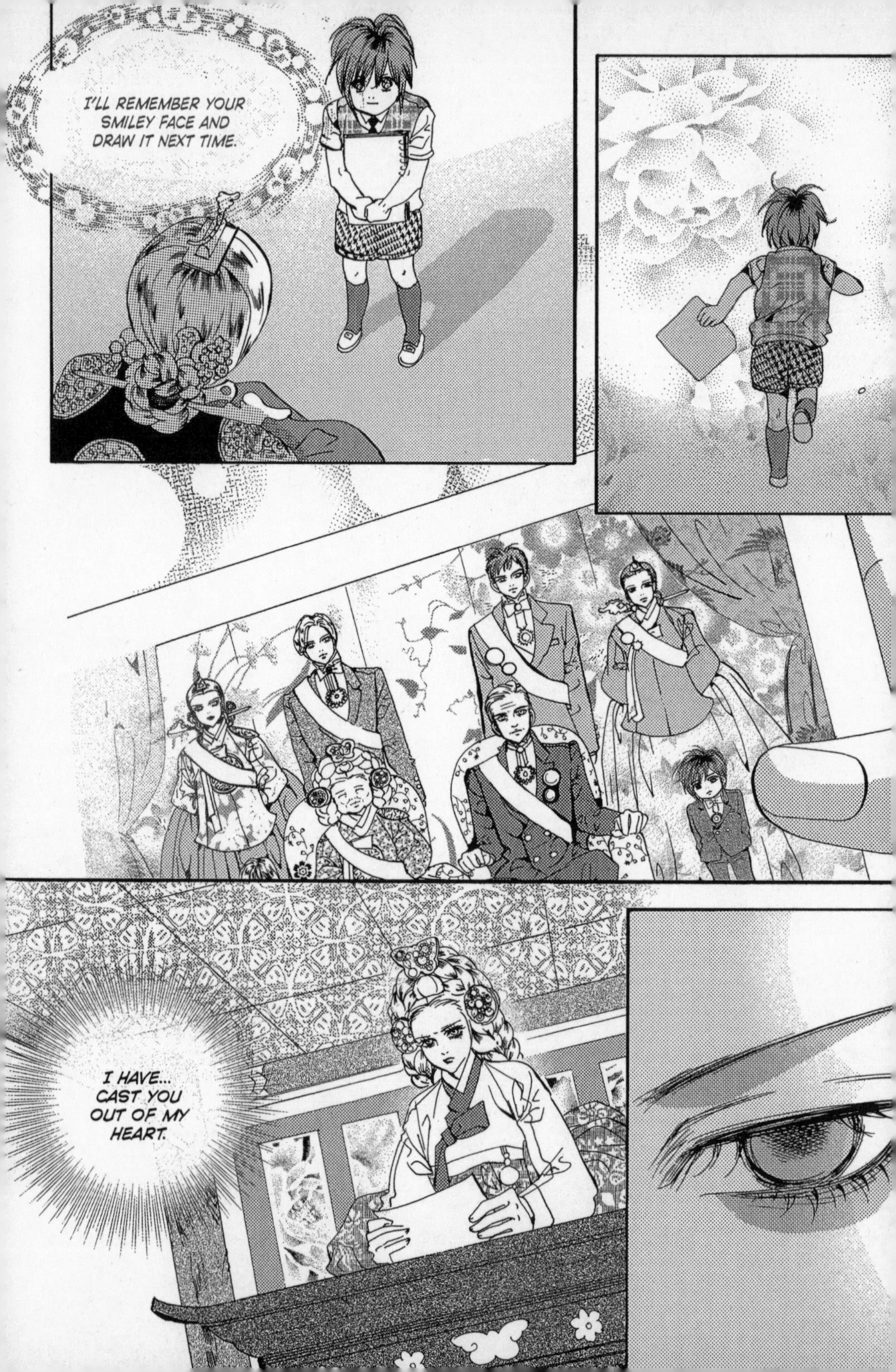
I'LL REMEMBER YOUR SMILEY FACE AND DRAW IT NEXT TIME.
I HAVE... CAST YOU OUT OF MY HEART.

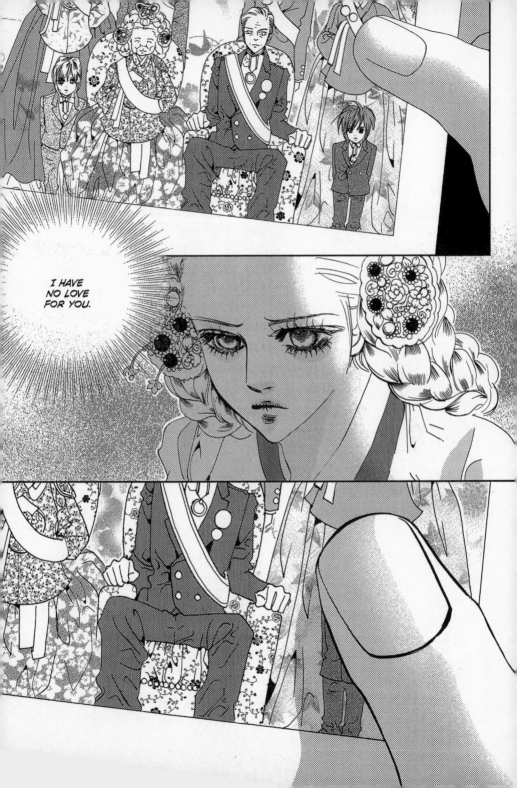

I HAVE
NO LOVE
FOR YOU.

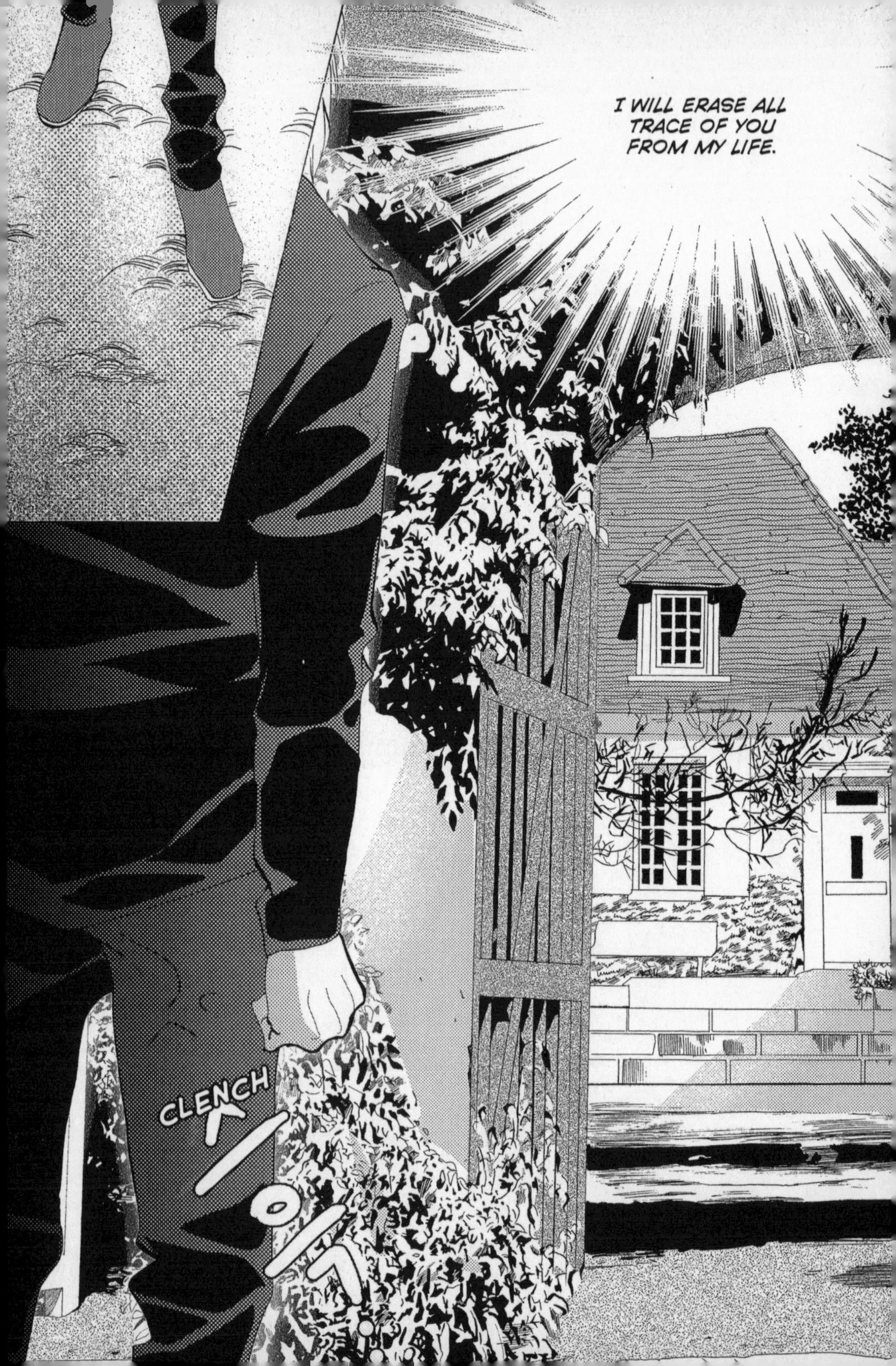
I WILL ERASE ALL TRACE OF YOU FROM MY LIFE.
CLENCH

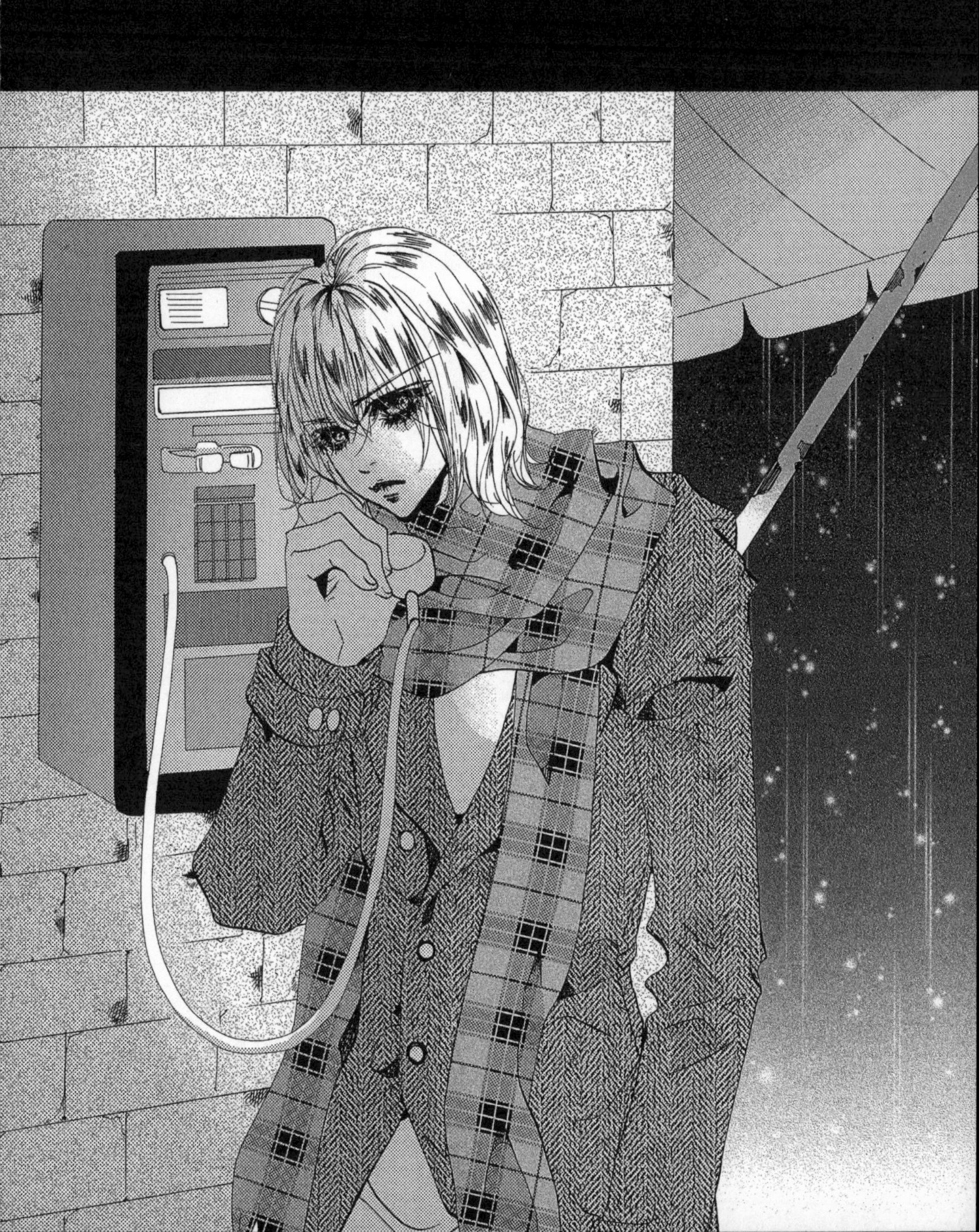

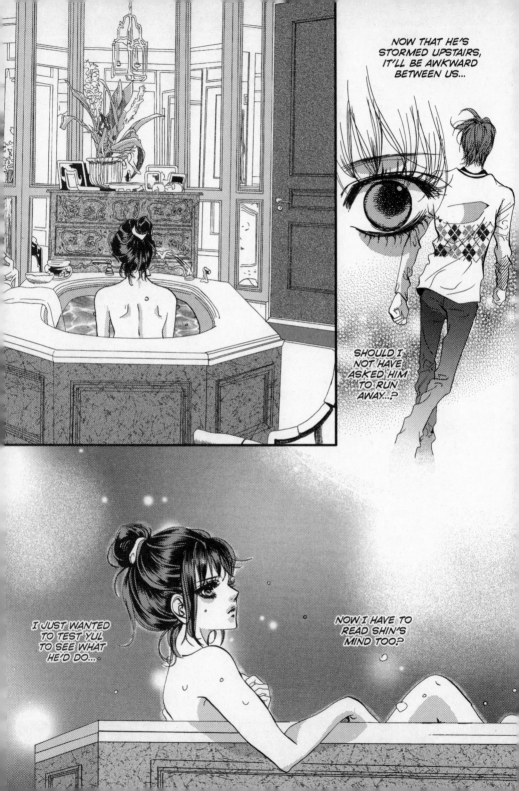

NOW THAT HE'S STORMED UPSTAIRS, IT'LL BE AWKWARD BETWEEN US...

SHOULD I NOT HAVE ASKED HIM TO RUN AWAY...?

I JUST WANTED TO TEST YUL TO SEE WHAT HE'D DO...

NOW I HAVE TO READ SHIN'S MIND TOO?

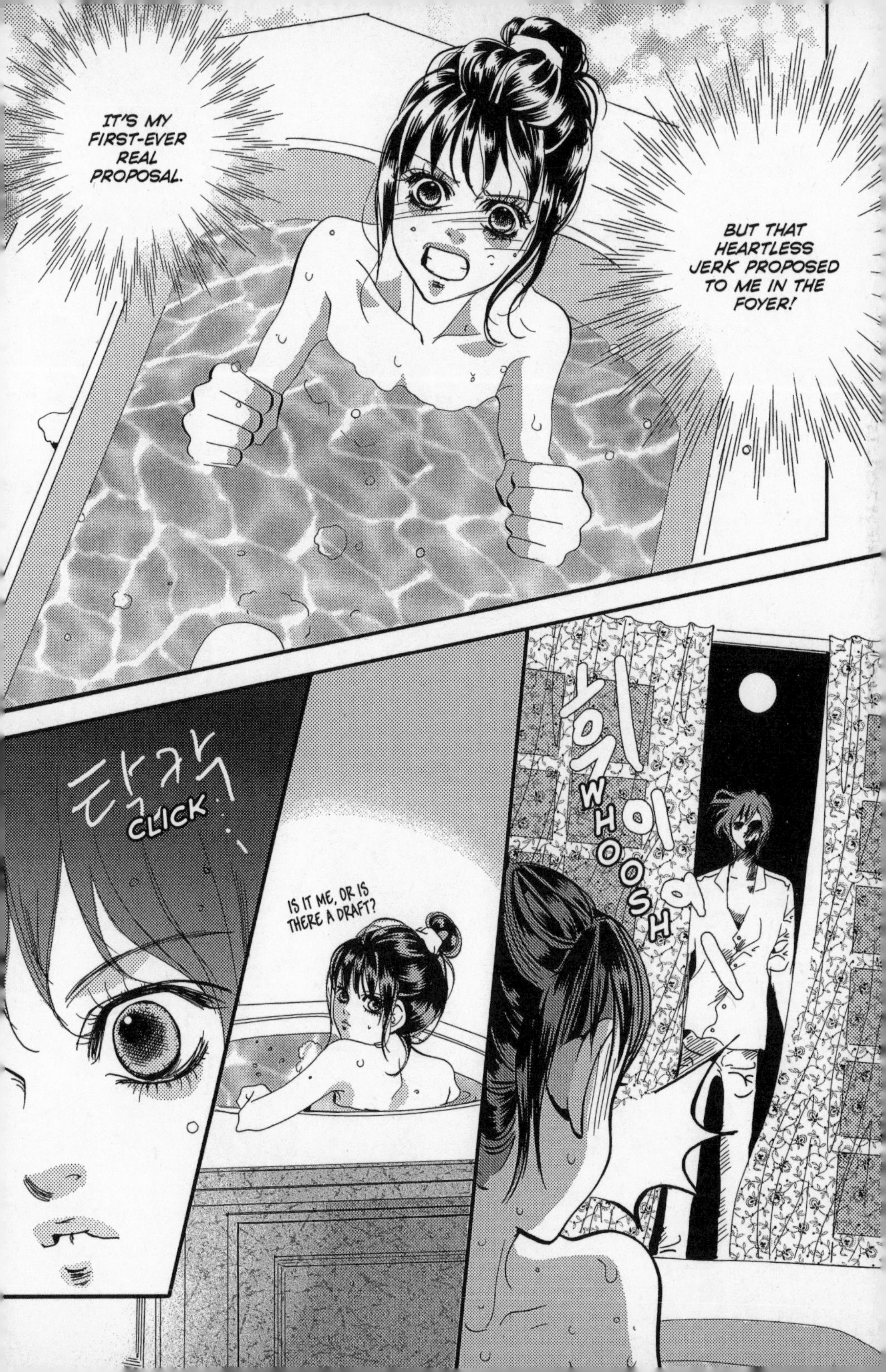
IT'S MY FIRST-EVER REAL PROPOSAL.
BUT THAT HEARTLESS JERK PROPOSED TO ME IN THE FOYER!
탈칵
CLICK
IS IT ME, OR IS THERE A DRAFT?
WHOOSH

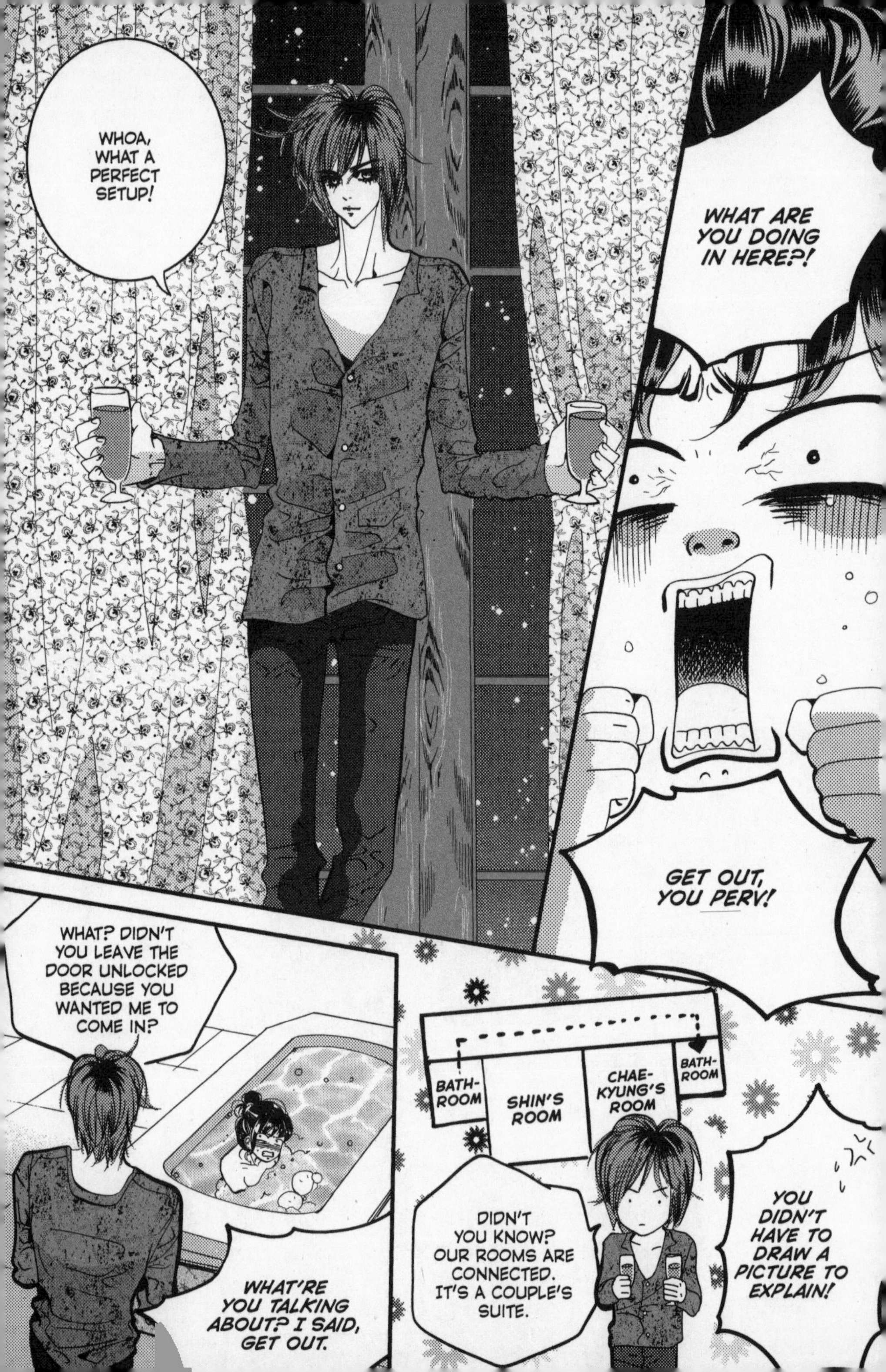
WHOA, WHAT A PERFECT SETUP!
WHAT ARE YOU DOING IN HERE?!
GET OUT, YOU PERV!
WHAT? DIDN'T YOU LEAVE THE DOOR UNLOCKED BECAUSE YOU WANTED ME TO COME IN?
WHAT'RE YOU TALKING ABOUT? I SAID, GET OUT.
BATH-ROOM
SHIN'S ROOM
CHAE-KYUNG'S ROOM
BATH-ROOM
DIDN'T YOU KNOW? OUR ROOMS ARE CONNECTED. IT'S A COUPLE'S SUITE.
YOU DIDN'T HAVE TO DRAW A PICTURE TO EXPLAIN!

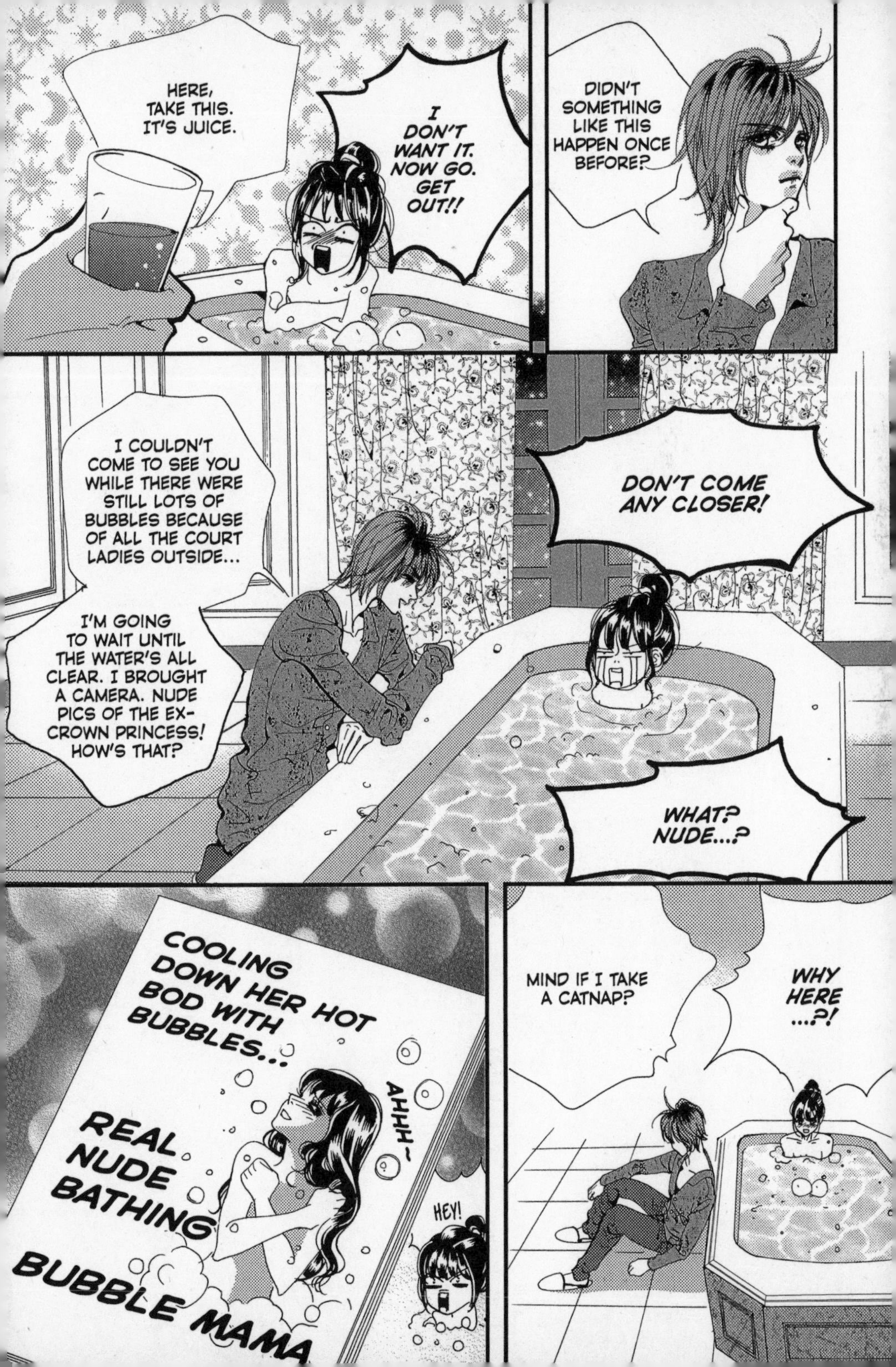
HERE, TAKE THIS. IT'S JUICE.
I DON'T WANT IT. NOW GO. GET OUT!!
DIDN'T SOMETHING LIKE THIS HAPPEN ONCE BEFORE?
I COULDN'T COME TO SEE YOU WHILE THERE WERE STILL LOTS OF BUBBLES BECAUSE OF ALL THE COURT LADIES OUTSIDE...
I'M GOING TO WAIT UNTIL THE WATER'S ALL CLEAR. I BROUGHT A CAMERA. NUDE PICS OF THE EX-CROWN PRINCESS! HOW'S THAT?
DON'T COME ANY CLOSER!
WHAT? NUDE...?
COOLING DOWN HER HOT BOD WITH BUBBLES...
REAL NUDE BATHING
BUBBLE MAMA
AHHH~
HEY!
MIND IF I TAKE A CATNAP?
WHY HERE ...?!

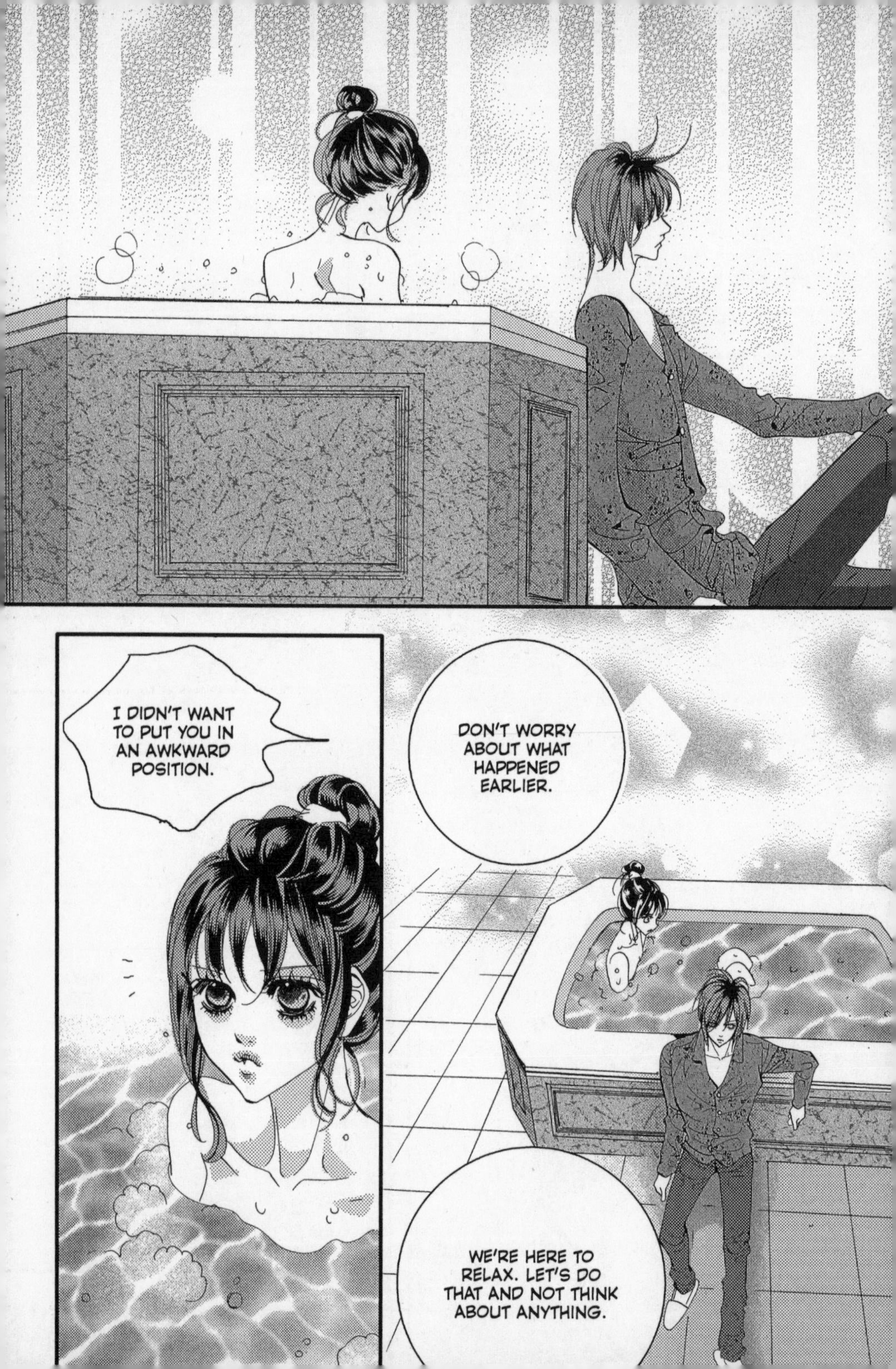
I DIDN'T WANT TO PUT YOU IN AN AWKWARD POSITION.
DON'T WORRY ABOUT WHAT HAPPENED EARLIER.
WE'RE HERE TO RELAX. LET'S DO THAT AND NOT THINK ABOUT ANYTHING.

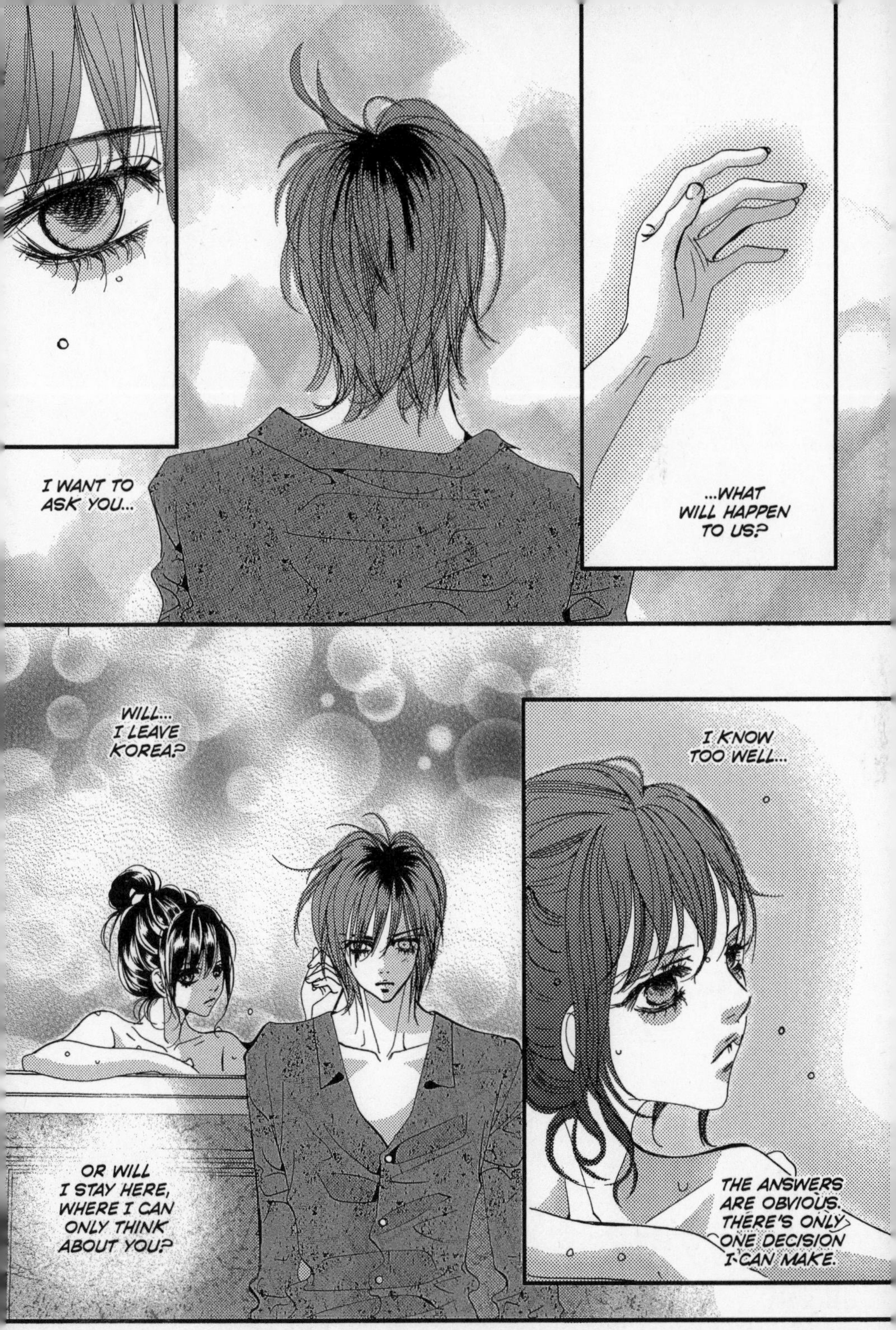
I WANT TO ASK YOU...
...WHAT WILL HAPPEN TO US?
WILL... I LEAVE KOREA?
OR WILL I STAY HERE, WHERE I CAN ONLY THINK ABOUT YOU?
I KNOW TOO WELL...
THE ANSWERS ARE OBVIOUS. THERE'S ONLY ONE DECISION I CAN MAKE.

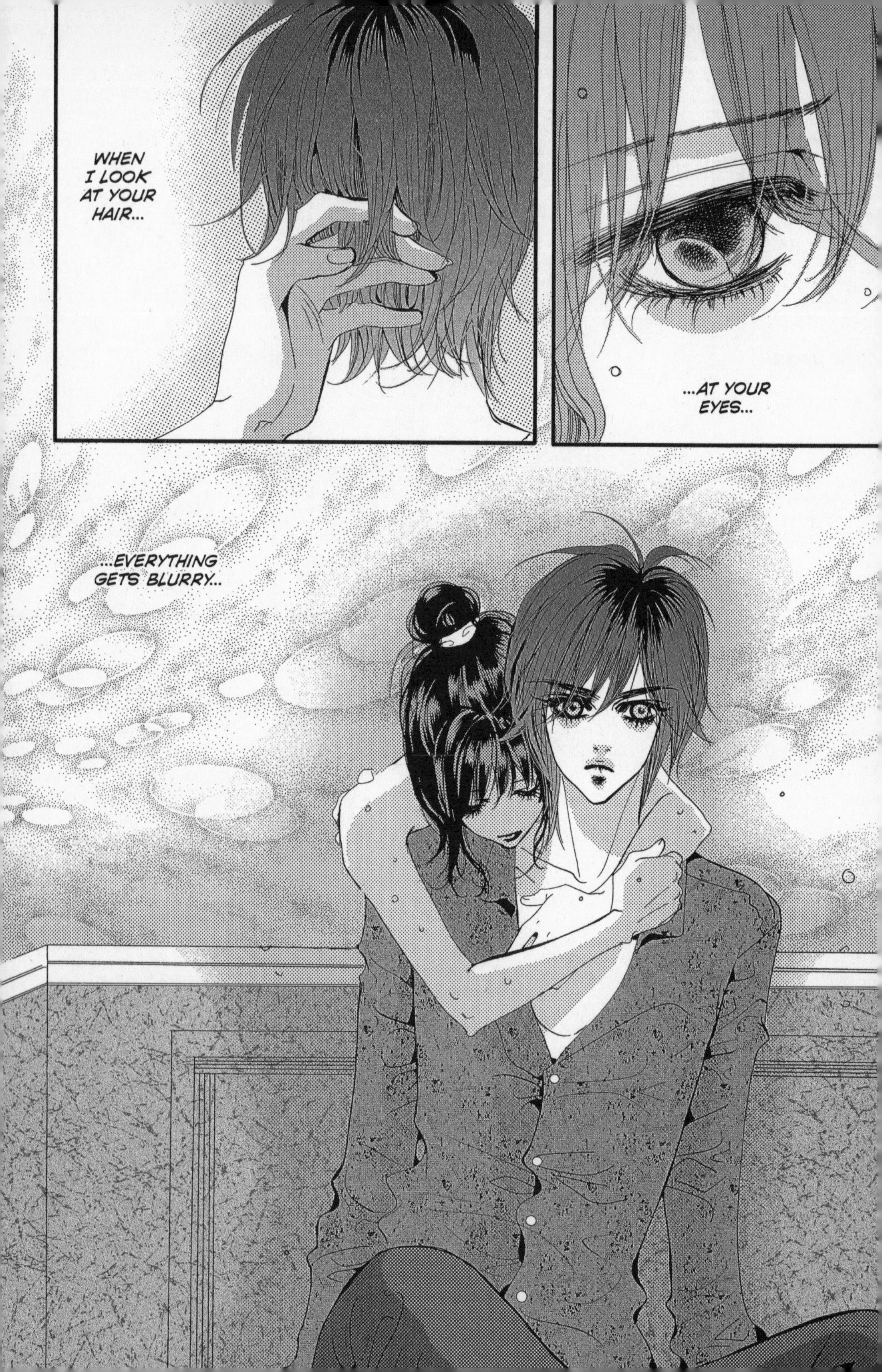
WHEN I LOOK AT YOUR HAIR...
...AT YOUR EYES...
...EVERYTHING GETS BLURRY...

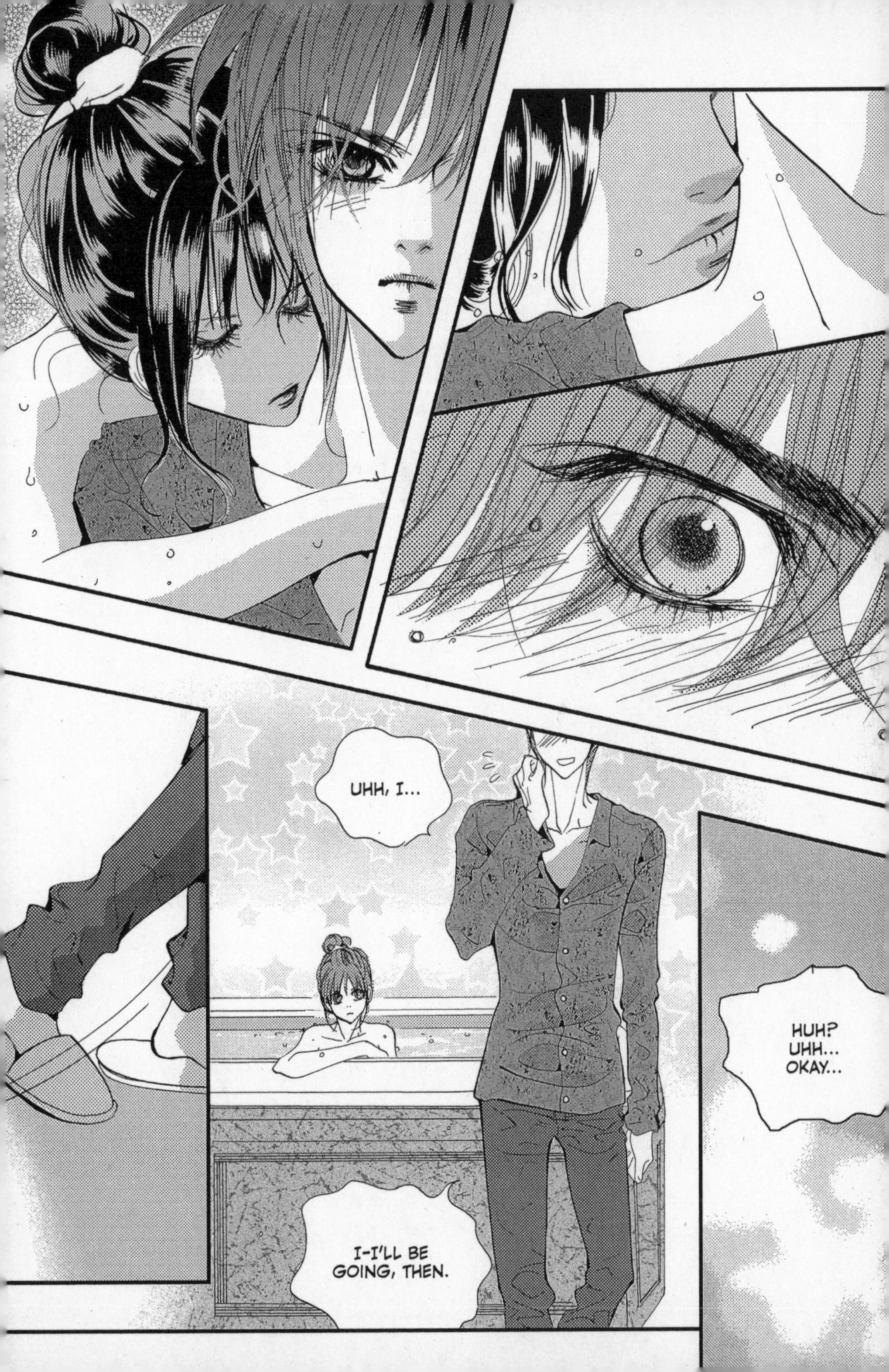
UHH, I...
I-I'LL BE GOING, THEN.
HUH? UHH... OKAY...

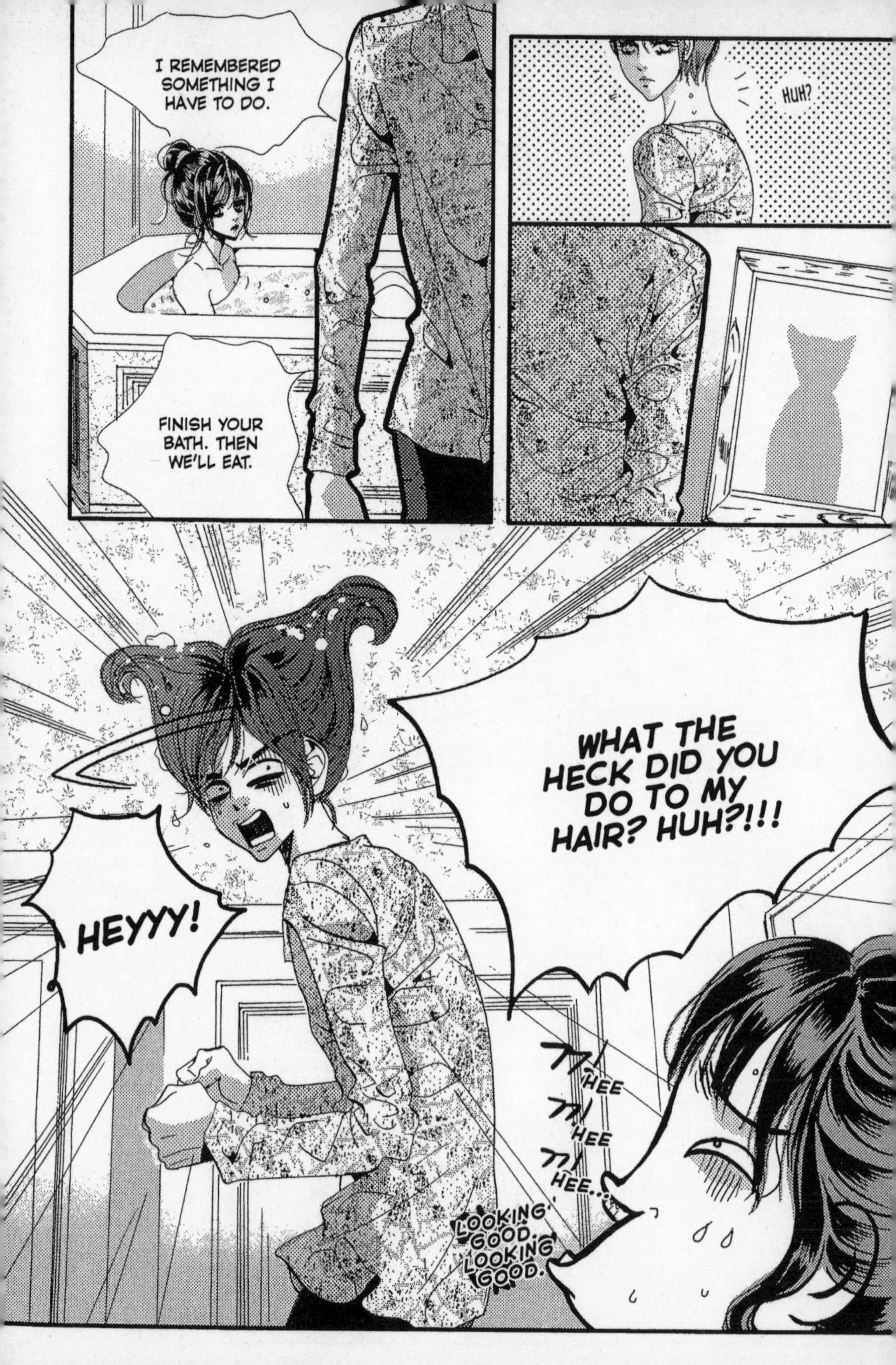
I REMEMBERED SOMETHING I HAVE TO DO.
FINISH YOUR BATH. THEN WE'LL EAT.
HUH?
HEYYY!
WHAT THE HECK DID YOU DO TO MY HAIR? HUH?!!!
HEE
HEE
HEE...
LOOKING GOOD. LOOKING GOOD.

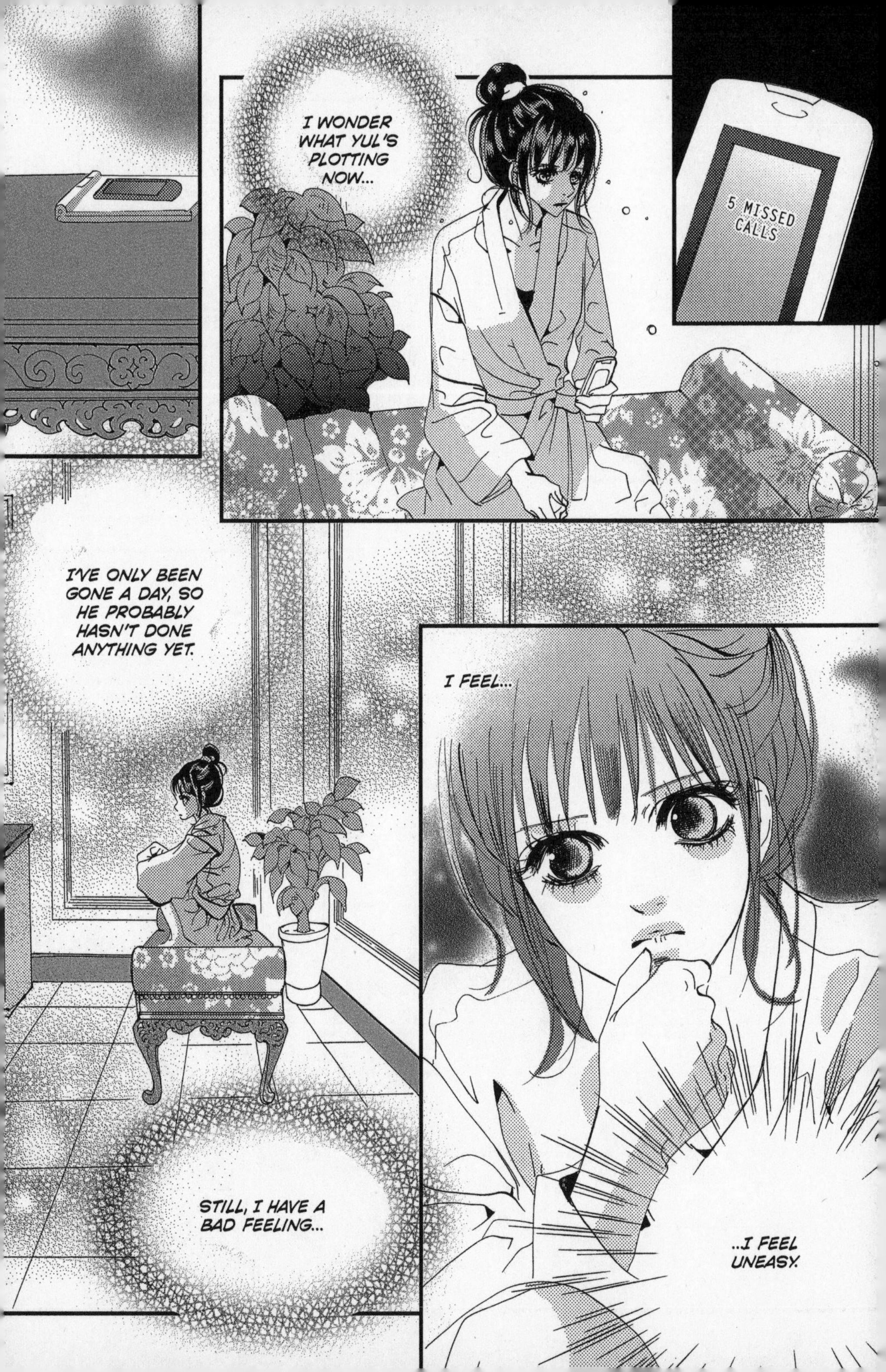
5 MISSED CALLS
I WONDER WHAT YUL'S PLOTTING NOW...
I'VE ONLY BEEN GONE A DAY, SO HE PROBABLY HASN'T DONE ANYTHING YET.
STILL, I HAVE A BAD FEELING...
I FEEL...
...I FEEL UNEASY.

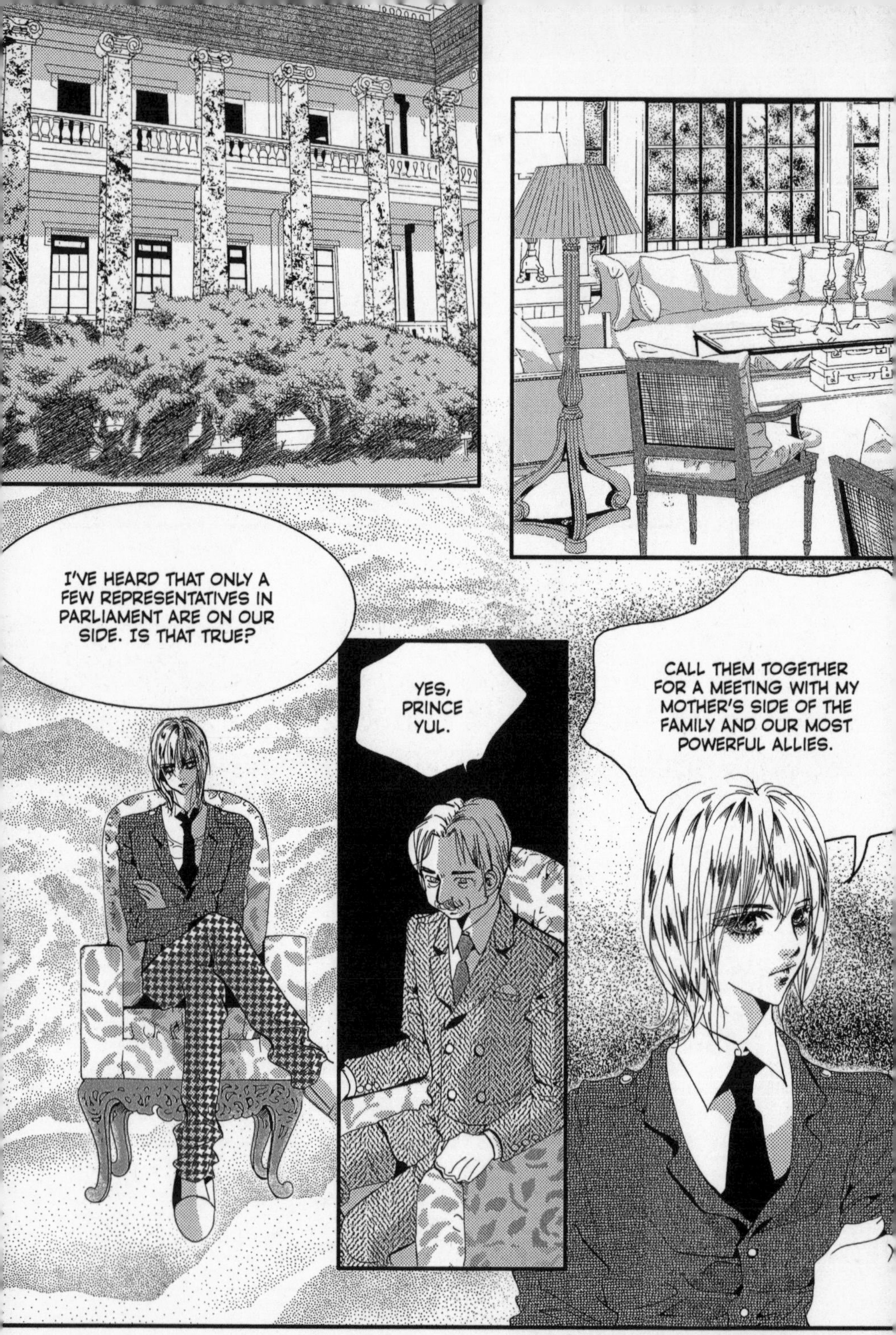
I'VE HEARD THAT ONLY A FEW REPRESENTATIVES IN PARLIAMENT ARE ON OUR SIDE. IS THAT TRUE?
YES, PRINCE YUL.
CALL THEM TOGETHER FOR A MEETING WITH MY MOTHER'S SIDE OF THE FAMILY AND OUR MOST POWERFUL ALLIES.

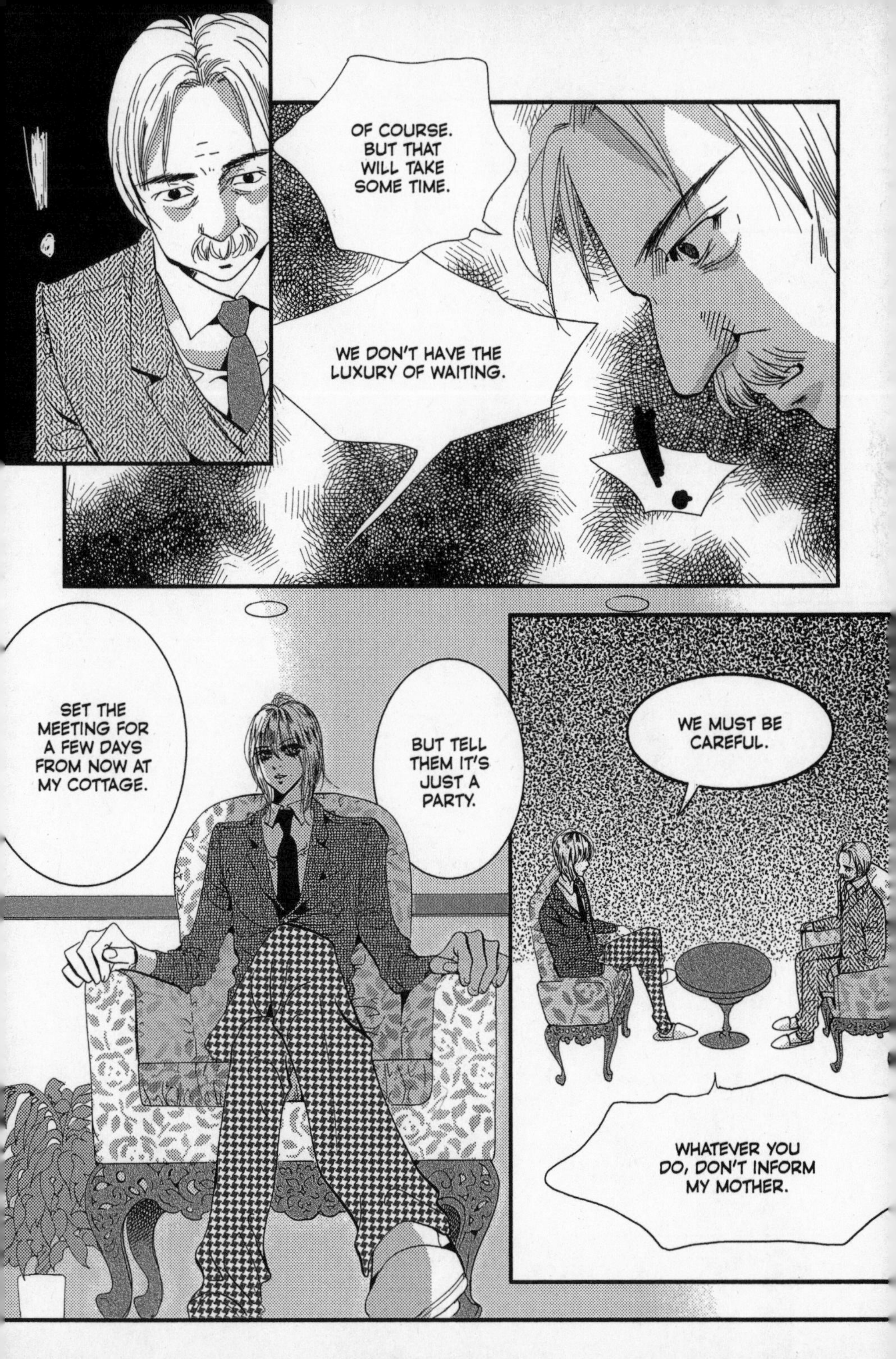
!
OF COURSE. BUT THAT WILL TAKE SOME TIME.
WE DON'T HAVE THE LUXURY OF WAITING.
!
SET THE MEETING FOR A FEW DAYS FROM NOW AT MY COTTAGE.
BUT TELL THEM IT'S JUST A PARTY.
WE MUST BE CAREFUL.
WHATEVER YOU DO, DON'T INFORM MY MOTHER.

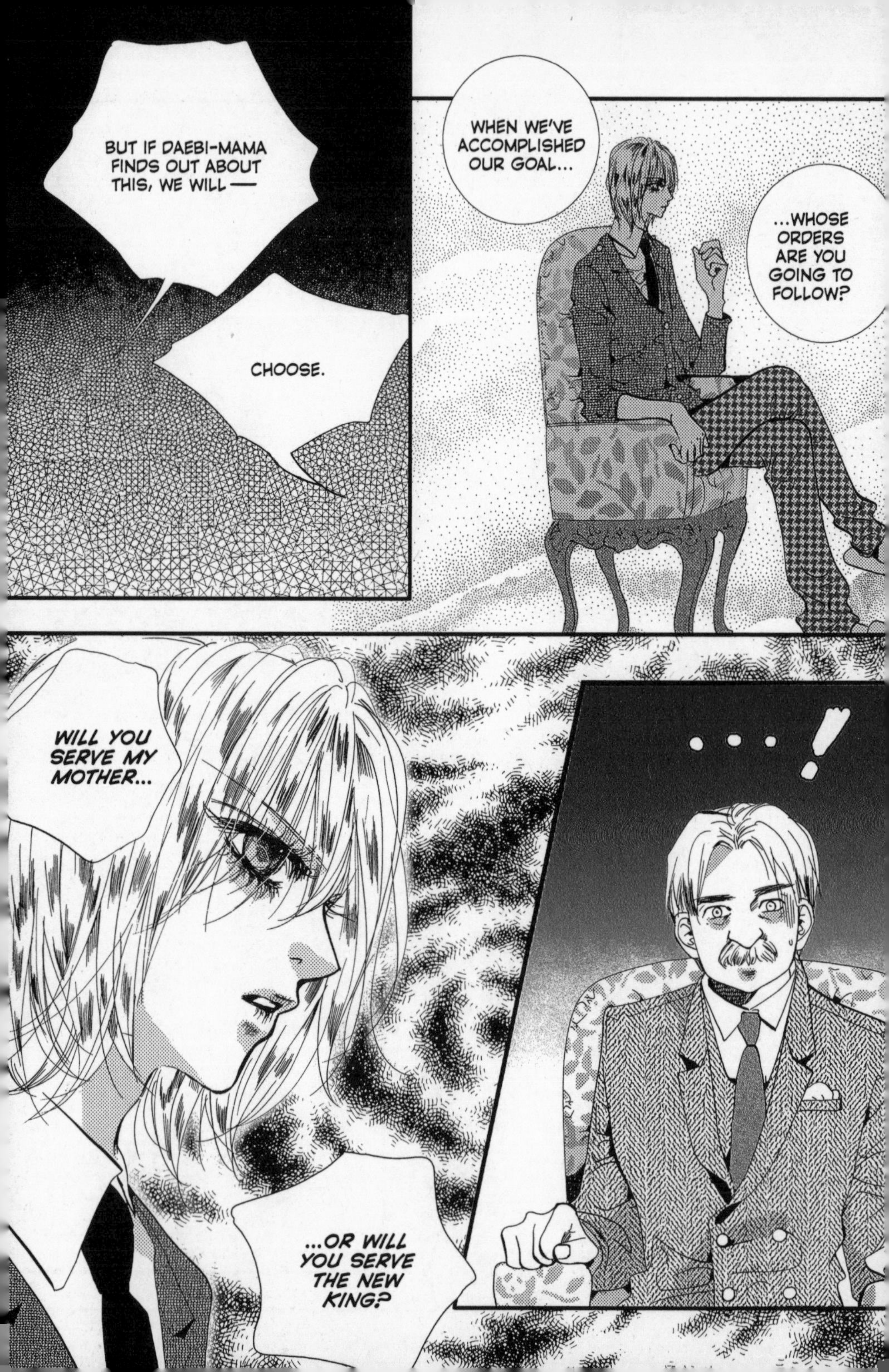
BUT IF DAEBI-MAMA FINDS OUT ABOUT THIS, WE WILL —
CHOOSE.
WHEN WE'VE ACCOMPLISHED OUR GOAL...
...WHOSE ORDERS ARE YOU GOING TO FOLLOW?
WILL YOU SERVE MY MOTHER...
...OR WILL YOU SERVE THE NEW KING?
...!

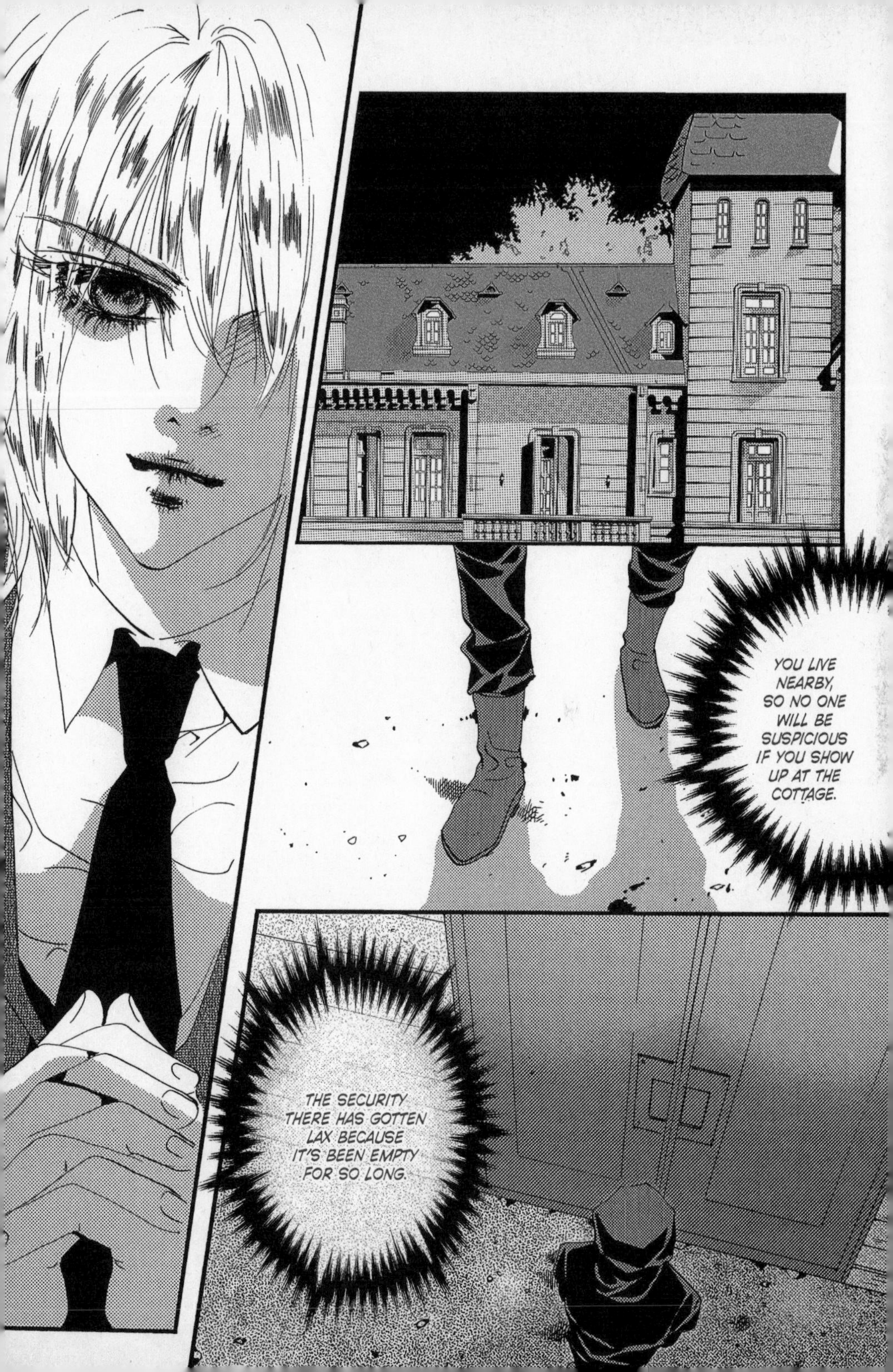
YOU LIVE NEARBY, SO NO ONE WILL BE SUSPICIOUS IF YOU SHOW UP AT THE COTTAGE.
THE SECURITY THERE HAS GOTTEN LAX BECAUSE IT'S BEEN EMPTY FOR SO LONG.

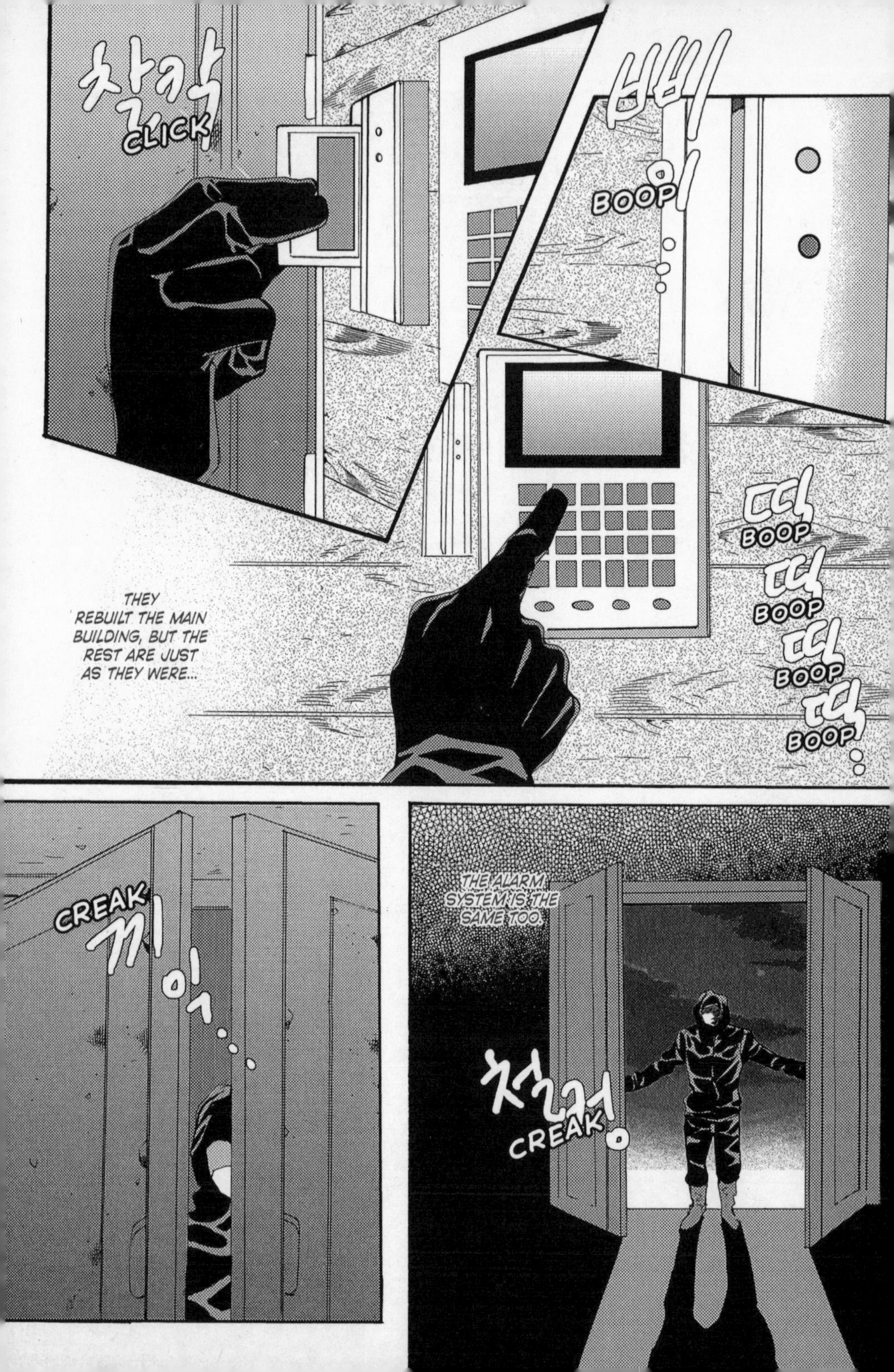

찰칵
CLICK
BOOP
THEY REBUILT THE MAIN BUILDING, BUT THE REST ARE JUST AS THEY WERE...
딱
BOOP
딱
BOOP
딱
BOOP
딱
BOOP
CREAK
끼익...
THE ALARM SYSTEM IS THE SAME TOO.
철컥
CREAK

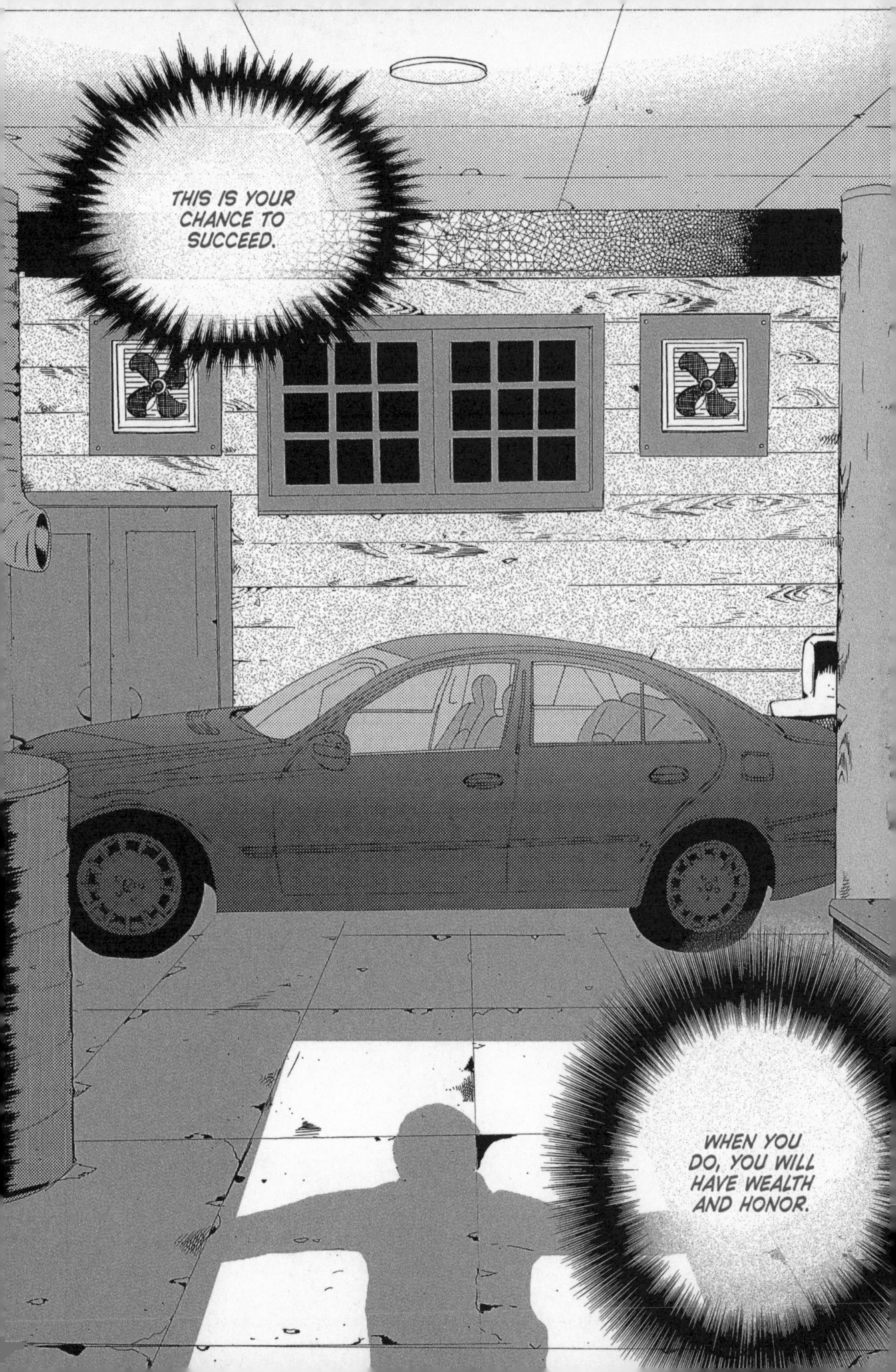
THIS IS YOUR CHANCE TO SUCCEED.
WHEN YOU DO, YOU WILL HAVE WEALTH AND HONOR.

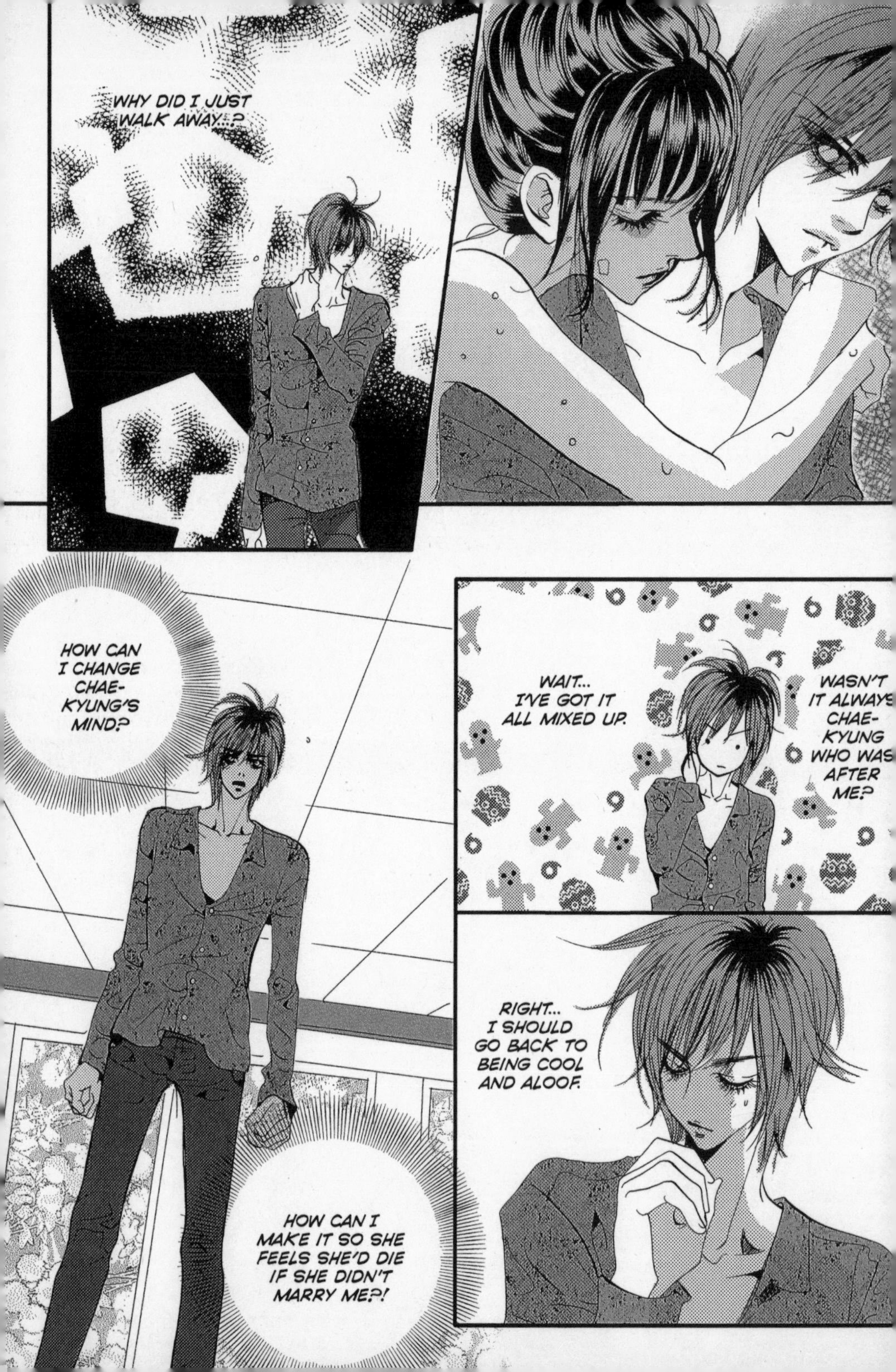
WHY DID I JUST WALK AWAY...?
HOW CAN I CHANGE CHAE-KYUNG'S MIND?
HOW CAN I MAKE IT SO SHE FEELS SHE'D DIE IF SHE DIDN'T MARRY ME?!
WAIT... I'VE GOT IT ALL MIXED UP.
WASN'T IT ALWAYS CHAE-KYUNG WHO WAS AFTER ME?
RIGHT... I SHOULD GO BACK TO BEING COOL AND ALOOF.

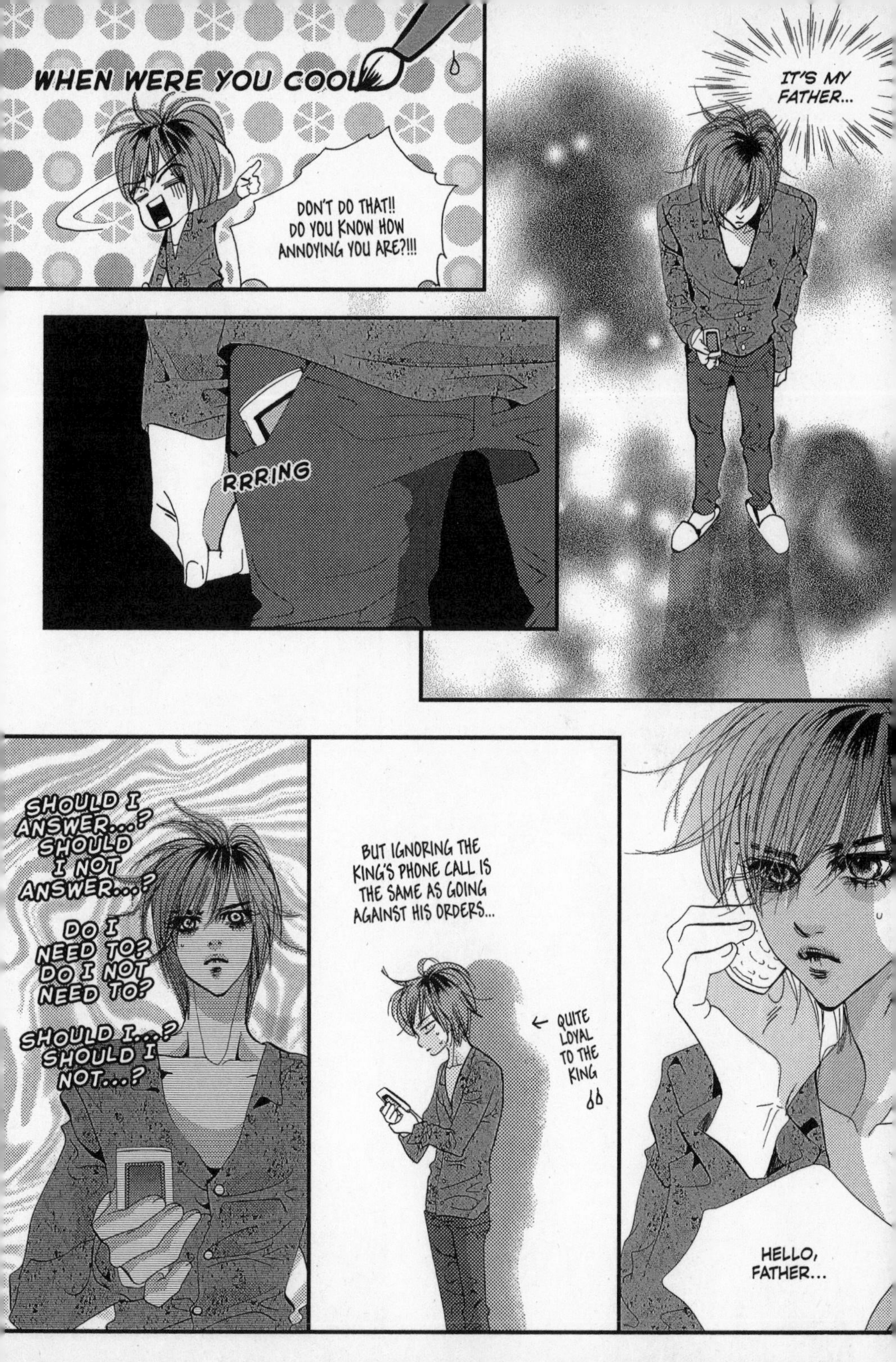
WHEN WERE YOU COOL
DON'T DO THAT!! DO YOU KNOW HOW ANNOYING YOU ARE?!!!
RRRING
IT'S MY FATHER...
SHOULD I ANSWER...? SHOULD I NOT ANSWER...?
DO I NEED TO? DO I NOT NEED TO?
SHOULD I...? SHOULD I NOT...?
BUT IGNORING THE KING'S PHONE CALL IS THE SAME AS GOING AGAINST HIS ORDERS...
← QUITE LOYAL TO THE KING
HELLO, FATHER...

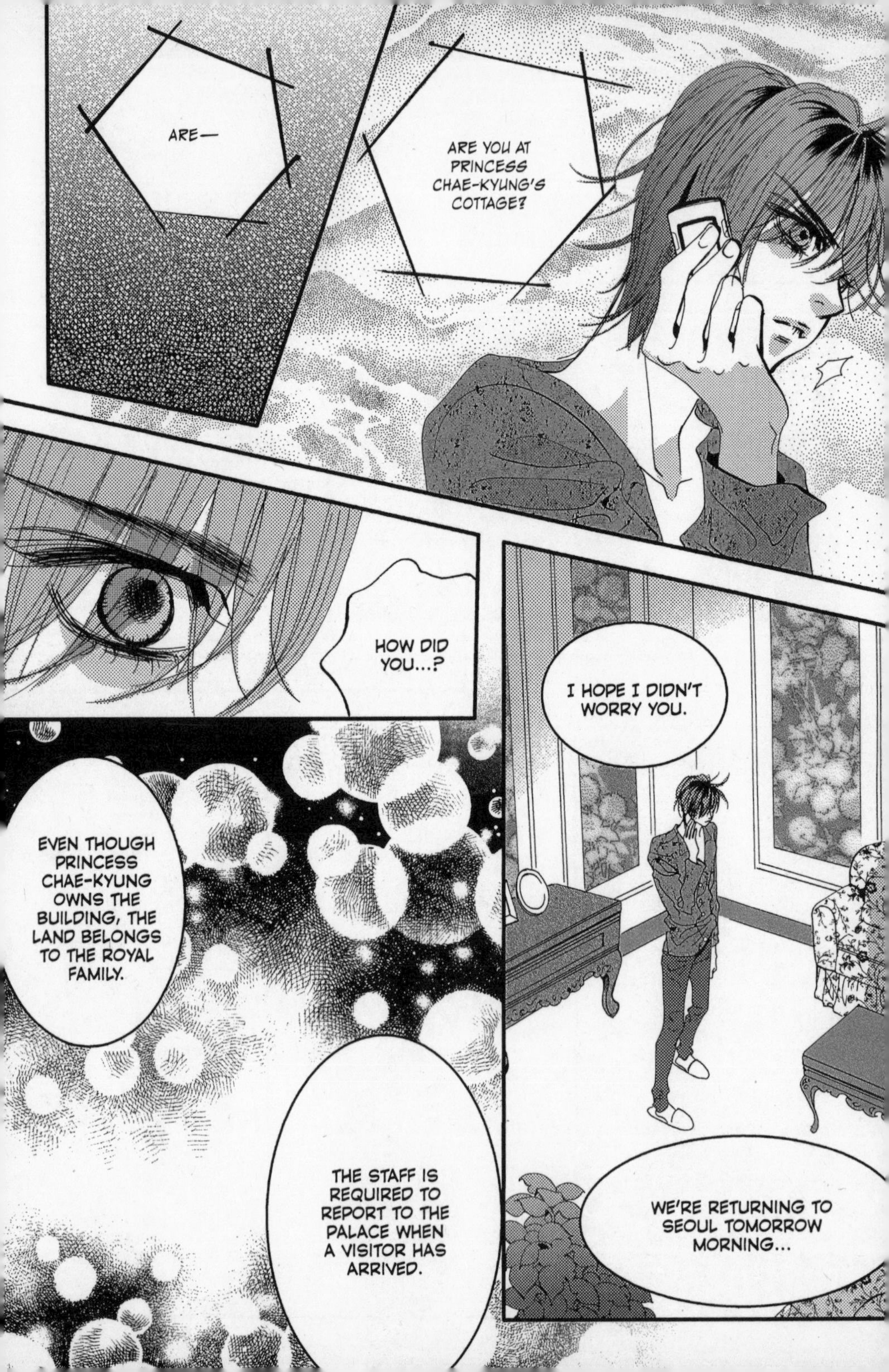
ARE—
ARE YOU AT PRINCESS CHAE-KYUNG'S COTTAGE?
HOW DID YOU...?
EVEN THOUGH PRINCESS CHAE-KYUNG OWNS THE BUILDING, THE LAND BELONGS TO THE ROYAL FAMILY.
THE STAFF IS REQUIRED TO REPORT TO THE PALACE WHEN A VISITOR HAS ARRIVED.
I HOPE I DIDN'T WORRY YOU.
WE'RE RETURNING TO SEOUL TOMORROW MORNING...

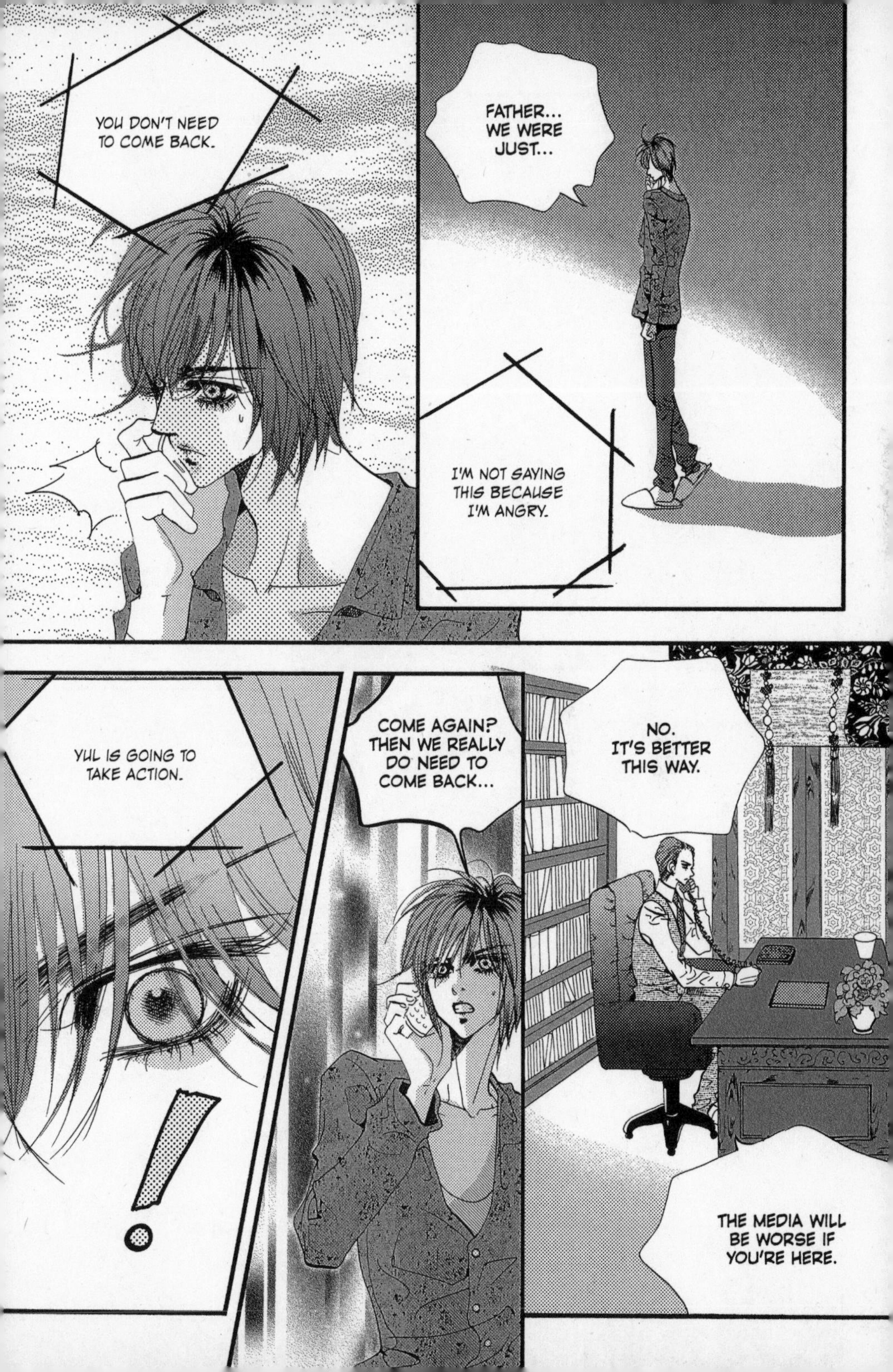
YOU DON'T NEED TO COME BACK.
FATHER... WE WERE JUST...
I'M NOT SAYING THIS BECAUSE I'M ANGRY.
YUL IS GOING TO TAKE ACTION.
COME AGAIN? THEN WE REALLY DO NEED TO COME BACK...
NO. IT'S BETTER THIS WAY.
THE MEDIA WILL BE WORSE IF YOU'RE HERE.

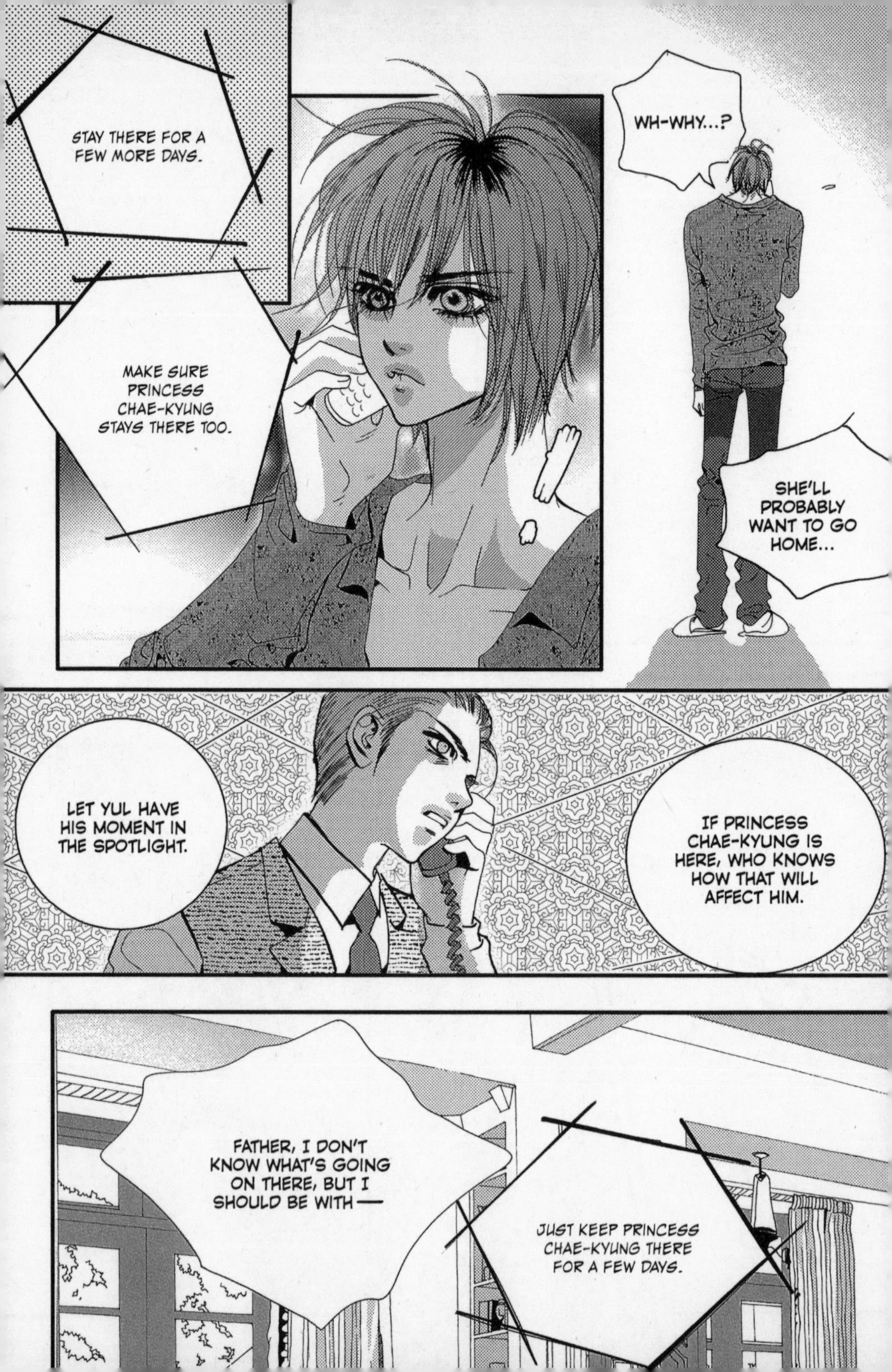
STAY THERE FOR A FEW MORE DAYS.
MAKE SURE PRINCESS CHAE-KYUNG STAYS THERE TOO.
WH-WHY...?
SHE'LL PROBABLY WANT TO GO HOME...
LET YUL HAVE HIS MOMENT IN THE SPOTLIGHT.
IF PRINCESS CHAE-KYUNG IS HERE, WHO KNOWS HOW THAT WILL AFFECT HIM.
FATHER, I DON'T KNOW WHAT'S GOING ON THERE, BUT I SHOULD BE WITH—
JUST KEEP PRINCESS CHAE-KYUNG THERE FOR A FEW DAYS.

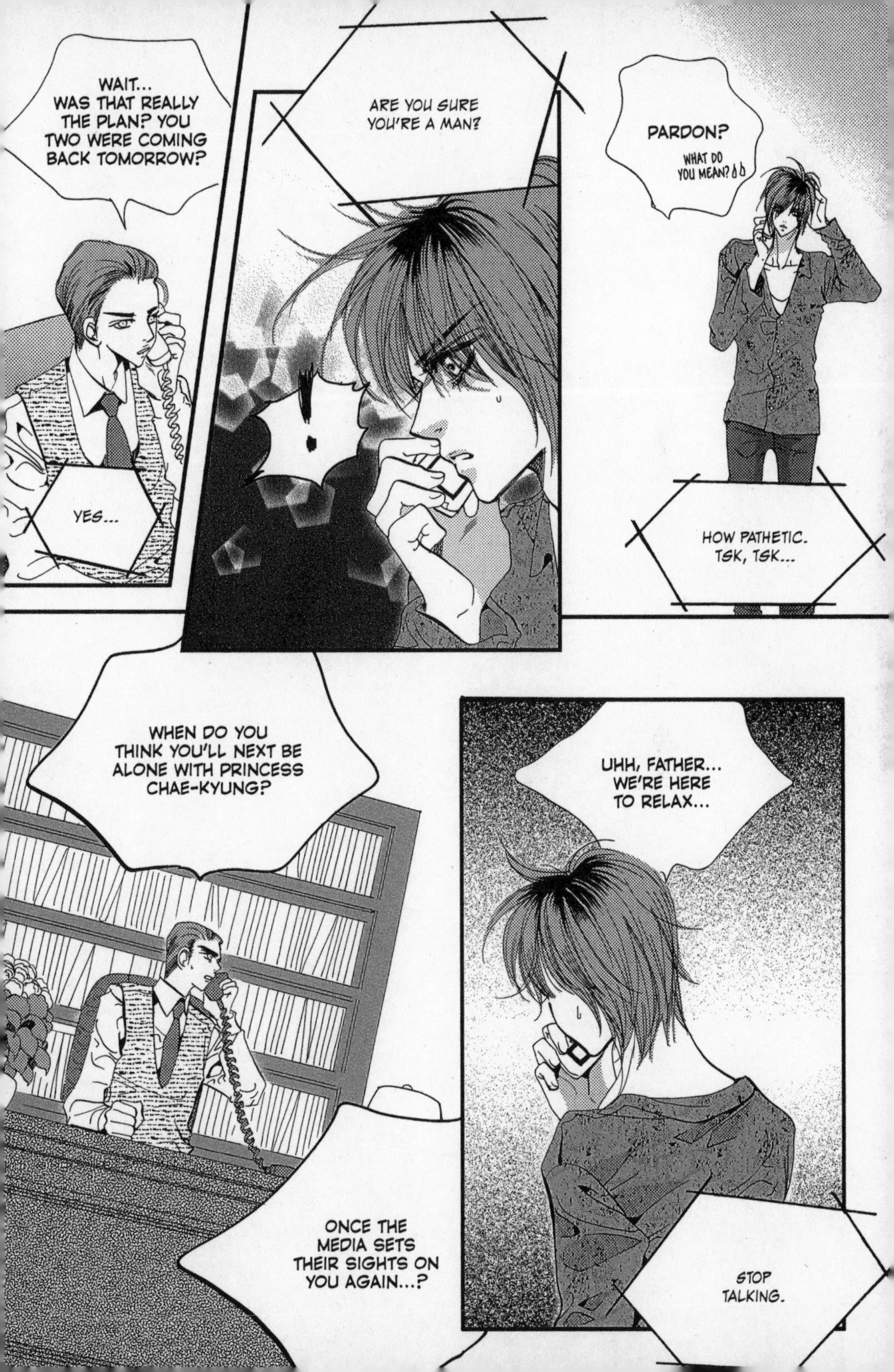
WAIT... WAS THAT REALLY THE PLAN? YOU TWO WERE COMING BACK TOMORROW?
YES...
ARE YOU SURE YOU'RE A MAN?
PARDON?
WHAT DO YOU MEAN?
HOW PATHETIC. TSK, TSK...
WHEN DO YOU THINK YOU'LL NEXT BE ALONE WITH PRINCESS CHAE-KYUNG?
ONCE THE MEDIA SETS THEIR SIGHTS ON YOU AGAIN...?
UHH, FATHER... WE'RE HERE TO RELAX...
STOP TALKING.

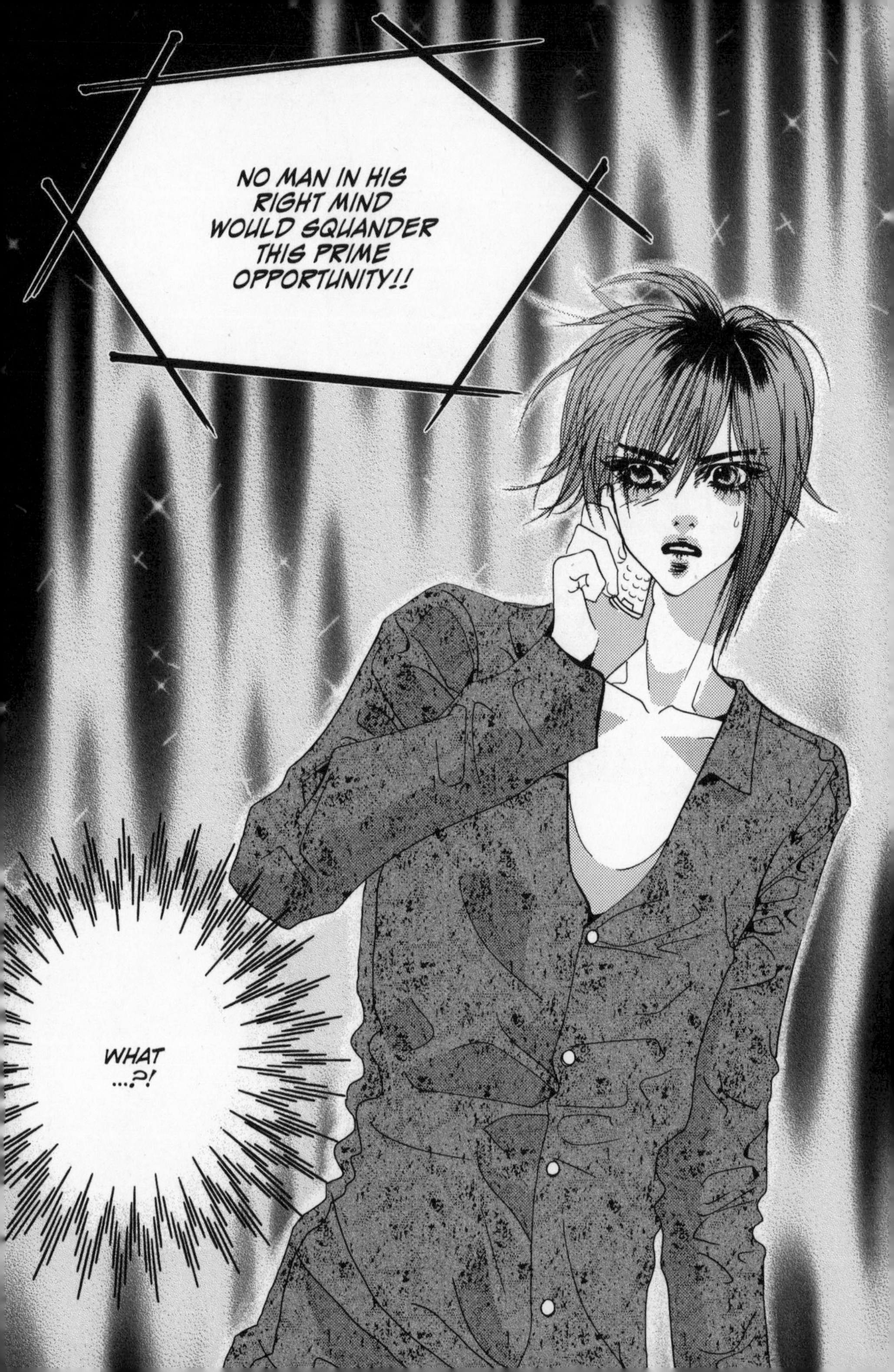
NO MAN IN HIS RIGHT MIND WOULD SQUANDER THIS PRIME OPPORTUNITY!!
WHAT ...?!

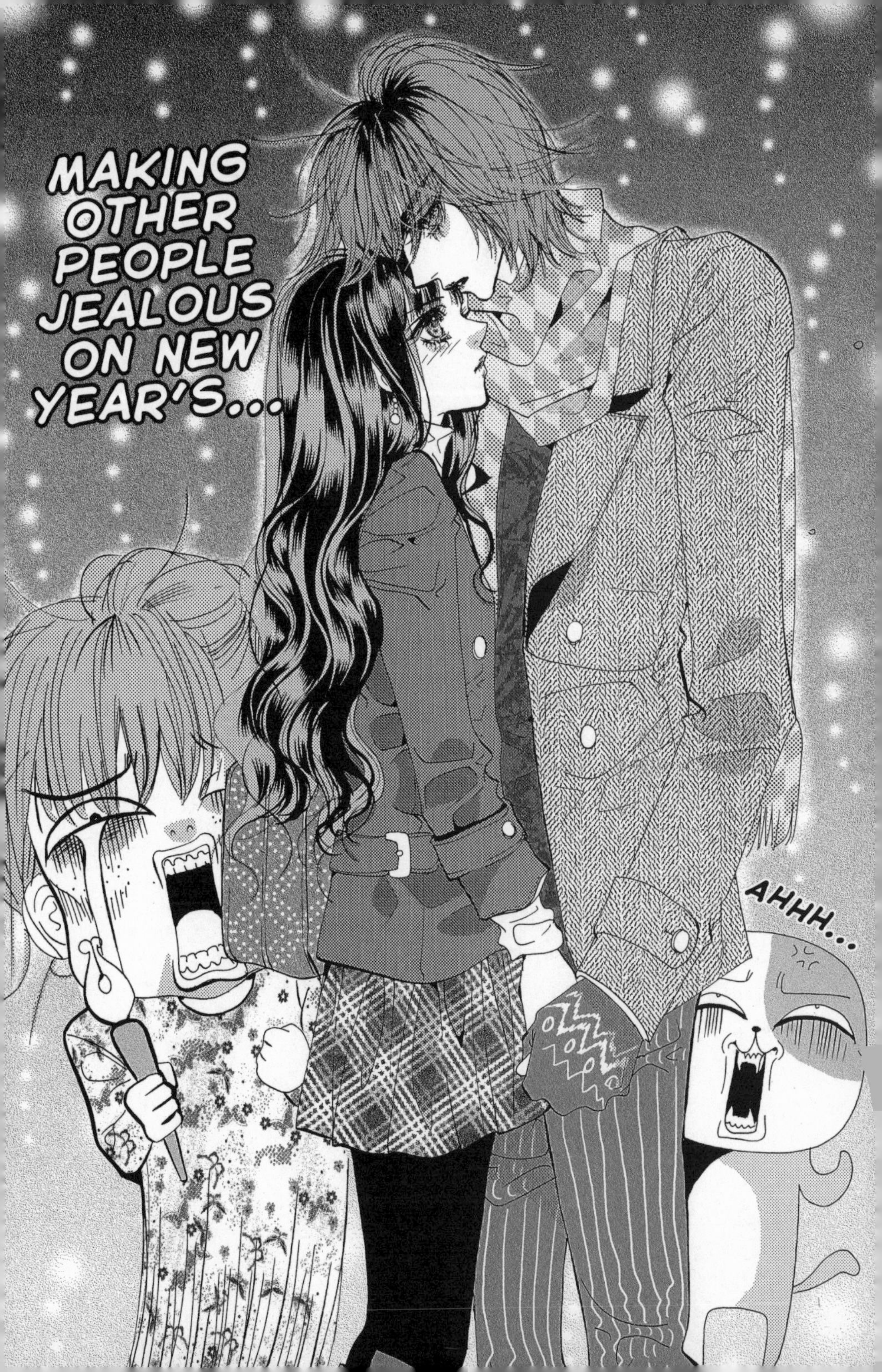
MAKING OTHER PEOPLE JEALOUS ON NEW YEAR'S...
AHHH...

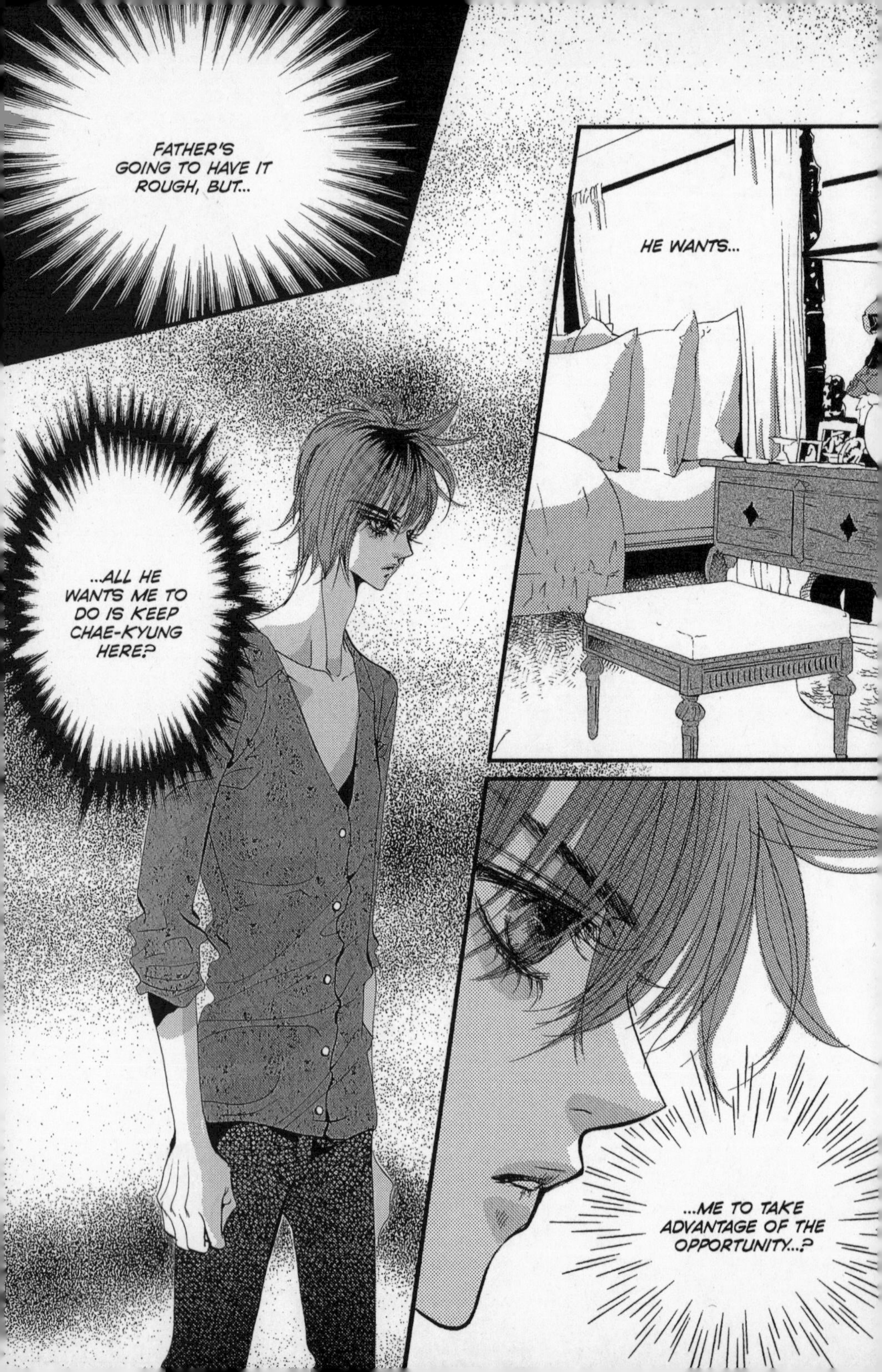
FATHER'S GOING TO HAVE IT ROUGH, BUT...
...ALL HE WANTS ME TO DO IS KEEP CHAE-KYUNG HERE?
HE WANTS...
...ME TO TAKE ADVANTAGE OF THE OPPORTUNITY...?

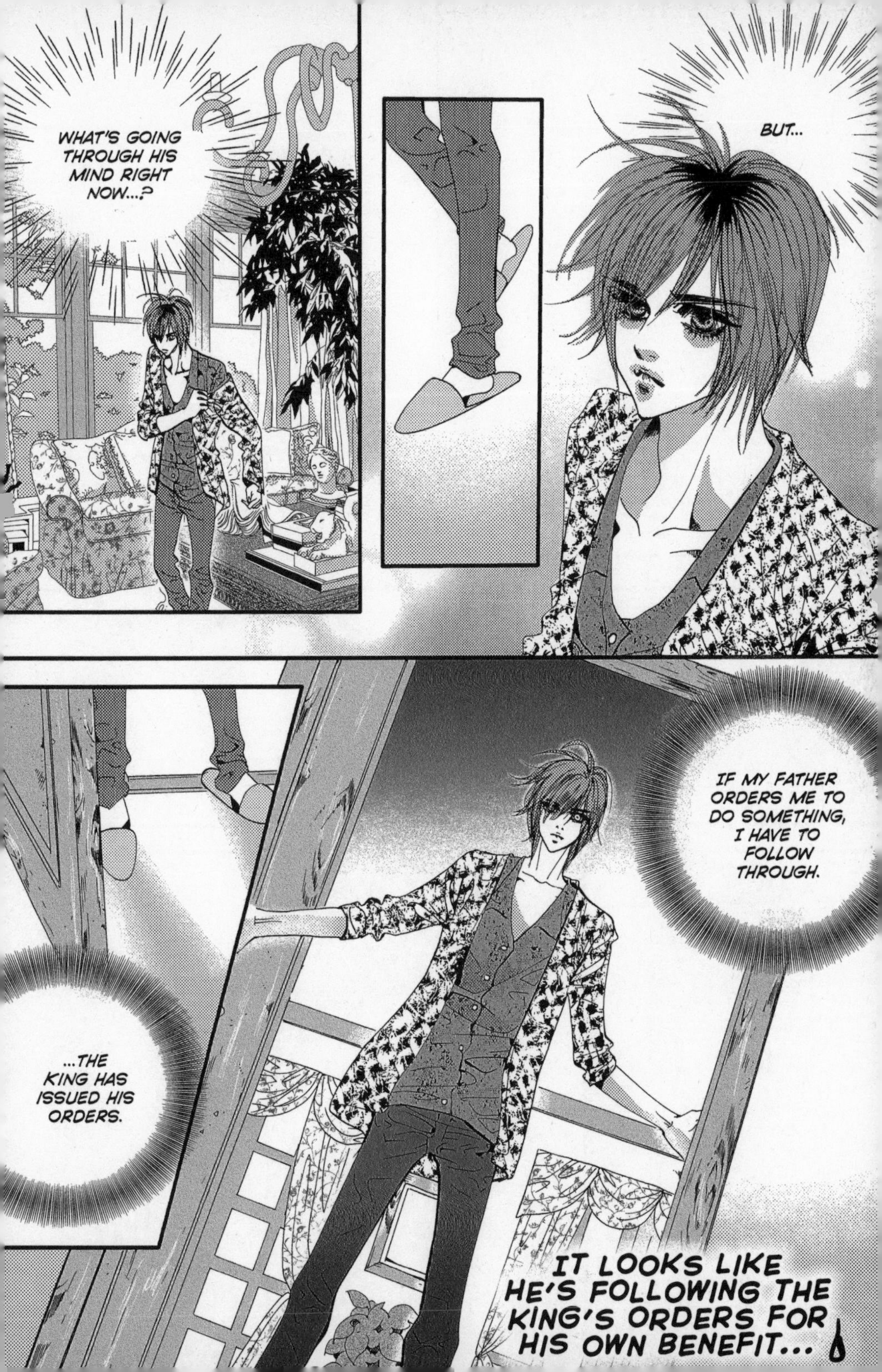
WHAT'S GOING THROUGH HIS MIND RIGHT NOW...?
BUT...
...THE KING HAS ISSUED HIS ORDERS.
IF MY FATHER ORDERS ME TO DO SOMETHING, I HAVE TO FOLLOW THROUGH.
IT LOOKS LIKE HE'S FOLLOWING THE KING'S ORDERS FOR HIS OWN BENEFIT...

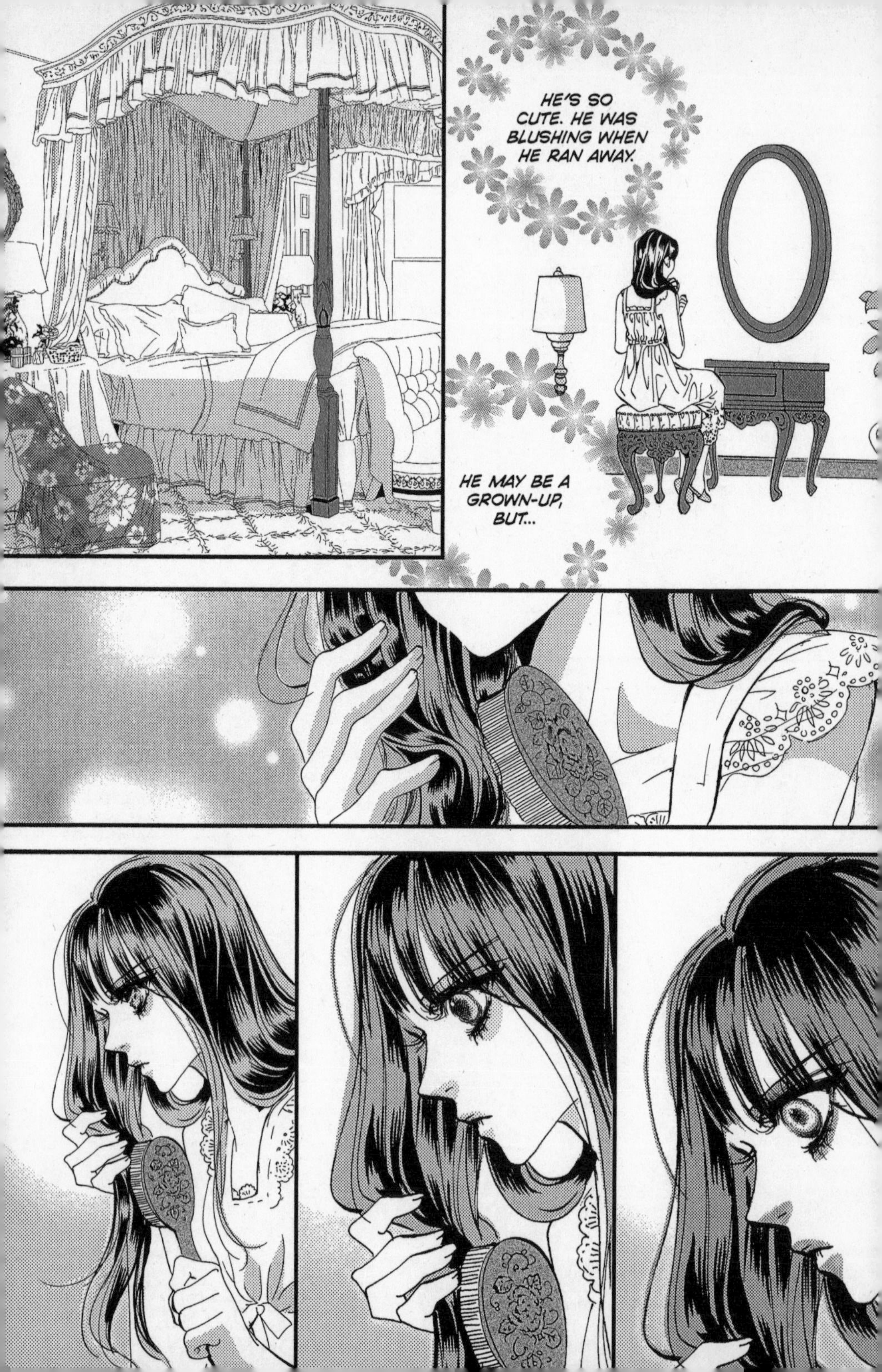
HE'S SO CUTE. HE WAS BLUSHING WHEN HE RAN AWAY.
HE MAY BE A GROWN-UP, BUT...

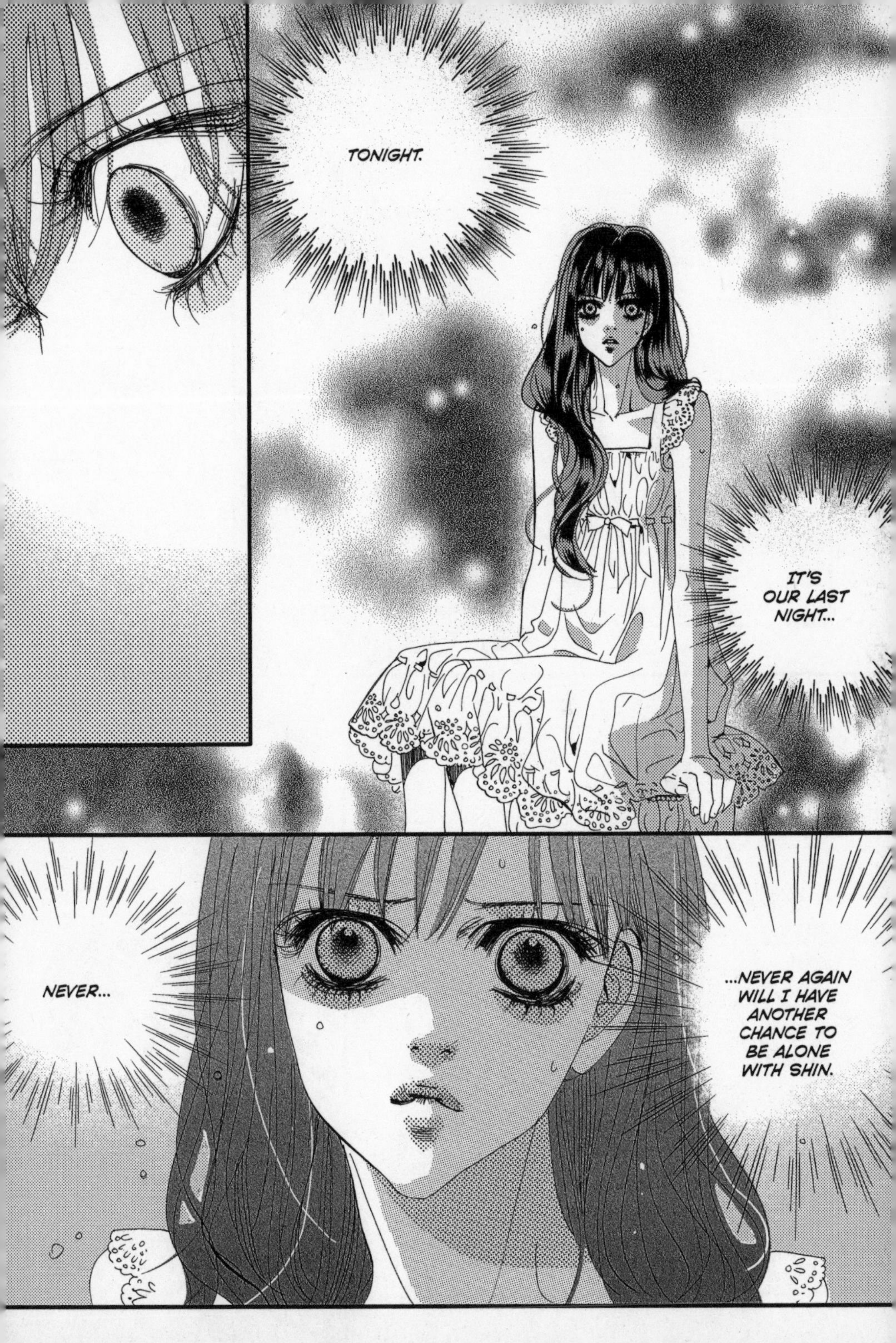
TONIGHT.
IT'S OUR LAST NIGHT...
NEVER...
...NEVER AGAIN WILL I HAVE ANOTHER CHANCE TO BE ALONE WITH SHIN.

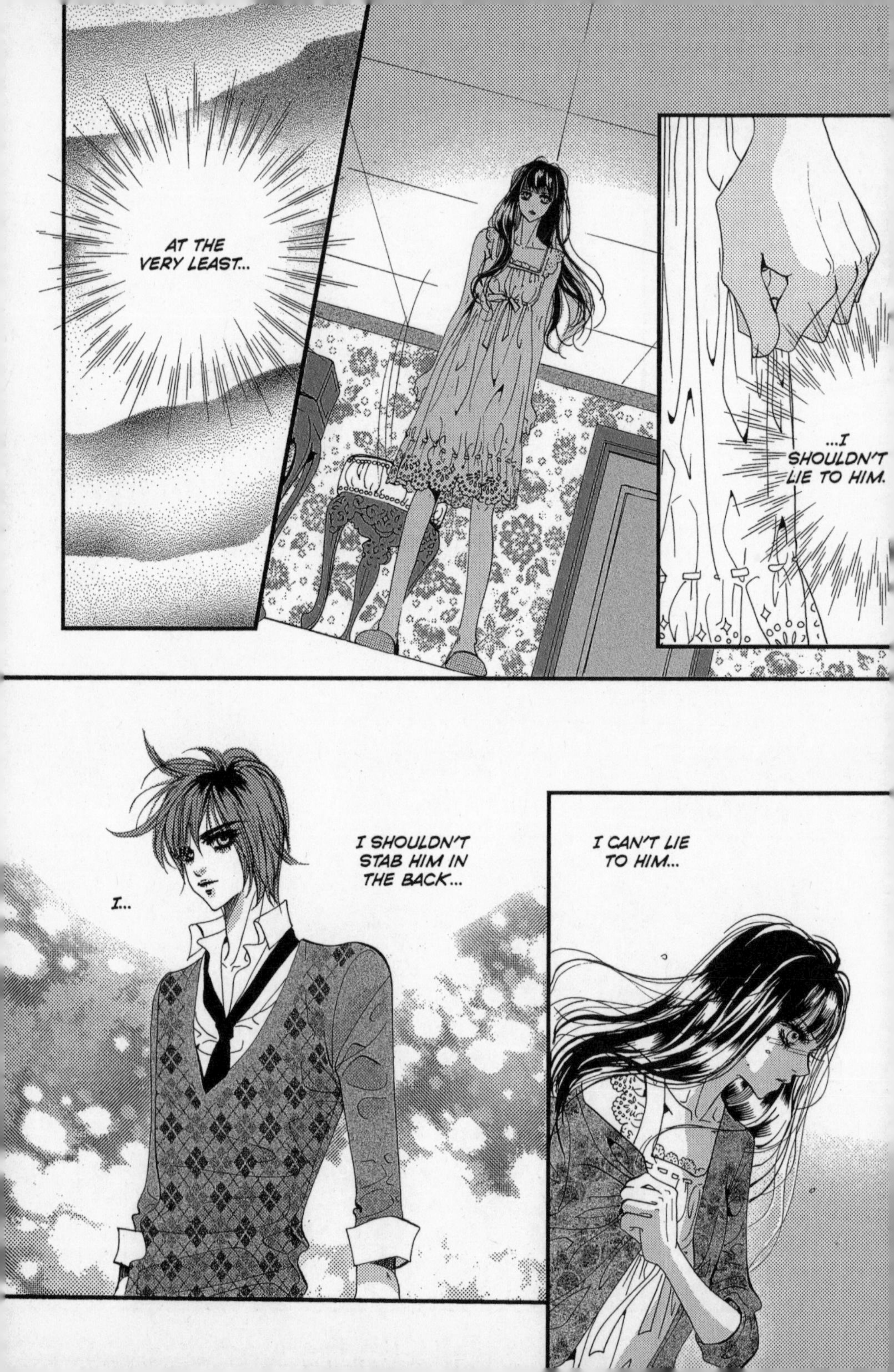
AT THE VERY LEAST...
...I SHOULDN'T LIE TO HIM.
I...
I SHOULDN'T STAB HIM IN THE BACK...
I CAN'T LIE TO HIM...

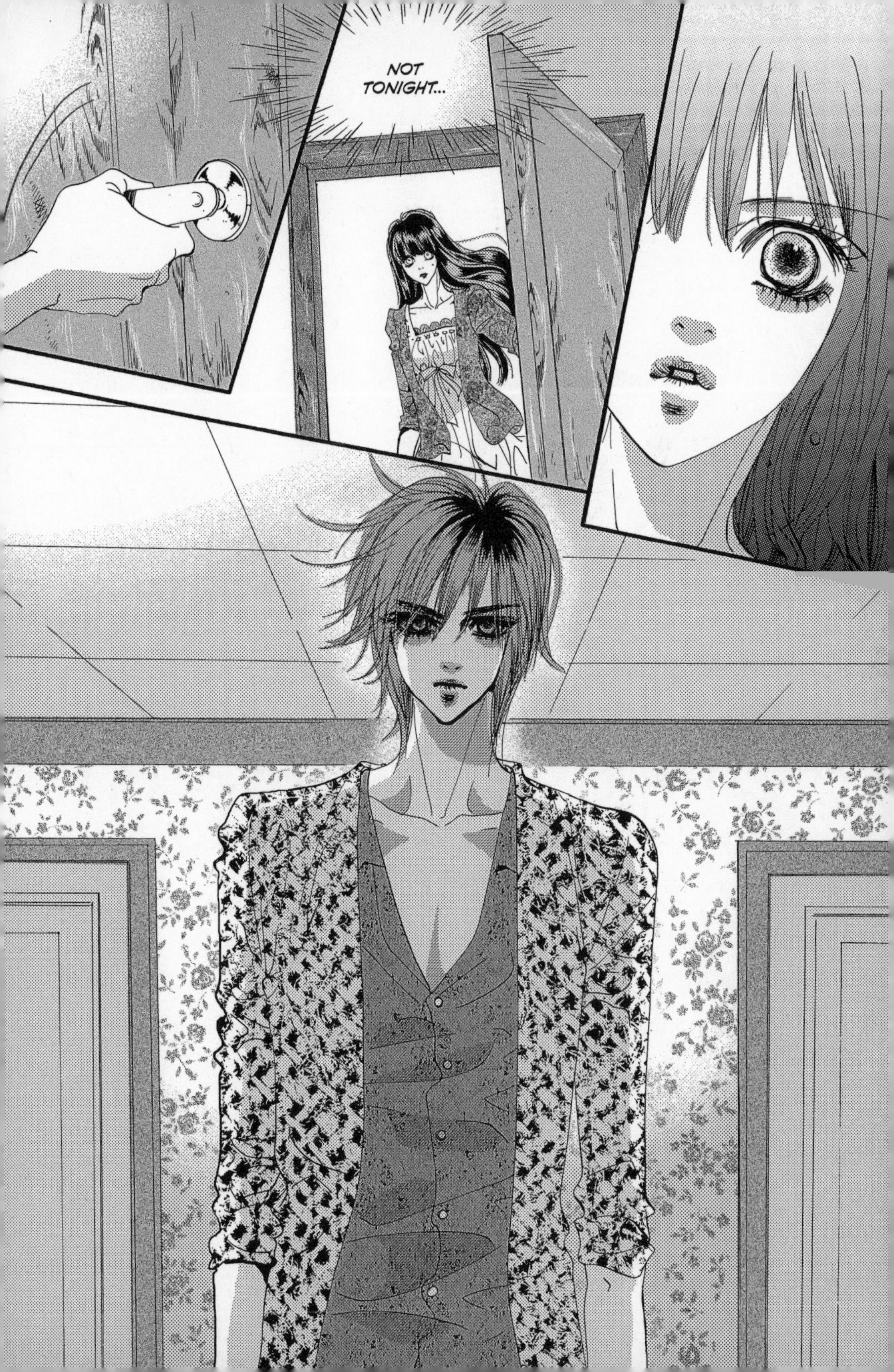
NOT TONIGHT...

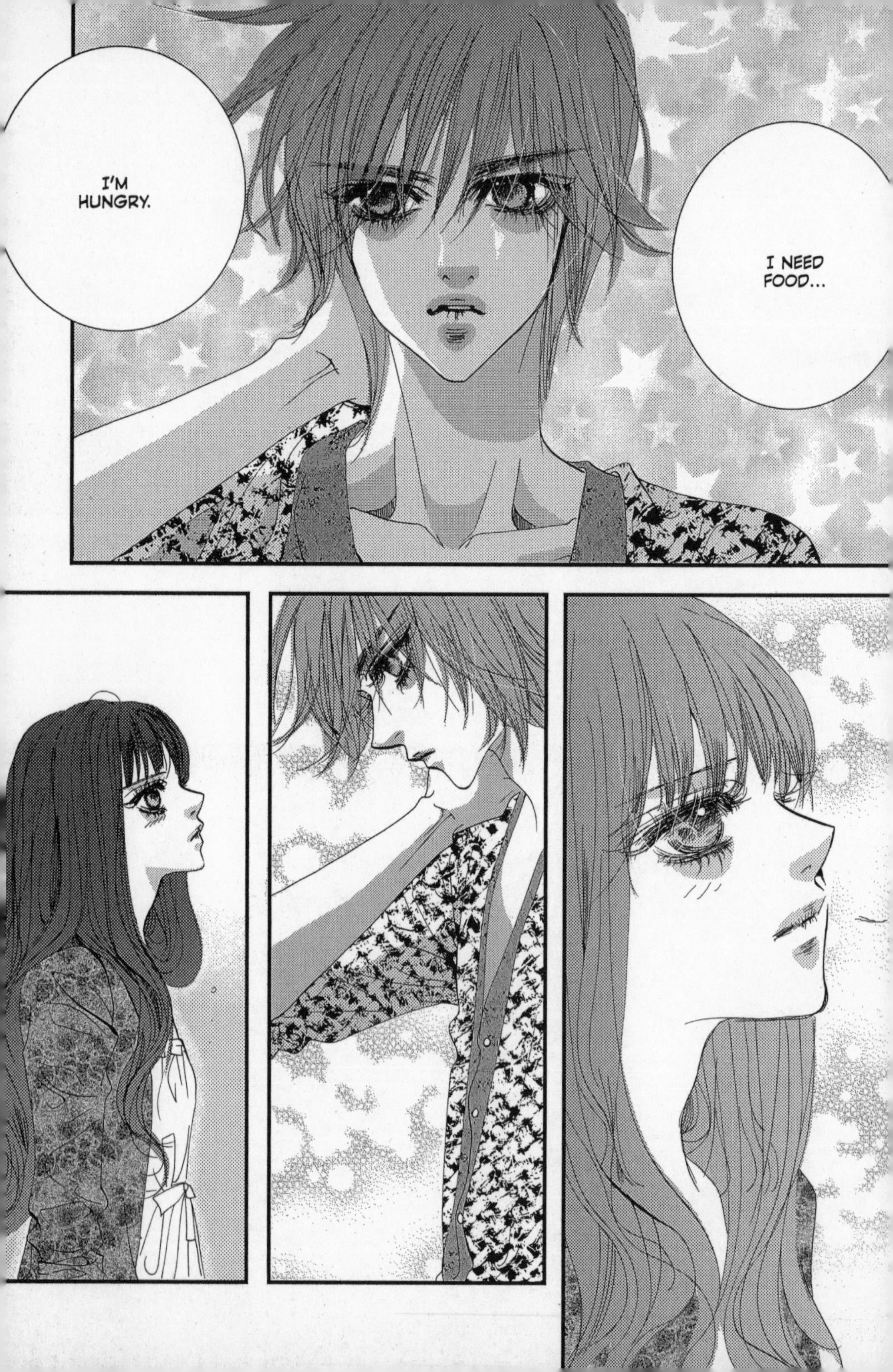
I'M HUNGRY.
I NEED FOOD...

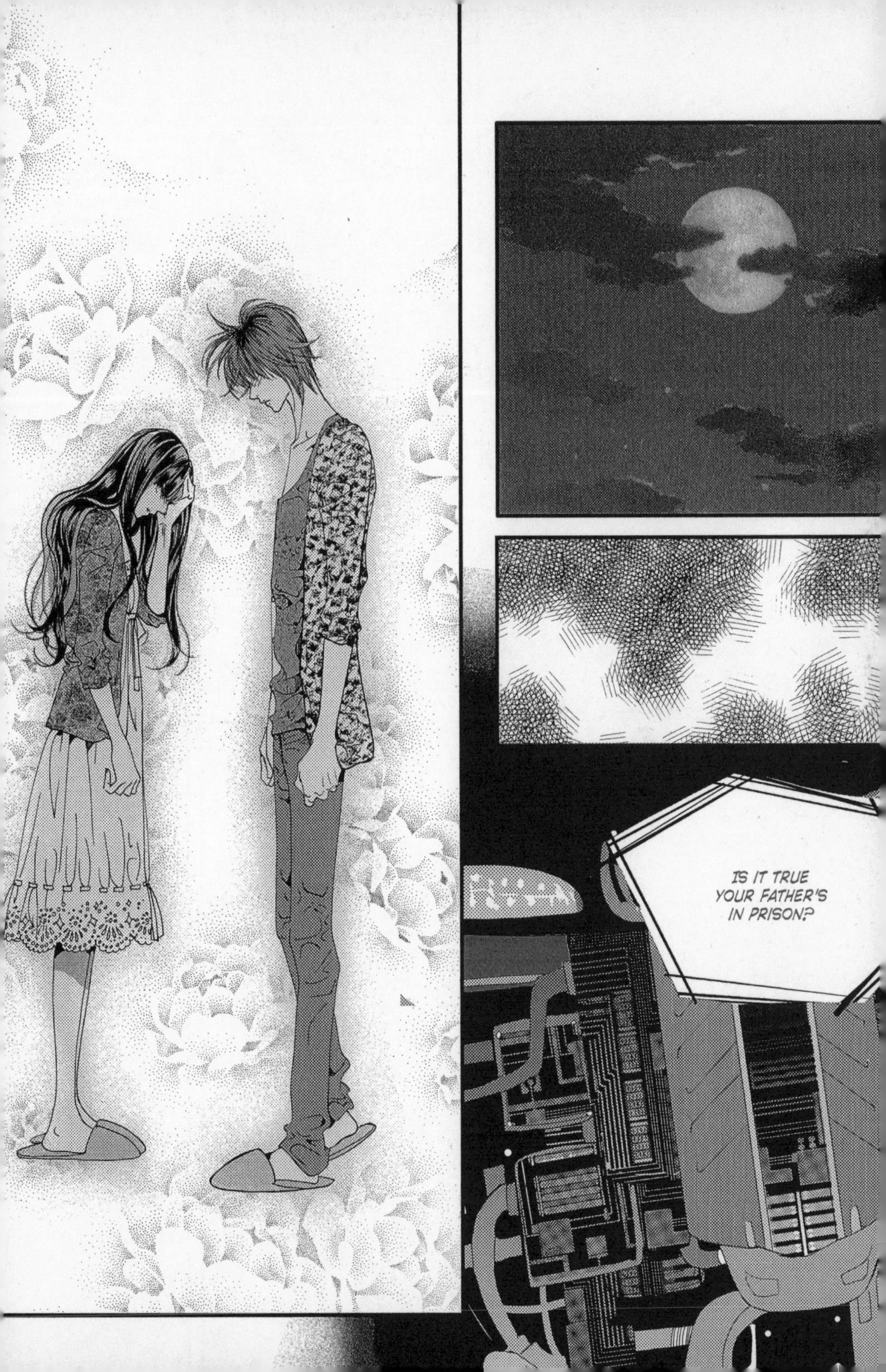
IS IT TRUE YOUR FATHER'S IN PRISON?

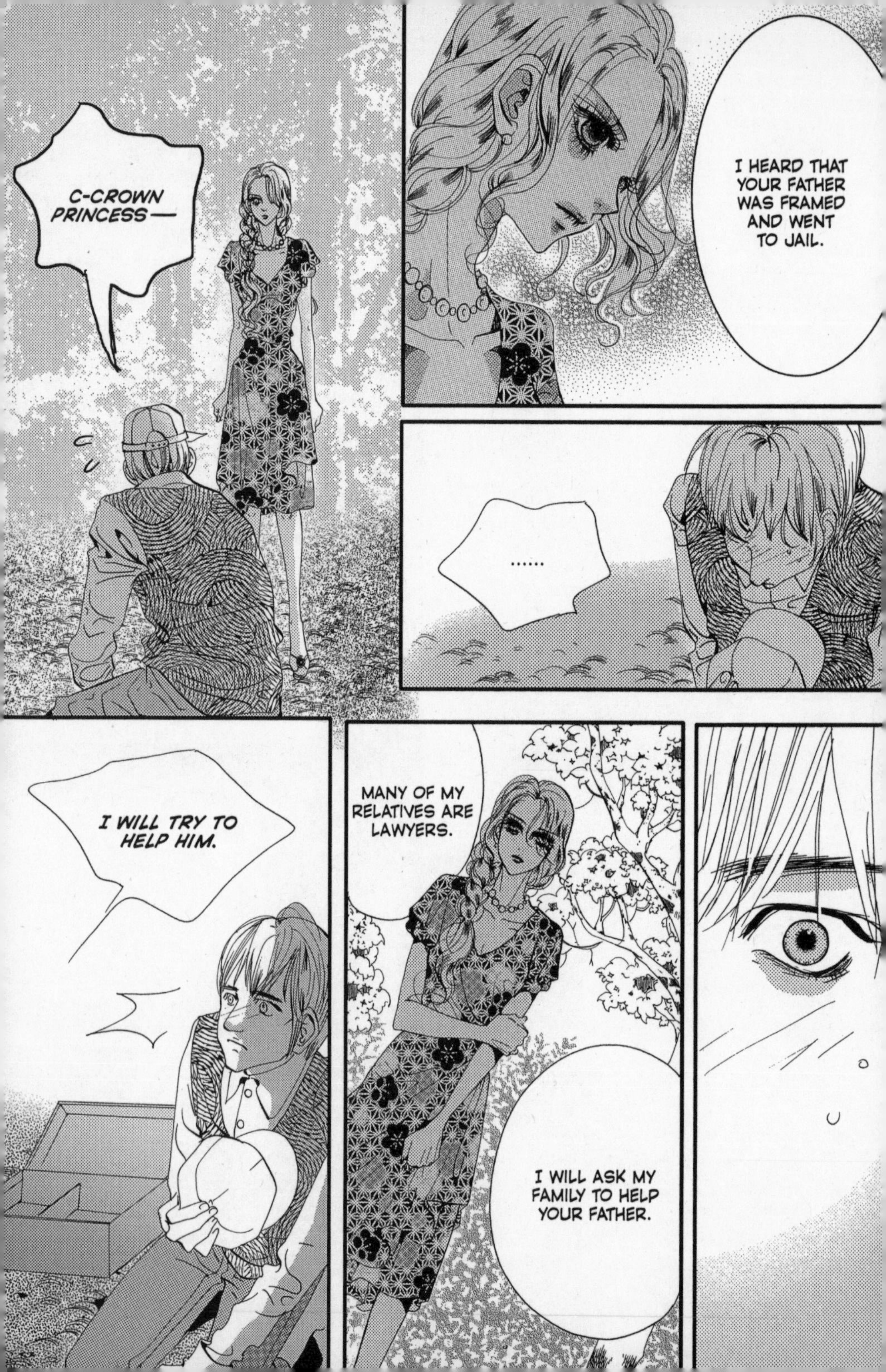
C-CROWN PRINCESS—
I HEARD THAT YOUR FATHER WAS FRAMED AND WENT TO JAIL.
......
I WILL TRY TO HELP HIM.
MANY OF MY RELATIVES ARE LAWYERS.
I WILL ASK MY FAMILY TO HELP YOUR FATHER.

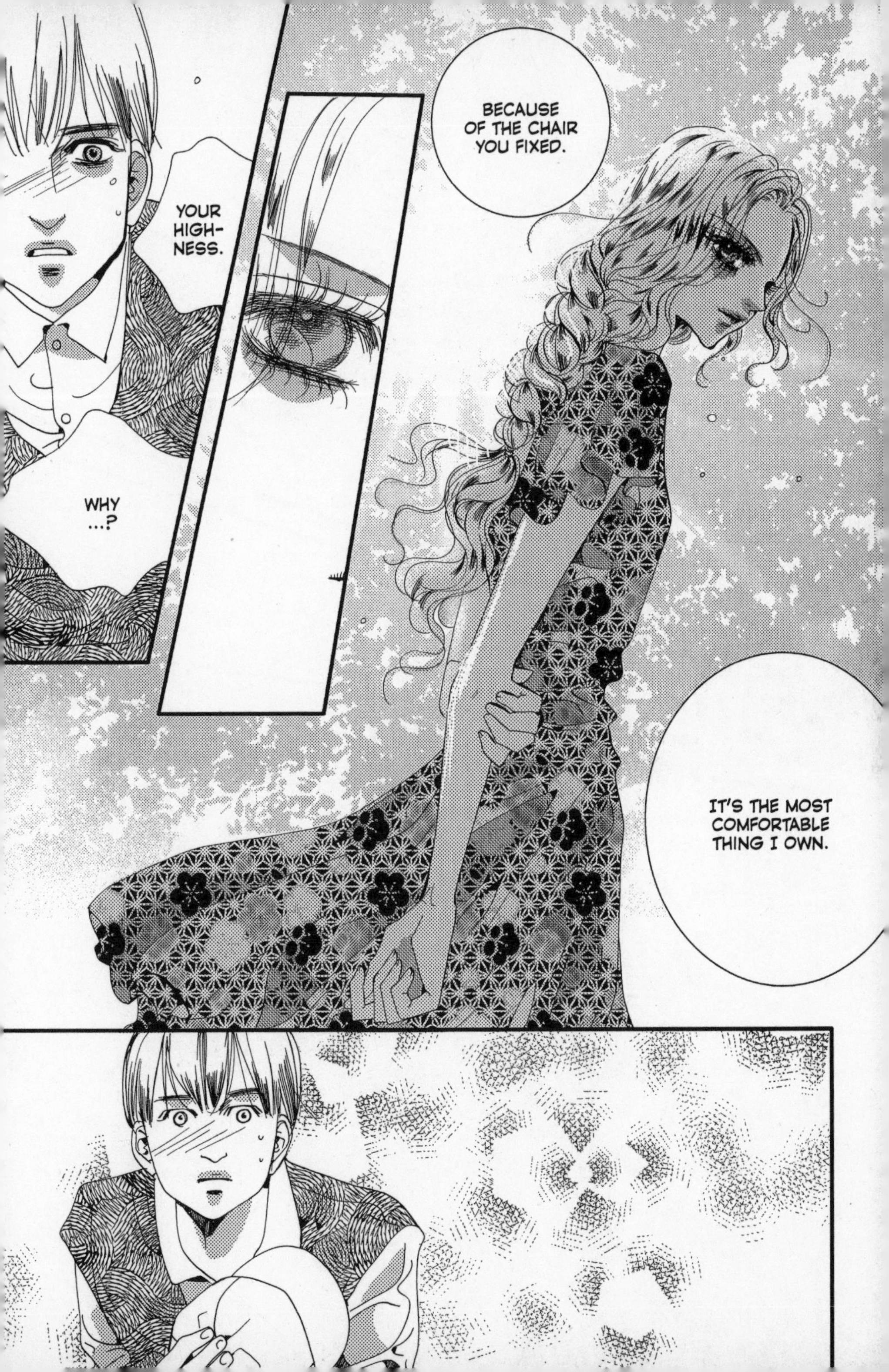
YOUR HIGH-NESS.
WHY ...?
BECAUSE OF THE CHAIR YOU FIXED.
IT'S THE MOST COMFORTABLE THING I OWN.

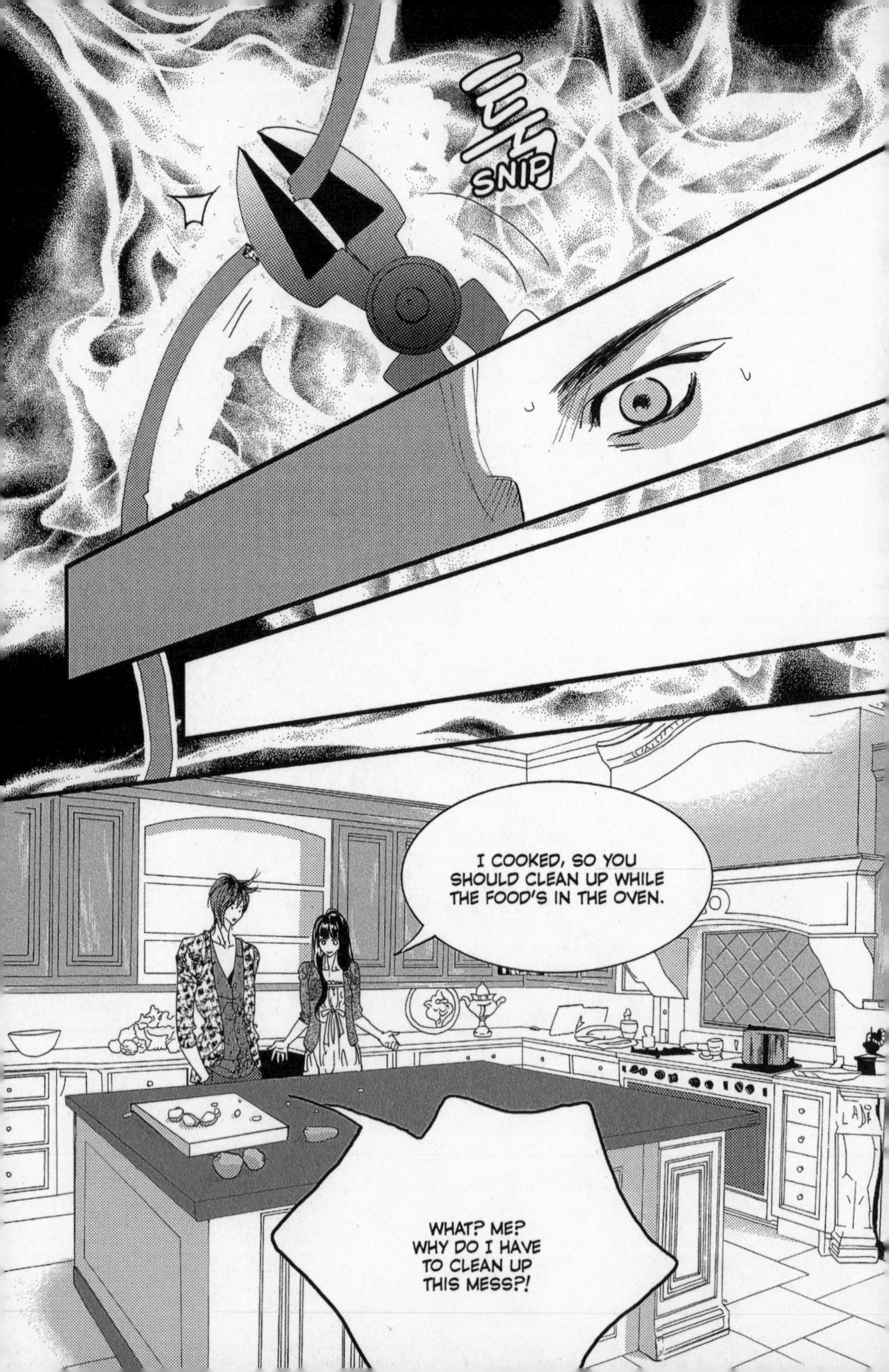
SNIP
I COOKED, SO YOU SHOULD CLEAN UP WHILE THE FOOD'S IN THE OVEN.
WHAT? ME? WHY DO I HAVE TO CLEAN UP THIS MESS?!

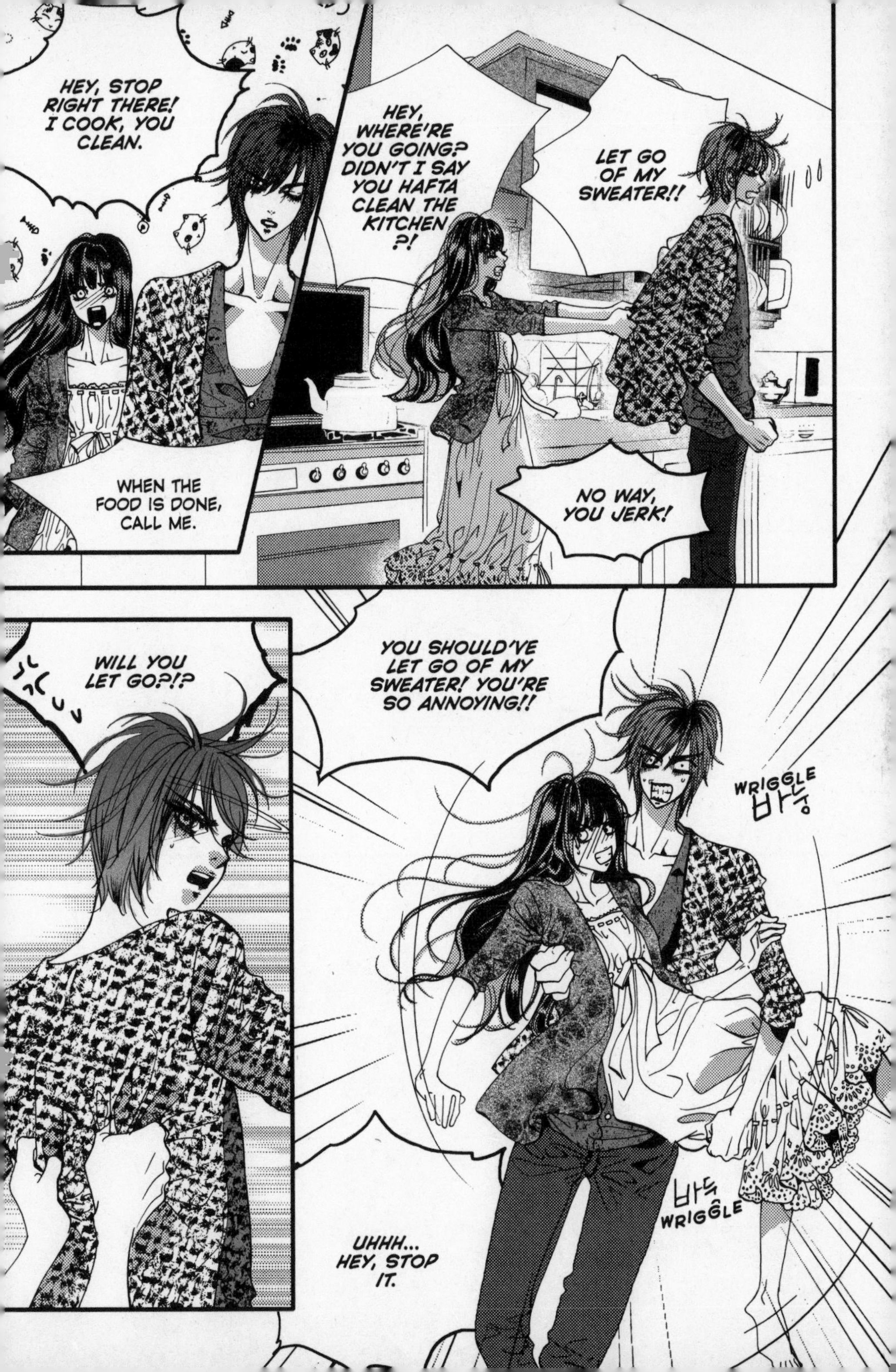
HEY, STOP RIGHT THERE! I COOK, YOU CLEAN.
WHEN THE FOOD IS DONE, CALL ME.
HEY, WHERE'RE YOU GOING? DIDN'T I SAY YOU HAFTA CLEAN THE KITCHEN ?!
LET GO OF MY SWEATER!!
NO WAY, YOU JERK!
WILL YOU LET GO?!?
YOU SHOULD'VE LET GO OF MY SWEATER! YOU'RE SO ANNOYING!!
WRIGGLE
바둥
바둥
WRIGGLE
UHHH... HEY, STOP IT.

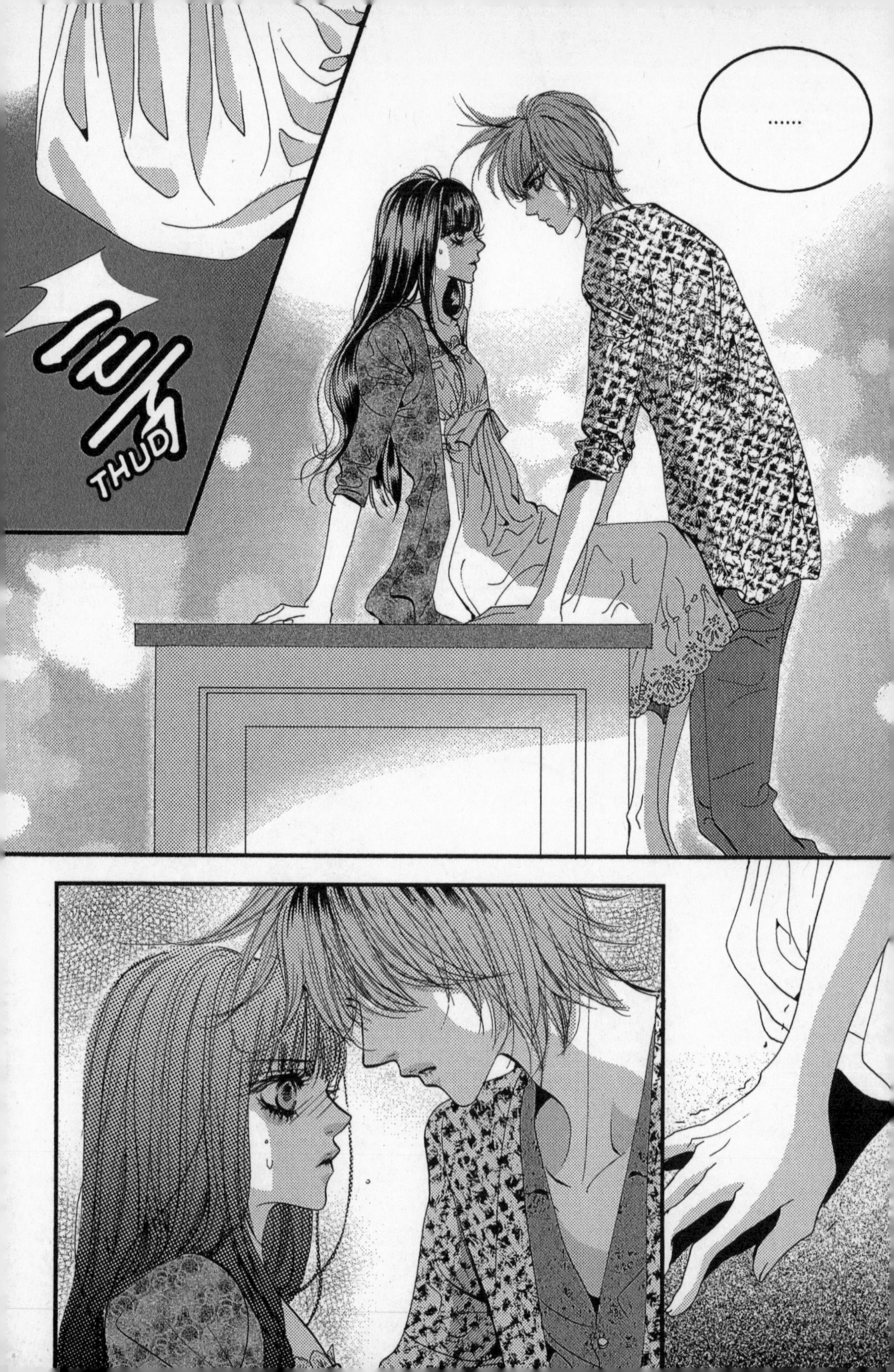
THUD
......

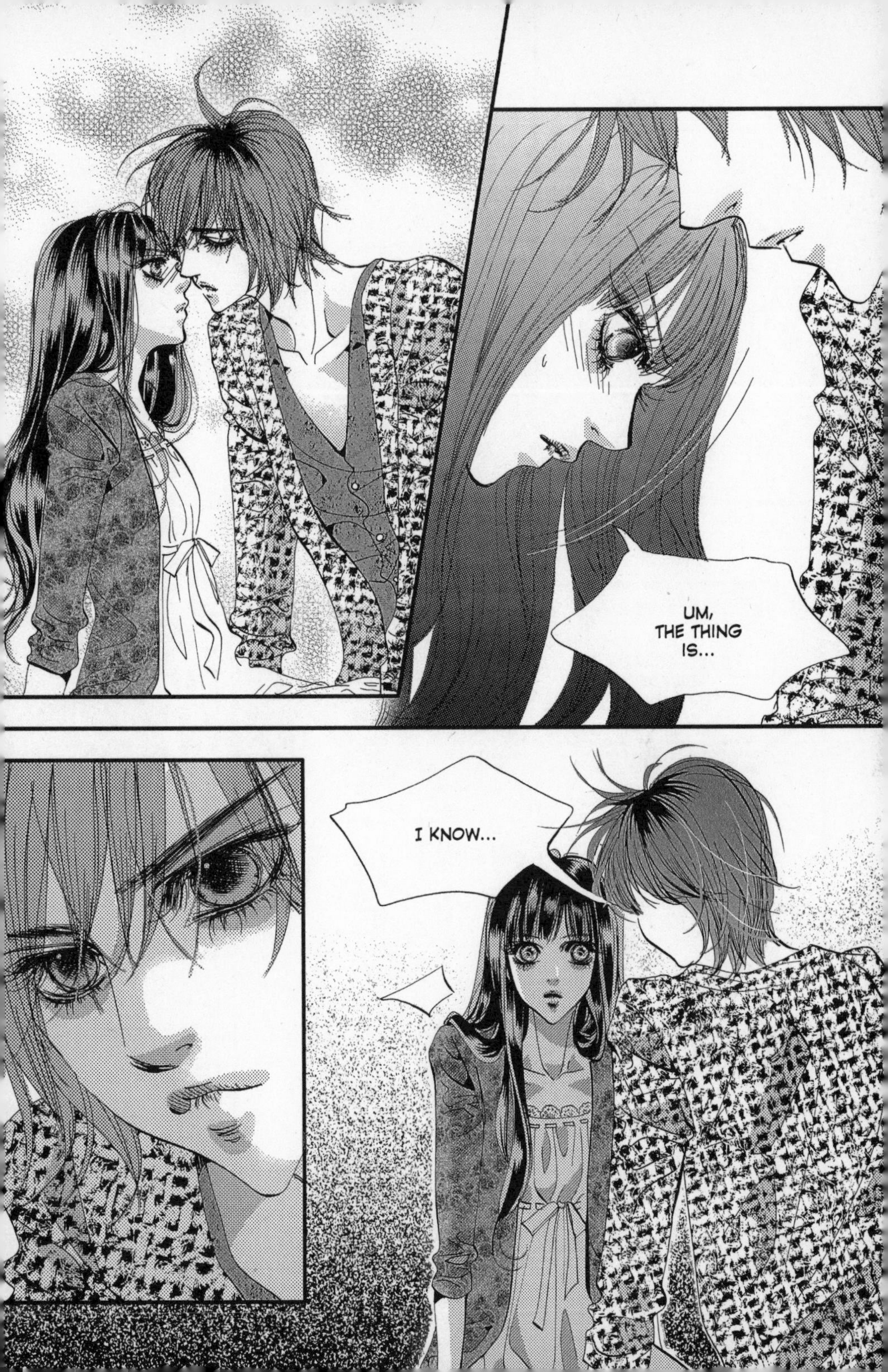
UM, THE THING IS...
I KNOW...

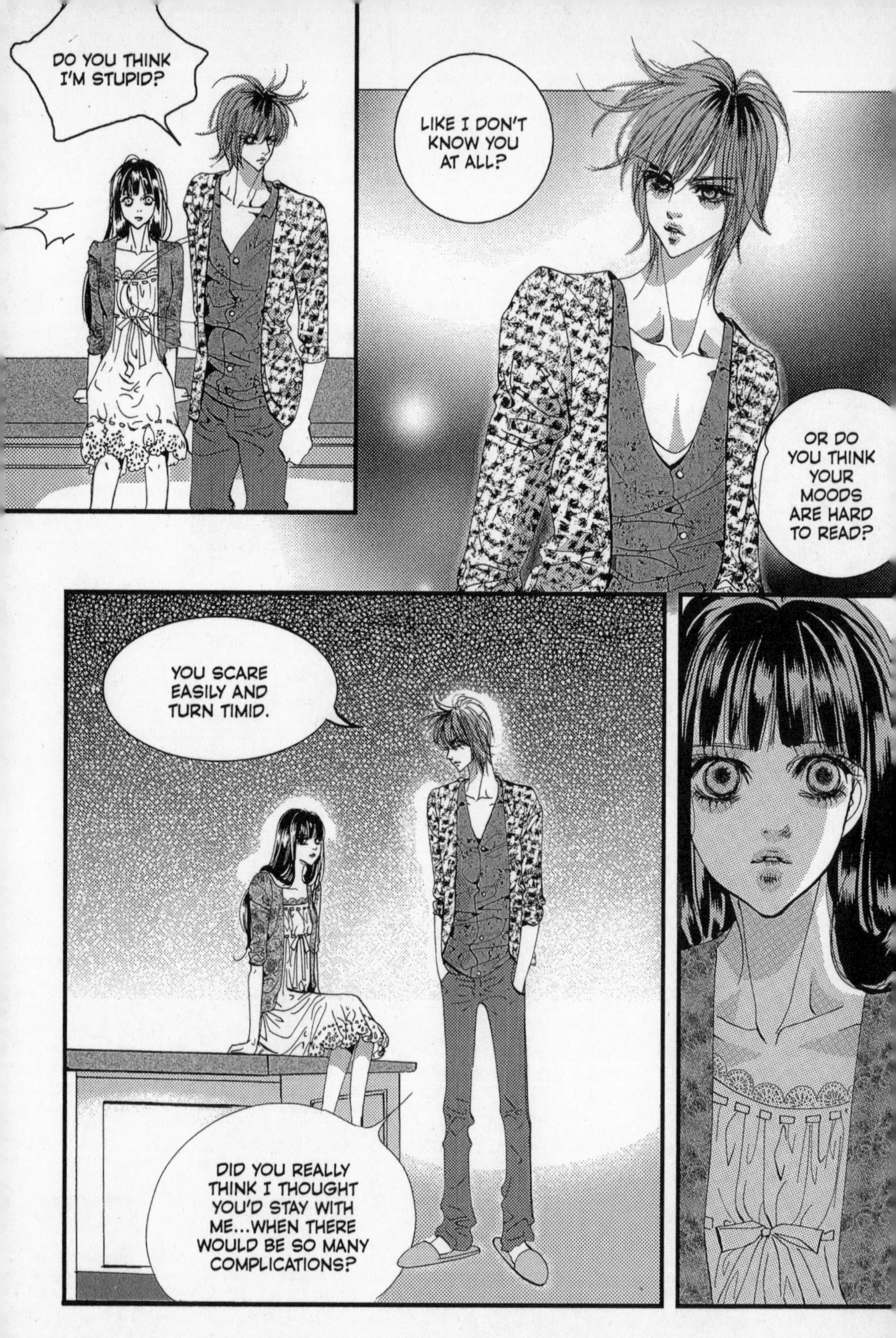
DO YOU THINK I'M STUPID?
LIKE I DON'T KNOW YOU AT ALL?
OR DO YOU THINK YOUR MOODS ARE HARD TO READ?
YOU SCARE EASILY AND TURN TIMID.
DID YOU REALLY THINK I THOUGHT YOU'D STAY WITH ME...WHEN THERE WOULD BE SO MANY COMPLICATIONS?

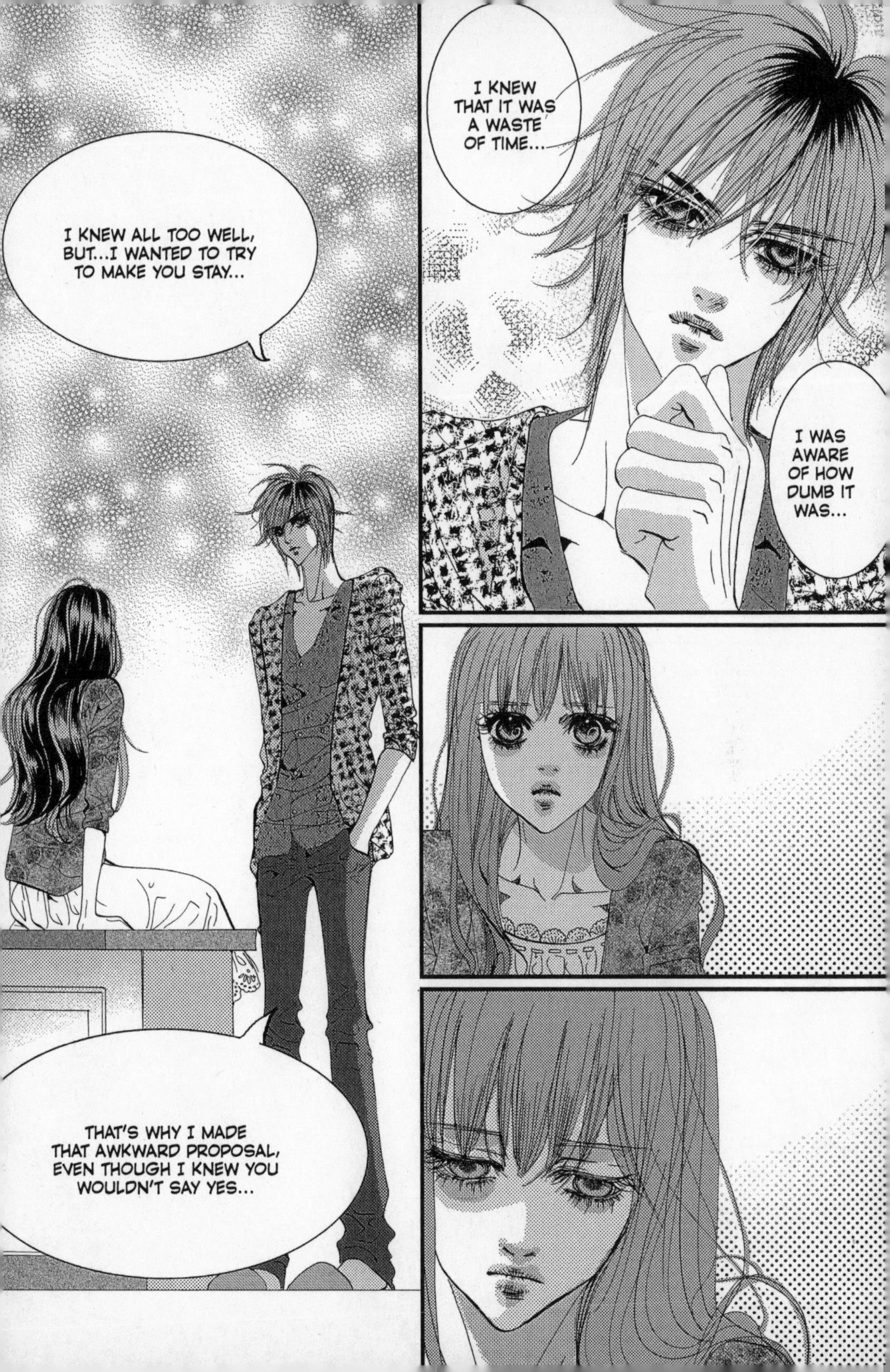
I KNEW ALL TOO WELL, BUT...I WANTED TO TRY TO MAKE YOU STAY...
THAT'S WHY I MADE THAT AWKWARD PROPOSAL, EVEN THOUGH I KNEW YOU WOULDN'T SAY YES...
I KNEW THAT IT WAS A WASTE OF TIME...
I WAS AWARE OF HOW DUMB IT WAS...

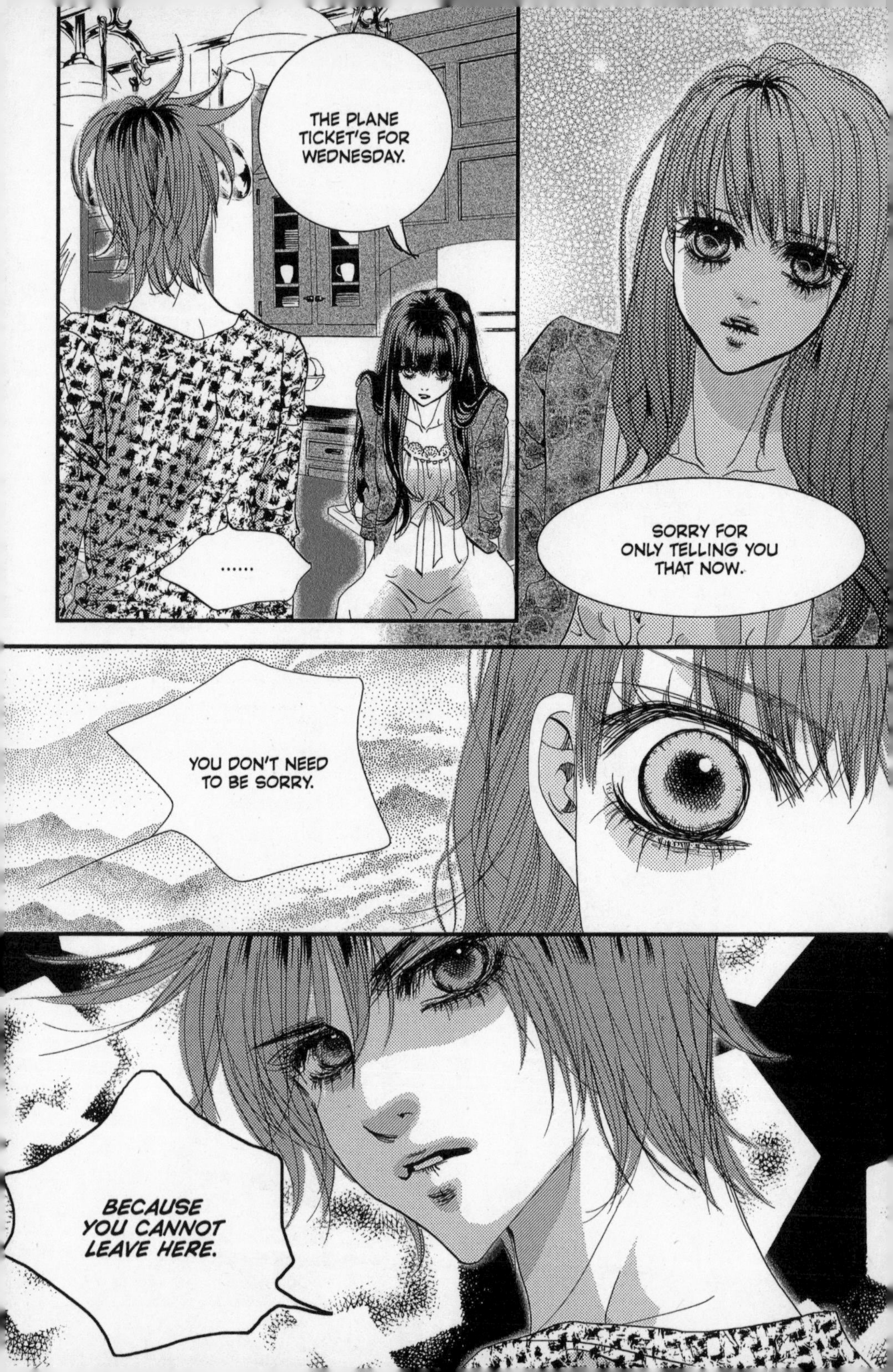
THE PLANE TICKET'S FOR WEDNESDAY.
......
SORRY FOR ONLY TELLING YOU THAT NOW.
YOU DON'T NEED TO BE SORRY.
BECAUSE YOU CANNOT LEAVE HERE.

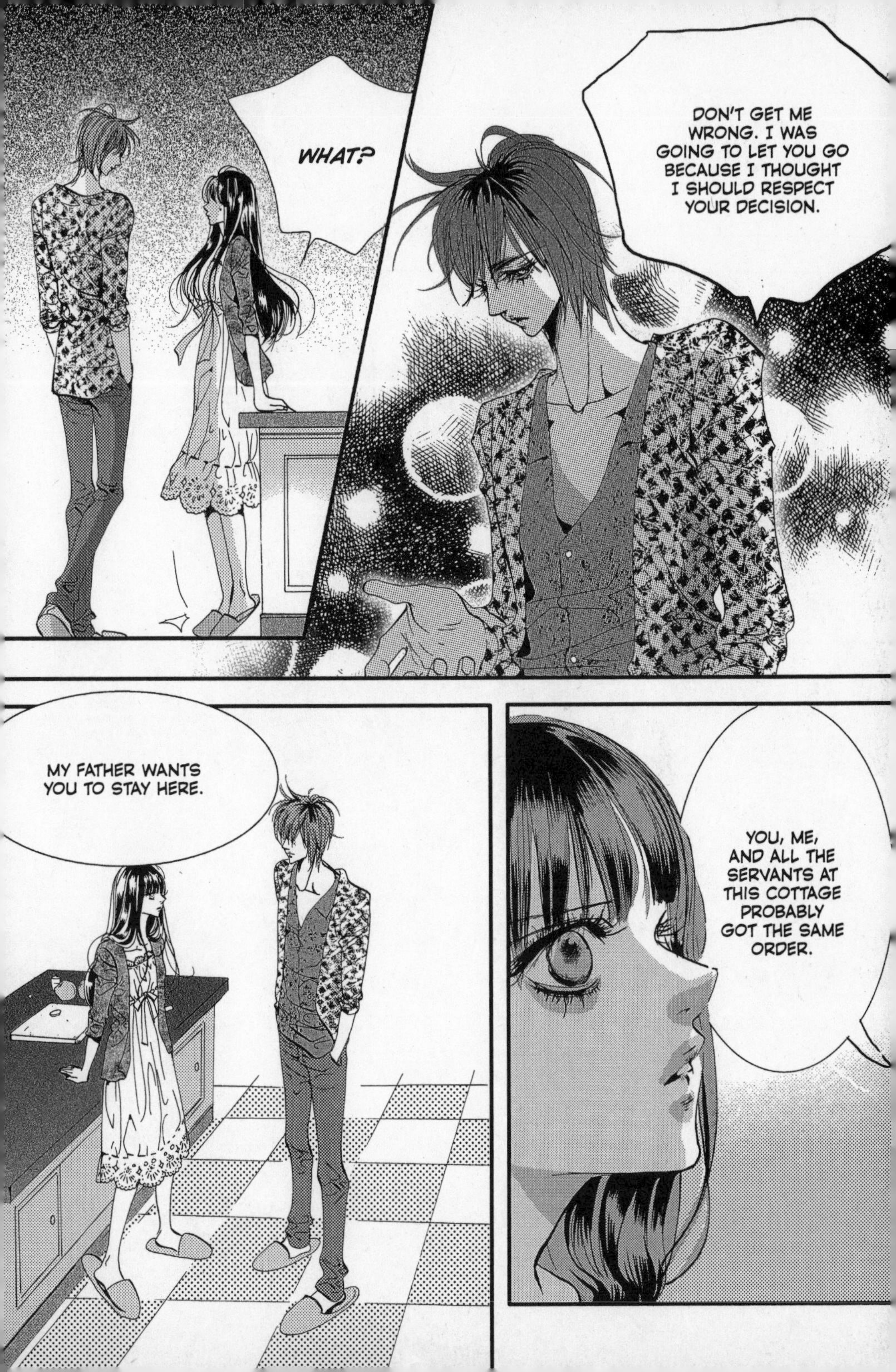
WHAT?
DON'T GET ME WRONG. I WAS GOING TO LET YOU GO BECAUSE I THOUGHT I SHOULD RESPECT YOUR DECISION.
MY FATHER WANTS YOU TO STAY HERE.
YOU, ME, AND ALL THE SERVANTS AT THIS COTTAGE PROBABLY GOT THE SAME ORDER.

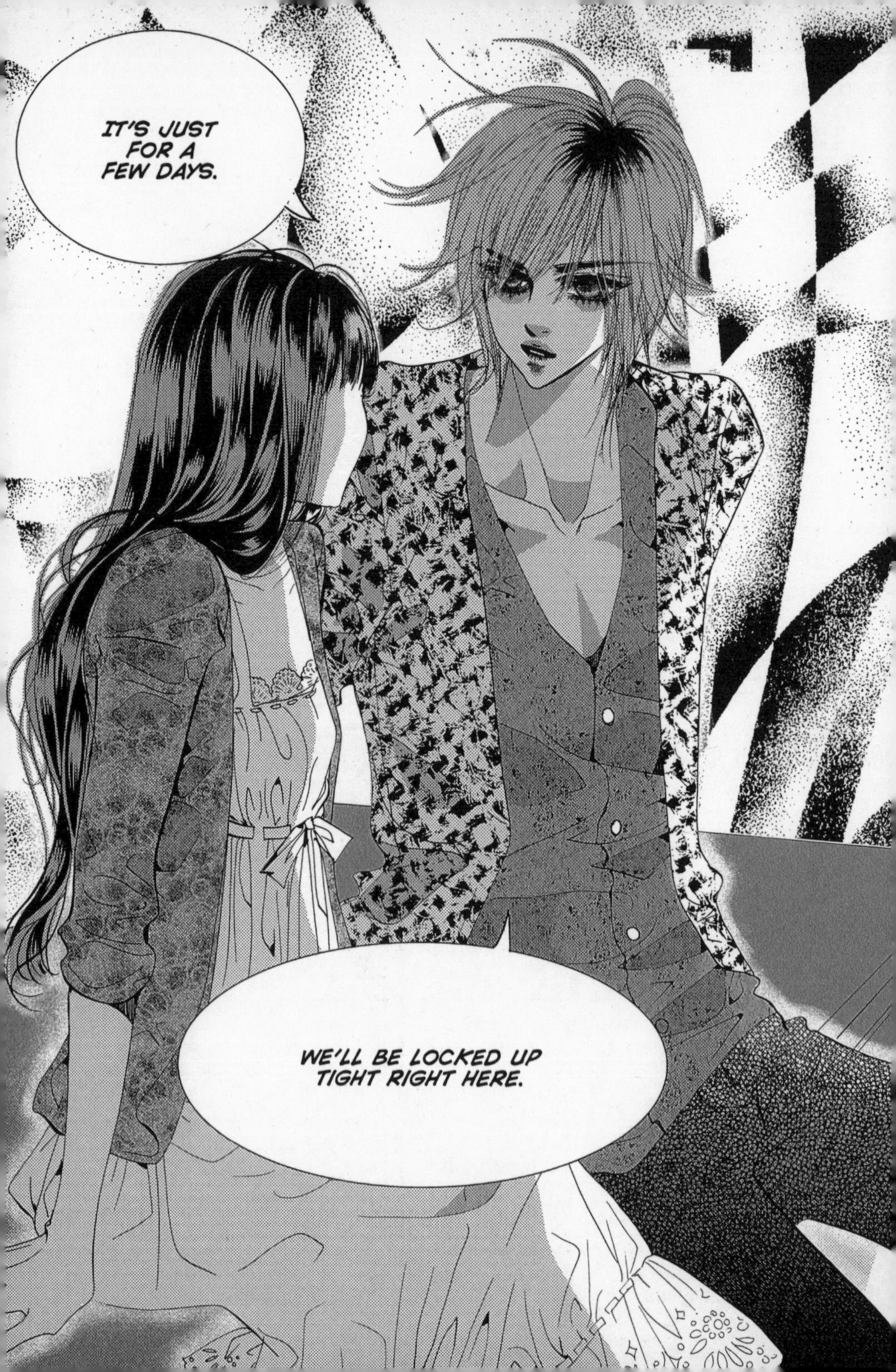
IT'S JUST FOR A FEW DAYS.
WE'LL BE LOCKED UP TIGHT RIGHT HERE.

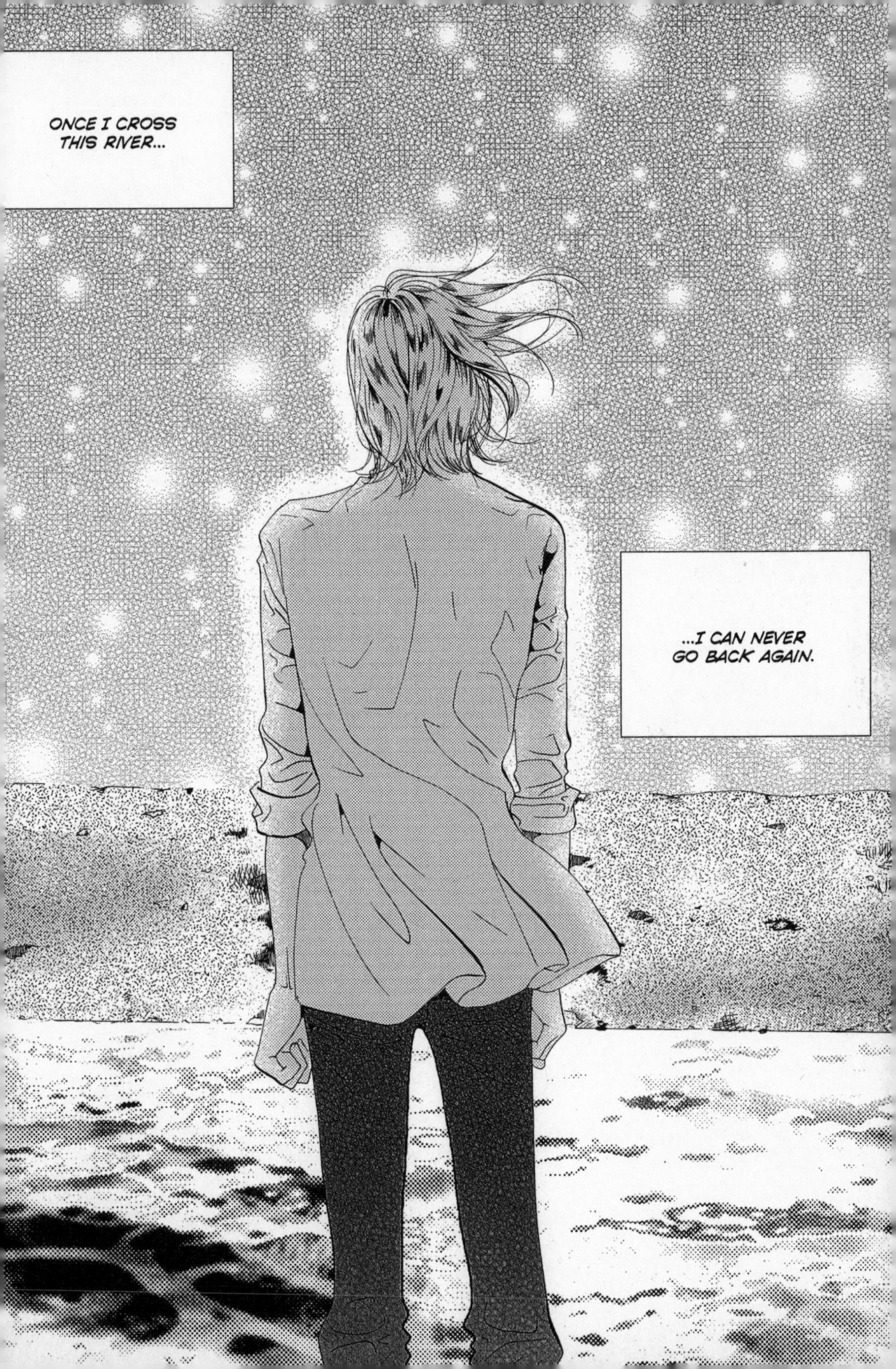
ONCE I CROSS THIS RIVER...
...I CAN NEVER GO BACK AGAIN.

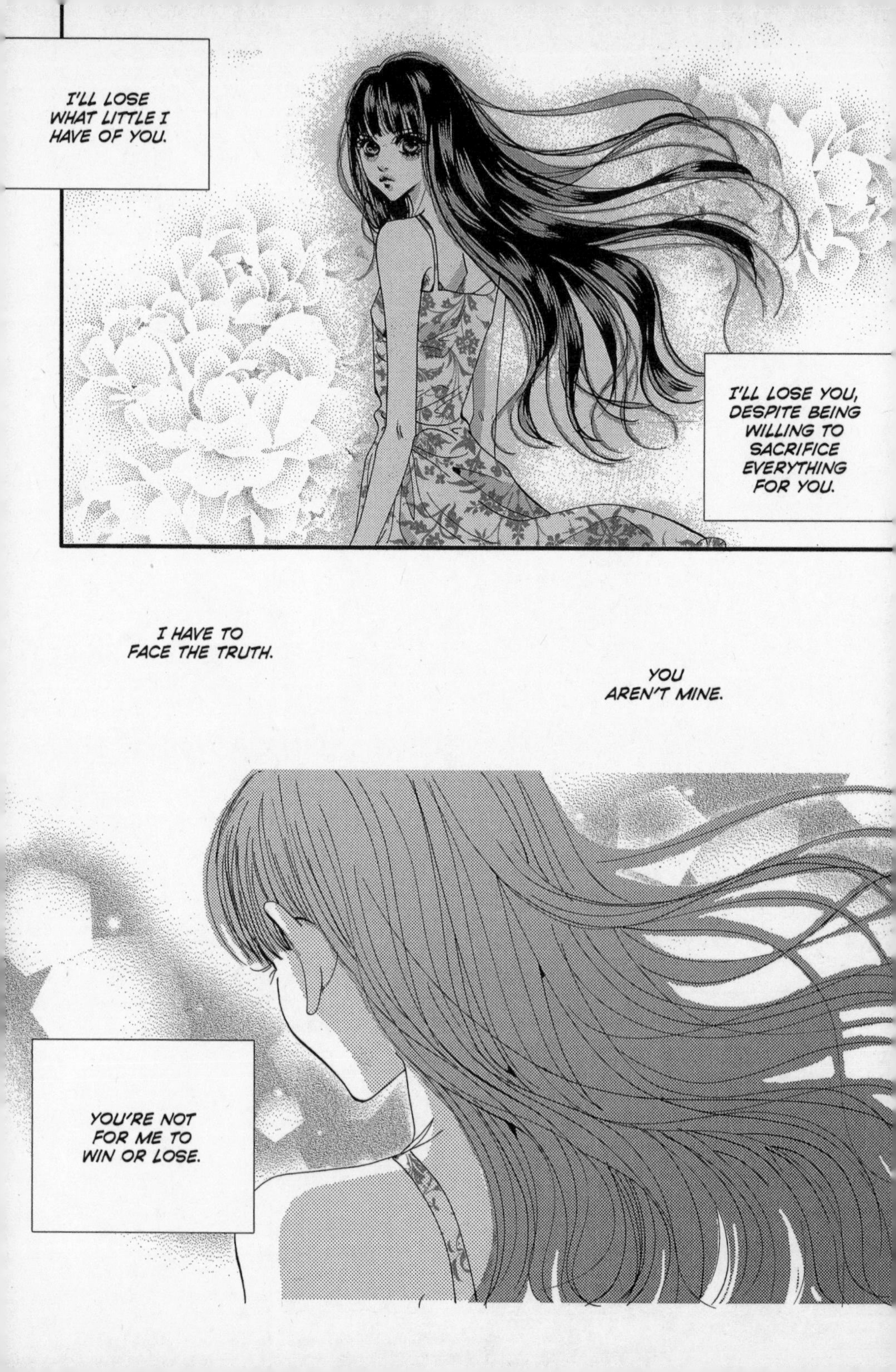
I'LL LOSE WHAT LITTLE I HAVE OF YOU.
I'LL LOSE YOU, DESPITE BEING WILLING TO SACRIFICE EVERYTHING FOR YOU.
I HAVE TO FACE THE TRUTH.
YOU AREN'T MINE.
YOU'RE NOT FOR ME TO WIN OR LOSE.

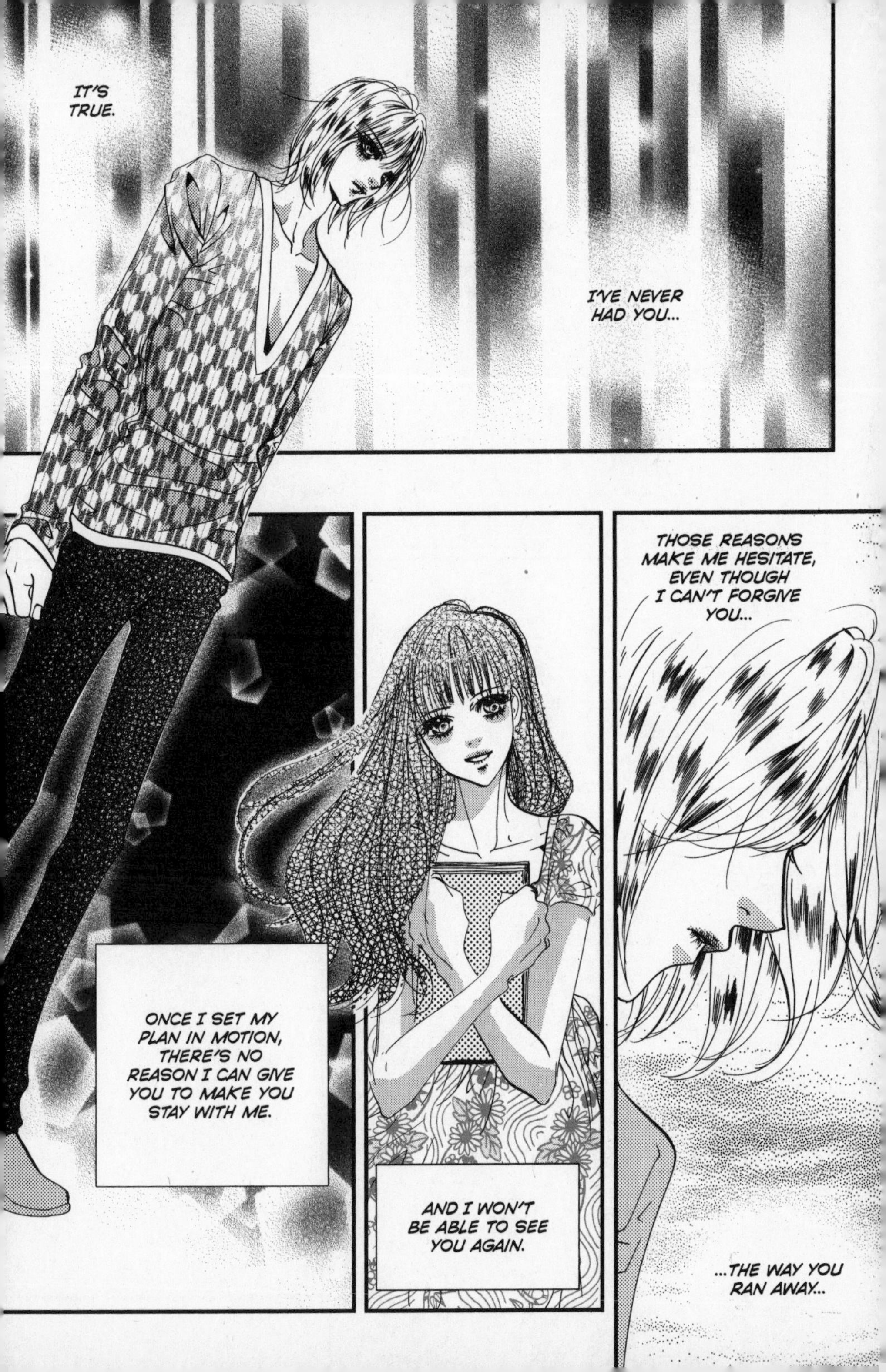
IT'S TRUE.
I'VE NEVER HAD YOU...
ONCE I SET MY PLAN IN MOTION, THERE'S NO REASON I CAN GIVE YOU TO MAKE YOU STAY WITH ME.
AND I WON'T BE ABLE TO SEE YOU AGAIN.
THOSE REASONS MAKE ME HESITATE, EVEN THOUGH I CAN'T FORGIVE YOU...
...THE WAY YOU RAN AWAY...

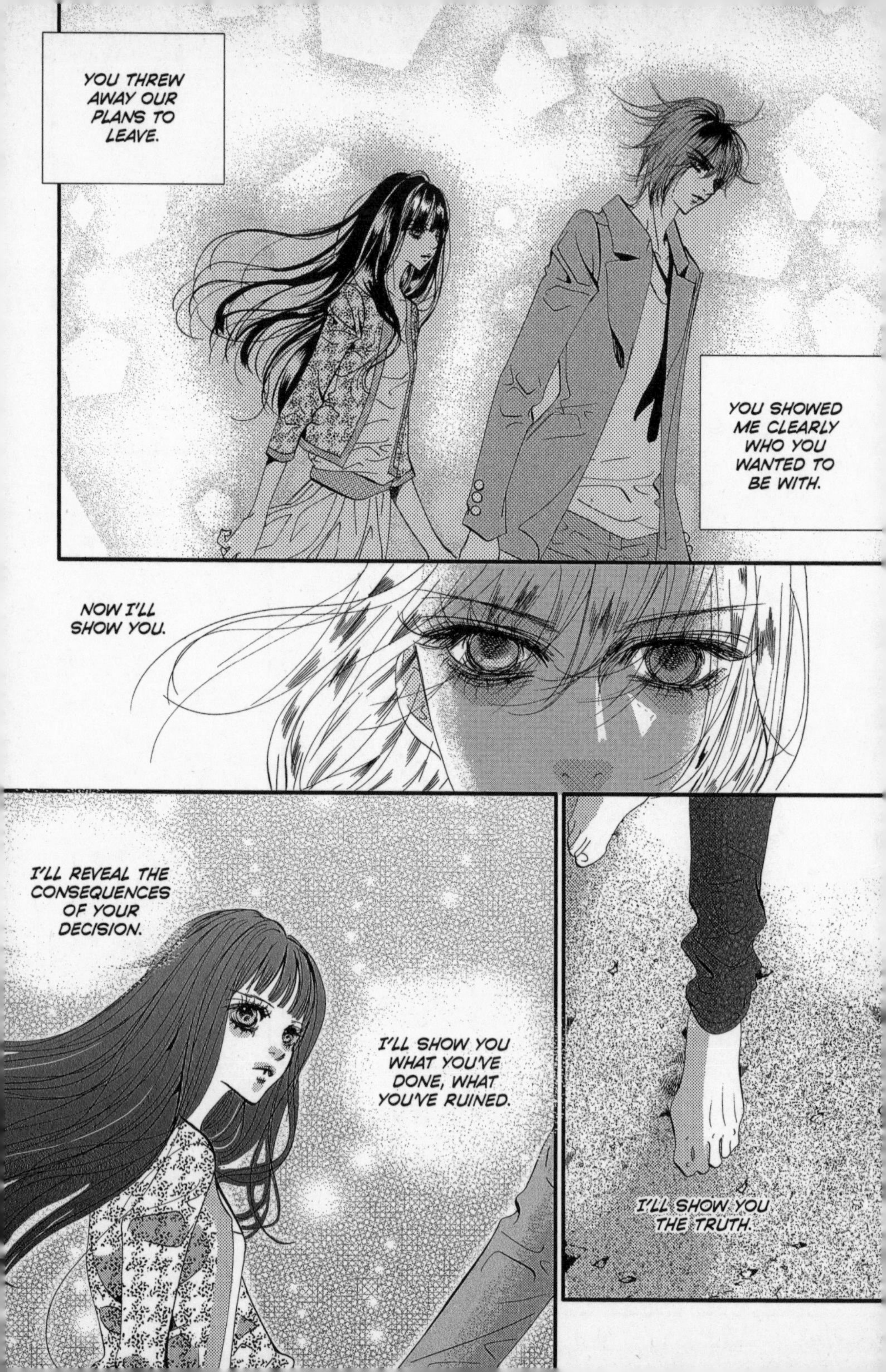
YOU THREW AWAY OUR PLANS TO LEAVE.
YOU SHOWED ME CLEARLY WHO YOU WANTED TO BE WITH.
NOW I'LL SHOW YOU.
I'LL REVEAL THE CONSEQUENCES OF YOUR DECISION.
I'LL SHOW YOU WHAT YOU'VE DONE, WHAT YOU'VE RUINED.
I'LL SHOW YOU THE TRUTH.

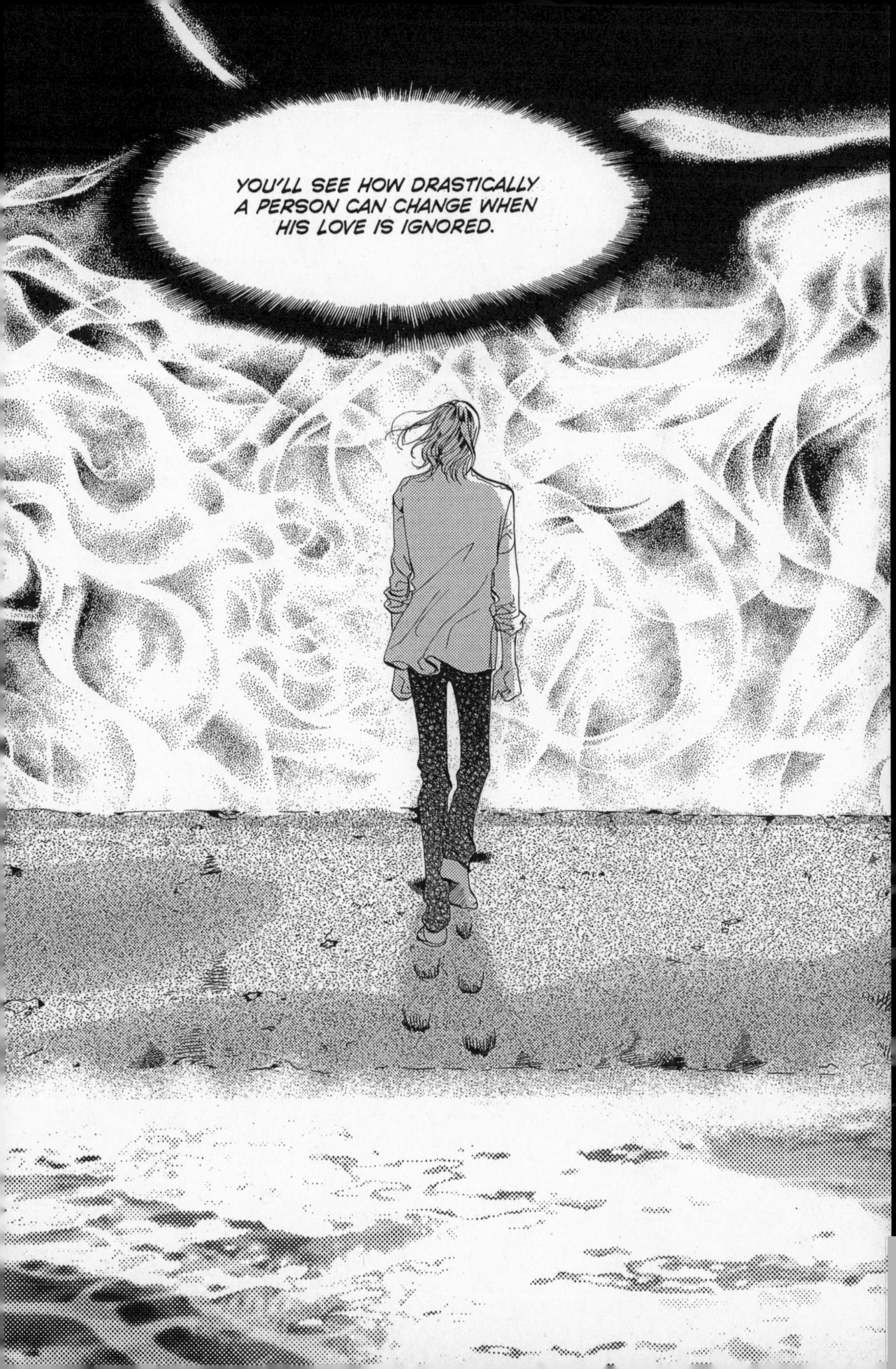
YOU'LL SEE HOW DRASTICALLY A PERSON CAN CHANGE WHEN HIS LOVE IS IGNORED.

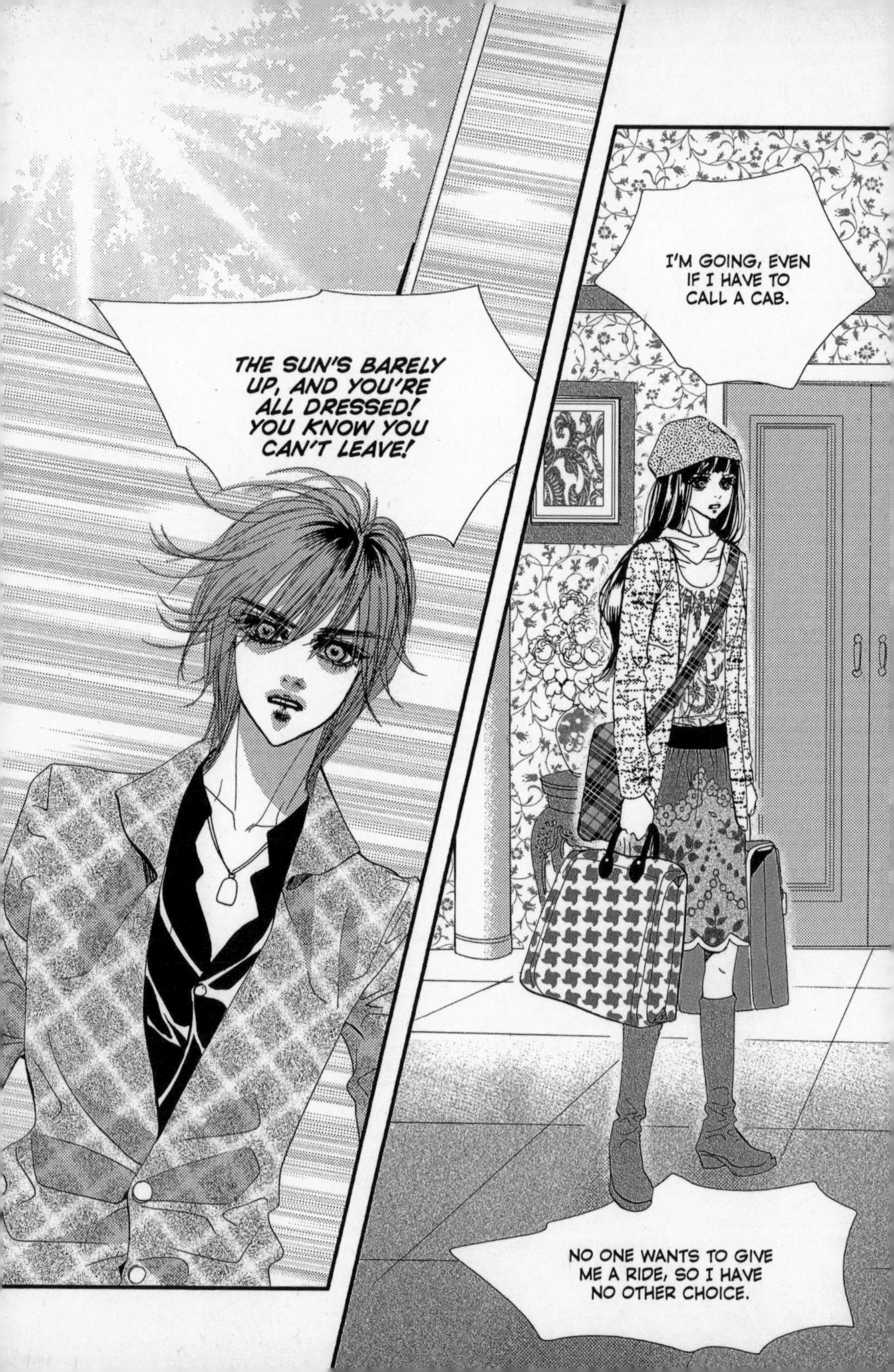
THE SUN'S BARELY UP, AND YOU'RE ALL DRESSED! YOU KNOW YOU CAN'T LEAVE!
I'M GOING, EVEN IF I HAVE TO CALL A CAB.
NO ONE WANTS TO GIVE ME A RIDE, SO I HAVE NO OTHER CHOICE.

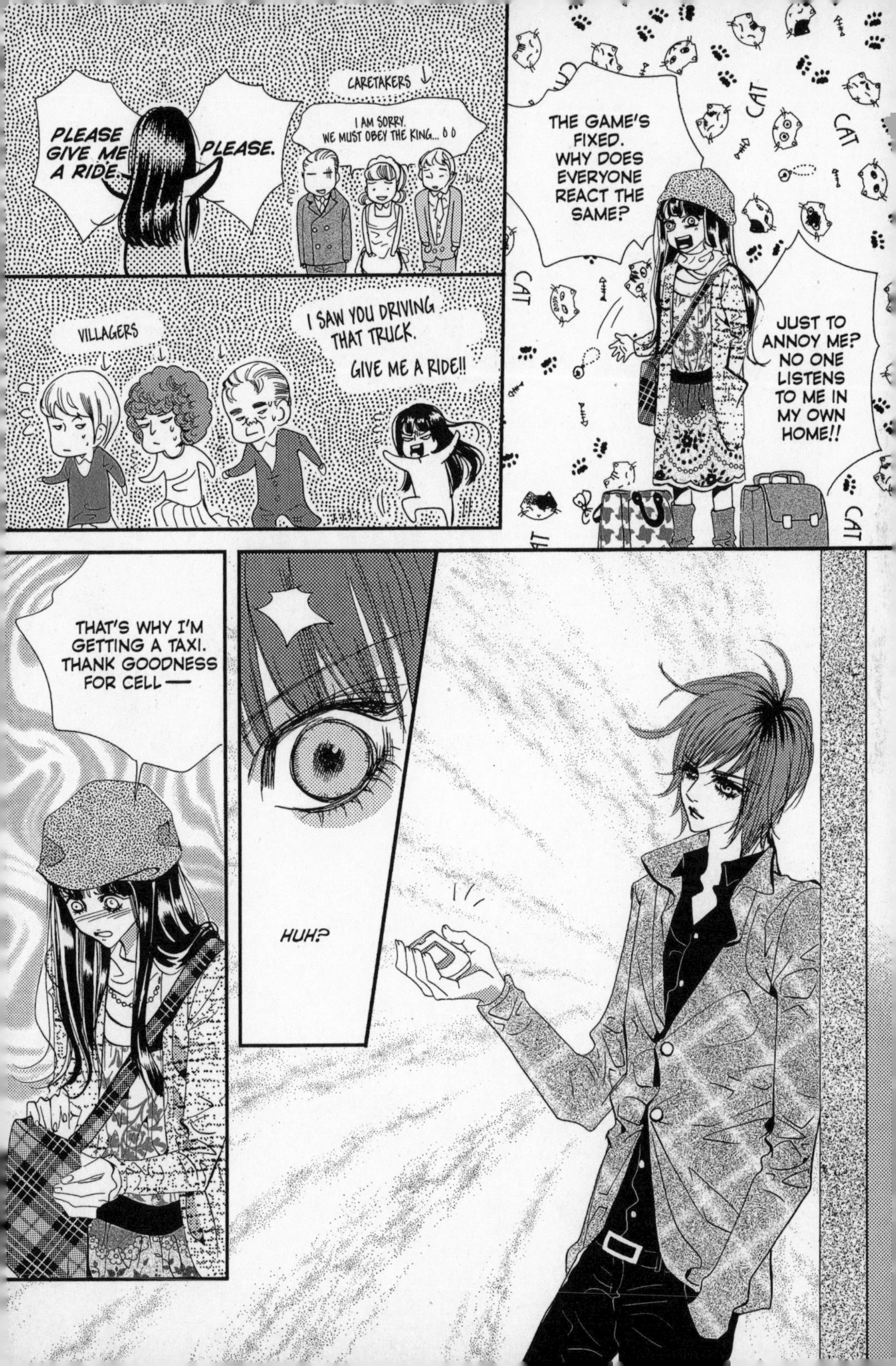
PLEASE GIVE ME A RIDE.
PLEASE.
CARETAKERS
I AM SORRY. WE MUST OBEY THE KING...
VILLAGERS
I SAW YOU DRIVING THAT TRUCK.
GIVE ME A RIDE!!
THE GAME'S FIXED. WHY DOES EVERYONE REACT THE SAME?
JUST TO ANNOY ME? NO ONE LISTENS TO ME IN MY OWN HOME!!
CAT
CAT
CAT
CAT
THAT'S WHY I'M GETTING A TAXI. THANK GOODNESS FOR CELL—
HUH?

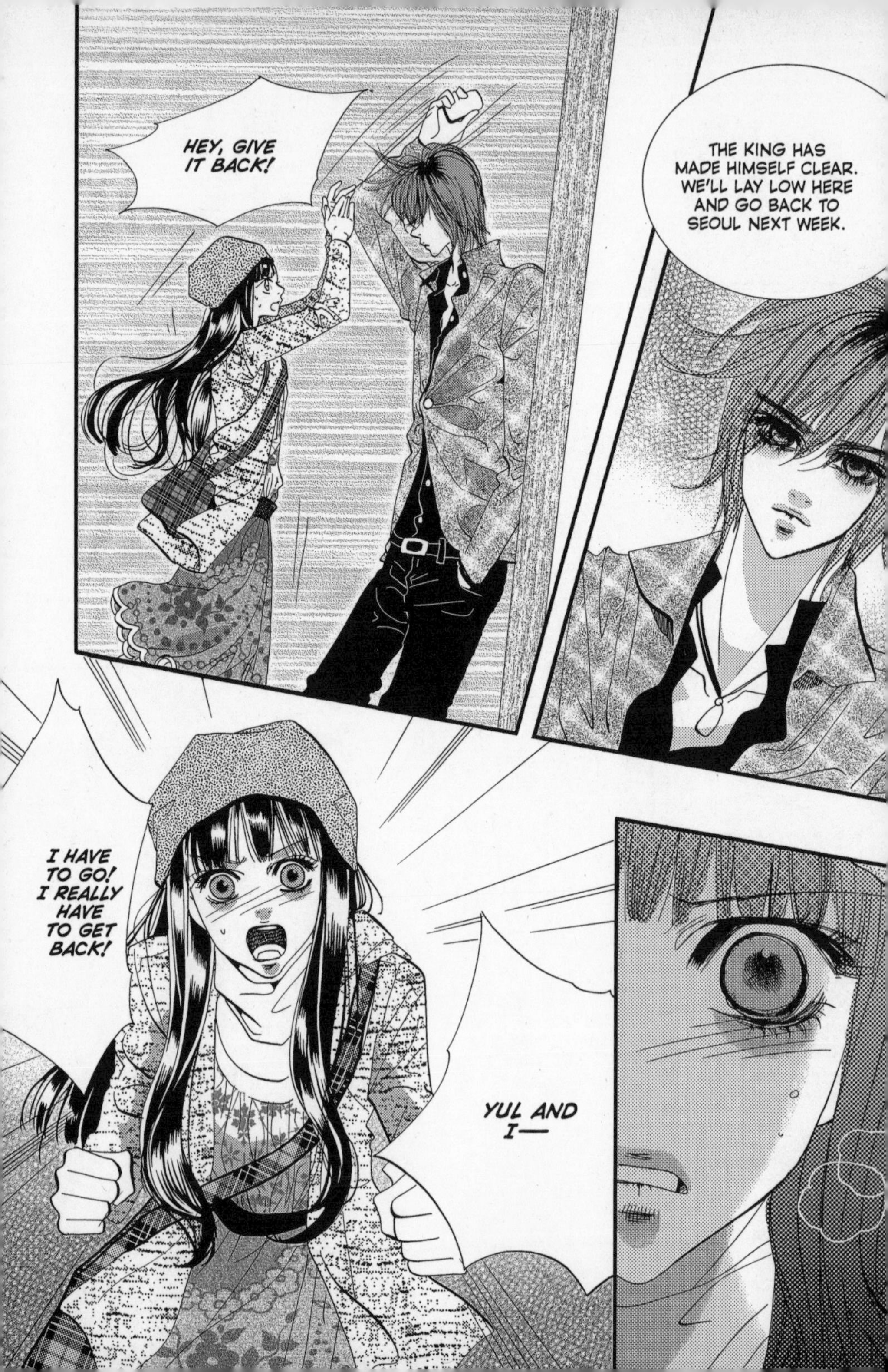
HEY, GIVE IT BACK!
THE KING HAS MADE HIMSELF CLEAR. WE'LL LAY LOW HERE AND GO BACK TO SEOUL NEXT WEEK.
I HAVE TO GO! I REALLY HAVE TO GET BACK!
YUL AND I—

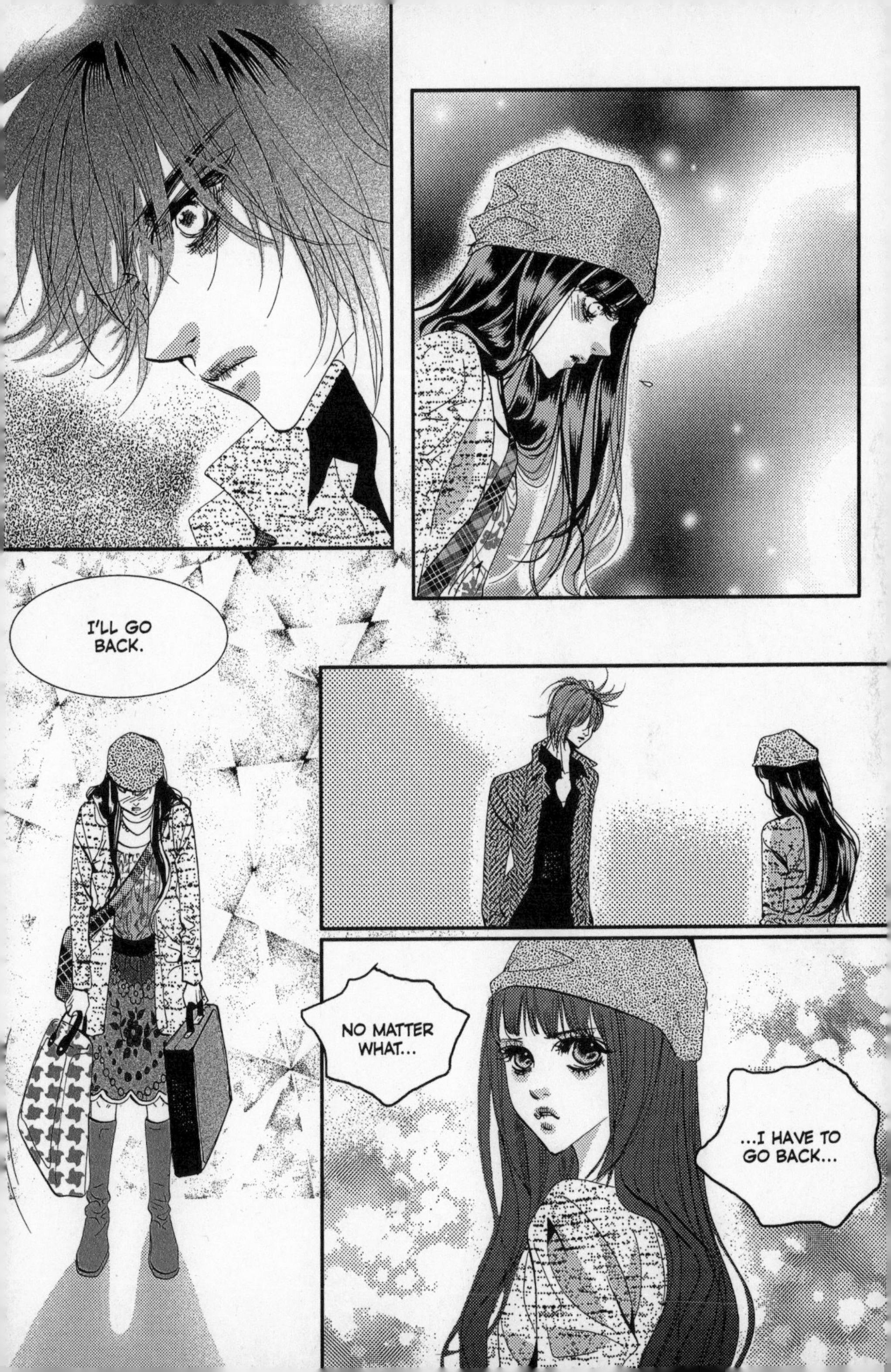

I'LL GO BACK.
NO MATTER WHAT...
...I HAVE TO GO BACK...

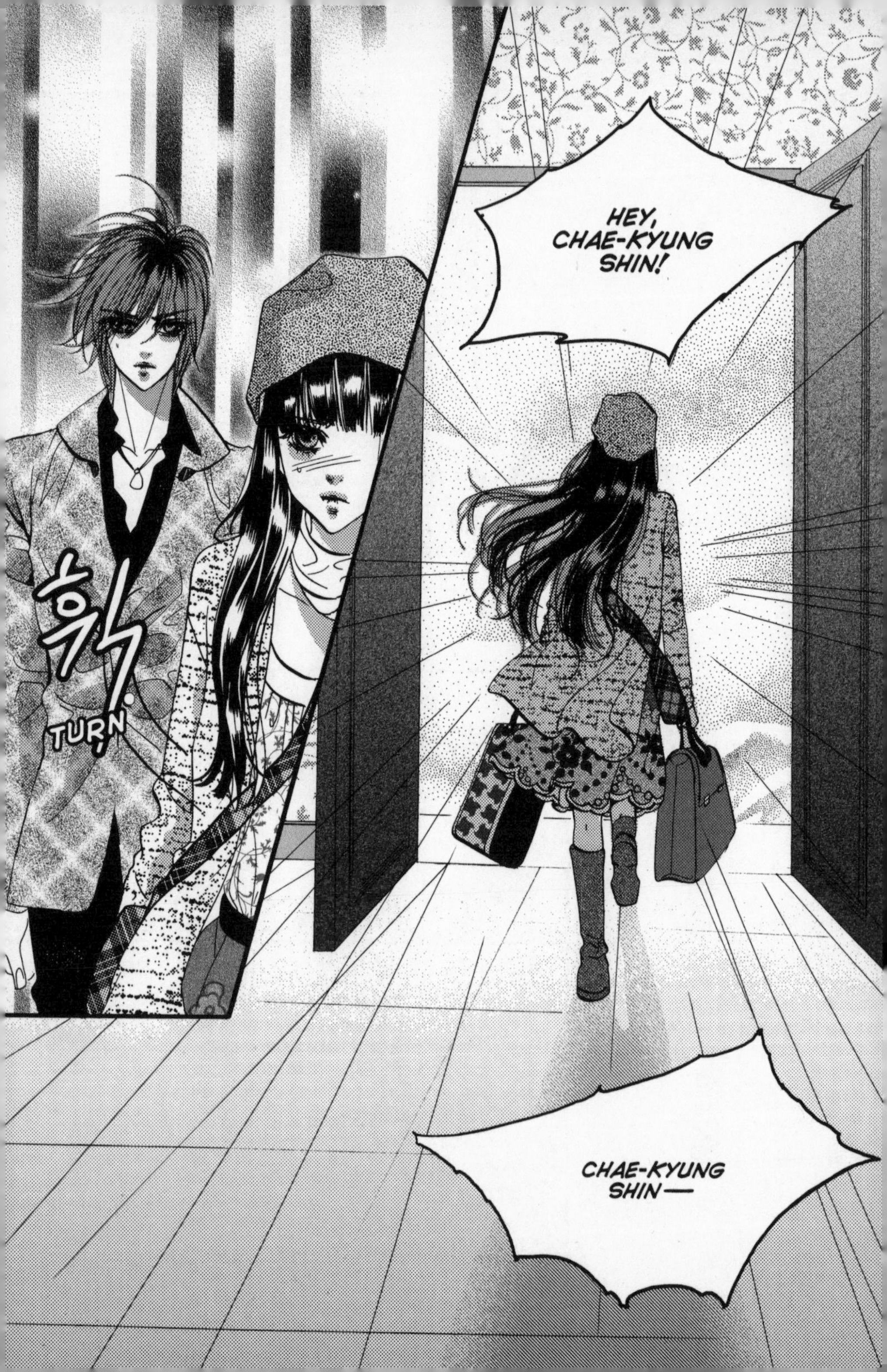
흑
TURN
HEY, CHAE-KYUNG SHIN!
CHAE-KYUNG SHIN—

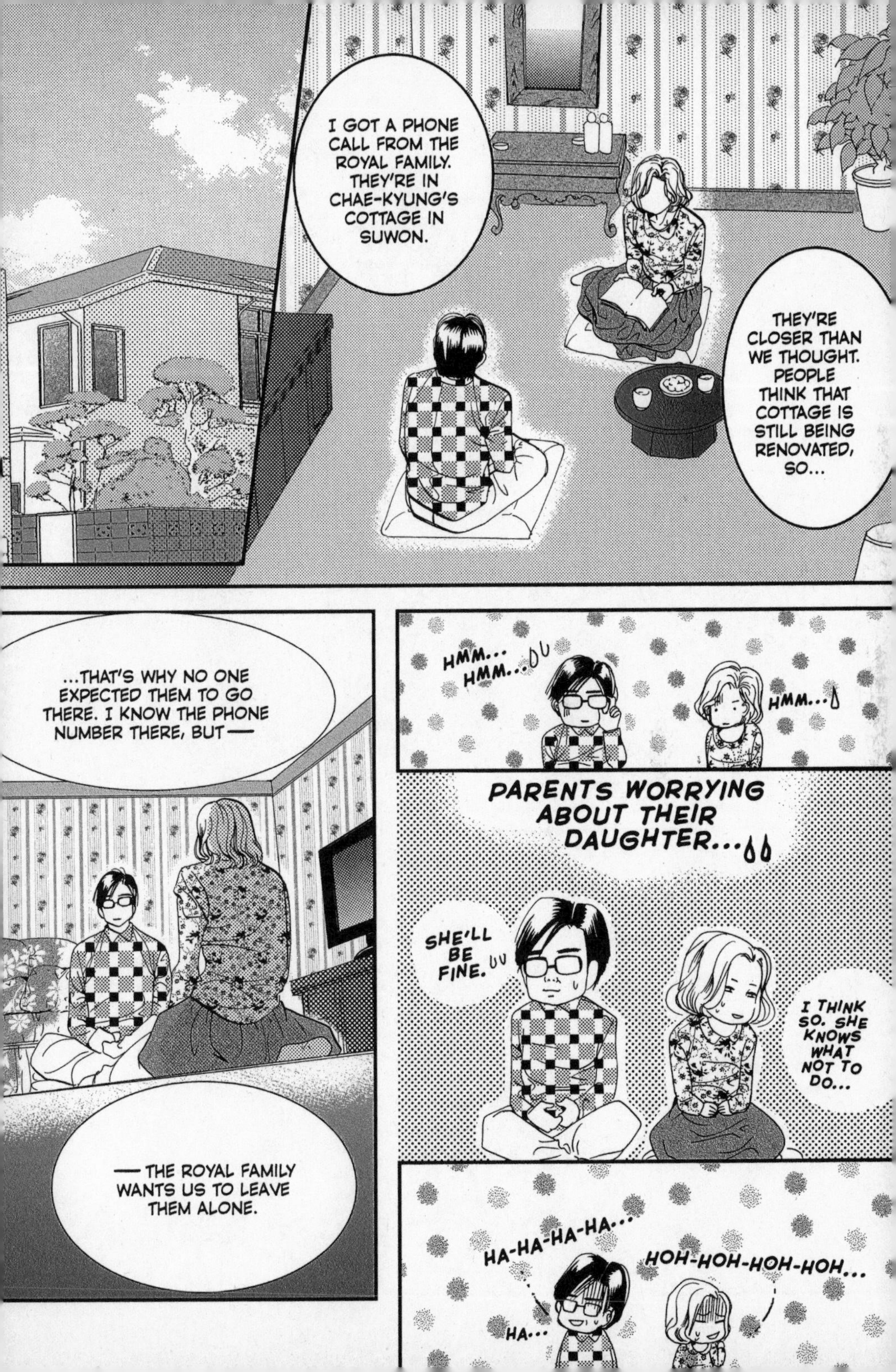

I GOT A PHONE CALL FROM THE ROYAL FAMILY. THEY'RE IN CHAE-KYUNG'S COTTAGE IN SUWON.
THEY'RE CLOSER THAN WE THOUGHT. PEOPLE THINK THAT COTTAGE IS STILL BEING RENOVATED, SO...
...THAT'S WHY NO ONE EXPECTED THEM TO GO THERE. I KNOW THE PHONE NUMBER THERE, BUT—
—THE ROYAL FAMILY WANTS US TO LEAVE THEM ALONE.
HMM... HMM...
HMM...
PARENTS WORRYING ABOUT THEIR DAUGHTER...
SHE'LL BE FINE.
I THINK SO. SHE KNOWS WHAT NOT TO DO...
HA-HA-HA-HA...
HA...
HOH-HOH-HOH-HOH...

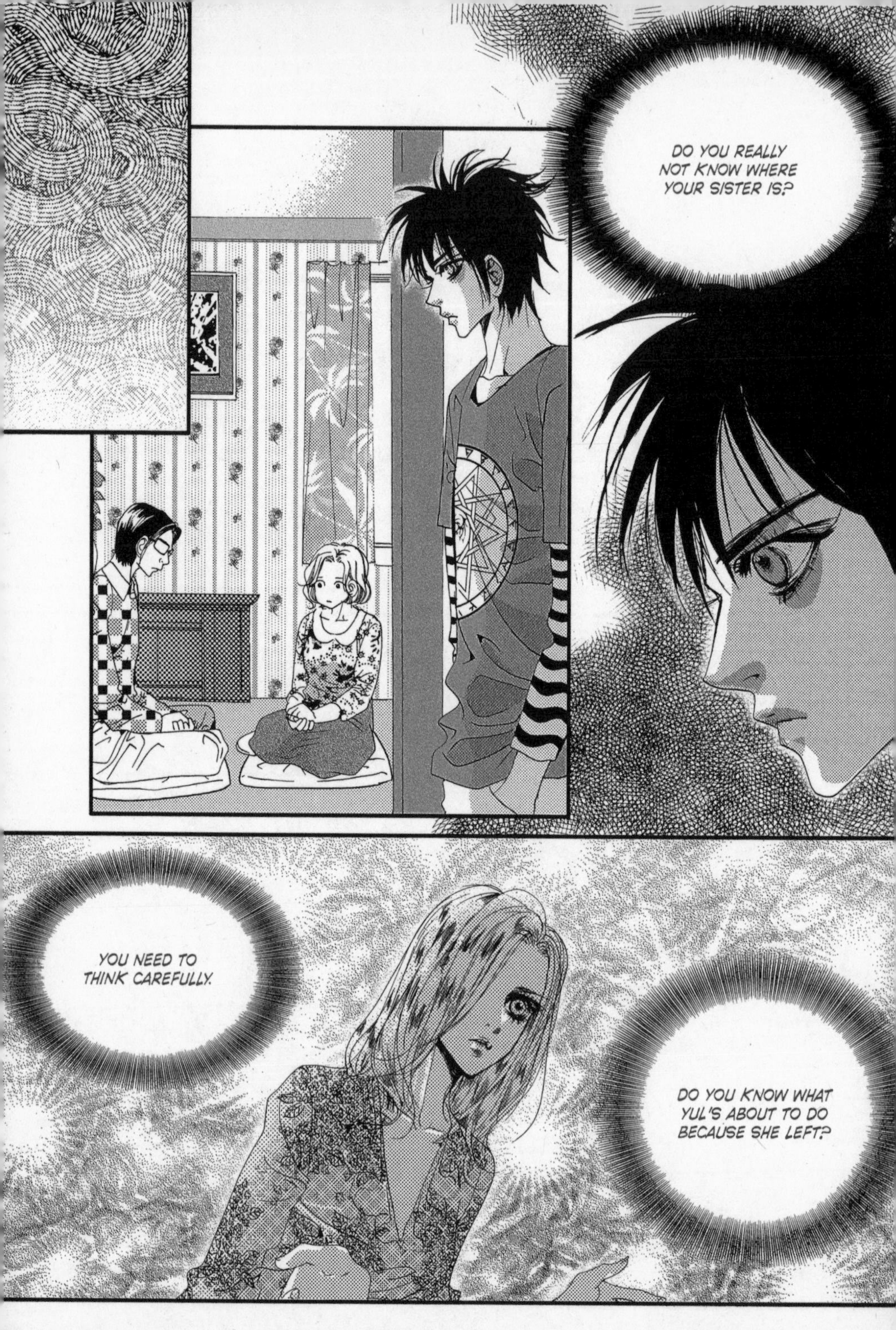
DO YOU REALLY NOT KNOW WHERE YOUR SISTER IS?
YOU NEED TO THINK CAREFULLY.
DO YOU KNOW WHAT YUL'S ABOUT TO DO BECAUSE SHE LEFT?

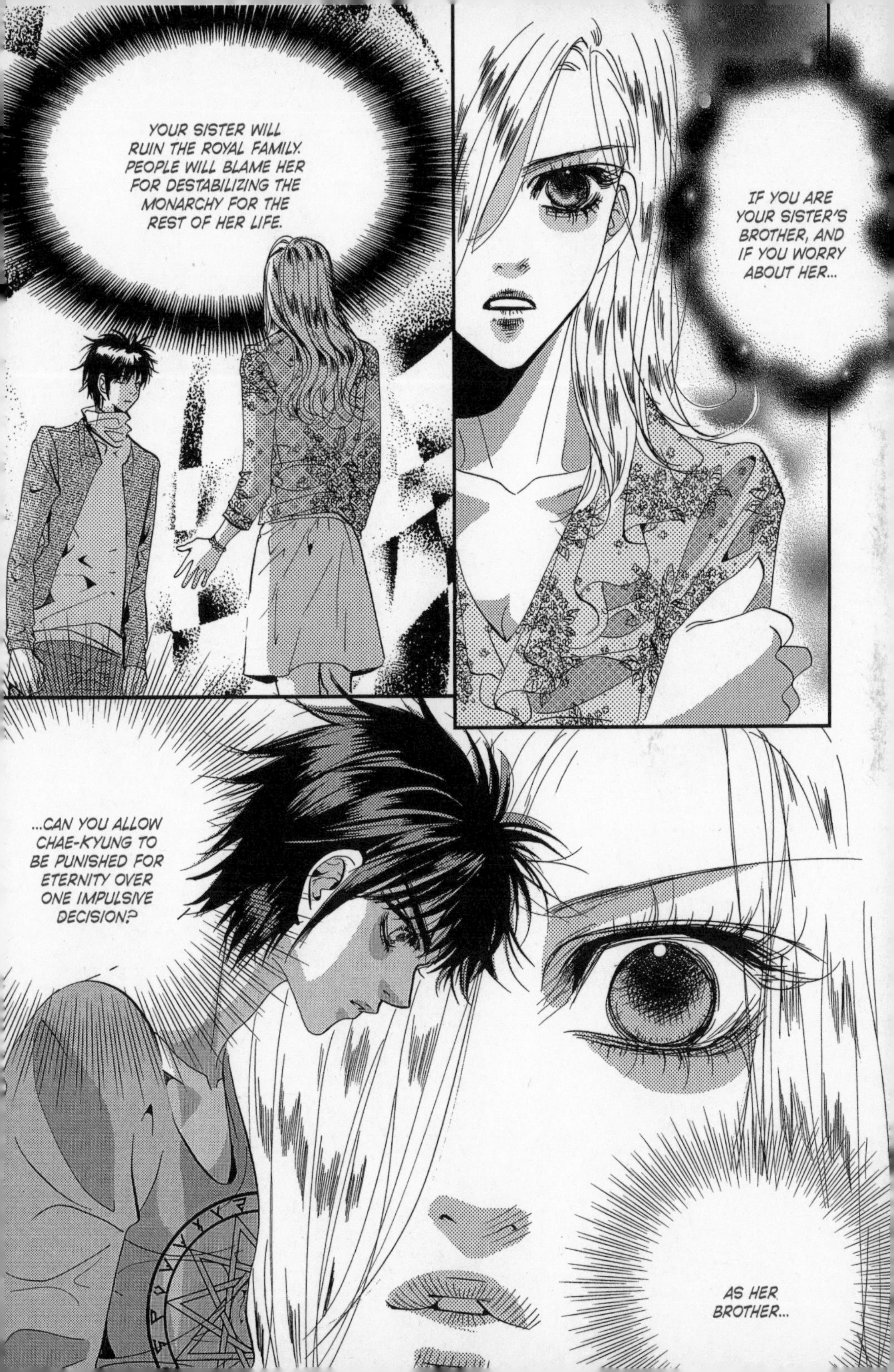
YOUR SISTER WILL RUIN THE ROYAL FAMILY. PEOPLE WILL BLAME HER FOR DESTABILIZING THE MONARCHY FOR THE REST OF HER LIFE.
IF YOU ARE YOUR SISTER'S BROTHER, AND IF YOU WORRY ABOUT HER...
...CAN YOU ALLOW CHAE-KYUNG TO BE PUNISHED FOR ETERNITY OVER ONE IMPULSIVE DECISION?
AS HER BROTHER...

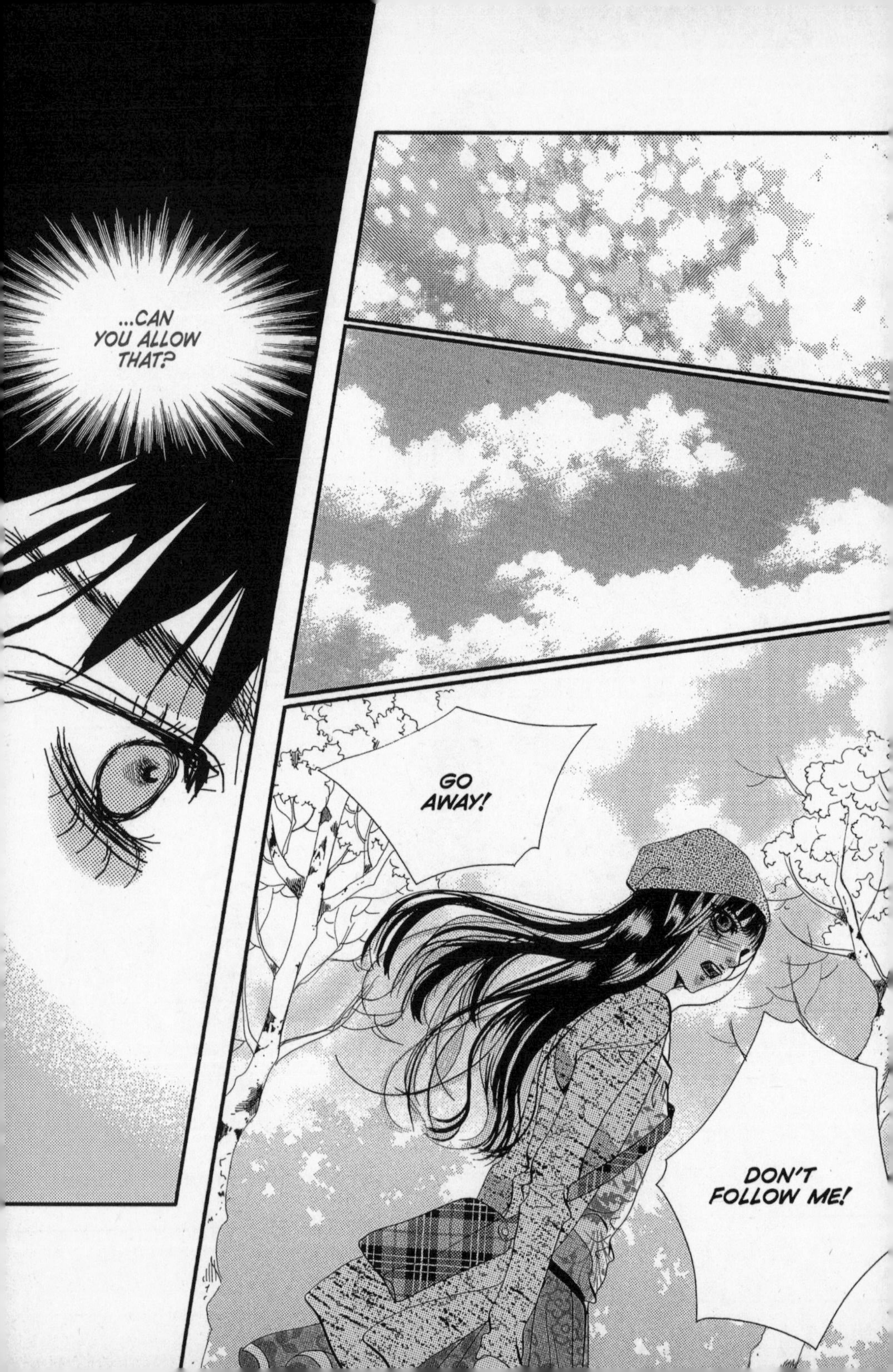
...CAN YOU ALLOW THAT?
GO AWAY!
DON'T FOLLOW ME!

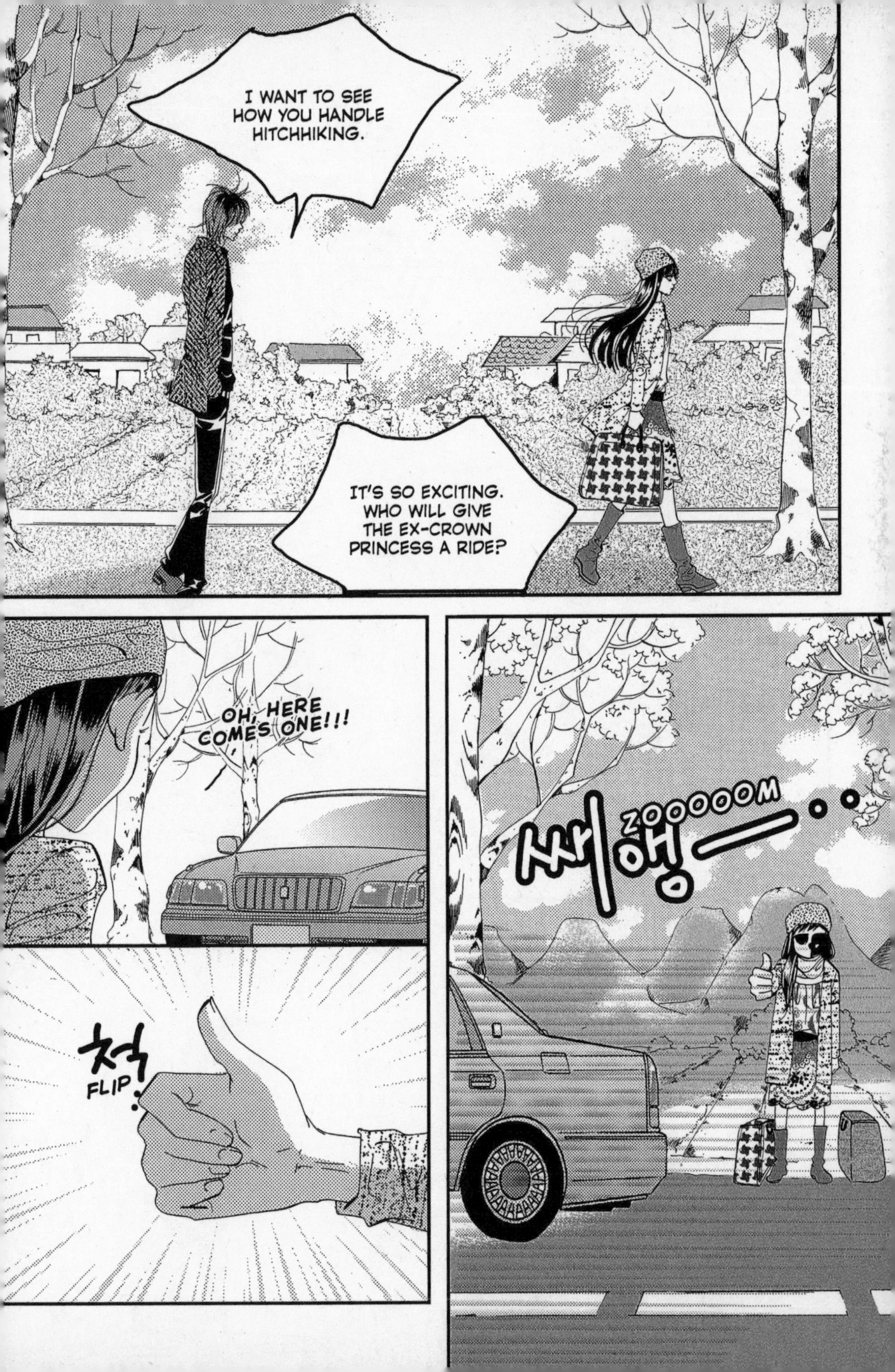
I WANT TO SEE HOW YOU HANDLE HITCHHIKING.
IT'S SO EXCITING. WHO WILL GIVE THE EX-CROWN PRINCESS A RIDE?
OH, HERE COMES ONE!!!
척
FLIP
쌔앵—
ZOOOOOM

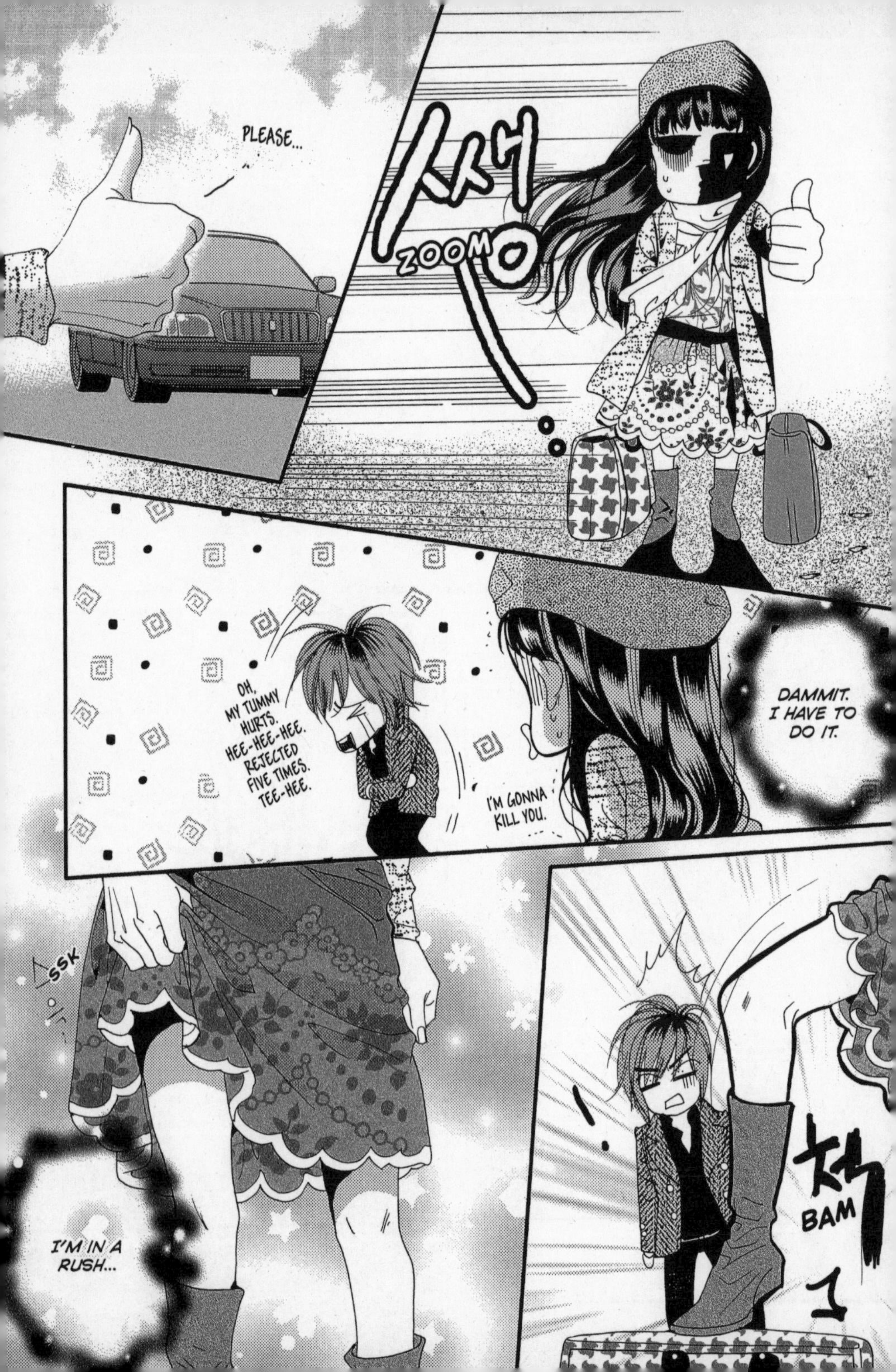
PLEASE...
ZOOM
OH, MY TUMMY HURTS. HEE-HEE-HEE. REJECTED FIVE TIMES. TEE-HEE.
I'M GONNA KILL YOU.
DAMMIT. I HAVE TO DO IT.
SSK
I'M IN A RUSH...
BAM

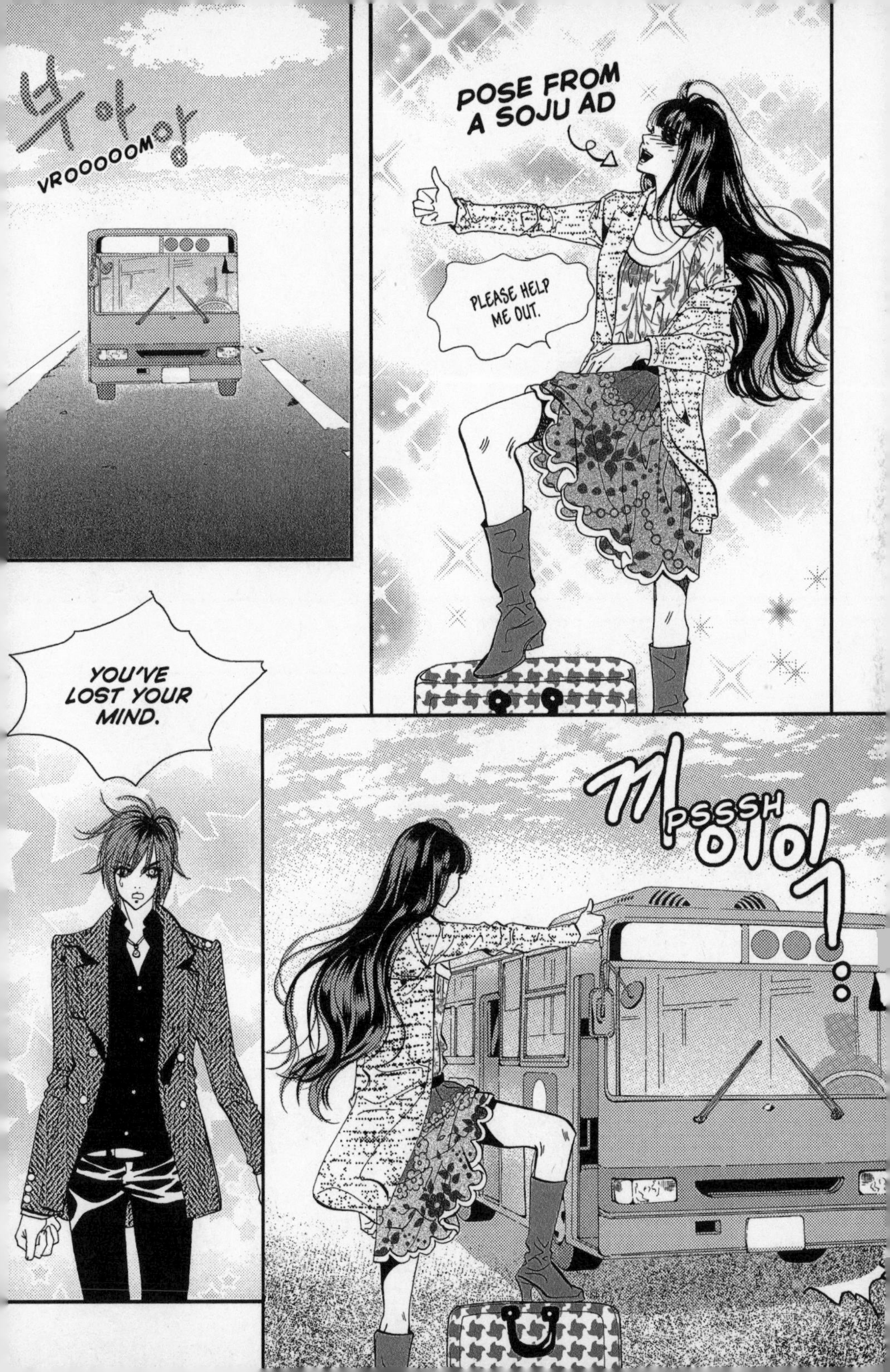
부아앙
VROOOOOM
POSE FROM A SOJU AD
PLEASE HELP ME OUT.
YOU'VE LOST YOUR MIND.
끼이익
PSSSH

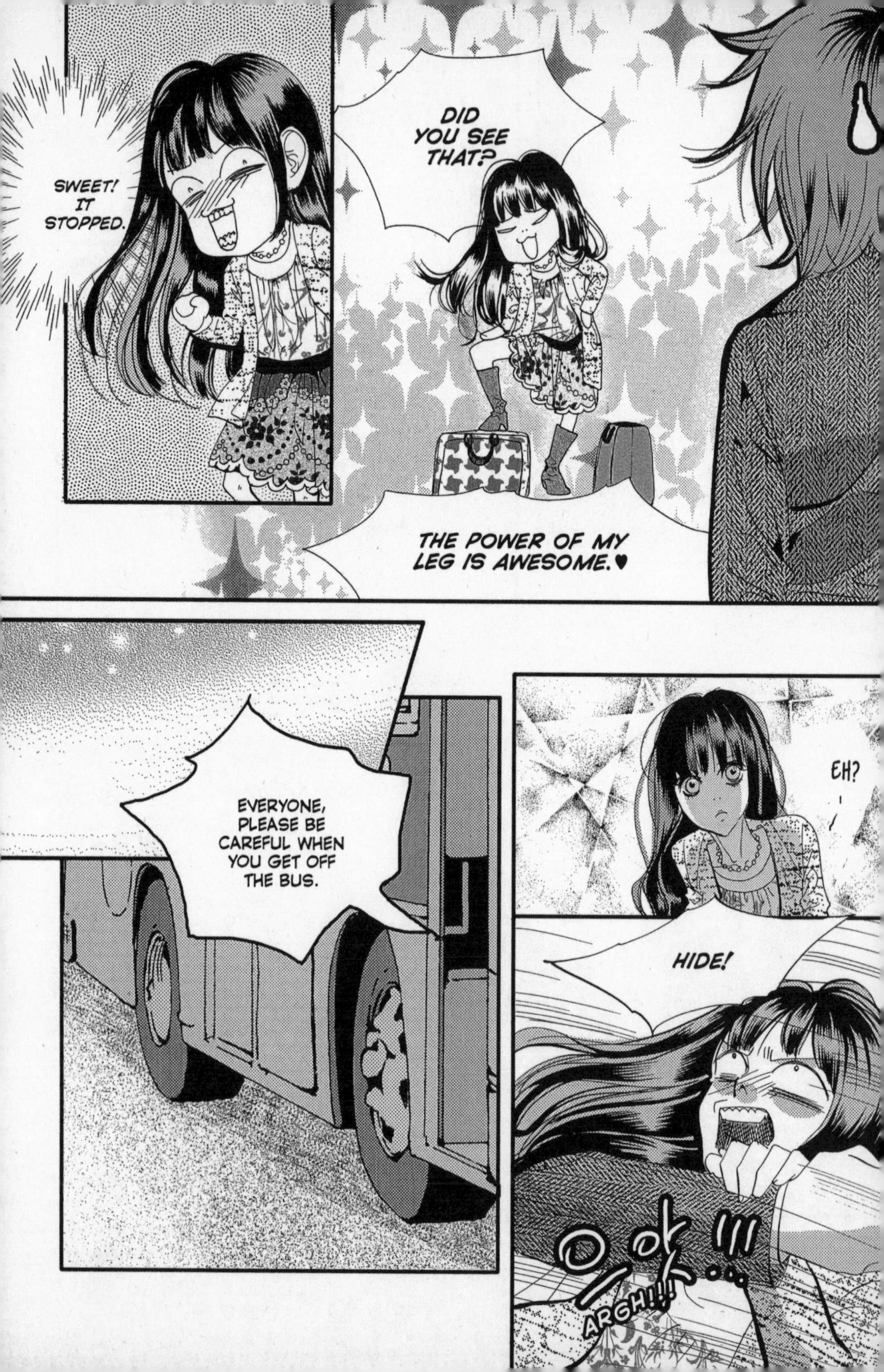
SWEET! IT STOPPED.
DID YOU SEE THAT?
THE POWER OF MY LEG IS AWESOME.♥
EVERYONE, PLEASE BE CAREFUL WHEN YOU GET OFF THE BUS.
EH?
HIDE!
으악!!!
ARGH!!!

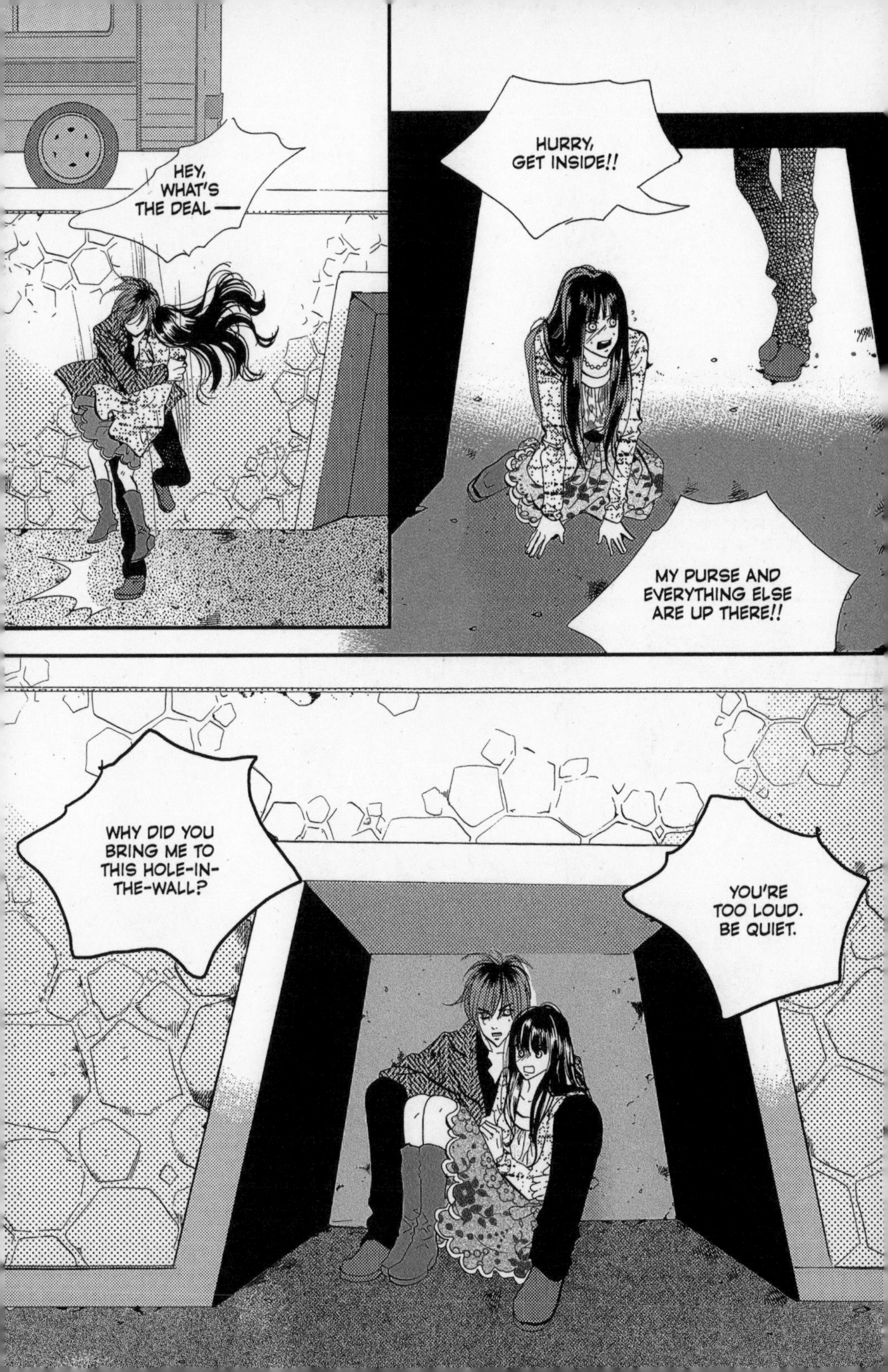
HEY, WHAT'S THE DEAL—
HURRY, GET INSIDE!!
MY PURSE AND EVERYTHING ELSE ARE UP THERE!!
WHY DID YOU BRING ME TO THIS HOLE-IN-THE-WALL?
YOU'RE TOO LOUD. BE QUIET.

DO YOU WANT PEOPLE TO SEE US?

YOU'LL BE SURROUNDED BY REPORTERS, AND THEY'LL CHASE YOU ALL THE WAY HOME.

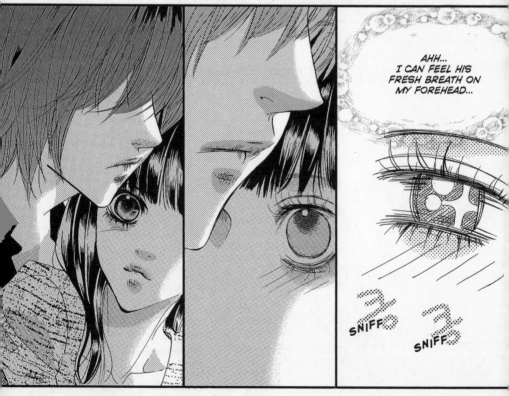

AHH... I CAN FEEL HIS FRESH BREATH ON MY FOREHEAD...

SNIFF

SNIFF

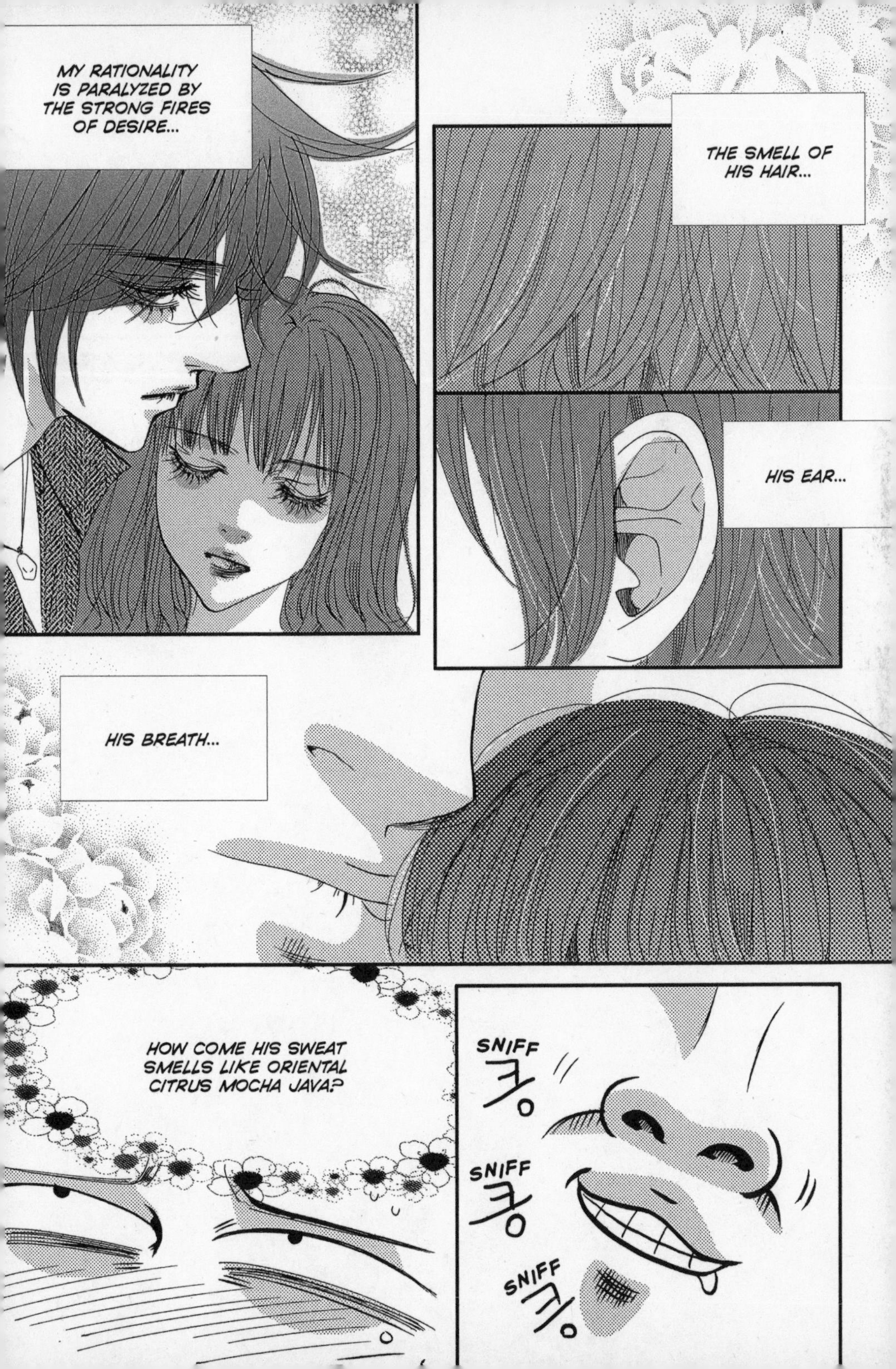
MY RATIONALITY IS PARALYZED BY THE STRONG FIRES OF DESIRE...
THE SMELL OF HIS HAIR...
HIS EAR...
HIS BREATH...
HOW COME HIS SWEAT SMELLS LIKE ORIENTAL CITRUS MOCHA JAVA?
SNIFF
킁
SNIFF
킁
SNIFF
킁

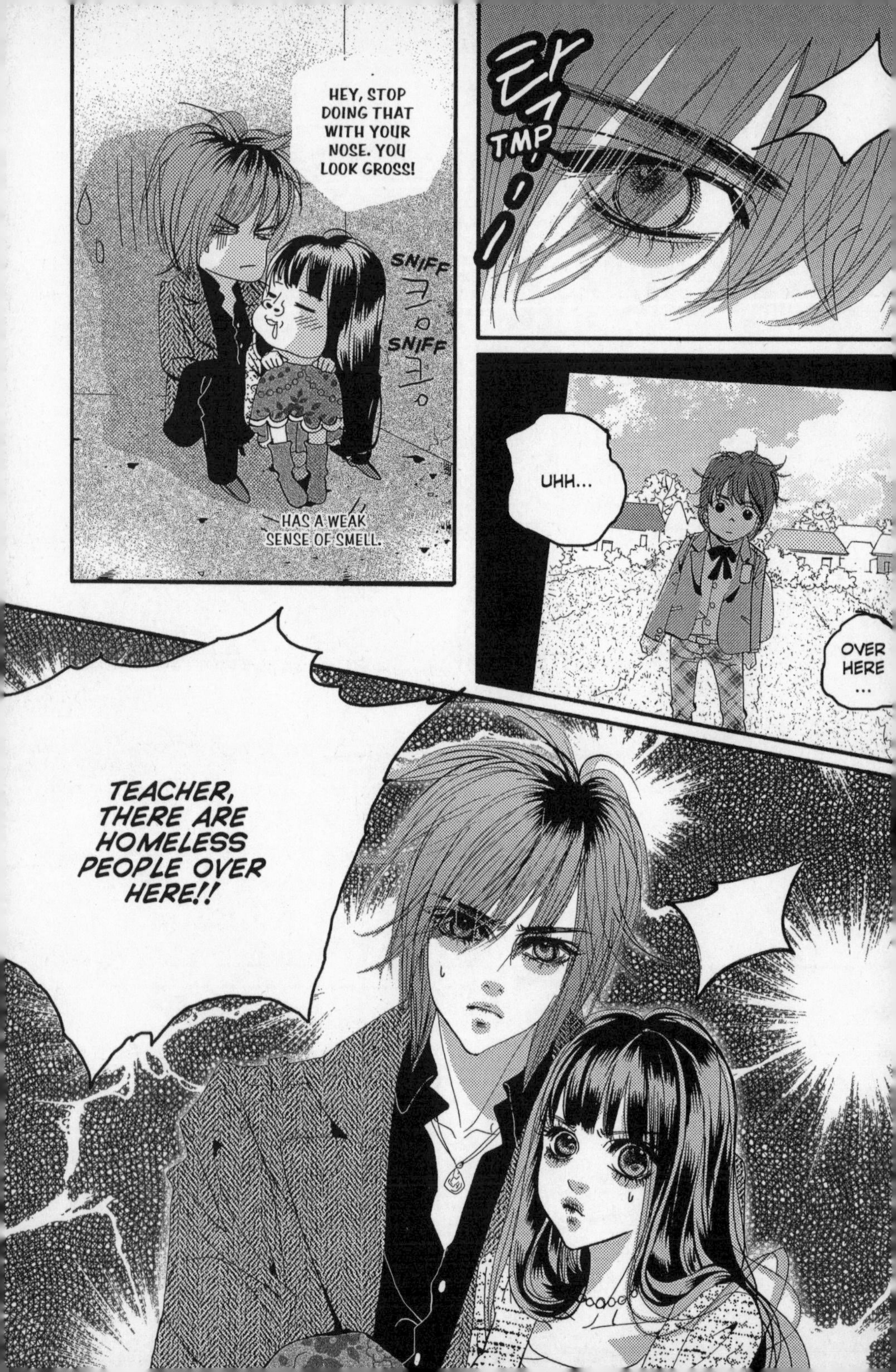
HEY, STOP DOING THAT WITH YOUR NOSE. YOU LOOK GROSS!
SNIFF
SNIFF
HAS A WEAK SENSE OF SMELL.
TMP
UHH...
OVER HERE ...
TEACHER, THERE ARE HOMELESS PEOPLE OVER HERE!!

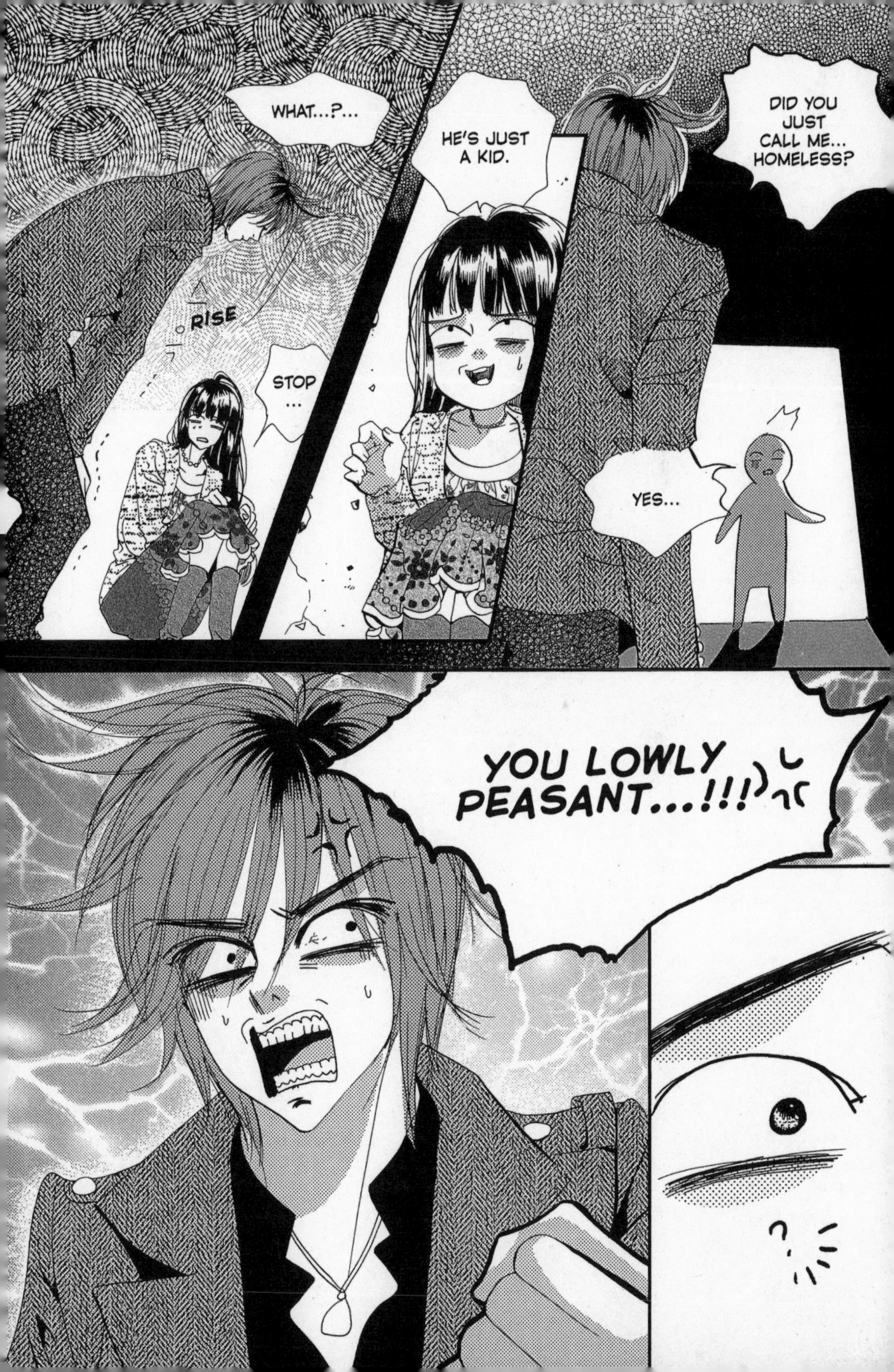

WHAT...?...
RISE
STOP ...
HE'S JUST A KID.
DID YOU JUST CALL ME... HOMELESS?
YES...
YOU LOWLY PEASANT...!!!

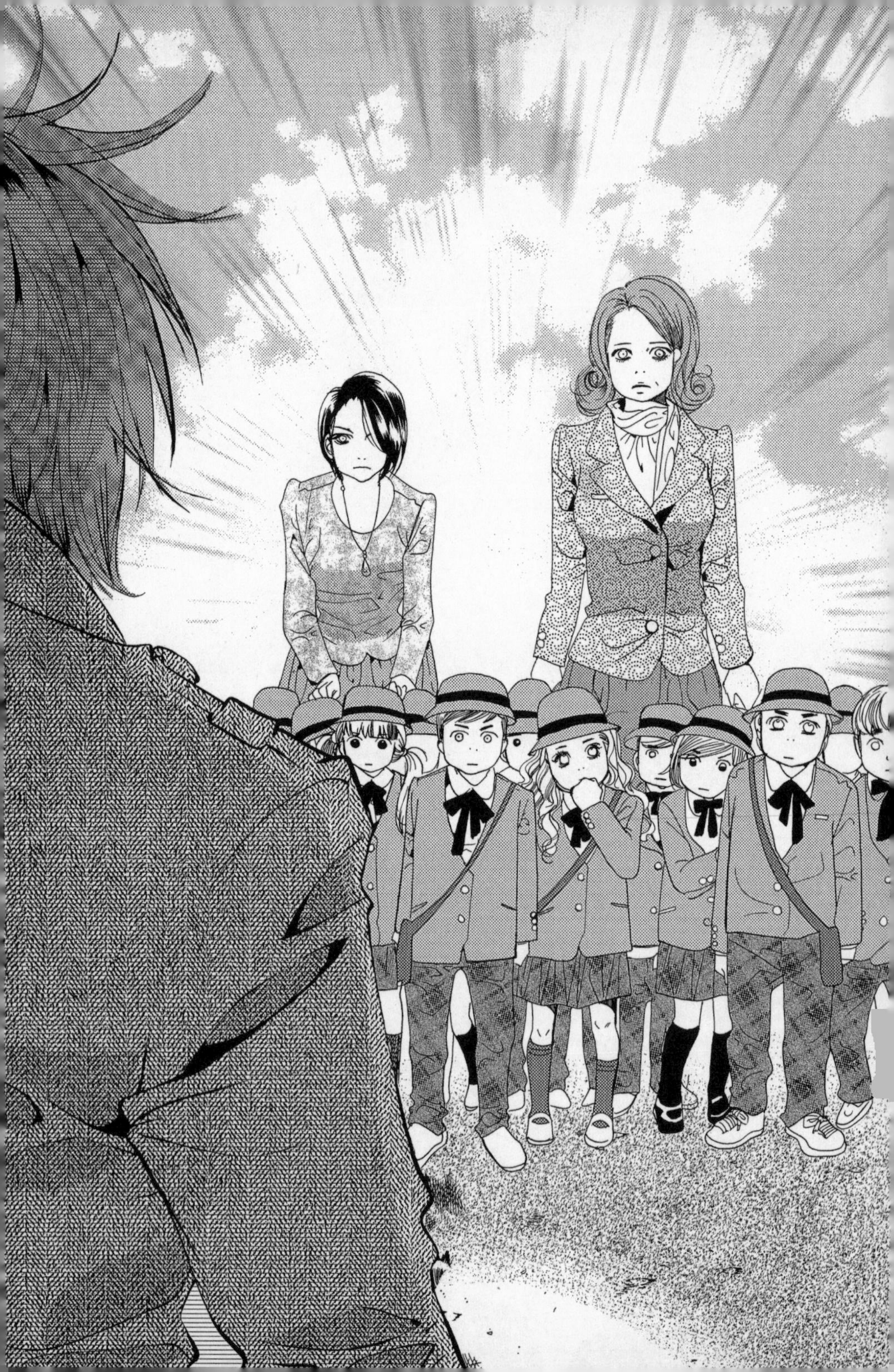

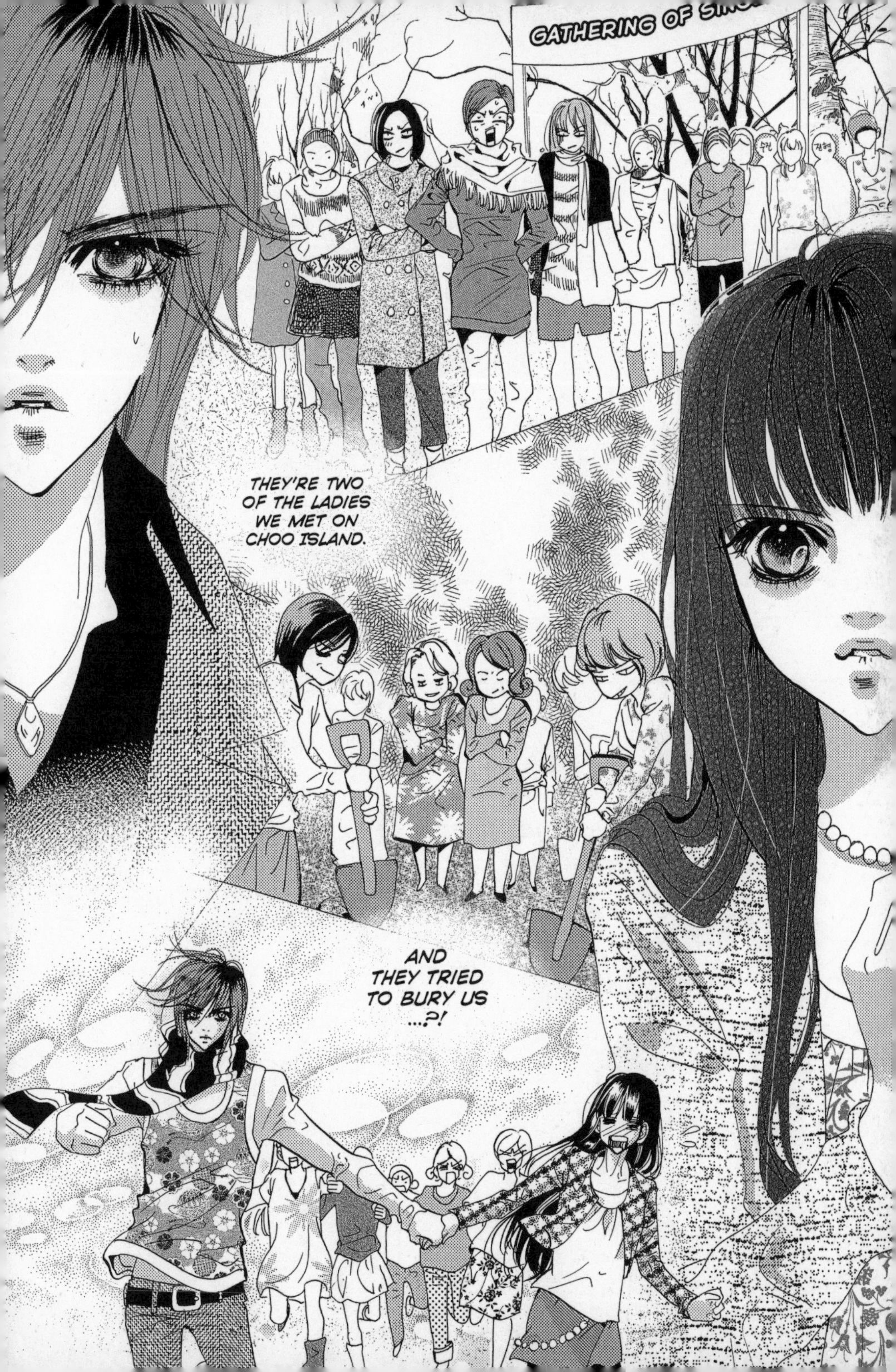
GATHERING OF
THEY'RE TWO OF THE LADIES WE MET ON CHOO ISLAND.
AND THEY TRIED TO BURY US ...?!

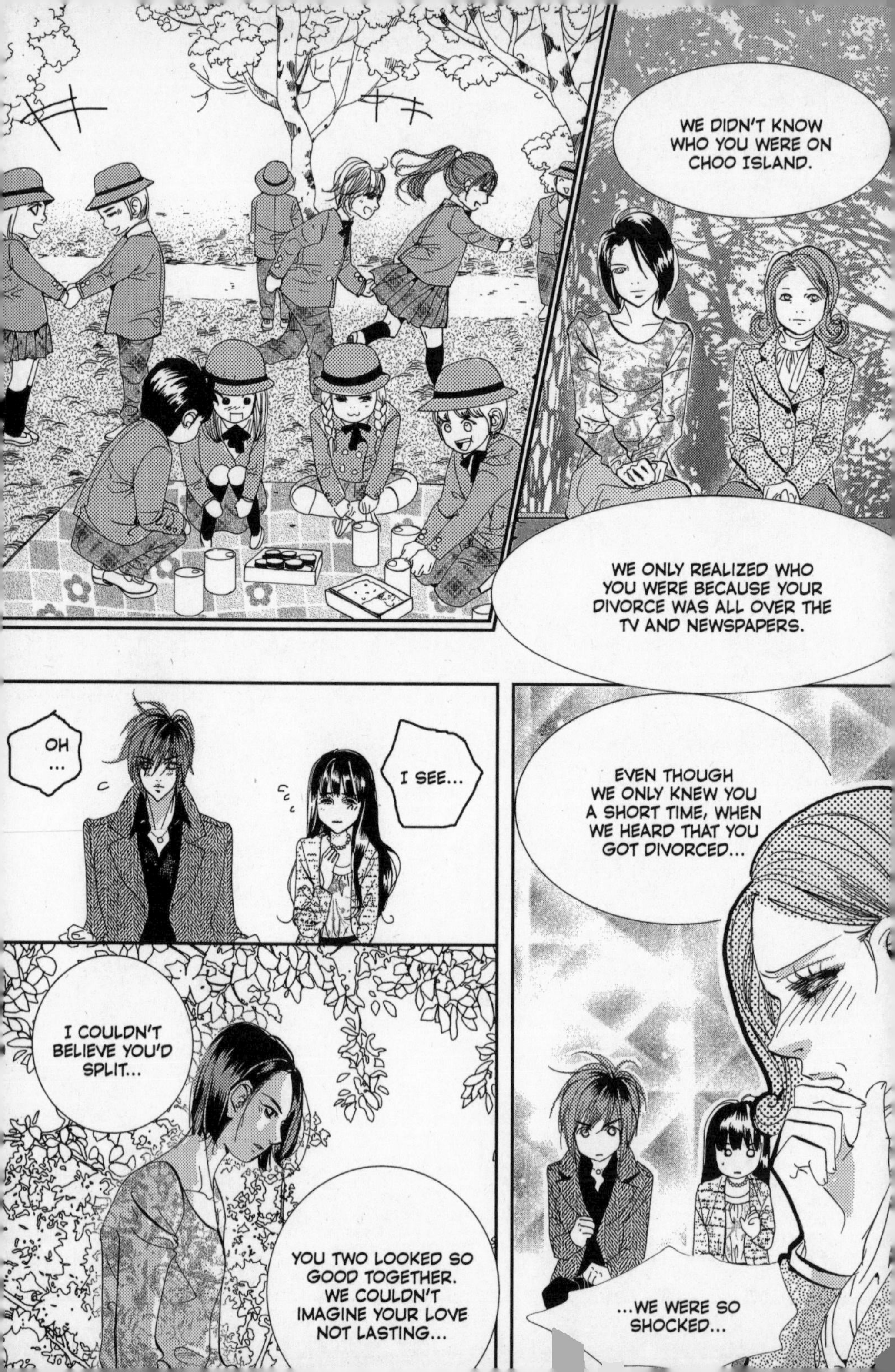
WE DIDN'T KNOW WHO YOU WERE ON CHOO ISLAND.
WE ONLY REALIZED WHO YOU WERE BECAUSE YOUR DIVORCE WAS ALL OVER THE TV AND NEWSPAPERS.
OH ...
I SEE...
I COULDN'T BELIEVE YOU'D SPLIT...
YOU TWO LOOKED SO GOOD TOGETHER. WE COULDN'T IMAGINE YOUR LOVE NOT LASTING...
EVEN THOUGH WE ONLY KNEW YOU A SHORT TIME, WHEN WE HEARD THAT YOU GOT DIVORCED...
...WE WERE SO SHOCKED...

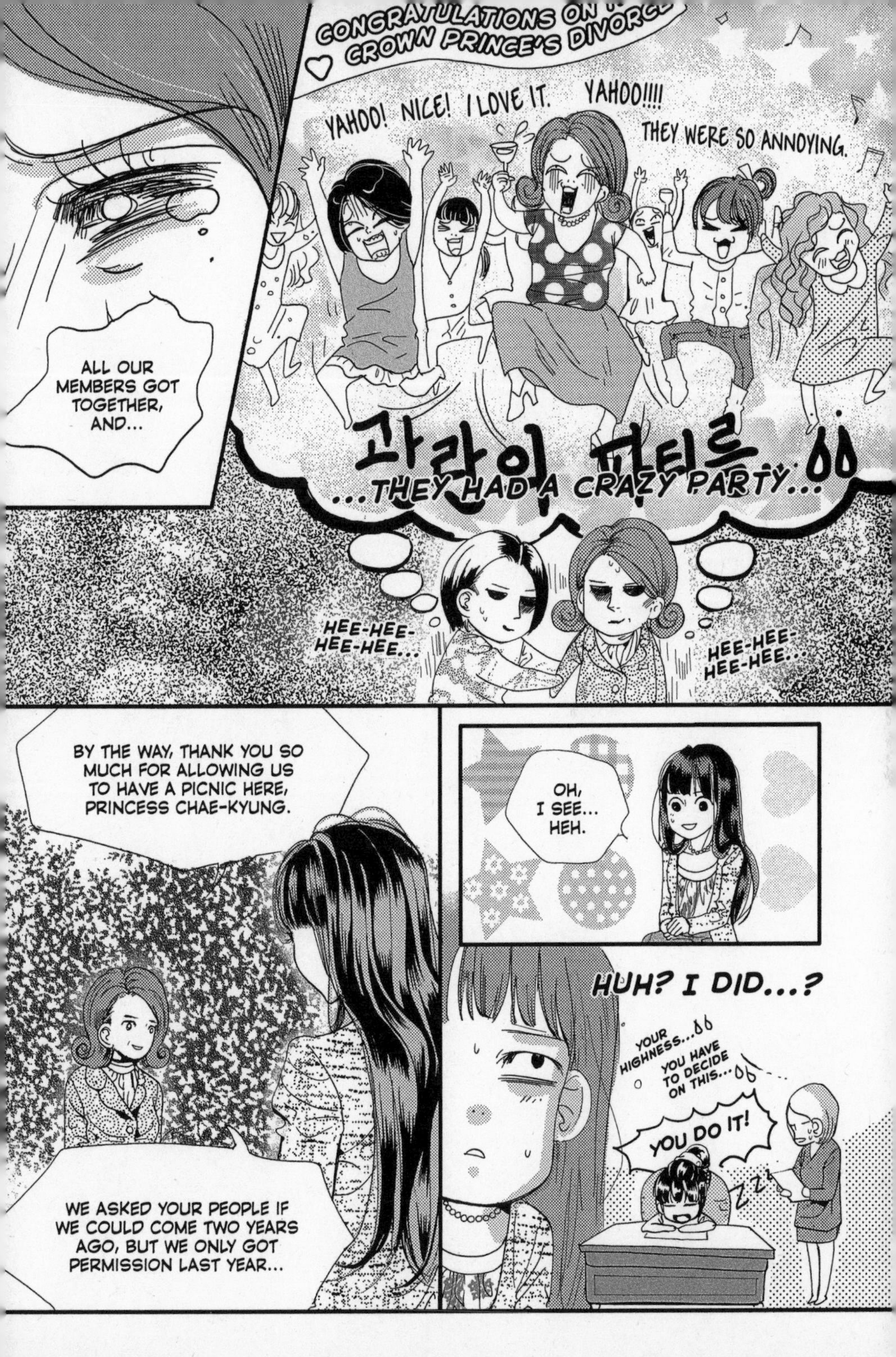

CONGRATULATIONS ON THE CROWN PRINCE'S DIVORCE
ALL OUR MEMBERS GOT TOGETHER, AND...
YAHOO! NICE! I LOVE IT. YAHOO!!!!
THEY WERE SO ANNOYING.
...THEY HAD A CRAZY PARTY...
HEE-HEE-HEE-HEE...
HEE-HEE-HEE-HEE...
BY THE WAY, THANK YOU SO MUCH FOR ALLOWING US TO HAVE A PICNIC HERE, PRINCESS CHAE-KYUNG.
WE ASKED YOUR PEOPLE IF WE COULD COME TWO YEARS AGO, BUT WE ONLY GOT PERMISSION LAST YEAR...
OH, I SEE... HEH.
HUH? I DID...?
YOUR HIGHNESS...
YOU HAVE TO DECIDE ON THIS...
YOU DO IT!

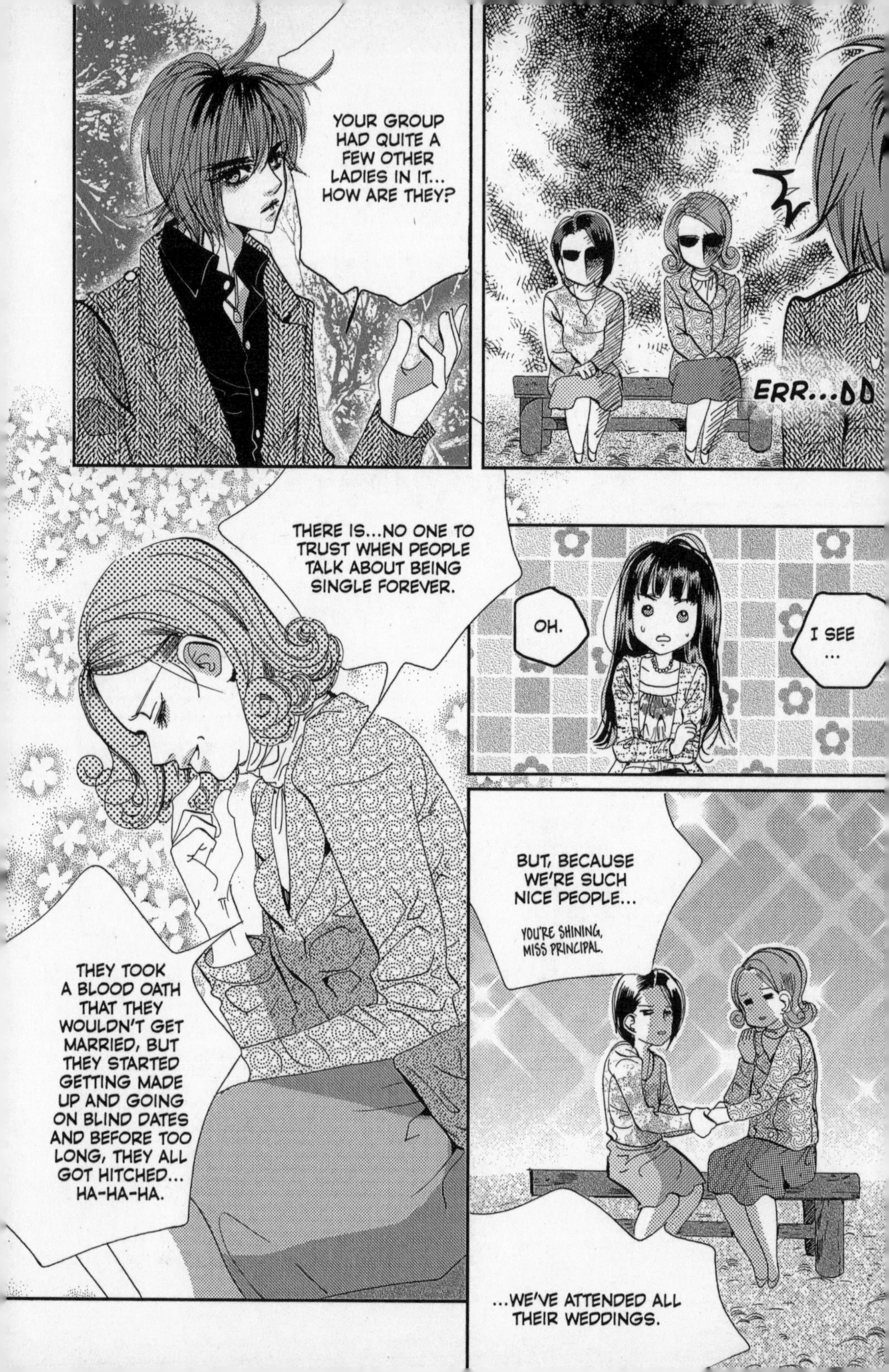
YOUR GROUP HAD QUITE A FEW OTHER LADIES IN IT... HOW ARE THEY?
ERR...
THERE IS...NO ONE TO TRUST WHEN PEOPLE TALK ABOUT BEING SINGLE FOREVER.
THEY TOOK A BLOOD OATH THAT THEY WOULDN'T GET MARRIED, BUT THEY STARTED GETTING MADE UP AND GOING ON BLIND DATES AND BEFORE TOO LONG, THEY ALL GOT HITCHED... HA-HA-HA.
OH.
I SEE ...
BUT, BECAUSE WE'RE SUCH NICE PEOPLE...
YOU'RE SHINING, MISS PRINCIPAL.
...WE'VE ATTENDED ALL THEIR WEDDINGS.

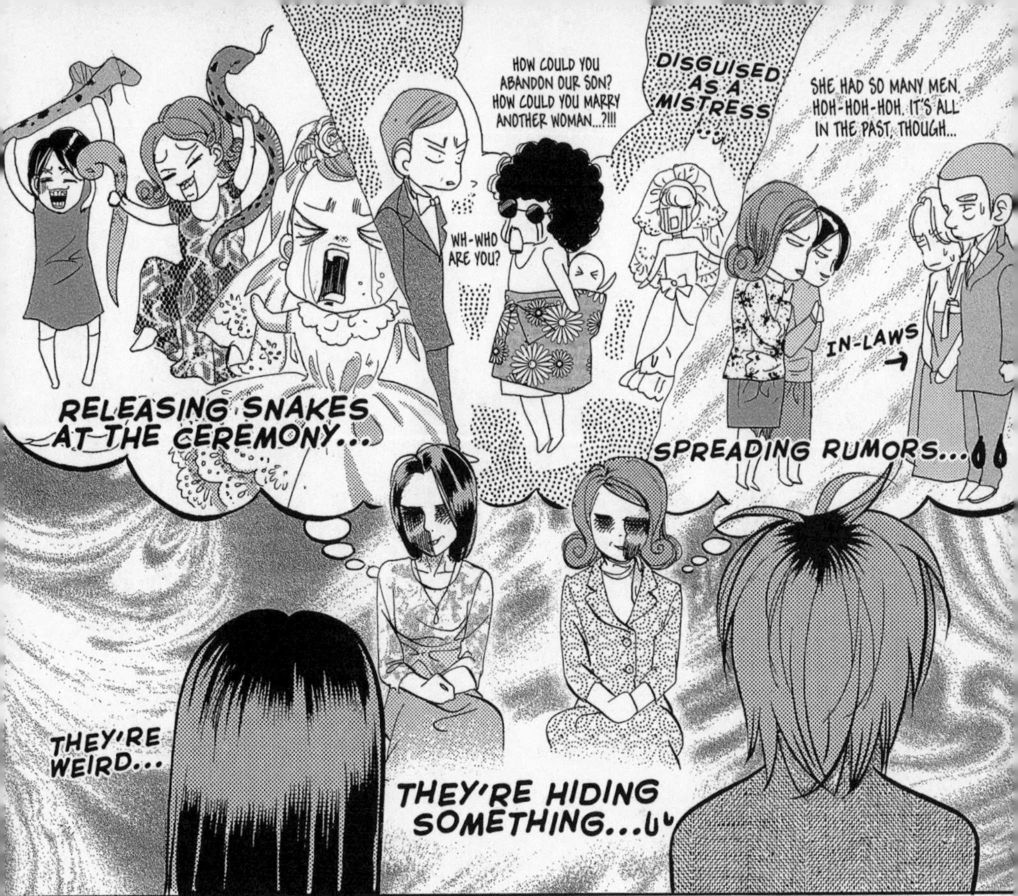
RELEASING SNAKES AT THE CEREMONY...
HOW COULD YOU ABANDON OUR SON? HOW COULD YOU MARRY ANOTHER WOMAN...?!!!
WH-WHO ARE YOU?
DISGUISED AS A MISTRESS
SHE HAD SO MANY MEN. HOH-HOH-HOH. IT'S ALL IN THE PAST, THOUGH...
IN-LAWS
SPREADING RUMORS...
THEY'RE WEIRD...
THEY'RE HIDING SOMETHING...

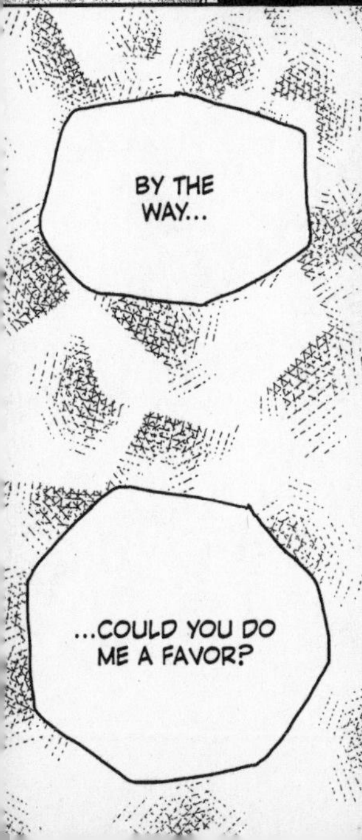
BY THE WAY...
...COULD YOU DO ME A FAVOR?

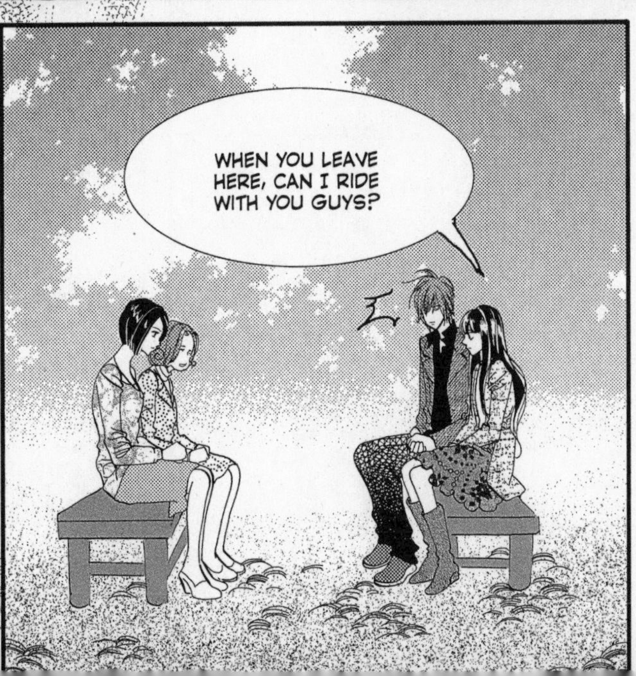
WHEN YOU LEAVE HERE, CAN I RIDE WITH YOU GUYS?

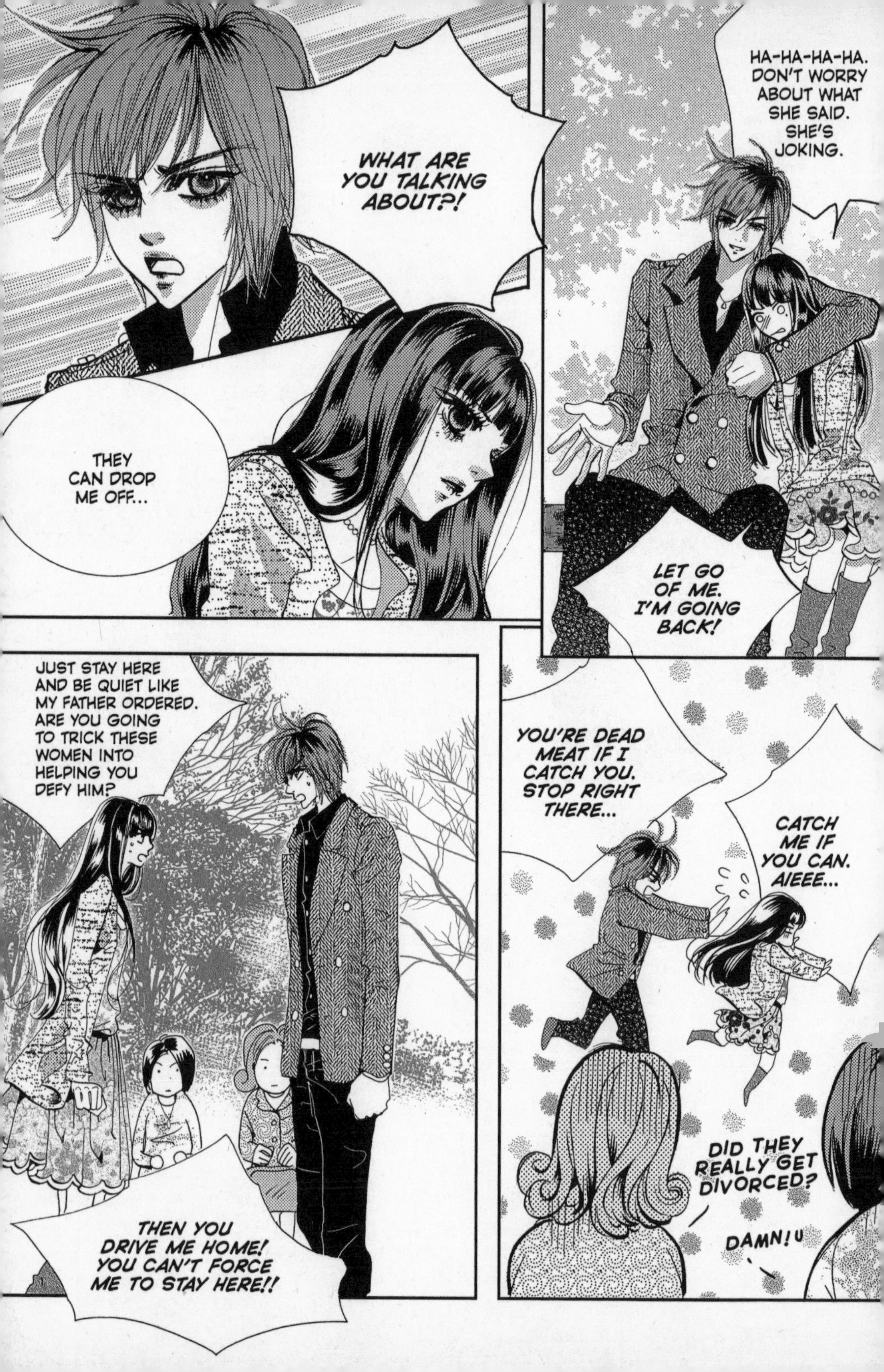
WHAT ARE YOU TALKING ABOUT?!
THEY CAN DROP ME OFF...
HA-HA-HA-HA. DON'T WORRY ABOUT WHAT SHE SAID. SHE'S JOKING.
LET GO OF ME. I'M GOING BACK!
JUST STAY HERE AND BE QUIET LIKE MY FATHER ORDERED. ARE YOU GOING TO TRICK THESE WOMEN INTO HELPING YOU DEFY HIM?
THEN YOU DRIVE ME HOME! YOU CAN'T FORCE ME TO STAY HERE!!
YOU'RE DEAD MEAT IF I CATCH YOU. STOP RIGHT THERE...
CATCH ME IF YOU CAN. AIEEE...
DID THEY REALLY GET DIVORCED?
DAMN!!

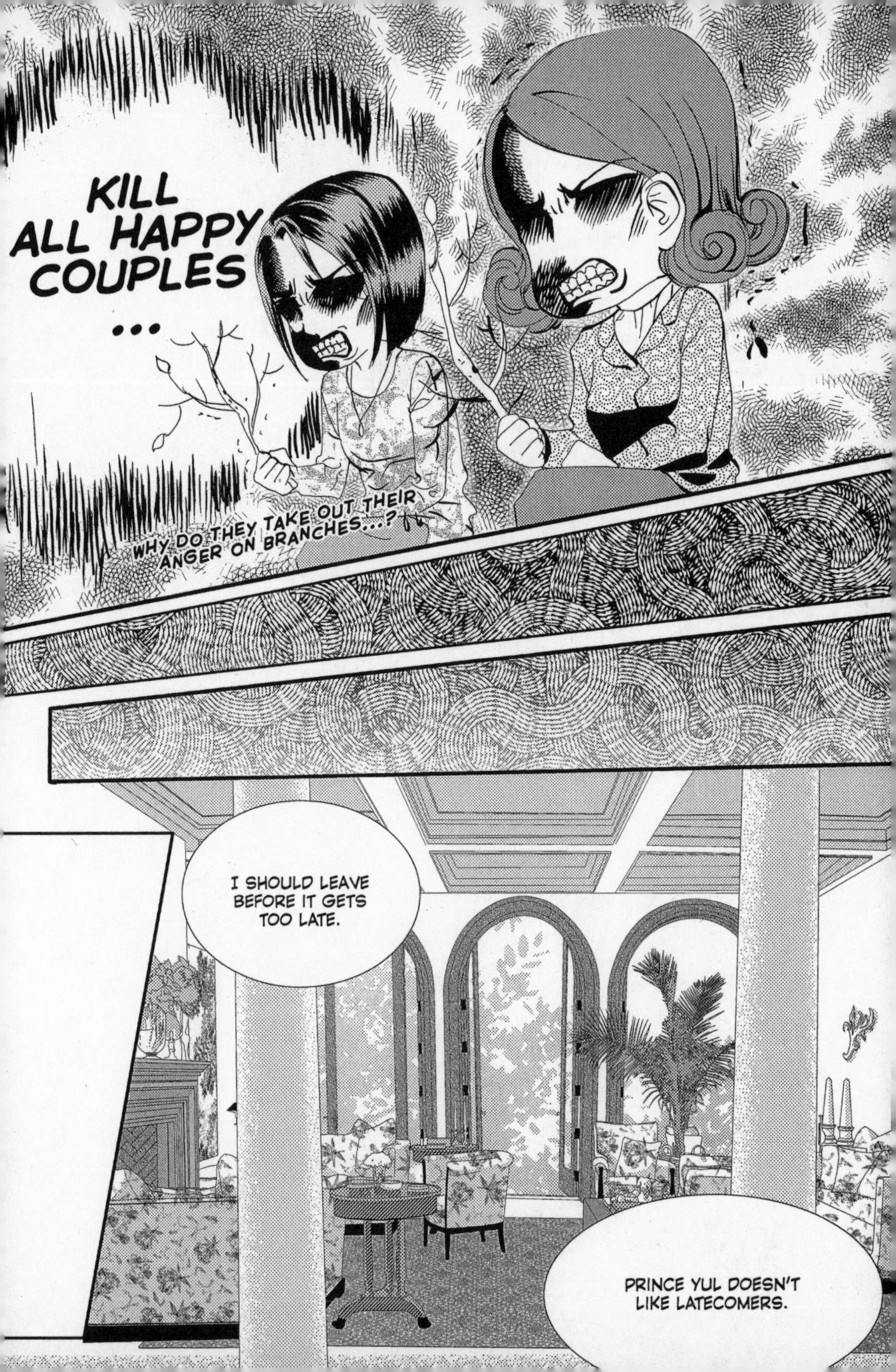
KILL ALL HAPPY COUPLES ...
WHY DO THEY TAKE OUT THEIR ANGER ON BRANCHES...?
I SHOULD LEAVE BEFORE IT GETS TOO LATE.
PRINCE YUL DOESN'T LIKE LATECOMERS.

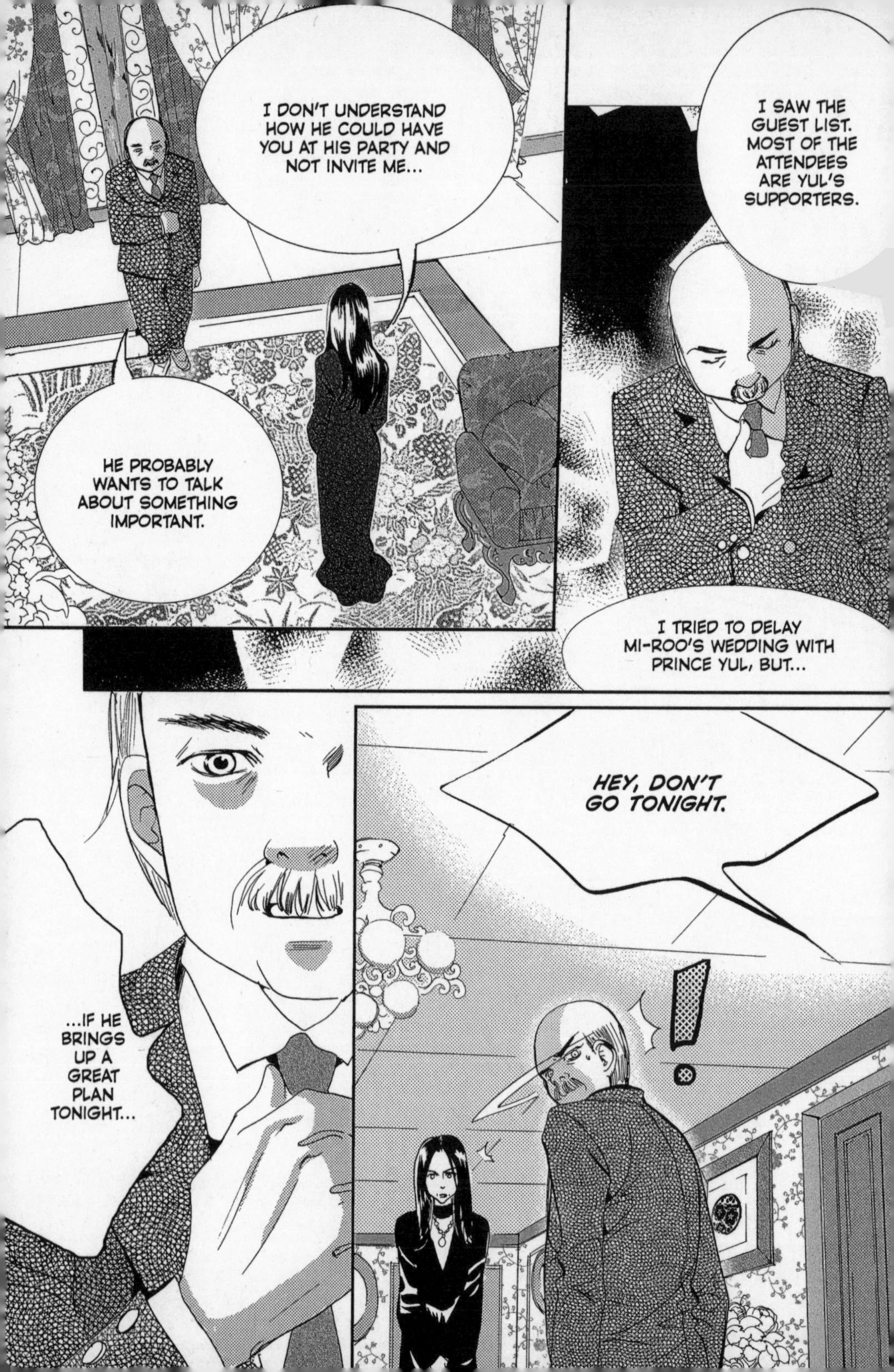
I DON'T UNDERSTAND HOW HE COULD HAVE YOU AT HIS PARTY AND NOT INVITE ME...
HE PROBABLY WANTS TO TALK ABOUT SOMETHING IMPORTANT.
I SAW THE GUEST LIST. MOST OF THE ATTENDEES ARE YUL'S SUPPORTERS.
I TRIED TO DELAY MI-ROO'S WEDDING WITH PRINCE YUL, BUT...
...IF HE BRINGS UP A GREAT PLAN TONIGHT...
HEY, DON'T GO TONIGHT.
!

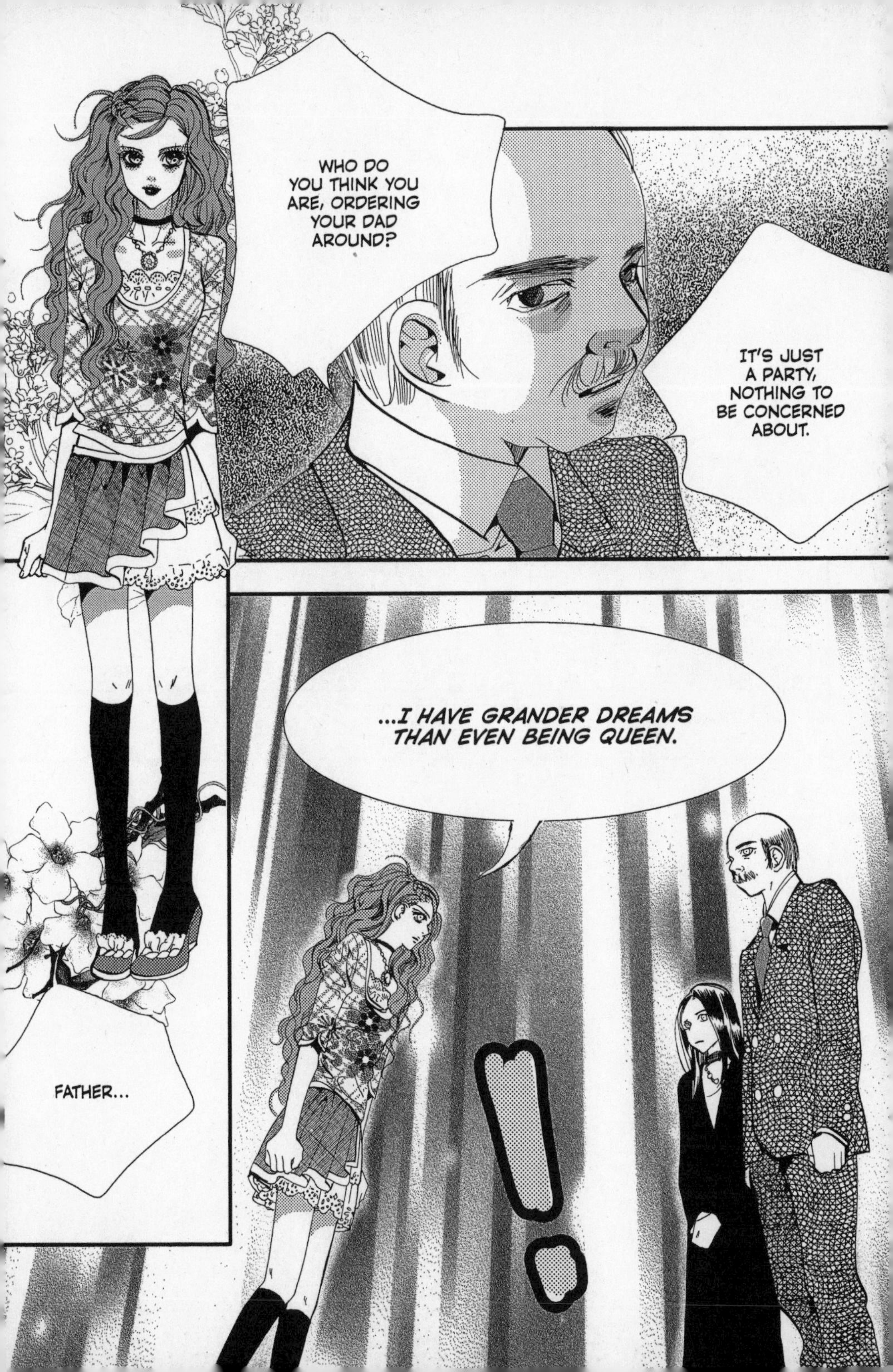
FATHER...
WHO DO YOU THINK YOU ARE, ORDERING YOUR DAD AROUND?
IT'S JUST A PARTY, NOTHING TO BE CONCERNED ABOUT.
...I HAVE GRANDER DREAMS THAN EVEN BEING QUEEN.
!

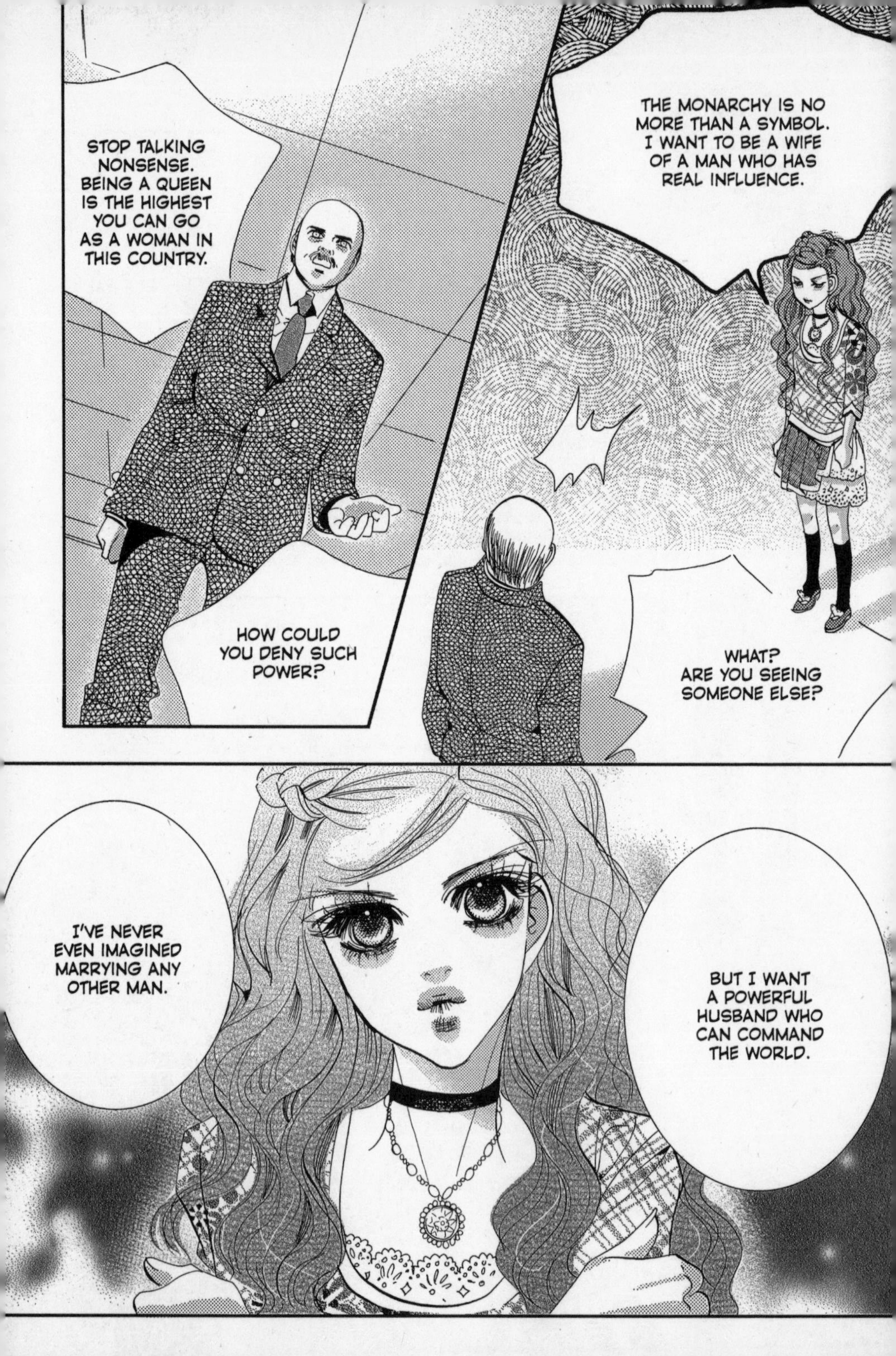
STOP TALKING NONSENSE. BEING A QUEEN IS THE HIGHEST YOU CAN GO AS A WOMAN IN THIS COUNTRY.
HOW COULD YOU DENY SUCH POWER?
THE MONARCHY IS NO MORE THAN A SYMBOL. I WANT TO BE A WIFE OF A MAN WHO HAS REAL INFLUENCE.
WHAT? ARE YOU SEEING SOMEONE ELSE?
I'VE NEVER EVEN IMAGINED MARRYING ANY OTHER MAN.
BUT I WANT A POWERFUL HUSBAND WHO CAN COMMAND THE WORLD.

......

THAT'S... WHAT YOU WANT?

THERE'S A BILL BEING INTRODUCED NEXT YEAR THAT WOULD ALLOW A MEMBER OF THE ROYAL FAMILY TO ALSO SIT IN PARLIAMENT.

IT'S GOING TO BE HARD ON HIM IF HIS PLAN BACKFIRES. BUT A PRINCE ABANDONED BY THE ROYAL FAMILY COULD TRANSITION INTO POLITICS.

IT'S A SAFE BET THAT THE BILL WILL BE PASSED. THEN IT'LL BE POSSIBLE FOR YUL TO BE THE PRIME MINISTER.

HE'D HAVE THE SUPPORT OF BOTH ADMIRERS AND DETRACTORS OF THE ROYALS.

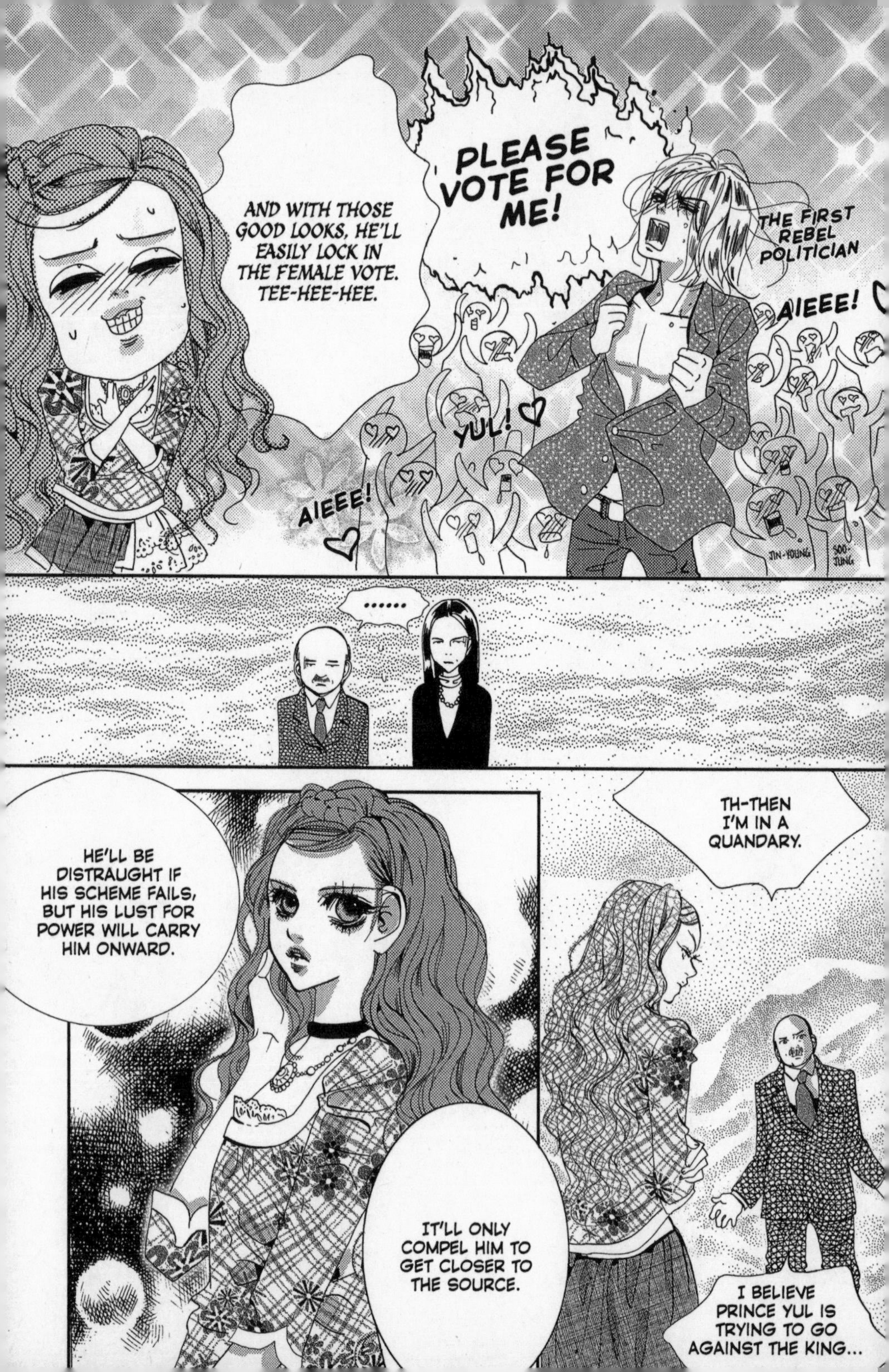
AND WITH THOSE GOOD LOOKS, HE'LL EASILY LOCK IN THE FEMALE VOTE. TEE-HEE-HEE.
PLEASE VOTE FOR ME!
THE FIRST REBEL POLITICIAN
AIEEE!
YUL!
AIEEE!
JIN-YOUNG
SOO-JUNG
......
HE'LL BE DISTRAUGHT IF HIS SCHEME FAILS, BUT HIS LUST FOR POWER WILL CARRY HIM ONWARD.
IT'LL ONLY COMPEL HIM TO GET CLOSER TO THE SOURCE.
TH-THEN I'M IN A QUANDARY.
I BELIEVE PRINCE YUL IS TRYING TO GO AGAINST THE KING...

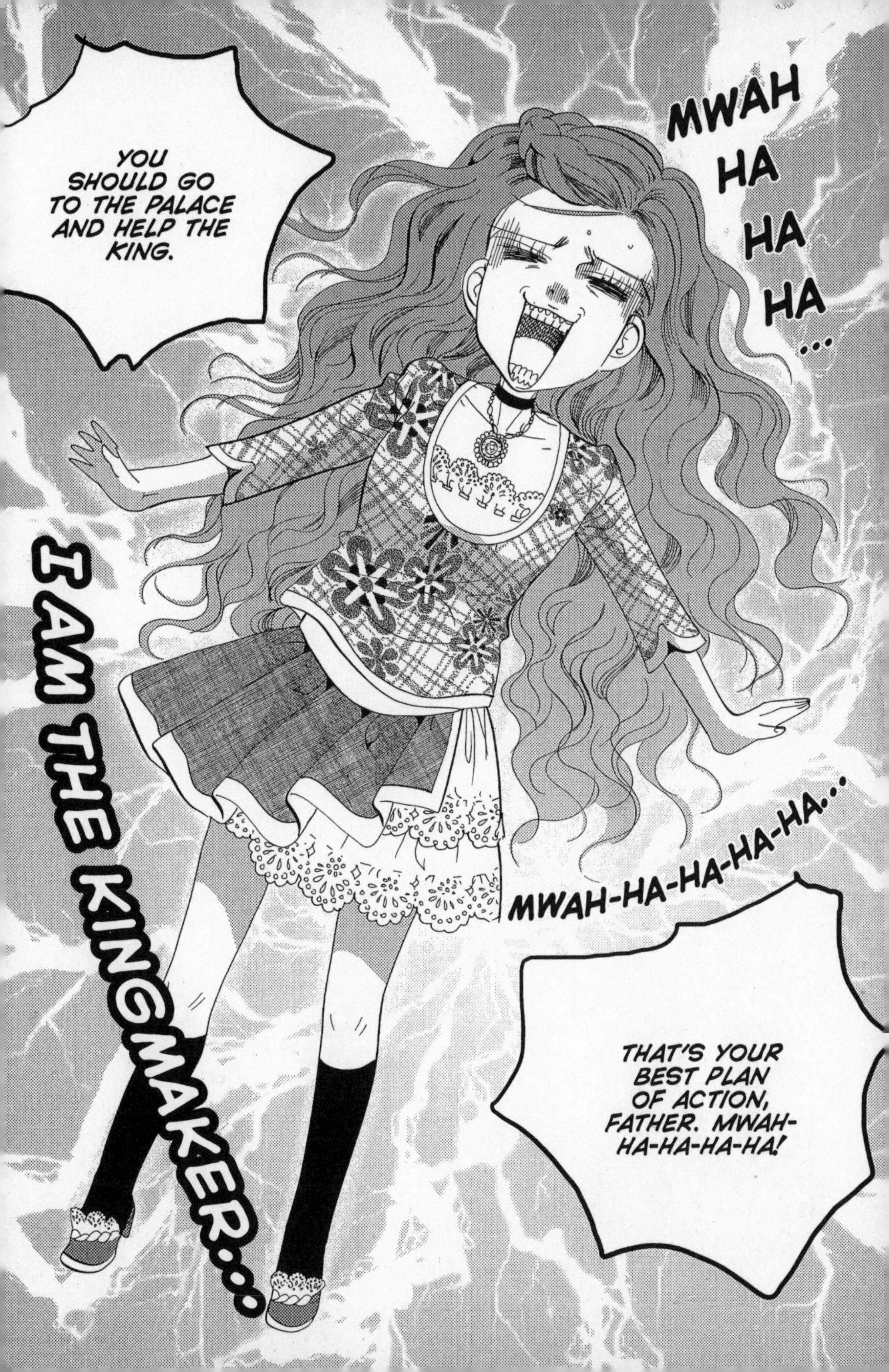
YOU SHOULD GO TO THE PALACE AND HELP THE KING.
MWAH HA HA HA...
I AM THE KINGMAKER...
MWAH-HA-HA-HA-HA...
THAT'S YOUR BEST PLAN OF ACTION, FATHER. MWAH-HA-HA-HA-HA!

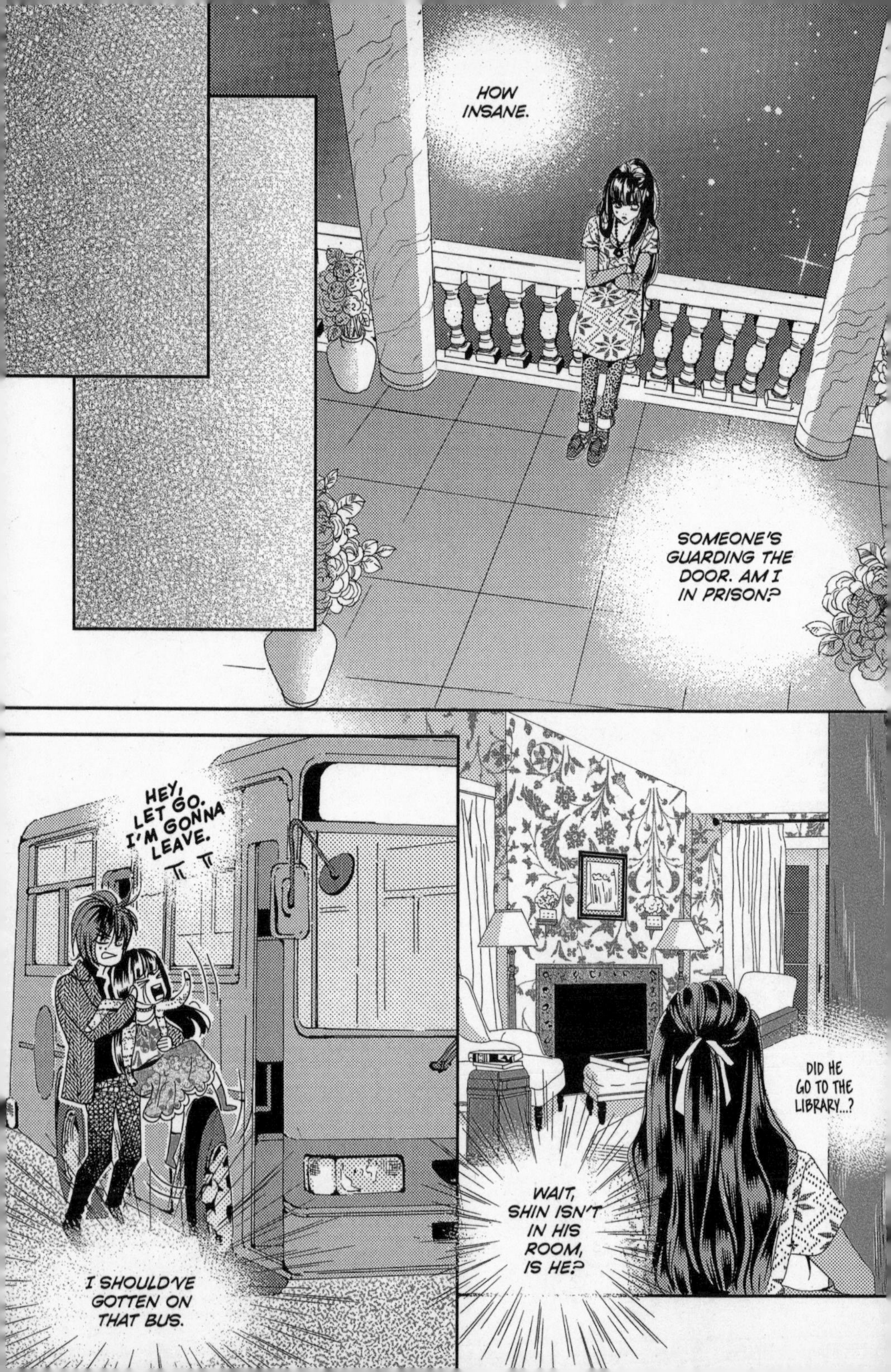
HOW INSANE.
SOMEONE'S GUARDING THE DOOR. AM I IN PRISON?
HEY, LET GO. I'M GONNA LEAVE.
I SHOULD'VE GOTTEN ON THAT BUS.
DID HE GO TO THE LIBRARY...?
WAIT, SHIN ISN'T IN HIS ROOM, IS HE?

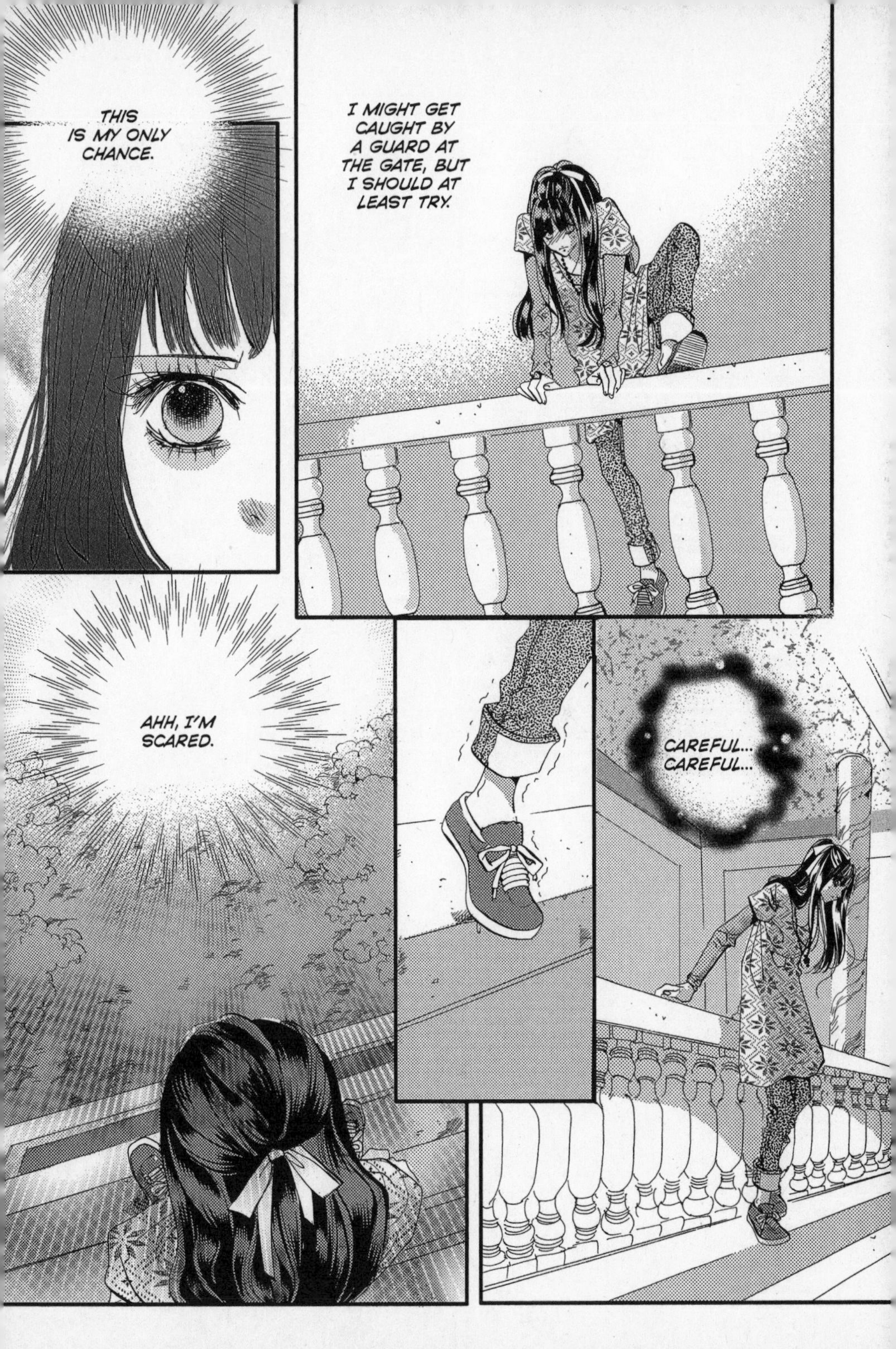
THIS IS MY ONLY CHANCE.
I MIGHT GET CAUGHT BY A GUARD AT THE GATE, BUT I SHOULD AT LEAST TRY.
AHH, I'M SCARED.
CAREFUL... CAREFUL...

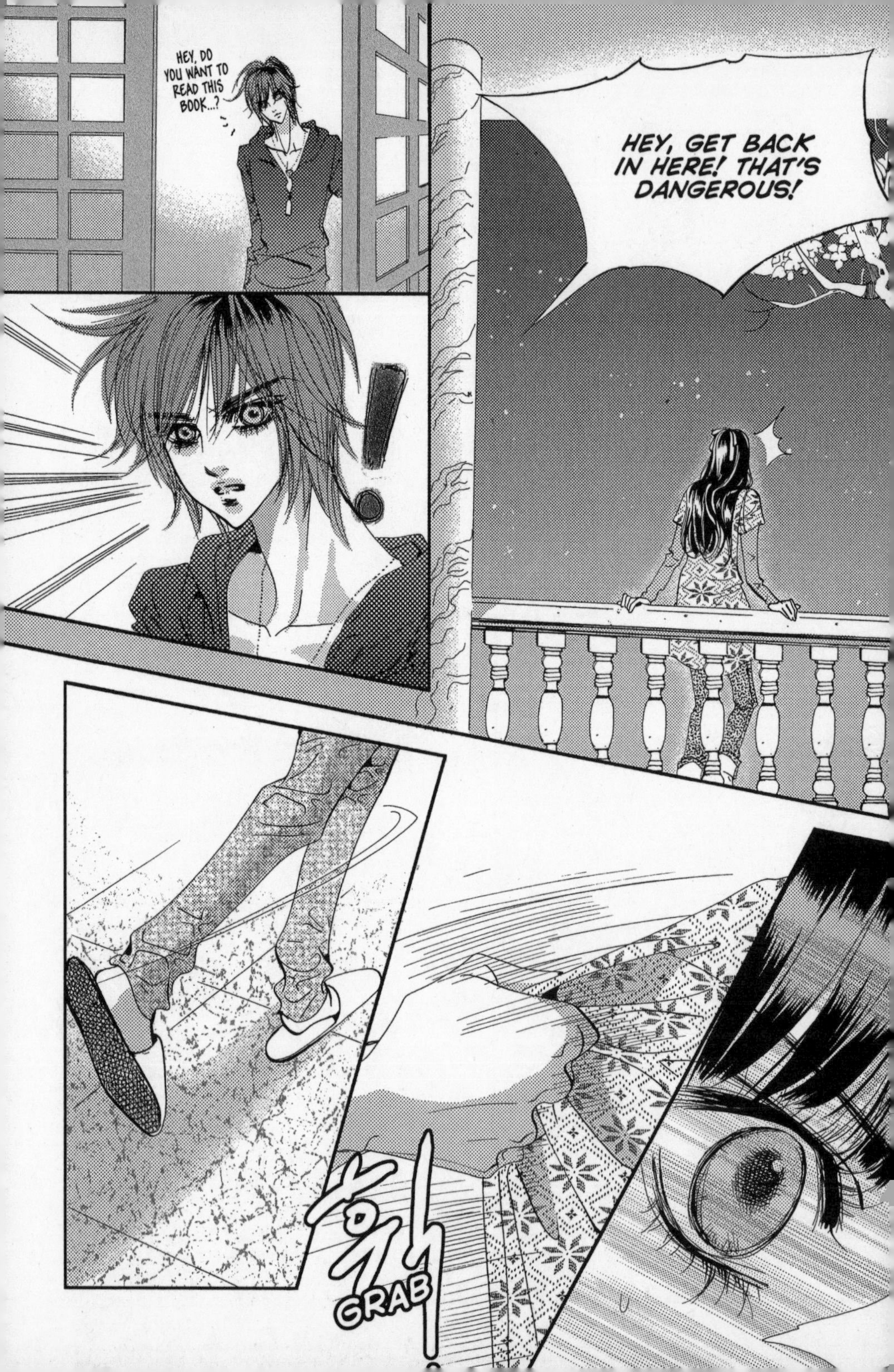

HEY, DO YOU WANT TO READ THIS BOOK...?
HEY, GET BACK IN HERE! THAT'S DANGEROUS!
GRAB

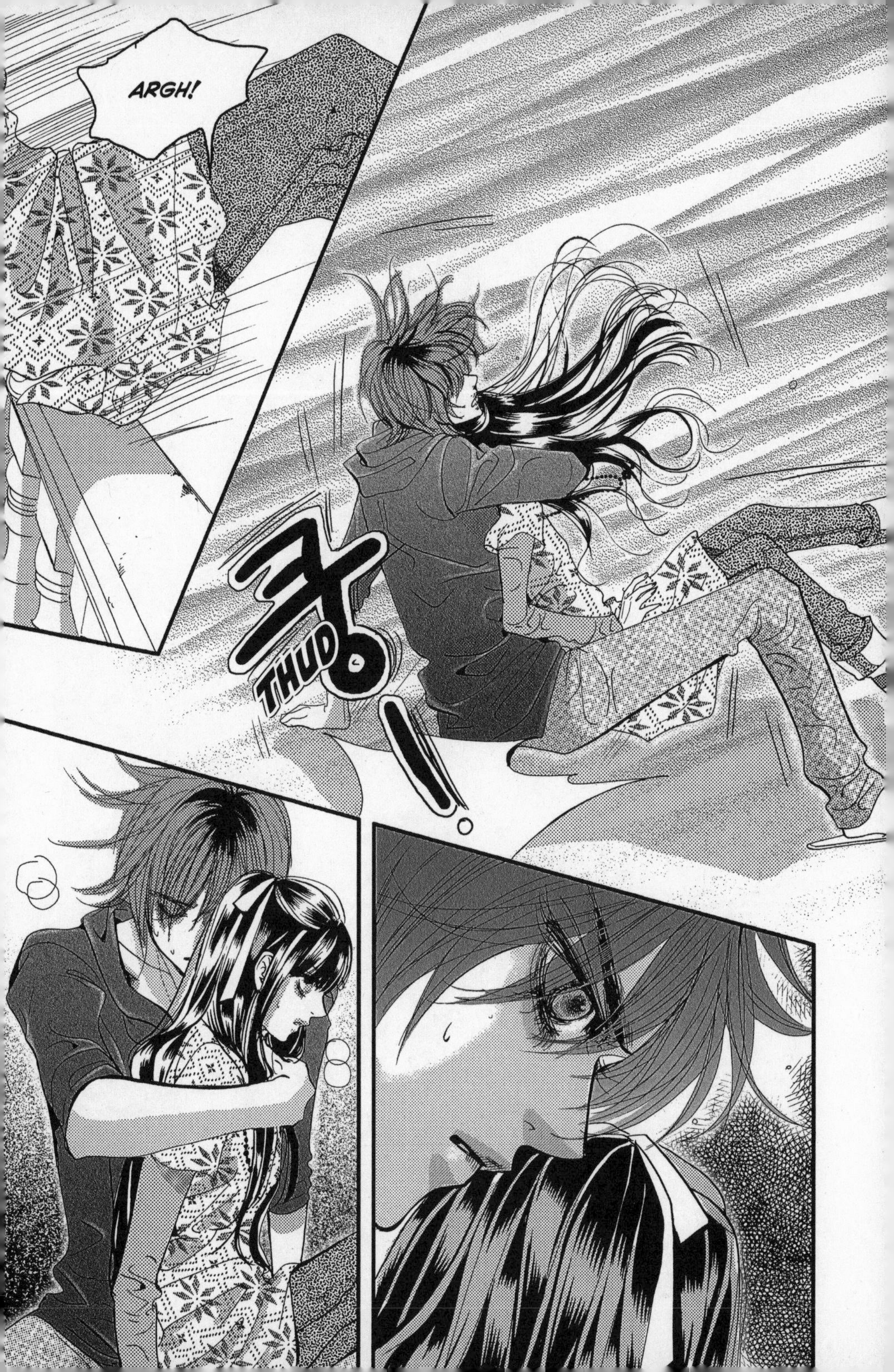
ARGH!
THUD
!

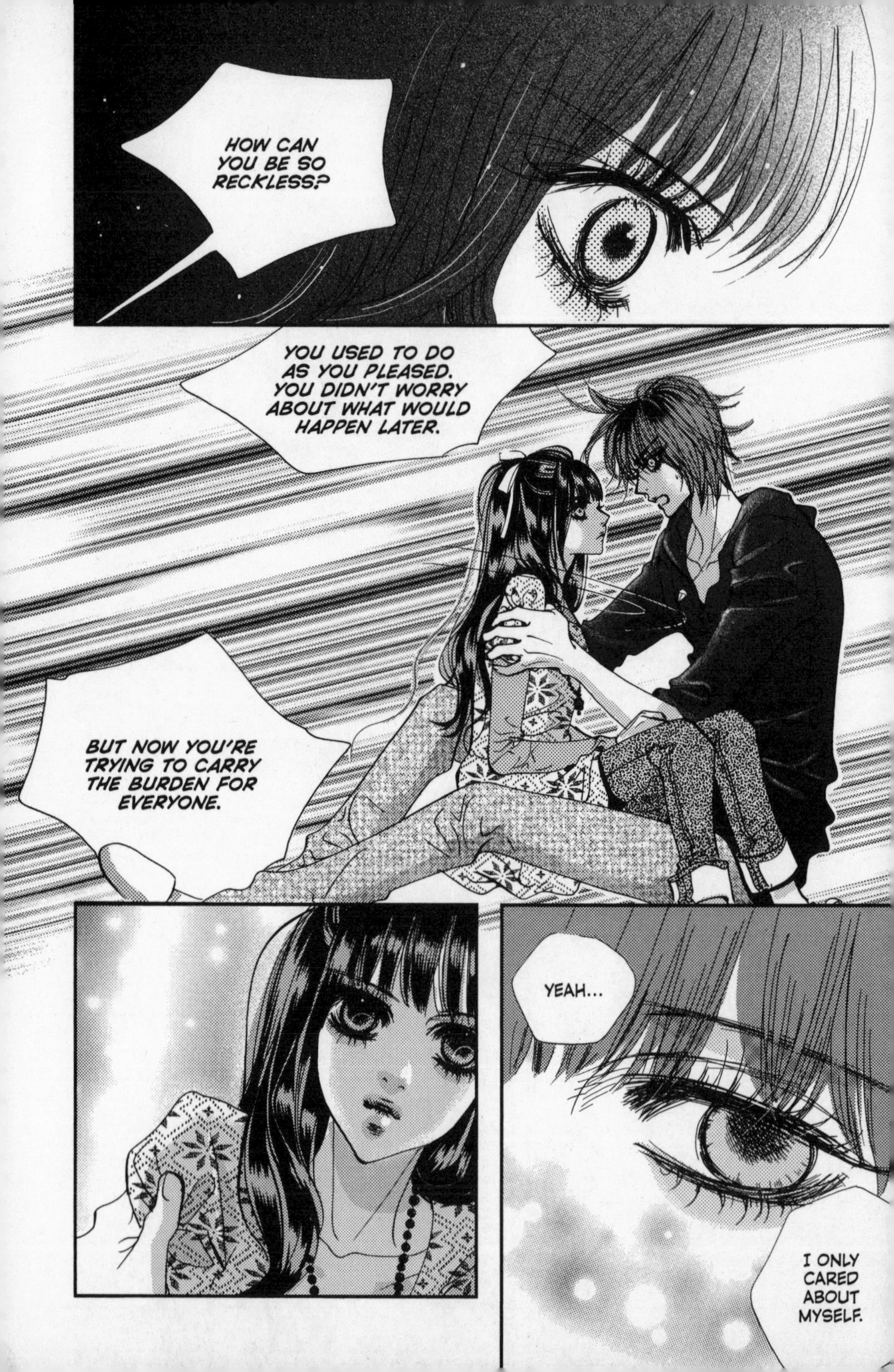
HOW CAN YOU BE SO RECKLESS?
YOU USED TO DO AS YOU PLEASED. YOU DIDN'T WORRY ABOUT WHAT WOULD HAPPEN LATER.
BUT NOW YOU'RE TRYING TO CARRY THE BURDEN FOR EVERYONE.
YEAH...
I ONLY CARED ABOUT MYSELF.

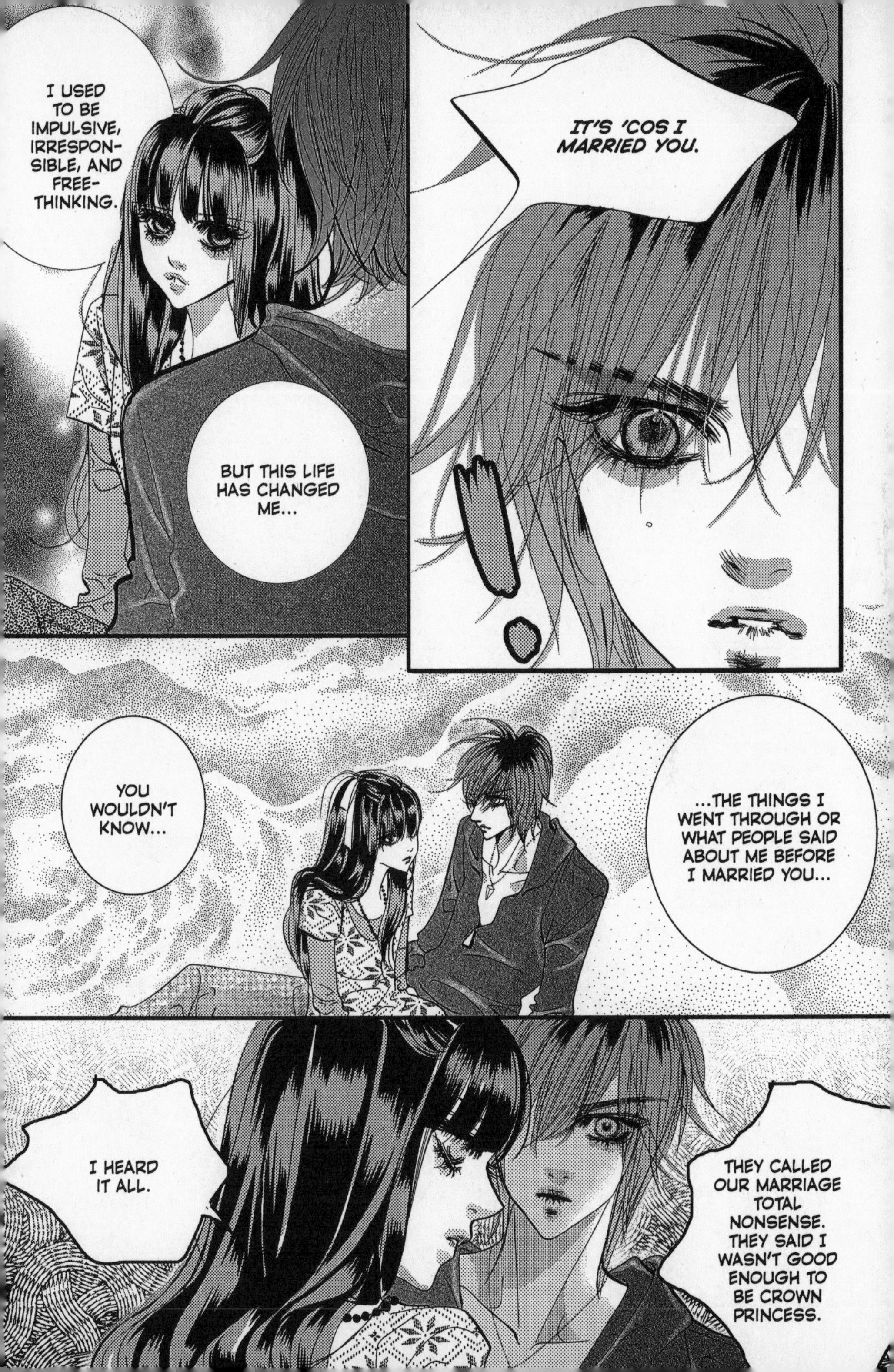
I USED TO BE IMPULSIVE, IRRESPONSIBLE, AND FREE-THINKING.
BUT THIS LIFE HAS CHANGED ME...
IT'S 'COS I MARRIED YOU.
!
YOU WOULDN'T KNOW...
...THE THINGS I WENT THROUGH OR WHAT PEOPLE SAID ABOUT ME BEFORE I MARRIED YOU...
I HEARD IT ALL.
THEY CALLED OUR MARRIAGE TOTAL NONSENSE. THEY SAID I WASN'T GOOD ENOUGH TO BE CROWN PRINCESS.

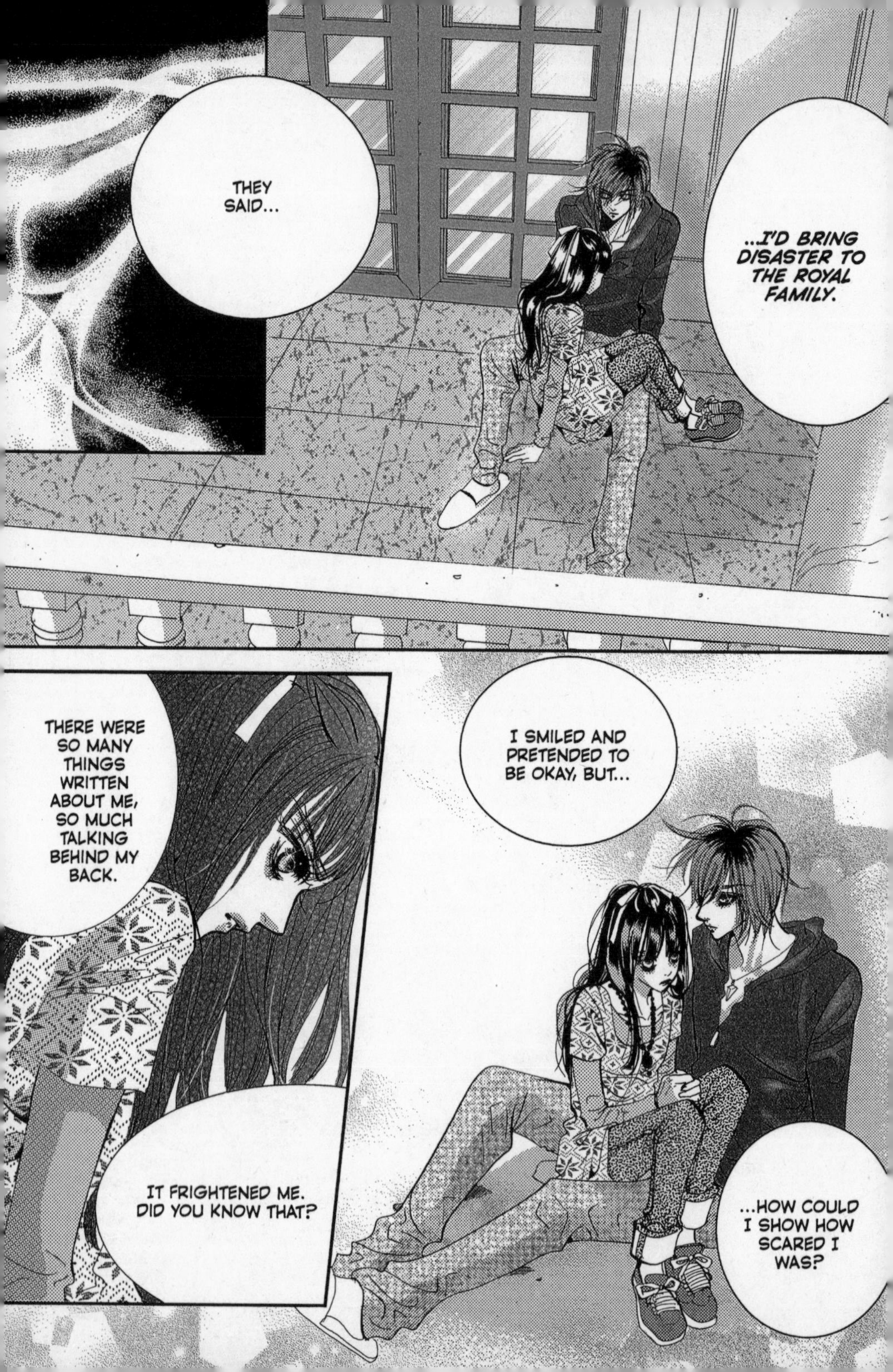
THEY SAID...
...I'D BRING DISASTER TO THE ROYAL FAMILY.
THERE WERE SO MANY THINGS WRITTEN ABOUT ME, SO MUCH TALKING BEHIND MY BACK.
IT FRIGHTENED ME. DID YOU KNOW THAT?
I SMILED AND PRETENDED TO BE OKAY, BUT...
...HOW COULD I SHOW HOW SCARED I WAS?

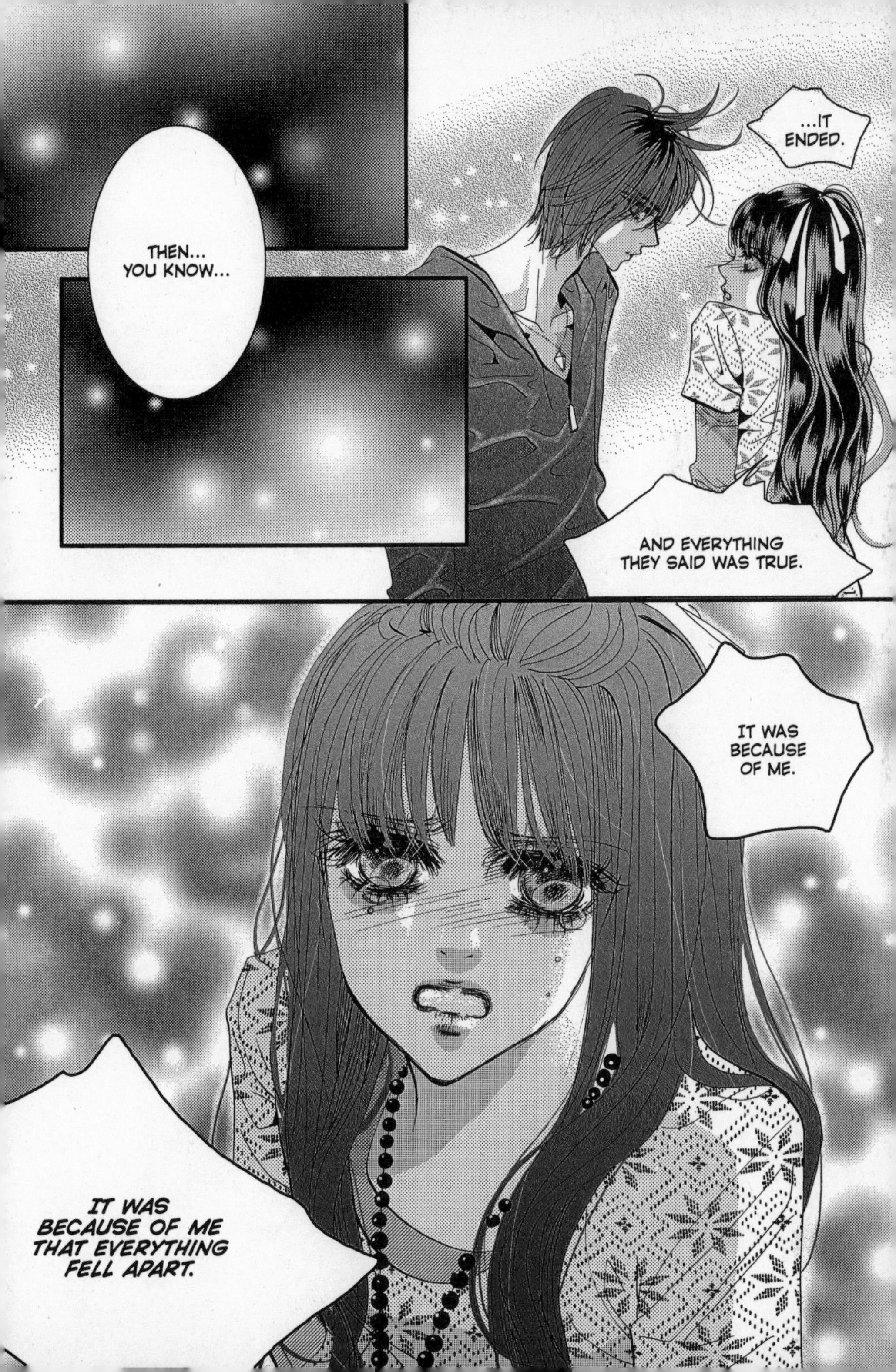
THEN... YOU KNOW...
...IT ENDED.
AND EVERYTHING THEY SAID WAS TRUE.
IT WAS BECAUSE OF ME.
IT WAS BECAUSE OF ME THAT EVERYTHING FELL APART.

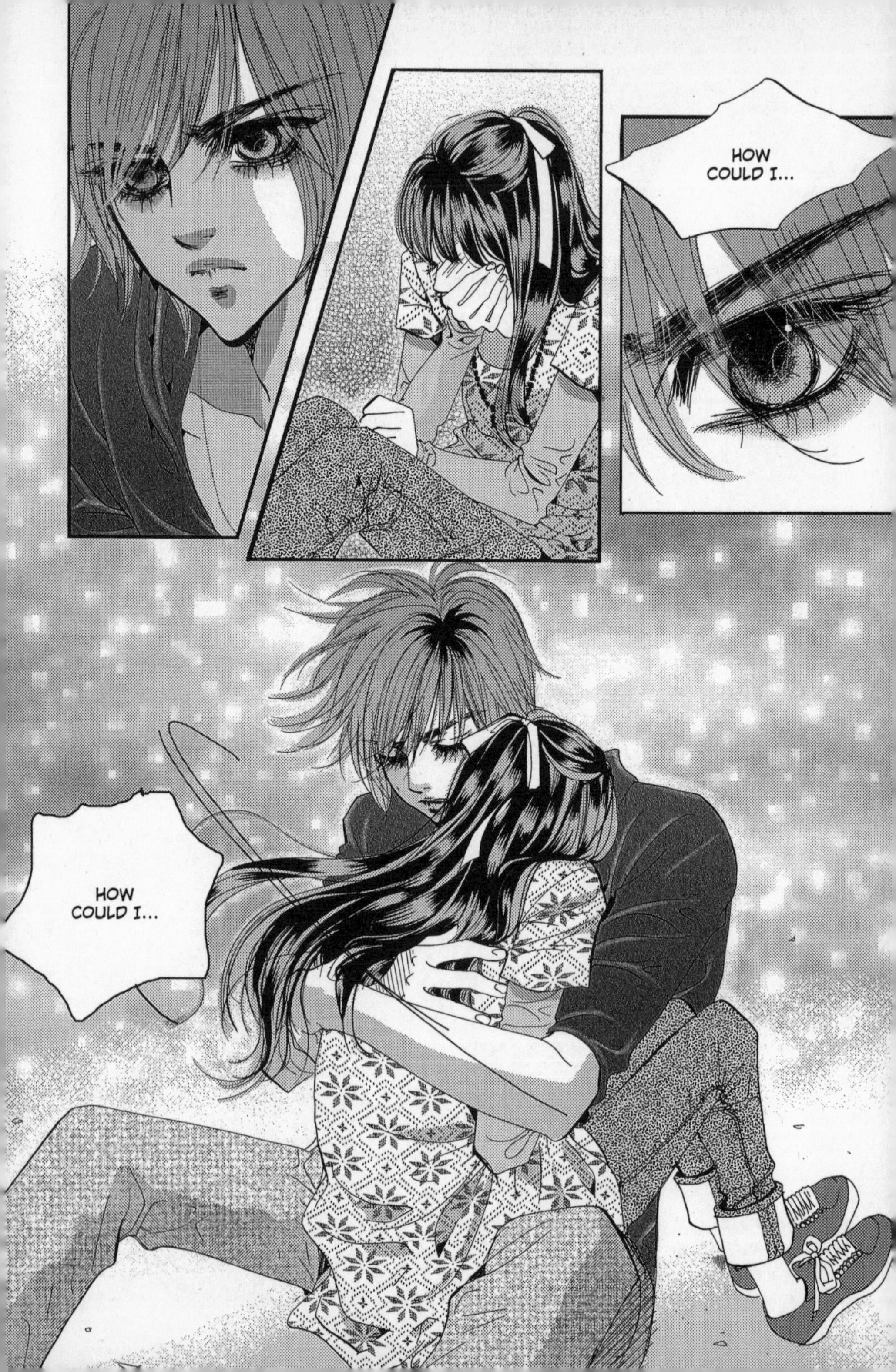
HOW COULD I...
HOW COULD I...

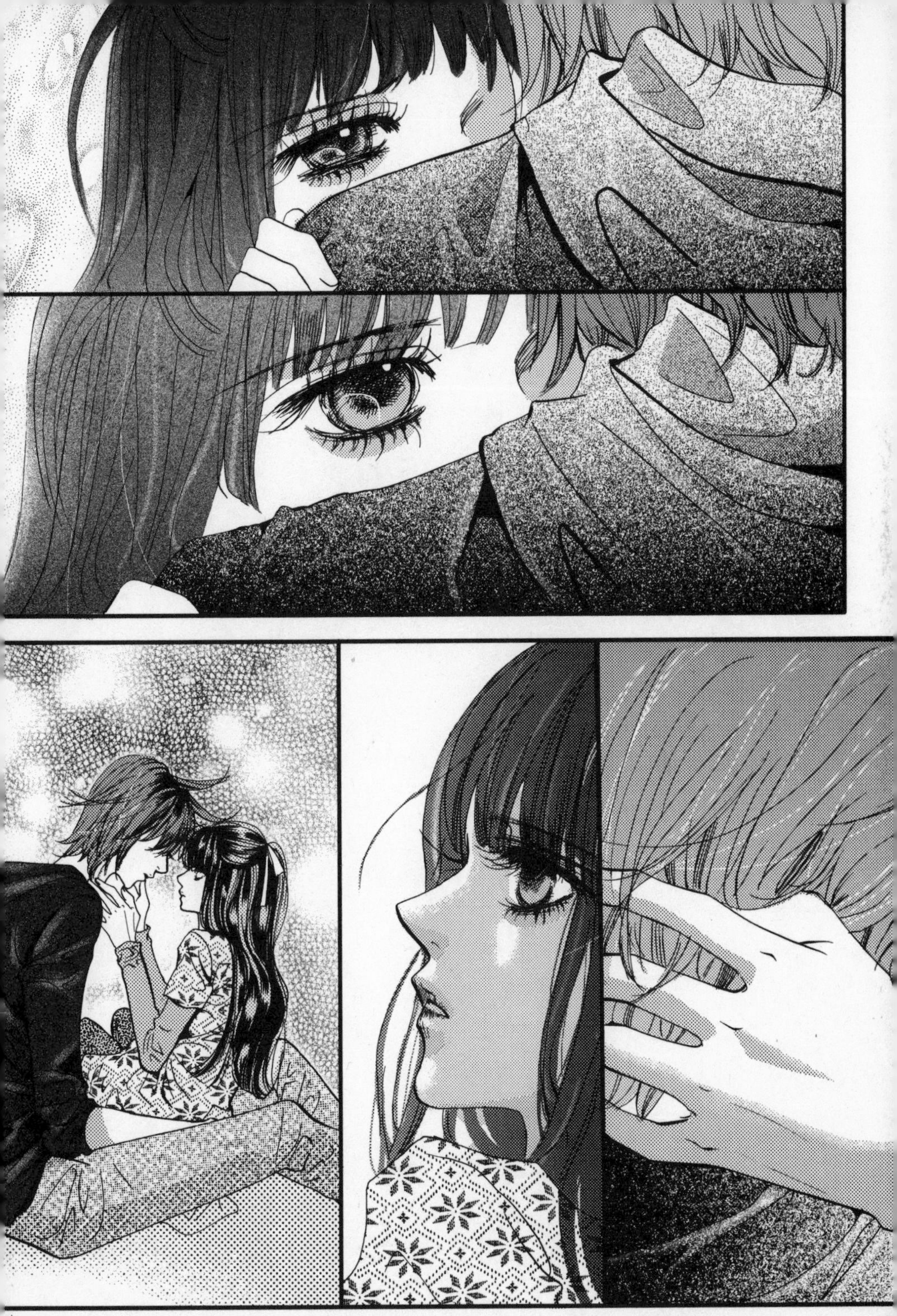

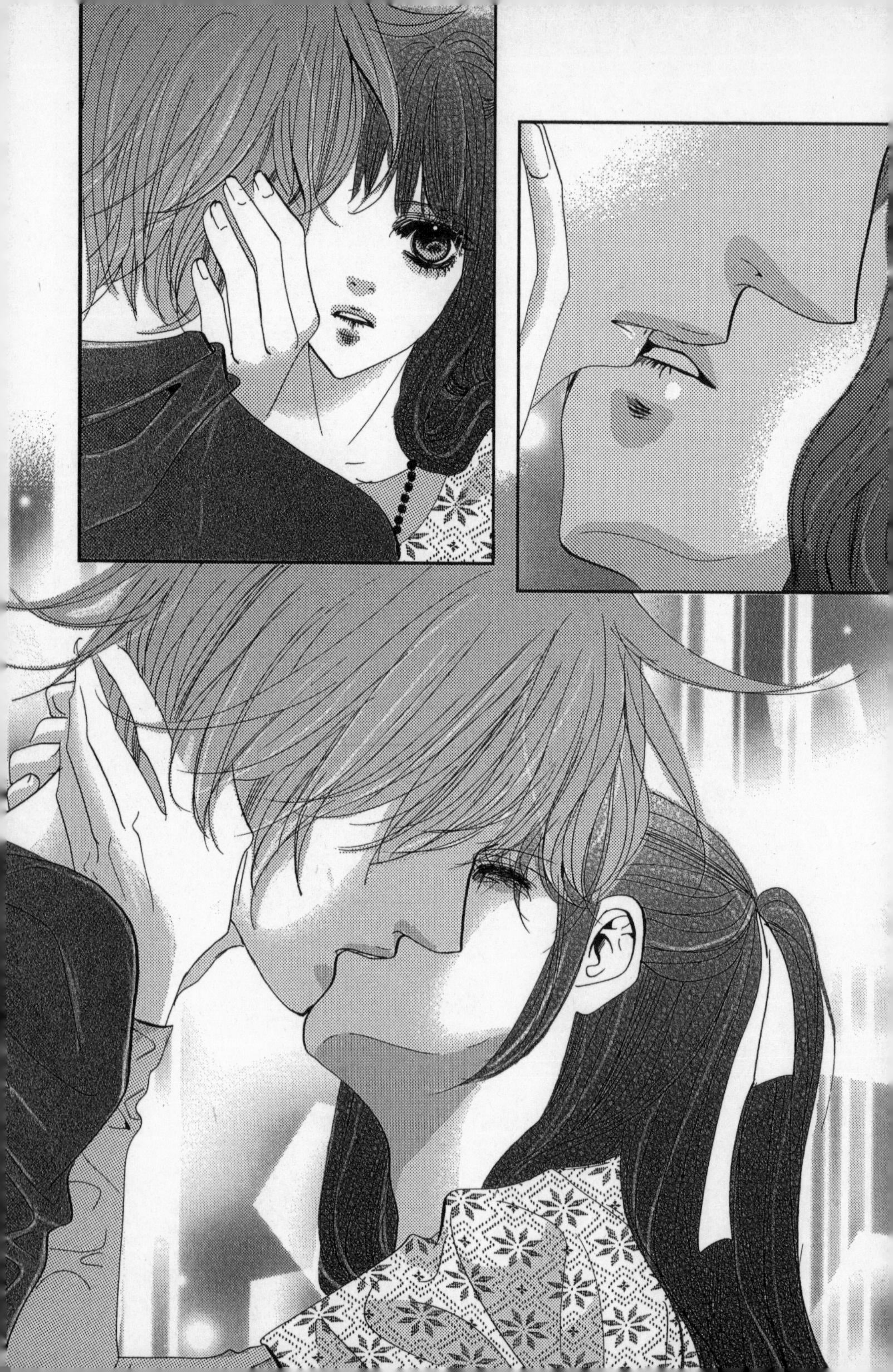

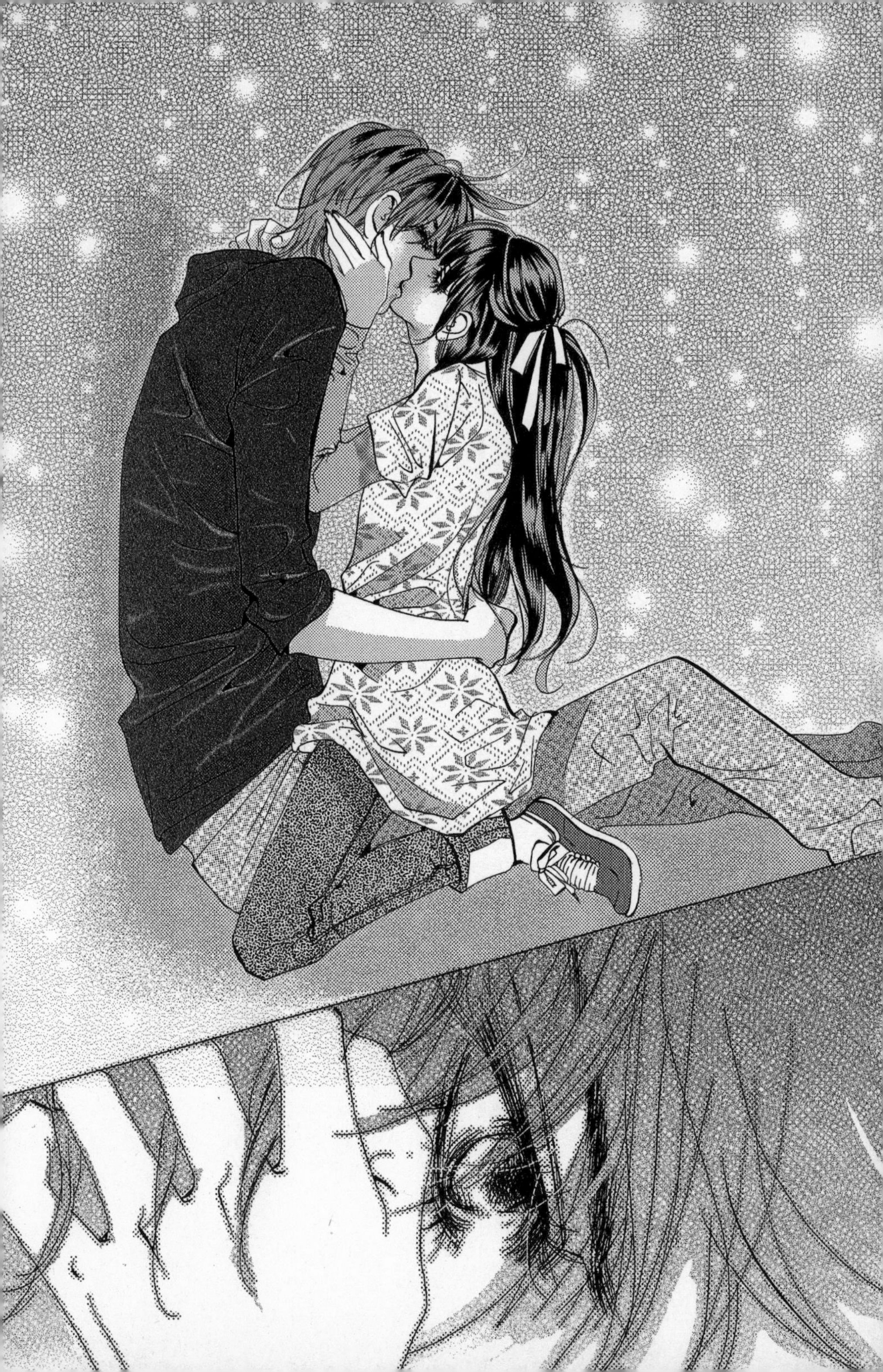

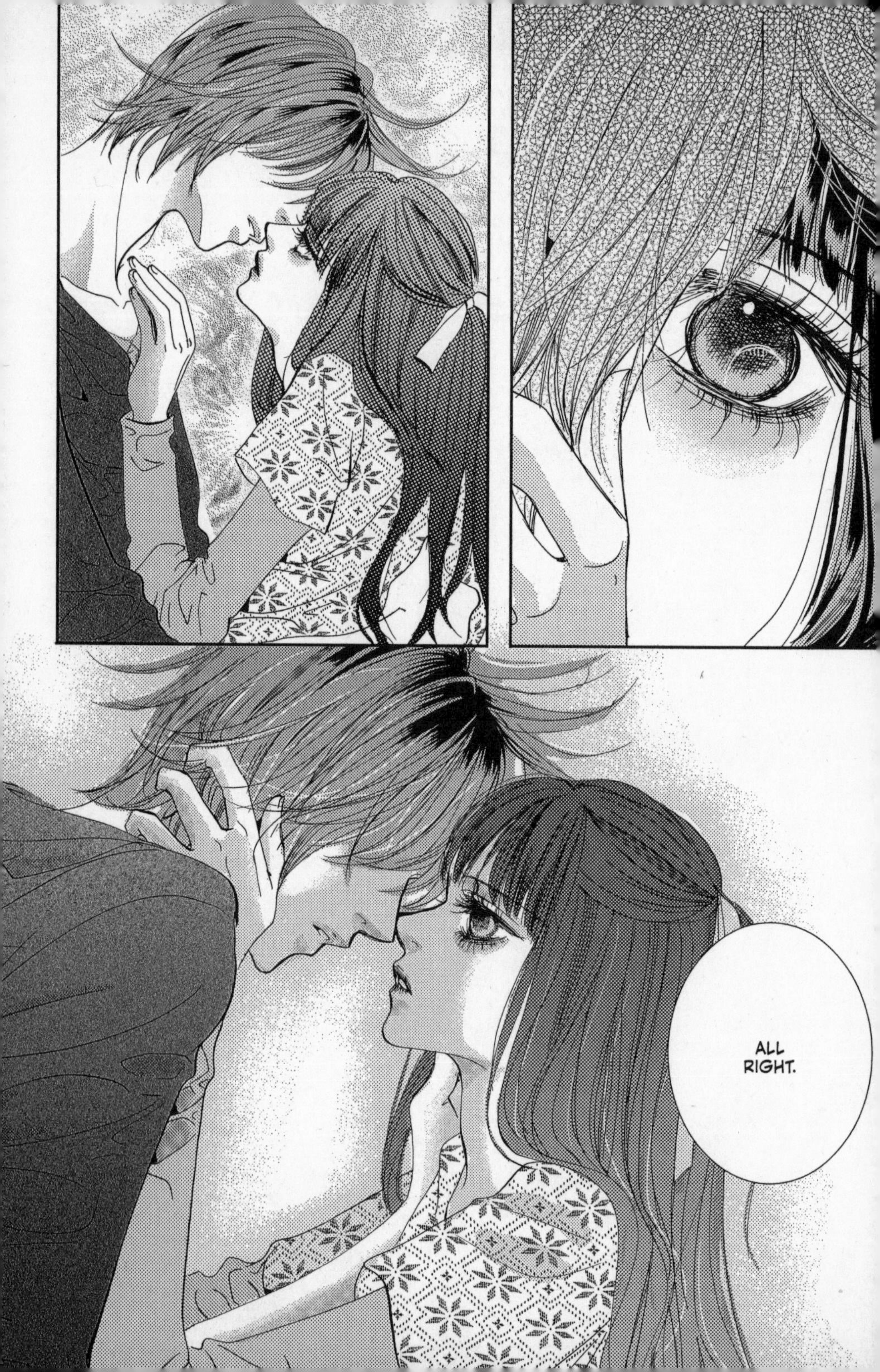
ALL RIGHT.

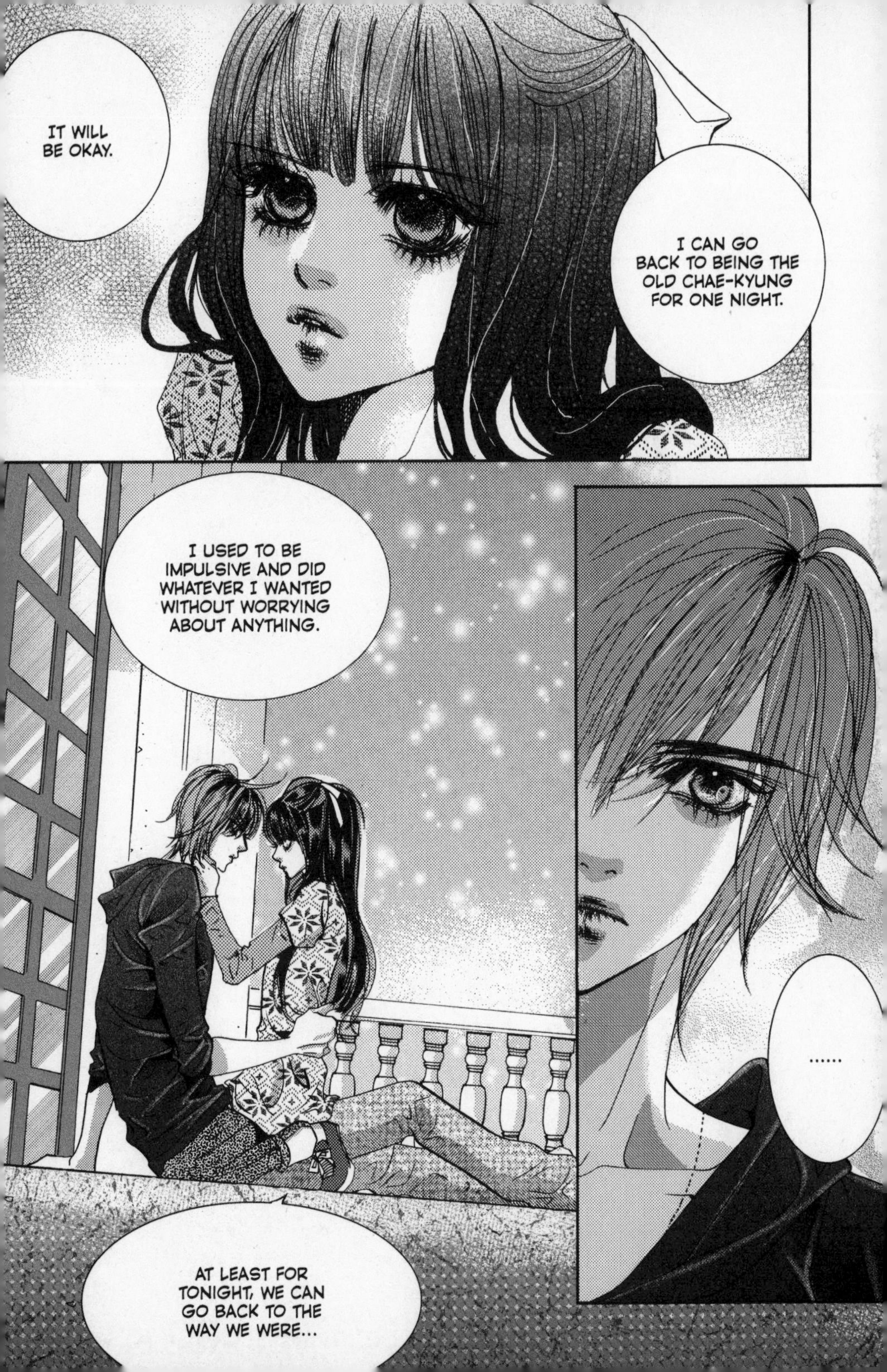
IT WILL BE OKAY.
I CAN GO BACK TO BEING THE OLD CHAE-KYUNG FOR ONE NIGHT.
I USED TO BE IMPULSIVE AND DID WHATEVER I WANTED WITHOUT WORRYING ABOUT ANYTHING.
AT LEAST FOR TONIGHT, WE CAN GO BACK TO THE WAY WE WERE...
......

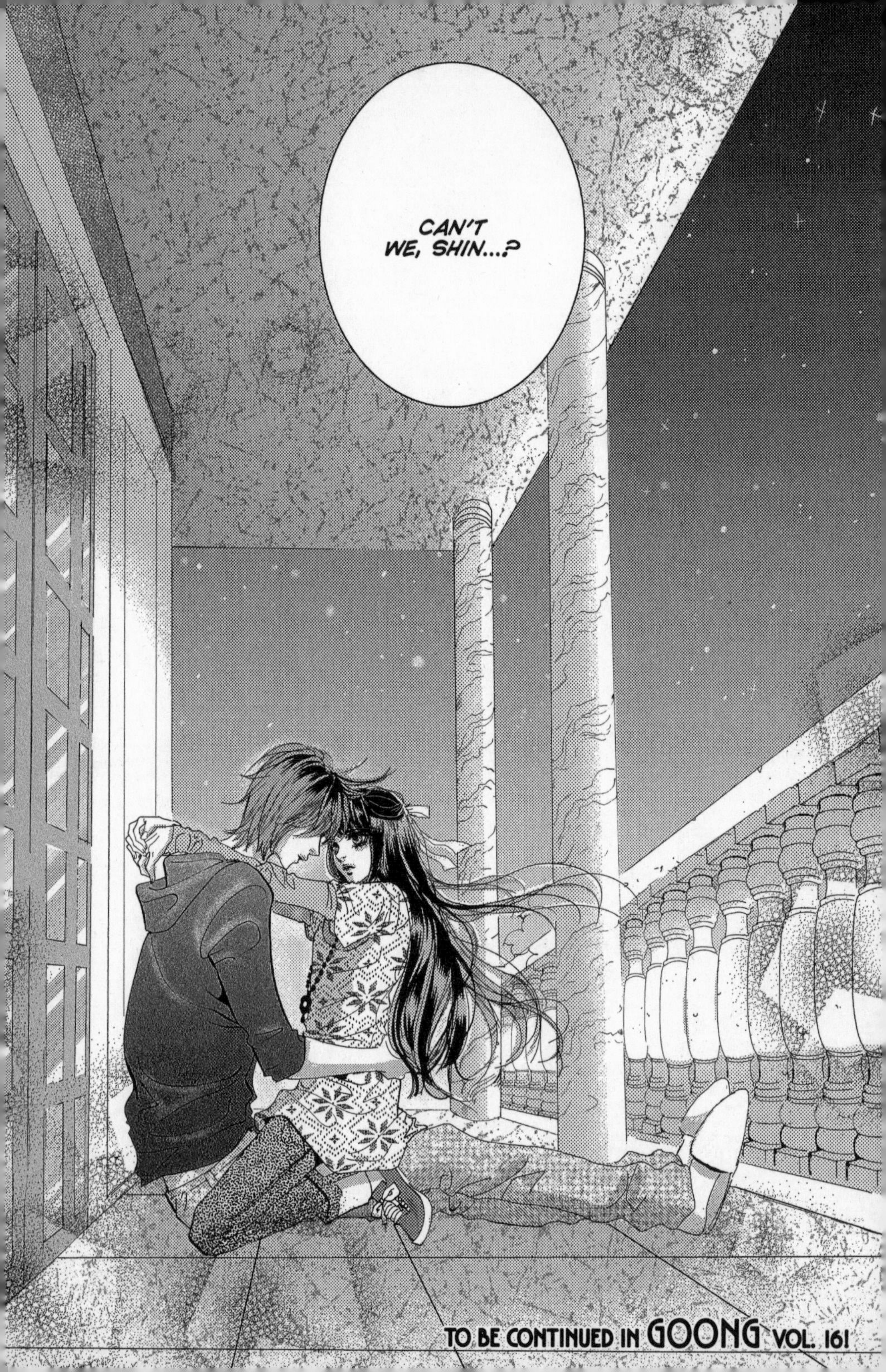
CAN'T WE, SHIN...?
TO BE CONTINUED IN GOONG VOL. 16!

THE ROYAL PALACE

Goong

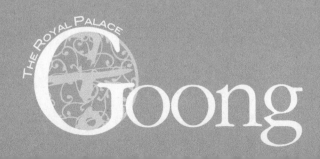

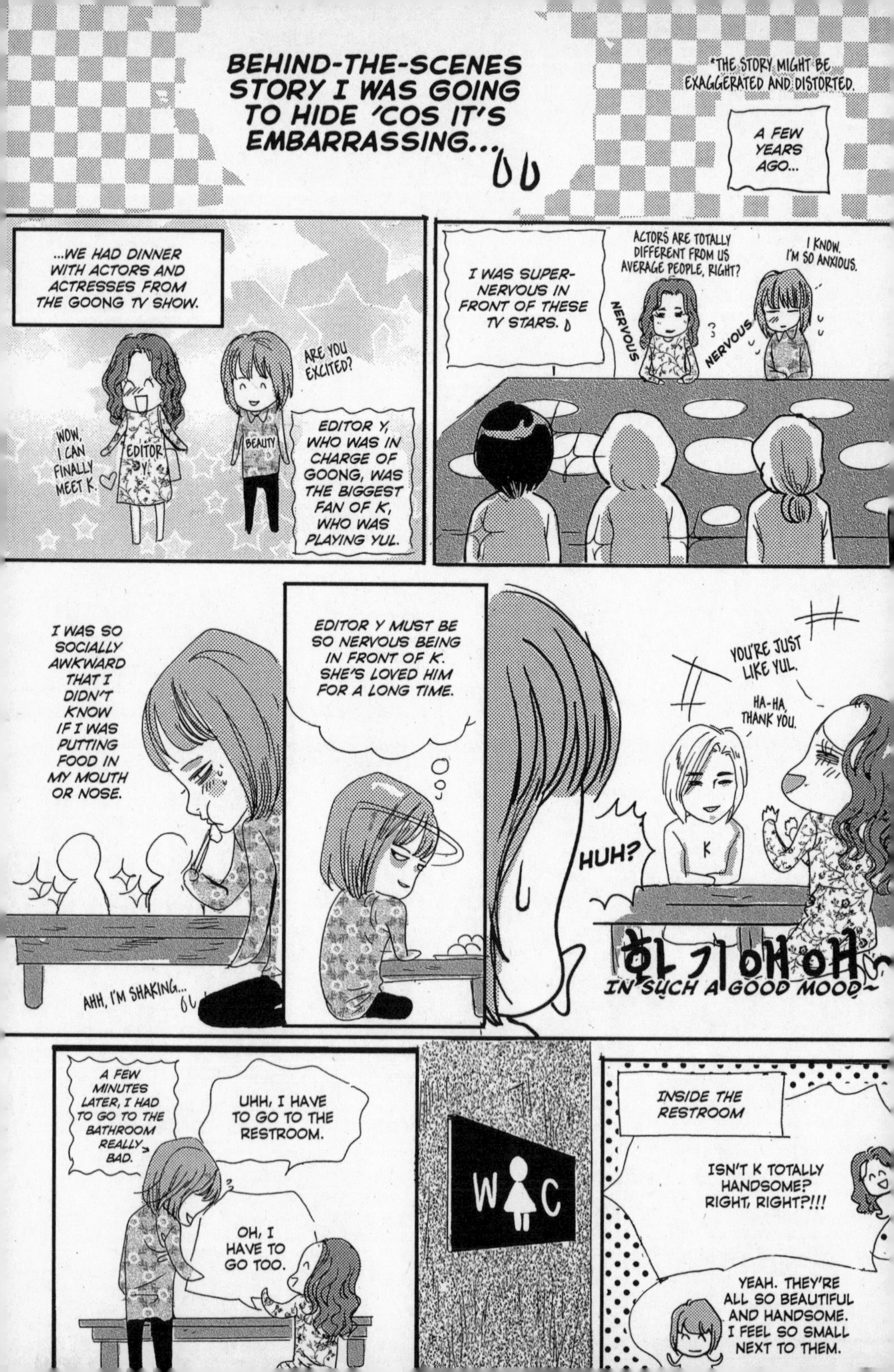
BEHIND-THE-SCENES STORY I WAS GOING TO HIDE 'COS IT'S EMBARRASSING...
*THE STORY MIGHT BE EXAGGERATED AND DISTORTED.
A FEW YEARS AGO...
...WE HAD DINNER WITH ACTORS AND ACTRESSES FROM THE GOONG TV SHOW.
ARE YOU EXCITED?
WOW, I CAN FINALLY MEET K.
EDITOR Y
BEAUTY
EDITOR Y, WHO WAS IN CHARGE OF GOONG, WAS THE BIGGEST FAN OF K, WHO WAS PLAYING YUL.
I WAS SUPER-NERVOUS IN FRONT OF THESE TV STARS.
ACTORS ARE TOTALLY DIFFERENT FROM US AVERAGE PEOPLE, RIGHT?
I KNOW. I'M SO ANXIOUS.
NERVOUS
NERVOUS
I WAS SO SOCIALLY AWKWARD THAT I DIDN'T KNOW IF I WAS PUTTING FOOD IN MY MOUTH OR NOSE.
AHH, I'M SHAKING...
EDITOR Y MUST BE SO NERVOUS BEING IN FRONT OF K. SHE'S LOVED HIM FOR A LONG TIME.
YOU'RE JUST LIKE YUL.
HA-HA, THANK YOU.
HUH?
K
화기애애~
IN SUCH A GOOD MOOD~
A FEW MINUTES LATER, I HAD TO GO TO THE BATHROOM REALLY BAD.
UHH, I HAVE TO GO TO THE RESTROOM.
OH, I HAVE TO GO TOO.
WC
INSIDE THE RESTROOM
ISN'T K TOTALLY HANDSOME? RIGHT, RIGHT?!!!
YEAH. THEY'RE ALL SO BEAUTIFUL AND HANDSOME. I FEEL SO SMALL NEXT TO THEM.

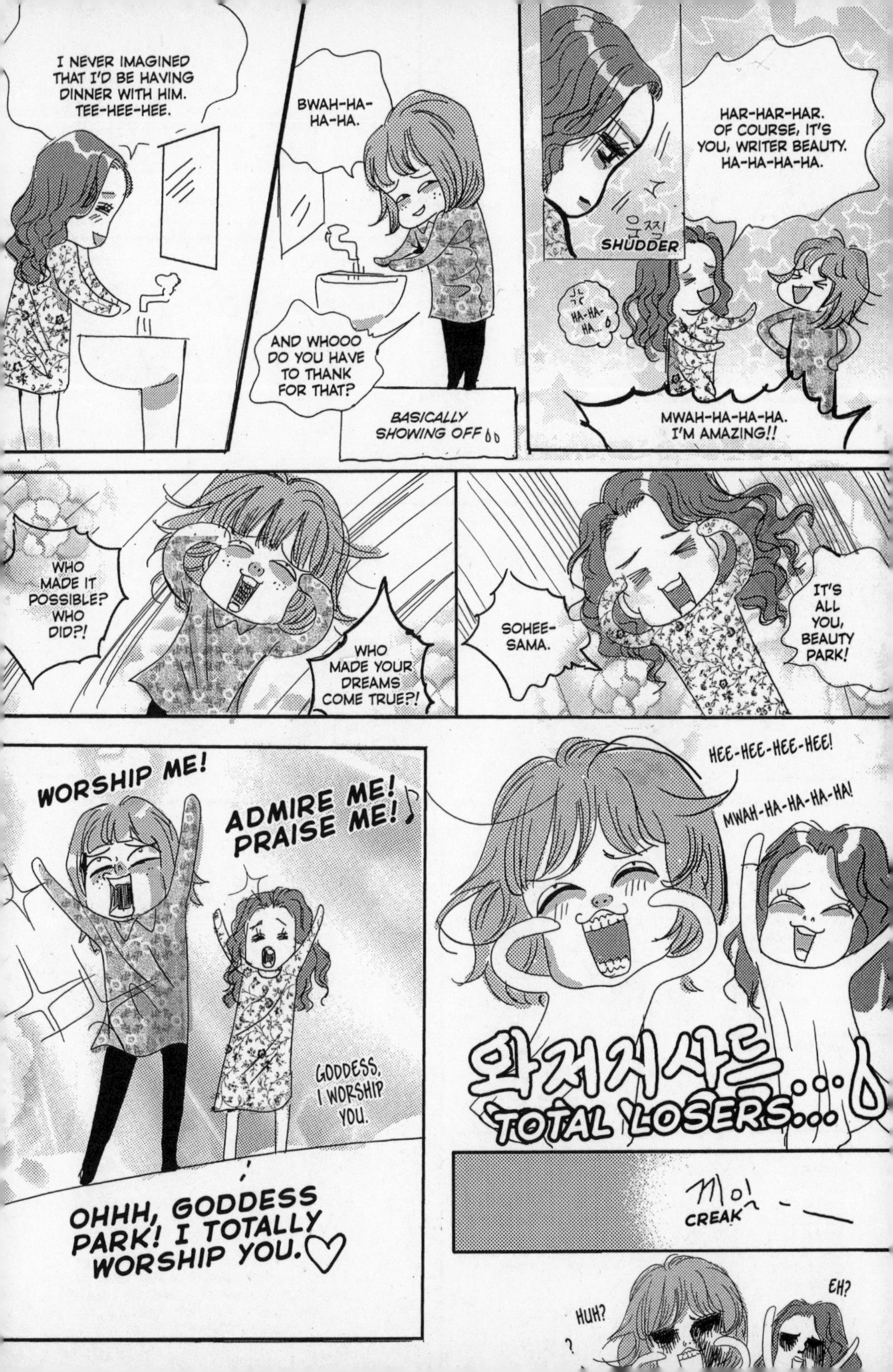
I NEVER IMAGINED THAT I'D BE HAVING DINNER WITH HIM. TEE-HEE-HEE.
BWAH-HA-HA-HA.
AND WHOOO DO YOU HAVE TO THANK FOR THAT?
BASICALLY SHOWING OFF
SHUDDER
HAR-HAR-HAR. OF COURSE, IT'S YOU, WRITER BEAUTY. HA-HA-HA-HA.
HA-HA-HA...
MWAH-HA-HA-HA. I'M AMAZING!!
WHO MADE IT POSSIBLE? WHO DID?!
WHO MADE YOUR DREAMS COME TRUE?!
SOHEE-SAMA.
IT'S ALL YOU, BEAUTY PARK!
WORSHIP ME!
ADMIRE ME! PRAISE ME!
GODDESS, I WORSHIP YOU.
OHHH, GODDESS PARK! I TOTALLY WORSHIP YOU.
HEE-HEE-HEE-HEE!
MWAH-HA-HA-HA-HA!
TOTAL LOSERS...
CREAK
HUH?
EH?

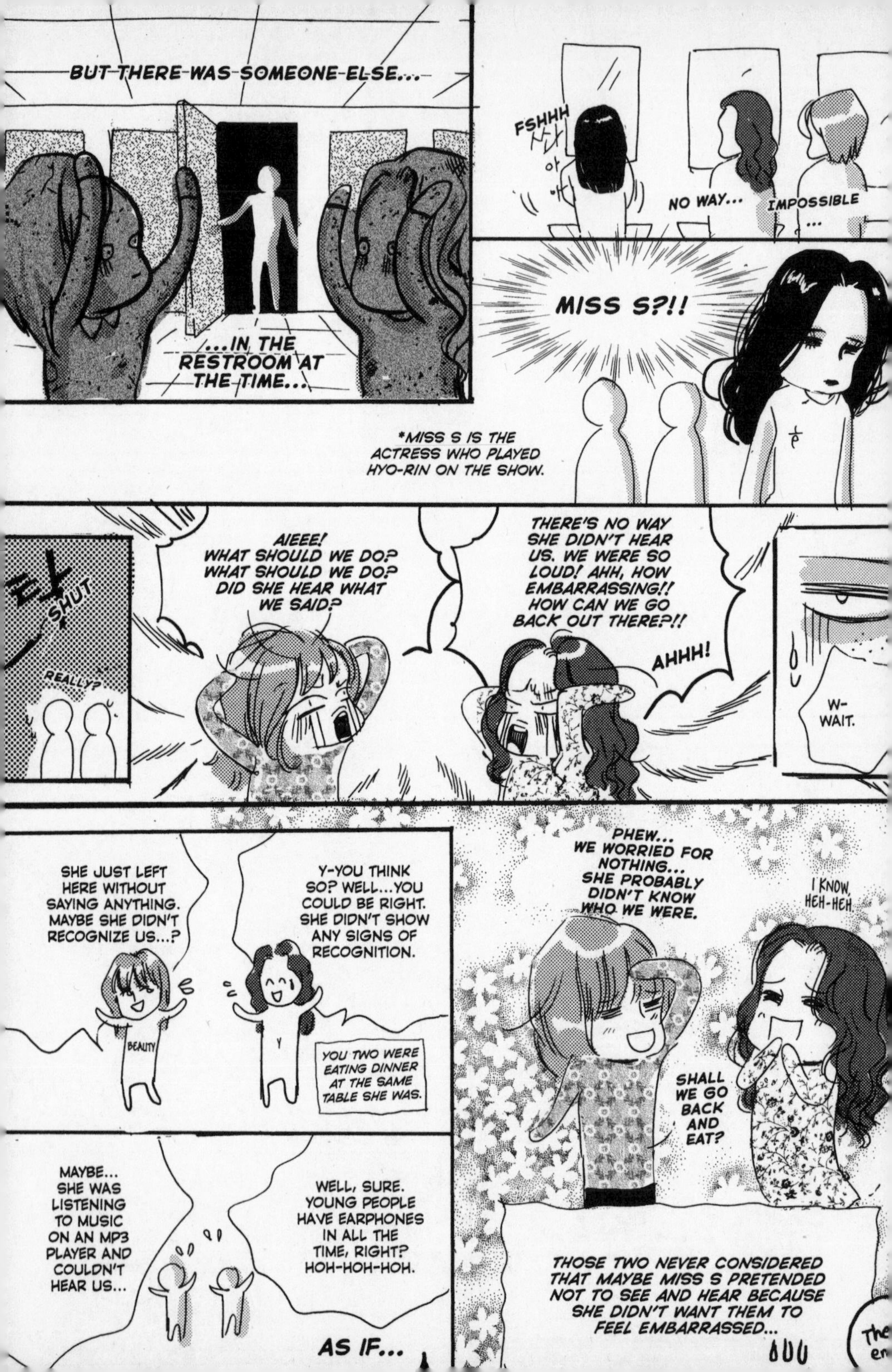
BUT THERE WAS SOMEONE ELSE...
...IN THE RESTROOM AT THE TIME...
FSHHH
NO WAY...
IMPOSSIBLE...
MISS S?!!
*MISS S IS THE ACTRESS WHO PLAYED HYO-RIN ON THE SHOW.
SHUT
REALLY?
AIEEE! WHAT SHOULD WE DO? WHAT SHOULD WE DO? DID SHE HEAR WHAT WE SAID?
THERE'S NO WAY SHE DIDN'T HEAR US. WE WERE SO LOUD! AHH, HOW EMBARRASSING!! HOW CAN WE GO BACK OUT THERE?!!
AHHH!
W-WAIT.
SHE JUST LEFT HERE WITHOUT SAYING ANYTHING. MAYBE SHE DIDN'T RECOGNIZE US...?
Y-YOU THINK SO? WELL...YOU COULD BE RIGHT. SHE DIDN'T SHOW ANY SIGNS OF RECOGNITION.
BEAUTY
Y
YOU TWO WERE EATING DINNER AT THE SAME TABLE SHE WAS.
MAYBE... SHE WAS LISTENING TO MUSIC ON AN MP3 PLAYER AND COULDN'T HEAR US...
WELL, SURE. YOUNG PEOPLE HAVE EARPHONES IN ALL THE TIME, RIGHT? HOH-HOH-HOH.
AS IF...
PHEW... WE WORRIED FOR NOTHING... SHE PROBABLY DIDN'T KNOW WHO WE WERE.
I KNOW, HEH-HEH.
SHALL WE GO BACK AND EAT?
THOSE TWO NEVER CONSIDERED THAT MAYBE MISS S PRETENDED NOT TO SEE AND HEAR BECAUSE SHE DIDN'T WANT THEM TO FEEL EMBARRASSED...

THE ROYAL PALACE

Goong

Seeking the love promised by destiny . . .
Can it be found in the thirteenth boy?

13th ★ BOY

After eleven
boyfriends,
Hee-So thought
she was through
with love . . .
until she met
Won-Jun, that is . . .

But when
number twelve
dumps her, she's
not ready to
move on to the
thirteenth boy just
yet! Determined to win
back her destined love,
Hee-So's on a mission
to reclaim Won-Jun,
no matter what!

COMPLETE SERIES IN STORES NOW!

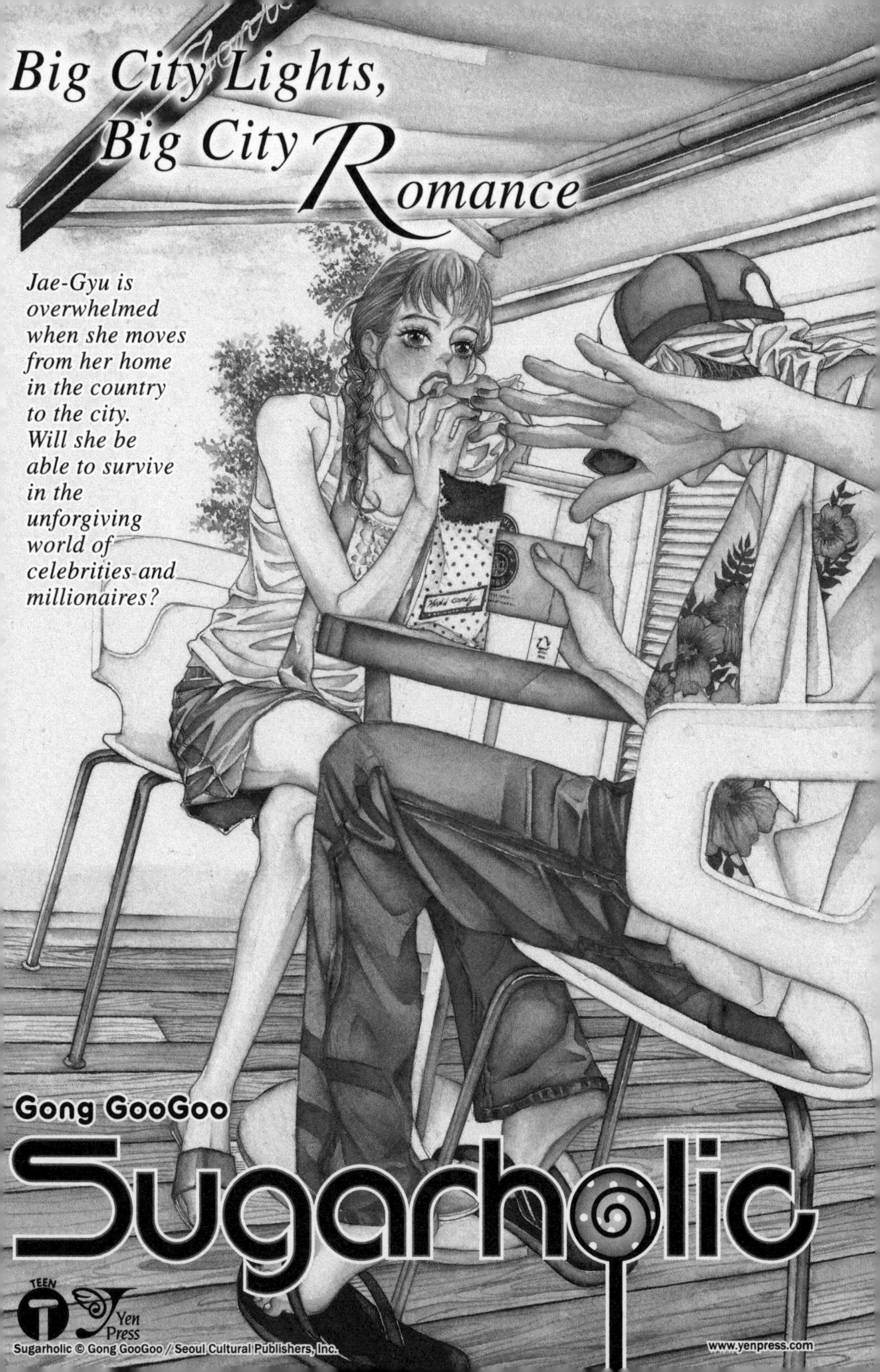
Big City Lights,
Big City Romance
Jae-Gyu is overwhelmed when she moves from her home in the country to the city. Will she be able to survive in the unforgiving world of celebrities and millionaires?
Gong GooGoo
Sugarholic
TEEN
Yen Press
Sugarholic © Gong GooGoo / Seoul Cultural Publishers, Inc.
www.yenpress.com

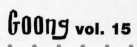

Goong vol. 15

Story and art by SoHee Park

Translation HyeYoung Im
English Adaptation Jamie S. Rich
Lettering Alexis Eckerman

Goong, Vols. 21 & 22 © 2009, 2010 SoHee Park. All rights reserved. First published in Korea in 2009, 2010 by SEOUL CULTURAL PUBLISHERS, Inc. English translation rights arranged by SEOUL CULTURAL PUBLISHERS, Inc.

English edition copyright © 2014 Hachette Book Group, Inc.

Yen Press
Hachette Book Group
237 Park Avenue, New York, NY 10017

www.HachetteBookGroup.com
www.YenPress.com

Yen Press is an imprint of Hachette Book Group, Inc.
The Yen Press name and logo are trademarks of Hachette Book Group, Inc.

First Yen Press Edition: May 2014

ISBN: 978-0-7595-3159-8

10 9 8 7 6 5 4 3 2 1

BVG

Printed in the United States of America